KU-302-769

EVELYN HOOD OMNIBUS

Looking After Your Own

McAdam's Women

EVELYN HOOD OMNIBUS

Looking After Your Own
McAdam's Women

EVELYN HOOD

timewarner
paperbacks

A *Time Warner* Paperback

This omnibus edition first published in Great Britain by
Time Warner Paperbacks in 2004
Evelyn Hood Omnibus Copyright © Evelyn Hood 2004

Previously published separately:
Looking After Your Own first published in Great Britain in 2002 by
Little, Brown
Published by Time Warner Paperbacks in 2003
Copyright © Evelyn Hood 2002

McAdam's Women first published in Great Britain in 1994 by
Little, Brown and Company
Published by Warner Books in 1995
Reprinted 1996, 1997, 1998, 2000
Copyright © Evelyn Hood 1994

A CIP catalogue record for this book
is available from the British Library.

ISBN 0 7515 3645 8

Printed and bound in Great Britain by
Clays Ltd, St Ives plc

Time Warner Paperbacks
An imprint of
Time Warner Books UK
Brettenham House
Lancaster Place
London WC2E 7EN

www.TimeWarnerBooks.co.uk

Looking After Your Own

To Alastair and Simon

Acknowledgements

My thanks go to Jessie McMaster and other former 'clippies' who took time to tell me about their lives as bus and tram conductresses; to Bill Peacock, who patiently explained the intricacies of playing the trumpet to one who has never been able to get a sound out of these elegant instruments, and to Assistant Divisional Officer Iain Glover, of Strathclyde Fire Brigade, for his advice on some aspects of fire-fighting.

1

The rich, warm smell enveloping the entire building, rising effortlessly through floorboards and swirling up the communal stairway, evoked memories of happier pre-war days, family gatherings, generous meals and full stomachs instead of making do with ration books and warm fires on cold winter nights.

Customers in the two shops on the ground floor sniffed the air as the aroma drifted down the flight of steps leading to the close, vying with the tang of paraffin, firelighters and soap in Binnie's the drysalter's, and even with the sweeter, fruitier aromas in Clark's sweetie shop.

'Is that dumplin'?' An elderly woman rested her basket on Mr Binnie's counter and sniffed noisily, distinguishing the smells of currants and raisins, sugar and spice and cinnamon. 'Who's got the makin's of dumplin' these days, with a war on?'

'It happens sometimes, in this building,' Mr Binnie said with a shrug, while his stomach, remembering the joy of homemade dumplings, gave a low rumble.

In the flat directly above the drysalter's, Julia McCosh, her face flushed with the heat from the big pot that had been simmering on the stove for the past two hours, wrapped a cloth about her hand to protect it against the steam and gripped a wooden ladle by the rounded spoon.

'Are you ready now?'

'I'm ready! Mum, it's nearly time I was back at the shop and I've not even had my dinner yet,' her daughter Chloe fretted.

'I know, pet, and I'll not be a minute. You're holding the plate tight?'

'Any tighter and it'll break. My hands are getting sore from gripping it and if you don't hurry up they'll go all weak and then I'll drop it.'

'Here goes, then.' As Julia took the lid from the pot she and her daughter leaned back to avoid the great gout of steam that rushed towards the kitchen ceiling. 'Now ...' Julia poked the handle of the ladle into the steam, blinking to clear her vision, and wiggled it until she managed to spear the knot fastening the cloth that gave the clootie dumpling its name. 'Got it. Ready ... ?'

'Mum! I'm ready!' Chloe snapped, tightening her white-knuckled hold on the plate as Julia braced herself and then began to ease the heavy bundle up from the boiling water, over the edge of the pot, and on to the plate.

'Down now ... put it down.' Julia held tightly to the ladle, trying to take some of the strain as the plate dipped dangerously beneath the weight of the huge dumpling.

'I've got it,' Chloe said through set teeth, and then gave a great sigh of relief as both plate and dumpling were settled safely on the shelf by the stove.

Duncan and Leslie arrived as though drawn by a magnet, leaving their toy soldiers to battle it out on the hearthrug. 'Can we try a bit now, Mum?' Duncan asked eagerly. He was thirteen, and his voice broke endearingly on 'now'. His mother eased the kink in her back and then ruffled his short brown hair.

'Later, pet, when it's cooled down and your dad's home.'

'And then we'll only get a wee scliff each,' mourned seven-year-old Leslie, the youngest of the three McCosh children, adding, reproach in the green eyes he had inherited from his mother, ''cos you'll be giving it all away to the neighbours again!'

'That's to keep them from minding the noise of the band practice. Anyway, it was Mrs Borland who gave me the ingred— is that the time?' Julia asked in alarm as the door-knocker thumped hard against the flat's outer door. She darted to the mirror, dragging at the ties of her wrap-around overall with one hand while the other dabbed at her auburn hair, her strong, flexible musician's fingers tucking errant strands deftly back into the neat roll about her head. 'Chloe pet, can you get yourself something to eat? There's bread, and some dripping in the pan from your daddy's sausage this morning. You could do a slice for the boys too. Keep an eye on that dumpling, will you, and don't let them lay a finger on it.'

'It's not fair,' Leslie groused as his mother whisked out of the kitchen. Chloe's heart went out to him. She had been only two years old when Duncan was born, too young and immersed in the pleasure and wonder of her own existence to bother much with him; but when Leslie arrived six years later, red-haired and green-eyed and with a smile fit, as Mrs Megson from upstairs said, to warm the heart of a water pump, eight-year-old Chloe had loved him at first sight. Now, she ruffled his hair in imitation of her mother.

'Nothing's fair, son, because there's a war on. If you're good,' she promised, 'you might get a bit of my slice too.'

'Just because he's wee!' Duncan stormed at once. 'You never gave me anything when I was wee!'

'I did so, but you were too little to remember it. Oh, all right, you can have a bit of my slice too.' At this rate, Chloe thought resentfully as she lit the gas cooker under the frying pan, she'd be lucky if there was a decent mouthful left for her. Sometimes being the oldest could be hard. She took the drab grey National loaf from the breadbin by the sink, listening to her mother's voice in the hall, and then the underlying murmur of the newly arrived music pupil.

'Quiet now, while Mum's teaching.' Keenly aware of the
two pairs of eyes fixed on the bread she was slicing and
the two snub noses sniffing in the aroma of the heating fat,
she shooed her brothers back to their game of toy soldiers
and pushed the cooling dumpling to the back of the shelf,
out of the reach of prying fingers. Then, with one eye on
the clock, she began to rub slices of bread over the frying
pan to mop up the dripping.

The tea had already been made and left to stew over a
low heat before she and her mother had taken the dumpling
from the pot. After putting the boys' food on the table Chloe
poured three cups of tea, dark and strong, then treated each
of them to half a spoonful of condensed milk.

Washing down her own bread and dripping with generous
mouthfuls of tea, she leaned against the sink, surrounded by
a wooden frame and known among Scottish tenement
dwellers as 'the jawbox', and stared down into the backcourt.
Once, it had been a pretty place, cared for by a tenant who
had been a former gardener with Paisley Council, but old Mr
Brown had died almost three years ago, just before Prime
Minister Chamberlain's promises of peace went wrong and
war was declared. And now his precious flowerbeds had been
dug up to make way for vegetable beds, mainly tended by
Chloe's father, Frank, and Dennis Megson, who lived with
his mother, brother and sisters on the top floor.

She took another bite of bread, another mouthful of tea.
When Mr Brown was alive she had still been a child; now,
in February 1941, she was months off her sixteenth birthday, almost two years out of the South School and earning
a weekly wage in Cochran's emporium opposite Paisley
Abbey. Now quiet, shy Mrs Fulton lived in Mr Brown's
flat, and everything had changed because of the war.
Nothing, especially the future, was certain any more.

The halting strains of 'To a Rose', played by small, uncertain fingers, trickled through the wall from the front room
as Chloe drained her cup and began to wash it and her plate.

She stared unseeingly at the sink, visualising the piano keys and her own fingers moving across them.

When she had first heard the old saying about the cobbler's children never getting their shoes mended she had been at a loss to understand it, but now she knew only too well what it meant. She herself would have loved to learn to play the piano but her mother and father, both talented musicians, never had the time to teach her. Instead, her mother taught other people's children, while Chloe was left to learn as best she could by watching and listening and picking out tunes on the rare occasions she found herself alone in the flat with nobody to hear her and laugh at her.

'If you want me to wash your cups you'd better hurry up,' she told her brothers, who were squabbling over possession of a comic. Then she sighed over what might have been, filling her nose and lungs in the process with the powerful scent of the cooling dumpling. Nobody could make dumpling like her mum, and this one, she could tell, was going to be one of the best. It was a pity that she had promised most of her slice to the boys. Still, the less she ate the slimmer she would be, and if she got really slim, then perhaps Dennis Megson might notice her. Her thoughts changed from imagining herself as a successful and talented pianist to Dennis, handsome in his Fire Brigade uniform, coming into the backcourt when she was helping her father to dig the carrot patch . . . no, wait, coming into the shop where she worked, though goodness knows what Dennis might want in the kitchen department . . . walking in, then all at once looking up to see Chloe standing at the counter, smiling at him, slender and smart and asking if she could help.

And then – Chloe's imagination had always been ripe – he would suddenly find himself looking at her as a woman instead of the way he thought of her now . . . wee Chloe McCosh who used to take his younger sister Amy out in the battered old pushchair.

It would be just like it was in the pictures. Imagining the

look in his eyes – wonder at first, mebbe, then dawning
recognition followed by admiration and then adoration –
Chloe sighed again, while across the hall, her mother's pupil
switched to scales, making them sound like an old, moth-
eaten teddy bear being dragged, bump-bump-bump, up a
flight of steep, badly lit stairs.

Dennis, gazing at her in awe and wonder across the pots
and pans and wooden ladles, suddenly vanished and Chloe
opened her eyes and found herself staring at the clock,
which was trying to tell her that she had five minutes to
get up the road. As she slammed the last of the cups on to
the draining board and scrambled into her coat, she ordered,
'Don't touch that dumpling, mind. If you do, Mum and
me'll kill you!'

Fergus Goudie, varnishing one of the two kitchen chairs in
his top floor flat, inhaled deeply and asked in wonder, 'Do
I smell dumpling?'

Cecelia, sitting on the other chair and polishing the
buttons on Fergus's khaki tunic, lifted her head and sniffed
the air. 'Surely not . . . but mebbe . . .' She looked at him,
puzzled. 'Who would have the ingredients for dumpling
these days? D'you think we're dreaming?'

'Not me, definitely, because when I dream, I smell you.'
Her husband of two weeks put down the brush and came
round the table to bury his face in her hair. 'But that's
because you smell like flowers.'

'I'll be smelling of peeled onions and boiled cabbage
when you get back for your next leave. Have you noticed
that this entire tenement smells of onions and cabbage?'

'It's an old building. It's absorbed generations of living,'
Fergus said in the lovely Highland lilt that still melted her
heart each time she heard it. He kissed the end of her nose
then went back to his work. After a while he straightened,
easing his back with one hand.

'Done. What d'you think?'

Cecelia glanced up briefly and then returned to the task of polishing the buttons, so intently now that her soft fair hair broke free of the restraining hairpins and flopped down over her forehead. 'It looks great.'

'I wonder if I could manage the other one before I go?'

'No, leave it. You're off tomorrow morning . . . we've only got tonight left and I don't want you to be working all the time. Anyway, we'd have nowhere to sit. It takes hours for that stuff to dry.'

'I'll do it on my next leave, then.'

'I can do it while you're gone.'

'But it's a man's job.'

'Lots of women are doing men's work now, or hadn't you noticed? I'll have to find myself a job when you're – when I'm on my own.'

'You could go back to the work you did before, in Glasgow.'

'I should probably be doing something more useful than working in an insurance office.' She was rubbing so hard at the buttons that her voice jerked involuntarily. 'A munitions factory, mebbe.'

'But that's heavy work!' he protested, and then jumped as she rose from her chair like a Jack-in-the-box.

'For goodness' sake, Fergus, there's a war on! Someone's got to do the bloody work, and all the men are busy figh—' her voice broke and she spun away from him, dashing the tears angrily from her eyes.

'Cecelia?'

She felt his hands on her arms and pulled away, but he insisted, turning her about to face him.

'Don't, darling, I can't bear to see you like this!'

'Blast and . . . and damn this damned war!' she wailed, clinging to him, her head buried in his chest. 'I don't want you to go away and leave me!'

'I don't want it either, but I'll be court-martialled if I don't. Shot at dawn or something.'

'Don't joke about a thing like that!'

'Sorry. Look, mebbe you should go back to Glasgow,' he said. 'I'm sure your father would like to see you back home.'

'The return of the dutiful daughter, you mean?' She stopped weeping at once, pulling herself back slightly so that she could glare up at him. 'Looking after him and his house, doing as I'm told and making sure that I'm home by ten o'clock every night?'

'It would only be for a little while.'

'Fergus, that's what people said when this war started, and it's gone on longer than anyone thought it would. And what would we do when you came home on leave? We couldn't . . . I couldn't . . .'

'Couldn't what?' he asked, and she punched him in the chest.

'You know very well what. And you know very well that we couldn't; not under my father's roof.'

'But we're married. Husband and wife.'

'Exactly.' Cecelia had forgotten her tears. 'And if I go home I'll stop being a wife and go back to being a daughter. I won't have that!'

'It might be for the best, sweetheart. I'm not happy, leaving you in a town where you don't know anyone.'

'I'll manage fine. I'll not give Father the satisfaction of thinking that I can't cope with being a married woman. Anyway, he's got that lady friend of his now, that Mrs McFadden. I'm sure they won't want me around to spoil things for them. So . . .' she said, letting go of him and returning to her work, 'we'll hear no more about that idea.'

'You're in danger of rubbing those buttons away to nothing.'

'I want you to have the brightest buttons in the regiment.'

'I'm sure the captain will appreciate it. I tell you what, let's go for a walk.'

'It's freezing outside!'

'We can wrap up well, and it'll give us a chance to cuddle without folk staring. Nothing wrong with trying to keep warm. We could go and have a look at those Fountain Gardens across the street. We've scarcely set foot outside the door since we arrived here. That's what happens when a man marries a demanding woman.'

'Fergus!' She put her hands to her face, glancing nervously at the walls as though afraid the neighbours might hear. 'You've been just as demanding as me.'

'I know, isn't it great? I'm so grateful to you for agreeing to marry me now instead of waiting until after the war like your father wanted,' he said, suddenly serious.

'I couldn't have waited a moment longer.'

'I noticed.' He grinned, pulling her up from the unvarnished chair. 'Come on, Mrs Goudie, let's catch a breath of fresh air before it gets too dark.'

When Chloe got home from work that evening her mother was cutting the cooled dumpling into slices.

'Busy day, pet?'

'Busy enough.' Chloe put her coat and hat away.

'D'you think you could give me a hand with this lot?'

The supervisor in Chloe's department insisted on all her staff standing at their counters even when there were few customers, and, young as she was, Chloe's feet and legs were aching. She shifted her weight from one foot to the other as she helped her mother to wrap most of the slices in greaseproof paper.

'There's not much left for us, is there? It doesn't seem fair, since you made it,' she mused wistfully.

'Better a wee bit than none at all, and we wouldn't have any if Mrs Borland hadn't got the ingredients for me.' Julia stacked the little parcels on to a battered tin tray.

'Mum, how can Mrs Borland manage to get things like that? Does she not have the same ration books as the rest of us?'

'She's thrifty, and after raising a big family on not

much money she knows how to make things stretch.'

'Even so—'

'I'll get the tea ready if you'll take the dumpling round,' Julia interrupted briskly. 'We'll eat early tonight because I've a lot to do before the others arrive for the practice. Your dad can have his dinner when he gets home from work.'

'Can Duncan not take the tray round tonight?' Chloe rubbed the calf of one leg with her other foot, and tried to keep the self-pitying whine from her voice.

'With his appetite? Are you daft? He'd have the lot eaten before it reached the first door. Go on now, there's a good lassie. Sooner started, sooner ended.'

With the stairs and landings only dimly lit because of the blackout a stranger would have found it hard to find his way around the tenement, but Chloe had lived there all her life and her feet knew the hollows of every single step. She hesitated outside her own door, working out a plan of action. It was only commonsensical, she thought, to cross the landing first and, balancing one edge of the tray on a raised knee, knock on the door that had once belonged to old Mr Brown, the gardener, and now belonged to Mr and Mrs Fulton. Then the next floor . . . the Borlands and old Mrs Bell; and finally, on the top floor, the new people and the Megsons, who would be saved till the last.

Even as a small child Chloe had made a point of saving the best to the last . . . opening the least interesting parcels first on Christmas morning, eating up all her boiled potatoes and turnip before starting on the fried sausage at dinner time. Now that she was grown, leaving the Megsons to the last on her dumpling round gave her the same pleasure.

After knocking on Mrs Fulton's door she waited for a reasonable length of time before knocking again. This time, her hand had scarcely left the door when it opened and Mrs

Fulton, her face almost ghostly against the darkness of the hall at her back, peered out.

'Yes? Oh, it's you, Chloe.' She frowned slightly and glanced back into the hallway.

'Sorry to bother you, Mrs Fulton.'

'It's all right; it's just that Mr Fulton's having a wee nap. He's going back to his regiment tomorrow morning.'

'Oh. Sorry.' Chloe lowered her voice to a whisper. 'My mother thought you might like a wee bit of dumpling.'

'Is there going to be a band practice tonight, then?'

'Uh-huh, but they'll try to keep the noise down.'

Mrs Fulton gave a wan smile. 'That's all right. I quite like the music they play, and George'll be up by then anyway.' Her fair hair was loose today; normally it was pulled back into a bundle on the nape of her neck, but Chloe had noticed that when Mr Fulton was on leave from the Army Mrs Fulton tended to wear her hair loose so that its natural curls framed her small neat-featured face. It made her look very young, not much older than Chloe's own fifteen years.

'It's not a very big bit because there's the whole tenement to go round, but I'm sure there's enough for Mr Fulton as well,' she volunteered.

'I'm sure there will be, dear. Thank your mother for me,' Mrs Fulton said, and closed the door very quietly.

2

'Lena!'

Lena Fulton, tiptoeing back along the hall, the small, greaseproof paper parcel warm in her hand, stopped in her tracks. Her shoulders drooped as she opened the door of the front room just a crack. 'Did you call, George?'

'Who the blazes was that at the door?'

'Only a neighbour handing something in. I'm sorry you were wakened. Go back to sleep.'

The bedsprings creaked as her husband surged up into a sitting position like a sea creature bursting through the surface from the depths below. 'I'm wakened now. Come over here.'

'I can't, I've left the kettle on and it'll boil dry.'

'Well, if it's on anyway you can make us a cup of tea. I'll be through in a minute.'

Back in the kitchen Lena hurriedly filled the kettle, keeping the flow from the tap low so that he wouldn't hear it and catch her out in the lie, then she lit the gas ring. She had taken advantage of George's afternoon sleep to do some work for a woman further along Glen Street who wanted a pair of curtains converted into a summer coat, and her old sewing machine was opened out on the big kitchen table.

Putting aside the small and fragrant parcel, Lena wiped her hands on a towel before gathering up the material. Once it and the machine had been put aside she began to unwrap the dumpling. The mingled smell of spices and fruit reminded her of happy hours spent during her childhood, helping her own mother to make a clootie dumpling. She could still recall the effort it took for her small hands to force the wooden spoon round in the rich mixture, and still hear her young brother Alfie clamouring impatiently for his turn, his little nose barely reaching the top of the kitchen table, even though he stood on tiptoe. It had been a red letter day for Alfie when he first saw over the table without having to strain every muscle. She remembered the three-penny bits wrapped carefully in greaseproof paper and stirred into the dumpling for special occasions such as Christmases and birthdays.

Tuberculosis had taken her father just before Lena left school, and her mother had died of the same disease fifteen months later. Alfie had been killed in the first months of the war and now there was only Lena left . . . though George didn't like it when she said that she had no family. She had him, didn't she?

'I'm yours,' he was fond of saying. 'And you're all mine, for always.'

He came into the kitchen just then, his hair still tousled from the pillow and his eyes heavy with sleep, snuffling loudly at the air as he entered.

'Dumplin', eh? You folks on Civvy Street know how tae look after yerselves.' He had pulled his trousers on and now, as he came to the other side of the table, he looped his thumbs below the braces to flip them over his shoulders.

'It's from Mrs McCosh across the hall. She'll have got the ingredients from Mrs Borland.'

'Borland? Oh aye, the black market woman up the stair.' He pulled his thumbs free and the braces thudded into place against his broad chest. Lena flinched at the stinging 'thwang' they made.

'George, she's not a—'

'Don't be so stupid, woman, of course she is. How else

does she get the nice wee cuts of meat and all the other
bits and pieces she doles out tae the rest of youse? It's not
by sellin' her body, that's for sure.'

'She knows a lot of folk, and she's well respected
throughout the neighbourhood. I'd not take anything from
her if I thought it was got illegally.'

'Yes you would, and that's an order, my girl.' He broke
off a piece of dumpling and tasted it. 'It's good,' he
commented, and picked off another piece between thumb
and forefinger. 'Now you listen tae me, Lena, you'll take
anything that's offered. You've got tae keep yer strength up
. . . ye're lookin' after my son now, don't forget that.'

Her hand flew to her flat belly. 'George, it might be a
girl, we'll not know for sure till after the summer.'

'It'll be a laddie.' George's voice took on the hectoring
tone that said he was right . . . and that if he was proved
wrong, there could be trouble. 'And you mind and look
after him while I'm away.' He broke off a lump of dumpling
and pushed it at her mouth. 'Eat up, it's good.'

'I thought we could have it for our tea. I could fry it with
what's left of the boiled potatoes.'

'Ach, there's not enough tae feed a sparrow here.' His
fingers pushed painfully against her lips. 'Go on, eat it.'

'I'll have mine la—' she began, and then choked as the
dumpling was forced between her teeth.

'There now; it's good, isn't it?'

Once, visiting Paisley Swimming Baths in Storie Street
with her school pals, Lena had almost drowned. Ever since
then she had had a mortal fear of choking, a fear that came
back as the wad of spicy dumpling almost went down the
wrong way. She doubled up, coughing vigorously.

'For any favour!' In two strides George was round the
table, thumping her hard on the back. 'What's the matter
with ye? Can ye never do anythin' right?'

'S-sorry.' She sucked in a long breath and recovered,
wiping the tears from her eyes.

'So ye should be. Eat it properly now. Good, isn't it?'

It was good. Lena chewed, swallowed, and smiled up at him. 'It's lovely.'

'Aye.' He picked up the last of the slice and popped it into his own mouth, then said, 'So what's the occasion, then? Someone's birthday, is it?'

'The dumpling? No, it's just that Mr and Mrs McCosh are having a band practice tonight. D'you not remember Mrs McCosh making a cake or some scones as a wee thank you to the neighbours for not complaining about the noise?'

'God, they're no' still at that, are they?'

'You used to like it.'

'Aye, but that was before the war, when I lived here all the time. I'm only able tae get home on leave now and again, and I'm off tae God knows where tomorrow,' he protested. 'I don't want that lot wastin' my last night at home.'

'They won't waste it. Their music's quite good.'

He scowled. 'If I'd known what the dumpling was for I'd have taken it back across and rammed it down their throats!'

'Don't make a fuss,' Lena begged. 'We could go to see Aunt Cathy if you want.'

'I suppose so,' he said slowly. Then, brightening, 'We could have our tea there. Use her rations instead of our own.'

'That wouldn't be fair, George . . .'

'Nothin's fair durin' a war, has nob'dy told ye that yet? It's not as if we can go to my parents, is it?'

Lena bit her lip and concentrated on folding the square of greaseproof paper neatly, so that it could be returned to Mrs McCosh. George always spoke as though it was her fault that his parents disapproved of his choice of wife.

'You could go and see them on your own. I'd not mind.'

'But I would.' He went on, emphasising every word as though speaking to an idiot for the umpteenth time, 'It's my last night, isn't it? And I'm damned if we're goin' tae spend it apart.'

'But you've only been to see your parents once during this leave.'

'That's their fault, not mine. Anyway, this nonsense of theirs won't last for much longer, will it?' A grin broke through. 'The old man's fair desperate for a grandson and it's lucky for us that our Neil and that wife of his have only been able to produce three lassies between them. I tell you, Lena, once our boy's here my old man'll be fallin' over himself tae welcome us . . . all three of us. He'll never be away from this door once the bairn comes, you wait and see!'

'Will he not?' Lena asked faintly. Her overbearing in-laws terrified her, and she had been secretly relieved when they told George that if he insisted on marrying beneath his station in life they would refuse to have anything to do with his wife.

'Oh aye, I know the way his mind works. I'll be the one callin' the shots once the wee one arrives.' Her husband's big hand clamped on to her belly, his fingers digging painfully into her hips. 'The bairn you're carryin' in there'll give me the upper hand all right. You wait and see!'

'Aye, whit is it?' Mrs Bell's voice screeched from behind her door as soon as Chloe rattled the knocker. 'Who's there?'

'It's just me, Mrs Bell . . . Chloe McCosh.'

'Who?'

Chloe sighed, and then put her mouth close to the door panel. 'Chloe McCosh!'

'Ye're on the wrong landin'. Mrs McCosh bides doon the stair.'

'I know, Mrs Bell. This is *Chloe!*'

'Who?'

'I've brought a wee bit o' dumpling for you, Mrs Bell.'

'Dumplin', ye say?' It was amazing how much the old woman could hear when she wanted to.

'Aye. My mother made it.'

The letterbox suddenly shot open against Chloe's hip. 'Doon here!' the old woman ordered, and Chloe obediently crouched down to peer into the open slit. Eyes glittered back at her.

'Oh, it's you. Wait a minute.'

There came the sound of a large key turning in a reluctant lock, and then the door creaked open just wide enough to reveal Mrs Bell, small and stooped, dressed as usual in a skirt and jersey beneath a wrap-over apron. All the garments were just a bit too large for her; according to Mrs Borland, Mrs Bell had been a big woman before age shrank her bones and wasted her muscles, and most of the clothes she wore had been bought in earlier, taller days.

'Aye, it is you right enough,' she said now.

'I said it was me, Mrs Bell.'

'Ye never know. Ye might have been one of thae German parashooters.'

'They're not coming, Mrs Bell. My father's in the Home Guard and he'll not let them come.'

'They're like cockroaches,' the old woman shot back at her. 'Gettin' in everywhere when ye least expect them.' Her eyes fastened on the tray. 'Dumplin', ye said?'

'Here.' Chloe balanced the tray on one raised knee so that she could lift a parcel. Mrs Bell's hand, made claw-like by arthritis, shot out to claim her packet.

'I'm partial tae a bit of dumplin',' she said, and began to close the door.

'My mum and dad are having a band practice tonight,' Chloe gabbled to the narrowing gap. 'They'll try not to be a nuisance . . .'

'If they are, I'll soon let them know about it,' Mrs Bell said tartly, and slammed the door.

Chloe, trying to rid her mind of the sudden image of the

old woman scurrying back to her kitchen like a spider scuttling along its web to devour its latest catch, crossed the landing and knocked on the Borland's door.

'Ellen!' a man's voice bawled from within. 'Someone's knockin'!' Then came the heavy tramp of feet before the door opened to reveal Mrs Borland, her head still bound in the scarf she wore for her work in the Anchor Thread Mill.

'It's you, Chloe hen.' Her voice was like the rest of her, big and confident. A mouth-watering smell of broth and liver and bacon and onions wafted out from behind her, and Chloe had to swallow a sudden flood of saliva back before she could speak.

'My mother sent you some dumpling, Mrs Borland.'

'Aw, did she? Is that not kind of her!' Mrs Borland always made it sound as if the dumpling was a surprise gift, when the whole tenement knew that she was the one who supplied most of the ingredients. With rationing biting as tightly as it did, nobody could afford to make a big dumpling without a lot of help.

'Ye'll come in for a minute, pet?' the woman asked as Chloe handed over the largest packet.

'I have to help my mother to get ready for tonight. They're having a band practice . . .' Chloe launched into her usual spiel and Mrs Borland nodded.

'That's nice, hen, me and my Donnie both like a wee bit of music. And our Chrissie's coming for her tea, with a friend. They'll be able tae enjoy it too.'

'Ellen . . .' Mr Borland's deep voice yelled from the kitchen. 'The soup's boilin' over, hen!'

Most women, including Chloe's own mother, would have shouted back, 'Well, turn the gas down then!' But Mrs Borland merely called, in the special soft voice she used for her husband, 'I'm just comin', Donnie pet.' Then, her eyes skimming over the remaining packages on the tray, 'Did ye bring some dumplin' for Mrs Bell?'

'She's got hers.'

'That's good.' Ellen Borland gave a brisk, satisfied nod. 'She needs all the nourishin' food she can get, the old soul. Just a rickle o' skin and bone, she is. I mind her as a big handsome woman when she was my mistress in the mills, hen, and now look at her.' She sighed gustily. 'Old age doesnae come itsel', pet. It brings all sorts of sorrows with it.'

'Yes, Mrs Borland,' Chloe agreed sympathetically, but she knew, as Mrs Borland went off to see to the boiling soup and she herself began to climb the stairs, that Mrs Bell would be getting a plateful of soup and whatever was cooking in the Borlands' kitchen. 'We all need tae look after our own,' was one of Mrs Borland's favourite sayings, and there was no disputing that she lived by it. Those she considered to be her own included the tenants at 42 Glen Street, especially Mrs Bell, who was so well looked after that Chloe couldn't understand why there was so little of her.

There was no reply when she knocked at the new tenants' door, and her heart began to flutter as she crossed the landing and prepared to make her final, very special call.

The Megsons' door looked just like the others, but as far as Chloe was concerned it was entirely different, because *he* lived here. She knocked upon its panels almost reverently, hoping that Dennis himself might answer, but the door opened to reveal Bessie Megson, with her younger sister Amy peering round her arm.

'Is it dumplin'?' Bessie asked eagerly. 'We could smell it when we came up the stair a wee while back.'

'Aye. We're having another band practice. Is your mum in?'

'She's still in her bed because she's been working at the hospital all last night. We're making the tea,' nine-year-old Amy said importantly.

'Is Dennis not at home, then?' Just saying his name made Chloe's heart skip a beat.

'Not yet. We're making scrambled eggs with fried

potatoes. And dumpling to follow.' Bessie seized the
package, held it to her nose, inhaled deeply with her eyes
closed, and then pushed it against her sister's face. 'Smell,
but don't touch,' she ordered. 'We don't want it all mashed
before we get it on to the table. And you'd best put it away
in the press where our Ralph can't see it, else he'll have it
down his throat before the rest of us get a taste . . .'

The door closed on the final sentence. Rejected now that
the dumpling had been delivered, Chloe turned back to the
stairs then hesitated when she heard footsteps coming up
towards her. There were voices too, a man's and a woman's,
and a lot of laughter. Then the couple who had just moved
into the flat next door to the Megsons' rounded the bend at
the landing, and began to come up the final set of stairs.

Cecelia and Fergus had walked all around the Fountain
Gardens, ending up in front of the huge, handsome fountain with its three carved and decorated upper basins from
which, in peacetime, water cascaded down and down and
down to splash, finally, into a large shallow pool occupied
by four life-sized sea lions. A statue close by depicted the
world-famed Ayrshire poet Rabbie Burns, dressed in the
good sturdy clothing of a well-to-do farmer, a broad-
brimmed hat on his head, and with one hand resting lightly
on a ploughshare.

'One of the best Burns statues I've ever seen,' Fergus
remarked, studying the figure. 'And by God, nobody's ever
been able to put words together the way that man could.'

'Shakespeare?' Cecelia ventured, but he shook his head.

'Shakespeare never penned anything like "Ae Fond Kiss".'

When they left the gardens they wandered hand in hand
about the town, walking first to the Cross, where they
strolled past the war memorial then leaned on the stone
balustrade by the handsome Town Hall to gaze down into
the river hurrying through the town on its way to join the
Clyde and eventually spill into the Irish Sea. After that they

walked to the west end of the town and then back again. By the time they returned to Glen Street it was dark and Fergus was getting hungry.

'Hello,' he said as they climbed the stairs and caught sight of the auburn-haired girl hovering uncertainly by their door. 'We've got a visitor, Cecelia.' Then, his eyes on the battered tin tray, 'Selling something, are you?'

The girl's dark eyes met his shyly and then darted beyond his shoulder to Cecelia. 'It's some dumpling. It's for you.'

'Ahh!' Fergus bounded up the last few steps. 'So you're the angel that makes it, are you?'

She flushed. 'It's my mum, not me. You're Mr and Mrs Goudie, aren't you?'

'Fergus and Cecelia.' He stuck out his hand, then laughed as he realised that she was holding the tray with both hands. 'Sorry. Here, give it to me.' He took it with his left hand and waited until she had gained the courage to put her own right hand in his. 'How do you do, Miss . . . ?'

'Chloe McCosh from downstairs. The first floor, above the shops.' Blushing furiously, she retrieved her fingers and snatched the tray back. 'My mum wondered if you'd like a wee bit dumpling for your tea.'

'Like it? You've saved our lives, Chloe McCosh from downstairs. That smell's been driving me crazy, hasn't it, Cecelia? I was getting desperate for a good slice of dumpling, and now here you are, sent from heaven like an angel, bearing gifts.'

Fergus was so good with people, Cecelia thought enviously as the girl giggled. He, who had been born and raised on a Highland croft, could talk to strangers as if he had known them for years, while she, a Glaswegian, hovered in the background trying to think of something to say. It was all topsy-turvy.

'The thing is,' Chloe was hurrying on, 'there's a band practice tonight, in our flat, and mum says that she hopes the noise doesn't bother you.'

'Band practice?' Fergus's eyebrows shot up.

'They've got a dance band . . . my mum and dad . . . and they play at dances and things, so they have to practice. They're quite good,' Chloe added anxiously. 'And they always try to keep the noise down.'

'I don't believe it.' Fergus's voice was suddenly hushed. 'I've found heaven on earth – this lovely new wife . . .' he drew Cecelia close to his side, 'a neighbour who hands out home-made dumpling to all and sundry, and a dance band.'

With his free hand he took the final wrapped bundle from the proffered tray, closing his eyes, just as Bessie and Amy Megson had done, to savour the aroma. 'And to think that I have to rejoin my regiment tomorrow and leave it all behind!'

'You don't mind the music, then?'

'Absolutely not. Are we allowed to dance?'

Chloe giggled again. 'If you want.'

'We want, don't we, darling?' He beamed at Chloe, digging into his pocket for his door key. 'Where did I . . . ah, here it is. Chloe, delightful bearer of delicious treats, can we offer you a cup of tea?'

'I have to get back to help Mum.'

'Well, thank her most kindly from us, and tell her that we're looking forward to the music.' Fergus fitted the key in the lock and the door swung open. 'Although I have to go and help to fight the war, you'll no doubt be seeing a lot of Cecelia.'

'Oh yes. If there's anything you need, or if you get lonely,' Chloe said, 'we're just above Binnie's the drysalter's. This is a nice tenement, very friendly.'

'I'm happy to know that I'm leaving my wife in good hands.' Fergus grinned at her, then ushered Cecelia into the hall and closed the door.

Looking at its panels, Chloe heaved a deep sigh. It was all so romantic . . . such a nice young couple, newlyweds, cruelly separated because he had to go and fight for his king and country. Just like something you might see at the pictures. She couldn't wait to tell her pal Marion about the new folk in the tenement.

Then all thought of the new residents fled from her mind as she heard more footsteps on the stairs . . . only one set this time, a man's boots taking two steps at a time. The fading blush bloomed again as she hurried to look over the railings, and the empty tray almost slipped from her fingers as she saw Dennis Megson breenging up towards her.

3

Dennis stopped short on the half-landing, leaning against the door of the water closet that served the residents on the upper floor. 'Hello, have you been up to play with the lassies?' The question was asked in all innocence, but if she had been closer it might have cost him a bang on the head with the empty tray.

Chloe drew herself up to her full height. 'No I have not!' Did he not realise that she was fifteen, and a working woman now? Did he not know that she was far too old to play with children like Bessie and Amy? 'I've just been taking some dumpling round to everyone,' she said haughtily.

'Oh aye.' His square, fair-skinned face broke into a grin. 'It's band practice tonight. What time does your dad want me there?'

'About the usual time, I suppose. Half-past seven.'

'Great!' He began to mount the final flight and as he came towards her she tried frantically to think of something to say . . . anything that would keep him there for even a moment longer.

Unfortunately, all she could come up with was, 'How was work today?'

'Fine. How was school?'

'For goodness' sake, Dennis Megson, I don't go to school now! I'm fifteen and I work in Cochran's, as you very well know.'

'Oh, sorry, I forgot.'

'Did you have to put out any fires?'

'Not today. Fires don't happen every day.' Dennis had followed his late father into the Fire Brigade.

'I'm glad.'

'So am I. We don't want folk to be hurt, you know, and there's always plenty to do at the station. Fighting fires is just part of the job.'

'Do they scare you? Fires, I mean,' she added as he looked perplexed.

'Oh. I'd not be much of a fire-fighter if I was scared of fighting fires, would I?'

'But they're dangerous.'

'So's crossing the road. See you tonight, then,' he said.

Angry tears filled Chloe's eyes as he vanished into his flat. Why couldn't he realise that she had grown up, that she was no longer a little girl, but a woman? And how was she ever going to have a fairytale life like Mrs Goudie's if the one person she yearned to share it with kept lumping her together with his wee sisters?

Anyway, she had never played with the Megson girls. She had taken Amy out in her pram and she had taught Bessie to play skipping rope, and peevers on chalked beds on the pavement outside the close, but she had always been far too old to play with them!

Dennis Megson's heart was singing as he went into the flat. Dumpling, and then band practice! It was a grand day!

He found both his sisters in the kitchen, the heart of the flat. Bessie was swathed in her mother's wrap-around overall, and being small for her age she had to gather up the hem whenever she moved about the small room to avoid tripping on it. Amy, only an inch smaller than her sister although she was two years younger, had pinned a dish-towel about her own waist for use as an apron.

'Mammy's still sleeping,' she told her brother in a loud whisper.

'Is Ralph not in yet?' Thirteen-year-old Ralph contributed to the meagre family income by working as a message boy for the Co-op branch at Number 4 after school and on Saturdays.

Bessie, carefully slicing cold boiled potatoes while her sister stirred the contents of a jug, pushed a wisp of reddish fair hair back from her forehead then clamped her fists on to her hipbones. 'Can you see him?' she asked irritably. 'If you can't, it means that he's not back.'

'He should be, by now.'

'I'm not bothered, we've got enough to do,' Bessie snapped, tottering against the table as the overall tangled itself round her legs. 'He'll be in when he's hungry.'

Dennis went into the small room he shared with his younger brother, where he knelt down and groped under one of the two narrow beds that took up almost all the floor space. Drawing out a battered case he opened it to reveal the trumpet within, and all thought of Ralph vanished as the instrument seemed to glide from the case and into his hands. Dennis had never had a girlfriend . . . between his music and being the man of the house, he had little time for lassies . . . but the silky coolness of the trumpet against his fingers, the soft yet firm touch of it on his lips, were surely better than any girl.

Mindful of his mother asleep in the room across the tiny hallway, he didn't breathe sound into the instrument; he didn't need to, for it was enough to hold it, closing his eyes and fingering the valves, and imagining the notes pouring into air. Mebbe Mr McCosh would let him play a solo tonight, but then again, mebbe not. He was young yet and there was a lot of learning to do, and plenty of time ahead for solos. For the time being it was enough just to be part of the band.

As he laid the instrument back in its case he heard the front door open. Leaving the case on the bed he hurried to the door then jumped back as it flew open, narrowly missing his face, and his younger brother breezed in.

Ralph gave a yelp of surprise as Dennis's hand clamped on to the lapel of his jacket. 'Here, what d'ye think ye're doin'?'

'It's not me, it's you.' Dennis tossed his brother on to his bed and closed the door quietly, mindful of his mother and the girls. 'Right, you, what have you been up to?'

'None of your business! You're not my dad.'

'No, but I'm the nearest you've got to one. D'you not think that that's just what he would be asking you if he was here right now? So what have you been up to?'

'Playin',' Ralph said sulkily, starting to get up from the bed, then as Dennis pushed him back down, holding him with one hand while the other foraged in his pockets, 'You've no right . . . you stop that!'

'Mum's sleeping, so keep your voice down or I'll shove that pillow in your mouth. What's this?' Dennis withdrew his fingers from his brother's pocket and held up the shilling he had found there.

'It's mine! I earned it!' Ralph made a grab for the silver coin, but Dennis stepped back, holding it out of reach.

'How did you earn it?'

'Some old lady gave it to me when I delivered her messages.'

'A whole shillin'? What did you do . . . put them all away for her and cook her dinner intae the bargain? And why are you home so late?'

'I told you . . . I was out playin'. I met some pals.'

'You've been runnin' for that Mrs Borland again, haven't you? Collectin' payments for her? She's the old woman that gave you this.'

'I have not!' Ralph blustered. 'She did not!'

'You'd better be tellin' me the truth, because if you're lyin' I'll find out. And after I've sorted you out I'll be havin' a word with Mrs Borland.'

'You'd not dare! Give me that . . .' Ralph struggled to his feet and tried to grab the money. Dennis closed his fist about it.

'Would I not? And this is for Mum.'

'It's mine! I earned it!'

'Mebbe the police would like tae know how. It's against the law tae have school bairns collectin' debts.' Dennis wasn't sure of his facts, but he knew how to subdue his cocky younger brother. 'Will I give it to her, or can you be trusted to do it yourself?'

'I'll do it,' Ralph mumbled, sticking his lower lip out.

'I'll be watching,' Dennis said as he relinquished the coin, 'so make sure you do. And no more workin' for that Borland woman, I've already told you.'

It was hard, he thought as he herded his brother out of the bedroom, to be the man of the house. He worried about Ralph, who was more interested in earning money than in being honest. His father wouldn't have tolerated the boy's behaviour, and his mother, if she had any idea that Ralph was working for their upstairs neighbour, would have fretted.

Nan Megson came into the kitchen, still heavy-eyed with sleep, her long fair hair loose about her shoulders. 'Oh, that's lovely,' she said when she saw the table set and the evening meal in progress. 'You're such clever lassies and I've been a lazy mum, lolling in bed and making you do all the work.'

Both girls beamed at the compliment, and Bessie said smugly, 'We can manage fine. It's almost ready and there's dumpling from Mrs McCosh for afters.'

'A band practice? I wish I could be here to listen to it.' Nan began to brush her hair out before the wall mirror. 'You'll be playing, Dennis?'

'If Mr McCosh lets me.'

'I'm sure he will. You're a grand musician.' Laying the hairbrush aside, Nan took an old stocking from her pocket

and fastened it about her head like a coronet. Dennis
watched, fascinated, as she began to twist thick strands of
hair around it. In no time at all the stocking was completely
hidden by a neat, continuous roll of hair and Nan had
reverted to her usual prim everyday self.

He could still remember how, as a little boy, he had loved
to sink his fingers into his mother's thick, clean-smelling
hair, and had been fascinated by the way it framed her face
like shining curtains. She had always been full of laughter
in those days; it was still there in the warmth of her smile,
but since his father's death and the coming of the war there
was more sadness than joy.

His mother, he realised with a shock of surprise, was
getting older. Then he comforted himself with the thought
that he, at least, had known the good days, the early days
when his father was alive and life was good. Not like the
others . . . Ralph had been eight years old and Bessie six
when their father died. At least they remembered him; Amy,
who had just reached her fourth birthday, scarcely recalled
him at all, though she pretended that she did.

Dennis had been the lucky one, and it was up to him to
carry on the responsibility that his father had laid down the
day the walls of a blazing factory had collapsed on top of
him as he followed his fellow fire-fighters to safety.

By the time Frank McCosh arrived home from work his
family had already started on their evening meal. Julia got
up at once to fetch his plate from the oven, where it was
keeping hot.

'We'd have waited for you, but we've not got much time
before the others arrive.'

'Quite right, love . . . and leave it,' he said firmly, putting
an arm about her and easing her back to her seat. 'I'll see
to it myself.'

'But—'

'Do as you're told, woman, and stop behaving as if I'm

your lord and master,' he ordered, cupping her shoulder in his big hand for a moment, smiling over her head at his daughter. 'She's a fusspot, your mother.'

'I'll see to Dad's dinner in a minute, I'm nearly finished here,' Chloe told her mother. From what she had heard from the other girls at school, their parents weren't as lovey-dovey as hers, she thought, and then, scraping up the last of the food from her plate, she corrected herself. Lovey-dovey wasn't the right phrase; they weren't always kissing and cuddling like the men and women she saw at the pictures, but they were both given to brief moments of contact and she had never known them to quarrel . . . which was very unlike what she had heard from the girls at school. Seeing them so happy together made Chloe happy. One day she and some lad . . . perhaps even she and Dennis . . . might be like that together, she thought as her father eased the canvas bag containing his gas mask and dinner tin from his shoulder and then began to unbutton his coat.

'I got held up . . . something that had to be finished before I left.'

'Frank, it's band night. Could someone else not have done it for you just this once?'

'It didn't take long.' He went into the hall to hang his coat in the cupboard that held his Home Guard uniform and rifle, while Chloe wrapped a dishcloth about her hands and drew two plates, one upended over the other to keep the contents as moist as possible, from the oven. She set them on the table and removed the cover, blinking as a waft of heat swept up and around her head.

'It's a cold night out and I'm a lucky man, with a nice warm home to come back to. Eh, lads?' Frank came back into the kitchen to stand between the boys, clapping a hand to the nape of each neck. They squealed and wriggled away from him.

'Your hands are freezing!' Duncan accused.

'And you're nice and warm. By Jove, Julia, that looks

good!' Frank enthused, rubbing his hands together. 'Sausage and onion, eh?'

'I've put some hot water from the kettle into the wee basin, Daddy. You can wash your hands in that.'

'Thanks, pet.'

Julia peered at the plate. 'It's begun to dry up.'

'I don't mind, I quite like it when it gets like that.'

'There's dumpling for after,' Leslie piped up.

'Dumpling too? It's at times like this I'm fair heartbroken for that poor wee Hitler man,' Frank McCosh said over his shoulder as he washed his hands at the sink. 'He's on the wrong side altogether, is he not?'

'Aye, well, if he came to us he'd get no dumpling, that's for sure,' his wife said tartly. 'Now then, boys, you can get washed as soon as you've eaten. You can stay up for some of the practice as long as you go to your beds when you're told, without any arguments. It's school tomorrow.'

'Did you manage to do the band parts?' Frank asked as he picked up his knife and fork.

'Aye, they're all through in the room.'

'Good lass.' The band consisted of Frank on the saxophone, Julia on the piano, Bert, an older man who ran a small hardware shop in the town and was also in the Home Guard, on the drums and Dennis Megson with his trumpet. A considerable pile of sheet music had been amassed over the years, but now, with it being wartime, printed music was hard to find, so Julia had taken on the arduous task of writing out the different parts for each member of the band.

'Is your dinner all right?' she asked anxiously as she watched her husband eat. She had had to augment the sausage and a half with a lot of vegetables.

'It's better than all right. I don't know how you manage on the rations we get. And I have a feeling,' Frank said, grinning at her, 'that it's going to be good band practice too.'

*   *   *

At Fergus's insistence he and Cecelia went out for a breath
of fresh air after they had eaten. As they left the flat a young
man already heading towards the stairs glanced up at them
and grinned. 'Evening,' he said, then, 'Sorry, in a hurry. I'm
late . . .' and he continued his headlong rush, taking the
steps two at a time, what little light there was glinting on
the rounded curves of the trumpet he clutched in one hand.
As the Goudies began to descend the stairs the youth gained
the landing below, catching the banister at the bottom of
the flight with his free hand and swinging round it so that
he gained momentum.

'He must be in this dance band we've heard about,'
Cecelia said, low-voiced, as they crossed the small landing
and prepared to follow him down.

'Must be.' They heard knuckles giving a smart double
rap on a door below. It opened and closed, and then another
door opened. As they left the next floor and turned at the
half-landing with its blacked-out stained-glass window, they
saw that the only people below were a small, fair-haired
woman and a burly young man. The man was glaring at
one of the doors, and muttering under his breath.

'Good evening to you,' Fergus said cheerfully. The
woman glanced up at them and then looked swiftly at her
companion, as though unsure about what to do.

'You're the new people, I suppose,' the man said.

'Fergus and Cecelia Goudie.' Fergus stuck out a hand as
he reached the bottom step. The man gave him a long hard
stare before offering his own large fist.

'George Fulton.' He twitched his head in his companion's direction. 'This is the wife. You're gettin' out before
the ruckus starts too, are you?'

'The band practice, you mean? We're quite looking
forward to it,' Fergus told him breezily. 'Just getting a breath
of air first.'

George Fulton snorted. 'Lookin' forward tae it? You're
welcome, pal. We're stayin' right out of this place until it's

over. It's a fine thing when a man cannae spend a peaceful evenin' in his own home. Come on, Lena,' he added impatiently, and hustled his wife down the stairs ahead of the Goudies.

Following, Cecelia noticed that the girl walked with a slight limp, but even so, her husband hurried her along and by the time Cecelia and Fergus had reached the close opening the other two had disappeared into the night.

'Now that's what I call a friendly neighbour,' Fergus murmured, drawing Cecelia's arm through his. 'A bundle of laughs.'

'She looked quite nice.'

'She probably is, when he gives her the chance to speak for herself. Which way would you like to go?'

'Are you sure you want to go out at all?' She hesitated, gazing into the chill dark night. 'I can't see a thing, and it's awful cold.'

'Your eyes will get used to the darkness,' Fergus slid an arm about her, 'And the blackout's great for kissing in closes.'

'We don't need to kiss in closes now that we're married.'

'We've only been married two weeks, though. Old habits die hard, and anyway, I like to kiss you in closes. It's romantic.'

They took only a short walk, along to Caledonia Street and then along to Greenock Road, which in turn led to the Paisley Racecourse, but it took quite a while because they had to feel about for the kerb each time they crossed a side street, and take care to avoid walking into the baffle walls that had been built in front of most closes to protect them from bomb blast. They were also slowed by Fergus's insistence on stopping frequently for a kiss. Despite her protestations, Cecelia didn't really mind because she was storing up memories to hold on to once he had gone back to his unit and she was alone. And there was truth in what he said about the romance of kissing in a dark close, she thought, tingling to the strength of his mouth on hers and the cool touch of his hands on the warmth of her skin.

'I wish the moon was out,' she said as they passed the Fountain Gardens on the way back home. Walking through such darkness was like wading across a river, with the ankle-turning kerbs like crocodiles lying in wait for the unwary.

'Don't wish that, for we'd be more likely to get enemy planes overhead if there was a moon to guide them. Listen to that,' Fergus added suddenly as the strains of 'Sweet Lorraine' wafted through the darkness. 'It must be the band started on their practice. That means that we're nearly home.' Then, as they reached the close, 'And they're not bad at all.'

Forty-two Glen Street, like its neighbouring tenements, was blacked out with not a chink of light to be seen, but the heavy, dark curtains couldn't muffle the sound of music. It grew louder as they turned in at the close entrance, and as they climbed to the first floor they could almost feel the throb of the drum and the haunting wail of the saxophone.

There was another noise . . . the shuffle and stamp of feet from above, and an occasional feminine giggle underlined by a man's laughter. Gaining the second landing, they saw, in the dim lighting restricted by war regulations, that a couple were dancing there.

Just as Fergus and Cecelia reached the top step the music halted suddenly in mid-flow, and the dancers came to a stop.

'That's the only thing about a practice,' the girl said. 'They keep stoppin'. Oh, hullo, you must be the new folk.'

'The Goudies from upstairs. Fergus and Cecelia.'

'I'm Chrissie and this is Marty. My mam lives in that flat.' The girl, a curvy blonde, nodded towards the well-polished door, letting her eyes flicker to Cecelia for a brief second before they returned to Fergus. 'D'ye like dancin', then?'

'I've got two left feet, but luckily for me Cecelia doesn't

mind. Bye,' he added as the music started up again and
Chrissie and Marty rushed back into each other's arms.
'Enjoy your dance.' Then, as he and Cecelia reached their
own floor, 'That's you met two of the neighbours now.
Mebbe you and Chrissie could be friends.'

'I think she'd prefer to be your friend, not mine.'

'Don't be daft.' Fergus unlocked the door and drew her
into the small hallway, and into his arms. 'You know that
you're the only one I've got time for,' he murmured against
her face. She clung to him.

'I don't want you to go away tomorrow!'

'And I don't want to go either, sweetheart, but it won't
be long now,' he comforted her. 'I'll soon be home for good.'

'Th . . . that's what they said when it all started, and it's
been two years, almost. Two years!' Cecelia wailed. 'And
who knows how much longer it might be? I can't bear it!'

'You can, we both can, because we must. Come on . . .'
He eased himself from her grip and began to unbutton her
coat. 'Let's go dancing.'

'I don't want to go back down where those other people
are.'

He hung up her coat and took his own off. 'You don't
need to, we've got our own dance floor,' he said, and led
her back on to the dim landing as the musicians, who had
halted once again, began to play 'Goodnight Sweetheart'.

They danced silently in the half-dark, holding each other
close, quite unaware of Bessie and Amy Megson, who had
fled from the stairs outside their own door at the sound of
the Goudies' approach and were now in their own hall,
peering at the new tenants from behind the part-opened
door.

As she moved about the dark landing in Fergus's arms
Cecelia wished that they could stay there, alone and safe,
for the rest of their lives.

Two floors below, Frank McCosh nodded to Dennis
Megson and lowered his saxophone as the lad, flushed with

excitement, took a deep breath and moved forward to take over the next chorus.

'Remember, son,' he had said earlier, 'no pressure on the mouthpiece. Gentle, like a kiss, no more than that.'

Duncan and Leslie began to snort suppressed laughter at the word 'kiss', and paid the penalty when their father, reminded of their presence and of the time, immediately halted the rehearsal and ordered them both to their minute bedroom.

Chloe, squeezed into a corner, hugging her knees, felt a pleasant little shiver as Dennis put the instrument to his lips. She drank in every golden note from the trumpet, and, like Cecelia Goudie on the landing above, wished that the evening could go on forever.

4

'Tell you what,' Fergus said, 'once this is over and the ration books have been burned, let's have dumpling every day. You know how to make it, don't you?'

'You're not still on about that dumpling, are you?' Cecelia drew her coat a little closer about her body in an effort to avoid the draught sweeping down the open platform. They were waiting at Gilmour Street Station, not far from Glen Street, for the train that would take Fergus away from her.

'I'm collecting and keeping every single memory of the past two weeks that I can, and last night's band practice is part of it, dumpling and all.'

'You'd get tired of it if we had it every day.'

'Right now I love the thought of getting tired of dumpling. What are you going to do today?' he asked. The words 'when I'm gone' hung in the air, unspoken, between them.

'I'll have to see about getting a job. We can't have able-bodied young women lounging about during wartime.'

'Desk work in a military establishment, mebbe. There's the Fleet Air Arm place out at Abbotsinch.'

'You think I could aspire to something as grand as that?'

'It's the sort of thing you did before.'

'I was a clerkess in an insurance office before. Fergus, isn't that the couple we saw in the tenement last night? There, further along the platform.' She craned to see through

and around the crowd, and caught another glimpse of the
burly man, in army uniform today, and the slight, fair
woman.

'Who cares? Listen, Cecelia, you have office skills and I
don't want you to be pushed into munitions, or into the services. If that happened they could send you anywhere, and
then we'd find it difficult to get together during my leaves.
Get yourself a job before the authorities do it for –' He
stopped, then asked, 'What's the matter?'

'Nothing.'

'Yes there is.' He bent to study her averted face. 'Oh, my
darling, I thought you'd done all your crying last night.'

'I can't help it.'

'Perhaps we should have listened to my parents and your
father, and waited until after the war was finished and done
with before we got married.'

'No!' she snuffled, knuckling back the tears. 'We wanted
to be together!' Then, passionately, 'Together, Fergus, not
you away fighting and me alone here, worrying about you!'

'Look, mebbe it would be best for you to go back to
your father's until I—'

'No! He's got his own life now, and anyway, I'm a grown
married woman and I shouldn't be behaving like this. I'm
Mrs Fergus Goudie, and proud of it.'

'Not half as proud as I am.'

'Want to bet?'

'Oh, Cecelia,' he said, kissing her wet face.

'Fergus, there's other people on the platform!'

'To hell with them,' he said, and kissed her again. She
clung to him, digging her fingers into the roughness of his
khaki greatcoat, and then pulled herself away as the clatter
of the signals told of the train's approach.

'You've got your sandwiches?' She had spread the meat
paste as thickly as she could, in an attempt to make the
dreary sandwiches a little more interesting.

'Yes, ma'am.'

'I hope there's enough of them.'

'They'll be fine, and so will I. There's nothing to worry about, honest. I'll be back before you know it,' he reassured her as the train, already filled with men and women in uniform, roared into the station.

In no time at all Fergus was on board, his final kiss still tingling on her mouth, his last tight hug still warming her. Up and down the platform people were leaning out of the train exchanging goodbyes with those about to be left behind, and then all too soon the guard's whistle shrilled, the green flag fluttered, and the train began to move.

As the back of the guard's van slid past the end of the platform Cecelia felt the fixed smile begin to slip from her face. The warmth of that last embrace vanished and she was suddenly aware of the wind rustling discarded scraps of paper against her feet. She waited until the train had disappeared from sight, then dug her hands deep into her pockets and turned to find that she was the last to leave the platform.

Going down the stairs to street level she saw her fair-haired young neighbour ahead, holding on to the banister and descending carefully, step by step. Cecelia caught up with her easily.

'Hello, I thought I saw you on the platform just now. We met last night,' she added as the girl turned and gave her a blank blue-eyed stare, 'at forty-two Glen Street. We've just recently moved into a flat on the floor above you.'

'Oh . . . yes,' the girl said, and went back to concentrating on the stairs. When they reached street level and walked out into County Square, Cecelia saw that she did indeed have a limp.

'Were you seeing your husband off?'

'Yes.' Cecelia was of average height, but this girl only came up to her shoulder. She was remarkably pretty, with a neat little face and hair like silk.

'Me too. It's a rotten business, isn't it? I'm Cecelia Goudie, by the way.' She thrust out her hand and after a moment a small, work-reddened hand clasped it briefly before being withdrawn.

'Lena Fulton.' Her voice was low and soft.

'Are you going back home? We could walk together.' And have a cup of tea together, and get to know each other, Cecelia thought, her spirits rising slightly. She had never felt so alone in her entire life and she longed to find someone she could call a friend. Lena seemed to be as shy as she herself, and was probably just as lonely now that her man, too, had gone back to the war. But to her great disappointment the other girl shook her head.

'I'm . . . I've got things to do,' she said, and turned away.

Cecelia bit her lip as she watched her only chance of companionship move slowly across the cobbled square and away from her. She wanted to offer to keep the girl company, but it was painfully clear that Lena Fulton wanted to be alone.

She sighed and turned towards Glen Street. She had intended to go straight to the employment office from the station, but instead she decided to wait until later, or perhaps the next day. At that particular moment, she could not face the thought of searching for work.

Trailing into the close, she realised that she was scuffing her feet just as she had done as a child on her way to school. In those days she had wanted to stay home; now, she hated the thought of returning to the empty flat. If only, she thought as she began to mount the stairs, her mother was there to nag at her for ruining her shoes. But her mother had been dead for years and her father besotted by a woman he had met only months before. Adult though she was, Cecelia had mixed feelings about this because it meant that for the first time in her life, her father no longer belonged only to her. In a way it felt as though he was rejecting not only his dead wife but the child they had created together.

'Get out of here!'

Startled, Cecelia stopped halfway up the stairs and then

jerked back against the wall as she saw a witchlike face, old and deeply lined, peering over the banister at her. A hooked nose jutted from the crumpled skin, and above it, two black eyes spat venom. At first it seemed as though the face had no mouth, for the nose and the sharp chin almost met; then they separated and a pink toothless crack appeared amid the mass of wrinkles as the old woman hissed, 'Get out of here, I'm sayin'. I'll no' have your sort comin' intae my hoose. I'll see tae ye!'

'But I live here. I'm—'

'Get oot, I'm tellin' ye!' The woman's voice rose to a screech on the last few words, and an arm as thin as a twig was thrust through the banisters towards Cecilia, who saw to her horror that the knotted fist at the end of the arm was clenched about the handle of a carving knife.

She retreated step by step, too terrified to argue, but clearly she was not moving fast enough, for the old woman began to descend the stairs towards her, the knife sawing viciously through the air.

'Go on with ye! Get oot of here!'

Cecelia almost fell down the last few steps, and had to slap a hand against the wall in order to keep her balance. A wail escaped as she suddenly pictured herself falling and the woman, who looked just like the witch in one of her old storybooks, rushing down the stairs to plunge the knife into her body again and again as she lay helpless on the ground. 'Fergus,' her mind screamed as she ran through the close. Why did he have to go away? Why wasn't he here, to look after her and protect her from witches?

As she erupted from the close entrance, panic-stricken, she ran into something large and soft on its way in. 'Here, here! What's the rush?' a voice boomed at her as she rebounded. 'Is the place on fire or somethin'?'

'It's . . .' Cecelia drew a swift, shaky breath and said to the woman standing before her, 'there's someone on the stairs . . . with a knife. She was going to kill me!'

'What? I'll have none of that in my close! Here, hold these.'

Two message bags were thrust at Cecelia. She took them, sagging at the knees as the weight of them jerked her arms down. As she managed to hoist them up and turned to peer into the close, her rescuer clumped along it and then set foot on the first step.

'What's goin' on up there? Is it you, Jessie?' Her voice floated back to Cecelia. 'Hold on, hen, I'm comin'.'

She disappeared up the stairs, and Cecelia, waiting anxiously on the pavement, heard the faint mutter of voices. After several minutes had passed she rested the bags on the step to rest her aching arms, and wondered what to do. Was her rescuer now in need of help herself? Should she fetch a policeman? She had been brought up to avoid making a scene in public, her mother's greatest fear. Calling for help or, even worse, for the police, was something she had never done before and never wanted to do.

She looked up and down the street, and was just beginning to wonder if she should go into one of the shops on the ground floor in search of assistance when she heard footsteps clumping back downstairs.

'See's my bags, then.' The woman took them from Cecelia then asked, looming over her from the single step that led up from the pavement to the close, 'And who are you?'

'Cec . . . Mrs Goudie. I live on the second floor.'

'Oh, ye're the new tenant, are ye? Why didn't ye say? Come on in, lassie, it's too cold tae be standin' on the step and I need tae sit down. I've been workin' all night.'

Cecelia hesitated. 'What about . . .?'

'Ach, don't fret about her. That's only Jessie Bell . . . Mrs Bell tae you. A harmless wee soul.'

'But she had a knife!'

'Ye didnae think she'd use it on ye, surely? Jessie wouldnae harm a fly. She thought ye were from the council, come tae take her intae the workhouse.'

'The workhouse?' Cecelia began to wonder if she had stumbled into some mad Alice-in-Wonderland fantasy.

'Aye, that's what I said.' The voice was suddenly sharp. 'In Jessie's younger days all the old folks with nob'dy tae look out for them were put intae the workhouse. Not that I'd ever let that happen tae her, as well she knows, but even so, strangers about the tenement make her nervous, poor old soul. For goodness' sake, will ye come on in afore the two of us turn tae ice right here on the step. I'm Mrs Borland, by the way,' she added over her shoulder as Cecelia followed her along the close. 'Mrs Ellen Borland that lives on the middle floor.'

'Cecelia Goudie.'

'That's a right fancy name.' Mrs Borland began to mount the stairs. 'Dae they cry ye Cissie for short?'

'My mother wouldn't let anyone call me that.'

'Would she no'? Well then, Cecelia, tae let ye understand, when I started work in the Anchor Mills I was just a wee skelf of a lassie scared tae say boo tae a goose. In these days Jessie was my mistress.'

'Mistress?' Cecelia asked the huge swaying backside going up the stairs before her.

'In the mills the women supervisors are cried mistresses. Anyway, Jessie was awful good tae me, so now that she's on her own I do the same for her. Ye have tae look after yer own, hen, 'specially in wartime.'

The old woman was waiting for them on the second floor.

'Is this her?' The malevolence had left her voice; now it was merely frail and creaky.

'Aye, this is the new tenant, Jessie. Mrs Cecelia Goudie from up the stair. Mrs Jessie Bell,' Ellen Borland introduced them primly, as though they were in a drawing room.

'Ye should have said who ye was,' the woman accused.

'Aye well, I'm sayin' now, for her.'

'How do you do?' Cecelia held out her hand, then drew it back as Mrs Bell, about half her height and bundled up in woollen jerseys and skirts, topped by a faded wrap-over apron, stared up at her and repeated, 'Ye should have said. How am I supposed tae know who bides here and who doesnae when they don't say?'

'Ye'll know her the next time, eh, Jessie? Come on, hen,' Ellen Borland said as Cecelia prepared to go on up to her own flat, 'come in and have a cup of tea.'

'I'd not want to take up your time . . .'

'I've got all the time in the world, hen. We'll get tae know each other, and ye can meet my Donnie. Come on,' Mrs Borland insisted, unlocking her door and sweeping inside with Mrs Bell scuttling in her wake like a dinghy bobbing behind a yacht in full sail. There was something in her voice that made Cecelia obey without further objection.

Her mouth dropped open as she entered the kitchen. She had expected the Borlands' home to be an ordinary tenement flat like her own, but instead she found herself in the most comfortable and richly furnished room she had ever seen. The chairs and sofa were deep and luxurious, and instead of being covered by the chenille cloth used in most houses, the highly polished table had a lacy runner pinned down by a beautiful china vase filled with artificial flowers. The rugs, soft underfoot, looked and felt expensive, and the shelves of the large and handsome dresser against one wall were crammed with decorative plates and ornaments. More ornaments filled a beautiful little corner display cabinet and stood cheek by jowl with a cluster of photographs in elaborate frames along the mantelshelf.

A canary chirruped a welcome from an elaborate cage on its own stand, and Mrs Borland made kissing sounds at it as she laid down her bags.

'Hello there, wee Tommy,' she crooned and then, turning to the man who was sprawled out on the sofa, 'Donnie, pet, this is Mrs Goudie, the new lassie from up the stair. She's come in for a cup of tea. This,' she added proudly, her voice suddenly softening and her eyes taking on the glow of a young girl in love, 'is my man, Donnie.'

'I could fair do with a cup myself, hen. I've been right parched, waitin' for ye tae come home.' Donnie Borland nodded at Cecelia. 'Hello, pet, sit yerself down.'

'Aye, sit down while I get my coat off. Jessie, mebbe you could put the kettle on for us.' Mrs Borland disappeared into the hall, reappearing for a moment to add, 'the nice china, Jessie, since we've got a visitor.'

'Not there,' Mrs Bell rapped as Cecelia made a tentative move towards an armchair. 'That's where I sit . . . and that's hers,' she added swiftly as Cecelia glanced at the other armchair. Meekly, she turned one of the upright chairs by the table and perched on its edge as her hostess returned, her coat off to reveal that she, like Mrs Bell, was wearing one of the all-covering aprons beloved of most working women. Her headscarf remained in place.

While the old woman, moving about with the ease of one who knew the flat well, filled the kettle, set it on the gas stove to boil, and began to set out fluted china cups and saucers, Mrs Borland lowered herself into one of the armchairs and removed her shoes, sticking her varicosed legs out in front of her and wriggling her toes.

'That's better. See standing at those machines all night? My feet were killin' me by the time I got off this mornin'.' She bent forward to give her feet a good rub. 'And then there was the shoppin' tae see tae before I could get home. There's chocolate biscuits in my bag there, Jessie, just put them out and all. I wouldnae mind a wee taste of chocolate,' she went on, fumbling beneath the chair and producing a pair of slippers, which she slipped on before relaxing back in the chair with a huge sigh of relief. 'Oh, that's better!'

'Ye're late, pet. I was beginnin' tae wonder where ye'd got tae.'

'Did ye miss me then, Donnie?' Ellen Borland asked

archly. It was amazing, Cecelia thought as she watched the woman lean over to touch her husband's hand, how she seemed to revert back to her love-struck youth every time she looked at him or spoke to him. She wondered if she would still be like that with Fergus when their middle years arrived. If this beastly war allowed them to grow older together, she suddenly remembered, a lump coming into her throat.

'Of course I missed ye,' Donnie Borland was saying. 'And I missed the wee *Express* tae. Did ye mind tae get it for me?'

'Of course I did, same as I do every day. And your cigarettes an' all. Here . . .' His wife eased herself forward in her chair so that she could reach into one of the shopping bags. 'That Jocky Beaton wanted away smart this mornin',' she said as she handed over the paper and the cigarettes, 'so I stayed behind tae finish off the job for him.'

'You're too good tae those men.'

'Ach, I don't mind. And it's worth it,' she added, then, to Cecelia, 'Donnie's got a bad back. He got hurtit at the shipyard and he's no' been able tae work since, the poor soul. No' even a decent bit of compensation, so we've just had tae struggle on as best we could.'

'You've managed to get the place very nice.' Cecelia waved a hand at the luxury all around them.

'Ellen's a great wee housewife,' Donnie Borland said proudly. 'And a great worker. She's always stayin' behind at the mill tae finish the men's work so's they can get off havin' tae work late.'

'Aye well, when ye have tae start wi' nothin' ye learn the hard way,' his wife chimed in. 'And ye learn tae work for what ye get, tae. Thanks, hen,' she added as Mrs Bell, clearly very much at home in this flat, brought her a cup of tea, then handed one to Donnie. 'Has Donnie's tea got two sugars in it?'

'Aye, and it's been stirred.'

'I'll have a couple of thae biscuits,' Mr Borland said, and they were brought to him on a plate.

Donnie Borland had once been a very handsome man; and as often happens with men, he still retained most of his good looks although his thick hair was now mostly grey, his square-jawed face slackening into lines and folds, and a paunch pushing the waistband of his trousers down almost to his hips. He was unshaven, and wearing an open-necked, collarless shirt, grey trousers and warm carpet slippers.

Cecelia got her tea last, and then the plate of chocolate biscuits went past so quickly that she only just managed to claim one. Mrs Bell glared at her as she put the plate back on the table and went to 'her' armchair.

5

'Now then, hen, you'll want tae know all about the tenement,' Mrs Borland began. 'On this floor it's me and Donnie
and Jessie. Our bairns have all grown up and married now.
We've got seven wee grandweans tae.' She pointed proudly
at a large photograph on the mantelshelf. It showed a small
girl in a white dress, with a white lace veil drifting about
her head. 'That's our Anne-Marie at her confirmation. She's
the oldest grandwean.'

Cecelia looked at the picture. 'She looks lovely,' she said
dutifully and then, to the old woman, 'Do you have grandchildren, Mrs Bell?'

The old woman had been licking the chocolate from her
biscuit as though it was a lollipop. Now she stared and said,
'Grandweans? Me?' and then she and Ellen Borland looked
at each other and broke into cackles of amusement. 'Me?'
the old woman said again. 'Cheeky bizzum!'

'Jessie was never married, hen,' Ellen Borland explained.
'In the mills, the mistresses were all called missus as a mark
of respect.'

'Oh, I see. I'm sorry.'

'I'm no', hen.' Jessie Bell wiped tears of mirth from
her eyes. 'I'd plenty offers, mind, but I never found a man
worth havin',' she said, and went back to licking the
biscuit.

Embarrassed, Cecelia returned her attention to the photographs, her eye lighting on a wedding photograph. The bride looked vaguely familiar. 'Is that your daughter?'

'Aye, that's Chrissie, the youngest.'

'We met her last night, dancing on the landing with her husband during the band rehearsal.'

'Her man's in the Navy, hen, that was just a friend she brought here for his tea. Chrissie's in munitions, workin' for Beardmore's, and in her spare time she works at a canteen for the poor young lads far away from their own folk because of this war. She's awful good tae them. Have ye met yer neighbours yet . . . the Megsons?'

'I've seen a young man on the stairs, and two wee girls, but I've not met their parents.'

'You'll no' meet him because he was killed in the line of duty years ago. He was a fireman. Now Mrs Megson's a widow, poor soul. She nurses at the Alexandra Infirmary, and her oldest lad's followed his father intae the Fire Service. There's another lad, Ralph, and two wee lassies, all still at the school. Nice, well-brought up family they are. On the first floor, above the shops, there's the McCosh family. He's not been called up because he does war work for the India Tyre Company. He's in the Home Guard and him and his wife's awful musical. The two of them run a wee dance band.'

'I heard them practising last night.'

'They've got two laddies still at school and a lassie workin' in Cochran's across from the Paisley Abbey. Mrs Fulton lives on the same landing as them. She's a quiet wee soul but very good with a needle if you need anythin' done. That's how she earns her keep while her man's in the army. I put some work her way because it's only right tae help yer own neighbours, d'ye not think so?'

'Yes, indeed.'

'You can use the drying green on Wednesdays, that's Mrs Fulton's day but with her being on her own she hasnae much washin' tae hang out. The same'll go for you, and

there's enough line for the two of you. And Friday's the
day for beatin' the carpets, so nob'dy puts out a washin' on
a Friday. You're no' from Paisley yersel', hen . . . ?'

Jessie Bell's long grey tongue took a final lick at the
biscuit and then, examining it closely and deciding that
there was no chocolate left, she dipped it into her tea before
sucking noisily at it. Cecelia was so mesmerised by the
procedure that before she knew it she had furnished Mrs
Borland with almost every detail about herself and Fergus.

The woman gave a satisfied nod. 'You'll fit in all right.
Now, what are you goin' tae do with yersel', hen?'

'I'll need to start looking for work tomorrow.'

'There's plenty tae be had but ye'd be best tae find the
right thing for yersel'. If ye don't, they'll decide for ye.'
Mrs Borland considered Cecelia with her head on one side
and her eyes narrowed. 'What did ye work at before?'

'Office work.'

'Ten a penny, hen, and anyway, it doesnae count. They
mostly use lassies straight from the school in offices these
days, and older women that won't be called up. Munitions
wouldnae suit you; too hard. And the same goes for the
mills. Can ye do sums?'

'I worked with money in my last job.'

'If I gave ye a shillin' tae pay for some things that cost
a sixpence halfpenny and a threepenny bit, what would you
give me back?'

'Twopence halfpenny.'

'Ye're probably right, hen. Ye should go on the buses.'

'Go where on the buses?' Cecelia asked, confused.

'Tae the terminus and back again, where else? Bein' a
clippie counts as war work.'

'Oh, I don't think I could . . .' The very idea of working
with the public and being at their beck and call terrified
Cecelia.

'Of course ye could. Ye can handle the money side of it
and ye look presentable. Donnie, where's yesterday's paper?'

With some difficulty Mr Borland heaved his body about so that he could scrabble down the side of the sofa. Eventually, after a lot of huffing and puffing, he hauled out a crumpled newspaper. 'Here,' he said and his wife ferreted busily through the pages.

'There, I thought so. Glasgow Corporation's lookin' for clippies. What age are ye, hen?'

'Twenty-one . . . and four months.'

'That's all right then, ye have tae be twenty-one tae work for them. Go on now,' Mrs Borland said above Cecelia's protests, 'you take the paper and write in tae them.'

There was something about Mrs Borland that made argument difficult, perhaps even unwise, Cecelia thought as she left the flat, the newspaper in one hand and the other clutching a small bag containing two pork link sausages.

'For yer tea,' Mrs Borland had said as she handed them over.

'But I can't take your rations!'

'Ach, we've got plenty. Go on now, they'll cheer ye up, after yer man goin' back tae the fightin'. And ye'll need tae keep yer strength up if ye're goin' tae be a clippie,' Mrs Borland had added before closing the door on her visitor.

The sausages were delicious, but even as she ate them, savouring every mouthful, Cecelia was determined that whatever her forceful neighbour said, she was going to find work for herself. She was not going to become a bus conductress just to please a woman she scarcely knew.

The bottle-green uniform issued to its bus and tram staff by Glasgow Corporation Transport was surprisingly smart, and fitted surprisingly well. Cecelia was amazed at how right it felt when she donned it.

She had sailed through the interview in the offices at Bath Street in Glasgow, then through the medical inspection. Even the test, strongly reminiscent of school exams, was quite easy, at least as far as the arithmetic section went. The worst question on the paper before her had been, 'What do you think are the four most important duties of a conductress?'

Panic mounted as she chewed at the end of her pen. Honesty? Sobriety? A love of travel?

A shadow fell across the paper on the desk before her and a voice whispered, so faintly that she wondered if she had imagined it, 'Efficiency.' Startled, she looked up at the overseer, who was slowly pacing along between the rows of desks. Their eyes met briefly, and he gave an imperceptible nod before moving on.

'Efficiency,' she wrote, and noticed that at each desk, as he passed, a head was raised sharply and then lowered as the applicant began to scribble busily.

On his next round he breathed out the word, 'Safety,' and next came 'Caution and courtesy.'

The four most important duties were further impressed on them the next day, when those chosen, including Cecelia, were required to attend a practice in a hall. Rows of seats had been laid out and the trainees spent half the day learning how to deal with passengers, how to give the right change and how to fill in their reports, known as waybills, at the end of the day, giving details of the different prices of tickets issued. They also learned how to cash in at the end of a shift and about the importance of memorising the different stages throughout a journey, and the need to alter the fare at each stage. They were also issued with a book of rules, which they were expected to know by heart.

Then, finally, the uniforms were issued, and suddenly Cecelia began to feel that being a clippie might, after all, be the right job for her; though her first run on a real bus was nerve-wracking. She was given into the care of an elderly woman called Anna, who inspected her from head to toe, said grudgingly, 'Aye, you'll do,' and showed her how to put on her money bag.

'There's three compartments, see? One for coppers, one for silver, one for notes. Not that ye'll get many of them, unless it's from the servicemen and women. They get a good pay. Ye'll see yer tickets all fixed intae that bar at the front of the bag . . . they're very important, the tickets. They're in the right order, from the halfpenny ones up, and ye mustn't get them mixed up because at the end of the shift ye'll be expected tae account for every one of them. And if ye're short with the money ye'll have tae make it up out of yer wages. You know how tae stamp the tickets?'

'Yes.'

'And mind tae give them out tae everyone. There's some that would slip off the bus without payin' if they got the chance, and ye never know when an inspector's goin' tae come aboard tae make sure ye're doing the job right. Come on then, time we were off.'

Cecelia watched, her mouth dry with nerves, while Anna took up her position directly behind their bus and guided the driver out of the depot. Then they both climbed on board and Anna pressed the bell.

'One bell means stop, two bells mean go,' she said briskly as the bus moved out on to the street. 'Three means the bus is full so yer driver cannae stop tae take on any more folk, and four bells means there's an emergency and the driver has tae stop quick tae help ye. Ye have tae remember that the driver cannae see what's goin' on behind his back, so he depends on the conductress and the bells tae let him know what tae dae.'

'Do you get many emergencies?'

'It's been known,' Anna said enigmatically. 'And ye don't sit down while ye're on duty, it's not allowed.' Then, plumping herself down on the seat by the door, 'Right then, here's the first stop comin' up, and there's folk waitin' tae get on. So ye'd better bell the driver. And get goin' with the tickets right away,' she added as a handful of people clambered

aboard and chose their seats, 'or ye'll fall behind and get
intae trouble if an inspector comes aboard.'

'I thought I was going to watch you first,' Cecelia faltered.

'Doin's a better way of learnin' than watchin',' Anna
informed her. 'You leave the watchin' tae me. And it might
be an idea tae give Harry two bells tae let him get started,
otherwise we'll be sittin' at this stop all day.'

It was a baptism of fire, especially as the bus began to
fill up, keeping Cecelia busy on the lower deck as well as
running up and down the stairs to the upper deck. Anna sat
where she was, like a Buddha in uniform, saying nothing
but giving the occasional grudging nod of approval, or,
sometimes, curling her lip in a sneer when Cecelia did
something wrong.

'How's it goin', hen?' the driver asked when they reached
their terminus and had twenty minutes to themselves before
starting back on the return run.

'All right, I think,' Cecelia ventured, and he gave her an
encouraging smile.

'Ach, ye'll be fine. At least ye've got the best driver on
the force, and the best teacher. Eh, Anna?'

'Stop yer nonsense, Harry Dobbs,' she said sourly, and he
winked at Cecelia. He was middle-aged, as were most of the
drivers now that the younger men were being called up, and
his calm friendliness cheered Cecelia. The worst was over;
she had done her first run and nothing drastic had happened.
Perhaps her new job was going to work out after all.

She started the next run with more confidence. The
passengers, swiftly realising that she was new to the job,
tended to be kind, waiting patiently while she found and
stamped the right tickets and then sorted out their change.
On the final run of the shift the bus was very busy; Cecelia,
having taken all the fares on the upper deck while keeping
an anxious eye on the mirror that showed when passengers
on the lower deck wanted to dismount, scurried downstairs
to pick up the few fares that had just got on.

A heftily built man who had been taking up the best part of a double seat at the furthest end from the door got up while she was stamping a ticket halfway down the bus and he stood behind her, waiting patiently for the chance to get past. It took her some time to sort out the change, and she could feel his impatience mounting until finally he said, 'Gonnae let us by, hen? My stop's just comin' up.'

Cecelia belled the driver to stop and then turned, pressing herself back against the seats in order to give the man as much space as possible, but he was so large that he really needed the entire passageway and more. Cecelia squeezed herself back even further, until she was almost sitting on the knee of the woman who had just paid her fare.

'Excuse me,' she said breathlessly.

'It's all right, pet,' came the reply, just as the man, squeezing by like a reluctant cork coming out of a bottle, got tangled with the leather money bag as he went. Cecelia felt the strap bite into her back and shoulder as the bag was dragged across her stomach in his wake, and then disaster struck as the bar holding the tickets unclipped and fell, showering small pieces of pasteboard in all directions.

'Oh no!' Cecelia wailed. 'Oh, my tickets! Look at them!'

'Awful sorry, hen,' she heard the man say above her head as she dropped to her knees on the floor, 'I'd give ye a hand, but I have tae get off here.'

'My tickets!' She snatched them up from beneath the seats as the bus halted at the stop. It was fortunate that nobody got on at that stop, because almost at once, most of the passengers on the lower deck were crawling about the passageway or standing up to peer under seats.

'There's one there, hen . . . hey, missus, there's one below your seat there, no, over a bit, aye, that's it.' Meanwhile, the driver, belled by Anna, continued on his way.

'Ye'll have tae sort them all out before ye can hand yer bag in,' the woman said sourly when Cecelia finally joined her on the platform, stuffing handfuls of tickets into her pockets. 'And look at yer skirt, the hem's comin' down.'

'Oh . . . !' Cecelia looked down at the dip in the line of her neat uniform skirt. 'Someone stepped on it just when I was trying to get up.'

'Lucky yer stockin's werenae torn and all. It's not easy gettin' new stockin's these days. Aw, come on, sit down,' Anna said gruffly, realising that her trainee was close to tears. 'I'll take the bus while you sort out yer tickets. And cheer up, there's worse things happen on a wet Saturday!'

The hem, Cecelia discovered when she finally got home, required quite a bit of sewing. She stared at it, chewing her lower lip. Needlework had never been her best subject at school, and she couldn't afford to make a mess of this job because the uniform belonged to Glasgow Corporation.

'Mrs Fulton's a quiet wee soul,' Mrs Borland had said, 'but very good with a needle if you need anythin' done.'

Lena Fulton's door opened just wide enough to let one blue eye peer through the crack. When Cecelia explained her business, the door opened further and Lena stepped back. 'You'd better come in.' Then, as Cecelia went past her into the hall, 'Go on into the kitchen.'

The kitchen table was covered with material, and a middle-aged woman was stitching busily. 'My auntie,' Lena said from behind Cecelia. 'Mrs Blacklock. Auntie Cathy, this is the new neighbour, Mrs . . .'

'Goudie. Cecelia.'

The woman nodded. 'How d'ye do?' she said briskly and then, putting the work down and getting to her feet, 'I'll be on my way then, Lena.'

'Please don't leave on my account. I just wondered if Mrs Fulton could put up this hem for me.'

'I was going anyway. I was just giving her a bit of a hand and a bit of company, but now you're here . . .' Mrs Blacklock peered at the skirt in Cecelia's hand. 'A uniform, eh?'

'I've just started work as a bus conductress,' Cecelia confessed with a mixture of shyness and pride.

'Now there's a job you could have done, Lena, if it hadn't been for your limp. Infantile paralysis,' Lena's aunt told the visitor as she buttoned her coat. 'When she was seven years old. We thought we were going to lose her, but devoted nursing pulled her through. Left her with a bad leg, though, so she can't do much. It's fortunate she's so good with a needle.' She picked up a message bag. 'I'll look in next week, Lena . . . and mind you eat well, you owe it to George to look after that bairn of his.'

When Lena came back after showing her aunt out there was an awkward silence between the two young women for a moment; then Cecelia thrust the skirt forward.

'I dropped my tickets on the bus and while I was kneeling down to get them someone stepped on the hem of my skirt. The stitching's come out and I think there's a wee bit of a tear.'

'Let me see.' Lena took the skirt and examined it closely, one hand reaching up to push back a lock of fair curly hair that had come loose and fallen over her face. She really was very pretty, Cecelia thought enviously. Her own fair hair was straight, and her eyes were an uninteresting grey. If Lena Fulton had more confidence in herself, she would be quite stunning.

She glanced about the kitchen, which was as plain and serviceable as her own. A wartime kitchen, she thought, then eyed the large wedding portrait in the very middle of the mantelshelf. Lena, in a plain dress and a small hat with a veil, clutched a posy of flowers. Her smile was hesitant, as though she was not sure that she had done the right thing, and one hand was looped through the arm of the tall, broad man Cecelia had seen on the night before Fergus returned to his regiment. George Fulton stared smugly into the camera lens with such an air of satisfaction that for an instant Cecelia felt as though Lena should have been on the ground with his foot planted on her back and a hunter's rifle in his other hand.

'I can sew this up, and mend the tear,' Lena said just then. 'D'you want to come back for it in an hour?'

'That would be grand. How much?'

'Oh . . . ninepence.'

'Are you sure that's enough?' Cecelia asked doubtfully, then, as the other girl ducked her head in a swift nod, 'Mrs Borland said that you did sewing for folk. It looks as if you're busy.'

'It's other folk that are busy these days, so they're pleased to find someone willing to take on some sewing for them.'

'That's pretty.' Cecelia fingered the patterned material on the table.

'It's for Mrs Borland's daughter.'

'She's lucky, finding such nice material when there's a war on.'

'Mrs Borland knows where to find things.'

Cecelia hesitated, then said, 'Your aunt said you're having a baby?'

'Not for months yet.'

'That's nice. You must be excited about it.'

'Yes,' Lena said flatly, moving to the door. 'You'll be back in an hour, then?'

When Cecelia Goudie had gone, Lena returned to the kitchen and pushed the pretty flowered material aside, then laid the green skirt on the table and began to hunt through her sewing box for thread of the right colour. Thread was as hard to get now as nice material, but Mrs Borland kept her supplied, in return for the sewing jobs she did for her and her family.

As she threaded a needle and settled down to repair the skirt she recalled the fleeting envy in the other girl's face as she said, 'You must be excited . . .'

Lena paused and looked down at her stomach, still not

rounded enough to be noticeable. 'You mind and look after that laddie of mine, ye hear me?' George had said, just before the end of his leave, his big hand clamped on her belly and his thick fingers biting into her flesh. 'You're in charge till I'm able tae come back and see tae him myself.'

She put her own hand on her stomach at the memory, but gently, not in the possessive way George had done it. During their courtship and marriage he had talked a lot about his parents and had painted a picture of his father as an obstinate, stubborn bully who dominated his entire family. She had seen at first hand the results of such an upbringing, and knew with a sick certainty that her child, if it were a boy, would almost certainly be forced into the same mould.

She hoped that it might be a girl . . . then began to wonder what George's reaction might be if he was deprived of the son he longed for. He might ignore a daughter, or he might insist on disciplining her as he would have disciplined a boy. Or, even worse, he might punish her for being born a girl.

It would have been better, Lena thought miserably as her deft fingers repaired the hem of the green skirt, if the child nestling comfortably and confidently in her womb had never been conceived.

6

———— ◆ ————

Chloe begged, pleaded, promised willing slavery for the rest of her life, sulked, and finally managed to coax her parents into agreeing that she could go to the dance they were playing at, in the Templar Halls.

'It means that I'll have to find someone else to stay with the boys,' her mother pointed out reproachfully.

'Mrs Norris in the next close said she would come in,' Chloe said at once.

'You've asked her already? Chloe . . .' Julia began, and then stopped as Frank laid a hand on hers.

'Since Chloe's asked and Mrs Norris has agreed, we'll leave it at that. But just for this once,' he added. 'You're not to do that again without your mother's permission, Chloe. You hear me?'

'Yes, Daddy, I promise. So I can tell Marion that I'll be able to go with her to the dance?'

'You can.' Frank avoided Julia's accusing gaze as Chloe threw her arms about his neck and kissed him.

'You spoil that girl,' Julia said that night when Chloe and the boys had gone to bed. 'She had no right to make arrangements with Betty Norris behind my back.'

'Ach, it's just this once. I'll not let her get away with it a second time. She's a good lassie, Chloe; she never complains about seeing to the boys when we're out playing anywhere.'

'And why should she?' Julia, who was drying the dishes, put the last cup into the cupboard by the sink, and shook out the dishcloth. 'Older children are always expected to look after the wee ones.'

'But she's not much more than a child herself.'

'She's earning a wage, and where are your eyes, Frank McCosh?' Julia turned to face him, resting her hands on the edge of the sink. 'Do you not see why she's so desperate to go to that dance? It's not to hear you, or me; it's so as she can be near young Dennis Megson. The lassie's daft about him.'

'Our Chloe?' He was stunned. 'But . . . what makes you think that?' he asked, suddenly gripped with the jealousy that most fathers feel when they discover that their daughters, so dear to them, have set their sights on another man.

'For goodness' sake, Frank!' Her lovely green eyes widened in mock despair. 'When we play, I'm at the piano with my back to the room, and you're standing right there facing her, and you've not noticed the way she never takes her eyes off him? The way she tingles every time he moves, let alone plays that trumpet of his? The way she feels about him is so strong that I can feel it in the air, even when I'm not looking at her.'

'Ach, you're havering, woman!' Frank returned to reading his newspaper, rustling it loudly.

'Maybe I am and maybe I'm not. Time will tell.'

'She's too young!'

'She'll be sixteen on her next birthday, old enough to get married if she wants to. So mebbe it's time to let her go to a dance. We can't hold on to her childhood, Frank, it wouldn't be fair.'

'D'you think young Dennis feels the same way about her?' Frank asked after a thoughtful pause.

'Him? He's too caught up in his music and being a fireman and trying to take his poor father's place as the man of the house. He scarcely notices our Chloe at all.'

'And her the prettiest lassie in the whole street? He's got a cheek . . .' Frank said hotly, and she started to laugh, a warm, genuine laugh that seemed to come from the tips of her toes and travel the length of her tall, almost boyish figure. He loved it when she laughed like that . . . it stripped the years from her, and reminded him of the day he had first set eyes on her.

'For any favour, man,' she said on the last breath of the laugh, 'will you stop your nonsense? Whether Dennis Megson notices our Chloe or not, it's none of our business. That's something they'll have to sort out for themselves, if they ever get that far. It's the way of the world. Though mind you, he's a nice lad and she could do a lot worse for herself.'

'Mebbe so, but . . . well, I suppose Chloe's special to me.'

'You shouldn't have favourites. Just because she's the only girl . . .'

'It's not that at all. It's because she brought us together, Julia, and I'll always have a special love for her because she happened.'

'Now don't put that sort of responsibility on her, Frank. Bairns don't ask to be born.'

'I'm glad this one was, though. Awful glad,' Frank said huskily. The newspaper he was reading fell from his hands, and he got up and went to stand behind Julia, who was mopping the draining board.

'Frank McCosh!' she protested as he slid his arms about her waist. 'What d'you think you're doing?'

'Holding the only woman I ever wanted to hold,' he said into the soft skin just below her ear. 'Come to bed.'

'I've got things to do yet.'

'They can wait.' He turned her about and kissed her, a long hard kiss.

'Remember that we're the parents of three growing bairns,' Julia protested faintly when he finally let her catch her breath.

'I do remember, and if they grow up to be half as happy as I am with you, lass, they'll do fine. Now,' he said firmly, 'stop your arguing, woman, and come to bed!'

Because most of the younger men had been called up, many of the couples stepping round the Temperance Halls dance floor to the tune of 'I've Got The World on a String,' were women, dancing with each other.

'We could do that, just to start with,' Marion said eagerly, her feet and shoulders twitching to the beat of the music.

'I'm not dancing with you!' Chloe cast a glance at the stage. What if Dennis was to look down and see her dancing with her pal? He'd think she couldn't get a lad of her own!

'Just to start with,' Marion begged. 'Come on, Chloe, what's the sense of coming to a dance if we just sit like a couple of wallflowers?'

'No. Well, all right, then.' Chloe changed her mind as she spotted two lads, clearly still school age and both of them a good head smaller than she was, edging through the crowd towards them. Better to dance with a girl than with someone the same size as her wee brother.

It took a few moments to sort out who was leading, then they were off, caught up in the crowd that circled round and round the hall. As they passed the stage Chloe kept her head down, hoping that Dennis wouldn't notice her. Looking back once they were clear, she saw that she needn't have worried, for the musicians were all too busy to look at the dancers. Her father stood at the front, eyes half closed as always when he was playing, and Dennis, to one side, watched him like a hawk, his trumpet halfway to his mouth in readiness. At the back of the stage Bert crouched over his drums, head nodding to the beat, while her mother, beaming and mouthing the words of the songs, vigorously thumped the piano. Julia McCosh seemed to her daughter to take on a new lease of life as soon as her hands came in contact with the ivory keys, and Frank joked more than once that she had taken him on only because his solid, square-shouldered figure and the strong white teeth revealed whenever he smiled reminded her of her beloved piano.

'We're not bad, are we?' Marion said into Chloe's ear.

'You've not stepped on my foot yet, if that's what you mean.' The two of them practised assiduously whenever they got the chance, usually in the McCosh's front room, following the steps as laid out on diagrams they had found in newspapers, and taking turns to lead as they danced to records played on the wind-up gramophone.

As the music took hold of their thoughts they both relaxed, letting it and the throng of people carry them along. Then suddenly they had reached the stage again, and without thinking Chloe glanced up and found herself looking straight into Dennis's eyes. He grinned and winked; she gaped and then, mortally embarrassed, tried to hurry Marion deeper into the crowd.

'Ow, my foot! It's all right,' Marion said, her voice heavy with irony, 'don't worry about my crushed toes, luckily I've got a spare foot at the end of my other leg.'

'Stop fussing,' Chloe snapped, heat flooding into her face. 'Come on, let's sit down.' She struggled through the dancers, Marion limping along behind her, and found two empty chairs. 'Your foot's all right, isn't it?'

'I'll live. What happened? We were doing so well.'

'I went over on my ankle,' Chloe lied.

'You've gone bright red.'

'It's hot in here.' She fanned herself with one hand. The music ended to a smattering of applause, then as it started again, she said, 'We'll sit this one out, eh?'

'I'm sure there's a lot of foreigners here.' Marion stared around the hall. 'Paisley's full of them. I wish one of them would come over and ask us to dance. It would be romantic, dancing with someone from another country. Look over there, Chloe, is that not Mrs Borland's daughter?'

'Where?'

'She's just coming past us now.'

Chrissie Harper's pretty face was heavily made up and her blond hair well styled. The best-dressed woman in the hall, she was laughing up into the face of the man who held her close.

'That's her, right enough.'

'She's beautiful,' Marion said wistfully. 'D'you think we'll ever look like that?'

'I don't know that I'd want to. Look at the colour of her hair, it's not natural.'

'You're just jealous. I wonder where she got that pretty frock, and that lovely man. Is it her husband, do you think?'

'He's away in the navy. Every time I see her she's with a different man. Mrs Borland says that she helps to keep the men from abroad from getting too homesick.'

Marion's elbow dug painfully into Chloe's side. 'Doing her bit for Britain, eh?' she said, and giggled so hard that she let out an unladylike snort. Clapping a hand to her mouth, she suddenly tensed and muttered from behind her fingers, 'Oh look, no don't look, there's two fellows coming over!'

Chloe glanced up. The youths bearing down on them were both around her own age, and both reasonably tall. 'They'll be on their way to someone the other side of us,' she said flatly, and then to her astonishment they stopped, and the red-headed one grinned at Marion.

'You dancing?'

'You asking?' she returned pertly.

'Aye.'

'I'm dancing, then.' The formalities over, she rose and scurried after him on to the dance floor, while the other boy smiled at Chloe.

'It looks like me and you, then . . . if you want to dance.'

'I don't mind.'

To her surprise, he held out his hand to draw her to her feet instead of simply strolling away and expecting her to follow, as most boys did. 'I'm glad of that,' he said as they walked the few steps to the floor. 'Because this is my favourite piece of music.'

'"Stardust"? It's nice, isn't it?'

''Specially with a band that knows how to play it,' he said, drawing her into his arms. 'And this one knows.'

It was lovely to be dancing with a boy instead of with Marion. They moved well together, Chloe thought as they circled the floor in silence.

Dennis got a chorus to himself, and the trumpet took over from the saxophone, its golden voice soaring through the melody. Chloe's heart sang in tune; this was turning out to be a perfect evening, though it would have been even better than perfect if Dennis could somehow have partnered her as well as being the trumpet player. Perhaps, she daydreamed, he could have leapt down from the stage between his solo pieces to dance with her . . .

The music ended, bringing her back to reality. 'Let's stay on the floor,' her partner was suggesting, and then adding at once, 'if you don't mind, that is.'

'That would be nice.' She smiled up at him shyly. He was a head taller than she was, slim built, with bright blue eyes and a tumble of straight black hair that flopped over his forehead. His mouth was wide and his chin strong. An interesting face, she thought.

'I'm Charles . . . Charlie Hepburn.'

'Chloe McCosh.'

'Are you enjoying the evening?'

'It's all right,' she said, then the music began again and they lapsed back into silence.

'They're all right, aren't they?' Marion said to Chloe as Charlie and his friend went off to fetch them some tea at the interval.

'I suppose so.'

'Don't be so picky, you! Mine's called Robert, what's yours?'

'Charlie.'

'Robert says they were at school together, and they work together too. D'you think they'll want to walk us home?'

'They can't, my mum promised yours that they'd see that you got home safely.' Marion lived in Caledonia Street, one of the streets overlooking the Fountain Gardens.

'Oh, bother,' Marion said. 'When are they going to realise that you and me are women now, not wee lassies?'

Secretly, Chloe was pleased when Charlie stayed with her for the rest of the evening. They danced well together and each time they passed by the stage she hoped that Dennis would notice what a perfect couple they made, and that he would begin to feel quite jealous.

'They're good,' Charlie said again as the band swung into 'Goodnight, Sweetheart' for the final dance. 'Have you heard them before?'

'All the time. They practise in our front room; that's my dad playing the saxophone, and my mum's at the piano.'

'Really?' Charlie stopped dancing so suddenly that the couple close behind bumped into them. When apologies had been made and they were moving around the floor again, he said, 'It must be wonderful, having parents that run a dance band. Do you play?'

'The piano, just a bit. My mother teaches piano.'

'I play the accordion. I'd love to be in a band.' Charlie's eyes were shining. As the dance finished and Chloe's father acknowledged the applause with a stiff little bow before stepping aside to indicate the other musicians with a sweep of his hand, Charlie Hepburn asked shyly, 'Can I . . . would it be all right if I walked you home?'

'Marion and I have to go home with my mum and dad.'

'Oh yes, of course. Well then . . . could we mebbe go for a walk on Sunday afternoon?' His face had turned quite pink and she suspected that hers had, too. Clearly, courtship was new to him, too.

'If you like.'

'Two o'clock at the war memorial?'

'Make it half-past.' She would have to help her mother to clear up after they had had their Sunday dinner.

It was only when she was in bed and half asleep that she realised that he had suggested walking her home after, not before he discovered that her parents ran the dance band. Her eyes flew open. Would he have asked her out if he hadn't known that?

'Going out with Marion?' her mother asked on Sunday as Chloe, the household chores done, pulled on her coat.

She had known that the question would be asked, and had been dreading it. 'No, not today.' She tried to keep her voice casual. 'I said I'd go for a wee walk with that lad I was dancing with the other night.'

'What?' Her father, in his Home Guard uniform, came into the room just in time to catch the last words. 'What lad's this?'

'Just someone I met at the dancing.'

'Where's he taking you?' Frank looked entirely different in khaki; taller and broader, and more stern, too. Chloe swallowed hard.

'Daddy, we're only going for a wee walk.' If he put his foot down and refused to let her go out, she would die!

'She's our daughter, not our prisoner. She is entitled to go out when she feels like it, Frank,' her mother said calmly.

'But we don't know this lad. She should bring him here first, so that we can have a look at him.'

'Daddy! Mum . . .' Chloe, horrified, appealed to her mother.

'It's broad daylight and I'm sure Chloe won't come to any harm. In any case, she's a sensible lassie . . . she was brought up to be sensible. If she likes this bo . . . this young man enough to meet him again,' Julia said, 'then I'm sure he's decent enough. You'll be back by five, won't you, pet?'

'Yes,' Chloe promised, and gave an inward sigh of relief when her father gave a reluctant nod.

'All right, then, but mind and look out for yourself,' he warned as he began to gather up his gas mask, cap, rifle, tin hat, and the box containing the sandwiches Julia had made for him. He would not be back until late that night, and then only if the air raid sirens stayed quiet.

'I'm not a child,' Chloe grumbled when he had gone.

'I know, but you're his only lassie and fathers worry about their daughters.'

'Did your father behave like that?' Chloe had never known her maternal grandparents; they had died before she was born. Frank's parents had both died before Chloe's twelfth birthday, but she remembered them clearly, and with affection.

'He did indeed.'

'But surely he must have realised that Daddy was a decent man.'

'I was his daughter, his wee girl, and men seem to want their daughters to be their wee girls for ever,' Julia said, a shadow crossing her face. Chloe suddenly wished that she had never brought up the subject.

'I'll have to go. Are you all right?'

'Of course I am.' Her mother smiled at her, the shadow gone as quickly as it had arrived. 'I'm looking forward to a nice peaceful afternoon, just me and the boys. Go on now, and enjoy yourself.'

Scampering out of the close, Chloe ran into Dennis Megson on his way in.

'Slow down or you'll meet yourself coming back,' he advised as they bounced off each other. Then, looking at her more closely, 'There's something different about you today.'

'D'you think so?' She had given her auburn hair an extra one hundred strokes of the brush, and lightly applied a touch

of her mother's precious lipstick; she had done it for
Charlie's benefit, but she would forego a hundred Charlie
Hepburns in return for a compliment from Dennis.

'I know what it is . . . you've washed your face, haven't
you?'

The glow within her withered and died under his broad
grin. 'Very funny. If you must know, I'm going out for a
walk with a lad I met at the dancing the other night.'

If she had hoped to arouse envy, or even interest, it did
not work. 'Good for you,' Dennis said cheerfully. 'Have a
nice time, then.' And he brushed past her and disappeared
up the close, leaving her fuming.

7

Charlie was already at the memorial, pacing back and forth. His long, expressive face lit up as he spotted her.

'I'm not late, am I?'

'No, I got here a bit early. You look nice.'

'Do I?'

'Yes. Where d'you want to go?'

She shrugged, suddenly shy. 'I don't care.'

'Up towards the West End?'

'All right.' She matched his long, easy stride as they headed along the High Street, half relieved that he had not taken her hand or her arm, but at the same time half annoyed.

As they gained the west end of the town and began to walk down Maxwellton Street, Charlie, nodding at a tenement building they were passing, said, 'My mum used to live there. We live in St James Street now.'

'St James Street? I live in Glen Street.'

'You don't! That means we're almost neighbours.'

'Nearly back to back.'

He laughed. 'Imagine us both walking up to the war memorial to meet when I only needed to go round the corner to fetch you! Where do you work?'

'Cochran's.'

'Where all the rich folk do their shopping,' he teased.

'What about you?'

'Craig's Engineering, in the drawing office.'

They crossed the junction with George Street, where a horseshoe set in the cobbles marked the spot where the Paisley witches had been burned at the end of the eighteenth century, then walked on past the swing park and round by West Station, where Charlie hesitated. 'Which way now?'

Before them, as they stood outside the railway station, lay the Ferguslie Mills cricket ground, dividing the road into two. The road on the right passed the great Ferguslie threadmill complex while the road to the left held large houses, and headed towards the Glennifer Braes. To their immediate left was a smaller road, Craw Road. 'D'you want to go up the braes?' Charlie suggested, but Chloe shook her head.

'Let's go up Craw Road to Brodie Park. It would be dark by the time we got to the braes.'

'You're right. We can go there later on in the year, when the lighter nights come in,' Charlie said, linking her arm in his as they started to walk again. The gesture, and his words were warming. Then, as they passed the small wooden gate that led to the big houses at Castlehead, he added, 'that's if I'm still here when the nights are longer. I turned eighteen last month, so I'll probably be called up in the summer.'

'How do you feel about that?'

'All right, but my dad isn't too happy. He was in the last lot and he doesn't believe in war.'

'Neither do I,' Chloe said drily.

He laughed. 'Nor me. What I meant was, he's against ordinary men fighting with ordinary men to please the power-hungry dictators that stay safe behind their desks when they should fight their own battles.'

Chloe gave it some thought, then said, 'I suppose he's right. What does your mother say?'

'She doesn't want me to go, but she says it's better than having me thrown into prison if I refuse. She says that she's had enough of visiting my dad in the jail without having to visit me there too.'

Chloe felt as though her stomach had just fallen through a hole in the pavement. What was her father going to say about this? In his eyes it was bad enough that she was walking out with a lad he didn't know, but the son of a jail-bird . . . !

'Your father's in . . . in prison?' Her voice had gone squeaky and she had to cough in mid-sentence before it got back to normal.

'Not just now. Not for about ten years. He isn't a criminal,' Charlie assured her hastily. 'He used to be put in prison because he took part in marches and made speeches and caused riots . . . according to the police. But he's more respectable now.'

'What does he do? My dad works at the India Tyre Company, so he's in a reserved occupation. He's in the Home Guard too.'

'You wouldn't catch mine in any sort of uniform. In any case, he's not at home much these days. He works for the trades unions and he's always away at meetings and making speeches and that sort of thing.'

'And are you going to do . . . that sort of thing too?'

'I'm not all that interested,' Charlie confessed. 'I think he's disappointed about it, but you have to care a lot about something before you're prepared to be slung into jail for it, or beaten up.'

'He's been beaten?'

'Oh yes. But not for a good while,' Charlie added hurriedly as they reached the great green expanse of Brodie Park.

As they wandered around the park, which was quite well populated on this dry February afternoon, they talked about schooldays, likes and dislikes, families. Like Chloe, Charlie was the oldest of his family, with a young brother and two sisters. He asked a lot of questions about the band, and when they reached St James Street some two hours later, he suggested, 'Why don't you come up and meet my family?'

'Is your father at home?' she asked nervously, and he grinned down at her.

'No, he's not, he's in Leeds or somewhere like that. And when you do meet him you'll probably like him. Come on.'

'They've got a very nice flat, and Mrs Hepburn's such a nice lady,' Chloe reported to her mother when she arrived home. 'They've got two Belgian refugees living with them, and Charlie says that half their furniture's gone because his mother's given it away to folk that were bombed out of their own houses. We had tea and lovely little biscuits that her brother and his wife sent from America. The Americans call them cookies. She sent you this, it came from America too.'

'Chicken?' Julia almost snatched at the tin, turning it round to admire it from all directions. Then, putting it down, 'But it's too much. You'll have to take it back, Chloe, we can't accept it.'

'I said you'd say that.' Just looking at the picture of a plump roasted chicken that decorated the tin made Chloe's mouth water, and she knew that it had had the same effect on her mother. 'But Mrs Hepburn said nonsense, we've to enjoy it. They get food parcels quite often, and Charlie says that she always shares them with folk.'

'But it's like taking charity!'

'Mrs Borland gives us things and you don't call that charity.'

Julia flushed slightly. 'But I know Mrs Borland . . . and don't you ever tell anyone about the things she gives folk.'

'You know Mrs Hepburn too, she says that you're in the Women's Voluntary Service together.'

'Hepburn . . .' Julia stared at her daughter, realisation dawning. 'Mirren Hepburn? Of course I know her, we were sorting out silver paper together last week. I didn't know she had a son your age.'

'Two years older than me,' Chloe confessed, then rushed on before her mother could object to the yawning age gap, 'and when I said that you taught piano lessons she wondered if you'd take on her wee girl, Daisy. She's coming round some time to talk to you about it. So we can keep the chicken then?' she finished hopefully.

'I suppose it would be rude to return it.' Julia put it into the cupboard. 'We'll keep it for a special occasion. And since Mirren Hepburn has entertained you, we'll have to invite your Charlie round here some time.'

'He's not my Charlie!'

'You like him, though, don't you?'

'He's all right. You can invite him if you want, I suppose. Mum,' Chloe ventured after a pause, 'he said that his dad had been in prison.'

'I seem to remember hearing about that, but it was before he became a town councillor.'

'Charlie's father was on the Council?'

'He was a Bailie for a few years, just before the war started. I mind there was quite a row about that, with him having a record himself. Bailies sit in court and try cases, but just for small things like fighting and being drunk and disorderly,' Julia explained, 'and some folk felt that it wouldn't be right for Mr Hepburn to try folk when he'd been had up in court himself. But he was so well thought of by most of the Paisley people that they let him be a Bailie. And a good thing too because he's done a lot for this town.'

'If he's such a good man, why was he put into prison?'

'Because he believed that ordinary folk have rights, and I suppose he still believes it. A lot of men who fought in the last war were thrown out of work in the thirties. Joe Hepburn used to speak at their rallies, and go on marches for workers' rights. Only, the authorities declared most of these meetings to be illegal, so he kept being arrested and put into prison for giving speeches. They saw it as inciting the workers.'

'So he's not really done anything wrong.'

'It depends,' Julia said wryly, 'which side you're on, pet.'

'Cecelia, here a minute!'

Cecelia Goudie, on her way out to her bus to start her shift, spun round and stared at the inspector beckoning her from the office doorway.

'Aye aye, been up tae mischief, have ye?' one of the other conductresses teased.

'No. At least, I don't think so.' She looked at her driver, panic-stricken. 'Have I done something wrong, Harry?'

'Of course not, hen, ye're a fine wee clippie. Come on, we'd best both go tae see what the man wants, since I cannae take the bus out without ye.'

Following Harry Dobbs's broad back across the yard, Cecelia suddenly wondered if the inspector had received bad news about Fergus. Her mouth went dry with fear, then she realised that the dreaded telegram would have been delivered to Glen Street and not to her work. Unless, her panicking mind clamoured, it had arrived at the flat and one of the neighbours, knowing where she worked, had brought it here . . .

'No need tae look as though ye were walkin' tae yer execution, pet.' Harry had turned to wait for her. She summoned up a smile, and a nod of the head.

A month had passed since she had first donned the uniform of a Glasgow Corporation 'clippie', and she had come to enjoy every minute of the job. She liked the passengers, many of whom travelled her route regularly, she got on well with Harry, her regular driver, and she loved being in control of her own bus. She still missed Fergus dreadfully, but work kept her so busy that she had little time to think of anything else while on the bus. But today her comfortable, safe routine had been broken, and the timid, self-doubting Cecelia she still was when out of uniform, was quick to take advantage of the fact and start worrying about the reason.

The inspector had gone ahead of them and was waiting in his office, together with another crew.

'Cecelia, I'm going to have to put you on to a different run for today. You're changing places with Nancy here.'

'Why?' Harry wanted to know.

'Because I'm not workin' with him, that's why!' Nancy, who had been standing glowering out of the window, jerked a thumb at Les, her usual driver.

'What's wrong with him?' Harry persisted.

'Nothin' wrong with me, pal, it's her. She's a thrawn wee b—' Les began, and Nancy, a pretty girl who had somehow managed to make her regulation uniform look as though it had been tailored especially for her, swung round on him, one red-tipped finger stabbing in the direction of his face.

'You use that word tae me, Les Nisbet, and I'll have yer eyes out!'

'Here here, I'll not have this in my office!' The inspector stepped between them, while Cecelia wondered where Nancy managed to get hold of nail polish. It was in very short supply, but her nails were always painted.

'Aye, well, tell him tae mind his tongue,' Nancy said sulkily.

'You'd better both mind your tongues or you'll be out of a job,' the inspector snapped, and the two of them subsided, glaring at each other.

'Ye've had a row, is that it?' Harry asked. The whole terminus knew that for more than a year Les and Nancy had been having an affair that was both intense and stormy. They also knew that Les had a wife at home.

Cecelia had heard the girl telling the other conductresses that she intended, by hook or by crook, to marry Les. But today it looked as though the romance was off.

'More than a row,' Nancy sniffed, while Cecelia went cold as the inspector's request sunk home.

'You want me to switch places with Nancy?'

'Just for today. This'll have blown over by tomorrow.'

'I'd not count on it,' Nancy said icily.

'Oh yes, milady, I would, because if you and him . . .' It was the inspector's turn to wag a finger, 'don't get yourselves sorted out by tonight you'll both be lookin' for another job. Now get your buses out and give me some peace.'

Les's bus went out first. Cecelia stood behind it, signalling him out, then as she jumped on to the platform and reached for the bell, Nancy came running across the yard and leapt on board.

'Watch it, you,' she said, her dark eyes flashing. 'Just behave yourself today, d'ye hear?'

'What else do you think I'd do?'

'I'm just warnin' you. He's mine,' Nancy's red mouth spat (where did she get the makeup? wondered Cecelia, who was hoarding her one and only lipstick for when Fergus came home) and then she reached past Cecelia, gave the double-bell that told the driver to start, and jumped off as the bus moved out of the depot.

It was a difficult shift. Cecelia, new to the run and its fare stages, had difficulty in keeping up. She didn't know the passengers and she soon got heartily sick of seeing faces falling as passengers waiting to board, mainly men, saw her on the platform, and asked, 'Where's Nancy, then?'

When they reached their turning point and had a ten-minute wait before setting off again, Les ignored her, and to cap it all, she discovered that she was on the special run that took Ferguslie Mill workers home for their mid-day break. They were waiting at the mill gate, a seething mass of mostly women, with their headscarves and coats covered in caddis, the flecks of cotton from the machines. They surged on to the bus in a steady stream, showering flakes of cotton on all sides, filling the bus almost at once and leaving angry faces behind with each stop Len drove past. There was another bus at their backs, but all the workers had only a short break and every second was vital to them.

When Cecelia went to collect the fares a hundred hands were thrust at her. 'Come on, hen,' one of the women said impatiently as she stamped tickets until she felt that she was wearing out the machine. 'I've got three weans and my mother tae feed, and the wean tae put tae the breast too. I'll never get it all done and get back for the next shift if you and your driver don't hurry up.'

Even though she worked faster than she had ever done before, at least a third of her passengers left the bus without paying their fares.

'How can one person collect all these fares and give out all these tickets in one short journey?' she asked Les, almost in tears, when they reached the end of the run.

He shrugged. 'Nancy manages.'

'Well, she's welcome to it!' And she was welcome to Les as well. He was one of the younger drivers, exempt from the Forces for some medical reason. He was undeniably good looking in a flashy sort of way . . . when she had time to think of it later, Cecelia realised that Les probably resembled Donnie Borland in his younger days. But even if Nancy had not warned her off, and even if Fergus's wedding ring had not been on the third finger of Cecelia's left hand, she would not have found him attractive.

As she belled him for the start of the next run it suddenly occurred to her that the quarrel might be more than a lovers' tiff. What if Nancy refused to work with Les again, and asked for a transfer? Most of the bus crews got on well enough, and if a driver and conductress found it impossible to work together they could get an exchange with another crew only if all four signed a form saying they agreed to it. What if Nancy continued to refuse to work with Les, and Harry agreed to keep her on his bus? Cecelia would have no option but to go along with the scheme. She didn't think that she could bear to continue as Les's clippie.

It was a great relief to her when the bus finally turned in at the depot. It had been a long hard day and she was glad to have reached the end of it. She never wanted another like it...but perhaps, she thought, the panic returning, she would have little choice.

Harry's bus was already in, and Nancy prowled around the yard. As their bus arrived she stood and watched it, fists rammed on to her slim hips, then she stalked forward to the driver's door.

'C'mere, you,' she ordered as Les climbed down. Running her arm through his she led him away, turning just once to glare back at Cecelia as though blaming her for the situation.

'How did it go, hen?'

'Oh, Harry!' She could have kissed his dear familiar face. 'I'm so glad to see you. I had a terrible day!'

'You only had Les,' he told her. 'I had Nancy, and Nancy in a rage is even worse. I'm the one that had the terrible day.'

'I thought she might want to stay with you and then I'd have to stay with Les.'

'Don't be daft,' he said kindly as they crossed the yard behind the tempestuous lovers. 'She just wanted tae teach him a lesson, that's all. And even if she'd gone down on her knees and begged, I'd as soon throw the job in as work with that yin every day. No, no, hen, you and me's a good crew and that's the way it's goin' tae stay.'

It was the highest praise that Cecelia had ever received, and as they went into the office she glowed with pleasure.

8

'As you can see, we have a piano.' Mirren Hepburn gestured to the small upright piano against the living-room wall. 'Joe bought it from a man who'd been threatened with bailiffs if he didn't pay his bills. He bought half the man's furniture too ... the half that he and his family could manage without,' she went on as Julia McCosh examined the piano, which had open fretwork panels over red silk, and candle holders. 'We'd precious little money ourselves, but a wee thing like that didn't matter to my husband. I found good homes for most of the furniture, but Joe insisted on keeping the piano because his mother had always liked music though she never had a piano of her own. He'll be pleased to hear when he comes home that it's going to come in useful at last.'

Julia ran her hands over the keys. The tone was mellow, and it could do with some tuning, but it was a good piano. 'Your husband's away from home just now?'

'In Liverpool for a trades union conference.' Mirren poured tea for them both then called, 'Tea, Magritte.'

The only answer was the whirring of a treadle sewing machine from elsewhere in the flat. As Chloe had already told her, the Hepburns had taken in two Belgian refugees; the mother, Magritte, a shy, gentle woman, had excused herself almost as soon as she and Julia were introduced, and gone off to do some sewing. Her daughter Anna, Mirren explained, was working in munitions at Beardmore's factory nearby.

'She can't hear me. I'll take some through to her,' she said now, and filled the third cup.

Left alone while her hostess delivered the tea, Julia sneaked quick glances about the living-room. The Hepburns' flat in St James Street was larger than her own home in Glen Street. It held a well-used but comfortable three-piece suite, several other chairs of assorted design, the piano, a large dresser with deep solid drawers and more bookcases than Julia had ever seen outside a public library. The walls were lined with them, some low, most tall. They were crammed with books; when the shelves had been filled to capacity, more volumes were fitted into the gaps between them and the base of the next shelf, and books were also stacked on top of the bookcases and in piles on the floor. She strained to see the titles on the nearest bookcase; they all seemed to be about politics and economics.

'I'd not be surprised if the tea goes stone cold before she thinks to stop and drink it,' Mirren bustled back into the room. 'She's busy repairing some of the clothing handed in to the WVS. I've never met a worker like her; if it wasn't for her being here to look after this place for me I'd not be able to do so much war work. Have another biscuit. Magritte made them.'

'To think that we've been working together in the WVS and I didn't even realise you were married to Bailie Hepburn,' Julia marvelled.

'To think that I'd no idea that you and your husband had a band, come to that. To tell you the truth, it's nice to be with someone who doesn't know about Joe. Those that do seem to think that I'm as passionate about politics as he is.'

'But you're not?'

Mirren leaned back in her chair with a sigh of content-ment. 'This is nice, just sitting here together after being on our feet all day, sorting out that stuff for refugees. I do care, of course I do, but not as strongly as Joe does, and not as much as he would like, either. When he first met me I was working in the Ferguslie Mills and he was all for me getting the women formed into unions to fight for their rights, and going to rallies and on marches, and even making speeches.' She laughed. 'Can you imagine me, standing on a platform, making a speech?'

'I think you could do it as well as anyone if you wanted to.'

'But I never wanted to, for that's not me at all. My job's to look after Joe and the flat and the children. He could live in a cave and eat wild berries and not give a jot about it, but that doesn't put food on the table.'

She took a sip of tea. 'We make a good team, though, between us. He looks after the working-class folk and I make sure that there's always a home for him to come back to. Not that he's here as often as I'd like, 'specially since the war started.'

Watching the soft smile that lingered round her mouth when she spoke about him, Julia realised that this woman was still in love with her man, just as she herself was still deeply in love with Frank. They were both fortunate.

Aloud, she said, 'You must be proud of him, though. He's done a lot for this area.'

'Yes, he has,' Mirren agreed. 'And I can't complain, for I knew what he was like before I wed him.' The smile deepened into a mischievous grin. 'And because of that, it took a lot of persuading before I said yes.'

'How did you meet each other?'

'My brother Robbie was one of his followers, so Joe was around our house quite a lot. I spent so much time patching the two of them up after they'd been to meetings that ended in fights that I could have been a nurse instead of a mill lassie. Or a prison visitor . . . I've had my share of that too.'

'That must have been a terrible worry to you.'

'There was no sense in worrying. Joe was so strong in his beliefs that being locked up was just a part of the man he was. Not that he's been in prison for . . .' She squinted at the piano, thinking, then said, 'My goodness, it's almost ten years now. Port Glasgow, that's where it was. Joe and a deputation of the unemployed shipbuilders there wanted to talk to the Public Assistance folk about the inhumanity of means testing, only they were denied a meeting, so they protested by marching through the town.'

'I don't blame them, if they were out of work and with families to feed.'

'Good for you,' Mirren approved. 'The thing is, someone broke a window while they were passing by one of the town's banks, then their band played the "The Red Flag" outside the Provost's house. That was enough to bring in the police with their batons, and off Joe went to the jail again. I've said to him that I've had more trouble with him fighting than with both my sons.'

'And you were a mill girl?'

'A twiner at Ferguslie, and proud of it. I ended up in the welfare department, and I still do some work for them when I'm needed. Now then,' Mirren set down her empty cup. 'The girls will be back from school any minute now so I'd best tell you about our Daisy. She's six years old and she's been on at me to let her learn to play the piano.'

'I'd be happy to take her on if you want. She might well decide that she doesn't want to learn after all, once she realises that it means practising regularly.'

'I doubt that. Once Daisy puts her mind to something she doesn't let go. I have to warn you, Julia, that she's a stubborn wee creature. Out of the four of them she's the one most like her father; I'd not be at all surprised to see her marching and demonstrating along with him in another ten years or mebbe less. And in a way I'd be quite pleased, for I think he's a wee bit disappointed that none of the others is of the same mind as him. Grace is a quiet lassie, and Bobby's never got his nose out of a book . . . that's the one thing he's inherited from his father, I suppose . . . and Charlie's looking forward to going into the Air Force if he can. He'll be old enough for call-up in June,' Mirren said quietly, the light leaving her face. She stared down at her hands. 'He can't wait, but I'm praying that the time will drag by.'

'Oh, Mirren . . .' Julia leaned forward and laid a hand on her friend's arm. 'Mebbe the war'll be ended by then,' she said, although she knew that there was little hope of that.

'Aye, mebbe,' Mirren Hepburn said, then drew a deep breath before looking up again, a smile pinned to her face. 'I like your Chloe, and so does Charlie.'

'I should warn you, I have a suspicion that she's got her heart set on a lad that lives upstairs, only he never seems to notice her.'

'Poor Chloe, and poor Charlie too, if he really fancies her. We'll just have to wait and see,' Mirren said as the outer door opened and feet came scampering along the hall. The living-room door burst open and a small girl erupted into the room.

'We did sums in our sand trays,' she announced, and then skidded to a halt as she saw Julia.

'Where's your manners, miss? Say how d'you do to Mrs McCosh. She's the lady who's going to teach you to play the piano.'

Daisy stuck out a hand. 'How d'you do, Mrs McCosh, I want to learn to play "The Blue Danube",' she said, all in one breath.

'You wee heathen,' her mother admonished. '"The Blue Danube" is a German piece.'

'It's music,' Daisy corrected her sharply, then, to Julia, 'Can you play it?'

'Yes, I can.'

'Will you teach me to play it?'

'You'll have quite a lot of learning to do before you get to that stage.'

'I don't mind. Can I please have a biscuit?'

'Just one.'

Daisy palmed the biscuit with the practised skill of a gambler and asked, 'Where's Magritte?'

'Through in the kitchen.'

'When can I learn to play the piano?'

'You can start next Tuesday after school, if your mother agrees.'

Daisy's head swivelled round towards her mother, who nodded.

'That's that settled then.' She took a bite out of her biscuit. 'I'm going to see Magritte now,' she said, spraying crumbs.

'Er . . . have you not got something to say to Mrs McCosh first? She's just agreed to give up valuable time to teach you how to play the piano.'

'Oh yes. Thank you, Mrs McCosh,' Daisy rattled out, and disappeared as swiftly as she had arrived.

'You're still willing to take her on? I'm beginning to think that if you can get her to sit still on a piano stool for more than thirty seconds it'll be a miracle.'

Julia laughed. 'I'm still willing.'

'Bless you. It might be Magritte that brings Daisy round for her lessons, or whoever's free at the time.' Mirren glanced at the door and called, 'Grace, come and meet my friend Mrs McCosh. This,' she went on as an older girl in school uniform came into the room, 'is my older and more respectable daughter.'

Daisy was dark-haired and dark-eyed and quite wiry, but Grace, Julia saw at once, probably looked just as her mother had done at her age. Tall and slender, she had long fair hair, striking features and her mother's air of serenity. Mirren Hepburn's body, like Julia's, had been thickened by child-bearing and years of hard work, and the light from the window glittered on threads of silver in the soft, fair hair drawn back into a loose coil at the nape of her neck, but the serenity was still there. Mother and daughter had the same quick smile and the same clear eyes.

'I must go,' Julia said a few minutes later. 'My own boys will be home from school at any minute.'

'Fetch Mrs McCosh's coat, will you, Grace? It's in the hall press. I won't be a minute,' Mirren said, and disappeared. When she came back a few moments later, she said, 'Put these in your bag, Julia. My sister-in-law Ella sent a food parcel and there's always more than we can eat.'

'I couldn't take all that!' Julia stared at the large tin of meat and the generous slab of cake that Mirren had wrapped in greaseproof paper.

'Och, away with you, woman, of course you could. Robbie and Ella send these parcels from America regularly and I like to share them out. That's what war's all about, isn't it?' Mirren said. 'Sharing the good as well as the bad.'

Chloe dreaded Charlie's visit to her home.

'I don't see why,' Marion said when she confessed. 'My parents liked Robert, and so did my gran and my auntie.'

'What did you invite the poor lad to . . . a family party?'

'No, but you know my Auntie Belle, she likes to stick her neb in when anything's happening. And when Gran heard that my auntie was going to drop in, she decided to drop in too. But Robert was neither up nor down about it, and we all had a great time. I don't know why you haven't asked Charlie over before this.'

'Why should I?' asked Chloe, who had resisted her mother's suggestions that Charlie be invited for tea for as long as she could. 'It's not as if we're walking out together.'

'But you are. You go for a walk with him at least once a week. I couldn't wait to get Robert to our flat. My sister's as jealous as anything!'

'Charlie Hepburn's just a friend, and I don't want my mum and dad to think that he's any more than that.'

'You know your trouble, Chloe McCosh?' Marion said. 'You're too choosy. You'll end up as an old maid on the shelf if you're not careful.'

Chloe had no idea that her father was even more reluctant to bring Charlie into the bosom of the family than she was.

'I thought you'd want to have a good look at the young man our Chloe's been walking out with,' Julia said when her husband asked if they really needed to invite Charlie for his tea. 'It'll give you the chance to decide whether he's worthy of her or not.'

'D'you mean that she's getting serious about this lad?' he asked, alarmed.

'He's not exactly a lad, Frank, he turned eighteen recently and he'll be called up soon.'

'Eighteen? She's too young to be courting a man of that age!'

'Frank!' She put her hand over his lips to silence him. 'Will you listen to me, man? I said they were walking out, and that's all they are doing. They enjoy each other's company, and where's the harm in that, while they're free to do as they want?' She gave a sudden shiver, then added almost grimly, 'Young folk have to take their pleasure where they can these days . . . they daren't look to the future.'

He freed himself, but kept her hand in his. 'And that's exactly why some of them try to grab life while they can. Who's to say that this lad Charlie isn't one of them?'

'I know his mother and I've been in their flat. He's as well raised as our bairns, and if you ask me, it's time you met him. You've built up a picture of some irresponsible lunatic in your mind and I want you to see how wrong you are.'

'Aye, I suppose you're right.' Frank gave her a rueful smile, and then kissed the tips of her fingers before letting go of her hand. 'I'm an over-possessive idiot.'

'You're a good, caring man, and I'll not let anyone say different. Chloe can bring him here, then?'

'Aye, she can,' he agreed, then just as Julia thought that the discussion was over, he added, a steely note coming in to his deep voice, 'I suppose it works two ways. I'll get the measure of him, and he'll get the measure of me. He'll see for himself that I'm not the man to let anyone treat my daughter lightly.'

It was difficult to decide, Julia thought with amusement when the two men met, which of them was the more nervous. Charlie looked quite pale when Chloe, who had been waiting for him at the close entrance, brought him in to the front room, but at sight of Frank he strode forward, his chin up and his hand stuck out.

'Mr McCosh sir, I like your music very much and it's an honour to make your acquaintance.'

For a moment Frank was nonplussed, then he shook the lad's hand. 'I've been interested in meeting you as well, son.' His steady brown eyes met and held Charlie's blue gaze for a long moment.

'You've got the look of your father.'

'You know him, sir?'

'You don't have to call me sir; you're not in the services yet, son. Plain Mr McCosh'll do. No, I can't say that we've ever moved in the same circles, Joe Hepburn and me, but I've seen him going about his civic duties. He's served Paisley Town Council well, though there's been times when he was over-zealous in expressing his views.'

Charlie laughed. 'That's what my mother always says, Mr McCosh. I know I have his looks, but I can't say that I have his political beliefs.'

'You could do worse, though it's understandable that you don't feel as strongly as he does about things. You're young, for one thing, and for another, you've had life easier than your da did, from what I've heard.'

'Until now, Mr McCosh.'

Watching, Julia saw a shadow come over her husband's face. 'Aye, son,' he agreed quietly. 'Until now.' Then, the shadow lifting, 'My daughter tells me that you play the accordion?'

'I do. I like music, 'specially the sort of music your band plays.'

Throughout the meal Julia and Chloe had prepared Charlie listened, spellbound, to the story of how the band was set up, and answered all Frank's careful questions openly, talking about his work, his hopes of ending up as an engineer and his intention, one day, to visit his relatives in America.

'I was supposed to go over there for a wee while when I left the school, but by then the war had started. But I still mean to go once it's all over.'

'Would you be thinking of settling there?'

'My uncle and aunt like it very well, and so do my mother's cousins, but I don't see me moving away from Scotland,' Charlie said. 'I'm mebbe not like my dad in ways that he would like, but I'm with him in wanting to stay in my own country. He's put a lot into Scotland, and I'd like to do the same, but in a different direction from him.'

When the meal was over Charlie, to the boys' disgust, offered to wash the dishes.

'I can be trusted not to break anything,' he assured Julia earnestly. 'My brother and I often wash the dishes at home. My dad had to look after himself for years and he says that a man should be able to turn his hand to anything.'

'Very sensible of him,' Julia approved. 'But another time, perhaps. Chloe can help me just now while the lads finish off their homework. Why don't you let Charlie have a look at some of the music we play, Frank?'

If her dad hadn't had his Home Guard duties to go to, Chloe thought when she found the two men later in the front room, talking animatedly and with their heads together over a bundle of song sheets, she might not have seen Charlie at all that evening.

'Mum says do you realise the time, Daddy?'

'Eh?' Frank glanced up, his face absorbed and then startled as he glanced at the clock on the mantelshelf. 'Good G . . . rief, I'm going to be late!'

'He's great,' Charlie enthused as his host rushed through to the kitchen, where Julia had spread his uniform out before the fire to take the worst of the chill off it. 'He knows so much about music.'

'I know,' Chloe said with smug modesty, as though she was solely responsible for her father's talent. She began to collect the sheets of music that had spilled over the floor and Charlie knelt by her side, helping.

'So . . . now do you feel better about me being here?'

'Feel better?'

'You didn't want me to meet your parents, did you? I could tell that as soon as you met me at the close entrance. You looked as if you'd been sent for by the headmaster.'

'I did not!'

'Aye you did. What was it . . . did you think I'd spill my dinner on the tablecloth, or scratch my backside?'

'Charlie!'

'Or say something rude, like I've just said, in front of them?'

'No, it was just . . . you're the first lad that's come for his tea. And your parents aren't anything like mine. Mine are just ordinary.'

'Ordinary? You think that musicians who have their own band are ordinary? They're great, Chloe, and so are Duncan and Leslie. You've got a great family.'

Chloe gathered up the last of the music sheets and tapped their lower edges on the floor to tidy them. 'I know,' she said, from the bottom of her heart as the door opened to admit Frank, in uniform.

'Very nice to meet you, son.' He held out his hand to Charlie.

'And you, sir. Thank you for your hospitality.'

'Any time, lad. The boys are getting ready for bed now,' Frank added to his daughter, 'so your mother says you and Charlie should just stay here. The kitchen's been turned upside down, the same as it is every night at their bedtime.'

'Let me hear you play the piano,' Charlie suggested to Chloe when her father had gone.

'I'm not good enough for that. We can play some records, though,' she offered before he could argue. They leafed through the great pile of records her parents had amassed, and when Charlie found 'Stardust' – 'My favourite piece of music!' – he wound up the gramophone and put the record on.

'It's grand, isn't it?' he asked as the first strains of music began. Then, holding out his arms, 'May I have this dance, madam?'

He was just the right height, and it was lovely, Chloe thought as they circled around her mother's good front-room carpet, to be dancing with him instead of with Marion.

She closed her eyes, and gave herself up to the music, and to the thrill of being held in a man's arms.

9

It had been a long, hard day, and as Cecelia dragged her tired feet along the street she promised herself that she was going to have a nice long bath when she got home, with as good a soak as anyone could have in the permitted five inches of water. Then she was going to eat a whole square of milk chocolate after her supper . . . perhaps instead of her supper, since she had not been able to find the time to join the queues at any of the food shops.

After getting her clothes ready for the next day, she was going to bed early, with a library book. And then would come the best part . . . dreaming about Fergus. As though on cue, as she reached Number 42, the strains of 'Stardust' came drifting through the cold night air from behind the McCosh's front-room window.

She climbed the first flight of stairs, almost having to feel her way in the weak light. Past the permanently blacked-out stained-glass window and the privy door, with its notices, 'Please keep clean' and 'Please bring your own paper', and up to the first landing, where she almost fell over a body, sprawled at the bottom of the next flight.

The fair curly hair identified the unconscious woman as Lena Fulton, her eyes closed and her face so white that it seemed to float in the dim light. When Cecelia put the back of her hand against the other girl's mouth she found that although the lips were cool she could feel the faint stirring of a breath against her own skin.

'Mrs Fulton? Lena?' There was no reply, no movement, but just then she heard someone coming into the close below, whistling cheerfully as they began to mount the stairs towards her.

'Hello?' Cecelia, still on her knees, pivoted round to clutch at the railings with both hands, pressing her face to the gap. 'Hello? Someone's been hurt! Can you help me, please?'

The whistling stopped at once. The man coming up the stairs craned his neck to look up at her, and then came up the rest of the stairs two at a time, hauling off his cap. 'What's happened?'

'I don't know, I was just coming home and I found Lena . . . Mrs Fulton lying here. I can't get her to waken up.'

The man knelt beside her, pushing Lena's soft hair back and laying two fingers gently against her neck. His own hair was fair, and when he looked up again Cecelia recognised him as a member of the Megson family. As yet, between shyness and work, she had not had time to get to know anyone other than the Borlands and Lena.

'She's still breathing, at any rate. Best not to move her.'

'Should I go and telephone for an ambulance, do you think?'

'My mother's a nurse; you stay here while I fetch her down. She'll know what to do.' He got to his feet and hauled off his jacket, then stooped to put it over Lena. 'Back in a minute.'

'It's all right, there's a nurse coming to see to you. You'll be fine,' Cecelia reassured Lena Fulton as she waited. Almost certainly the girl couldn't hear her, but it helped Cecelia to talk.

The young man returned almost at once. 'My mother's coming directly, she says we've to leave her as she is.'

'I feel so helpless! Thank goodness you came when you did. I don't know anything about first aid.'

'I know a bit, from the Boys' Brigade and the fire station. I work there,' he added in explanation, then, 'You're Mrs Goudie, aren't you? We live on the same landing. I'm Dennis Megson . . . and here's my mother coming now.'

'What happened to her?' Mrs Megson had brought a few towels; she laid them aside as she knelt down by Lena.

'I just found her like this. I don't know if she fainted, or tripped,' Cecelia said helplessly, watching as the woman ran her hands swiftly over Lena's limbs.

'No bones broken at any rate, and no head wound that I can see. Mrs Fulton?' She tapped her fingers gently against Lena's cheek. 'Can you hear me, dear?' Then as she was answered by a faint moan and a slight movement, 'It might just be a faint. Best to get her into her own place. I'll have to go through her pockets for the key.'

'No need, it's still in the door,' Dennis had stayed on his feet, out of the way. Now he pushed the door and it swung open. 'And it hadn't been turned, so she didn't mean to go far. I can carry her in if you think it's safe, Mum.'

'Best to do that.' His mother began to ease Lena over on to her back, and then stopped suddenly and nodded to the towels she had brought with her. 'Just give me one of these, will you? The big one on the top.' She took it from Cecelia and wrapped it tightly round Lena's still body. 'There now, be careful with her, Dennis. Mebbe you'd go on ahead and make sure the blackout's in place before you switch on the light,' she added to Cecelia. 'We don't want him blundering into furniture and dropping the poor lassie.'

The flat was exactly like Cecelia's and she tried to remember, from her one brief visit, what the kitchen had looked like. She edged round the big table, tripping on a chair that had been pulled out from beneath it, and fumbled her way to the sink to find that a blackout curtain already covered the single window above it. Feeling her way back to the kitchen door she called, 'It's all right, I can put the light on once you're in.'

'Follow me, Dennis,' she heard Mrs Megson say in her calm, firm voice. 'Once we get inside I'll close the door and then we can get a light on.'

A moment later they were blinking at each other in the sudden burst of light.

'Is there a bed in the kitchen?' Mrs Megson wanted to know, and Cecelia darted back in to look.

'She's got a big cupboard in the recess.'

'Can you wait for just a minute longer, Dennis,' his mother asked, 'while I make sure that it's safe to put on the bedroom light?'

'I could wait all night, for there's nothing to her. She's as light as a wee bird,' the boy said in awe, looking down at the fair head against his shoulder.

'Good lad.' His mother threw the words over her shoulder as she went into the dark bedroom. There was a pause, then a muffled thud followed by an exclamation.

'Mum?'

'It's nothing, I just walked into the corner of the bed.' The light went on. 'You can bring her in now.'

Cecelia followed Dennis into the room as his mother pulled back the bedclothes, and she watched as the boy laid his burden down carefully. Then, straightening, he said sharply, 'There's blood on the towel, Mum! She's hurt!'

'She'll be all right, son, just you leave her to me and . . . er . . .'

'Cecelia Goudie.'

'Me and Cecelia. You don't mind staying, do you, dear?'

'No, if I can be of help.'

'Good.' Nan Megson eased her son's jacket free and returned it to him. 'You go on upstairs, Dennis, and see to the others. I don't want them coming down here to find out what's happening.'

When Dennis had gone Cecelia moved closer to the bed, a shiver running through her as she saw the red stain blossoming on the towel that had been wrapped about Lena Fulton.

'Did you know she's expecting?' she asked Mrs Megson.

'I thought she might be. Mebbe not any more, though, poor lassie. Would you boil some water for me, dear, and find some clean towels or pillow cases?' Mrs Megson rolled up her sleeves and bent over her patient as Cecelia hurried to obey.

'She's lost her bairn,' the older woman said when Cecelia brought in a basin of hot water and a face cloth and towels. 'But at least she'll be all right.'

'Should I try to find a doctor?'

'There's no need. She just needs to take things quietly for a week or so.'

'D'you think it started to come away, and she ran out to get help and fainted?'

'I doubt it. Look at that bruise, and this one . . .' She had undressed the unconscious girl and now, as she washed her, she pointed to the bruising. 'And she's going to have a black eye to add to her troubles. It's my guess that she fell down a flight of stairs. It's all right, pet, you just had a wee bit of a tumble,' she soothed as Lena's eyelids fluttered and then opened.

At first the young woman tried to fight off the hands that were tending her, and then, as she recovered her wits, she lay back and let the two women get on with their work. When Mrs Megson said, 'We'll need to get a nightdress for you,' she was able to tell them where one could be found.

'My bairn?' she asked faintly as they raised her up to slip the gown over her head and she saw the towelling swathed, tucked and pinned about the lower part of her body.

'I'm sorry, love, it's gone,' the older woman said gently, and Lena let out a long, tired sigh.

She took some bread and milk and sipped a little tea, then fell into a deep sleep.

'She'll be fine,' Nan Megson said. 'It's just a matter of

getting her strength back now.' Then, giving Cecelia a tired smile, 'I'm on night duty in an hour and I wouldn't mind some hot tea before I go upstairs to get ready.'

'Mrs Megson ...' Cecelia ventured when they were drinking their tea in the kitchen.

'Call me Nan. My mother-in-law's been gone these four years now but even so, whenever folk say "Mrs Megson" I still think it's her they're speaking to and not me. You're our new neighbour, aren't you?' Then, when Cecelia nodded, 'I should have looked in to make you welcome, but I've had that much to do.'

'So have I. I'm working on the buses now.'

'D'ye like it?'

'More than I thought I would. It was Mrs Borland who suggested it to me.'

'Aye, that sounds like Ellen all right.' Nan Megson gave her tired smile again. She was fair, like her son, with the same steady gaze, but the similarity ended there, for Dennis was broad-shouldered, and his face strong and square, while his mother was thin, probably too thin, with permanent worry-lines between her eyebrows.

'About Lena,' Cecelia pressed on. 'You say that she must have tripped and fallen downstairs, but we found her on her own landing. Mebbe she fell down the stairs on her way out then managed to crawl back up again. But why would she go out and leave her door unlocked?'

'Well now, dear, that's not really important, is it? All that matters,' Nan went on as Cecelia opened her mouth to speak again, 'is that the poor girl's lost her bairn and she needs our support in her time of—'

Sirens began to wail, the sound climbing towards the night sky. Hob-nailed boots hastened by in the street below and far away, someone shouted something. Nan clattered her cup on to the table.

'A raid. I'd best get the girls downstairs before I go off to the hospital. And Dennis'll be wanting to get to the fire station.' She hesitated at the door, biting her lip. 'I don't think Lena should be moved out of her bed tonight.'

'I'll stay with her.'

'Are you sure?'

Cecelia nodded. 'What about your younger children?'

'Julia McCosh takes them downstairs with her children if me and Dennis are away during a raid. I'll get her to tell the rest of them that Lena's not well and you're staying with her. Good luck,' Nan said, and went.

In the distance, Cecelia could hear the rumble of enemy planes approaching, and from much nearer came the thud of feet, the banging of doors and the sound of voices as the tenement's occupants hurried down to the storeroom behind the drysalter's shop, where a space had been cleared and some bits and pieces of furniture set up to create a makeshift shelter.

Very quickly, the human noises were drowned out by the drone of wave after wave of planes passing over, and by the thud of anti-aircraft guns. Cecelia glanced at the ceiling nervously, only too aware that the night sky overhead must be filled with enemy aircraft. She looked in on Lena, who was still sound asleep, and then returned to the kitchen to pour out the last of the tea.

The building was silent now; she thought of her neighbours all huddled together in the ground floor storeroom, and of the other flats, all empty. Picking up her cup, she took it to the bedroom, where she pulled a low chair close to the bed, and the only companion she had.

The raid seemed to go on for hours. Cecelia, remembering that she had a late shift the next day, managed to doze, her head on the bed. Once, she was startled awake by the muffled thump of an explosion, but after a while sleep overtook her again, and she heard nothing more until someone knocked on the door.

Jumping up to answer it, she ran into a dresser just where

she had expected to find the door. Befuddled, she stared around at the unfamiliar room, and then as Lena stirred in the bed and murmured something in her sleep, the previous evening's events came rushing back to her. The knocking sounded again, louder this time, and she fumbled her way to the door, opening it to find grey daylight flooding the landing.

Dennis Megson stood before her, in his uniform and with his face anxious beneath smears of dirt. 'Are you both all right?'

'We're fine.' She blinked at him. 'What time is it?'

'Just after eight o'clock.'

'In the morning?'

'Aye. I'm just back from the station and I thought I'd look in to see if there was anything I could do to help.' His hazel eyes flickered past her to scan the hall. 'How's Mrs Fulton?'

'Still asleep.'

'That's good. She didnae get disturbed when the bomb fell, then?'

'Bomb?' Cecelia was fully awake now. 'We were bombed?'

'A tenement in Seedhill Road got it. Two dead. It's been a busy night.'

Cecelia suddenly remembered waking during the night with the echoes of some noise in her head. But she had heard nothing else, and fallen asleep again. 'Is Seedhill Road near here?' she asked nervously. It could have been their tenement, and if it had been . . . Suddenly the war seemed to be much closer than before, and much more threatening.

'It's by the Anchor Mills, on the other side of the river. Near enough. I could mebbe clear out the kitchen grate and light the fire for you,' he offered eagerly. 'She'll need to be kept warm till she's better.'

She was suddenly aware of her untidy hair and rumpled clothes. 'What about your own family?'

'Ralph can see tae himself, and Mrs McCosh took the girls into her flat after the All Clear. She says she'll get them off to the school.'

'Well, if you're sure you've got the time. Thanks.' She stepped back to let him in, then went to the bedroom, where Lena was trying to sit up.

'Just lie back for the moment. Remember me?' Cecelia asked as the other girl stared at her warily. 'Cecelia Goudie from upstairs. You mended my uniform skirt for me the other week when I got it torn.'

'What's happened?' Nan Megson had been right, Lena did have a black eye, and one side of her face was badly bruised. Cecelia winced at the livid rainbow of colours marring the girl's white skin.

'You took a tumble down the stairs in the dark last night. Mrs Megson got you to bed and I stayed with you during the night.'

'Oh.' Lena fell back against the pillow, the bedclothes tangled about her waist, and asked in a voice so faint that it was a mere whisper. 'I lost my bairn, didn't I?'

Cecelia wished that Nan Megson were there to take charge. 'Yes,' she admitted awkwardly. 'Yes, my dear, you did.'

Tears came swiftly to Lena's blue eyes and she reached down to lay one hand lightly on her stomach.

'Poor wee thing,' she whispered. 'God rest its wee soul.'

Cecelia laid a hand on Lena's, and felt it flutter beneath her touch like a terrified moth trying to escape. 'You're young yet; there'll be other wee ones for you and your man.'

'No.' Lena said the word with finality, as though she knew it to be true. She pulled her hand free and turned her head away. Cecelia straightened up, feeling helpless.

'I'll make some tea, and fetch some warm water. You'll feel better when you've been washed and had something to eat.'

Lena said nothing, but when a sound came from the kitchen her head whipped round. 'Who's that?' Her voice was suddenly strong and her undamaged eye opened wide with alarm. 'Is it George? Did someone send for him?'

'It's Dennis Megson from upstairs, making up the fire for you.'

'Oh.' Lena fell back as though exhausted, and her eyes closed. When Cecelia returned to the bedroom, balancing a large tray that held tea and toast and a small bowl of hot water, she was almost asleep again.

10

'Best thing for her,' Nan Megson said when she arrived later that morning, still wearing her uniform. 'Rest's what she needs . . . and nourishment. You managed to get her to eat something?'

'Yes, and I've made some soup for later. I washed her, though I didn't know what to do about the . . .' Cecelia flushed, one hand gesturing about her own hips.

'I'll see to that. It was good of you to stay up here with her. I'll just go and have a word.'

Cecelia took advantage of the other woman's presence to run upstairs to her own flat, where she changed hurriedly before returning to find Nan in the kitchen, stirring the soup.

'I've made some tea and taken a cup to Lena. Pour some out for yourself.'

'I'll have to go in an hour or two, to start my shift.'

'You've done more than enough as it is, and she's on the mend. She can manage on her own, though she's very weak. We'll all have to keep an eye on her for a wee while.'

'Your Dennis came in this morning to take down the blackout and light the kitchen fire, and Mrs Borland handed these in.' Cecelia indicated the jar of calves' foot jelly and the bottle of tonic wine on the kitchen table. 'She said to let her know if Lena needed anything else.'

'I thought they must have come from her.' Nan's voice was a touch dry.

'Where did she get them?' Cecelia marvelled. 'I'm hard pressed to find a stomach powder these days.'

'Oh, Ellen Borland can get anything you need . . . and she will, if you care to ask, for she's a great believer in looking after all the folk that live in her tenement.' Nan smiled wryly as she emphasised the word 'her'. 'She works in the mill dyeworks. It's a hard, dirty job, but she's more than fit for it, and if any of the men she works beside wants to avoid doing overtime Ellen'll always do it for him . . . for a price.'

'What sort of price?'

'A few coupons here, a shilling or two there, or mebbe a favour to be called in.'

'Is that why her flat's like a palace?'

'That's why.'

'But that's black-marketeering, surely!'

'Lassie, I'm normally as law-abiding as the best of them, but the thing that's really wrong these days is that we're all fighting for our lives in a war we never wanted. If the likes of Ellen is willing to make it a bit more comfortable for herself and her family and the folk about her, I'll not criticise that. Would you prefer it if that lassie lying in the bedroom didn't get these to help her recover?' Nan indicated the tonic wine and calves' foot jelly.

'No, of course not, but . . .'

'Then best just keep your own counsel, for Ellen Borland's not a woman who takes well to being critici— now who's that?' Nan asked as a determined hand plied the doorknocker.

'I'll go,' Cecelia volunteered.

As soon as she opened the door the elderly woman on the landing outside slapped the flat of her hand against it and pushed. She barged in, past Cecelia, and then stopped in the hall, staring. 'Who are you?'

'Cecelia Goudie from the top landing. And you're Lena's aunt. We met the other week when I came in to see if she would mend a skirt for me.'

'Aye, I mind. So what are you doing here now, and where's my niece?'

Cecelia, never good with strangers, began to panic. 'Come on through and we'll explain.' She shepherded the woman into the kitchen, where Nan was rinsing the cups.

'This is Mrs Megson from the next landing; she's a nurse, and—'

'Another neighbour?' the woman interrupted. 'Is the whole tenement making free with George Fulton's home while he's away? And where's my niece? What have you done with her?'

'I'm Nan Megson, Mrs . . . ?' Nan said easily.

'Blacklock. Cathy Blacklock. Where's Lena? What's happened to her? Oh my God . . .' Mrs Blacklock dropped her shopping bag on the floor and fumbled for a chair, pressing her free hand against her chest. 'It's that bomb, isn't it? The one in Seedhill Road. What was she doin' there at that time of the night?'

'Lena's fine, Mrs Blacklock, and it's nothing to do with the bomb. She's not very well, that's all. Cecelia, pour out some tea for Mrs Blacklock. No, wait,' Nan said, taking up the bottle of tonic wine. 'Just give me a cup.'

As she poured out a half-cupful of wine she told the distraught woman about Lena's miscarriage, finishing with, 'but she's fine, I've just changed the dressings and all she needs now is rest and building up.'

'Poor George!' Mrs Blacklock took a deep drink of wine. 'He was fair delighted about that bairn, and now it's all come to nothin'. He's been so good to her . . . she was lucky to find a man like that, and her crippled the way she is.' She took another drink, then asked with sudden suspicion, 'Is that what made her lose the bairn? Bein' a cripple?'

'Lena's not a cripple, Mrs Blacklock, she's just been left with a weak leg after having infantile paralysis, and it had nothing to do with her losing the baby. It certainly won't stop her having children in the future. It seems that she tripped and fell in the blackout, and that brought it on. Nobody's fault,' Nan said firmly, pouring some wine into another cup. 'Now then, I have to go and see to my own place, and Cecelia here has her work to go to, but if you can stay with Lena today I'm sure she would be pleased to have your company.'

'Of course I'll stay, I'm her auntie! I'm the only blood kin she's got. It's my duty to stay with her,' the woman said self-righteously, then added, 'but I can't be here all the time though; I've got a job cleaning for some very nice professional families and I'm just a widow woman so I need the money . . .'

'Of course you do, and you can be sure that we'll be keeping an eye on your niece until she's better, won't we, Cecelia? So no need to worry about that,' Nan soothed as she put on her coat. 'Cecelia, mebbe you'd go through with Mrs Blacklock and let Lena know that someone'll be in during the evening to make sure she's all right. Seeing you will do her a lot of good,' she added to the woman.

Cecelia wasn't so sure that seeing her aunt did Lena Fulton good. As soon as she saw her niece's black eye and bruised face the woman skirled, 'Dear God in heaven, lassie, what have ye done tae yerself?'

'I . . . nothing . . . I didn't do anything,' Lena whimpered, for all the world, Cecelia thought, like a naughty child. One hand flew up in an attempt to cover the bruising. 'I . . .'

'Like we said in the kitchen, Lena lost her footing last night and fell down the stairs,' Cecelia broke in. 'It's happening all over the town, folk getting hurt in the blackout.'

'Ye should have been more careful, when you knew ye were expectin',' Mrs Blacklock lamented. 'And there's poor George far away an' fightin' for his country, with only the thought of that bairn tae keep him goin'. I've never seen a man so pleased about becomin' a father,' she added to Cecelia, and then, turning back to her niece, 'and now you're goin' tae have tae write and tell him that the wee soul's gone afore it got the chance tae take in a lungful of air . . .'

'No!' Lena reared up in the bed, her voice frantic. 'I don't want George told!'

'What d'ye mean, ye don't want him told? He's goin' tae notice somethin's amiss when he comes home on his next leave, isn't he?'

'I mean, let me tell him in my own way, Aunt Cathy. Like you said, he's away fighting for his country, and I don't want him to start fretting about what's happening here. He's got enough to think of,' the girl pleaded.

'Aye well, right enough. I'll leave it tae you tae do what ye think best,' her aunt conceded. 'Now then, drink yer tonic wine and I'll stay here for today. We'll not be needin' you now, Mrs . . . er . . .' she added firmly to Cecelia.

Cecelia wondered on her way to work if Lena Fulton was afraid of her husband. The girl had gone into a real panic when her aunt mentioned George Fulton's reaction to the news of her miscarriage. Then she realised that she herself had no right to question or criticise Lena, for she had not yet told Fergus that she was working as a clippie on the buses.

Fergus's family were crofters, and he himself would have become a crofter if the 1930s depression hadn't driven him, and many other young men like him, south to the industrial towns and cities in search of work.

He had found a job as a tenter in the Paisley thread mills, and when he and Cecelia first met, he had been so impressed to discover that she worked in a Glasgow insurance office that he became convinced that he was not good enough for her. It had taken some time before she managed to get him to change his mind, and even then he had felt guilty when she gave up her job in order to marry him and move to Paisley.

He had assumed that his wife would find an office job just as important, or perhaps more so, in Paisley, and when she was taken on by Glasgow Corporation, Cecelia had found it difficult to tell him the whole truth. Better, she told herself cravenly, to wait until his next leave, when she could explain things face to face. In the meantime, telling herself that she had not really lied, but had merely blurred the truth a little, she had given him to understand that she was working in the transport department's offices.

In a way, she thought ruefully, she and Lena were sisters under the skin.

Dennis Megson, on his way to work, hesitated when he reached the first landing, glancing over at Lena Fulton's door. He hadn't seen her since that night he and Cecelia Goudie had found her lying in a crumpled heap at the bottom of the stairs; his mother said that she had made a full recovery, but Dennis would have liked to have seen her for himself, just to make sure. Each time he passed her door he hoped against hope that it might open, and she might come out, but today, as always, it remained stubbornly closed.

Dennis sighed, and continued on down the stairs to the close, remembering the softness of her limp body in his arms, the tumble of fair curls against his shoulder, the curve of her cheek pale against the dark material of his jacket.

He was still thinking of her when he stepped down on to the pavement and turned to see his younger brother coming along the pavement towards him. The boy was scowling, and he was being escorted by a police constable.

'Ralph?'

'You know him, son?' the policeman asked.

'He's my brother Ralph. I'm Dennis Megson.' Dennis's mouth had gone dry.

'Is yer faither in?'

'He's . . . he's dead.'

'Sorry tae hear that, son. Yer mammy then?'

'She's at work,' Dennis lied. 'I'm in charge. What's he done?'

'He's been runnin' for one of the street bookies. You know that's illegal. What age is he?' the man asked, speaking across Ralph.

'Thirteen.'

'Is he, now? Telt me he was fifteen, didn't ye, son? Mind you, he could get away with it, for he's big for thirteen.'

'What's . . .' Dennis's mouth was dry with fear. If Ralph had to go to court, what would it do to their mother? 'What's going to happen to him?'

'A lot of bad things if he doesnae learn a lesson from this,' the constable said. 'But for now, seein' as he's never been in trouble afore, I'm inclined tae let him off with a warnin' . . . providin' you make sure he behaves himself in future.'

'I will, I can promise you that!'

'Aye, right, then. Ye hear yer brother?' the man asked Ralph, who was staring sullenly at the ground. 'You behave yersel', laddie, and we'll say no more about it. But I know yer face now, and I'll be watchin' out for it. Take one step out of line, and I'll have ye. And I'll not be so lenient the next time. Are ye listenin' tae me?'

'Aye.' Ralph spat the word out, screwing up his face around it as though it tasted bitter.

'Fine, then. I hope I don't have tae meet up with ye again.' The man's voice was grim, but at the same time the wink he gave Dennis said 'Laddies will be laddies.' Then he wheeled round and strode off up the street.

'Come here, you!' Dennis grabbed his brother's arm and threw a swift glance about the street before hustling the younger boy into the close. There were no loiterers around, no women out sweeping their own stretch of pavement or down on their knees whitening the edges of the close steps. No sign of anyone watching, but goodness knows how many sharp eyes might have been spying on them from behind curtains and through the tape that criss-crossed every window.

'Mum's at home,' he said, pulling Ralph back when he began to mount the stairs. 'She mustn't know about this. Through here.'

They went out into the backcourt, then into the small washhouse, where Dennis closed the door and leaned his back against it, while Ralph took up a stance by the big double sink and growled, 'Get it over with, then.'

'Is that all you have to say? Ralph, you were lucky that it was that policeman that caught you. Another one might have had you in the cells and then up before the sheriff officer.'

'I'm too young tae be treated like a criminal. They cannae touch me.'

'Who told you that?' Dennis asked sharply, then as his brother shrugged and stared at the opposite wall, saying nothing, 'Whoever it was, they're wrong. You couldnae be sent tae the jail, but there's always the Kibble School for bad boys in the Greenock Road, and that would be just as hard for ye. And what d'ye think it would do to Mam if you were locked away? Did ye never think of that? What if I hadnae been comin' out of the close just now, and she'd seen you brought home by a policeman when you should be in the school?'

'She didn't see me, so there's no harm done.'

'Mebbe she didn't, but who's to know which of the neighbours were watching from behind their curtains? Mam could still hear about it from them. Where's the money?' Dennis wanted to know.

'What money?'

'The policeman said you'd been runnin' for a bookie.'

'He took all the money I had on me. And some of it was mine!' Ralph said, aggrieved.

'It serves you right. Who were you running for?'

'Mind your own business.'

'You are my business, Ralph, though I wish you weren't. Look, I've got my work to go to,' Dennis said, suddenly aware of the time. 'Come on, I'm going to walk you to the school and see you inside before I go to the fire station.'

'What? I'm not going in late, I'll get into trouble!' Ralph began, then yelped as his brother shot across the small space and grabbed him by the arm so roughly that he was swung round to land with a painful thud against the big mangle.

'You're already in trouble! And you'll only make it worse if you don't get to that school!' Dennis snarled, almost beside himself with worry.

'You hurted me,' Ralph snivelled, rubbing at his shoulder.

'That's nothing to the hurt you'll get if you don't behave yourself from now on. Now get moving!' Dennis roared, and opened the door.

He was sick with worry as he stood at the North School gate watching Ralph stamp across the playground towards the entrance. The collapsing wall that had killed his father had also sent Dennis's future crashing down about his ears. Alex and Nan Megson had decided, when their firstborn showed promise in his schoolwork, to encourage him to stay on at school and then, if the money could be found, go to university. But when Alex died, Nan had had no option but to return to work at Paisley Alexandra Infirmary, and Dennis had immediately rebelled against the idea of university.

'But you can't miss out on the chance to get to the university, son,' his mother had protested on the day he told her that he was leaving school to get a job. 'Not many boys from tenement families manage it; that's why your father wanted it for you.'

'But I never said that it was what I wanted,' Dennis protested in a voice that, at that time of his life, was still uncontrolled and given to soaring from top to bottom of the scale during one short sentence. 'And I'm the one that would have to go through it. I just want to work.'

'Doing what?'

'Doing what my dad did. I want to be a fireman.'

The last sentence came out in a defensive mumble, and Dennis, unable to meet his mother's eyes, stared at the fading pattern on the well-scrubbed linoleum. There was a pause, then, 'No!' Nan almost shouted the word at his bent head.

'But, Mum, when I went to the evening classes the station held for the Boys' Brigade I learned a lot about—'

'I said no and that's an end of it!'

Two days later, Tom MacIntosh, her late husband's colleague and close friend, called to see her. 'Dennis has asked you to come and talk me round, hasn't he?' she said when she saw him standing on the doormat.

'I'll not lie to you, Nan, he did.'

'Then you've had a wasted journey.' She began to close the door, but the man put a big hand, calloused from years of hard work, on the panels.

'At least give me a hearing, lass.'

She bit her lip, staring up at him. He had been Alex's best friend for years; it was Tom who had come to tell her that her man would not be coming home at the end of his shift, or ever again. She knew that it had not been an easy task, but he had insisted on doing it because he knew that if things had gone the other way, Alex would have done it for him.

'Come on in then,' she said at last, turning and going into the kitchen, leaving him to close the door and follow her. When he did, she faced him squarely and went straight into the attack.

'Who do you think you are, Tom MacIntosh, coming here to ask me to throw my boy's life away the way his father's went? If you need recruits, why don't you go to some woman who's not suffered already?'

'Nan ...' He twisted his cap between his hands. 'The lad wants to join the service.'

'He wants to go to the university!'

'And I want tae be King of Britain but it's not goin' tae happen. You cannae afford tae pay for him tae go tae the university, hen.'

'There's scholarships and ...'

'I know that, but he'd not get enough money tae cover everything, and even if ye could afford tae help him out, he'd not let ye. He sees himself as the man of the family now, and ye've got tae let him be just that. D'ye want tae destroy his pride, when it might be all he has tae keep him goin' in the sort of future we've just pushed our bairns intae? We won the last war, but who knows what's goin' tae happen in this one?'

'You could be jailed for defeatist talk,' she said wryly.

'Aye, mebbe so, but it's the truth I'm sayin' and you know it.'

'Even if I do agree to Dennis going to work instead of the university, I'd never agree to the Fire Service. You've got a right cheek on you, Tom, asking me to even consider it.'

He grinned fleetingly. 'You know me well enough to know that cheek's just about all I've got goin' for me,' he said, and then became serious again. 'But let's be practical about this, Nan. In two years' time, if the war's still on, your Dennis is goin' tae be called up and sent tae God knows where. But if he comes intae the Service now and we start trainin' him up, he'll be in a reserved occupation.'

'I don't want to see him making the Fire Service his life, not after it was his father's death,' she said bitterly.

'I'm not talkin' about the rest of his life, Nan, I'm talkin' about now ... and that's as far as we should be lookin' these days. He could work as a messenger to start with, and a general a'things. There's always somethin' needs doin' at the station and he's a clever lad, he'd learn fast.'

'Too clever to be picking up and cleaning up after a bunch of firemen!'

'We're trainin' up auxiliaries now, because of the war,' Tom said patiently. 'Why not let him apply for that, and see how it goes? He needs tae start earnin', Nan.'

'Are you saying that I can't provide for my children?' she flared at him. 'They're as well fed and well clothed as they ever were!'

'Wheesht, woman, you don't have to bite the face off me every time I try tae explain somethin'.' He held out his hands towards her, palms up as if to ward off her anger. 'I was never good with words but I'm doin' my best, and I'm sayin' that your Dennis needs tae to know that he's bringin' in a wage now. He needs tae feel that he's a man, and no' a wee laddie dependent on his mother. He's worried about you and he wants tae help.'

'There's no need to worry about me, I'm managing fine.'

'He's worried anyway,' Tom said, his eyes on her pale, tired face. 'He sees you workin' hard at the infirmary and then comin' back here and bein' mother and father tae him and the wee ones, and it's breakin' him in two, Nan. He's desperate tae help.'

'He does help. He looks after the others when I'm working.'

'But he needs tae do more than that. He wants tae be the man of the house, because he thinks that that's what his father would expect of him. And before ye say anythin' more, Nan,' Tom added swiftly as she opened her mouth to argue, 'he knows fine that Alex was out workin' when he was twelve years old tae support his own family after his father was hurt and had tae leave the pits. Times have mebbe changed, but not that much. And folk don't change as fast as the times.'

'I don't know, Tom . . .' Her shoulders slumped.

'Give him a bit of rope, Nan. Show that ye trust him enough tae let him make his own decisions. I'd look after him, I promise you. For your sake, and for Alex's, I'd lose my own life before I'd let your laddie get hurt, as God's my witness!'

'You're taking on a lot, making promises like that.'

'They're not made lightly, and I'll keep them, ye've no fear of that. I've always felt as though he was my son as well as Alex's, what with him talkin' about his bairns so much, and me not havin' any lads of my own,' said Tom, father of three girls.

He had won her round, and Dennis had no regrets about his decision, for he loved the work and was hungry for more and more experience.

And now, he realised as Ralph, with a final backward glance to see if he was still under observation, disappeared into the school building, he was going to be late. He took to his heels and ran all the way to the fire station in Gordon Street, where he had to endure a tongue-lashing from the officer in charge.

11

———⋅———

True to his promise, Tom McIntosh had taken Dennis under his wing when the boy started work at the fire station in Gordon Street. Every man in the brigade had a trade apart from his fire-fighting skills, and under Tom's guidance Dennis had started attending night classes at the Paisley Technical College as the first step to becoming an engineer. His mother may not have liked the situation, but she learned to tolerate it, which was all that Dennis asked of her.

Today, he was put on to helping Tom with some maintenance work. 'It's not like you to be late, son,' the man said after a while. 'Everything all right at home? Is your mother well?'

'Everything's fine. I was doing some reading for tonight's class and I forgot the time,' Dennis said brusquely.

'Classes goin' all right, are they?'

'Aye, they're fine.' Now that the subject had changed Dennis relaxed. 'I'm enjoying the course. We've got a good teacher.'

'You're certainly comin' on. Yer father would be proud of ye,' the older man said, then added carefully, as Dennis glowed at the compliment, 'You know that if you ever need a bit of advice, or a bit of help, ye can come tae me, don't ye?'

'I know. You've told me often enough.'

Tom nodded, wiping his oily hands with a rag. 'Mebbe

more than ye care tae hear, eh? But your faither and me were good friends, and I think well of your mother. You and her are doin' a grand job between ye, raising the younger ones; but you're still young yersel', Dennis, and there's times when ye might feel that need tae speak tae someone like me. Anytime, lad, that's all I wanted tae say.'

'Thanks, Tom.' Dennis swallowed back a sudden rush of emotion as the man put a paternal hand on his shoulder. Tom had helped to some extent to fill the hungry black hole that had been left in his life after his father died, and that, together with the knowledge that he was bringing a wage into the house, gave Dennis the strength and confidence he had badly needed.

He would have dearly loved to tell Tom MacIntosh about Ralph, and to ask his advice; but at the same time he could not bear to tell anyone about his younger brother's behaviour. Ralph's love of money and, perhaps, the loss of his father's authority in the house had led him to the edge of a precipice; if things went on as they were, he could well start the long slide down towards a life of shame, carrying his family with him.

By the time Dennis got home from work that night Ralph was in bed and, apparently, asleep. The next morning the younger boy bolted down his breakfast and left the flat without a word for anyone.

'What's the matter with him?' Nan fretted.

'Nothing, he's just in a thrawn mood. Best leave him tae work himself out of it,' Dennis advised. Nothing had been said about the previous day's escapade, which meant, with any luck, that nobody had seen the policeman and tattled to Nan.

'If you ask me,' Ellen Borland pronounced, 'thon lassie didnae lose her bairn out of misfortune. She flung hersel' down thae stairs on purpose.'

It was Saturday afternoon and she was sitting at one side

of the table, dusting the photographs from the mantelshelf and some of the ornaments from the corner cupboard, while Jessie Bell, sitting opposite, rubbed up the silver tea set that was kept on the bottom shelf of the kitchen cupboard, out of sight. Saturday afternoons were always put aside for cleaning.

'For one thing . . .' Ellen waved the duster at Jessie for emphasis, 'she was found on her own landin' and that means that she must have fallen down from the flight above. Now what was she doin' up there?'

'Mebbe she was visiting,' Chrissie suggested from one of the armchairs where she sat with one heel propped on the knee of her other leg so that she could paint her toenails. She wore slacks and a blouse, and curlers peeped from beneath her headscarf. She was going dancing that night with a young serviceman she had met at the La Scala Picture House a few evenings before.

'Or mebbe she was borrowin' a screw o' tea or somethin',' her father put in from his own chair.

'Lena Fulton doesnae visit and she doesnae borrow. She went up these stairs just tae throw herself down them again. And it worked.'

'Why would she want tae lose her bairn, but?' Donnie persisted, deciding that this conversation was more interesting than the newspaper in his hands. He spent most of his time alone when his wife was out working, and he enjoyed a wee bit of a crack at the weekends, even if it was only woman talk.

'That's what I'd like to know,' Ellen said. 'She's got a ring on her finger, and a decent enough man. He did this place up lovely.' She looked around at the expensive paper on the walls and the glossy varnish on the doors and skirting boards, and then added, lowering her voice, 'Unless, of course, it's not his.'

Chrissie had been concentrating so hard on painting a little toe that her eyes were squinting and her tongue sticking out from between her teeth. Now she stopped, and looked up at her mother. 'That quiet wee limpy lassie . . . seein' another man? Who'd look at her twice?'

'Her husband, for one,' her mother pointed out, and Chrissie nodded.

'Aye, right enough, he's a fine good-looking fellow. I don't know what men like him see in the likes of her. She's too timid to say boo to a goose.'

'And there's better ways of getting rid of an unwanted bairn. She could have hurtit hersel', goin' down the stairs like that,' Jessie Bell contributed in her wavery, raspy voice. 'There's knittin' needles, for one, and a good bottle of gin and a hot bath for another. I've seen them both used more than once in my time as a mistress in the mills.'

'I know you have, Jessie, and the church is right, it's a terrible sin!' Ellen's eyes flashed. 'That's one thing I agree with!'

Raised in the Catholic faith, Ellen had made the mistake of falling in love with Donnie, a Protestant. When both families opposed their marriage the couple had retaliated by renouncing families and religions. 'And never regretted it once,' Ellen had said frequently during the years between, gazing fondly at her husband. She still loved him passionately, and ever since the accident that had damaged his back she had been happy to work every hour of the day to keep him in comfort. Sometimes people wondered if his injury had really been as permanent as he claimed, but none ever dared to voice their doubts to Ellen.

Now, when Donnie, losing interest in female gossip and turning to the racing pages, said, 'See's over that pencil, hen,' she was more than ready to abandon her work and fetch the pencil, which had fallen from the arm of his chair and rolled just out of his reach.

'There you are, pet.' She returned it to his hand before going back to her seat. The pieces before her included some statues of saints, because even though she had not set foot inside the chapel since her marriage Ellen had not been able to make a complete break.

Now, she had no sooner started work again than the door-bell rang.

'Chrissie . . .'

'My nails are still wet.' Chrissie waggled her foot about in the air to dry the varnish, adding when her mother had trudged out into the hall. 'It'll be for her anyway.'

Sure enough, they heard the front-room door open and then close almost immediately. Ellen Borland had a finger in many pies and when the doorbell rang, which happened quite often, it was always for her.

The three left in the kitchen lapsed into silence and after a while the room door opened and closed again, then the front door closed and Ellen came back, remarking as she sat down at the table again, 'It's all go, so it is. Helpin' folk tae get through this war's wearin' me away tae a shadow.'

Chrissie, still brooding over the interrupted conversation, cast a glance at her mother's ample form and said, 'I don't ever want to have weans.'

'Of course you'll have them . . . eventually, when the war's over and Stanley comes home.'

'I don't know, Mam. I don't fancy losin' my figure and drippin' milk and havin' tae stay in at nights tae look after them.'

'I'd help you,' Ellen coaxed. 'You'll come round to the idea once Stanley's home for good. It's not natural not tae have bairns, is it, Donnie?'

'Eh? Aye, I suppose so. Ye'll find that they just keep on comin', pet,' Donnie Borland explained to his daughter. 'And there's not much ye can do about it.'

'There is,' Jessie muttered, rubbing hard at the elaborate teapot in her hand. 'There's knittin' needles and gin and—'

'You'll make a lovely wee mother when the time comes, Chrissie,' Ellen broke in. 'And ye'd not begrudge me and your daddy some grandweans, would ye?'

'You've got plenty, Mam!'

Ellen and Donnie had raised five children, all married now and out in the world doing quite well for themselves. 'Only seven,' Ellen said now, 'and only one of them a wee lassie.' She picked up the elaborately framed photograph of a little girl in a snowy white Confirmation dress and veil and began to polish it lovingly. 'Isn't she a wee angel?'

The split with her church had meant that Ellen had missed out on the joy of watching her three daughters take Confirmation. It had broken her heart, and she had been secretly delighted when her eldest daughter married a Catholic, became one herself, and had her own daughter confirmed. Chrissie, too, had married into her mother's faith.

'Mebbe she looks like a wee angel there, Mam, but ye know well enough that she's a right wee bugger the rest of the time.' Chrissie said now, starting on her other foot. 'I'd drink all the gin in the world if it spared me from havin' a wean like that one.'

'You'll change your tune, lady, when Stanley comes home and the priest calls round to find out what's wrong between you that ye've no bairns.'

'Stan'll do what he's told and the priest'll get a flea in his ear if he tries tae tell me what tae do.'

'That's no way to speak of the church!'

'I've heard you say worse.'

'Donnie, tell her!'

'Put the kettle on, Chrissie,' Donnie said without looking up from his newspaper, 'and make some tea.'

'But, Daddy, my nails aren't properly dried yet!'

'I'll do it,' said Ellen, putting down her work and hauling herself out of her chair again.

Being the youngest and newest recruit at the Gordon Street fire station, Dennis Megson came in for a lot of teasing

from the older men. 'Not got yerself a girlfriend yet?' they
would ask. 'You want tae get a move on, son, afore all thae
servicemen going about the town in their smart uniforms
drain the place dry. Paisley lassies for Paisley men, eh,
Dennis?'

He had learned to grin and to hold his tongue. No sense
in telling them that he had quite enough to do looking after
the women already in his life . . . his mother and two little
sisters. And right now he didn't have any time to spare for
courting and walking out with girls. As well as work and
studying for his night-school class, there was the backcourt
vegetable garden, too.

Dennis enjoyed the manual labour on the vegetable beds,
finding that it freed his mind to think over his text books
and all the things he had to memorise at work. He was
turning over a section that had recently been cleared of
winter turnips when he heard the clash of a metal bucket
being set down on flagstones. Glancing up, he saw Lena
Fulton making her way towards him, carrying a cup and a
plate.

'I saw you from my window,' she said shyly, 'and I
thought you might like some tea and something to eat.'
Then, as he stared at her, her voice began to falter. 'Or
mebbe you don't want it.'

'No! I mean, yes, I do.' He found his tongue at last, just
as she was about to retreat to the tenement. 'It's very kind
of you.'

Her pale face went pink as she thrust the cup and plate
at him. 'It's just a wee thank you for what you did the other
week, when I fell and hurt myself. I've never seen you to
thank you since then.'

Dennis rammed the spade into the earth and dusted his
hands together before he accepted the proffered cup and
plate. 'Och, that was nothing.' He took a big swallow of
tea to cover his embarrassment.

'It was more than that,' she insisted, and then, as he

glanced from the cup to the plate, trying to work out how he could lift the jam sandwich without dropping the cup, 'Here, let me.' She took the plate, leaving him free to lift the food from it. 'I should have brought a tray.'

'No, it's fine,' he assured her through a mouthful of bread and jam, recalling the moment when, gently laying her on her bed, so as not to add to her hurt, he had seen the blood, red and wet, staining the towel his mother had tucked around the young woman. He had thought that she was dying, but his mother had explained later, embarrassed and unable to look him in the eye, that Mrs Fulton had lost the child she was carrying.

'You were all very kind,' she said now. 'Mrs Goudie too, and your mother.'

'That's what neighbours are for. It's as well that my mother was at home, and not at the hospital when you fell. She's a good nurse.'

'Yes, she is. And a kind woman too.' She looked around at the vegetable beds. 'Do you like digging?'

'I don't mind it. The vegetables are worth it.' Frank McCosh had a colleague with an allotment, and he was fortunate enough to get seeds and even seedlings now and again. The whole tenement, following Ellen Borland's edict that in wartime folk should look after their own, shared in the produce, whether they worked in the garden or not.

'I miss the flowers,' Lena said. 'They were nice to look out on.'

'Aye, they were. I sometimes think,' he confessed, ' that it's a good thing old Mr Brown went when he did, for it would have broken his heart to see what's happened to this place.'

'That's what I think too, only I've never liked to say it because we're all supposed to put food first now.'

'I've never said it to anyone either.' Dennis beamed down at her, delighted to discover that they shared a secret. He broke off a corner of his sandwich and tossed it to a bird that had been hopping about close by ever since he started turning the earth over. 'It's not really waste when it's eaten and enjoyed,' he said apologetically, watching the bird snatch at the offering. 'Birds need food too, and he's been working hard.' Then he rammed the last of the sandwich in his mouth, washed it down with tea, and held out the empty cup. 'Thanks.'

She nodded and turned back towards the tenement. Instead of going in she put the cup and plate down on the ground and picked up a bucket she had brought downstairs.

'Are you fetching some coal?' Dennis called over, leaving the spade where it was and hurrying across to her. 'I'll see to it for you.'

'You're busy. I can manage.'

'Ach, I'm dirty already, I might as well do it for you.' He held out his hand and after a moment's hesitation she relinquished the bucket.

'Half full will do me.'

There wasn't much in her bin, Dennis noticed as the lumps clattered into the bucket. He straightened, shaking his head when she reached out for the handle. 'I'll take it upstairs for you. It won't take a minute, and I can finish the digging when I come back down. '

'Well . . .' she glanced around as if to see if anyone was listening, then said, 'If you're sure it isn't a bother...'

'It's not!' Dennis said fervently. 'My mother would want me to.' A stupid remark worthy of a kick in the backside, he thought at once, his face reddening as he followed Lena Fulton into the close and up the stairs.

There was something missing in the Fultons' flat and at first Dennis couldn't think what it was. True, there was little furniture other than the basic requirements, but that was common enough in these tenements. He glanced around the kitchen as he put down the coal bucket, and realised that not only was the room cold to the point of being chilly; it also gave off a bleak air of something he couldn't quite understand. Then it came to him . . . the flat felt lonely.

'Thank you for your help,' Lena was saying. Her voice had become animated when she'd talked about old Mr Brown and the way he had filled the backcourt with flowers; now it was flat, as though she, too, was affected by the atmosphere in her own home.

He glanced at the small grate, neatly laid with twists of paper and a few sticks. 'Will I light the fire for you before I go?'

'It's too early. I always wait until it gets dark outside. It's comforting to have a fire then.' Lena wore a shawl over her jersey and skirt, and now she drew it closer about her shoulders. For some reason the gesture reminded him of that moment on the dark landing, when he had gathered her into his arms and carried her to her flat. He recalled it vividly; it was as though she had left a physical imprint of herself on him.

'You surely need a bit of warmth, though, for your sewing.' He indicated the material spread over the table, and the open sewing machine standing to one side.

'I manage fine. I have a pair of mitts, and this jersey's warm.'

'You know, this room feels colder than it should.' He lifted his head, testing the chill air against his face, then glanced over at the window. 'It's the window.' He went over to it, reaching across the small chipped sink to run the tips of his fingers round the edge of the pane. Gentle though his touch was, a chip of dried putty came free to rustle down into the sink. 'The glass is loose in the frame, and letting in a draught. All it needs is some fresh putty.'

'Does it?' Her voice was anxious, and when he glanced back at her he saw worry in her blue eyes . . . the same deep colour, he saw now, as the bluebells under the trees in Donald's Wood, where he sometimes went walking. 'Does that mean that the window could fall out?'

All that held the glass in place was the criss-cross pattern of sticky paper which covered everyone's windows these days, to protect people from shards of glass should the pane be shattered by a bomb explosion, but Dennis, unwilling to frighten her, said reassuringly, 'No, but there's quite a draught getting in round the edge of the glass. I could fix it for you if you like.'

'You know about windows?'

'My dad could turn his hand to anything,' he boasted. 'I used to watch him working about the flat and then I helped him when I got older. One of the men at the fire station served his trade as a builder; he'd be able to tell me what to do.'

'I wouldn't want you to go to any trouble . . .'

'It wouldn't be a bother,' Dennis assured her. 'And it wouldn't cost you either, because he'd probably be able to give me the putty too.'

'If you're sure . . .'

'I'm sure,' he said firmly.

12

————— ◆ —————

Cecelia jumped off the bus that had brought her back to Paisley from the Ibrox depot, gave the driver a wave as she passed his cab, and started the walk home from Paisley Cross. It was the end of her shift and she was tired, but even so she stepped out briskly because that was what the uniform demanded. Every time she put it on she felt herself turning into a different person. The old Cecelia was quiet, diffident, a little unsure of herself, but Cecelia the bus conductress was confident and able to take on the world.

Glancing down at the green jacket and skirt, wondering if wearing different clothes could really make a person different inside as well as outside, she reached the end of Moss Street and crossed the junction, heading towards Love Street.

'Hello.'

A young woman, also turning into Love Street, had paused to wait for her. As Cecelia blinked at her, the girl's smile faltered a little.

'Mrs Goudie, isn't it? I'm Chloe . . . Chloe McCosh.'

'The clootie dumpling!' Cecelia suddenly remembered. Then, as the girl started to laugh, 'I don't mean you, I mean . . .'

'I know what you mean. I thought it was you coming along the street.'

'With my mind far away,' Cecelia admitted as they fell

into step together. 'I've been up since just after four this morning. We have to be early to catch the service bus that takes us to the depot so that we can run the workers' buses. Hello.' She smiled at the little girl clutching Chloe's hand. 'Is this your wee sister?'

'No,' the child said firmly. 'I'm Daisy and I'm Grace's wee sister.' She tugged Chloe onward. 'Come on, I'll be late!'

'Daisy lives in St James Street,' Chloe explained as they hurried along. 'My mother's giving her piano lessons and I said I'd fetch her today. It's my half-day; I work in Cochran's.' Her voice, as she mentioned the big emporium, was filled with pride.

'Magritte usually brings me, but she's got toothache,' Daisy piped up. 'and my mummy won't believe that I can come through the streets perfectly well on my own. She's taking Magritte to the dentist to have the tooth pulled out but Magritte doesn't want to because the dentist will leave a big hole in her mouth and it'll bleed and it'll hurt and hurt and—'

'Yes, all right,' Chloe interrupted. 'We don't want to hear any more about poor Magritte. She's a right wee talker,' she confided in a lower tone to Cecelia. 'The only time she shuts her mouth is when she's playing the piano. She's not worked out yet how to do both at the same time, but I'm sure she will. Are you settling in all right at Number forty-two?'

'I like it fine, though I've not had much time to meet my neighbours. Well, there's you, and I've been to the Borlands' flat, and I've met old Mrs Bell and Mrs Fulton, and Mrs Megson and her son . . .' Cecelia's voice tailed away as she realised that one way and another she had met almost everyone without realising it.

'That'll probably be Dennis.' There was a certain ring to the girl's voice as she said the name. 'There's Ralph Megson, but he's still at school. It'll be Dennis you met.'

'That's right. A nice boy, very kind.'

'Oh, he is! And he's a great musician too, he plays the

trumpet in my father's band.' This time there was no mistaking the hero worship in Chloe's voice, or the glow in her eyes as she beamed at Cecelia. The girl was head over heels in love.

'We enjoyed hearing the band practising. Are there any more evenings planned?'

'Next Friday, for a dance on Saturday night. There'll be dumpling,' Chloe said, the dimple in her left cheek deepening.

'I'll still be on the early shift, so I can look forward to the music. And to the dumpling,' Cecelia said as they turned in at their close. Once inside, Daisy shook off Chloe's restraining hand and raced ahead of them and up the stairs. As they began to climb the first flight they heard her small hands slapping impatiently at the door panels, and by the time they gained the first landing the door of the McCosh's flat was ajar and Daisy's shrill voice could be heard chattering away in the depths of the flat.

'I'd invite you in, but with Mum having a piano lesson . . .'

'I'm too tired to be a proper visitor anyway,' Cecelia assured the girl, and began to climb the next flight, wishing, as she often did when returning home after a long and busy shift, that she lived on the lowest floor.

Chloe was a nice lassie, she thought as she climbed, and pretty, too. She hoped that Dennis Megson liked her as much as she clearly liked him.

Ellen Borland was standing at her own door, talking to a youth. Their heads were close together, and Ellen seemed to be giving him low-voiced instructions. As soon as they became aware of Cecelia, Ellen said something to the boy, who immediately bolted across to the stairs leading up to the top floor. As he went, he stuffed something into his jacket pocket.

'It's you, Cecelia hen,' Ellen Borland said easily. 'Just gettin' home from work, eh? How's the job goin', then?'

'Very well. I like it more than I thought I would.'

'I thought it might be your cup of tea. Here, talking of tea, I've got a nice wee bit of cold ham that would just do you a treat. Come on in.'

'If you don't mind, Mrs Borland, my feet are aching and I'd like to get these shoes off . . .'

'Wait here a minute, then,' the woman said, and hurried into her hallway, to reappear almost at once.

'There you are.' She proffered a small greaseproof parcel.

'I can't take it, Mrs Borland!'

'Ach away, you need the nourishment and thae rations books scarce give ye enough tae feed a cat. I'm just lucky, havin' friends that can help me out.' Ellen thrust the parcel into Cecelia's hands. 'And I believe in passin' luck around. That way, it comes back tenfold.'

'There's not much I can do in return, though.'

'Ach, you can always let me off my fare if I get on to your bus some time,' the woman said cheerfully. 'Don't worry about it, pet, those that can help me do help me, and I'm grateful. Young Ralph Megson, that you just saw me talkin' tae . . . he goes messages for me now and again. A nice lad, well brought up. I like tae see young ones with good manners.' Ellen was in the process of settling her shoulder comfortably against the doorframe for a good chat when a voice called from within the flat.

'Ellen hen, what about that tea ye were supposed tae be makin'? My throat's parched!'

'Better go and see tae Donnie,' Mrs Borland said. 'Enjoy the ham, pet.'

It was a day or two before Dennis got the chance to return to Lena Fulton's flat. When he tapped on the door he had to wait for so long that he was beginning to think she had gone out. Then, hearing soft movement from the other side of the panels, he knocked again.

'Who is it?' a voice asked timidly,

He squatted down and opened the letterbox. 'It's me, Dennis Megson.'

'What d'you want?'

'I'm here to mend that window of yours. I've got everything I need for it.'

There was another pause, then he straightened as he heard the snib being lifted.

'Come in,' Lena said as the door was opened wide enough to admit him. Then, as he stepped into the dark hallway, 'Go on into the kitchen.'

Glancing back as he obeyed, he saw the woman peering out on to the landing as though making sure that it was empty.

'We're neighbours, Mrs Fulton,' he said when she followed him into the kitchen. 'There's no harm in me coming to do a wee bit of work for you. I'd do the same for Mrs Goudie if she needed help, and for old Mrs Bell . . . only she sent me off with a flea in my ear the one time I tried to offer to do something for her. Anyway, Mrs Borland looks out for her.'

Lena leaned against the doorframe, huddling the shawl about her thin shoulders as usual, and chewing at her bottom lip. 'I'd not want anyone thinking that I'm takin' advantage of your kindness,' she said at last.

'It's not kindness, it's . . .' he fumbled for a word, and could come up with nothing better than, 'neighbourliness. I'm always happy to fetch some messages for you, or bring up coal, or . . .' he indicated the canvas bag in his hand, 'do a bit of repair work.'

'George doesn't like us to be obligated to folk.'

'I know that Mr Fulton would see to your window himself if he was here, but he's away just now and so it makes sense for me to help out. I'd never want you to feel that you owed me anything for my help.' Dennis wished that he could get her to understand. 'He'd surely be pleased to know that your neighbours were there for you when you needed them.' Then, as she said nothing, but just stared at him, worrying, 'I'll just get on with mending that window, eh?'

After a while, she went back to her own work. Dennis found the whirring of the sewing machine pleasant to listen to.

'There now,' he said as he stepped back, 'that didn't take any time at all, and I'm sure you'll feel this place much warmer now.'

The whirring stopped and he felt Lena's shoulder brush his as she came to look at the window. 'It looks grand.' The admiration in her voice made his chest swell with pride.

'Ach, it wasn't any bother at all.'

'Are you sure I can't pay you something for your time?' she offered hesitantly, and he grinned down at her.

'My charges are a wee bit steep; I usually ask for a cup of tea, but if you can't manage that you can always owe me till another day.'

The first part of the sentence had made her frown anxiously and catch her lower lip between her teeth once more; when he mentioned the tea, she blinked at him for a second or two, then laughed before she could stop herself. He had never heard her laugh before . . . come to think of it, until recently he had not even heard her speak.

'I think I can manage that.'

'Good. I'll just wash my hands first.'

'There's some hot water in the kettle.' She poured it into a basin sitting within the old, chipped sink, then refilled the kettle, and stepped out of his way. He spread his hands out before him, eyeing them and then the small piece of yellow washing soap by the edge of the sink doubtfully.

'D'you have anything I can use to get the worst of this stuff off first? Turpentine, mebbe?'

'There might be some in the big cupboard in the lobby.' Lena was lighting the gas stove. 'George . . . my husband . . . keeps some of his things there.'

'Right you are.'

In the small hallway, lit only by the fanlight, Dennis had to drop to his knees and rummage about amongst the clutter on the floor of the cupboard. He pulled out a small tool bag first, then some tins of paint and varnish.

When he returned to the kitchen he was holding a bottle. 'I found this Ligroin. It's a white spirit that painters use to thin down paint and varnish.'

She nodded. 'It'll be for George's work.'

'Did you know that it's inflammable?'

'Is that bad?'

'It's best to keep it away from naked flame.'

'It's quite safe in that cupboard, surely. Nobody's going to strike a match in there.'

'I know, but . . .' he hesitated, reluctant to frighten her by talking about the possibility of fire during an air raid, then said, 'It's just that this sort of stuff's best kept outside. I could take it all down to the shed for you, if you want. It would be safe there.'

'But it's George's,' she said again. 'He'd not like his things to be touched.'

'He surely wouldn't want anything to happen to you.'

'It won't, will it? Not if I leave it alone.'

Dennis went to the sink, where he carefully tipped a little of the liquid into the palm of one hand. 'I'll screw the top on tight and put it right at the back, out of the way,' he said as he cleaned his hands, 'but you should mebbe ask him in your next letter to let you store it outside, just to be on the safe side.'

He returned the Ligroin to the cupboard, checking the other tins and bottles to make sure that they were well sealed, then went back to the sink, where he picked up the sliver of yellow soap.

'Mr McCosh is working in the garden,' he said, glancing through the window. 'I'll go down and give him a hand.'

'After you've had your tea. Here.' Lena handed him a

small towel as he shook the water from his hands. 'Have you not done enough for today?'

'It's all right. I get peace tae think when I'm digging. There's not much chance of that in our place, with five of us.'

'When I was a wee girl my father had an allotment. He gave me a corner to myself and I planted flowers in it.' A slight smile warmed her pale mouth at the memory.

'Have you never thought of working down there yourself?'

Her eyes widened and then narrowed as she frowned, thinking the proposal over. Finally she said, 'I'd just get in the way. I don't know much about planting and pruning.'

'You don't need to, there's weeding, and earthing up the potatoes and that sort of thing. And you'd not be in the way, the more folk helping the better. Mr McCosh does most of it and I try to help him as much as I can. Mrs McCosh does a bit now and again but she's busy with housework and piano lessons and her WVS work, and my mother works hard enough at the infirmary as it is.'

'She's a good woman,' Lena said. 'You're right, she does enough. Mebbe I should take my turn at working in the garden.' Then, shyly, 'Could I work alongside you? I don't know Mr McCosh very well. You can show me what to do.'

'I'll knock on your door the next time I'm going down there and if you've got the time, you can come with me.'

Leaning back against the sink as he dried his hands, he watched her gather up the cloth strewn over the table, shaking it out then folding it again and again until it was small enough to put aside, on the top of the dresser in the recess that had once held a bed. Then she covered the treadle sewing machine, gathered pins and spools of thread, and put them into an old box. The kettle boiled, and she turned her attention to making tea in a battered metal pot, still with the same swift, deft movements.

'I can feel a difference,' he said, and when she looked

at him, puzzled, he jerked his head in the direction of the window at his back. 'No draught.'

'Oh. You're right, it makes a real difference. You're a good neighbour,' she said, and he felt his face redden.

He was further embarrassed, when he sat down at the table, to find that she had made up a cheese sandwich for him.

'But that's your ration. You mustn't go giving it away to folk!'

'You deserve something to eat after the work you've done.' She indicated the window. 'I'm going to be warmer now, thanks to you. Anyway, I don't eat much.'

That, Dennis thought, studying her thin arms and wan face, was obvious. A bit of gardening in the fresh air, or as fresh as the air was allowed to get in Glen Street, would do her good. Aloud, he said, 'Can we not share? Then I won't feel so greedy.'

She laughed, ducking her head shyly and glancing up at him from beneath her lashes, 'If you insist.'

'I do.' He took the knife she offered, and cut the sandwich in two, offering her half.

For a moment they ate in silence, then she asked, 'Have you lived here long?'

'I was born here. My parents moved in when they got married. I like Glen Street, it's a great place to live.'

'Are you still at the school?'

He felt his face redden. 'Not for a long time. I'm training to be a fireman.'

'Oh! I forgot . . .' A soft pink flush came over her pale face. 'How stupid of me.'

'It's all right. I said just the same thing to Chloe McCosh a few weeks back. Now I know why she glared at me. Not that I'm glaring at you,' Dennis added hurriedly, and almost choked on a mouthful of bread and cheese. He took a swallow of tea to wash it down.

'A fireman?' She looked impressed.

'My father was a fireman,' he told her proudly. 'I'm following in his footsteps.'

'George . . . my husband . . . followed in his father's footsteps too. His father has his own painting and decorating business in Well Street.'

'Fulton's . . . I've heard of them. I didn't realise that it was your man's da that owned it. It must be useful to have a painter . . .' His voice died away as he looked round the shabby room.

'You know what they say about a cobbler's children never having any shoes. The business keeps George and his father and brother busy, so he never found the time to do this place. He's always promising, but . . . .well, he did start varnishing the woodwork in this room when we first moved into the place, but then he was called up before he got round to finishing it. I thought he might manage to finish that the last time he was home on leave, but he couldn't be bothered.'

'I'll do it for you if you want.'

'It's good of you to offer, but George wouldn't like it.' She drew the shawl closer as though protecting herself against something. 'Anyway, you've got enough to do. You play the trumpet in that band, don't you?'

'Mr McCosh's band? Yes, I do.'

'I saw you taking it into their flat a while back, when they were having a practice.'

'Aye, I remember.' She and her husband had been coming up the stairs at the time, and in his haste, Dennis had almost bumped into George Fulton. He could still remember the scowl the man had given him.

'D'you like playing?'

'It's grand!'

'Where did you learn?'

'In the Boys' Brigade. Trumpet and cornet,' he told her proudly. 'I played the cornet mostly while I was in the BB, because it's best for marching music. The trumpet's best for a dance band.'

'It must be very difficult.'

'Not once you realise that you don't want to put pressure on the instrument. Most folk,' he explained, 'push the mouthpiece against their lips and blow into it, but that only makes their muscles ache. The way to do it is to just rest your lips against the instrument and use them to shape the notes.'

'How do you make the music go up and down?'

'Tonguing . . . using your tongue to shape the notes. And there are three valves as well. I use my fingers to operate them.' Then, as she frowned and pursed her lips in her attempt to follow the explanation, he added, 'I could bring the trumpet down some time, if you like, and show you what I mean.'

'Would you?' Her face lit up, and then suddenly she was solemn again. 'I'd not want you to go to the trouble . . .'

'It wouldn't be any trouble at all. I'd like to,' Dennis said. 'It's not often that anyone's interested in hearing about music.'

13

'I'd not want Charlie to think that there's anything special between us,' Chloe told Marion. 'He's a nice enough lad, but I'm too young to get serious about that sort of thing.'

'You speak for yourself.' They were in the McCosh kitchen, ripping down an old jersey of Julia's. It was evening, and Chloe was in charge of her brothers because her parents were both out, her mother on WVS work and her father on Home Guard duty. 'I really like Robert,' Marion went on dreamily. 'I'd not mind getting serious about him.'

'Don't be daft, he'll be getting called up soon and there's no knowing what might happen then.'

'That's right, tell me that he's going to get himself killed. That's a nice thing to say!'

'That's not what I meant. I'm just saying that folk change a lot when they go away from home. He might be a different person when he comes back, or he might have met someone else. Or you could meet someone else,' Chloe tried to explain. Although they were both working women, it seemed to her that she and Marion were still poised on the verge of adulthood, not quite ready to plunge in, because once they did there would be no turning back, ever.

'Robert says we were meant for each other.'

'Are you sure he's not just telling you that because he . . .'

'He what?'

'You know,' Chloe hinted, then as her friend continued to stare blankly, 'him going away to fight and all; he isn't trying to get you to do anything you shouldn't, is he?'

Marion's uncomprehending stare lasted for a few more seconds, then realisation set in, swiftly followed by shock. 'Chloe McCosh, how could you even think of such a thing? What d'you take me for? What d'you take Robert for?' Her voice rose to a screech, and Leslie, who had been playing in the front room with his train set, put his head round the door.

'Is everything all right?'

'No it is not!' Marion snapped, while Chloe smiled at her brother and said, 'Everything's fine. We were just singing.'

'Oh. Can I have a biscuit?'

'No, you know you're not supposed to.'

'I'm hungry!'

'You've not long had your dinner. Go and play.'

'I'm tired of playing on my own. I'm going out the back to play with Duncan.'

'It's getting dark, and it's nearly time for bed.' Chloe cast a glance at the kitchen clock. 'I'll be calling him in any minute now.'

'But I want to go out . . .' His voice took on a nasal whine, and Marion shot an irritated glance at him.

'Mebbe just the one biscuit,' Chloe capitulated, laying down the half-unravelled jersey sleeve and going to fetch the biscuit barrel. 'And only if you go back to your train set.'

'There's times,' Marion remarked pointedly as the door closed behind Leslie, 'when I'm glad that I'm the youngest of my family.'

'Mebbe now you know what your big sisters have had to put up with.'

'So what's wrong with Charlie Hepburn, then, that you won't get serious about him?' Marion wanted to know as they got on with their work.

'Nothing's wrong with him. He's a pleasant, decent lad and I like him, but I don't think I like him as much as he likes me. He's got his mother to ask me round for my tea on Saturday. His father's going to be home and Charlie wants me to meet him.'

'Oh, that sounds serious,' Marion mocked.

'I wish he hadn't, with his father being the way he is. An important man,' Chloe explained as Marion raised her eyebrows. 'Travelling round the country and making speeches the way he does.'

'What are you going to wear?'

'I thought my navy dress with the puff sleeves and the wee flowers all over it.'

'It might be cold for short sleeves.'

'I can wear my good pale blue cardigan over it.'

'Mmm.' Marion considered for a moment. 'I think that would be all right,' she agreed; then, holding up the ball of wool she had just created from one sleeve of the jersey, 'D'you think that this would knit up into a decent hat?'

'You'd suit the colour. And you could use this sleeve to make mitts, or mebbe a wee scarf.'

'You're not thinking of making a hat from it too, are you? We couldn't both wear the same colour.'

'I was wondering about a sort of waistcoat. You could borrow it, if you want, when you wear the hat.'

'And you could borrow the hat when you wear the waistcoat,' Marion said, and the quarrel between them was over.

When the jersey had been converted to four balls of crinkled wool Chloe dragged herself back to her duties as babysitter, instructing Leslie to tidy away his train set and then going downstairs to fetch Duncan in.

He was squatting down, a bucket by his side, grubbing happily in the border of the big vegetable bed, while Dennis Megson, stripped to his shirtsleeves although the wind was keen, dug a trench. Someone else was working in the far corner, huddled down over the earth, but as it was getting dark, Chloe couldn't make out who it was.

'Ach, do I have to go up?' Duncan whined when his sister arrived. 'I'm helping Dennis.' He shook the battered pail at her. 'I'm weeding.'

'And making a good job of it.' Dennis drove the spade effortlessly into the earth and straightened, wiping the back of an arm over his forehead. 'But it's time for us all to call it a day, son. It's getting too dark to see what we're supposed to be doing. We don't want the carrots and potatoes to be growing down the way by mistake because we couldnae see which way up to plant them.'

'You're not planting, you're weeding and digging,' Chloe pointed out.

'Le . . . Mrs Fulton's putting in onions.' Dennis indicated the far corner, where the third gardener still worked, apparently oblivious to the conversation, then raised his voice slightly, 'We're going in now, Mrs Fulton, it's getting too dark to work on.'

As the woman rose and turned, Chloe saw that she had been sitting on a low stool. Dennis hurried over to lift it in one hand, offering his free arm to Lena to help her over the uneven earth and on to the flagged path. Once there, she released her hold on him and scurried into the tenement, with a murmured 'Good evening,' as she passed the others.

'I didn't know she was interested in gardening,' Chloe said as they turned to follow her.

'She's doing her bit, same as young Duncan here.' He fetched his jacket from the top of one of the coal bins as they passed, and slung it over his shoulder.

'Can I help you next time?' the lad asked eagerly.

'Any time. We can always use a good strong set of muscles. Good night, then,' Dennis said when they reached the first landing.

'Go on in, Duncan,' Chloe ordered her brother, and then, to Dennis, 'Are you working tonight?'

'Not at the station, but I'm fire watching.' He had volun-teered to become part of the street team. 'My mother's on duty at the hospital so I'm keeping an eye on the rest of them as well,' he added.

She glanced round to see if Duncan had gone indoors, and was irritated to find him breathing on the brass letter-box then writing on it with one finger. 'Duncan McCosh, will you stop that at once and get indoors when I tell you? Now I'll have to fetch a cloth and polish it up again.'

'I'll do it,' he said, and disappeared into the flat. Chloe turned to Dennis, pinning a tolerant, older-sister smile on her mouth, only to find that he was already halfway up the flight leading to his own home.

There was nobody at home when Dennis returned on Thursday after working an early shift. He took the trumpet from its box beneath his bed and carried it downstairs.

'I brought it,' he said when Lena Fulton opened the door. Then, as she looked blankly from his face to the instrument he was holding out in his two hands, as though it was an offering, 'My trumpet. You said that you'd like to see it, but if you're busy I can come back another time.' He should have thought, he told himself, sick with embarrassment; he should have realised that she was just being polite when she said she wanted to hear him play.

Then, just as his heart was hurtling down towards his sturdy boots, she blinked the blankness out of her eyes and said, 'Oh, your trumpet! Of course I want to hear it. Come on in.'

In the kitchen, he looked at the open sewing machine and the materials strewn about the table. 'You're busy.'

'Not too busy, though.' Already, she was gathering up the cloth with those swift, neat feminine movements that fascinated him. 'I'm lucky, I'm getting plenty of work from folk these days; now that things are hard to get, they're all wanting their clothes made over. But I can make time for myself when I want. And for you.'

She listened solemnly as he explained the trumpet's functions, then asked hesitantly, 'Do you mind if I . . . can I hold it?'

'Of course.' He put it into her outstretched hands and watched as she ran her fingers over it. A slow smile broke over her face.

'It feels . . . comforting.'

Dennis grinned in return. 'That's what I think too. Try playing it. Don't push it against your lips,' he cautioned as she lifted the instrument to her mouth. 'Just lay them gently against the mouthpiece, as though you were giving it a kiss, then breathe into it.'

She made several tries at it, but had to give up and return the trumpet to him. 'You play it for me,' she said, and he put the mouthpiece to his lips and played the opening bars of 'The Way You Look Tonight', softly, so that nobody outside or upstairs would hear it. Lena listened, entranced, and when he stopped, after a long, hushed pause she said, 'That was lovely.'

'It's not too difficult when you know how.'

'It sounds as though you're part of the trumpet when you're playing, and it's part of you.'

He beamed at her. Nobody else had put it quite so well. 'That's exactly what it feels like.'

'What happens if you hurt your mouth?'

'Then I can't play. I mind once when I was supposed to play the cornet for a Boys' Brigade parade, and I got the toothache. I couldnae bear the touch of the mouthpiece and I'd tae miss the parade.' He grinned. 'My mother says the good thing about it is that I'd never let myself get mixed up in a fight, for fear of hurting my mouth. And she's right. Would you like tae hear something else?'

She nodded, then as the final notes of 'The Talk of the Town' died away, said, 'That's lovely.'

'You can hear more tomorrow night. We've got another

practice. You could open your door and listen to it, everyone else does that. Sometimes folk from outside come in and sit on the stairs to listen.'

'Mebbe I will,' she said.

Somewhat against her husband's wishes, Julia had invited Charlie Hepburn to sit in on the band practice.

'There's little enough room for the four of us as it is, and you know what a practice is like . . . all stops and starts. We have to be free to concentrate on getting it right.'

'That's exactly what Charlie wants . . . to see musicians working at getting things right. And he'll not take up all that much space,' she coaxed.

'I suppose you've already told the lad he can come.'

'I might have mentioned it.'

'Oh, all right,' said Frank McCosh, realising that he had already lost the battle. 'But just this once, mind'

'We'll not be playing the way you've heard us play in the dance hall,' he cautioned Charlie when the boy arrived. 'This is a practice so we'll be stopping and starting and stopping again to get things right. You'll soon get fed up listening to the same bits over and over again.'

'I'll be interested in seeing how you all work at things to get them just right.'

'Well, as right as we can,' Frank was saying drily as a knock came to the outer door. Chloe rushed to open it.

'Charlie's come to watch the practice,' she told Dennis as he came into the hall.

'Your boyfriend?'

'He's a friend, not a boyfriend!'

'He's a friend, and he's a boy, so does that not make him a boyfriend?' Dennis said maddeningly, and then turned as slow heavy footsteps began to trudge up the stairs from below. 'Hello, Bert. Grand evening.'

'It is if ye only have tae come down the stairs tae get here,' Bert grumbled as he appeared. 'Some of us have tae walk further than that, and it's bloody cold out. Oh sorry, hen.' He whipped his cap off as he reached the landing and saw Chloe in the doorway. 'Never noticed you there.'

'Think yourself lucky that you didnae have to carry your drums and all,' Dennis said cheerfully. The drums shared the McCosh's big hall cupboard with Frank's Home Guard uniform and kit. 'We've got a visitor tonight. He's a friend of young Chloe's and he's a boy, but he's not a boyfriend.'

'Eh?'

'Oh, for goodness' sake,' Chloe snapped, exasperated. 'Are you coming in or are you not?'

'What are the two of you on about?' Bert asked, bewildered, as she flounced back into the flat.

'Don't let it bother you, I was just enjoying a bit of a tease. After you, sir!' As he stepped back to let the elderly man precede him into the flat, Dennis glanced across the landing and smiled as he saw that Lena Fulton's door was very slightly ajar.

Lena had pulled a chair from the kitchen into the hall, where she sat in the dark, waiting. She heard someone running down the stairs from one of the flats above, then the sound of knocking followed by the murmur of voices. She recognised Dennis Megson's laugh, and then there were more footsteps, this time coming up the stairs, and a deeper voice joined in the conversation. Then the door closed, and about five minutes later the music began.

She rose very quietly and opened her own door a little wider, peering through the crack to make sure that the landing was empty. Satisfied that it was, and that anyone passing was unlikely to notice her door ajar, she was about to return to her seat when the small band began to play 'The Way You Look Tonight'.

Lena paused, listening, unaware that she had begun to lean slightly towards the source of the music, her good leg going on tiptoe. Her thin body began to sway gently in time to the rhythm.

In his front room, Frank McCosh lowered his saxophone and tossed a brief nod at Dennis, who took a half-step forward, raising the trumpet to his lips. 'This,' he thought to himself, 'is for Lena.'

And across the landing, safe within the darkness of her narrow hall, Lena Fulton danced to the trumpet's golden, rounded notes, her body dipping each time her weight transferred to her shorter leg. The music stole in through the narrow space at the door to wrap itself about her like a soft, warm shawl. For the first time in months, perhaps years, she was happy, and at peace.

'They're holding another band practice downstairs,' Cecelia wrote, 'and I can't stop thinking about the last time, when we danced out on the landing. Oh, Fergus, I can't bear being so far away from you . . .'

The writing paper suddenly blurred, and she knuckled her eyes with a fist, then tutted with irritation when she realised that she had succeeded only in releasing the tears to splash on to the letter. She tried blotting them with her sleeve, but that only smeared the ink. Sighing, she crumpled up the page and threw it into the meagre little fire she had allowed herself, and then fumbled in her pocket for a handkerchief.

Once her eyes were properly dried and her nose blown hard she pulled the writing pad over and dipped the pen into the bottle of ink. Fergus had enough on his mind without her moaning and weeping all over his letter.

'They're holding another band practice downstairs,' she began again, 'which meant that I got a nice bit of dumpling, which I enjoyed for my tea. Not that they need to bribe me on practice nights, I love listening to the music. The people in the tenement are all friendly, and I am getting to know them and to feel at home.

'You'll never guess what happened the other day at work. We always have to check the buses after each shift and hand in anything that has been left behind. And I found a whole, unopened bottle of whisky, in a paper bag under the seat! When I showed it to him, Harry said that I didn't have to hand it in, I could keep it and nobody would know. He was desperate to get his hands on it. Well, *I* would know for one, and so would the poor soul that had left it behind by accident, so I took it into the office when we got back to the depot. The inspector was impressed, I think. He said that not every clippie would have done that. Harry isn't speaking to me at the moment, and some of the other drivers are being very offhand with me, but that can't be . . .'

'Oh, blast and bother!' she suddenly said aloud, staring down at the page she had almost covered with her neat writing. She had completely forgotten her decision to wait until Fergus's next leave before telling him the truth about her job, and now she had almost given the game away in a letter!

'Stupid woman!' she muttered as the second page flared up in the fireplace. At this rate, she would run out of writing paper, and it was hard enough to find these days.

Sighing, she started afresh on a new page. 'They're holding another band practice downstairs . . .'

14

'Here, let me help.'

Lena Fulton flinched as a hand came out of nowhere and took hold of the handle of her shopping basket. Then, peering up at the man who had stopped her on her way along the pavement, she said in relief, 'Oh, it's you.'

'Only me, on my way home like yourself. Did you think you were being robbed?' Dennis asked with a grin.

'No, it was just . . . I can manage,' she said. 'There's not much in it.'

'You're right there.' He glanced down at the two small parcels in the basket. 'But I'd like to carry it for you anyway.'

He had turned to walk alongside her, the basket already in his hand, and so she had no option but to let him accompany her. It was a moment before she realised that he had, indeed, turned before falling into step with her.

'You weren't on your way home, you were walking in the other direction.'

'Was I? I must have been going somewhere else then, but for the life of me I can't think where, so it can't have been important. So I might as well walk back to the tenement with you. Did you hear the music the other night?' he asked, before she could argue.

'Aye. It was good to hear music again.'

'Again?'

'My brother used to play the violin. Are you sure you can't remember where you were going when you saw me?' Walking along the street like this, in broad daylight where anyone might see them together, worried her. What if Aunt Cathy decided to call in and saw her with Dennis Megson? What if she mentioned it to George when he was next home on leave?

'I'm quite sure,' he said, and she quickened her step and kept as far away from him as she could, so that nobody could mistake them for a couple.

Dennis sensed her nervousness; he couldn't do otherwise because it radiated from her like spokes from the axle of a wheel. He fell silent until they were nearing Number 42, then as Lena reached out and almost snatched the basket from him, he asked, 'D'you ever go walking in the Fountain Gardens?'

'I've been there, but not often.'

'I go quite a lot. I wouldnae mind going there now, for it's a nice day. D'you fancy a wee stroll?'

'No, I couldn't! I'm far too busy!'

'Oh well. I'm going anyway,' he said, 'so if you change your mind, we'll mebbe meet up.'

Lena scurried up the stairs, head down as usual, and rushed into her flat. In the kitchen she put the basket down on the table and stood gripping the handles tightly until her breathing slowed. Then she started to unfasten her coat, looking round the four walls of the kitchen. They might as well be the walls of a cell, she thought, suddenly sickened by the limitations of her daily life. At least when George was home there was shopping for two and not just for herself. And on those days when he was in a good mood, they sometimes went out for a walk together. When he was gone, it never occurred to her to go anywhere other than to the shops for essential supplies, or to return work she had completed or, occasionally, on a visit to her aunt's flat in William Street, in Paisley's West End. She stopped unbuttoning her coat and went to the single window. Dennis was right, it was a nice day. The April sky was blue, with little white puffs of cloud floating across it.

Lena drew a deep breath, but only stale air filled her lungs. She bit her lip and turned to stare round the kitchen and then, making up her mind, she hastily buttoned her coat again and hurried from the flat and down the stairs, anxious to return to the fresh breezy day before she lost her nerve.

The large stretch of land bordered by Glen Street, Caledonia Street and Love Street had originally been the Hope Temple Gardens, created in the eighteenth century by Paisley manufacturer and florist John Love 'for the pleasure of the people of the town'. Over a hundred years later the area was bought by Thomas Coats, a member of a large family that had sprung from humble beginnings to become a local employer and benefactor. The Coats family had built the huge Ferguslie Thread Mill complex in Paisley's West End, and had then spun its web world-wide, with Paisley as its centre.

After creating a splendid park fit to grace the largest and most sophisticated city in the realm, Thomas Coats had in May 1868 handed it over to the townsfolk to enjoy as their own, a haven of peace and greenery within the busy industrial town.

Still in a hurry, afraid that if she slowed down she would lose her nerve and bolt for home, Lena went through the gates and along one of the wide walkways that radiated from the centre. Dennis was sitting on a bench beside the magnificent fountain; hesitating, she turned to look at the gate, with some idea of scuttling back home to safety, then she dug her fists into her coat pockets and made herself walk on.

'I was thinking . . .' he said without turning his head when she sat down beside him, 'that it must be a grand feeling to be able to make a place like this and just give it away for folk to enjoy.' Then, turning to bathe her in one of his wide grins, 'On the other hand, the man that did it lived in a fine big house with a garden mebbe twice this size, all to himself.'

'It was still a good thing to do.'

'Aye, you're right.' He nodded at the nearest of the four huge sea lions in the bottom pool. 'I wonder what that fellow thinks of all the changes he's seen in the past seventy years.'

Lena, her racing heart beginning to slow at last, studied the beast's raised head. 'Whatever he thinks, he's keeping it to himself,' she said, and Dennis gave a bark of laughter.

'You're right. I wish, though, that that man over there had written something about it all.' He glanced over at the statue of Rabbie Burns close by.

'It's nice here, isn't it?' Lena drew in a deep breath, and sat back, looking round at the broad stretches of grass, the flowerbeds, the lush trees stirring in the breeze. 'I should come more often.'

'I come in quite a lot. It's a great place if you just want to sit and think about things. You'd scarce know you were in the town.'

For a long time they sat in comfortable silence, content to study the fountain and the statue. Lena finally broke it. 'I enjoyed the band practice very much,' she said. 'You're all very clever.'

'You should come to a dance some time and hear us properly. Lots of folk come just for the music,' he hurried on as he saw her beginning to shake her head. 'You don't have to dance, you could just sit at the side and listen.'

'George wouldn't like it, not while he's away.'

Dennis almost asked if George was opposed to his wife having any sort of life at all, but he stopped himself just in time. It was none of his business. Instead, he asked casually, 'That brother of yours who's musical; does he live in Paisley too?'

'He did, until the war started. Then he went into the navy and his ship was torpedoed almost at once.'

'I'm sorry.'

'So am I,' Lena said. 'But these things happen when there's a war.' Then, while he was still wondering what to say next, 'Alfie. He was christened Alfred, after my grandfather, but we always called him Alfie. It suited him better. Alfred always sounds like a middle-aged name to me.'

'I suppose that was because it was your grandfather's name.'

'You're right,' she said, surprised. 'D'you know, I never thought of that before. Alfie liked to play the sort of music you'd hear at concerts. He used to take me to concerts. I liked that.'

The fresh air had coaxed some colour into her face, and memories had softened and curved her mouth and given her blue eyes a soft, dewy look. The breath caught in Dennis's throat as he realised that he was probably seeing the young Lena that George Fulton had fallen in love with.

'Is it your mother that sometimes visits you?' he asked, and then, wondering if she would think that he had been spying on her, 'I've seen her at your door once or twice when I was going up and down the stairs.'

'That's my aunt. She looked after me and Alfie after our parents died of the consumption. Though I was working by then. We could have managed fine between us, but I think my aunt still saw us as bairns.'

'Folk do that; my mother for one. To hear the way she speaks sometimes, you'd think that I was still a child and she had to look out for me, when she's got more than enough on her plate.'

All at once Dennis began to pour out his worries about his mother, who never seemed to get enough rest. 'She works hard at the infirmary, and now she's taken to doing extra work at one of the First Aid Posts as well. And she tries too hard to take my father's place on top of everything else.'

'She's a fine woman. She was very kind to me when I had my accident.'

'My dad used to say that she'd a heart the size of Glasgow.' Dennis laughed at the memory. 'But it's true, for she cares about everyone. She'd look after the whole world if she could, but she needs someone to look after her, the way my father did The girls are good, though. Bessie's become a right wee housewife; she doesn't even seem to mind standing in queues after school to get the messages, and she knows everything there is to know about coupons and money. Amy's a great help too, and at least I'm bringing in some money now. I wish I earned enough to support all of us.'

'You will, one day,' Lena said, and then got to her feet. 'I have to go now. I've got work to do.'

'I'll walk back with you.'

'No!' she said sharply. 'Best not.'

He watched her walk away from him, head down, and was glad that she had stopped him before he mentioned Ralph. Speaking of his growing suspicions about his brother to anyone, even Lena or Tom McIntosh at the fire station, would have been a betrayal.

Ralph was without doubt the most intelligent member of the family; unlike Dennis, a steady plodder who enjoyed learning for its own sake, the younger boy had a quick-silver mind that learned quickly, then grew bored just as swiftly. To Ralph, school was a prison and he couldn't wait to be free of it. He thirsted continuously after adventure, and his main hope these days was that the war would continue until he was old enough to become involved. He had already made one attempt to enlist in the army, and had been furious when the recruitment officer told him kindly to go back to his mammy and give it a year or two yet.

It was Ralph's hunger for the material things of life, and for the money to buy them, that concerned Dennis the most.

There were ways to satisfy such a hunger, and for folk like the Megsons, folk who had very little to begin with, most of these ways were illegal.

Lena had disappeared from sight now. Dennis began to walk towards the gate nearest home, deep in thought.

Chloe, standing at the other side of the gardens and almost hidden from Dennis by the fountain, watched him walk away. She was fond of strolling through the gardens, and did it frequently, but this was the first time she had ever seen Dennis there with Mrs Fulton.

The two of them had looked so cosy, with their heads close together as though discussing something very important. But what could Dennis and Mrs Fulton possibly want to discuss? Chloe wondered, confusion, unease and a stab of jealousy mingling within her.

The children were shabbily dressed and not as clean as they might have been, and the woman's eyes were red and swollen in an ashen face. When they boarded the bus at Paisley's West End the older girl steered the woman to a seat, sitting beside her and patting her shoulder now and again, while the younger children, a girl and a boy, claimed the seat in front and immediately knelt up on it so that they could look at the other two over its back. Their small faces were tight with worry, their eyes solemn.

Going to collect their fares, Cecelia wondered if they had received that most dreaded of visitations, a telegram. These days, all telegrams meant bad news; a husband, father, son, brother or fiancé lost in action, taken prisoner, killed. Every time she herself saw a telegraph boy in the street her heart retreated into such a knot of fear that it almost stopped.

'Are you all right?' she asked as the woman fumbled in a purse that looked as worn as herself, bringing the money out coin by coin. 'D'you need help?'

'Nothin' you can help with, hen, though it's kind of you tae ask. It's my sister in Glasgow that's been taken ill and

I've been sent for. Her man's in the forces and she's ...'
she glanced at the children, then leaned forward slightly to
mouth the words, 'havin' a baby.' Then, aloud, 'And she's
on her own so I'll have to go on the train.' The words rattled
out as though once started, they refused to stop. 'She's had
a lot of trouble that way before, poor soul. And my own
man's away too, and when I took the weans to his mother's
she was out so I'll have to take them with me and the wee
ones are both under five so I don't pay for them,' she ended
in a rush, indicating the two smallest children.

The girl was certainly less than five years old, but as for
the boy ... Cecelia opened her mouth and then closed it
again. One missed fare wouldn't hurt, she told herself as
she stamped the ticket, and the poor woman had more than
enough to cope with as it was. In any case, the clippies had
to use their own discretion where youngsters were concerned, for it was a company rule that no child should be
put off a bus, even if he or she did not have the money to
pay the fare. In this case, Celia decided, she was using her
discretion.

When she had handed over the tickets she dug into her
pocket and brought out a small bag of sweets. The children's eyes lit up and the smaller ones each dipped an eager
fist into the paper bag then crammed the sweets into their
mouths.

'What d'ye say tae the kind lady?' the woman prompted
them, and they murmured a dribbly 'Thank you' round their
sweets. The older girl shook her head shyly, and then as
her mother nudged her, she took a sweet and thanked
Cecelia before popping it into her mouth.

'Have one yourself.' She held the bag out towards the
woman.

'It's very kind of you, but no thanks. They're chewy
sweeties, and my teeth are nae too good. I don't want the
toothache on top of my other worries, hen.'

The bus filled at the next stop, and Cecelia noticed on

her rounds that the woman had gathered her brood together, squeezing the four of them into the one seat so that other people could sit down. At least she was more considerate than some.

'Move right into the bus, sir, please,' Cecelia said to a man who had remained on the platform. The Kilbarchan to Abbotsinch run ended at the Fleet Arm installation, and so she was used to dealing with airmen and navy men of all nationalities . . . Australians, Free French and Poles as well as British. This particular passenger was in a uniform unknown to her.

He stayed where he was. 'One ticket to Abbots-inch, please,' he said in careful English.

She told him the fare, and he searched through a handful of change then proffered a few coins.

'You need more than that, sir.'

'Not on the platform, madam.'

'You shouldn't be on the platform, sir, you should be inside the bus.' She pointed, trying to speak as clearly and slowly as he had. 'There are empty seats inside.'

'Madam, in Poland is only half the price to stand on the platform.'

'In Scotland, you have to go into the bus and pay the full price.'

He was a dapper little man, a good two inches shorter than she was. Now he pouted up at her and said, 'Madam, I prefer to stand here, so that I may enjoy your company.'

'In Scotland, sir, that is not allowed.' They were being so formal with each other that at any minute, Cecelia thought, the two of them might break into a minuet, or an old-fashioned waltz. But dancing was the last thing on the man's mind.

'You go out with me tonight?' he asked hopefully. 'You go to the pictures with me?'

'I beg your pardon, sir?'

He beamed up into her face, revealing several gold fillings

in his teeth. 'You go out with me?' he repeated, and then, with a hopeful lift of the eyebrows, 'You be naughty with me?'

She felt the colour rush up into her face from beneath the collar of her crisp white blouse, and realised that she must look like a tomato on the vine, ready for plucking.

'I . . . I . . .' she stammered, looking over his head at the passengers seated on the long seats nearest the doorway. Thank goodness none of them seemed to have heard a word, but as the bus neared its next stop several people had begun to make their way down the aisle towards her.

'I'm sorry, sir, but fraternising with a Glasgow Corporation uniform is not permitted,' she gabbled, slamming a rigid forefinger on the bell push. 'Please clear the platform, passengers wish to alight.'

He went to a seat, shoulders drooping, and each time she caught his eye after that he looked at her sorrowfully with big dark eyes.

Most of the passengers got off at the next stop, Paisley Cross. The red-eyed woman was among them, but when she tried to shepherd her little flock from the bus, the children hung back, arguing. Cecelia sighed, and went to investigate.

'Is there something wrong? Only we've got a timetable to keep to, and I can't hold the bus back.'

'You've been very kind already,' the woman said, then bit her lip. 'They don't want to go to my sister's and I don't blame them, it's just a single room with nothing for them to do. And what with her being . . . in a delicate condition, it's no' really fittin' for them to be there.'

'Well . . .' Cecelia looked at the little family helplessly. 'Is there nobody you can leave them with?'

'There's his mother when she comes home but I can't leave them outside in the street to wait for her, can I? She should be home by the time the bus gets back to Broomlands,' the woman said, struck by a sudden thought.

'You could put them off there, couldn't you, on your way back? Sadie here has the address, she'll keep an eye on them if you'd just let them stay on the bus till it gets back there.' Then, as Cecelia stared speechlessly, still trying to make sense out of the sudden flow of words, 'Oh thank you, you're a very nice person! Be good now, and do what the lady tells ye,' she warned the children. And before Cecelia knew what was happening, she had gone and the few people boarding the bus had already seated themselves.

'Go and sit down,' she told the children, and belled Harry. Then she gave her bag of sweets to the eldest girl. 'Divide them out fairly,' she said.

15

At the terminus, the Polish man paused on the platform on his way out. 'No?' he asked.

'No!' Cecelia told him firmly, and he sighed, and dismounted.

'What are they doing here?' Harry wanted to know when he came round for his break before the bus set off again. Cecelia explained in a rush, finishing with, 'So on the way back, could you stop in Broomlands Street near King Street, and give me a minute to take these three to their gran's?'

'We can manage,' Sadie said at once. 'I know where she lives.'

'I need to make sure that you've been handed over safely.'

'I don't know,' Harry grumbled. 'This is a public transport service, not a nursery for abandoned weans!'

'Ssshhh!' She shot a swift glance at the children, lowering her voice. 'Don't say such things in front of them, they'll start to worry.'

'They're not the only ones. I've got enough to do just drivin' the bus from one place tae the other without havin' tae stop here and there while my clippie nips out tae see if someone's granny's at home.'

'It's all right for you, sitting in your cab all the time,' Cecelia shot back at him, her nerves beginning to fray. 'Nobody can pester you there. I'd a wee Polish passenger trying to get half fare by travelling on the platform. Then he wanted me to go out with him.'

'You should have gone,' Harry told her. 'And told him that the three weans were part of the deal. And you'd better hope we don't get an inspector on the bus on the way back!'

'Won't be a minute,' Cecelia told the startled passengers on the lower deck as the bus drew in at its unscheduled stop. She hustled the children off and ran with them up the nearest close. Sadie flew ahead, and when they caught up with her she was fishing about inside the letterbox.

'She usually leaves the key on a string if she's at home,' she said, then straightened, dismay in her round blue eyes. 'It's not there.'

'What does that mean?' Cecelia asked, her heart sinking, but the girl had already darted across to knock on the door opposite.

'D'you know where my gran is?' she asked the old man who finally opened the door.

'Eh?' He bent down and peered into her face, then said, 'Oh, it's you, hen. Come tae see yer granny?'

'She's not in.'

'I know that, I met her goin' down the stair this mornin' when I was on my way out mysel'. She's gone tae see some friend that's awful no-weel. She'll be back in the mornin', though, because it's her turn tae wash the stairs.'

'In the morning?' Cecelia asked, aghast.

The old man looked at her, taking in her uniform and ticket bag, then asked wheezily, 'Lost yer bus, hen? It's no' here. I'd have seen it if it had come up thae stairs.'

'Is there anyone who could look after the children until their grandmother comes back tomorrow?' Cecelia asked desperately over his gasping laughter.

'Eh? No' that I can think of, hen,' he said, and shut his door.

Three pairs of eyes fixed on Cecelia.

'Back to the bus,' she said.

*   *   *

'What am I going to do?' she asked Harry as they sat in the bus at the Kilbarchan terminus.

'Don't ask me. You wouldnae share that whisky you found below one of the seats,' he said huffily, 'so why should you expect me tae share these three? Ye'll have tae hand them in tae the office.'

'I can't hand in children!'

'Why not? Their mammy did. Here,' he said, relenting a little in the face of her despair, 'have half of this sandwich.'

She chewed on the unappetising sandwich, made of slices of national bread thinly spread with some sort of paste. The children had eaten all her sandwiches and now the girls were playing peevers on the pavement, on beds marked out by a stub of chalk Sadie had produced from her pocket, while the boy, Tommy by name, was busy with a handful of marbles.

The three of them travelled back and forth on the bus for the rest of the shift, and caused a lot of interest when Cecelia led them into the depot. Some of the clippies found food for them, while Harry, to his fury, had to put up with a lot of joshing from the other drivers about his new family. Then the inspector arrived.

'What are those kids doing here?' he wanted to know.

'Cecelia here found them on her bus,' Nancy smirked. 'She's handing them in to the lost property department and if they're not claimed in six months she'll have 'em back.'

'Their mother had to go and look after her sister and their grandmother won't be home until tomorrow morning,' Cecelia explained, colour rushing to her face.

'Well, you can just take them out of here . . . and don't come back until you're got rid of them.'

'I'm on late shift tomorrow, they'll be with their grandmother by then.'

'You make sure of that,' the inspector snarled. 'Come back with these kids in tow, lady, and you'll be gettin' your books.'

* * *

There was nothing else for it but to take the children back to Glen Street with her. As they trailed along the street Cecelia tried to work out how she would manage to feed and accommodate them, and came up with only one answer . . . she must throw herself and her charges on Mrs Borland's mercy.

The woman was at home, and more than willing to take over. 'Och, the poor wee things,' she crooned, sweeping them and Cecelia into her flat. 'Come away in, now. Donnie, see what we've got here,' she added as she opened the kitchen door.

'Oh aye? Come in, come in,' Donnie Borland said charitably from his usual armchair. 'Put the kettle on, Ellen.'

'If I could just borrow some milk, and mebbe some bread . . .' Cecelia began.

'They need more than that. A wee bit of sausage, eh? And mebbe an egg? And none of that nasty powdered stuff,' Ellen added as the children's eyes brightened. 'Fried bread an' all. It's what we were going to have for our own tea. Plenty for everyone. And they can sleep in our wee room tonight, it's where my own grandweans stay when they're here.'

'It's very kind of you, Mrs Borland, but I don't want to be a nuisance . . .'

The woman patted Cecelia's arm. 'Don't you worry, hen, there's no nuisance about it. We're happy tae do this for you, aren't we, Donnie? And mebbe some day,' she added, beaming at Cecelia, 'you'll be able tae do somethin' for me. We should always look after our own, pet.'

'That's a nice lady,' Sadie said when Cecelia collected her and her siblings from the Borlands' flat the next morning, their faces so clean that they shone, and each head of hair well brushed.

'We had porridge, ' Tommy boasted as they set off up the street, while wee Molly added in awe, 'With syrup on it!'

All three children, full of porridge, golden syrup and high spirits, scurried ahead of Cecelia, who was hard put to keep up with them as they made their way up Gilmour Street then along the High Street into Wellmeadow and then, beyond, to Broomlands Street. She was relieved, when she reached the top of the stairs, to see Sadie opening the door. The missing grandmother had come home, just in time to save Cecelia's job.

'Wait a minute,' she called as they rushed into the flat, 'what's your grandmother's name?'

'Gran,' Molly, the last of them, shouted back. 'Come on in!' Then she vanished, leaving Cecelia to look in vain for a nameplate.

'Gran ... Gran, we've come to stay!' she heard them shouting as she ventured in through the open door. The children were all leaping about the small kitchen, talking over each other and waving their arms at the elderly woman who stood blinking at them. The noise was terrible.

As Cecelia appeared in the doorway, the woman's eyes widened, and she gathered the excited children to her.

'Who are you? What are you doin' in my home? I never invited ye in here!'

'Mrs ... er ... I'm Cecelia Goudie, and your daughter-in-law asked me to look after the children ...' Cecelia began, but the woman was having none of it. She pushed the children behind her then moved towards Cecelia, her face set in grim lines.

'If ye're from the Social ye can just get out! These are my grandweans and they're not goin' tae be taken away by you or anyone else!'

Cecelia took a step back, into the tiny hallway. 'I'm bringing them back, not taking them away,' she said frantically. 'Their mother had to go and help her sister in Glasgow so I took them for the night because you were out. A neighbour helped and they've been quite safe. We made sure they did their homework and ...'

The children, ignoring their grandmother's attempts to stay between them and Cecelia, had followed her, and were still leaping about like a pack of excited puppies. Now Sadie calmed down and said in a grown-up, matter-of-fact way, 'She can't hear you because she's deaf.'

'Stone deaf,' Molly agreed, nodding vigorously.

'It's all right, she'll make you a cup of tea when I've explained it all to her,' Sadie urged as Cecelia hesitated on the verge of flight. 'She's just glaring at you because she doesn't know why you're here. You have to talk to her like this . . .'

She tapped her grandmother's arm to get her attention, and then deftly, her hands moving at speed, she started to use sign language.

'I've never seen anyone speaking with their hands before,' Cecelia said to Harry that afternoon during their stop at Kilbarchan. 'It was really interesting to watch. The woman was very pleasant once she realised what had happened. And there was me thinking she was just ignorant because she kept waving at me to get out of her flat.'

He took a bite of his sandwich, then said, spraying crumbs, 'So the bairns are all right now? She's lookin' after them?'

'They'll be fine with her until their mother gets back.' Cecelia brushed crumbs from her skirt as unobtrusively as she could. 'You don't need to worry about them.'

'Worry about them? Me? If I was worried at all, it was that you'd bring them back with you today. Damned wee pests!'

'So you were just forcing yourself to play marbles with Tommy yesterday, then?'

'I wasnae doin' it for pleasure,' Harry said loftily. 'I used tae be the bools champion in our street, and I was just showin' the bairn how tae play properly. He was goin' about it all the wrong way.' Then, with a note of satisfaction in his voice, 'But now he'll be able tae give his wee pals a right trouncin' the next time he plays them at bools!'

'Chloe. Chloe!'

She had been dreaming about work, and about Dennis coming into the shop. He wanted to buy something and he was angry with her because she couldn't find what he wanted. As Chloe searched the shop someone kept getting in her way; a woman who kept her face averted, but seemed to be wherever Chloe turned. She had only just realised that it was Mrs Fulton from across the landing when Dennis started shouting at her so loudly that the shop began to tremble with the force of his voice.

'Chloe! Wake up, we have to go downstairs!'

She shot upright in bed as Dennis's angry voice was replaced by the wail of the air-raid siren and the ominous rumble of approaching planes. 'Wha'?'

'Can you not hear the planes? We have to go downstairs! Are you awake now? I have to get the boys.'

'I'm wakened, Mum.' Chloe threw the bedclothes aside and reached for the chair by the bed, where warm clothes were set out every night in case of a raid. Because of the blackout the bedroom was so dark between dusk and daylight that she had to put her clothes out in the proper order so that she could dress without having to look.

The sirens were still wailing, and people were shouting in the street outside. The thunder of the enemy bombers, wave upon wave of them, was frighteningly loud now. There must be hundreds, coming fast.

She tied a scarf over her hair, which had been wound round rags, and felt for her bag and the torch she kept beside it, then snatched up her quilt and pillow and made her way out into the hall. The boys were already there, their eyes bright with excitement in the light from her torch.

Every evening before going to bed Julia made up some

sandwiches, which, if they were not needed in the shelter, were used for packed lunches the next day. Now, each of the boys carried a big message bag holding the food and some books and games to keep them occupied, while Julia rummaged in the big hall cupboard for the canvas bag that held the spare blankets.

'Are we all ready?' she asked as she closed the door. 'Come on, then, fast as we can.'

'What about Dad?' Leslie quavered.

'He's gone to the Home Guard.' Julia opened the door.

'But . . .'

'He'll be fine,' Duncan told his little brother gruffly. 'He's got his rifle with him.'

Voices and hurried footsteps echoed up and down the stairwell as their neighbours all made for the room at the rear of the drysalter's shop on the ground floor. As the McCosh family emerged from their flat Chloe heard Mrs Borland's voice as she shepherded her husband and old Mrs Bell down to the ground floor. Dennis was coming down from the landing above with his brother and sisters, and at the sight of him, Chloe began to pray that her headscarf completely covered her shameful rag curlers.

But Dennis had other things on his mind. 'D'you think you could look after the weans, Mrs McCosh? I'm supposed to be firewatching, and my mother's workin' at the hospital tonight.'

'Of course, son.' Julia smiled at the two girls. 'We'll all look out for each other, eh?'

'I'm not a wean!' Ralph grumbled, half under his breath.

'If you're that grown up, why couldn't you get the girls up and ready instead of leaving it to me?' Dennis snapped, then asked, 'What about Mrs Fulton? D'you know if she's gone downstairs yet?'

'I've not seen her,' Julia said, and he lunged across the landing, almost knocking Ralph out of the way, and began rapping on the door.

'Mrs Fulton? Are you wakened? You have to go down to the shelter!'

'She's down there already,' Cecelia Goudie said from halfway up the last flight of stairs, 'and so are the Borlands and Mrs Bell. I came back up to see if I could help anyone.'

'That's everyone, then,' Dennis said with relief. He shepherded them all down to the close entrance and saw them into the shelter before going off to join the group of fire-watchers set up from Glen Street residents.

There were two rooms behind the drysalter's; the smaller room was used during the day by the owners, and held a tiny gas cooker, some chairs and a table, as well as shelves packed with goods. The larger room at the rear of the building had been used solely as a storeroom before the war, but now the boxes and cartons and sacks were piled against the four walls so that there was an open area in the centre. At first, the residents had donated what they could spare – stools, boxes, sagging and collapsing chairs that they had finally managed to replace in their homes – but after one particularly long and uncomfortable night in the shelter Ellen Borland had taken charge, and now there were three sets of metal bunk beds and several deckchairs in residence. Where she obtained them nobody knew, and nobody asked. They were just grateful for the modicum of comfort.

When Julia McCosh ushered in her charges, Donnie Borland, wrapped so tightly in warm blankets that he resembled a Swiss roll with a head at one end, was stretched out on a lower bunk while Jessie Bell occupied one of the two comfortable armchairs, knitting so fast that her veined, almost skeletal hands were little more than a blur.

Ellen's knitting bag and the old leather bag containing family photographs and papers were on the other chair, while the lady herself was talking quietly to Lena Fulton. As the others came in Ellen moved to her armchair while Lena stayed where she was, in an upright chair on the edge of the group, her head bent over some sewing.

'Here we go again, eh?' Ellen said cheerily. 'Your man out with the Home Guard tonight, Mrs McCosh?'

'That's right, and Mrs Megson's working too.' Julia immediately began making up beds with help from Cecelia and Chloe. 'Come on now, you've got school tomorrow,' she told the children, 'so into bed with you. Amy and Bessie can share one bunk and Duncan and Leslie can share another, and that leaves one for you, Ralph.'

'I'm not goin' to any bed,' the boy announced. 'I'm no' a bairn.'

'You'll be tired in the morning,' Cecelia told him, and he shrugged his broad shoulders and said, 'I can handle that!'

'Fancy a game of Snakes and Ladders?' Chloe suggested, pulling the box from the bag her mother had brought with her. Ralph sneered, then said dismally, 'might as well, there's nothing else to do.'

The hours dragged by. The Megson and McCosh children finally managed to get to sleep despite Donnie Borland's snoring, while his wife dozed in her armchair, her head twisted to one side and her mouth falling open. Lena Fulton stitched busily at the work she had brought down with her, replying to anything Julia and Cecelia said with a brief 'yes' or 'no'. Julia and Cecelia both knitted, and talked a little as they waited for the All Clear to sound.

Chloe and Ralph played game after game of Snakes and Ladders, and more than once the boy had to be talked out of going into the backyard to see what was happening.

'It's not fair,' he grumbled. 'Why can't I be a firewatcher like our Dennis? He has all the fun!'

'I'd hardly call it fun,' Cecelia said dryly. 'What if an incendiary bomb comes down and sets fire to the place?'

Ralph's eyes glowed. 'Puttin' it out would be a lot better than sharing this damn . . .'

'I beg your pardon?' Mrs Borland boomed from her chair.

They all jumped. 'What did you say, my lad?'

'Dice,' Ralph muttered, his ears going red. 'I said that putting out fires would be better than shakin' this dice.'

'That's just as well, for I'll not abide bad language in my shelter,' Ellen said grandly. 'I'll not abide it anywhere, as you well know. And you can just stop complaining and get back to your game, for your mother would never forgive us if we let anything happen to you while she was away ministering to the sick and the dying.' And she settled down again, closing her eyes, while Ralph scowled across the rickety card table at Chloe and shook the dice as though he held it by the throat.

Gradually, Julia and Cecelia talked less and less. Their fingers stilled and their eyelids began to close. Chloe left the card table and started flicking through a magazine, holding it close to her eyes in the poor light. Ralph moodily threw the dice over and over again, while Lena Fulton stitched away at her work, to the muffled drone of plane engines and the thud of anti-aircraft guns.

16

They had been in the shelter for over three hours when Julia jerked awake, then said, 'Listen . . . I think the planes have gone.'

Cecelia and Chloe strained their ears. It was difficult to be sure above Donnie Borland's snoring, but it seemed to the three women that the drone of engines had all but ceased. Then they jumped when the door opened and a tall, burly figure strode in. His face was in shadow, the features hidden between the brim of his tin hat and the upturned collar of his khaki greatcoat. Ellen Borland, startled awake by the gust of cold night air that billowed in through the open doorway, shot upright in her chair and yelped, 'Oh my heavens, it's the Germans come tae get us all!'

Chloe, Cecelia and Julia stared transfixed while Ralph jumped to his feet and picked up the wooden kitchen chair he had been sitting on, holding it before him as a weapon.

Then the figure in the doorway said, 'Aye, that'll be right, Mrs Borland. Hitler asked me tae drop by when I was passing on my parachute and invite you all back tae Germany for your tea.'

'Frank!' Julia jumped up. 'Oh, Frank, you gave us the fright of our lives! What are you doing here? Has something happened?'

'Aye, it has, but not in this area. They're sayin' that the

First Aid Post at Woodside's been hit. I came to make sure you were all right, and to tell you that I don't know when I'll be back, Julia. We've got to go up there now.'

'I'll come too,' she said at once. 'The WVS'll mebbe be needed.'

'You'll stay where you are, woman. You're not on duty and the All Clear's not been sounded. Now do as you're told, for once,' he added sternly as she began to protest. 'The bairns need you tonight, and those livin' nearer the West End will be the ones tae help out. I'll be back as soon as I can.'

Then he went, as quickly as he had come, leaving them staring at each other.

'A First Aid Post?' Ellen said, stunned. 'God help the poor souls that were in it if it's true.'

'Mebbe there's been a mistake,' Cecelia suggested.

'I certainly hope so,' Julia agreed, as the All Clear sounded.

'Well, that's another raid gone by . . . for us, at any rate.' Ellen struggled to her feet and started shaking her husband, who had slept through the panic caused by Frank's sudden arrival. 'Come on, Donnie son, let's get you to your bed, then you can have a proper sleep.'

'I thought that was what he was having already,' Cecelia commented when the Borlands had left; Donnie, still half asleep, had been leaning on his wife, who carried the big bag containing their belongings. 'Should we waken the children now?'

'I suppose so. Poor wee things, this is no life for them,' Julia said as they set about the task while Lena folded her sewing.

The young Megsons and McCoshs were stumbling about, rubbing their eyes, when Dennis arrived.

'Any fires?' Ralph wanted to know.

'Just the one, from an incendiary. But we caught it early, and got it out before any damage was done.'

'You were in the wrong place,' the younger boy said excitedly. 'Mr McCosh was just in and he says that the First Aid Post at Woodside's been hit!'

Dennis stared, and then grabbed his brother's arm. 'Don't make jokes like that!'

'It's true! Ask them, they all heard it the same as me!' Ralph wrenched his arm free.

'Is it? Is it true?'

'We don't know for sure, but the Home Guard's been sent up there,' Julia began, and was cut short.

'My mother,' Dennis said frantically. 'I think my mother was there tonight!'

'Surely she's working at the infirmary?'

'She was due to finish at midnight. Sometimes when there's a raid on and she's not needed at the infirmary, she goes to help out at one of the First Aid Posts. She's not come back here, has she?'

'No, but—'

'Ralph, get the girls upstairs and into their beds.' Dennis swung round on his brother, barking, 'Just do it!' when Ralph began to object.

'Where are you going?' Julia asked as he made for the door.

'To the West End, to see if it's true!'

'But if it is, there's folk there that know what to do for the best. Stay here until the morning at least—'

'It's my mother!' Dennis shouted at her, and ran.

Paisley's West End was seething with people and vehicles, and as Dennis Megson neared the site of the First Aid Post a soldier blocked his path.

'Can't go along there, sonny. No civilians allowed.'

'Is it true?' The words wheezed out of Dennis's tortured lungs. 'Was the post hit?'

'Look, lad,' the man said. 'I'm here to keep folk away. I cannae tell ye what's happening, even if I knew it myself.'

'But my mother . . .' Dennis crouched against a wall, hands on knees, trying to catch his breath. 'She's a nurse. She might have been working there tonight.'

'I'm sorry, son.' There was rough kindness in the voice now. 'You cannae go past, and they're all too busy up there tae answer any questions. Best go home and wait for word.'

'Go home? How can I just go home and wait when I don't know what's happened to her? If you won't help me, I'll go to the infirmary and find out from them.'

'They've got enough tae do tonight without you . . .' the man began, but Dennis was off again, his heart hammering and his lungs labouring.

Paisley's Royal Alexandra Infirmary was near the Cross, which meant that he had to go all the way back through the town, moving against the tide of people beginning to hurry to the West End as word of the bombing spread. Dawn was lightening the sky as he reached the infirmary, an imposing Victorian building. The entrance was seething with ambulances and people, and he had to fight his way through them.

The interior was just as busy as the exterior. Dennis tried to catch someone's attention, asking any porters, nurses or doctors that hurried by, 'Nurse Megson . . . Nan Megson. D'you know if she's here?' But each time, they just looked at him blankly, as though he was speaking a foreign language, and then hurried on, too busy to think of anything other than the work to hand.

He finally managed to struggle as far as an inner door, where a porter stopped him. 'What are you doin' here, lad? What's your business?'

At last someone was willing to listen to him. 'I'm looking for my mother, she's a nurse here and she might have been working in the First Aid Post,' Dennis gabbled. 'Nurse Megson.'

'Don't know anythin' about her, son.'

'Can you not go and ask someone?'

'I've got more tae do than that. Anyway, I can't go roamin' about the infirmary and botherin' busy folk at your biddin'.'

'Then I'll go and look for her myself.'

'You won't!' The man put a big hand on Dennis's chest as he tried to push past through the doorway.

'I need to find out if my mother's all right!'

'What ye need tae do is, you need tae sit down over there and wait until someone's got the time tae find out for ye!'

'For pity's sake . . . !' Dennis made another bid for the door, and this time the man grabbed his shoulders, his fingers biting painfully into the muscles.

'You'll do as ye're told, sonny boy, or ye'll be thrown out and not allowed back in,' he was saying when the door behind him opened and Nan Megson hurried through, almost colliding with the two struggling figures.

'What's going . . . Dennis?' Her face, already pale with fatigue, turned grey. 'It's not the girls, is it? Or Ralph?'

'No, it's you. I thought . . .' he began, then gulped as the words tangled themselves in his throat. To his horror, he felt hot and heavy tears pressing against the backs of his eyes.

'Get him out of here,' the porter growled at Nan, 'before I call the polis and have him escorted off the premises for gettin' in the way of folk with work tae dae.'

'It's all right, he's my son. I'll see to him.' She took Dennis by the arm and hurried him into a corner. 'What's wrong?' Her voice was frantic.

'We heard about the First Aid Post. I thought that . . .' he gulped again, and blinked rapidly. 'When you didn't come home, I thought you might have been working there.'

'No, I had to stay on here because . . .' she began, and then understanding dawned. 'You thought that I . . . oh, Dennis! I'm fine, just very busy. What about the younger ones?'

'Mrs McCosh is seeing to them. I'll get back to them

now.' All at once he felt slightly foolish, and in awe of her. She always changed for work when she got to the infirmary and so he had never before seen her in her uniform. Exhausted though she looked, the starched white cap and apron, the stiff white collar and the watch pinned to her bib gave her an air of authority and turned her into a stranger.

'You do that. Get to your bed and stop worrying about me. I'll be home as soon as I can.' She patted his face and managed to find a faint smile for him before vanishing into the milling crowd.

As Dennis left the hospital he passed an elderly couple on their way in, the man supporting his weeping wife. 'Mebbe it'll be all right,' he was saying. 'Mebbe he wasn't there at the time . . .'

As he forced his aching legs to carry him back to Glen Street, Dennis was almost overwhelmed by a thick black cloud of despair. He had thought until then that he was managing to deal with the triple burden of taking responsibility for his family, learning to be a fire-fighter and coping with his engineering classes. But the sudden shock of believing, for one terrified hour, that he had lost his mother had brought it all to a head. She had escaped death or injury this time, but it could so easily happen . . . a bomb landing on the hospital when she was on duty, or a sudden raid when she was out in the night streets, making her way to and from work. The blackout had hurt and even killed folk who had fallen down unlit stairs or walked into the concrete baffle walls built in front of the town's tenement closes to protect them from shock waves. Death seemed to lurk around every corner, watching and waiting, and ready to pounce.

If anything happened to his mother, he doubted if he could manage to work and look after Ralph and the girls at the same time. Visions sprang to mind of Amy and Bessie pining in an orphanage, and Ralph going to the bad because his older brother did not have the time to watch out for him.

Dennis had thought that at eighteen years of age he was a man, but as he walked through the night, the years fell from him, and tears of fear and loneliness poured down his face.

The tenement was quiet when he got back, its residents snatching what sleep they could before morning took them off to work or school. In the close, he used his cap to scrub the tears from his eyes and his cheeks before taking a deep breath and ascending the stairs, pulling himself up by the handrail, moving like an old man instead of taking two steps at a time as he usually did.

Hesitating on the first landing, he glanced at Lena Fulton's door. He would have given anything to see her at that moment, to talk to her and find comfort in just being with her. But she would be in her bed by now, and fast asleep. Dennis started climbing the next flight of stairs, one by one.

Within her flat, Lena was sitting at the kitchen table, fingers curled around a cup of tea that had gone cold long since.

Mrs Borland had drawn her to one side as soon as she had gone into the room used as a bomb shelter.

'Nice tae see you, dear. Listen, I've got some work for you. A lassie at the mill's gettin' married, and she needs a dress for herself and one for her bridesmaid. I said you'd do them for her.'

'I don't know,' Lena faltered. 'I've got an awful lot of work just now, Mrs Borland, and . . .'

The woman's smile hardened a little. 'She's no' gettin' wed for three months yet, you've got plenty of time.'

'There's the material, and the time . . . I'd need to charge for that as well.'

Ellen Borland's mouth thinned out and her voice took on an ominous undertone. 'I'll supply the material, same as I usually do, and as for cost, the lassie's a workmate of mine, and an awful nice girl too. You'd surely not expect her to pay you? After all . . .' she added with meaning, 'if she pays you, you'll only have tae give the money tae me, won't you, tae cover what ye owe me already? And that wouldn't help you at all, hen, would it? Best to stay with the nice wee agreement we've already got between us.'

Then, as the door opened to admit the McCosh family and the Megson children, the woman ended the conversation with, 'So I'll let ye know when she can come tae be measured, all right?' and turned away abruptly.

Lena put down the cup then got up from the table and went to fetch the large bag that held scraps left over from work already done. Sometimes, when life began to overpower her, it helped her to sort through the bits and pieces of cloth.

She shook the remnants over the table and began to put them into piles according to size, her mind still circling desperately round and round, seeking an answer to her problems. It would have made such a difference to her if only George had behaved like most servicemen and arranged for his Army pay to go to his wife. Instead, deciding that Lena was not capable of handling money without guidance, he had opted to have it paid to his father. The arrangement between the two men was that old Mr Fulton would put some of the money into the bank each month, and give the rest to his daughter-in-law, who was to augment it with the small sums she earned as a seamstress.

The scheme should have worked, and at first, it did. Mr Fulton senior stumped into the close at 42 Glen Street at the beginning of every month, climbed the stairs, and pushed the envelope through the letterbox without knocking on the door; but after the first six months the payments became sporadic, and the man had not once made the journey to Glen Street since his son's last leave.

Lena could not summon the courage to complain to

George in her weekly letters; instead, in desperation, she had been forced to borrow from Mrs Borland, not realising that she was backing herself into a corner. In return for the occasional small payment, Ellen Borland expected Lena to do work for her family and friends at half the price she could charge others, and when Ellen supplied the material and threads, as she usually did, Lena had to do the work for nothing. Her timid attempts to reason with the woman had met with a sneering smile and a reminder that if she chose to, Ellen could go to George's father and demand full repayment of his daughter-in-law's debts.

'And I doubt if that would go down with your man, hen. After all, he's havin' a difficult enough time fightin' the Jerries without the shame of knowin' that his wife's spendin' money that's not hers by rights. We'll just keep it between ourselves, eh?' she always urged, taking Lena's roughened hand in her own and slipping two half-crowns or a ten-shilling note into it. 'Between friends. That's the way tae do it.'

The remnants had been sorted into neat piles according to size; now Lena began to divide each pile according to type and colour. She could remember where every scrap came from, and what she had made from that particular material. Now she picked up a piece of cream linen, rubbing it between her fingers. Her aunt had chosen the sleeveless cream dress for Lena to wear at her wedding to George. He had approved, though Lena herself would have preferred something softer and more romantic for what she had thought would be the most important day of her life. The dress had been taken apart to make a skirt for another girl's trousseau.

She reached out and picked up a soft brown patch that had come from a skirt a young mother had had cut down for her little daughter. Lena put the two fragments together, admiring the way they contrasted with each other.

Then she threaded a needle, reached for her scissors, and,

oblivious to the dawn chorus outside the window, began to cut and stitch.

In the kitchen of his own flat, Dennis stopped short, staring. 'What are you doing here?'

Chloe, already flushed from the heat of the ironing she was doing, felt her face grow even warmer. 'I was just keeping them company till you got back.' She nodded at Amy and Bessie, huddled together on one of the two sagging armchairs flanking the range. 'They wouldn't go to bed until they knew about their . . .'

The girls, roused from sleep by their voices, struggled from the chair and ran to Dennis, their eyes dark with fear, while Chloe rested the iron on its base.

'What are you two doing up at this hour?'

'Is Mam all right?' Bessie asked anxiously as he knelt to put his arms about them. 'You don't need us to be brave, do you?' It was a term that children with fathers fighting in the war had become used to, a term that always preceded bad news.

'No, I don't need you to be brave. She's all right,' he assured them. They seemed so young and vulnerable, in their long nightdresses and with their hair carefully rolled up in rag curlers by Chloe.

'She'd to stay on at the infirmary, that's all, because of the raid.' He could feel the warm bodies within his embrace suddenly slump as the tension left them.

'Good,' Amy said, then, after a massive yawn, 'Does that mean we can go to bed now?'

Dennis looked at the two small faces, almost grey with fatigue, and with shadows under their eyes. 'You should have gone to bed ages ago.'

'They wouldn't, not until they heard that their mummy was safe and well. But now that we know, let's get you two settled down.' Chloe shepherded them out while Dennis sat down on the chair and began to take off his boots.

'Ralph?' he asked when Chloe returned.

'He went to his bed as soon as we came in. Would you like some tea?' She picked up the kettle and moved over to the sink, but he shook his head.

'I'm fine. You should be in your bed.'

'My mother was worn out, so I said that I'd stay with the girls until you got home.' She glanced at the clock. 'There's still time for an hour or two's sleep.' She added then, 'Are you sure you don't want some tea? You look awful tired.'

'I'd just as soon get to my bed. You didn't need to do this.' He gestured towards the small pile of neatly ironed clothes at one corner of the table.

'I had to have something to keep me occupied.' She began to fold the old blanket and sheet that turned the table into an ironing board. 'Was it the First Aid Post right enough?'

'I think so. Something's happened, but nob'dy would tell me anything. There were soldiers and police all over the West End, and the infirmary was busy too.'

'I hope there's not been too many folk hurt,' Chloe said soberly; then, putting the basket of ironed clothes in a corner, 'I suppose I'd best get off home now . . . if you're sure there's nothing else you need.'

'No, you've done more than enough already. Thanks for your help.'

'Och, it was nothing,' she said. 'I'll let myself out.'

When she had gone he looked in on the girls, both sound asleep already, then went quietly into the small room he shared with Ralph, who didn't move or speak. Dennis thought he was asleep until, just as he was sliding into bed, his brother said from the darkness. 'Is Mam all right?'

'She's fine. She'd just had to stay on at the infirmary.'

'You saw her?'

'Aye. And I spoke to her. She's fine,' Dennis said again,

and heard his brother's breath being released in a faint sigh. Less than a minute later, he could tell by the slow and even breathing that Ralph was asleep.

17

The whole town was abuzz with the news of the night's disasters. A mine dropped by parachute had made a direct hit on the First Aid Post at Woodside, killing ninety-two people ... doctors, nurses, pharmacists, first-aid workers, clerks and clerkesses, ambulance drivers and messengers. Had the wind carried the parachute and its deadly load a little to one side it would have landed and exploded in Woodside Cemetery, just over the wall from the post.

Another mine had exploded in a yard in Newton Street, close by the Woodside site, setting fire to an Auxiliary Fire Service vehicle, and killing two more men, both Fire Service personnel. Rescue workers had had to work through the night to release the dead and injured. More than twenty people had been seriously injured. Another bomb had fallen in the neighbouring town of Renfrew, killing two people and injuring half a dozen more.

The raid had then spread westwards from Paisley, culminating in the Clydeside shipbuilding towns of Port Glasgow and Greenock, which had been particularly damaged.

Almost everyone in the town had some story to tell in the next few days. Chloe's friend Marion's cousin had narrowly escaped death; a mill worker who had gained her certificate at the first-aid classes in Ferguslie Mills, she was among the personnel at Woodside, and should have been on duty that night, but another girl had agreed to change duties with her so that she could go to the pictures to see her hero, Clark Gable.

'My uncle and auntie near died of shock,' Marion told Chloe. 'When they heard about the bomb they thought they'd lost her . . . then she walked in large as life and said, "Hello, I'm back." My uncle started giving her such a telling off for going to the pictures instead of being on duty before he realised that it had saved her life.'

'I can't be doing with this, Lena.' Cathy Blacklock stirred the spoon round and round in her teacup as though trying to grind the bottom of the cup away. 'My nerves won't take it.'

'It's war, Aunt Cathy,' Lena said from the sink, where she was doing some washing. 'None of us likes it, or wants it, but we have to put up with it.'

'Not me. I near died of fright last night when I heard the bang,' said Mrs Blacklock, who lived not far from the stricken First Aid Post. 'I said to Mrs Wilson that was under the stairs alongside me, I said, "It'll be us next time, you wait and see."'

'But it might not be.'

'There's plenty of next times to come, Lena. Look at me . . .' The woman lifted the cup from its saucer and held it up, 'I'm shakin'! I'm an old woman and I cannae be doin' with this. I'm going to write to my friend Effie Galbraith in Millport to say that I'm goin' over tae stay with her. She's asked me often enough.'

'There's warships in the Clyde, Aunt Cathy. It was the Clyde that the bombers were making for. They might come back while you're living on the island.'

'Mebbe, but Cumbrae's such a wee island that there's a fair chance of the bombs missin' it. And you'd best come with me.'

'Me?' Lena turned from the sink, soapy water dripping on to the linoleum from her hands. 'I'm not going to live in Millport.'

'Why not? You'll be safer there, and George would be easier in his mind, knowing that you were with me.'

'And what about when he comes home on leave? He'll expect to find me here, looking after the place.'

'Surely if you write to him and explain what it's like living in a town, he'll see sense. Give me his address and I'll write to him myself.'

'No,' Lena said swiftly. 'I'll do it. You make your own arrangements to go to your friend in Millport, and if George agrees, I'll join you later.'

'I'm sure he will agree.' Cathy Blacklock drank down her tea then put the cup back on to its saucer and got to her feet. 'I'd best go, there's a lot to be done and the sooner I'm safe in Millport the happier I'll be.'

When the woman had gone, Lena scooped the wet and soapy clothes from the sink into a basin, washed the teacups, and then returned to her sewing. She would wait until her aunt was settled in Millport and then write to say that George preferred her to stay where she was, in their own home. She had no intention of asking him if she could accompany her aunt; it suited her fine to be here, within her own four walls, with her own things around her and without her Auntie Cathy buzzing around like a tiresome fly, asking if she was eating properly and going on about George.

The mood at the fire station was bleak. 'It makes ye realise how lucky this town has been up until now, compared tae some,' Tom McIntosh said to Dennis as they worked on an engine. 'Not that what happened the other night is anythin' like as bad as what these poor souls in London and places like that have had tae go through. Even so, when it hits close tae home, and it's folk that you know . . .' He stopped, shaking his head, then went on after a pause, 'And it makes ye wonder what else might be in store for us before this damned business is over and done with. But what's happened can't be changed, so we just have to get on with it the best we can. Pass me that spanner, lad.'

Getting on with things as best they could was what the people of Paisley did, once the funerals were over. There was still food to be queued for, ration books to be clipped, children to be educated and, always, work to be done.

Cecelia and Harry were moved from the Kilbarchan–Abbotsinch run to a Glasgow Clyde Street–Paisley Cross route, and this time Cecelia was experienced enough to deal efficiently with the task of memorising new stage fares and tickets. Most of the passengers were easy to get on with, and she had discovered that the occasional troublemaker or inebriate could usually be handled with a mixture of tact and firmness. Where drunk men were concerned, she discovered that a touch of firm motherliness went down well.

Her only problem, as the summer set in, was the heat. Her uniform was an asset in the winter, but on lovely summer days it could become unbearably hot. Some of the clippies found ways of subtly altering their uniforms to compensate, and as always, Nancy went a stage further. She tilted her cap to the back of her head and managed to push up her sleeves, as well as unfastening the top buttons of both jacket and blouse.

'I don't know how she gets away with it,' Cecelia said to one of the other conductresses. 'What if an inspector sees her like that?'

Inspectors were the bane of the conductresses' lives. Like birds, they seemed to travel in flocks; when they were spotted in an area the drivers flashed their lights at each other as a warning and each driver would then flash the bus's interior lights to put his conductress on her guard.

The woman shrugged. 'Les'll let her know if he sees an inspector waitin' at the next stop, and she'll be all smartened up and lookin' as if butter wouldnae melt in her mouth by the time the man sets foot on her bus.' She fanned herself with one hand. 'I wouldnae mind bein' on a run tae some nice seaside place like Largs in weather like this. I was on that run before the war when I worked for Youngs of Paisley; we used tae have a long turn-around there, so we'd time tae buy an ice-cream from Nardinis and take a wander round the town lookin' at the shops afore we had tae get back on the bus. Sometimes there was even time tae sit on the promenade an' watch the steamers comin' in and out. It was like havin' a wee holiday, the Largs run. There arenae any bus stops once you get right intae the country, so the folk just wait by the roadside and wave the bus down. And they sometimes brought a few eggs or some turnips or potatoes from their farms for the conductress and the driver. See this damned war? It's got a lot tae answer for.'

The Glasgow to Paisley run was a busy route, which suited Cecelia because keeping busy made the time pass faster. Under local regulations, buses running between Glasgow and Paisley and therefore crossing the city boundary could not drop passengers before the halfway stage at Crookston, and on the return trip they could not pick up passengers after Crookston.

On one particularly hot day the bus filled up rapidly and by the time Cecelia came downstairs after collecting fares it had reached the last stop before the boundary, where a considerable number of passengers waited.

She sped down the stairs and took command of her platform. 'Still seats upstairs,' she shouted. 'Upstairs if you can manage it, please. Give these to me, madam . . .' She relieved a harassed young woman who was carrying a small baby and trying to cope with a toddler as well as her heavy shopping bag. A heftily built man who was sitting on one of the long side seats by the door glanced up from his newspaper as Cecelia stared fixedly at him, and then got up hurriedly and offered the woman his seat.

'Thank you, sir, very kind of you. Move up to the front

of the bus, please,' Cecelia called out as people continued to cram on to the platform. Then the line came to an abrupt stop. Craning her neck, Cecelia saw that one woman had paused halfway up the bus instead of moving as far up as she could. Irritation swept over her.

'Move up the bus, please!' she yelled, then as the woman, chatting to someone in one of the seats, paid no heed, she threw all the strength she could find into her voice. 'Would the lady in the red hat please move right up the bus NOW!'

A man in an officer's uniform had started up towards the top deck. Now he paused and said, 'Good God, woman, with a voice like that you should be a sergeant major in the army!'

'Thank you, sir, but I prefer my own command,' Cecelia shot back at him while the guilty passenger, her face turning as red as her jaunty hat, rocketed up to the very top of the passageway, thus making just enough room to accommodate everyone who wanted to get on.

Cecelia slapped the bell push twice and then, as Harry drew away from the kerb, set about the difficult task of squeezing by the standing passengers to collect fares. They had passed the halfway stage, which meant that some passengers alighted at the next few stops, easing the pressure for those remaining. There were still a few straphanging, one of them a man in army uniform.

'Fares please, sir,' Cecelia said briskly, and he started to manoeuvre round to face her.

'How much is it from Cessnock to . . . Cecelia?' Fergus Goudie said. 'What the blazes are you doing here?'

She gaped at him guiltily, then, remembering her mother's adage that attack was the best form of defence, said, 'Never mind me . . . what are *you* doing here?'

'I asked first!'

'And this is my bus!' Cecelia rapped back at him and his eyes widened.

'I'm on leave . . .' he began, then altered the explanation

to, 'Never mind that just now, what the dickens are doing
in this bus, wearing that uniform and carrying that ticket
machine?'

'What d'you think I'm doing? I'm working. I told you
that I'd got a job with Glasgow Corporation Transport.' She
was hugging the ticket machine close, as though ready to
use it to defend herself.

'In the office, you said.'

'I didn't say that exactly, I just . . .'

'You just let me think you were. D'you mean to tell me
that that was you, yelling at that woman just now?'

'I'm allowed to yell, it's my bus.'

'But I've never heard you raise your voice like that,'
Fergus said, stunned.

'That's because I've never had to move you further up
the bus,' she said stupidly, still unable to believe that he was
really there, pressed tightly against her in the narrow aisle.
'On leave, did you say? You never wrote to tell me.'

'They didn't give us much warning.'

'Excuse me,' the woman in the red hat said from behind
him. 'This is my stop and you've not collected my fare yet.'
She glared. 'I'd not like to get off without paying, because
that would break your rules, wouldn't it?'

'Look here . . .' Fergus said heatedly, and then winced
as one of Cecelia's strong practical shoes kicked him in the
ankle.

'That's very conscientious of you, madam. Did you see
the look she gave me?' Cecelia said to Fergus after she had
rung up a ticket, given the woman change, and belled Harry
to stop and then start again. 'You can sit down now, there
are empty seats,'

'I think I need to.' Fergus sank into a seat, and then
fumbled in his pocket. 'How much is the fare?'

'Don't be daft, you don't need to pay a fare on my bus.'

'Cecelia, what possessed you to become a bus conductress?'

'It was Mrs Borland's idea. She lives up the stairs from us. So I applied and I sat the exam and they took me on.'

'But your office experience . . .'

'It was the buses or munitions or mebbe the Forces or the Land Army. As Mrs Borland said, better to choose them before they chose me.'

'It seems such a waste!'

'You being in the army is much more of a waste. Anyway, I like it.' Glancing ahead she saw a knot of people waiting at the next bus stop. 'I'll have to go,' she said as she stabbed at the bell. 'I've got work to do.'

She collected fares from the latest passengers then had to return to the platform to usher some people off at the next stop. One of them was the young woman with the two small children and the bag of messages. Again, Cecelia took charge of the bag, and offered her free hand to the toddler. 'Oh thanks, that's kind of you,' the young woman said gratefully as they all arrived on the pavement.

'That's all right,' Cecelia said, then glanced up to see a uniformed figure hurrying along the pavement towards her. She leapt back on to the platform and scurried along the lower deck to where Fergus sat. 'Give me twopence ha'penny!'

'What?'

'For your fare!'

'But you said . . .'

'Just give me twopence ha'penny,' Cecelia ordered, low-voiced, as the inspector jumped on to the platform and belled Harry. She stamped the ticket with trembling fingers and stowed the proffered fare in her bag. 'You got on at the last stop, right? And you don't know me,' she hissed as the inspector began to patrol the aisle, intoning, 'Tickets, please!'

'That's me finished my shift now, but I have to go back to the depot at Ibrox,' Cecelia explained to Fergus as most of the passengers, including the inspector, got off at Paisley Cross. 'Then I'll come back to Paisley on one of the other buses. You go on home now and I'll see you later.'

'Can you not come home with me now?'

'I have to cash up and put in the takings,' she was saying when Harry came round from his cab.

'Havin' a problem, hen?' He eyed Fergus, who glared back at him.

'Harry, this is my husband Fergus.'

'Oh aye? Home on leave, are ye? That's nice. Ye never said he was comin' home, hen.'

'I didn't know till I saw him on the bus.'

'Ye've got a canny wee wife there,' Harry grunted, sticking out his hand. 'She's a quick learner and she's fairly taken tae the work.'

'Has she indeed?' Fergus took the older man's hand, looking from him to Cecelia, then said awkwardly, 'Well, I suppose I'd best get off now. I'll see you back home, then?'

'I'll not be long. Oh . . .' she fished in her pocket, 'here's the key.'

'He doesnae seem tae be very happy,' Harry observed as they watched Fergus walk away. 'Ye've never had a quarrel already, have ye?'

'It's just . . . he didn't know that I was working on the buses,' she explained, and his brows shot up.

'Ye never told yer man what ye were doin'? Ashamed of the job, are ye?'

'No, it's nothing like that! It's just that I used to work in an office, and he thought that I was going to get the same sort of job again.'

'Someone should tell him that there's a war on,' Harry said, with just the glimmer of a smile tickling at the corners of his mouth.

On the way back to Ibrox Cecelia practised all the arguments she could think of in favour of her choice of work.

If only Fergus had written to let her know that he was getting leave, she could have worked out a way of telling him the truth in a letter, instead of letting him find out as he had.

If only she had been honest with him from the start, she thought miserably as she alighted at Ibrox and began the task of directing Harry as he reversed the bus into its slot. In hindsight, that would have been the best thing to do. She held up a hand and Harry, watching her in his mirror, braked and then turned the steering wheel in answer to her next signal.

If she had only had the sense to write, he could have got used to the idea while he was far away, with his regiment. As it was, the two of them would probably spend what precious time they had together arguing and . . .

'Look out!' someone yelled, but it was too late. Cecelia snapped out of her reverie and watched in horror as the back of the bus caught a corner of the terminal building with a nasty scraping sound. A crowd gathered as Harry almost threw himself out of the cab and came running round to inspect the damage.

'Ye daft wee bitch, what the blazes were ye thinkin' about?' he yelled at her.

'I'm sorry . . . I'm so sorry . . . !' Cecelia bleated, staring at the dent in one corner of the bus, and the scraped paint-work. 'I didn't realise . . .'

'Are youse two tryin' tae knock down the whole termi-nus?' One of the inspectors bulldozed his way through the crowd. 'Look at that! That's going to cost good money to repair!' Then, glaring at Harry and Cecelia, 'Intae the office . . . right now!'

'I cannae leave the bus like this,' Harry protested.

'I don't see why not, since you're the one that got it like this! Les, Nancy, you take it in where it belongs.'

As Les climbed into the cab and Nancy, smirking, took up her position behind the bus, Cecelia and Harry were

marched into the office, where they stood side by side before
the desk like naughty children hauled up before the headmaster for talking in class. Only this was much more serious,
Cecelia thought miserably. She had managed to damage a
Glasgow Corporation bus that had cost goodness knows
how much to buy. And she had got Harry, one of the best
drivers in the depot, into trouble. Not to mention having to
face Fergus when she got home.

'Well?' the inspector demanded, hurling himself into the
chair behind the desk.

'I was—' Cecelia began, but Harry spoke over her.

'It was my fault. A damned great bumblebee flew intae
the cab just as I was takin' the bus back. It hit against my
face and I got such a fright that my foot skidded off the
brake.'

'You expect me to believe that?'

'It's the truth. Have I ever damaged a bus before, in all
the years I've worked for this corporation?' Harry asked
heatedly.

'No, but—'

'Have I ever been late on a run, or not turned up for
work apart from havin' tae get my appendix out fifteen
years ago?'

'No, but—'

'Come on, Charlie, it's just a scratch, you know it is.
And mebbe a wee dent too. But it can be sorted. And there's
no harm done tae yer precious building.'

'Listen you to me,' the inspector began, glaring from one
to the other. Then he sagged back in his chair. 'Oh, what
the hell! You'll both have to fill in forms before you go off
duty. And if you ever do a thing like this again you're in
real trouble!'

'Aye, the next time a bumblebee comes intae my cab I'll
swallow it whole and keep drivin',' Harry said sarcastically.
'Come on, Cecelia, let's get these forms filled in.'

As soon as they were out of earshot he rounded on her.

'Don't you ever let your mind wander when you're directin' my bus again!'

'I'm so sorry, Harry,' she said wretchedly. 'You should have let me tell him the truth instead of taking the blame. I'll go back in now and tell him if you like.'

'And make me out tae be a liar? Ye will not. Ach, the company owes me a wee slip, given the loyalty they've had from me. Let's get on with the forms and then you can go home and make a fuss of that man of yours.'

18

———————

School was out by the time Cecelia reached Glen Street. Boys were kicking a football about the street while girls, the Megsons among them, played peevers and skipping ropes, or bounced a ball against any windowless wall they could find.

Reaching Number 42 she sucked in a deep breath and squared her shoulders. Fergus was waiting for her and now, for the second time that afternoon, she had to face the music.

'Excuse me,' someone said as she made her way along the close, and she turned to see a man hovering in the entrance.

'Yes?'

'I'm looking for a woman called Julia . . .' He hesitated, gave a rattly cough, then said, 'McCosh, I think her name is.'

'Mrs McCosh lives on the first floor. To the left.'

'Thank you.' The light was behind him and all she could make out was a tall, very thin figure with longish hair.

'I don't know if she's in . . .'

'Thank you,' he said again, dismissively this time, as though used to being obeyed. She shrugged and turned away. She had her own problems to deal with.

'Wait there,' Fergus ordered as soon as he opened the door.

'What do you . . . Fergus!' she squeaked as he stepped

outside and swept her up in to his arms. 'What are you doing?'

'Carrying my wife over the threshold.'

'You did that when we first came here!'

'And I'm doing it again. And again, if I want to, or if you want me to.' He turned as if to carry her out again, and she hastily reached over to shut the door.

'Just the once is enough. You can put me down now,' she said as he negotiated the small hallway.

'Not just yet. D'you know something?' he said when they arrived in the kitchen, where the table was set for two and the radio was tuned into a programme of dance music, 'I like the way you feel in that uniform.'

'Fergus, about the uniform, and the job—'

'It it's what you want, that's fine with me. Life's too precious and time's too short to argue. You look good in the uniform too.' He kissed her, then said, 'I made a sort of pie thing with mashed potatoes on top. It's in the oven. I just used what I could find.'

'It smells lovely.' He had probably used up all her rations for the week, but she didn't care. Fergus was back, and nothing else mattered. 'How long have you got?'

'Five days.'

'Five whole ... oh, Fergus,' she wailed, 'I'm working for the next four days!'

'We'll manage.'

'And I smashed the bus against a wall this afternoon.'

'What? Are you all right? Did anyone get hurt?'

'Nobody, it happened in the depot, when I was directing Harry while he took it in to its slot. I was so busy thinking about you ... about us ... that I forgot what I was doing and he scraped the bus against the side of the building.'

'And they let you keep your job?'

'Harry took the blame.'

'Harry,' said Fergus, 'is a gentleman.'

'And I'm on early shifts!'

'What does that mean?'

'It means that I have to catch the service bus at the Cross at ten past four in the morning.'

'Damn,' he said. Then, cheering, 'Early bed, then. That sounds fine to me. Come on, I'll help you to take your uniform off.'

'What about the pie in the oven?' she asked as he carried her in to the bedroom.

'It'll keep,' he said, and kicked the door shut with his heel.

Julia McCosh had spent the morning in the WVS shop, sorting out donations of clothing and furniture. Returning home via the shops, where she had to queue for food as always, she had snatched a ten-minute rest in an armchair with a hasty cup of tea and a slice of toast before starting on the housework. When Leslie and Duncan came home from school she was peeling potatoes for the family's dinner.

'I've put out a sandwich and a cup of milk for each of you,' she said as they came raging into the flat like two runaway trains. 'And mind and change your clothes before you go out to play. You can do your homework after dinner, since it's a nice day.'

Leslie, always in a hurry, crammed his 'piece' into his mouth, washing it down with gulps of milk, then tore off his school clothes and battled his way into his old jersey and patched trousers. Duncan, the elder and more serious of the two, took time to hover about his mother for ten minutes, fiddling with bits of potato peelings as he told her all about his day. Then he too got changed and headed for the street, where a football game was already in progress.

He came back almost at once. 'Mum, there's a man outside wants to speak to you.'

'Who is it?'

'I don't know.' His round face was frowning, uncertain. 'He just asked if Mrs Julia McCosh was in.'

Julia's stomach clenched, as it always did these days when anything unusual happened. Had there been an accident at the India Tyre factory? Was Frank hurt? She hurried to the door, Duncan at her heels.

'I'm Julia McCosh. You were looking for me?' she began, and then the words died in her throat as the man on the landing pulled off his hat, revealing a balding head fringed with straggly, overlong hair.

'I was,' he said. 'And now I've found you.' Then, as she stared, speechless, 'D'you not know me, Julia?'

Duncan looked doubtfully from the stranger to his mother. 'Mum?' He tugged at her apron.

'Away you go and play, son.' Julia's dry tongue rasped against the roof of her mouth as she spoke.

'I'll stay here if you want.'

She wrenched her eyes away from the dark gaze holding them, and smiled down at the boy. He was Frank's child in every way; thoughtful and caring, and quick – sometimes too quick – to sense her moods.

'No need. On you go now, and get some fresh air.' She gave him a slight push towards the stairs, saying to her unexpected visitor, 'Come on in.'

He walked past her, and as she closed the door she saw Duncan, going down the stairs step by slow step, staring at her through the banisters. She smiled and flapped her hand at him, then closed the door. 'Through to the door at the end.'

'So this is where you're living,' he said, putting his hat on the kitchen table and looking around the small room with the piercing, taking-everything-in gaze she remembered so well.

'How did you find me?'

'I used to be a policeman, remember? I know how to find folk when I want to.' His gaze turned on her, raking her from head to foot and back again. 'You've changed, Julia. You're more confident than I remember.'

'I'm happier.' She put her hands on the back of the chair Frank usually sat in, curling her fingers tightly round the top spar.

'I suppose I should be glad about that, though I would have preferred it if you had found your happiness with me,' he said. 'After all, I am your husband.'

'Not any more. I've been with Frank for over sixteen years now.'

'Which makes you man and wife under Scottish common law, I'll grant you. But naturally, I prefer to follow the King's law.'

'Did you say that you *used* to be a policeman? You've left the force?' It was difficult for her to think of the police force and Thomas Gordon as two separate entities, for they had suited each other so well.

'A year past, when . . .' He began to cough, a deep, harsh sound that went on and on. One hand fumbled in his pocket for a handkerchief while the other reached out to clutch at the edge of the table. Alarmed, Julia hurried to take his arm and ease him into a chair.

'Sit here. I'll fetch a cup of water.'

The paroxysm was over by the time she brought the water. Her eye caught a splash of bright red as he stuffed the handkerchief back in to his pocket.

'What's the matter with you?' she asked sharply.

'Just leave me be for a minute.' He fumbled in another pocket and produced a small bottle. Opening it, he shook a few drops into the cup and then drank it down.

Julia seated herself opposite, watching him. His long narrow face, thinner than she remembered it, had been pale when he came in; now it was grey and he looked ill to the point of collapse. She wondered if Nan Megson was at home.

'Thank you,' he said after a long pause.

'Would you like some tea?'

'Isn't your . . . isn't he due home soon?'

'There's time for a cup before you go back to Glasgow. Just sit quiet and get your breath back while I see to it.' Thank goodness, Julia thought as she filled the kettle and put cups and saucers out, Frank's working late. And thank goodness Chloe had been invited to the Hepburns' for her tea.

Setting the cup before him and resuming her own seat, she saw with relief that the frightening grey tinge had left his skin, though he still looked ill and drained. He had always been lean, with no fat on him, but now he was painfully thin.

'What's wrong with you, Thomas?'

'Oh, just some trouble with my chest.' His mouth twisted in a rueful smile. 'All those cold wet nights out on patrol have caught up with me.'

Julia remembered that smile; at one time it had charmed and attracted her, but that had been before she realised that behind it lay a cold man, incapable of giving any woman the warmth and love she needed.

Remembering the red stain she had seen on his hand-kerchief she asked, 'Is it bad?'

'Bad enough, apparently.' He took a sip of tea. 'Why else would I be here?'

'What do you mean?'

He leaned across the table, his deep-set eyes holding her. 'I mean that I'm dying, Julia. I've got the consumption and I've left Glasgow and the life I knew there. I've found lodgings here in Paisley because you're still my wife and it's up to you to look after me.'

'I have tae hand it tae our Charlie,' Joe Hepburn said, leaning back in his chair, 'for once he's brought an intelligent lass home to meet his old father.'

'Dad!' Charlie's open, honest face went red. 'You'll have

Chloe thinking that I fill the place with girls. You know full
well that she's the first!'

'I know it, son, and you know it.' His father gave Chloe
a wink. 'But you don't want to have young Miss McCosh
here thinking that no lassie's ever fancied you before.'

Chloe had been worried about meeting Charlie's father.
Everything she had heard about him – a speaker for workers'
rights, a demonstrator, a man who had been thrown into
prison several times for his political beliefs and finally won
through to become a respected Bailie – had, in her mind,
built him up into a terrifying image. Instead, she had found
a family man who, with his thin face, good bone structure,
blue eyes and black hair, greying at the temples, looked like
an older version of Charlie. Even the slight twist to the
bridge of his nose made him look more distinguished than
frightening.

'I'm not bothered about what the other girls think of
Charlie, Mr Hepburn,' she dared to say, 'though I'm sure
that plenty have fancied him. It's not as if we own each
other. I don't believe in men and women being possessive.'

Joe Hepburn raised his brows at her. 'Better and better,
son, you've found yourself an independent thinker intae the
bargain.'

'Behave yourself, Joe,' Mirren Hepburn said firmly, while
Chloe felt herself turn red. 'What my husband is trying to
say, Chloe, in his own wordy political way, is that he likes
you.'

'That's very true, but as my wife would be the first to
tell you, I've never been very good at making compliments.
Am I being too hard on you, lassie?'

'Mebbe a wee bit. I don't like being made to blush,' she
said, and he laughed.

'You're right as usual, Mirren. Here, Chloe, give me your
cup.'

She watched in amazement as he poured tea and added
milk and a spoonful of sugar before bringing the cup back

to her, together with a plate of biscuits. Although her own father helped a little about the flat, it was always her mother who looked after visitors. And her father rarely poured his own tea, as Mr Hepburn was doing now.

'Oh, I've got him well trained.' Mirren Hepburn had been watching her guest's reaction. 'Chloe's more impressed by your housewifely skills than by your wit, Joe.'

'One day, lass, women like you will take it for granted that their menfolk should do more for themselves in the house.' He settled himself back in his chair. 'And the men will just have to accept it.'

'I should think so,' Grace said sharply. Bobby, the younger boy, was off on some ploy of his own, but Grace and Daisy were at home.

Now Joe smiled over at his daughter before going on, 'I looked after myself entirely before Mirren here took me under her wing, Chloe, and I still have it to do, when I'm travelling about and living in lodgings.'

'D'you like moving about all over the country?'

'I don't care for living out of a suitcase, but it's a job worth doing and it has to be done. And it's always grand tae come back to Paisley, and tae my own home.' As he said the final words, he gave his wife a smile that wiped the years from his face.

The door flew open and young Daisy rushed in. 'I'm going to practise,' she announced, and made for the piano.

'No you're not.' Grace, sitting near the piano, put her hand on the lid to hold it down.

'I am!' Daisy scowled at her, her face going pink as she tried in vain to open the lid.

'Mother, tell her!'

'Not while we've got a visitor, dear.'

Daisy turned and swept the room with clear blue eyes. 'That's not a visitor, that's Chloe,' she said, and whirled back to the piano.

'Chloe's been invited here for her tea, so today that makes

her a special visitor. And she doesn't want to hear you playing the piano at the moment,' her father said. Then, ignoring Charlie's mutter of 'I'm sure she hears more than enough of your playing when you're at her flat,' he held out a hand to his youngest child.

'Come and sit on my knee and help me to eat this bit of cake,' he suggested, and Daisy eyed the cake and then the piano several times before opting for her father's lap, where she demolished most of the cake before kneeling up on his thighs and rubbing her face against his.

'Mr Bumpy Nose,' she said affectionately.

'Not my fault, Daisy. I just happened to get in the way of a policeman's stick during a peaceful law-abiding demonstration,' he said, and his wife rolled her eyes.

'It was probably peaceful enough before you started rousing them up with your speech.'

'You know, Chloe, my wife would have made a wonderful politician, probably better than me. But I could never get her to do anything about it.'

'I had more sense,' Mirren said drily. 'Anyway, if I'd gone on the march the way you did, who would have been around to bandage you up and visit you in the jail?'

'Aye, I suppose you're right. Were you shocked at the thought of meeting a man who'd been a lodger in His Majesty's Prisons, Chloe?' Mr Hepburn asked suddenly, catching her off-guard. She took a moment to think out her answer.

'Not shocked, but a wee bit worried, mebbe,' she said at last, and he laughed.

'There's nothing wrong with going tae prison, lass, if it's in a good cause.'

'It's still breaking the law,' Charlie pointed out.

'Aye, but sometimes when the laws are unfair they need tae be broken because that's the only way tae make folk realise how unfair they are.' Joe Hepburn settled his younger daughter against his shoulder and said over her head, 'This country of ours has always had wealth, Chloe, more wealth than you or me could ever imagine, but it's kept in the hands of just a few fortunate folk. They like it that way and they've always taken it for granted that, for them, life was going to keep on like that. Nice and cosy for them and to blazes with the rest of the folk. When I fought for them – the rich and the powerful – in the Great War, I fought because I thought that things would change afterwards; that they would appreciate what the ordinary folk had done for them, and make things fairer. But not a bit of it. We ended up with mass unemployment and misery. Now we're fighting again, and if you ask me, it could all go the same way once more after this war's been settled. The only difference is that this time my own lad's havin' tae go and fight for them.' His voice was suddenly serious, and Chloe, glancing over at Mrs Hepburn, saw the pain in her eyes.

'I'm not complaining, Dad,' Charlie said. 'I'm willing to do my bit. In fact, I'm looking forward to a bit of a change from the same old life.'

'I know you are, but this time we need to make sure that things really do get better for you and all the lads like you.'

'They will,' Charlie said confidently.

'We're off to a good start, I grant you that,' his father agreed. 'In the war I fought, the working classes were the foot soldiers and the gentry were the officers, with swords at their waists. You'd have thought at times that we were still in the Middle Ages! But this new conflict's thrown all the classes together for the first time, like a big crucible. It's just a damned shame that it took a war to do it.'

'Language, Joe!'

'Sorry,' he said, and then, returning to his theme, 'And it's not just happening in the Forces, for civilians from different walks of life are gettin' together and learnin' new skills. Women are discoverin' that they can manage very well without having to lean on their menfolk . . .'

'We always knew that,' Mrs Hepburn put in, and was
ignored.

'. . . and the people of this country are showing that
they can work together to get things done. And when it's
over . . .'

'Dad, it's time Chloe was going home,' Charlie interrupted gently.

Once they were outside, he tucked Chloe's hand through
his arm. 'He can go on a bit, but he's all right really.'

'I like him. I like him very much. He's like my own dad,
only my dad doesn't talk as much.'

19

Chloe returned home to find her mother putting the final touches to the dinner. She set the table, talking all the time about her visit to the Hepburns, and it was a while before she noticed that her mother was very quiet.

'Mum, are you all right? You look pale.'

Julia summoned a smile. 'I've got a bit of a headache, that's all.'

'And here's me nattering away and making it worse!'

'No, it's all very interesting. I'm glad that you got on so well with Mr Hepburn.'

'I was surprised at how nice and ordinary he is. And he talks a lot of sense too. He says . . .' Chloe stopped, then said, 'Sit down, Mum, and I'll make you a cup of tea.'

'But your father'll be in at any minute, and there's the boys to fetch.'

'I can do that.' Chloe was already filling the kettle. 'And I can dish out the dinner.'

'This is supposed to be your afternoon off.'

'And I've had a very nice time. Imagine, Mum, Mr Hepburn actually gave me a second cup of tea . . . poured it out with his own hands! And him a former Bailie, too!' Chloe put the kettle on the stove and fetched a clean dish-towel, which she folded and held under the running tap. 'There now, I'll just give this a good squeeze out, and then I'll put it on your forehead.'

'You're a good lassie, Chloe,' Julia said when she was resting in an armchair, her feet on a stool, the cold compress on her forehead and a cup of tea on a small table by her hand. 'A good lassie.'

And Chloe was startled and alarmed to see tears glistening in her mother's lovely green eyes.

Lena and Dennis were working on the vegetable garden when Fergus Goudie appeared and asked cheerfully, 'Need a hand?'

'We could always do with extra help.' Dennis straightened up and leaned on the handle of the fork he was using. 'You're Mrs Goudie's man, aren't you?'

'Fergus.' He held out his hand. 'I'm home on leave but my wife's had to go to work, so I'm at a loose end.'

'Dennis Megson.' They shook hands, and Dennis introduced Lena. She put her fingers into the newcomer's fist for a second or two then withdrew them and scuttled off to the furthest corner, where she sat down on the small wooden stool Dennis had found in the shed, and got on with some weeding.

'That corner looks as though it could do with a bit of digging.' Fergus nodded to a neglected patch.

'The soil's not so good there and we've not had time to tackle it yet.'

'Leave it to me.' Fergus spat on his hands and picked up a spade that was leaning against the wall. 'I'm in the mood for a bit of hard work.' He drove the spade deep into the hard earth and levered a compacted lump free, then moved a spade's width to the side and started again. 'Last time I was home on leave there was a right good band practice going on the night before I left. Are they still playing?'

'Aye.' Dennis forked the soil round a blackcurrant bush. 'That's Mr and Mrs McCosh's band. I play the trumpet in it.'

'Do you indeed? Where d'you play?'

'All over, wherever we're wanted. We're playing at a dance in the Templar Halls on Saturday, so there'll be a practice on the Friday night.'

'A dance?' Fergus's eyes lit up. 'I think I'll take my missus to that. It beats travelling on the buses.'

'The buses?'

Fergus completed the row and started another. 'With Cecelia working and me on leave, the only way I can see more of her is by sitting on her bus all day, going back and forth and back and forth. It's not my idea of a proper leave.' He grinned over at Dennis. 'I got so fed up with it that I called off for today. I'd much rather be doing something like this.' He lifted another two spadefuls of earth then asked casually, 'Waiting to be called up, are you?'

It was a question Dennis was used to hearing. 'I'm training with the Fire Service. This is my day off.'

'Ah. You'll be kept busy.'

'Busy enough.'

By the time he had to leave to meet his wife coming from work, Fergus Goudie had turned over the entire corner, and broken up the solid clumps of soil.

'A good raking over and a bit of horse manure and it'll be as good a piece of ground as the rest,' he said, rubbing his hands together to remove the worst of the dirt. 'It was grand to get back to some diggin' again.'

'You're used to having a garden?'

'I was brought up on a croft. There was always digging of some sort to be done there. When this business is over I want to find a nice wee house for Cecelia and me with a nice wee garden that I can work in. Vegetables, mebbe a tree or two, some nice flowers for show and for the house . . . that sort of thing. See you on Saturday, then.'

When Fergus had gone, Dennis put the fork and spade away. 'I think we've done enough for the day, too,' he said, then gave a low whistle as he inspected the corner Lena had been working on. 'You've got this bit looking like part of the gardens at Buckingham Palace.'

She gave her shy smile. 'It'll do. D'you want to come up for a cup of tea?'

When the two of them had washed their hands in her kitchen Lena nodded at the usual clutter of material on the table. 'Push that stuff out of the way while I make the tea.'

'Is there anything I can do for you while I'm here?' Dennis asked, and she shook her head. 'He's a nice man . . . Mrs Goudie's husband,' he went on idly as he began to gather up the cloth strewn over the table. 'A grand worker too.'

'Yes.' Lena's voice was tense, just as she herself had tensed when Fergus appeared. Men made her nervous, Dennis thought, then his chest swelled with pride as he realised that she was different with him. She trusted and liked him, and that made him feel protective in a way he had never felt before, even towards his mother and sisters. He wanted to look after Lena, to banish the anxiety from her bluebell eyes and the worry lines from her mouth. He wanted . . .

'Ow!' he yelped as a sharp pain stabbed through one finger.

'What's wrong?'

'A needle, just.' He put the injured hand up to his mouth. 'I should have thought to look out for them!'

'Keep away from the sewing machine,' she said at once, 'I mustn't have blood on that material!'

'It's all right, it didn't drip on to anything.' He went to the sink and turned on the single cold tap so that the water could trickle over the bright bead welling from a tiny puncture mark. 'It's stopped bleeding already,' he said after a moment, fishing his handkerchief from his pocket and dabbing the finger dry.

He turned to smile at her, and saw that she was standing by the stove, clutching the battered tin teapot in both hands and staring at him, her eyes large in her stricken face.

'It's all right, no harm done.'

'You got hurt and all I could think to say was keep away from the work. You must think I'm a terrible person!'

'Of course I don't. You didn't want me spoiling that nice material.' He nodded in the direction of the sewing machine and the blue dress draped over it.

'Let me see.' Lena put down the teapot and came over to him, taking his hand in hers and turning it over in search of the wound.

'I told you, it's stopped bleeding. You can't even see where the needle went in.' Her hands were small and cold, the nails cut or bitten short, the skin rough. And yet there was something about her touch that made Dennis tingle from head to toe. Suddenly embarrassed, he cleared his throat and turned away from the sink so that their hands fell apart. Two steps took him to the sewing machine and the blue tulle dress lying across it.

'That's pretty.' He made sure to keep both hands well away from the delicate material.

'It's a bridesmaid's frock. A lassie that works with Mrs Borland's getting married and I'm doing the dresses.'

'That's a lot of work surely,' he asked, and when she shrugged in reply, 'I hope you're paid well for it.'

'Mrs Borland brought me all the materials, and bobbins of thread and things like that. They're difficult to get these days, and expensive too.'

'She can probably get them from the mill for nothing.'

Lena put cups on the table. 'That's something I don't ask about. Better not to know.'

'But even though she gets thread for nothing and supplies the cloth, she still pays you well for your time, doesn't she?'

'I think the tea's ready now. Sit in. Oh ... I got some

biscuits,' Lena remembered, beaming at him. 'The kind you like.'

The flat was silent when he let himself in half an hour later. Time to do some studying in peace before the others got home, Dennis thought, stripping off his jacket as he went through the small hall.

He opened the bedroom door and halted in the act of tossing the jacket on to his bed. 'Where the hell did you spring from?'

Ralph, also taken by surprise, gaped up at him from where he sat on his bed, and then managed to pull himself together. 'I came in through the door, where else?'

'What are you doing here? School's not over yet.'

'Our teacher had the toothache, so we got sent home early while he went to the dentist.'

'I don't believe you. And what's that you've got?' Dennis pounced, and managed to grip his brother's wrist, dragging Ralph's hand out from beneath the pillow.

'Nothin'! Let go of me!'

'Open your hand.'

'No!' Ralph tried to lash out as Dennis threw himself on to the bed so that his body pinned the younger boy down.

'Open your hand!

'No!'

'Do as you're told!' Dennis began to peel his brother's clenched fingers back one by one. Ralph, struggling hard, managed to pull one knee up so that it was wedged between them, then lunged it forward, breaking Dennis's grip and throwing him against his own bed, only some eighteen inches away. He rebounded and came straight back, reaching out for the boy's wrist again, but as Ralph squirmed round, trying to escape, Dennis's outspread hand slammed against his face, the tip of a finger prodding into his eye. As he uttered a howl of pain, both hands flying to his face, the money he had been guarding so jealously showered over the bed and the floor, coins jingling and notes fluttering.

'What the . . . ?'

'You've hurt my eye,' Ralph whimpered, then dragging himself upright as his brother bent to collect the money, 'You leave that alone, it's mine!'

'There's . . . there must be five pounds or more here. Where did you get it, Ralph?' Then, as his brother glared at him in silence, one eye streaming tears, 'Have you been runnin' for some street bookie again?'

'No.'

'You must've got it from somewhere. Did you steal it?'

'No I didnae steal it. It's mine, I earned it.'

Dennis put the pile of notes and coins on his own bed, out of reach. 'If you earned it then you have to give it to Mam. All of it. And she'll want to know the same as me . . . how could a schoolboy earn money like that?'

'I was goin' tae give her some of it, but I've got the right tae keep some for myself,' Ralph muttered, tears from his injured eye beginning to spill down his face.

Light was beginning to dawn. 'This has come from Mrs Borland, hasn't it? You've been goin' round doors, collectin' debts for her.'

'Mind your own business!'

'This is my business! The woman's a money lender and there's folk round here living in misery because of her.'

'She's good tae us. She's good tae all the folks that live in this buildin'.' Ralph knuckled his face, smearing the moisture from his eye all over.

'She's good to folk when it suits her, and if it doesn't suit she can be a right old devil. If you keep on working for her you'll turn out to be just as bad as she is!'

'It'd be better than livin' the way we are now,' Ralph snarled back at him. 'What's wrong with havin' money and bein' able to do what you want?'

'Nothing, if you've earned it fair and square.'

'And I earned that, so give it back!'

'Not a penny of it.' Dennis used his old pay packets to save money – coppers in one, threepenny bits in another – and now he pulled open the drawer of the small locker standing at the head of his bed and drew out an empty packet. He poured the money into it and then folded the top over. 'I'm giving this back to old Ma Borland, and I'm going to tell her—'

Ralph kicked at his brother's hand, a vicious upswing that Dennis had not expected. As his arm jerked up with the force of the kick the packet flew from his grasp and landed on the floor. Before it could be retrieved, Ralph bunched his fists and went for his brother in earnest, his face twisted with rage.

Although Dennis was the older by five years and half a head taller, Ralph was sturdy and square built. He was also out of his mind with rage, and although they had often sparred before this was the first time they had fought seriously. Ralph's clear aim was to hurt his brother as quickly and as severely as possible, and Dennis was driven back on to his own bed, trying to defend himself from a barrage of hard, painful blows that landed on his head, shoulders and body.

Breathing heavily, grunting with effort, they struggled against each other, Dennis still in shock at the ferocity of the attack and Ralph, straddling his older brother's body, punching as hard and as fast as he could, pinning Dennis down on to the bed. He had gained the upper hand and Dennis could tell by the ferocious grin on the face above his that Ralph knew it, and was out to take full advantage of the situation.

'For God's sake, Ralph!' he gasped, and then gurgled as one of Ralph's hands clamped across his windpipe. The other hand was raised, slowly this time, the fingers clenched into a club of bone and muscle. Ralph's grin grew wider.

'Got ye, ye bastard,' he said softly. 'And now I'm goin' tae make sure that ye'll not play that precious trumpet of yours for a good long while. That should teach ye tae leave me alone!'

'No!' Dennis managed to wheeze the word out. His greatest fear, as Ralph well knew, was damage of any kind to his mouth. He thrashed his body about on the bed, desperate to dislodge the weight that pinned it down. Just as his brother's clubbed fist began to plunge towards him he managed to wrench his head to the side, despite the tight grip on his throat. Pain ripped through his neck and then exploded along his jawline and up into his skull as Ralph's fist came down hard, just below his ear.

Lights flashed before Dennis's eyes and for a moment he thought that he was going to black out; instead, as the grip on his neck eased slightly, he managed to find enough energy to heave his body upwards, throwing Ralph off balance.

They were so intent on their struggle that neither heard the door open, and it was not until Nan Megson's shocked voice asked, 'What in the name of heaven is going on here?' that they were aware of her arrival.

They immediately broke apart. Dennis, a hand to his bruised throat, fought to get his breath back, while Ralph whined, 'He nearly put my eye out!'

'For goodness' sake, have the two of you not got an ounce of common sense between you? Dennis, you're the man of this family now and you should know better. So should you, Ralph. You're thirteen years old and it's time you learned to act like it. Let me see.' Nan took the boy's head in her two hands and tilted his face up to catch what light there was from the narrow window. 'It's inflamed, but no harm done. Now put this place to rights, the two of you . . . look at the mess you've made of your beds.'

Ralph scurried to obey, tossing a smirk at Dennis as he knelt to tuck in the bedclothes. 'Sorry, Mam,' he said as he got to his feet.

'So I should think. Now get into that kitchen and start peeling potatoes. As for you,' she said to her elder son as Ralph slunk out, 'there's to be no more of this fighting. I know that Ralph can be annoying at times but if you can't discipline him without having a fight you'd be best to leave it to me to deal with him if he misbehaves in future.' Then her voice changed as he pressed his fingertips gently against the hinge of his jaw, wincing. 'What's the matter, son? Did he hurt you?'

He opened then closed his mouth gingerly. 'He got in a lucky punch, just.'

'Away through to the kitchen and soak a bit of rag in vinegar and water, that'll help to keep you from getting too much of a bruise,' his mother ordered, unfastening her coat. She turned to go out of the room, then stopped as he said, 'Mam?'

'What is it, son?' She had put in a long shift at the hospital and then walked home; wisps of hair escaped from beneath her hat and she looked tired, as always. She had enough to worry about without him adding to it, Dennis thought guiltily.

'I'm sorry,' he said. 'I know that I shouldnae let Ralph anger me the way he does sometimes.'

She smiled, and put her hand lightly on his head. 'It's all right, Dennis. I've not been fair on you, expecting you to grow up so fast and be responsible for the younger ones. You've got your own life to lead.'

'I don't mind. I want to take my father's place. It's what he'd want too.'

'You're doing fine and he'd be as proud of you as I am. But no more fighting! Now, come through to the kitchen and I'll get the vinegar out.'

Before following her, Dennis looked down at the floor,

then got on to his knees and felt about in the darkness below each of the narrow beds.

The packet of money was gone. Ralph must have taken it when he was tidying his bed.

20

Fergus was waiting when Cecelia arrived at Paisley Cross at the end of her shift. He kissed her, heedless of the people milling about, then tucked her hand into his arm as they turned to walk down Smithhills. 'Busy day?'

'Nothing special. I missed you.'

'I needed a day off. Travelling up and down between Glasgow and Paisley's not my idea of a perfect leave, sweetheart. Half the time you're too busy to speak to me.'

'I don't think Glasgow Corporation would like it if I refused to let passengers on to my bus just because they get in the way of us speaking to each other.'

'I know. The only excitement I get is when Harry spots an inspector waiting to board, and you've to rush up to me and demand my fare. Although I've learned something interesting about the woman I married.'

'What's that?'

'You can be surprisingly bossy when you're on that bus, and quite loud too. And yet when you're at home you're the same quiet, shy Cecelia I fell in love with and married.'

'I've noticed that too. It's got something to do with the uniform. Don't you feel different when you're wearing yours?'

'That's different,' he said. 'When I'm in uniform I'm just one part of a unit; if anything, I get quieter and more obedient. But you're in charge of your own bus, so you have to give the orders and see that the rules are obeyed. You love that job, don't you?'

'I do. I never thought I would, though. The war's taught me something about myself,' Cecelia said, surprised by the realisation. 'So what did you do with your day while I was bossing the passengers about?'

'Nothing much. A bit of reading, a bit of housework. And in the afternoon I saw that young fellow Megson working in the backcourt so I went down and gave him a hand. There was a woman doing a bit of weeding, a pretty little thing, very shy. She had a bit of a limp.'

'That's Lena Fulton; we met her and her husband on the stairs once, remember? He was on leave the same time as you. She was working in the vegetable garden?' Cecelia asked with surprise.

'Yes, but she kept herself to herself. There's going to be a band practice on Friday,' Fergus remembered, 'and young Megson said that they're playing at a dance in the Templar Halls on Saturday night. Fancy going?'

'I'd love it.'

'Good.' He withdrew her hand from the crook of his elbow so that he could put his arm about her. 'Come on, let's get you home and out of that bossy uniform.'

Cecelia knocked on the door, waited, and was wondering if she should knock again when she heard movement in the hall beyond. A moment later the door opened slightly and Lena Fulton peered out at her.

'Lena, I wondered if you had time to look at this skirt for me. The problem is, I need it in a bit of a hurry, for tomorrow evening.'

The other girl hesitated, and for a moment Cecelia thought that she was going to refuse. Then the door opened wider and Lena said, 'Come in and show me what you want done.'

'I've put on a bit of weight,' Cecelia explained in the

kitchen, taking off her coat to show the skirt she wore underneath. 'I've managed to get the button in to the buttonhole, but it won't zip up, and Fergus is taking me dancing at the Templar Hall tomorrow. I wanted to wear this with a nice wee blouse I have, but when I tried it on . . . it's all these slabs of bread and margarine I eat when we get to a terminus,' she babbled on as Lena examined the skirt, 'but I get so hungry, specially when I have to start early in the morning . . .'

'Take it off, will you?'

Cecelia slipped off the skirt and stood in her petticoat, watching as the seamstress examined the darts and the waistband.

'There's a bit of room left in the waistband, so I can let it out a little. And there are darts that could be opened.' She put it aside and took a tape measure from the table. 'Lift your arms away from your sides . . .'

While Lena fussed around with the tape measure Cecelia studied the work laid out on the table. 'What's that you're making?'

Lena cast a look over her shoulder. 'A patchwork quilt.'

'Are you making it for someone?'

'No, it's just something I'm trying for myself whenever I have a spare minute.'

'Can I have a closer look?' Cecelia asked when Lena finished taking her measurements and returned to study the skirt.

'If you like.'

The quilt was only the size of a large pillow as yet, but even so the combination of colours and textures gave Cecelia plenty to look at. 'Where did you get the material from?' she wanted to know, running her fingers over the beautifully stitched sections.

'All sorts of places,' Lena said vaguely. 'Clothes I altered for myself and bits left over from work I've done for other folk.'

'Would you do one for me when you've finished this one?' Cecelia dared to ask, adding hastily when Lena looked uncertain, 'I'd pay you whatever you wanted. I can see that there's a lot of work in something like this.'

'Mebbe . . . yes, when I've got the time,' Lena said.

'I'd like that. It would be something to keep for ever, a memento of all the different frocks I had, and what they meant to me. Is that what you're doing yours for?'

'Yes, it is,' Lena said, after a brief pause, then held up the skirt. 'I think I can let it out just enough to fit you. Saturday, you said?'

'Fergus is going away on Sunday and he wants us to go to this dance on Saturday. Mr McCosh's band is playing . . . you know, Mr and Mrs McCosh and Dennis Megson.'

'I know.'

'D'you want paying now, or when I fetch the skirt?'

'When you fetch it will be fine.'

'What about your own man?' Cecelia asked as she put on her coat, wrapping it about her and pulling the belt tight in case she met anyone on the stairs on her way back to her own flat. 'When's he going to get some leave?'

'I don't know. He's overseas just now, so not for a while.'

Cecelia hesitated, then said, 'Why don't you come to the dance with me and Fergus?'

'I couldn't! I'm . . . I'm not very good at dancing.'

'You don't have to dance at all, you can just sit and enjoy listening to the music. We could have a nice night out.'

'No,' Lena said, her voice almost panic-stricken. 'I've got too much work to do.' She opened the door and waited for her visitor to precede her into the hall.

'Well, if you change your mind you know where we live,' Cecelia said at the front door.

'Aye, I do. Thank you for thinking of me.'

'It's a pity about your husband,' Cecelia said, stepping on to the landing. 'You must miss him.'

'Aye,' said Lena. 'I do.'

When her visitor had gone, she lifted the quilt and then laid it back down on the table, running her hand over it and letting her fingers rest on each of the patches. When she first started work on it she had used whatever material she picked up, but as the work began to gain importance to her, she had become more selective.

The centrepiece was the large patch from her wedding dress, the day she had given herself to George, not fully realising at the time just what 'giving herself' entailed. A silky turquoise patch came from a blouse she had been particularly fond of. She had been wearing it on the day she and her aunt got the telegram telling them of her brother's death in France, and she had never worn it again. Here was a piece from the scarf George had given her when she agreed to marry him, and there was a section from the blouse her aunt had worn when she attended their wedding.

A small bag of specially selected pieces lay beside the quilt; Lena chose one and sat down, drawing the quilt towards her and picking up a needle. She would stay up late tonight, working on Cecelia Goudie's skirt. For the moment, the quilt took precedence.

Frank McCosh had had a difficult day at work, and for once, he did not feel up to a band practice.

'It had better be a good rehearsal,' he told Julia as they got the front room ready, 'for I'm not in the mood for stops and starts all night.' Then he paused and eyed her closely. 'Are you all right?'

'Why wouldn't I be all right?'

'You look pale. Is it a headache?'

'I'm fine. Just a bit tired.' Her tone was dismissive as she began to lay out the sheet music she had laboriously copied.

'D'you want me to cancel the practice? I will, if you don't feel up to it.'

'For goodness' sake, Frank, don't go sympathising with

me or you'll only make me feel even more sorry for myself! Everyone's tired just now, with interrupted nights and rationing and this constant worry about what's going to happen to us . . .'

He took the papers from her hands and put his arms about her. 'It'll be all right, love, I promise you. We'll not let that Hitler get the better of us.'

She drew away, biting her lip, and then said, 'I suppose I'm feeling down because Mirren came round to tell me that Charlie's call-up papers have arrived.'

'Already? They must be keen to get recruits in the Air Force.'

'I think they're getting desperate for new recruits in all the Forces. At least we're still a few years away from that worry as yet, and with any luck it might never happen to us. Now then, let's get on with it or Bert and Dennis will be here and nothing ready for them.'

Bert arrived just as they got everything set up, but Dennis Megson kept them waiting, and incurred Frank's displeasure when he finally arrived.

'It's not as if you've got a distance to travel,' Frank pointed out coldly as the young man stammered out apologies. 'Two floors away, that's all. Bert lives over in Orchard Street and he's been cooling his heels along with the rest of us for the past half-hour, waiting for you.'

'I'm sorry, I'd things to do and I didnae realise the time was passing,' Dennis stuttered, his face bright red apart from a slight shadowing along his jawline, just below the ear. Frank's hand shot out to catch the lad's chin and turn his face to the light.

'And what's this? Have you been fighting?'

'Just a wee scrap with our Ralph . . .'

'I hope it doesnae interfere with your playing.'

'It won't, Mr McCosh, honest!'

'For goodness' sake, Frank, the lad's here now,' Julia interrupted, 'so can we not just get on with the practice instead of spending more time talking about why he was late?'

Her tone was unusually sharp, and when they all looked at her, surprised by her unexpected anger, she swallowed hard and added in a more reasonable voice, 'Let's just start work, shall we?'

Unfortunately, everything that could go wrong that night did go wrong. Time and again Frank lowered his saxophone and ordered them to stop. They had to go over small sections again and again before they got them right, and to make matters worse the air-raid siren started to wail just when they were into the final hour of the rehearsal.

'Damn and blast!' Frank exploded as feet clattered on the stairs outside and Chloe and her mother ran to waken the two boys, long since in their beds. As they got the youngsters up and were helping them to get dressed the two women heard the door of the flat open and then close. They stared at each other.

'Surely that's not your father going to the Home Guard?' Julia asked. 'He's not on duty tonight, and neither's Bert.'

'Mebbe it's Dennis gone to see to his own family,' Chloe suggested, but as they led Duncan and Leslie, blinking sleepily in the light and clutching their 'shelter bags', into the front room Dennis and Bert were still there.

'Where's Frank gone?'

'Just away to find out what's happening,' Bert said. 'He told us tae stay here and the mood he's in tonight, I'd not want tae cross him. Anyway, I'm not wantin' tae walk home in the middle of a raid.'

'Dennis?'

'My mother's home tonight and she knows where I am if she needs me,' the young man said as Frank returned.

'Right, I got hold of a warden and it looks like just the one fighter plane that's mebbe got separated from his squadron. They're tracking him now.' From a distance, as he spoke, they could hear the dull thumping of anti-aircraft guns. 'He doesnae think the raid'll be a long one unless it turns out that this chap's mates are behind him. So here's what we'll do ... you take the boys down to the shelter, Chloe, and the rest of us'll keep on with the practice.' He glared at the members of his band. 'Any objections?'

There were none, and so Chloe was sent off in charge of her brothers while the others picked up their instruments and Julia returned to the piano stool.

As the rest of the tenement folk settled into the drysalter's the faint strains of 'Marie' filtered down from above to make a pleasant background to Donnie Borland's snores.

Ellen, Jessie Bell and Nan Megson talked quietly together while Lena Fulton, on the edge of the group as usual, worked at some sewing. Fergus Goudie had dreamed up a variation on Ludo to keep the McCosh and Megson children occupied, and even Ralph joined in.

'Come and have a game, Chloe,' Cecelia Goudie suggested, and when Chloe squeezed in at the small card table, she whispered, 'your parents will be safe, I'm sure. If your father thinks there's any danger he'll bring them all down here.'

Chloe smiled wanly, and tried without success to concentrate on the game. Cecelia was right, her father wouldn't let any harm come to her mother, or to any member of his beloved band. But she was fretting about her mother, who had not been her usual self for the past few days, and she was still trying to take in the news that Charlie had been called up. Somehow, she had not thought that it would really happen, and she was still confused about her own reaction.

The music changed; she had learned to recognise a tune from just a few notes, and now she realised that on the floor above they were playing 'All I Do Is Dream of You.' Her father would start it off, she knew, and then give Dennis a nod so that the trumpet could come in for a verse.

Thinking of Dennis reminded her of the dark smudge of

a bruise on his jawline, faint but definite, as though a sooty finger had been run lightly along the length of the bone. He, like her mother, had something on his mind, and it surely wasn't the fight he had had with his brother. Brothers fought all the time, she knew that well enough.

She glanced over at Lena Fulton. Had his preoccupation anything to do with Lena? Something was going on there; Chloe had seen them working in the garden companionably, and sitting together in the Fountain Gardens. And once, on her way out, she had even seen Dennis coming out of Lena's flat, looking pleased with himself. She had stepped back into her own hallway unnoticed, and waited until he was gone before venturing out again.

Were he and Mrs Fulton . . . ? Surely not! Mrs Fulton was a lot older than him, and besides, she was a married woman. It must be something else, something innocent. But what?

Now she could just make out Dennis playing the solo section. She closed her eyes and dreamed that she was stroking the tips of her fingers over his face, and smoothing away the faint bruise that had shadowed the line of his jaw.

'I'm going to miss dancing with you, and listening to your parents playing,' Charlie Hepburn said as he steered Chloe round the Templar Halls dance floor. Saturday night dances were popular in Paisley, and the place was crowded. As well as the local folk there were foreign servicemen based at the Fleet Air Arm station at Abbotsinch and even some seamen from the Clyde base at Gourock, who had become friendly with Paisley girls.

'You'll be coming home on leave. We can go dancing then.' Chloe knew that she should be trying to make the evening enjoyable for him, but her mind was on other matters. The band was playing well enough, but not as well as it usually did; although she wasn't as musical as her parents, Chloe had heard enough practices to know how it was doing.

'. . . a drink of juice?' Charlie asked from above her head.

'What?' Chloe started from a daydream and realised that she and Charlie were now at the side of the dance floor, which was clear except for people standing in small groups, talking. The band members were laying down their instruments. It must be the interval already.

'For the third time of asking, d'you want a drink? It's flattering,' Charlie said with mock annoyance, 'to know that my presence is so riveting that you don't even hear a word I'm saying.'

'Sorry, I was thinking about something that happened at work.'

'See what I mean? Even work is more interesting than being with me.'

'Don't be daft, and yes please, I would like a drink of juice.'

'Won't be long,' he said, and pushed his way into the crowd gathered around the counter, where women were serving tea and cold drinks to the thirsty dancers.

Chloe waited, perched on the edge of a seat, her hands clasped in her lap, missing Marion. Usually they had a good gossip during the interval, but tonight was Robert's grandmother's birthday, and Marion, now 'going with' Robert in a serious way, had been invited to the family celebrations.

On the stage, her father was talking earnestly, both hands gesturing and the tea someone had brought for the band in danger of flying from the cup he held. Chloe could tell by his face that he wasn't pleased with the night's performance.

'Here you are.' Charlie thrust a tumbler into her hand and took a seat by her side. 'The music's good, isn't it?'

'Not as good as usual. My mother hit a couple of wrong notes.'

'Did she? I didn't notice,' he was saying as Cecelia Goudie and her husband came towards them.

'Hello, mind if we join you?' Cecelia asked.

'No, that would be nice.' Chloe introduced them to Charlie, who leapt to his feet to offer his chair to Cecelia. Almost at once he and Fergus were talking about Charlie's call-up.

'I sometimes think,' Cecelia said into Chloe's ear, 'that men still treat the war as a game.'

'Mebbe it's as well they do, otherwise they might not be able to keep going.'

'I hadn't thought about it like that. You're probably right.' Cecelia eyed the younger woman with a new respect, then said, low-voiced, 'But it's nothing like a game for us, is it? If you ever feel that you want to talk to someone once your boyfriend's gone, you're welcome to come to my flat anytime.'

'Thanks, Mrs Goudie.'

'Call me Cecelia . . . "Mrs Goudie" makes me feel old!'

'Cecelia.' Chloe smiled, still young enough to be thrilled by the thought of having a mature, married woman as a friend. Then she added hurriedly, 'Not that Charlie's my boyfriend, really. Just a friend.'

'Quite right, you're both young to get too serious. Or is there someone else on your mind?'

'Nobody,' Chloe lied, only just stopping herself from glancing up at the small stage, where the band was taking its place in readiness for the second half of the evening.

Fergus Goudie had noticed them and now he held out his hand to his wife. 'Come on, Cecelia, we don't get the chance to dance together often, so I want us to dance every dance tonight.'

21

'What happened to you?' Lena's hand fluttered towards Dennis's bruised face, and then she drew her fingers back, trapping them in her other hand. 'Have you been in a fight?'

'Aye . . . with Ralph.' He wished that she had not pulled back, for he ached for her soothing touch. He needed it; he needed her, he suddenly realised.

'You fought with your brother? Why?'

'He's up to his tricks again.' Dennis gave her a brief description of the scene with Ralph and the money he had found in the boy's possession, ending with, 'I told him already that he had to keep well away from her, but he's disobeyed me. When I tried to take the money away from him, he went for me.'

'He might not have got it from her.' She sat down at the kitchen table and reached for the patchwork quilt, which she had been working on when he came to the door.

'He did. Who else would pay so much money to a lad of his age? The woman's a money lender.' Dennis sat down opposite. 'The whole street knows about it, and it's her business, not mine. But it's another matter altogether when she brings our Ralph into it. Ralph likes money and he likes to feel important, but he's only thirteen. She's paying him for the errands he runs, mebbe even to collect debts for her, and that's a bad thing.'

She glanced up at him, a swift flick of the eyes from

beneath her tumble of fair hair. It was a glance that made
him shiver in a pleasant way; he wondered if she realised
what an attractive woman she was, or if that husband of
hers had ever told her. Probably not.

'Why tell me about it?' she asked.

'I have to speak tae someone, and you were the only one
I could think of.'

Lena made a few more tiny stitches before raising the
work to her face and biting off the thread. Then she selected
another needle to be threaded with a different colour. 'What
about your mother?'

'That's the last thing I want to do! She's working long
hours at that hospital and she worries enough about the four
of us as it is. Are we happy, are we getting enough to eat,
what's going to happen to us if this war goes the wrong
way . . . she tries to cover it up, but I know fine that she
worries, day and night,' Dennis said helplessly. 'And if she
knew what Ralph was up to she'd only worry even more.
I have to sort it out for myself. Mebbe I should go and have
it out with old Ma Borland.'

Lena had been trying to introduce the end of the thread
through the needle's minute eye. Now, she paused for a
moment and looked across the table at him, her face
suddenly tense. 'Best to leave things as they are for a wee
while. You don't want to cause trouble with neighbours.
That might be worse for your mother.'

'D'you think so?'

'You say you've told your brother to stop whatever it is
he was doing. Give him the chance to do it.' She blinked
and then rubbed at her eyes as though they were sore. 'Don't
do anything that'll cause trouble for anyone.'

'Mebbe you're right. Here, let me try . . .' He took needle
and thread from her, and after a few tries managed to ease
the end of the thread through the needle's tiny eye.

'There!' he handed it back, and watched as she began to
stitch. It was a relief to talk to someone, and to make the

decision to just let things go for the time being. Dennis reached out and touched the quilt, which now spilled over most of the table. 'That's growing fast.'

She smiled at him. 'I like working on it. It soothes me.'

To his eye it appeared sombre, with few of the bright patches he would have expected, but it seemed to satisfy Lena. 'D'you have to buy the bits of cloth specially?'

'I just cut down scraps left over from work I've done . . . mostly from clothes I used to wear.'

For the next few minutes they enjoyed one of the companionable, comfortable silences that they had grown into, with Lena sewing and Dennis studying the quilt. Finally, he stirred and said reluctantly, 'I'd better go. Is there anything I can do for you before I go? Wash the cups, mebbe?'

'I can't have you washing my dishes. That's not a man's work.'

'Aye it is. My father washed dishes and he was a man. I wash them and I'm a man. Look . . .' He thrust his arms towards her, hands outspread. 'I've got two hands the same as you. That's all that's needed for dish-washing.'

'It's kind of you to offer, but I can see to the cups.'

When he had gone, Lena finished working on the patch she had cut from a pretty handkerchief George had bought her, and sifted through the bag of pieces.

Finding nothing there to suit her, she walked about the flat restlessly, opening drawers and cupboards, fingering clothes, bedding, everything she could find.

One of the drawers in the large bedroom dresser held nothing but a baby's pale lemon romper suit and a little bib. 'For my son,' George had said with pride on his last leave, as he unwrapped them and held them up for her inspection.

'You went into a shop and bought clothes for a baby?' she had asked in disbelief.

'Not just for a baby, ye daft woman . . . for my son! I

told the woman in the shop that. I said to her, I only want the best you have because it's for my son. We'll get more things the next time I'm on leave, so save up your clothing coupons,' he had ordered.

She had tried to do as he said, but as her debt to Mrs Borland mounted, and no more money arrived from old Mr Fulton, the coupons had gone to Ellen Borland in part payment of her debt.

Now, she took the bib out of the drawer, hesitated, put it back, and lifted the romper suit instead. The material was silky soft against her rough-skinned fingers and she caressed it as she carried it back to the kitchen.

Sitting back down at the table, she picked up her scissors and carefully cut a large piece of cloth from the front of the rompers. There was still enough left, she noticed happily as she re-threaded the needle, for another patch. They would help to brighten her precious quilt.

A fragile sense of contentment stole over Lena as she tied a knot on the end of the thread and began to stitch at the silky yellow patch.

It didn't get any better, Cecelia thought drearily as she tapped the bell twice and the bus drew away from the stop. The missing and the longing only seemed to get worse with each parting.

Twenty-four hours had passed since Fergus's leave had ended, and she had scarcely slept on the previous night. Once or twice she had dozed, then reached out in her sleep to touch the warm solid body that should have been in the bed with her, only to be awakened by the realisation that he was not there any more.

As she collected fares from the two housewives who had just boarded, one of them said encouragingly, 'Cheer up, hen. Worse things happen at sea.'

'What?'

'Ye look as if ye'd hung yer best knickers out on the

washing line and gone back tae find a pair of flannel drawers. Cheer up, you're too young to look so worried!'

'I'm fine.' Cecelia summoned up a smile.

'Here . . .' The other woman delved into her pocket and produced a small crumpled paper bag. 'Have a sooky sweetie.'

'I can't take your sweet ration.'

'Aye ye can,' the first woman told her, jerking her head sideways at her companion. 'She made me wave the last bus by just so's she could get on yours and give you a sweetie. So you take it, hen.'

'Thanks.' With some difficulty Cecelia prised a round black-and-white striped sweet free of its companions and put it into her mouth.

'That's for bein' such a nice wee clippie,' her benefactor said, as Harry, spotting an inspector at the stop ahead, flashed the interior lights in warning and slowed down.

The sweet helped Cecelia to cheer up a bit, but the inspector, unsmiling and officious, did not do her spirits any good at all. He trudged up and down the aisle checking tickets, then came back to the platform to go over the day's takings with Cecelia

'Seems in order,' he admitted at last, sounding faintly put out. Then he lifted his head, sniffing the air. 'What's that?'

'What?' Cecelia, who had been doing her best to conceal the fact that she was sucking a sweet while on duty, tucked it hurriedly into her cheek and prayed that she wouldn't swallow it or inhale it by mistake.

'That!' He sniffed again. 'For pity's sake, lassie, you're not goin' tae tell me that ye can't smell anythin'!'

Cecelia suddenly noticed that the passengers sitting on the long side seats nearest the door were screwing up their noses and eyeing each other furtively. She stepped up into the main section of the bus, sniffed, and then recoiled at the stench that hit her.

'I don't know . . . it didn't smell like this a wee while

ago when I was taking the fares,' she told the inspector, who turned red.

'Are you saying that that ... stink ... came on to the bus with me?'

'No, of course not. I just meant . . .'

More passengers were beginning to notice that something was amiss. Up and down the length of the bus heads were turning, noses lifting and sniffing, people doing their best to edge away from each other.

'Open a window, for pity's sake,' the inspector muttered, and as Cecelia hurried to obey she heard the first ominous murmurings from the passengers.

A woman who had brought a small baby on board glared at those nearest to her and then whipped the infant out of the shawl that had been wrapped about her own body to act as a carrier. Turning the child about, she sniffed noisily and energetically at its little rump.

'Whatever it is, it's no' her,' she announced to all and sundry, and then, shoving the baby at the man sitting next to her, invited, 'Here you, have a good sniff, why don't ye?'

When he declined, choosing instead to leap to his feet and head for the exit, she went on loudly, 'An' it's not me neither, so it must be one of youse!'

As Cecelia paused in her window-opening and reached for the bell to signal Harry to stop the bus, the woman who had given her the sweetie turned round in her seat at the front of the bus and shouted cheerfully, 'Keep your hair on, everyone, it's just me.' She dipped into her bag and brought out a small glass jar, which she flourished in the air. 'I got a bad egg from the grocer yesterday and I'm takin' it back and gettin' a fresh one. With eggs on the ration I cannae afford tae throw out a bad yin.'

The entire bus seemed to heave a collective sigh of relief. 'I'd one just last week, hen,' a respectable-looking woman in the seat across the aisle said. 'I took it back an' all. It's a disgrace, so it is. It's bad enough, being expected to manage with just one fresh egg each a week, but it's a right insult when you get one that's not even fit to eat. And nobody can tell me that that powdered stuff can replace a real egg from a real hen.'

As the entire lower deck settled down to a cosy discussion about the merits of shelled and powdered egg, and another woman began to impart the secret of how to make two cakes from one 'proper' egg, the bus began to slow for the next stop.

'D'you really want to get off here, sir, or would you prefer to stay on until you reach the right stop?' Cecelia heard the inspector murmur to the man who had previously decided to alight.

'I think I'll stay on.' The man scurried gratefully back to his seat as the first of the new passengers put one foot into the main section then hesitated, sniffing.

'Bad egg,' Cecelia heard the inspector say as she finished opening the windows. 'Going back to the grocer's. There'll be another bus along in five minutes if you'd prefer to wait.'

He belled the bus back into motion, and then beckoned her down to join him on the platform.

'I was just going to collect the new fares,' she protested as she reached him.

'You can do that when I get off the bus at Paisley Cross,' he said. 'For now, lassie, you can just stand here beside me, for I prefer the smell of the sweetie you're sucking to the stink from that addled egg.'

22

'I kept hoping that the war would suddenly turn our way,' Mirren Hepburn said wistfully, 'and that my Charlie wouldn't have to go. But I suppose every poor soul who's had to watch a son or a brother or a husband go off to war has prayed for the same thing without success.'

'I suppose they have,' Julia agreed, 'but that doesn't make your worry any the less. Are you sure you don't just want to go home again? I could see to this work on my own.'

'It's kind of you, Julia, but I'm better to be occupied. Would you look at this?' The two women were sorting out clothing that had been donated to the Women's Voluntary Service, and now Mirren held up a strapped evening blouse consisting of layers of glittering beads. 'I can just imagine some poor woman bombed out of her home and left with nothing but the clothes on her back wanting something like this! On the other hand, it might cheer someone up, who knows?' She put it to one side, shaking her head. 'I wish the better off folk would give a bit of thought to what they donate.'

'Perhaps they don't have much that's useful for ordinary people,' Julia offered.

'They must have warm coats and skirts . . . good woollens and tweeds that would keep the women we're trying to help warm and decently covered. And proper under-clothes. It makes a difference to a woman, doesn't it,'

Mirren said, 'having decent underclothes?' Then, with the ghost of a smile, 'I meant to tell you, when I was giving out clothing last week one woman who came looking for help was telling me that her husband sent her a beautiful pair of silk drawers from Singapore with a note saying "Please fill and return." Isn't that a lovely, romantic gesture? It fairly cheered her up, and the dear Lord only knows she needed it, because she'd just heard that she'd lost two brothers in France.' She shivered, and Julia knew by the darkness of her eyes that she was thinking of Charlie again.

'He'll be all right, Mirren. I'm sure he will.'

'Of course he will.' They worked in silence for a while, then Mirren said, 'One of my brothers was killed in the Great War. The older one. He was married, with a wee boy. My mother's health was never the same after she heard that our Crawford was gone. It's a hard thing, losing a child. You expect them to live on after you.' She sighed, and then held up a skirt with a frayed hem. 'This is past mending.'

'Give it to me and I'll put it in the sack for the ragman. What happened to your brother's wife?' Julia asked as the garment changed hands.

'Agnes? She married a good man that cared for wee Thomas as much as for the bairns that came later to him and Agnes. Not that Thomas is wee now; of course. He's married with two children of his own. And he's in the navy, but so far he's survived and please God he'll come home safely.'

Mirren paused, then added with a sidelong look, 'You're awful quiet, Julia. Are you not feeling well?'

'I'm fine.'

'You don't look fine,' Mirren said bluntly. 'In fact, you look right poorly. Is there something wrong with your man, or the children?'

'No, not a thing.'

'It's not . . . another bairn on the way?'

'What? Of course not!' Julia was startled in to an abrupt laugh.

'It's not all that impossible. You're young yet, and you seem to be happy enough with your man.'

'Oh, I am,' Julia said from the heart.

'There you are, then, you still enjoy a wee cuddle together in bed at night. So what's wrong?'

'You're beginning to sound like a gossipy schoolgirl instead of a respectable married woman, Mirren Hepburn!'

'Those were the days, eh?' Mirren heaved a nostalgic sigh. 'I mind the chats me and my pal Ella had when we worked in the mill together, about clothes and the dancing . . . and about lads, and what we were going to be when we were properly grown up.'

'Did your dreams come true?'

'Not the way we expected at the time. In those days, right after the Great War, I was all set to go to America to join my sweetheart Donald. He'd gone out there with his family to build a new life for us. And Ella . . . well, she was never going to tie herself down to marriage. But I'd my mother to look after, and then Donald found someone else.'

'He jilted you?'

'He did that. It was terrible at the time. Then after a while he decided that it was me he wanted after all and not this other lassie. But by that time I'd met Joe, so the upshot of it is that I'm still here in Paisley. And the same Ella that wasn't ever going to get married changed her mind too. She wed my brother Robbie, and now she's the one living in America. They're doing very well for themselves; it's them we get the food parcels from. My cousin Grace sends them too; she left Paisley not long after the war and now she's married to an American. It's funny how things turn out, isn't it?' Mirren folded a pair of trousers neatly and put them on top of the growing pile of acceptable clothing.

'Not so funny, sometimes.'

'Look, Julia, you're going to have to tell someone what's bothering you or the misery of it will make you ill. And surely we're friends enough for you to tell me. You know it won't go any further.'

'I've no doubt of that, but . . .' Julia hesitated, then said in a rush of words, 'Oh Mirren, I've done such a terrible thing and I know we're good friends but, if I tell you, you'll not want to be my friend any more and—'

'I doubt if that could happen, for I know the sort of woman you are, Julia McCosh, and I like you; and unless you've committed some terrible murder my liking won't change. If you can't tell me, then at least tell your husband.'

'Frank? He's the last person I'd want to tell . . . though he might have to know, and perhaps it should come from me first and not from . . . Oh, Mirren, what am I going to do?'

Mirren took the blouse that Julia was fumbling through her agitated fingers and put it to one side, then said slowly and firmly, 'You're going to tell me what this is all about before you destroy yourself completely with the worry. Two heads are better than one and mebbe I can help you.'

'It's my husband.'

'Frank? Is he ill?'

'No, not him. Frank and me . . . we're not married,' Julia said in a shamed whisper. 'We couldn't marry because when we met each other I already had a husband.'

'Oh, my dear. And the two of you have kept your secret all these years? I think that's very brave of you,' Mirren added when Julia nodded.

'Brave?'

'It must have taken courage to leave your legal husband for someone else. I presume that he deserved to be left, for you don't strike me as the sort of woman who would just go off with another man on a whim.'

Mirren's matter-of-fact acceptance made it easier for Julia to tell her friend about her marriage to Thomas Gordon, and the realisation within months that she had made a mistake.

'He was a hard man to live with . . . or perhaps I was just the wrong woman for him, I don't know. Thomas had been a military man and when he left the army he went into the police force. He was good at it, firm but fair, someone once told me, and he was made up to sergeant not long after we married. But he was the same in the house as he was in the police office . . . everything had to be just so, and he'd no time for what he called slacking.'

'In other words,' Mirren said crisply, 'he was a bully.'

'Oh no! Well, he never hit me, if that's what you mean; he didn't have to because he had other ways of showing his disapproval when I did something wrong. And he didn't like me to be out of the house unless I was at the shops or with him. He used to make out a list of housekeeping duties . . . a rota, he called it,' Julia recalled with an inward shudder. 'He worked out the exact time it should take me to do each task, and he wrote down when I should start it and when it should be completed. That way, when he was on duty he knew exactly where I was and what I was doing.'

'He sounds a bit like my Joe's family. From what I've heard, they were strict, humourless folk. I'd a hard struggle teaching him how to be a proper father, I can tell you, once the bairns came along. I wasn't going to let him raise them the way he had been raised. Or the way I had been raised, if it comes to that.'

'To be fair to Thomas, he didn't just show his annoyance when I got things wrong, he also had ways of rewarding me when I pleased him,' Julia hastened to explain.

'A lot of men follow that line, but it's usually with their dogs or their horses, not their wives,' Mirren said drily. 'So, where does Frank McCosh come into the picture?'

'Through music, what else?' The shadow of a smile tugged at Julia's strained mouth. 'I had taught piano lessons from home before we married, and since it brought in some money, Thomas allowed me to go on with that. Then about a year after we married, the mother of one of my pupils asked if I would play the piano for a fund-raising concert. And Frank was there, playing the saxophone. After that I was asked to play at other events, and Thomas agreed to let me do it. He was quite proud of me, poor man,' Julia went on, too involved in her story to notice Mirren's sharp, angry intake of breath at the thought of Thomas Gordon 'agreeing' to allow his wife to play at concerts. 'And each time I was asked to play at some function I found myself hoping that Frank would be there too, that I would see him again. Then a few months later . . .' The shadows came back into Julia's striking green eyes. 'Thomas was away for a few days on a course and I agreed to stand in for a pianist who had taken ill. And Frank was there in the audience, because he had heard that I was playing that night. He walked home with me, and . . .' her voice faltered.

'Julia, my dear, we're two grown women, no need to be coy with me. In any case, it all happened many years ago.'

'You're right. We started meeting whenever we could . . . with Thomas working some nights it made it easier for me to see Frank. I knew it was wrong, but I couldn't help myself. Frank was so kind, so easy to talk to. I just lived for the times I would see him again. Then someone told Thomas. They must have seen me and Frank together, though we tried to be careful.'

'What happened?'

Even after all those years Julia flinched at the memory. 'He was very angry, of course, but he said that he forgave me, and we would say no more about it. I wished that he would put me out of the house, disown me, for then I could have gone to Frank, but mebbe he knew that that was what I wanted, so he wouldn't do it. He stopped my piano lessons, of course, and he made me watch while he burned all my music in the fireplace then smashed up the piano. He had to bring in a man to take the pieces away and he was angry with me because the man had to be paid.'

'It must have broken your heart,' Mirren said quietly.

'My spirit more than my heart, because I knew what Thomas was like, and all the time I was seeing Frank I knew what might happen if I was found out. But I went ahead anyway because once I met Frank, I couldn't help myself.'

'He . . . Thomas . . . didn't hit you, then?'

'Oh no, he wouldn't hit a woman. Anyway, he knew that destroying the piano and the music would hurt me more than any blows could. Bruises fade faster than memories. It was Frank that he hurt,' Julia's voice trembled and tears glittered on her lashes. 'He came in one night and told me that my "friend" had got himself hurt on his way home from work the night before. An unfortunate incident, he called it. He was smiling when he said it. Thomas had been on duty that night, and he had been patrolling the area near where Frank lived.' Julia's hands twisted tightly together in her lap. 'He said that I'd best stay well away from Frank in future, because he must be prone to accidents and it could easily happen again. The next day when he'd left for work I went to Frank's lodgings and got his landlady to tell me what hospital he was in. I went there out of visiting hours and they didn't want to let me into the ward, but I made such a fuss that they had to give in. I scarce recognised him, Mirren, he was in such a bad way. But they said it looked worse than it was . . . he said that too, bless the man. And it turned out to be true.'

'What did you do then?'

'I told him about the baby I was carrying . . . that was Chloe . . . and oh, Mirren, I've never seen such joy in a man's face! Then I went back home and bided my time for a whole month while Frank got out of hospital and found a new job here in Paisley, and a room where the two of us could be together.'

'Could the baby not have been your husband's?'

Julia shook her head. 'Thomas had an illness in his early twenties, before we even met, and he was told afterwards that he could never father children. I didn't know about that until his sister told me, not long after we were married.'

'That means that if Frank had turned his back on you, you couldn't have stayed with Thomas and pretended the child was his. What would you have done?'

'Found work as a servant, mebbe, somewhere where I could have kept the wee one. But Frank did want her, and he wanted me too, and one day when Thomas was at work I packed my things, wrote him a note and left. It was a cowardly way to do it.'

'But wise as well, given the man's temper. He never tried to find you?'

'I didn't expect him to. He was a very proud man; I knew that once he found out that I'd . . . betrayed him with another man, he wouldn't have taken me back if I had begged him on my bended knees. Chloe was born several months later, and she's always been special in Frank's eyes, because he says that she was the one that brought us together in the end.'

'But now something's happened, or else why would you be telling me this?'

'Last week,' Julia said quietly, 'Thomas came to see me.'

'What?' Mirren sat bolt upright in her chair. 'But you said that he would never want you back!'

'He's ill, Mirren, very ill. And he's got nobody to look after him.'

'He surely doesn't expect you to do it after all these years?'

'He says that I owe it to him. He's taken a room in Clarence Street and he wants me to go there and stay with him until he . . . until he dies.' Julia looked up, her eyes haunted. 'I don't know what to do!'

'You must have no more to do with him!'

'Julia, the man's ill, and he's still my legal husband. He's got the right to expect me to care for him.'

'That's what he told you, I suppose? He's got a damned cheek on him,' said Mirren Hepburn emphatically. 'So what's supposed to happen next?'

'He gave me a week to get myself ready, and it's almost up. I'm supposed to go to his lodgings the day after tomorrow, to stay there for as long as I'm needed.'

'Let me go to see him. Just to talk to the man and get the measure of him,' Mirren added as panic flared in Julia's eyes. 'Then you and me can decide between us what's best for him, and for you. And no arguing, for I'm used to sorting things out for folk, and thanks to Joe having been on the Council I've got to know some very useful people. I'll visit this husband of yours, and there's no more to be said on the matter.'

'Need some help?'

Dennis turned to see Chloe McCosh hovering on the path, eyeing him hopefully.

'Not at work today?'

'It's Tuesday. Half-day.'

'Oh. You could earth up these potatoes if you want.'

Her smile faltered slightly. 'How do I do that?'

He rammed the blade of his spade in to the earth and made his way over to where the gardening tools leaned against the wall. 'You use the hoe . . . this is the hoe . . . to scoop the earth up against the plants on both sides. Like this, see? Now you try it.'

She plied the hoe vigorously. 'Like this?'

'Aye, that's fine, but you don't have to work so hard at it. Just draw it up nice and easy, then you won't tire yourself out.'

He went back to his own digging, and for a while they worked in silence. Then Chloe asked, 'Why am I doing this?'

'Because the potatoes grow in the ground. When you earth the plants up, the main stem starts to throw out more roots, then you have layers of potatoes. And it's a good way of keeping the weeds away too.' He straightened and eyed the section of ground he had been working on, then dragged a heavy sack over and opened it. Chloe wrinkled her nose.

'Phew! What's that?'

'Horse manure. This ground's getting starved and it has to be built up for the winter vegetable crop.'

'You're going to grow things to eat,' Chloe asked, horrified, 'in horse dung?'

'It's the best thing there is if you want to enrich the soil.'

'You mean that I've eaten food that was grown in dung?' Her face paled, and he laughed.

'Not pure dung . . . it changes once it's dug in. And the vegetables are washed and cooked.'

Chloe said nothing, though as she went back to work she was thinking of the time when she and Marion had filched a young carrot each from the vegetable plot, rubbing the soil off and eating the sweet flesh with relish. Never again!

'How d'you know so much about gardening?' she asked after another pause.

'Your dad taught me some of it, and Tom MacIntosh – he's one of the firemen – told me a lot. He's got an allotment, and he's given us a lot of cuttings and seeds and stuff for this place.'

'Are you still enjoying working at the fire station?'

'Aye.' Dennis forked manure from the bag.

'Have you been to many fires?'

'Some, though I'm still learning. Most of the fires I've seen are wee things,' he admitted, 'like chimneys going on fire, and folk being careless in the house. Fire doesnae start on its own, you know, it's always someone's fault. Being careless with matches and cigarettes and pipes, and inflammable stuff like paraffin.' As he spoke, he made a mental note to remind Lena that the tins and containers her husband had used in his peace-time job as a painter were still waiting to be brought out to the shed.

'Have you ever been in danger?' Chloe was asking now.

'No. We're taught to do the job properly. Putting ourselves in danger doesn't help to put out fires, does it?'

'That's good,' she said in a small voice. 'I'd not like to think of you getting hurt.'

'That's nice of you, Chloe, but don't worry. I'll be all right.'

Another silence fell, then she said, 'That's the first row finished. Did I get it right?'

Dennis straightened and looked over at the potatoes. 'You did a grand job.'

Chloe felt a self-righteous glow sweep over her. 'Would it be all right,' she asked as she started earthing up the next row, 'if I helped you in the garden some other time?'

'Of course. You know what they say, many hands make light work. And your father would no doubt be pleased at getting some help when he's out here as well.'

'I'd not be in the way? Only,' she hurried on as he shook his head, 'I've seen Mrs Fulton helping you and I wondered if you . . .' her voice almost gave out on her, and she had to clear her throat before continuing, 'if you'd rather have her working with you than me.'

Dennis shot her a swift glance, but she had anticipated it, and she was apparently concentrating on the work in hand, her auburn hair falling forward to hide her face.

'We all eat the vegetables,' he said, 'so what difference does it make who works with them?'

'Who you work beside might make a difference to you.' She took the plunge. 'You like Mrs Fulton, don't you?'

'I like everyone. I even like you, when you're not pestering me with daft questions.'

'You know what I mean.' Chloe stopped work and leaned on the hoe, using her free hand to tuck a strand of hair out of the way, behind her ear. 'I've seen you, Dennis,' she said.

'I've seen you going in and out of her flat, and talking to her in the Fountain Gardens.'

'You've seen me going in and out of your flat as well,' he said shortly.

'That's for band practice, and there's plenty of folk in our flat when there's a practice on. But it's just Mrs Fulton and you in her flat, and she's a married woman, Dennis . . .'

'I know she's a married woman. Her husband's away fighting for his country and she needs someone to see to things for her now and again.'

'What sort of things?'

'Clearing drains and mending things, and . . .' He threw the spade down and turned to glare at her. 'What sort of things did you think?'

'Dennis, it's mebbe not wise to get too friendly with a married woman . . .'

His face flamed with anger. 'And it's mebbe not wise to push your neb into other folks' business.' He picked up his jacket and slung it over his shoulder. 'I'll go where I want, Chloe McCosh, and I'll see who I please. And you'd best mind your tongue in future!'

She was watching him march away from her and back to the tenement when tears suddenly flooded her eyes. As Dennis's figure seemed to shimmer and then dissolve she blinked hard, but it was no use; the tears overflowed and began to trickle down her face. She spun round just in case he happened to turn and see her weeping, and gulped back a sob as she picked up the hoe and got on with her work. She had tried to help him, to warn him that folk might notice as she had, and might begin to talk. Instead, she had turned him against her.

23

As Dennis stormed up the stairs and gained the first landing he saw Ellen Borland standing in her open doorway talking quietly to a woman who stood humbly before her on the landing, her head nodding and bobbing as though it was on a spring.

'You mind now,' Dennis heard Ellen say as he reached the top of the stairs.

'Aye, I promise, missus,' the woman said in reply, then turned, her eyes widening at the sight of Dennis. Hurriedly, she buried her hand, fisted round something, deep into her pocket.

'Hold on there, Mrs Borland,' Dennis said as the door began to close. 'I want a word with you.' He couldn't bring himself to take out his anger on Chloe McCosh, but Mrs Borland was fair game.

The other woman, a stranger to him, ducked round him with her head well down, and went scudding down the stairs, her shoes clattering and flopping as though they were too big for her feet, or the soles were parting company with the uppers. Either could be possible in these days of wartime shortage when shoes were hard to find and folk had to make do with what they could get.

'Aye, what is it, son?' Ellen Borland folded her arms. She was dressed in her usual wrap-around pinny and her greying hair, which was always pulled into a bun at the back of her head, was escaping in wisps.

'It's about our Ralph and the way you've got him working for you.'

The woman's gaze didn't flicker. 'Don't know what you're talkin' about, son.'

'Aye you do. He's only thirteen, still at the school, and if he's going to make anything of his life he'll have to work harder at his lessons instead of running around the town collecting debts for you.'

'Debts?' Ellen's voice rose slightly. 'I don't know anythin' about debts. I pay my way and if other folk won't do the same, it's got nothin' tae do with me.'

'You lend them money, Mrs Borland,' Dennis said levelly. 'You charge them interest on the loans and because they're desperate they agree. Then when it's time for them to pay, you send someone round to collect the money. Ralph's big for his age, and strong too. Folk wouldn't want to deny him when he's at their door with his hand out, saying Mrs Borland sent him.'

'Ye're haverin'!' the woman snapped. 'And I've got more to do than stand here listenin' tae ye!'

Dennis moved swiftly as she began to shut the door, slapping one hand on the panels while a booted foot landed on the threshold.

'Tell Ralph that you've no more need of his services, Mrs Borland.'

'Listen you tae me, son,' the woman said, her voice low and sharp. 'Your mammy's a decent widow woman that works herself half tae death for her family. I respect that, because I've had tae work my way up from nothin'. I've seen folk lookin' at me as if I'm no more than the dirt under their shoes and I've toiled all my life tae prove them wrong. I've no quarrel with your mother and I've no quarrel with you, and if yer brother wants tae earn a bit of money so's he can help his poor mammy out, it's none of my concern.'

'It is your concern, and I'm telling you that I don't want him being part of whatever you're doing!'

'Then speak tae him about it, or tae yer mammy.' The woman's face was ugly now, her tone menacing. 'Just don't tangle with me, son, or you'll be sorry!'

Dennis was seeing a side to Ellen Borland he had never seen before. Possibly the only people to witness it were those poor souls who found themselves in her debt and unable to pay what they owed. He swallowed hard, then said, 'It's not me that'll be sorry, Mrs Borland. I'm sure the factors would be interested to hear what sort of business is being carried on in their tenement.'

'Threatenin' me, are ye? Well mebbe ye should just remember, sonny, that two can play at that game.'

'If you do any harm to my brother, I'll—'

'Don't be daft, I'm not talkin' about your Ralph. I like Ralph, he's a civil lad with a good brain in his skull. He could go far. No, I'm thinkin' about someone closer to you than he is.' The woman gave Dennis a cold-eyed smile. 'Before you come accusin' decent folk of breaking the law, you should think about your own secrets. A young laddie messin' about with a married woman whose man's away fightin' for his country ... it's not seemly,' she reproved, her mouth turning down at the corners in distaste.

Colour flooded into Dennis's face as he caught her meaning. First Chloe and now old Ma Borland. 'There's nothing goin' on between me and her!'

'I'm sure there's no', son, but other folk might not be as decent-minded as me. I thought you were a fine upstandin' young man but now I'm beginnin' tae wonder if ye're such a fine example to that wee brother you're so concerned about. I've been wonderin',' Ellen Borland said, gazing at a spot just past Dennis's left ear, 'if someone shouldnae let that poor Mr Fulton know what's goin' on behind his back.'

'You mind your own business. And when it comes to Mrs Fulton,' Dennis said, recovering, 'I know that you don't pay her for the work she does for you. That's as good as theft!'

'Did she not tell you about our wee agreement? It suits her, and it suits me, and that's all that matters. Now, if you're quite finished . . .'

One minute she was standing there, arms folded, and the next, a large hand was on Dennis's chest, pushing him away from the door. Taken by surprise, he stumbled back, and by the time he had recovered himself the door was closed.

As he turned, shaken by the encounter, he heard a low cackle, and looked across the landing to see that Jessie Bell's door was ajar. Something stirred in the darkness beyond the open space; a tangle of white hair, a glittering eye, a sharp chin. Then the door closed and he was left wondering how much the old woman had seen and heard. How much, indeed, she had already known?

'Good afternoon,' Mirren Hepburn said pleasantly, 'I believe you have a Mr Thomas Gordon lodging here?'

The woman who had opened the door gave her a suspicious stare. 'Aye, mebbe. Who wants him?'

'He won't know my name, but I think he'll want to see me all the same. Is he in?'

'Aye, he is, but he's sleepin'. He's not well.'

'I know that, it's why I came to see him.'

'Are you a nurse?'

'No,' Mirren said, 'just a friend of a friend. Someone who might be able to help him.'

'Ye'd better come in, then.' At last the woman stepped back, and Mirren followed her into an untidy kitchen that smelled strongly of boiled cabbage and urine. A baby slept in a pram pushed into one corner, and a toddler playing before the range scrambled up and snatched at his mother's skirt, hiding his face when Mirren smiled at him.

'Give it five minutes, he'll probably be awake by then. He gets intae a right temper if he gets wakened before he's ready. I've had a terrible time tryin' tae keep the weans quiet enough tae please him. Ye'd think he owned the flat instead of just bein' the lodger.' The woman indicated one of the chairs at the table. 'Just push the stuff off it. D'ye want some tea, then?'

'No thank you.' Mirren picked up the jumble of bits and pieces and put them on the table before sitting down. The baby woke and began to cry, and her hostess took the infant from the pram, sat down in a sagging fireside chair and unbuttoned her blouse. The toddler, brushed away from her skirt, settled on the shabby rug at her feet.

'Has Mr Gordon been here long?' Mirren asked.

The woman produced a breast from within the unbuttoned blouse and pushed it in to the baby's face. Tiny hands shot out of the bundle of wool, the squalling mouth fastened on a nipple, and the room became blessedly silent.

'Not long. About two weeks. And if I'd known how ill he was I'd never have said he could have the room. But I need the money, see, with my man bein' away in the army.' She indicated the small head buried in the softness of her breast. 'He's never even seen her yet and I'm just wond'rin' if he ever will. My sister's man was torpedoed on the way back from Dunkirk . . . left her with three weans tae feed and house. But nobody ever thinks about the wives and bairns when there's a war, do they?'

'No, they don't. If Mr Gordon's ill, shouldn't he be in hospital?'

'I wish he was, but he says there's someone comin' soon tae take him away and look after him. It that you?' the woman asked hopefully.

'I know who he means, and perhaps I can do something for him instead.'

'I'd be right pleased if ye could, missus! I thought it'd be nice tae have the wee bit of money comin' in, but it's no' worth it. Sometimes he's so bad that I worry in case he dies on me. I'd not know what tae dae if he did.' The woman raised her head, then plucked the child from her breast and struggled to her feet. 'I think I heard him, so he's mebbe wakened now. Here . . .' She thrust the baby at Mirren, 'you hold her while I go and see.'

The baby's milky mouth was moving, seeking the food source it had suddenly lost. Blue eyes gazed up at Mirren, puzzled, then as she rocked the little bundle and crooned to it, the eyes began to glaze with sleep and the lids lowered.

The wee thing's clothing was damp, and the sharp smell of ammonia brought tears to Mirren's eyes. The pram mattress was probably soaked through. She longed to strip the little creature and bathe her, then dress her in dry clothing, but, knowing that even if there had been fresh clothing readily to hand, such behaviour by a mere visitor would mortally offend the young mother, she had to content herself with rocking the baby in her arms.

Her lap and her sleeves were beginning to feel distinctly damp by the time the woman returned, the toddler in tow.

'He says tae go in.' She took the baby and returned her to the pram.

'I think she needs changing,' Mirren ventured.

'She always needs changin'. It goes in at one end and out the other all the time. I'll see tae her later. Ye'd best go on through now; he wants his dinner so ye'll have tae be quick. He doesnae like tae be kept waitin'.'

The most that could be said for the small bedroom where Thomas Gordon lay was that it was not covered with clothing and it did not smell of permanently wet baby. It did, however, smell of ill health.

'Who are you?' The hoarse voice was unfriendly, as were the piercing dark eyes set in the hollows and caverns of a gaunt face.

'Mrs Mirren Hepburn.'

'Never heard of ye.'

'I'm a friend of Julia's.'

'She sent ye here? I told her tae come herself!'

'She couldn't do that. She has a family to care for.'

'And a husband that she swore before God tae love and honour and obey for the rest of her life!'

'A husband who also swore before God to love and cherish *her*, Mr Gordon. Marriage isn't worth much unless both parties keep to their vows. Once one breaks them, the other has to work twice as hard to keep them.'

'What's she been tellin' you?' Mirren could tell by the wrists and the big hands protruding from his pyjama jacket that this man was probably tall, and had once, when the bones were overlaid by muscle and fat, been burly, but now face and body were wasted, the flesh all but gone. His eyes were the strongest part of him, and they burned his dislike and resentment at her.

'Enough,' she said calmly. 'She had to talk to someone, and she knew that she could trust me to keep her secret . . . and your secret as well, if it comes to it.'

'She couldnae tell that man of hers about me, could she?' There was a sneer in his voice, and the tell-tale patches of red on the sharp ridges of his cheekbones flared momentarily.

'She's feared about what he might do if he knew you were here, in Paisley.'

'Get his revenge, you mean? He's welcome tae it now. I'm past carin'.'

'From what I know of Frank McCosh, I doubt if he'd stoop to harming a defenceless invalid,' Mirren said levelly, and got some satisfaction in seeing him wince, though whether it was her reference to Frank or her description of him that caused it, she had no way of knowing.

'Julia should be here, lookin' after me!' he said harshly. 'It's her duty tae care for me in my last days.'

'Julia owes you nothing, man, and even if she did, she couldn't possibly care for you now. You're sick, very sick . . .' Her eyes flickered to the shabby, slightly lopsided table by the bed, and the crumpled blood-smeared cloth on it, 'and you need proper nursing.'

'Goin' tae fetch a private nurse in for me, are ye?' he jeered.

'The care you need can only be got in hospital and we have a very good institution here in Paisley ... the Royal Alexandra Infirmary.'

'I'm not goin' tae any infirmary!'

'Don't be a fool, man, you can't stay here. Your land-lady has more than enough to do with caring for her children, and you're probably a threat to their health into the bargain. You'd be more comfortable in hospital, being properly looked after.'

'Aye ... by strangers! I'll not die among strangers!' He began to cough, and almost at once he was doubled over, what little breath he could catch whistling through his diseased lungs.

Mirren caught up the bloodied cloth and pushed it into his hands before hurrying through to the kitchen. 'D'you have a wee bowl of cold water?' she asked. 'And a clean cloth?'

'Is that him away again?' The young woman's eyes were bright with fear. 'Honest, missus, when he starts on like that I'm that scared he's goin' tae die right there in my spare room!'

'He won't die. Give it to me.' Mirren snatched at the basin the woman had picked up from beneath the table; moving to the sink she turned on the leaky tap and half filled the basin. 'A cloth, if you have one.'

'Er ...' The woman grabbed something from a pile and handed it over, and Mirren hurried back to the bedroom, where Thomas Gordon lay exhausted, the pillow he lay against as grey as his face. Fresh spots and streaks of red glistened on his chin.

'Here.' Mirren put down the basin and picked up a cup from the table. It was half full of water, and it looked reasonably clean. She held it to his lips and he took a few sips before waving it away. His eyes, the only part of him with any life in them, closed, and she thought that without their strong, angry gaze, he did indeed look as though it would take very little to push him over the fragile line between life and death.

The cloth she had been given was a dish-towel, smelly and stiff with dirt; she put it aside and used her own clean handkerchief instead, dipping it into the water and wringing it out before wiping his face and neck and hands.

'There now,' she found herself soothing them both as she worked. 'There, that's better, isn't it?'

She dried his face as best she could with the edge of the tattered quilt that covered him, then sat down and waited. When his eyes finally opened, she said, gently but firmly, 'You'll surely agree with me now, Mr Gordon, when I say that you cannot stay here. You must get proper care. Somewhere where you will be much more comfortable. And you'll not be among strangers. I'll visit you, and so will Julia.'

'You'll get me in there and you'll leave me tae rot.'

'We'll do nothing of the sort; you have my word on that. I think I can speak for Julia as well as for myself; she's worried about you and she wouldn't just leave you.'

'She did before.'

'That was because she couldn't stay. For one thing, you made it impossible for her to go on living with you, and for another, she loved Frank McCosh. She still does and she always will,' Mirren said with brutal honesty, 'but as you say, she made vows on the day she married you, and I know that she'll want to keep them as best she can.'

'Mebbe ye won't be able tae get me intae this infirmary of yours just as easy as that. Not the way things are these days.' His voice was very weak and the intensity had gone from his eyes; the bout of coughing had drained him.

'I think I'll manage. Just leave it to me.' No sense in

telling him that she had a certain influence, and knew which strings she could pull. She got to her feet. 'I'll be back tomorrow to let you know what's happening.'

And she would be bringing some decent food with her, and clothes for the children. It wasn't just those who had been bombed out of their homes that needed help; the woman in the kitchen, probably a good ten years younger than she looked, had donated her most precious possession – her husband, the father of her children, the bread-winner of the house – to this war that had been set in motion by men with wealth and power, men who often cared for the warriors they sent to the trenches as little as young boys did for their lead and tin soldiers.

Joe was right, she thought as she left the flat and returned to the street outside. War was the ultimate obscenity, and it should never be part of a decent society. And soon it would swallow her own precious firstborn up in its hungry maw.

Forcing thoughts of Charlie from her head for fear that she might end up weeping, she found herself thinking instead of the man she had just left. Tyrant and bully though he had been in his prime, there was something pathetic about Thomas Gordon's fear of dying alone among strangers; he appeared so vulnerable, perhaps for the first time in his life, that Mirren could not let it happen to him.

24

'Goin' somewhere nice?' one of the other clippies asked Cecelia when she arranged her first week's holiday.

'Nothing special. There's no chance of my husband getting home, so I'll just catch up on my sleep and get the flat put to rights,' she said vaguely. It would arouse altogether too much interest if she were to reveal to anyone, even Harry, that she had arranged the time off in order to attend her father's wedding.

His letter had come as a complete surprise; not the news that he and his lady friend, a widow named Elspeth McFadden, were going to be married, but the fact that after such a long silence between them, broken only by the occasional single-page formal letter, he wanted Cecelia to be there.

Clothing coupons had just been introduced, and Cecelia used up most of her first allowance in Cochran's, where she bought a dark green two-piece costume, to be worn over a cream blouse she already owned.

'And I'll need a hat . . .' she said to the shop assistant, who immediately disappeared and came back with a tiny pillbox creation, the same colour as the suit.

'This would finish off the ensemble perfectly, madam.'

Cecelia, who was given to wearing sensible hats with nice brims, eyed it with misgivings. 'I don't know . . . it's not really my sort of hat.'

'Try it on. No, madam, like this . . .' The woman took it from her, and pinned it into place with a few deft movements. 'There now. Have a look in the mirror.'

The hat, a velvet creation, was perched on Cecelia's fair hair, inclining rakishly over one eye. It made her look completely different. 'Oh,' she said, half in surprise, half in horror, then, 'I don't know. Have you got something in straw, with a nice brim?'

'This goes very well with the costume, madam, and you did say that it was a wedding.' The woman reached up and tweaked at the hat, and when she stood back, Cecelia discovered that her vision had gone slightly misty, with dots. 'It has a very pretty little half-veil,' the woman was chirruping, 'which can be worn up or down.'

Cecelia edged closer to the mirror and peered at her own reflection. Whether the mistiness deceived her or the hat really did suit her she didn't know, but she was beginning to like it.

She gasped a little when she heard what it cost, but told herself that it was after all to be worn at a wedding, and she could afford it, thanks to the good money that bus conductresses earned. And she would have something nice to wear the next time Fergus came home, she pondered as she carried her new clothes home. She would think of somewhere nice for them to go, some outing in keeping with the smart costume and hat.

Still trying to justify the outlay, she scuttled upstairs to her flat, flushing guiltily as she encountered Dennis Megson coming down the second flight.

'Hello,' she said breathlessly, and kept on climbing. As she went, she heard him tap at a door below. Going to see Mrs McCosh about something to do with the band, she thought, then forgot Dennis as she gained her own landing and rushed to open her door before anyone else saw her and asked about the parcels she carried.

*   *   *

Instead of standing back to let Dennis in, Lena hesitated when she saw him on the doorstep. 'I'm busy.'

'I need to talk to you,' he said urgently. 'It'll not take long. Please,' he said as she began to shake her head, 'it's important.'

She stepped away from the door to let him pass, and when he moved into the hallway and glanced back, he saw that, as usual, she was peering out of the door to make sure nobody had seen him. With good reason, he thought bitterly, since they seemed to live in some kind of an ants' nest where everything that happened was spied on and immediately passed from door to door.

In the kitchen, he gestured to the sewing machine on the kitchen table, and the floral material lying on it. 'Is that something else for Mrs Borland?'

'Why should you ask that?'

'Most of the work you do these days seems to be for her.'

'She knows a lot of people. She brings in work for me.'

'Work that doesnae pay.'

'Sometimes it does.' She sat down at the machine, fidgeting with the cloth. 'What did you want to talk about?'

'I've just been telling Ma Borland to stop giving work to our Ralph.'

Lena paled, and one hand – she seemed incapable of sitting still these days, he realised – went to her throat. 'You've had a row with her?'

'I'd no choice. We all know that she's into black market coupons and money lendin' and goodness knows what else. As far as I'm concerned that's up tae her, but I'll not have her draggin' my brother into her web.'

'But now she knows that you know what she's up to.' Lena's eyes were frightened. 'She might find a way to make things difficult for you and Ralph, and your mother.'

'Is that what she does when folk try to defy her?'

'How would I know?' She plucked at the material in the

sewing machine. 'I have to get on with this, Dennis.'

'Lena, are you in debt to Ma Borland?'

Her already pale face went bone white. 'Me? She mentioned me?'

'Not in so many words.' It was a lie, but he couldn't tell her the truth. 'It was just the way she was rantin', that's all, about how she helped folk. Bartering, and that. And I remembered you saying that you don't charge her for the work you do for her because she gives you thread and cloth.'

'Yes, she does, and it's good of her. It would be difficult to do my sewing if she didn't help out.' She was breathless now, as though she had been running.

'So I'm asking . . . is it just sewing stuff, or has she loaned you money as well?'

'That's got nothing to do with you!'

'It has. I care about you, Lena. I . . . I care for you, and I don't want to see you caught up in that woman's trap.'

'You've no right to come in here, questioning me.' Two bright spots burned in her cheeks, and her eyes were glittering sapphires. 'My life is none of your business!'

'I thought we were friends. If you need help, Lena, I'm earning, and I could mebbe . . .'

'I can manage fine, and anyway, you've got enough to do with your own family.' She clasped her head in both hands. 'I've got a headache coming on; it's the heat, I think. I'll need to go and lie down.'

'Lena . . .'

'I need to lie down,' she repeated. 'You can let yourself out, can't you?'

When he had gone and she had the flat to herself, Lena walked from room to room and up and down the narrow hallway, rubbing her hands up and down the sides of her skirt and trying to control her shaky breathing. 'Pity,' she said aloud several times, her voice harsh. 'I can't be doing with pity!'

The sewing for Mrs Borland's niece was waiting in the

machine, but when she returned to the kitchen Lena ignored it, going instead to the cupboard where the patchwork quilt lay waiting for her. She shook it out with trembling fingers. It was time for a new patch.

She went in to the bedroom and looked at the bed, her marriage bed, made up just the way George liked it, with not a crease or a wrinkle, then she began to work her way through the drawers. There was nothing there to catch her eye. She opened the wardrobe, which was half empty now; George's best suit was in a pawnshop, and every Monday Lena paid a small deposit to ensure that instead of being sold, it would stay where it was, to be redeemed, somehow, as soon as she got word that he was coming home on leave. Her own clothes took up little space, for most of them had already been cut up for the quilt.

She hesitated, then took down George's favourite shirt and carried it into the kitchen, where she reached for her big scissors and got to work.

'It was a good film,' Chloe said when she and Charlie finally reached her close. 'That Will Hay's very funny.'

Even though it was summer, the day had been overcast and the night was dark.

'I enjoyed it, but I thought you'd have chosen to see *Mark of Zorro*,' Charlie said, 'with it being Tyrone Power. Girls think he's handsome, don't they?'

'That would have been a good picture, but I like the Regal . . . it's more comfortable than the Astoria. And me and Marion might—' She stopped suddenly, wishing that she could bite her tongue out.

'If you and Marion do go to the Astoria later in the week,' he said, 'you can write to me and tell me all about Tyrone Power and Linda Darnell.'

Chloe's right hand fingered the silver bracelet on her left wrist. Charlie had given it to her a few days earlier, for her sixteenth birthday, and before tonight's film he had treated her to her tea at Cochran's handsome restaurant before they walked along to the Regal.

'Mum said I should ask you up for your supper.'

'D'you think they would mind if I didn't?' he asked. 'I hate goodbyes. I've had to go through all that at work, and I'll have to go through it tomorrow at home.'

'It'll be all right. She said, if you felt like it, just.'

'Your mother's very understanding. Come here . . .' He seized her hand and drew her into the close.

'I thought you didn't want to go up to my house.'

'We're not. I'm just looking for somewhere more private than the street. Will the washhouse be open?' he wanted to know as they emerged into the backyard.

'It's kept locked and our key's in the kitchen.'

'Let's try the wee shed, then.'

She pulled back as he tried to draw her across the back-court. 'It's probably locked, and in any case, it'll be dirty and full of stuff to fall over. I'm not going in there wearing my good cloth—' The words were cut short as he eased her against the house wall and kissed her.

Chloe had not had much experience of boys, but from what she had heard in the school playground, and from Marion, she was quite sure that Charlie Hepburn was a good kisser. She enjoyed being kissed by him, and responded with enthusiasm, but when his lips moved from her mouth to her neck and his hands began to rove she pushed him away.

'That's enough, Charlie!'

'Chloe, this is our last time together till goodness knows when!'

'I don't care, I'm not going to let you do that!'

'Other girls probably do, when their boyfriends are called up.'

'I'm not other girls, I'm me, and you should be ashamed of yourself, expecting me to . . . to do whatever you want, just because it's your last night in Paisley!'

'But I really like you, Chloe!'

'And I like you, you know that.'

'How much do you like me?'

She drew him back towards her. 'This much,' she said, and kissed him on the mouth. 'And this much.' This time the kiss was longer, warmer.

'Enough to be my proper official girlfriend?' he asked hopefully when he could speak again.

'I've told you, I'm too young to make promises like that.'

'You're sixteen now, old enough to get married.'

'Old enough to make up my own mind about whether or not I want to be tied down. Charlie, your whole life's going to be changed; you could easily meet someone else while you're away.'

'I won't, because I don't want to.'

'I could meet someone else!'

'There isn't anyone now, is there?' he asked sharply.

'No, of course not.' Dennis Megson popped into her mind, and was pushed away. 'I only said that I might. We never know what's ahead.'

'All the more reason for us to have an understanding, then.'

'An understanding won't make any difference if one of us meets someone else, can you not see that? Can we not just stay best friends?'

'But you'll write to me, won't you? Every week?'

'Of course I will. Not that I'll have much to tell you. Nothing ever happens round here.'

'Write about the ordinary things,' he said, 'like what you're doing, and thinking, and what's happening with the band, and your family. I want to go on being part of your lives even though I'm away.'

'I wish you weren't going away, Charlie.'

'I'll be back on leave, lots of times. You're sure you just want us to be best friends and nothing more?' Then, when she nodded, her head bumping gently against his shoulder, 'You're a tease, Chloe McCosh.'

'I am not! A tease is someone who lets a man think he's going to get more but he doesn't.'

His breath was warm on her cheek as he laughed. 'How do you know that?'

'I read the women's magazines.'

'Oh, Chloe,' he said, against her lips. 'I'm going to miss you!'

'And I'm going to miss you,' she said from the heart.

They lingered for another ten minutes before the coolness of the night signalled the end of the evening.

A few minutes after they went inside, hand in hand, to enjoy a final, chaste kiss outside the McCosh's door, Dennis Megson stepped cautiously out of the little tool shed, where he had been smoking a cigarette.

For a moment he stood in the backcourt, looking up at the darkness of the building. It was too dark to make out Lena's windows, but he knew exactly where they were anyway. She would be in her bed by now.

He sighed, and went into the close, almost bumping into a youth on his way down the first flight of stairs. As the lad brushed past, muttering a greeting, Dennis gave an answering mutter and continued to climb, slowly, still thinking about Lena.

'Charlie?' a voice said from the landing above. 'Is that you coming back?'

'Chloe?'

There was a little gasp, then she said, 'It's you, Dennis! I thought it was . . .'

'The lad I met in the close?' He had gained the landing now.

'We were at the Regal to see the Will Hay picture.' She looked at him warily; it was the first time they had spoken since he had stormed off and left her weeping in the backcourt. 'Is this you just coming home from your work?' she asked, desperate to find a way to apologise for what she had said about him and Mrs Fulton.

'No, I've been having a smoke out the back.'

'The backcourt?' They had been speaking in whispers, mindful of the people already asleep in the flats, but now her voice rose. 'You've been in the backcourt?'

'Aye, the tool shed. I sometimes go there when I want some peace to think.' He grinned down at her. 'Some courtin' couple came through from the street for a bit of privacy and I was stuck in there waitin' until they went away.'

'Courting couple?' Chloe said faintly. 'Who was it, d'you know?'

'How would I know, in the dark, and with them over by the doorway. It happens sometimes, but usually they don't come in further than the bottom of the stairs . . .'

'Oh!' she said, then, 'Oh!' And she turned and ran through the partly opened door of her flat, leaving him alone and puzzled on the landing.

The Royal Alexandra Infirmary was a honeycomb of large high-ceilinged wards and long, tiled corridors housed in an imposing Victorian building on Neilston Road, on the south side of the town.

By the time he had been wheeled along corridors and around corners and along more corridors and, once, into a large and clanking lift, Thomas Gordon, who had only just managed to glimpse the exterior of the large building while being taken from the ambulance, had no idea whether he was at the rear or the front of the place, or perhaps in a side wing. All he had been able to make out on his long journey was high ceilings, rushing towards, over and then past him like a moving ribbon.

Finally the porter stopped the trolley and a woman in a starched white apron and cap bent over Thomas. 'Mr Gordon? We'll get you into bed now, and get you comfortable.'

'I can manage it mysel'.' He tried to sit up, but the effort made his head swim and it was almost a relief when she pushed him down gently and said, 'I'm sure you can, but why don't you just lie still and leave it to us?'

When he had been manhandled on to the bed, albeit gently, the porter trundled the trolley away without as much as a glance at him; for all the world, Thomas thought with feeble anger, as though in his illness he had become no more than a parcel that required delivering. He lay still, staring up at the ceiling, avoiding eye contact with the nurses who efficiently stripped him and then washed him before dressing him again, this time in pyjamas. Finally they went away; all except one, who drew up the bedclothes around him and tucked them in.

'There now. Are you comfortable, Mr Gordon?'

'As comfortable as I can be under the circumstances.'

'Would you like a drink?' When he nodded, she raised him up and held the spout of an invalid drinking cup to his lips, then eased him back down again and wiped his mouth. 'The doctor will be coming round in about an hour, and there'll be a cup of tea for you before that. I don't know if they told you already, but you're in Ward—'

'In prison, that's all I have tae know. The number of the cell makes no difference tae me.'

'This is a hospital, Mr Gordon, not a prison.'

'So when can I expect tae get out of your . . . hospital?' For the first time since the ambulance men had tramped into the little bedroom in Clarence Street to collect him, he allowed himself eye contact with another human being. Rather than being some young thing on the threshold of life, this nurse was much his own age, which was something of a comfort. Her face was pleasantly homely, and lined, reflecting that she had had good experience of the ups and downs of life, and her hazel eyes were serious as she said quietly, 'I think you already know the answer to that one, Mr Gordon.'

'Aye, I do. I've been handed a death sentence . . . and

you're tryin' tae tell me that I'm not in a prison?'

'It's only a death sentence if you give up hope, surely. I tell you what . . .' To his surprise, she leaned forward, her breath tickling his ear as she whispered, 'on my next day off, I'll bake you a cake with a file in it.'

For a moment Thomas was taken aback, then he rallied. 'Put a map of the place in it an' all,' he grunted, 'for I've got no idea where tae go once I get out of this room.'

She laughed, her eyes lighting the whole of her face. 'You'll do,' she said. 'Do you need anything before I go?'

'My health back again?'

'If I could do that for you, Mr Gordon, I would, with pleasure,' she said as she swept the screens away, revealing the row of beds opposite, some of the occupants reading, some sleeping, some talking to their neighbours.

'I have to go and torment some other poor patient now. I'd appreciate it if you could behave yourself till I come back. No rioting allowed in my cell.'

He watched her go off down the ward, shoulders back and head up despite the exhaustion that cast shadows beneath her eyes, then he took stock of his surroundings, wondering if that bossy friend of Julia's would tell her where he was, and wondering, too, if Julia would visit him, or decide to let him rot on his own.

25

'I've got a job for you.' Dennis closed the bedroom door and leaned back against it.

Ralph, sprawling on the bed, looked up from the latest copy of the *Beano* comic. 'What is it?'

'A real job, I'm talking about, for an hour after school and on Saturday mornings, and through the holidays. When I was passing Coghill the ironmonger's today I saw a notice in their window, advertising for a message boy, so I went in and had a word with the manager. There's shelves to stack too, and a bit of sweeping, and mebbe the chance of helping behind the counter when they're busy. You could work your way up the ladder. '

'What?'

'They were looking for someone a bit older, but I managed to persuade the manager to give you a chance. You start tomorrow, right after school. Five shillings a week, so we'll make it four to Mum, and one for yourself. I think that's fair enough.'

'I'm already workin' for the Co-op.'

'I had a word with them and all,' Dennis said blandly. 'Told them you'd found something better. They didn't seem to mind. It seems that you weren't all that reliable, but you'd better smarten up for the new place because I'll be keeping a check on you.'

'I'll not do it!' Ralph squirmed off the bed, his face red with anger.

'Aye you will. You wanted to be kept busy and you wanted to earn money, and you'll be doing both . . . and keeping out of old Ma Borland's clutches as well.'

'Five shillin's? You think I'd be satisfied with that after—' Ralph started, and then suddenly shut his mouth.

'Five shillings made legally is better than fifty for workin' against the law. I've not said to Mum because I thought you might like to pretend that it was your own doing. She'll be pleased.'

'I'll not do it,' Ralph said. 'You can't make me!'

'I can, because until you're old enough to leave school, you have to do what you're told. If you don't take that job, Ralph, I'm going to tell on you, and on Ma Borland. And if that happened it would mean that you wouldn't be able to go on working for her anyway. And there's another thing . . .'

Before Ralph knew what was happening his brother had swooped down and slid one hand under his pillow. It emerged with the newspaper Dennis had seen the boy push out of sight when he came into the room.

'I thought so . . . the horse racing. Well . . .' He crushed the flimsy sheets into a ball and stuffed them into his jacket pocket. 'You'll not be needing that any more, will you?'

Ralph sat upright, his face burning and his eyes damp with childish frustration. 'Just you wait, Dennis Megson. Just you wait until I leave the school and get tae be my own boss!'

'I'll be waiting, and I'll be ready. But until then, you'll do as you're told. And now I'm going down to do some work in the backyard. I could do with a hand, when you've finished your homework. I'm sure you've still got some to do.'

'Go tae hell!'

'And that's another thing . . . you mind your language in

future. Don't forget to let Mum know about your new job,'
Dennis said, opening the door. 'She'll be right proud of
you.'

Julia, who had been blessed with a healthy family, had had
to venture within the Royal Alexandra Infirmary only once
before, when Duncan, an adventurous three-year-old at the
time, had managed to get a large seed jammed in one ear
on a family picnic, and had to have it syringed out.

There was something about infirmaries, she thought as
she walked down the long corridor leading to one of the
men's wards, that struck fear, or at the very least nervous
anticipation into the hearts of those who entered. It might
be to do with the smell of disinfectants, or the silent-but-
echoing size of the rooms and passageways, or perhaps the
very title, suggesting as it did that it was a place only for
the infirm. Whatever it was, she glanced longingly at the
high windows as she passed, envying those outside on the
street, going on with their everyday lives.

The visiting hour had already started by the time she
reached the ward.

'Mr Gordon. Third bed on the left,' the uniformed nurse
at the desk said in a voice as cool and starched as her crisp
cap and apron.

'Thank you.' Julia hesitated and then laid a small parcel
on the desk, well clear of the large ledger the nurse was
studying. 'I didn't know what to bring . . . I thought an egg
for his tea . . . ?'

'Oh.' The nurse looked at the package for a moment, then
picked it up gingerly. 'I'll have it sent to the kitchens. They
will prepare it for Mr Gordon,' she said.

Most of the beds already had men and women seated by
them; all were perched on the edge of their chairs, craning
uncomfortably towards the men lying in the high narrow
cots so that they could converse in low murmurs. The
various colours of the visitors' outdoor clothing seemed

incongruous, intrusive almost, when set against the muted white, blue and grey shades of the ward and Julia wondered, as she began to traverse the great expanse of polished floor, if the nurses secretly resented the general disharmony that visiting hours must cause to their ordered, disciplined hospital routine.

The first bed on the left from the door had two people by it, an elderly woman and a young man. A young woman murmured at the second bed, but there was nobody at the third. Julia hesitated, swallowed hard in an attempt to subdue the butterflies swarming around in her stomach, and then moved forward.

She had not seen Thomas for two weeks, because after her own first visit to the flat in Clarence Street, Mirren had persuaded Julia to stay away until he was settled in the infirmary. 'It's worrying you sick, seeing him in that state, and in that place,' she had said.

'But when all's said and done, we used to be married, him and me. In the eyes of the law we still are. I can't just abandon him for a second time.'

'You'll not be abandoning him, because I'll be visiting in your place, and letting you know how he is. And I doubt if he'll thank you for your concern in any case. We've got the measure of each other, Thomas Gordon and me, I can see for myself that he's not an easy man to get on with. He's the sort that would think nothing of using your guilt and your sense of responsibility to keep you by him until he draws his final breath. He needs to be properly looked after, and I've half convinced him of that. It's best for you to stay away until I get him out of that wee flat.'

'You've got enough to do without taking on my worries.'

'What's a visit here and there, to help out a friend?' Mirren had asked. 'Lassie, if you only knew what's already been in my life . . . and I'm not just talking about years of marriage to a man who'll always put others before himself and his entire family . . . you'd know that my shoulders are broad enough for anything. If they hadn't been, I'd have given up the fight long since.'

As she approached Thomas's bed Julia saw that he was asleep, his head lolling to one side on the immaculate pillow, and the sheets drawn up and tucked neatly in just below his shoulders. The illness had progressed rapidly since she had last seen him; there seemed to be no muscle or tissue beneath the skin of his face, only bone, and when he opened his eyes, sensing her presence, they were dull and listless.

'So.' His voice was a shadow of the deep, hectoring tones she had known so well. 'You decided to visit after all.'

'Did you think I wouldn't?'

'I didnae know if ye'd the courage.'

'I've got courage all right, Thomas. I'm older and I'm wiser, and I know who I am.'

His eyebrows rose, laboriously, as though they had had to be cranked up from behind the skin of his forehead. 'So who are ye, then?'

'I'm Julia McCosh.'

'Julia Gordon.' A spark of anger lit his face, but it was only a spark, and although she sensed an echo of the fear his anger had once roused in her, she was able to suppress it almost at once.

'Not for years, Thomas. You said it yourself . . . I'm Frank McCosh's common law wife now, with the right to bear his name. Me and my children. And if you're going to start on at me about Frank, I might just as well get back to them now.'

'Sit down, woman. I don't get many visitors and I suppose I cannae afford to chase away those I do get.' Feebly, but with determination, he began to fight his arms free of the sheets. 'These damned nurses, they never seem tae be done tuckin' folk in. Ye'd think we were parcels instead of human beings.'

'Here, I'll do it.' Julia cast a swift glance at the stern nurse on duty, and seeing that the woman was writing busily, she stooped over the bed and loosened the sheet, then helped him to free his arms. She could feel the bones and sinews and loose skin through his pyjama jacket, and although he smelled of carbolic soap it was underlain by another aroma . . . one, she thought, of sickness and impending death.

'Is that better?'

Aye,' he said, exhausted by his struggle. Then, almost forcing the word out, 'Thanks.'

Julia drew up the chair that stood at the bottom of the bed, and sat down. 'How are you?'

'You can see that for yerself.'

'You're surely better here, being looked after, than where you were.'

'I suppose so. Though it's hard tae think that this is where I'll be for the rest of my days. Dyin' in Paisley instead of Glasgow.'

'You didn't need to come to Paisley.'

'I came because I'd nob'dy else tae turn to but you.'

'What about your sister?' Thomas's sister Kate had been just like him; sturdily built, strong and totally convinced of her own righteousness.

His pale mouth twisted in something that might have been a smile, and might have been a grimace. 'She moved tae Clydebank last year after her man died, tae be near her daughter and her grandweans.'

'But Clydebank's not far from Glas—' Julia began, and then stopped short, remembering the terrible raids on the shipbuilding town in March. Scarcely a house left undamaged, Frank had told her. 'The blitz?'

'Aye, the blitz. Kate and the rest of them went quick, I was told. Never knew what hit them, and that's the way she'd have wanted it. She was luckier than me, I'll tell ye that.' Then, his mouth giving that brief twist again, 'And I'll tell her that when I see her.'

Julia put a hand on his. The skin was icy cold beneath her warm palm. 'Thomas, I . . .' She hesitated, not knowing what to say, then ended lamely, 'I brought you an egg for your tea. The nurse said she'd see that it was cooked for you.'

'What'll your man have tae say about his rations goin' tae the likes of me?'

'It's my rations, and anyway, he'd not object.'

'Does he know that I'm here, in Paisley? That you're visitin' me?'

'Not yet.'

'Scared tae tell him, are ye?'

'I've never had to be afraid of Frank,' she said clearly and deliberately.

He looked away from her gaze, while his hand eased itself out from beneath hers. 'You never needed tae be afraid of me.'

'Oh, I did. And I was. That's all you knew, Thomas, frightening folk into doing as you wanted and behaving as you expected. I'm not blaming you; it was the way you were taught in the army, and then in the police force. It just became part of you. You should have married someone stronger than me, someone able to stand up to you.'

He ran his tongue over his chapped lips, then said, 'I married you because you were the one I wanted.'

'And I thought it was what I wanted too. I would never have said yes otherwise. I meant it to be for the rest of my life.' This was the first chance she had had to explain things to him. 'But things turned out differently.'

'That woman you sent, the one that got me put in here.'

'Mirren Hepburn. She's a friend of mine.'

'She's a strong one.'

'She's had to be.' Mirren had told Julia something of the way she had had to combine her job as a twiner in Ferguslie Mills with caring for her invalid mother and working in a chip shop in the evenings in order to save up towards the day when she had expected to join her fiancé in America.

'She visits me.'

'And I'll visit too, whenever I can, if that's what you want.'

'It passes the time,' he said, then turned his head on the pillow so that his eyes were on the locker by his bed. 'There's an envelope in there.'

She opened the locker, drawing out the long brown envelope within. It was quite bulky, and the flap was sealed. 'D'you want me to post it? It's not addressed to anyone.'

'That's because it's arrived where it was goin'. You take it and keep it safe. It's got all my papers and all the instructions ye'll need.' He raised himself up slightly and said emphatically, 'I want tae be buried in Glasgow.'

'Time enough to talk about that sort of thing when you're a bit stronger . . .'

'I'm not a bairn, Julia, and I'm not a weakling either. This is where I am and this is where I'll stay for as long as it takes. I want you tae see tae my . . . tae things afterwards. It's not much tae ask of my own wife, is it?' His eyes had found a new intensity, and now they were burning into hers.

'No, it's not much to ask.' She put the envelope into her bag and then said as he fell back, suddenly exhausted, 'Mebbe I should go. You're tired out.'

But his gaze was now on a spot just beyond her arm, and a slight smile was lifting the corners of his pale mouth. 'Here's my nice nurse comin' tae chase ye away.'

'You've been overdoing it, Mr Gordon, I can tell.' The nurse swept past Julia and bent over the bed, one hand going to his wrist to take his pulse. 'Now lie quiet for a minute.'

Julia wanted to leave, but as she hadn't said her goodbyes properly she felt that she had no option but to wait until the woman was finished with her patient.

'As I thought, a bit over-excited. A wee sleep, I think.'

'Aye, I'm ready for a sleep. Nurse, this is my wife.'

'So she came to see you right enough. That's good.' The

woman straightened from the bed and turned towards Julia, who was horrified to discover that she was face to face with her neighbour, Nan Megson.

'He's been waiting for you, Mrs . . .' Nan was saying, and then she faltered, but only for a moment. 'Mrs Gordon,' she went on smoothly. 'I'm so glad you were able to visit, but I think your husband needs to rest now.'

'I was just going.'

'You'll come back?' Thomas asked.

'I will, I promise,' Julia said, and almost ran from the ward.

'There's a girl at work,' Chloe said later that afternoon, her voice subdued, 'who had to be fetched home by a police-man today because her brother got killed. Blown up in the trenches, they said.'

'Are you all right, pet?' Julia, summoned from a piano lesson in the front room by a concerned Duncan, was alarmed by her daughter's pallor.

'I'm fine. I just . . . it's the first time I've known someone that's been killed like that, in the war. I didn't know him, of course,' Chloe gabbled on, 'but I know his sister well and she's talked about him. So I felt as if I knew him, and I suddenly thought, what if it happened to Ch-Charlie . . .'

'Sit down, Chloe.' Julia took the girl by the shoulders and eased her into her father's chair, the most comfortable chair in the flat. Then she knelt on the fireside rug, taking the girl's cold hands between her own. 'Duncan, put the kettle on, there's a good lad. Your sister and I could both do with a nice cup of tea.'

She certainly could, she thought as she massaged Chloe's hands. Her head had been aching ever since she came back from the hospital. Somehow, she had to see Nan Megson on her own, tell her the truth, and persuade her not to say a word to anyone. And that, Julia thought miserably, would be yet one more person to share the secret that she and Frank had kept so well for so many years.

'What about your piano lesson?' Chloe asked, recollecting the tune that had been thudding rather than dancing from behind the closed door when she arrived home.

'I'm not bothered,' Daisy Hepburn's clear little voice said from the doorway, where she stood surveying the scene. 'If you want me out of the way, I could always go down to the backcourt and play with your Leslie,' she went on hopefully.

'It's not what your mother's paying me for, but just this once, off you go,' Julia agreed, and the little girl skipped off, her face wreathed in smiles.

'She drives Leslie mad, you know she does, Mum,' Duncan said from the stove, where he had just lit the gas.

'You go as well, then, and keep the peace between them. Just until I come to fetch Daisy. I'm taking her home today. Chloe,' Julia said gently to the figure huddled in Frank's big chair when Duncan had gone, 'you must know that folk get hurt and killed in a war. Not just the soldiers and the sailors and the airmen either; there's all these poor souls that were killed in Greenock and Clydebank and other places. And here in Paisley too.'

'I know that, but it's all too much to take in!' Chloe's tone was almost irritable, and she glared at her mother with eyes bright with unshed tears. 'Up to now it's been lists in the newspaper, and folk saying things, and I always knew that it was real, but I didn't know any of the people. And now I do! Well, almost.'

'We've been lucky so far.' Julia got up to make the tea, spooning in more of her precious stock of tea-leaves than she would have used normally. 'This whole tenement's been lucky, though there's been telegrams delivered to quite a few of the other families in Glen Street.'

She set the teapot back on a low gas to mash, then after a moment's hesitation she went to a corner cupboard and took out the small bottle of brandy kept for emergencies and slipped it into the pocket of her cardigan.

She poured out the tea and added a double spoonful of sugar, then just before carrying it over to Chloe, she tipped some brandy into both cups. 'Drink this up, it'll make you feel better.'

Chloe clutched the cup in both hands. 'It's not right, is it, Mum? That boy had just finished serving his apprenticeship at Fleming and Ferguson's shipyard. Young men like him shouldn't have to go and fight wars they didn't start!'

'It's the way life is, pet.'

'Can they not just use the men that are soldiers anyway, instead of making lads like Pearl's brother join up, just to get killed?' Chloe's voice began to wobble on the last few words, and she dipped her face into the warmth of the steam coming up from her cup. Julia stroked her pale auburn hair.

'They *have* used those soldiers, Chloe, but when they get killed, they need to find more men.'

'It's not fair!'

'I know, but life isn't always fair. We have to make what we can out of it.'

'Mr Hepburn fought in the Great War, and he doesn't believe in lads like Charlie and Pearl's poor brother having to fight for their country all over again.'

'I can understand his way of thinking.'

Chloe took a drink of tea and then, without looking at her mother, said, 'Before he went away, Charlie asked me to be his girlfriend and I said no.'

'Well, you're both young yet, and mebbe it's not a good thing to get tied down like that. You don't know how you'll feel in two years' time, or even in two months.'

'That's what I said. We're friends, but that's all.' Chloe took another drink. 'This tastes different.'

'I made it strong and put extra sugar in.'

'Is that what it is?' The girl took a deeper drink, and then gave her mother a faint smile. 'It's nice.' A little colour had come back into her cheeks and her eyes were clear again.

'Take your time with it,' Julia said over her shoulder as she took her own cup to the sink. 'I'd better take Daisy home. I have to get back in time to get the dinner ready.'

'I'll start it while you're away. Mum?' Chloe said as her mother went to the door.

'What is it, pet?'

'I wish I had told Charlie that I would be his girlfriend. Mebbe I should say it in my next letter.'

'Would you have meant it?'

'No. Yes. I don't know!' Chloe said frantically. 'I don't even know what it feels like to love someone, so how can I know if I really love Charlie or just like him?'

'It's not something you recognise,' Julia said. 'It's just . . . a feeling. It happens when it's ready, and when it does, you'll know. And that's all I can tell you.'

'Then I don't think I do love him.' Chloe's voice was forlorn. 'I wish I did, Mum, it would make things much easier.'

'Better to be a good friend than a fickle sweetheart.' Julia hesitated, then said tentatively, 'Chloe, pet, is there someone you like better than Charlie Hepburn?'

The girl opened her mouth, closed it, and opened it again to say, 'No.' Then she buried her face in the teacup.

'I'll not be long,' Julia said, and went to fetch her coat.

26

As Julia and Daisy reached the Hepburns' close they met Mirren on her way home. Daisy gave her mother's thighs a warm hug before racing into the close and up the stairs, leaving the two women to talk on the pavement.

'It's understandable,' Mirren said when she heard about Chloe. 'I was a bit younger than her when the Great War started and now that I think of it, it wasn't until my own brother was lost that I realised just what war can do to ordinary folk. She'll be all right.'

'She's got no choice, has she? It's hard, seeing our children getting caught up in something as terrible as a war . . . something that has nothing to do with them.'

'I know, but there's nothing we can do but thole it and hope for the best, and make up our minds,' Mirren said grimly, 'that we're never going to let it happen again.'

'I'm sorry about Daisy's lesson being spoiled.'

'Och, a break now and again does no harm.'

'I'll not charge for this time.'

'Whether you charge or not you'll be paid for it, and don't argue. She's enjoying her lessons, so you must be a good teacher. It's the first time in her life that our Daisy has kept on with anything. And she practises every day, no matter how much Grace and Bobby and their daddy go on at her to stop.' Mirren looked closely at her friend. 'Is there something wrong, Julia? Something other than Chloe? You look shell-shocked.'

'I went to visit Thomas this afternoon, in the infirmary.'

'Is he still managing to upset you? Mebbe you should just leave the visiting to me.'

'It wasn't that. One of the nurses came over just as I was leaving. Mirren, it was Mrs Megson who lives on the top floor of our tenement.'

'Did she say anything?'

Julia shook her head. 'Thomas introduced me as his wife, and she called me Mrs Gordon and behaved as if she'd never seen me before.'

'That's a blessing.'

'But now I'll have to go and see her. I'll have to ask her not to say anything to the other folk in the building. Her son plays in our band . . . what if Frank found out about Thomas from him, or someone else?'

'All the more reason to make sure he hears it from you first,' Mirren pointed out gently.

'He's working so hard just now, and as often as not he has to go out again at night to the Home Guard. I never seem to find the right time to break it to him. Thomas looks a lot worse than the last time I saw him,' she hurried on, 'for all that he's more comfortable, and well cared for.'

'Aye, poor man. I doubt he'll last much longer,' Mirren said.

'I just want to pop up to see Mrs Megson for a minute,' Julia said after she and Chloe and the boys had finished their evening meal. 'If I go now, I'll be back before your dad comes home. Could you make sure that the boys do their homework? They can go out for a wee while once they've finished.'

'All right.' The girl was still listless.

At the Megsons' door, Julia knocked and then waited, rubbing her hands down the sides of her skirt. When the door opened she shied back, her heart hammering.

'Yes?' the younger Megson boy said, sticking his chin forward aggressively.

'Is your mother in?'

'Aye.'

'Could I have a wee word with her?'

He stared at her suspiciously, as though wondering if the wee word was about him, then turned and went along the hall to the kitchen, leaving her on the doormat. 'It's for you,' she heard him say. 'That woman from down the stairs.'

'What woman? And for goodness' sake, laddie, why didn't you invite her in?' Nan Megson's voice came nearer and then she appeared, no longer crisp and cool in her nurse's uniform, but flushed and wrapped in a large apron, with her hair wisping out from the loose bun at the back of her head.

'Mrs . . . McCosh, I'm so sorry you were kept standing. Come on in.'

Julia shook her head. 'I've only got a minute. I wondered . . . could I speak to you out here?'

Nan cast a swift glance back into the hall before stepping on to the landing and drawing the door to behind her. 'Of course.' She led Julia to the top of the stairs, well away from both doors on the landing.

'I wanted to explain about what happened this afternoon.'

'My dear,' Nan said swiftly, 'there's no need for you to explain anything to me. It's none of my business.'

'It is, now that you're nursing him. And I'd like to tell you, for if I don't, he probably will.'

'Patients tell us all manner of things,' Nan said, 'but we know how to keep their confidences.'

'Even so, I want to explain.' Julia took a deep breath and then, realising that her carefully prepared and rehearsed story had vanished, she told the other woman the truth as swiftly as she could, finishing with, 'and now that he's ill and has nobody to care for him he's come to Paisley, looking for me to help him. But I couldn't care for him by myself; apart from having Frank and the children to think of, I wouldn't know how to nurse him properly.'

'Of course you couldn't,' Nan agreed. 'The man's in the final stages of his illness, as you've probably realised, and there's no doubt that he needs constant nursing.'

'D'you think there's a chance he can ever be well enough to leave the infirmary?'

'No, my dear, no chance. But you can be sure that he'll get the best possible care for the time left to—' She stopped short as heavy footsteps were heard from below, then went on, 'I would suggest a cold compress, Mrs McCosh. That's the best thing for bringing down a lump on the head. And if the laddie seems to be all right otherwise, no need to trouble the doctor.' Then, as Ellen Borland peered up at them from the lower landing, 'Good evening, Mrs Borland.'

'I thought I could hear voices.' The woman, dressed in her working clothes, clutched at the newel post. 'Thae stairs are goin' tae be the death of me. The sky's awful clear out there, I hope it doesnae mean another air raid the night for I'm fair desperate for my own bed. I don't know when I last had a decent night's sleep. If we're no' havin' tae go down tae the shelter, we're lyin' awake waitin' for the sirens tae start.'

She paused, then, as the two woman above said nothing, she added, 'This war's goin' tae be the death of me,' and disappeared in the direction of her own door.

'As I was saying, lumps on the head usually look worse than they are,' Nan said. 'And if the skin's not broken the compress should do the trick. And if you feel that you want a second opinion, you know that I'll come and have a look at the wee chap.'

'I think he'll be fine,' Julia said, and then, as a door on the landing below opened and closed, 'Thank you.'

'Best not to spread things around, eh? And kind though Mrs Borland is to the rest of us, I sometimes feel that she

takes too much interest in what goes on in our lives.' Nan
put a cool, firm hand on Julia's. 'Don't worry, my dear, if
there's anything you should know, I'll make sure to tell
you.'

Frank was coming up the stairs just as Julia reached her
own door. His face lit up at the sight of her, as it always
did. 'Where have you been?'

'Just having a word with Nan Megson.' She went into
the flat ahead of him.

'I'm going to my bed,' Chloe said as soon as they went
in.

'Already? Are you sickening for something?' her father
asked anxiously.

'No, I just had a busy day.'

'Are you sure she's not ill?' Frank asked his wife as he
took off his jacket and began to roll up his shirt sleeves.
'She doesn't look right to me.'

'One of the other girls at work was fetched home because
her brother's just been killed. It gave Chloe a bit of a turn,
with Charlie going away recently.'

'I can see that it would. Charlie Hepburn's a decent young
fellow, but I hope Chloe doesnae start moping and worryin'
about him. Not at her age. Where are the lads?' he asked,
pouring water from the kettle in to a basin and getting down
to the business of washing away the day's grime.

'If you didn't see them playing in the street, they'll probably be down in the backcourt. We've all had our dinner.'
Julia fetched his plate from the oven, where it had been
keeping hot. 'It's shepherd's pie but it's been in too long,'
she said, vexed. 'It's dried up, Frank.'

'I quite like it that way, with the gravy well soaked into
the potatoes.' He soaped his face vigorously and then tossed
a double handful of water over it, sending drops showering the surrounding area. 'It's been a bugger of a day. Thank
God I'm not on Home Guard duty tonight. With any luck
there won't be a raid.' He scrubbed water from his eyes

with one hand, fumbling about with the other, and showering more water about the place. 'Where the dickens has that towel got to now?'

'It's right there, beside you.' Julia handed it to him and as he dried himself he glanced out of the window to the yard below.

'Young Dennis is working out the back, and the boys are down there pestering him. I'll mebbe give him a wee hand after,' he said as he sat down to his meal.

'I thought you were tired. Can you not just take an evening to yourself, for once?'

'Working out in the fresh air will be just as good as a rest. And Dennis could probably do with a hand. He's a good lad, and a fine musician too.' Frank forked up a load of meat and vegetables and mashed potato and then grinned at his wife. 'But don't tell him I said so. I'd not want him to get too big headed.'

'I don't think he's the type to get big headed. That young brother of his, though . . . he's completely different from Dennis. I still think that it's Dennis that Chloe really fancies.'

'Ach away! I've said before that he's too old for her.'

'He's only about two and a half years older than her, Frank. That's not a big difference.' Thomas Gordon was five years older than Julia herself, but Frank was her senior by only six months.

Frank pushed away his empty plate with a sigh of contentment. 'That was good. What's for after?'

'I managed to get some stewing apples, and there's custard to go with them.' Julia set the bowl on the table, together with a small jug of custard. 'The tea might be too strong, I'll make fresh.'

'Never bother, what's in the pot will do me fine. Sit down for a minute,' he urged, 'you look worn out.'

'I spent most of the day queuing, and there was WVS work to do as well.'

Frank spooned up apple and custard. 'What was it you were speaking to Mrs Megson about when I got home?'

'It was nothing special.'

'The two of you aren't usually pally, are you?'

'We get on fine, her and me; it's just that we don't live in each other's pockets. We're both busy people.'

'She's a nurse, isn't she?'

'Yes, at the RAI.'

He reached across the table and took her hand in his. 'Are ye ill, Julia?'

'Me . . . ill? What put that notion into your head?'

His eyes were suddenly dark with fear. 'You've not been looking well these past few weeks. I should have made you go to the doctor's, but I've been that busy at work . . . and now you're having wee talks with the nurse that lives up the stair. What's wrong, Julia?'

'Nothing's wrong. We're all tired these days because we're worked off our feet, and life's not exactly easy, is it? And as for Nan Megson, I was asking her advice for a woman who works alongside me in the WVS. She's got a bit of trouble, ' Julie said carefully, knowing that he would construe that as some female problem, and probe no further, 'and she's too scared of the outcome to go to see her own doctor. Mrs Megson was very helpful.'

'Are you certain that was all?' His fingers tightened on hers and his voice deepened as he said, 'Julia, if anything happened to you I don't think I could bear it.'

'Don't be daft!'

'I'm not being daft, woman. You're my whole life, you know you are, and all I want is for you to be well, and happy.'

'Oh, Frank . . .' For a moment she was tempted to tell him about the dying man in the infirmary, to let him share her burden. Then, telling herself that he had enough to deal with, she went on briskly, 'You're a good man, and if there

was anything to tell you, I would. Now, can we drink our
tea before it goes cold?'

On the day of her father's second marriage Cecelia Goudie
went into Glasgow by train rather than by bus, just in case
she met a driver or conductress she knew.

Two men were standing outside the registry office when
she arrived; they turned as she paused on the pavement, and
with a sudden stab of panic, she realised that the smaller
man was her father, almost unrecognisable in a suit.

'Cecelia?' he asked tentatively, peering down at her.

'Father. I'm not late, am I?'

'No, not at all. We're just waiting for . . . for the others.'
He began to hold out both hands towards her as she climbed
the few steps, then hesitated and made as though to shake
her hand formally. Then he changed his mind again, his
face reddening. To her astonishment, Cecelia realised that
he was just as nervous about their meeting as she was. 'This
is Jack Liddell,' he said, putting his hands behind his back.
'He's agreed to be one of the witnesses. Jack used to work
alongside me in the engineering works. You'll mind me
mentioning him, I'm sure.'

'Yes, of course I remember,' she said, although she didn't.
Her mother had had a great memory for names, but Cecelia
needed to be able to link them to faces. She shook hands
with Mr Liddell, and then her father took her arm, the first
contact between them in a year.

'D'you mind watchin' out for the others, Jack, while I
take my daughter inside?'

In the foyer, he said hurriedly, 'I just wanted the chance
to thank you for comin', Cecelia. I know you're not too
pleased about me marryin' again.'

'You weren't pleased about my marriage either, Father,
but even so, you gave me away, so I felt that I owed it to
you to attend your marriage.'

'Aye, well, I appreciate it.' His eyes, the same shade of

grey as her own, travelled to the smart hat perched on her head. She had pushed the veil back because the tiny velvet dots stitched all over it kept making her feel as though she was turning faint. 'You look very nice,' he said. 'Very grown up.'

'I am grown up, Father,' she was saying when the outer door opened and Mr Liddell ushered two women into the foyer. Turning towards them, Cecelia was taken aback as she saw that the motherly woman in a grey silk dress and matching coat, being introduced to her now as the bride, bore a striking resemblance to her own mother.

The other woman, who, like Jack Liddell, was standing as a witness to the ceremony, was Elspeth McFadden's cousin. It seemed that the five of them made up the entire wedding party.

'I was an only child,' Elspeth said to Cecelia, 'like your father. And since my two boys are in the navy, and neither of us has close family apart from our children and my cousin Netta here, we decided to make it just the five of us. After all, at our age, we don't need to make a fuss about it.' Then, as they were summoned through the inner door, she clutched the small bunch of roses she had brought with her, and smoothed her hair – pepper and salt hair, just like Cecelia's mother's – with fingers that were suddenly nervous.

The ceremony was over almost as soon as it began, and afterwards, they went back to the large, high-ceilinged second-floor flat that had been Cecelia's home all her life until she left it to marry Fergus. Her stomach began to flutter as she climbed the stairs and waited on the landing for her father to put his key in the lock. At least the registry office had been neutral ground, but this was different.

The others were joking about the groom carrying the bride over the threshold. 'Only if I was willing to let the poor man wrench his back,' Elspeth said, and then, briskly, 'Come on now, let's get inside and get something to eat.'

For some reason Cecelia had got it into her head that her

father, egged on by the new woman in his life, would have
replaced everything that he and her mother had bought, but
it was all still there . . . the upright chairs, the big polished
parlour table, now set out for the wedding breakfast, the
big comfortable sofa that had doubled as a house, a boat,
a shop or whatever Cecelia wanted it to be when she was
small, the dresser with the ornaments on its shelves . . .
even the curtains and carpet were familiar.

'Mebbe you'd give me a hand with the tea, Cecelia,' her
stepmother suggested and then, to the others, 'The rest of
you can just sit down and have a glass of sherry. We'll not
be long.'

In the kitchen, which was also just as Cecelia remembered it, the woman pulled off her hat and scratched her
head vigorously. 'Oh, that's better. D'you mind if I get rid
of these shoes, dear? My feet are killing me!' She sat down
on a chair and eased off the smart, square-heeled shoes,
then stretched out her plump legs and wriggled her toes. 'I
only bought them this morning,' she confided, 'so I'd no
time to get my feet used to them. Could you put the kettle
on? The cups and plates are all laid out and there are trays
of sandwiches in the pantry. Netta helped me to get them
ready before we got dressed for the registry office.'

She sat watching as Cecelia moved about the kitchen.
'You look very smart, dear, and so slim! I bet you don't
have to wear corsets.'

'No, I don't.' Cecelia found the tea caddy in its usual
place, and measured tea-leaves in to the pot. 'There's
another teapot in this cupboard; I'd best use it as well.'

'I think so. Corsets are so uncomfortable,' Elspeth
confided. 'I never wear them if I can help it, but I couldn't
have got into this dress without one.' She looked ruefully
at her shoes. 'D'you know, I don't believe that I could bear
to put them on again. It'll have to be my slippers.' Then,
as she eased her feet in to a pair of shabby slippers, 'Daniel
tells me that you're a clippie.'

'That's right. He wasn't very pleased when I wrote to tell him about it. Just like Fergus . . . my husband. He wanted me to find the sort of job I'd done before, in an office.'

'Not nearly so interesting, though. It's great, isn't it, being a clippie? Did your father not tell you that that's what I did myself, before my boys came along?' the woman asked as Cecelia turned to stare at her.

'He did not.'

Elspeth gave a warm, full-bodied roar of laughter. 'That's men for you. I was on the trams myself. That's where I met my husband . . . my first husband, I should say.'

'He was a driver?'

'An inspector,' Elspeth said, with a grin. 'My cousin'll tell you that I always did have ideas above my station. Come on through to the parlour, I'm sure we're both ready for a glass of sherry.'

'Is everything all right with you?' Daniel asked his daughter an hour or so later.

'Everything's fine. The only thing I need is for this war to be over and Fergus to come back home.'

'So the marriage is working out, then?'

'Didn't I tell you that it would? You shouldn't have doubted me, Father.'

'That's because I couldnae believe what I was hearin'. A wee shy lassie like you, always afraid of her own shadow, wantin' tae get married tae a farm laddie from the back of beyond? What father in his right mind would agree tae that?'

'Plenty, surely, but there's no sense in arguing over that now, for it's all water under the bridge and we've both made our own decisions.'

She glanced across the room at her new stepmother, sitting on the big sofa with her stockinged feet planted on the familiar carpet. She had thought all along that, by courting another woman, her father was supplanting her mother. But Elspeth, though more relaxed and easy-going than

Cecelia's mother, was so like her in looks that it had suddenly became clear that far from forgetting his first wife, Daniel had sought to bring her, or at least a strong reminder of her, back into his life.

'You and Elspeth must visit me in Paisley,' she said.

'Paisley?' Her father, a Glasgow man born and bred, considered Paisley to be beneath his notice. Fergus's decision to work there, and take her to live there, had been yet another bone of contention between them.

'Yes, Father, Paisley. It's not a bad place at all, as you'll see for yourself if you come to visit me.'

Daniel gave his daughter a long, probing look, then nodded.

'Mebbe we will, at that,' he said.

27

Cecelia, returning to work after her week off, heard the latest gossip as soon as she got on to the service bus taking her into work her first shift.

'That Nancy's moved in with her driver,' the conductress she sat beside breathed into her ear.

It was just after four o'clock in the morning, and despite the walk from Glen Street to the Cross, Cecelia was still half asleep, but astonishment stopped her in mid-yawn. 'With Les? But he's married, isn't he?'

'Oh aye, well married. But his wife's had tae go off tae nurse her mother, and she was no sooner on the train that Nancy was in there. One of the clippies got it from a cousin who's a friend of one of Les's neighbours. Not that it was a secret anyway; the bold Nancy comes in with him at the start of their shifts, arm in arm, and they go off together when they've finished work, as cosy as if it was all legal.'

'But what'll happen when his wife comes back?'

'Nancy says that she'll move out when they get word that the woman's comin' home.'

'But a neighbour could easily tell his wife what's been going on.'

'Exactly. If you ask me – and I'm not the only one that thinks this – Nancy wouldnae mind if the woman did find out. Then she'd get Les tae herself for good.'

'Are you sure that that's what Les wants?'

'He's that daft about her that he's not even thinkin' straight. And it must be a temptation for a man, havin' a bonny young lassie like Nancy after him. You mark my words, hen,' Cecelia's informant said with relish, 'there's goin' tae be sparks flyin' before this is over!'

At the depot, she was warmly welcomed by Harry.

'I'm right glad tae see ye, lassie. They gave me this clippie, then that clippie . . . whoever they could spare, and not one of them comfortable tae work with.'

Cecelia glowed. It was good to know that she was appreciated. 'Never mind, Harry, I'm back.'

'Aye, ye are, and it'll be like puttin' on a nice old pair of slippers that have shaped themselves tae fit a man's bunions instead of all thae tackety boots I've had tae work with,' he said. Then, as Nancy entered the canteen, hanging on to Les's arm, 'There's been fun and games while you've been away, hen.'

'So I heard, on the service bus. It's true, then?'

'Oh, it's true, right enough. The man's taken leave of his senses, that's all I can say.'

Cecelia looked at Les. The man's face was glowing with embarrassed pride, while Nancy smirked to left and right, well pleased with herself. 'He's in love, Harry.'

'If that's love then you can keep it.'

'You're married, aren't you? You must have been in love once.'

'I'd a boil on the back of my neck once, tae,' Harry said, 'and I still mind that well, but for the life of me I cannae mind anythin' that could be cried love. I just got married because the wife wanted it that way and it was easier tae give in than tae argue. That's the secret of a successful marriage.'

It was the school summer holiday, and the streets were filled with youngsters; boys playing football or testing their skill with marbles, girls deftly spinning their skipping ropes, or

bouncing balls against tenement walls or sitting on the steps
at the close entrance with their dolls. Pavements blossomed
with chalked peever beds, tops spun, hoops rattled, and
parents' wardrobes were raided for costumes for backcourt
concert parties.

With the technical college closed for the session, Dennis
threw himself into his work and also spent long hours in
the vegetable garden, stopping every now and again to look
up at Lena Fulton's kitchen window and wonder if she was
watching him. She no longer came down to help when she
saw him digging, and on the few occasions he had tapped
on her door, there had been no sound from within.

Ralph, even more sullen and withdrawn than usual,
worked at his new job as messenger boy, hating it but afraid
to skive off in case his brother caused trouble. 'Keep yer
head down, son,' Mrs Borland had advised him when he
complained to her. 'I cannae afford trouble and neither can
you. Ye'll be out of the school by the end of the year and
able tae go yer own way. And then you and me can do business together, eh?'

Cecelia wrote long letters to Fergus and suffered the
misery of wearing her sturdy uniform on hot days. She
became involved in the lives of her regular passengers,
sharing their sorrows when the news from the front was
bad, and their joy on the occasions when word came that
a son or brother or husband who had been reported missing
was still alive. Some were in hospital, some in prison camps,
but always the women said, their tired faces glowing, 'At
least he's still breathin', hen, and where there's life there's
hope.'

And the war dragged on.

'What's it like outside?' Thomas Gordon asked his favourite
nurse.

'Nice. A wee bit of a breeze, just enough to keep me
cool as I was walking to my work.' Nan Megson wiped his

face and neck gently, so as not to hurt the paper-thin skin, then dipped the facecloth into the basin and squeezed out the surplus water before wiping away the soap.

Thomas, who had been staring out of the ward's high windows at the blue sky and fluffy clouds, all he could see from where he lay, transferred his gaze to the strong hands twisting the cloth and coaxing every last drop from it. 'I missed you yesterday. The other nurses are all right, but they don't have your gentleness.'

'I'm sure they do, Mr Gordon.'

'Thomas.'

'Mr Gordon.'

The glimmer of a smile touched his mouth, and she smiled faintly in return. This gentle argument over whether or not it was seemly for a nurse to call a patient by his first name had become something of a game between them.

'So what did ye do on yer day away from this place?'

'I cooked and I cleaned the flat and I went along the street to watch my daughters singing and dancing in a back-court concert. Then at night I washed their hair and then my own, and did some darning and went to my bed. Nothing very exciting, but it suited me well enough.'

'Was it a good concert?'

'The bairns put a lot of work into it. They're trying to raise funds to buy a battleship.'

'Is your man in the navy, Nurse?'

Nan put the basin of water aside and began to dry his face with gentle dabs of the towel. 'He died a few years ago,' she said levelly. 'He was an officer in the Fire Service and he got trapped in a fire.'

'I'm sorry tae hear that. It must be hard for ye, raisin' a family on yer own.'

'There's plenty other women in the same boat, Mr Gordon, especially these days, but fortunately, most of us have got broad shoulders.' She raised him slightly, one arm firm behind his back while with her free hand she plumped up his pillows. Soon, she would leave him, and go to minister to some other patient. His mind beat about in search of something, anything, to keep her by his side for a few minutes longer.

'Can I have a sip of water?'

She raised him again, holding the spout of the cup to his lips, then lowering him and wiping his mouth when he had finished.

'I was in the Great War myself,' he said. 'I mind once in France, early on, going through a deserted village in search of wood so's we could make a bit of a fire, and comin' face tae face with a German soldier. A lad in his teens, like myself. I hadnae thought that there would be any of the Boche still there, and he was as surprised as I was.'

'What happened?'

'We just looked at each other for a minute, not knowin' what tae dae. It was my first sight of the enemy close up, and probably his, too. Then I minded what I'd been telt time and again when we were in trainin' . . . kill him afore he kills you. So I lifted my rifle, and he lifted his, but I fired first.'

'You killed him.'

'The bloo . . . the thing had jammed,' Thomas managed a wry smile. 'So I couldnae do anythin' but stand there and wait for him tae kill me. But he didnae. He just lowered his gun and gave a sort of a shrug as if tae say, what's the sense? And then he turned away.' He was silent for a moment, then said bitterly, 'I wish tae God he'd put an end tae me there and then.'

'You can't wish away your whole life like that!'

'Aye I can, and I do.' His eyes were suddenly angry. 'If that lad had done his duty like a proper soldier should, he'd have killed me there and then. But he didnae, and so I'm lyin' here like a bairn, dyin' inch by inch and gettin' in everyone's way. If I was a dog I'd have been put down, but because I'm a man I have tae suffer!'

'You mustn't talk like that,' Nan Megson said firmly. 'You talk about your training . . . well, don't forget that I'm trained too . . . trained to look after you and make you comfortable, and show you that there's always someone who cares. So no more of that wishing, d'you hear me?'

Then she patted his hand as someone further along the ward called for her. 'I'll look in on you in a wee while, Mr Gordon. Try to get some sleep now.'

Left on his own, Thomas Gordon, the all-pervasive stink of hospital disinfectant in his nostrils, stared up at the patch of blue sky showing in the window opposite his bed and wondered if his wife, the wife he had lost to another man, would visit him later.

His eyelids began to close, and as he drifted off into a restless sleep he saw the young German soldier shrugging, half smiling at him, and then turning his back. Dereliction of duty, that was. 'Remember, lads, if you don't kill them, they'll kill you,' the sergeant had told them time and time again; and 'It's your duty to wipe out the enemy.'

Duty had been the backbone of Thomas Gordon's life, all his life. It had helped him to serve with honour in the army and then in the police force. Duty. The word still had a good strong ring to it. That German boy deserved to be punished for his negligence in lowering his own rifle when he had had the enemy in its sights. And punished he was, by having his brains dashed in by the butt of Private Thomas Gordon's jammed rifle.

'What do you want?' Lena Fulton asked through the narrow space between door and frame.

'I thought you might like some carrots.' Dennis held out his cupped hands. 'I've just dug them up.'

'I don't know . . .'

'Carrots are good for your eyes, and with your job that's important. I'll wash them for you,' he offered, and at last the door swung open wide enough to let him through.

'They've done well,' he said as he followed her through the hall. 'You'll enjoy them.'

'I'm not fond of vegetables.'

It had been a while since he was last in her flat; as usual, there was material spread over the table, and Lena immediately went back to work while he washed the carrots in the sink, asking over his shoulder, 'What are you going to have for your dinner tonight?'

'I don't know yet.'

'Tell you what, my mum used to grate carrots and let us eat them from a saucer, with a spoon. Why not try that? D'you have a grater?' he forged on, as she said nothing.

'I think there's one in that cupboard.'

He found it, and dried the vegetables before starting to grate them. 'Still got lots of work, have you?'

'Yes.'

'Me too. We're kept going at the fire station.' He chattered on about work until the few small carrots had been grated on to a plate, then found a spoon and sat down opposite her. 'Here you are, try that.'

The golden-red carrot glowed in the dim room. With a slightly impatient air, Lena put a spoonful into her mouth and chewed slowly.

'Nice and fresh, isn't it?'

'Yes.' She took another spoonful, then another.

'I've knocked on the door a few times but there was no answer.'

'I might have been out, or sleeping. Or just busy with the quilt . . .' She gestured towards the alcove that had originally been used for a set-in bed. In the Fulton flat, where only one bedroom was required, the recess held a chest of drawers, and when she was not working on the patchwork quilt, Lena draped it over the big piece of furniture. Dennis glanced at it, and then gave a low, surprised whistle.

'It's fairly come on. You must have put in hours of work.

If you ask me,' he said, turning back to study her, 'you're overdoing it. You don't look well.'

'I'm fine, and I like my work.'

'There's more to life than work. I've got tomorrow morning off, so why don't the two of us go out for a walk? We could meet at the West End,' he added swiftly as she opened her mouth to object. 'The top of Maxwellton Street at ten o'clock, say, then we could go to the braes, where nobody from round here would see us.'

'There's too much to do. I have to get ready. I'm thinking of going away.'

'Away where?'

'To Cumbrae, on the Clyde. My aunt's staying in Millport with a friend and they want me to go too.'

His heart sank. 'When would that be?'

'Any day now.'

'When will you be back?'

'After the war finishes, mebbe.'

'But that might not be for years yet!'

She got up and took the empty saucer and spoon to the sink. 'I'll be back some day, when George comes home for good.'

'But then he'll . . .' Dennis got to his feet and took her shoulders to turn her about from the sink. She felt fragile beneath his big hands. 'Lena, I don't want you to go. I . . . I care about you and I need to know that you're not far away.'

She had been glancing everywhere but at his face, but now she looked full at him, her blue eyes narrowed and bisected by a frown. 'That's one of the reasons why I have tae go away, d'you not see?'

'No, I don't see! I know you belong to . . . to him, and there's nothing I can do about that, but where's the harm in us seeing each other sometimes, having a wee talk . . .'

'No.' She twisted away from him. 'I've got enough to think about, I don't want the responsibility. Go home, Dennis. Leave me be.'

'But . . .' he began, and she rounded on him.

'Leave me! If you care for me at all you'll do what I ask,' she said sharply, and he had no option but to turn away from her and walk out of the flat.

Julia knew as soon as she opened the door to Nan Megson why the other woman had called. She turned without speaking and led the way into the kitchen, relieved that the boys were playing out in the street.

'Sit down. You'll have a cup of tea?'

Nan nodded, lowering herself slowly and carefully into the chair as though her bones ached. Then she sat quietly, watching Julia busy herself about the cooker, waiting until the other woman was ready to hear more.

'When?' Julia asked as she put the teapot down on the table between them.

'Early this morning, during the air raid. He haemorrhaged, very suddenly, and then . . . it was over. I'm sorry.' There were tears in Nan's eyes.

'God rest his soul, he's at peace now.' Julia lifted the teapot and then put it down suddenly. 'Would you mind . . . ?' She looked at her hands, which had started to shake.

'Of course.' Nan poured tea for them both and spooned sugar into Julia's. 'I told the Matron that I'd break the news to you. I'm sorry to have to bring it up so soon, but there's the question of the funeral . . .'

'Oh . . . yes, of course. He left instructions; an envelope. I'll start seeing to things today.'

When the other woman had gone, Julia fetched the brown envelope from its hiding place and sat down to open it. Thomas Gordon had organised the last few months of his life with his usual efficiency; there were details of the family lair in a Glasgow cemetery, where he would be laid to rest beside his parents, and a fat envelope which proved to be stuffed with bank notes held together by a piece of twine. A piece of paper included with the notes turned out to be

Thomas Gordon's last will and testament, a brief statement declaring that all debts had been met in full, and that the balance of any money left after his funeral expenses were paid to go to, 'Julia Alice Gordon, née Wallace, my wife.'

Their wedding certificate was the only other document in the envelope. Julia smoothed it to flatten the deep folds, and studied Thomas's bold signature, then her own, small and tidy. The witnesses had been his brother-in-law and her best friend of that time, a young woman whom Thomas had effectively removed from her life once they were married.

'I can't feel anything,' she told Mirren an hour later. 'I wish I did, because everyone deserves to be mourned. Nan Megson had tears in her eyes when she told me that he'd gone. She said that she had come to like Thomas in the short time she nursed him. Everyone should have someone to mourn them, and yet I can't feel a thing.'

'I know we're not expected to speak ill of the dead, but for myself, I think that they need to earn that right while they're still with us. Be grateful that Mrs Megson thought kindly of him. You'll have to tell your man now, surely.'

'Tonight. I'll tell him tonight. In the meantime . . .' Julia looked at the envelope she had brought round to Mirren's flat.

'In the meantime there's a funeral to arrange. D'you want me to help?'

'Would you? I've never had to do anything like this on my own before.'

'I have,' Mirren said briskly. 'Come on, sooner started, sooner done.'

28

For once, Frank McCosh was home from work at a reasonable time that evening, and as luck would have it he was
not on Home Guard duties. One of Chloe's workmates at
Cochran's was getting married, and her friends were celebrating the occasion with a night at the La Scala Cinema,
where a Robert Taylor film was showing. Duncan and Leslie
were playing football in the street with their pals, and Julia
and Frank were alone in the flat.

'Let's leave the dishes for a wee while,' she said when
he began to run water into the sink.

'We always do them straight off, between us.'

'Tonight I'd like to have a talk. I could make more tea,
if you want.'

'What I want is to know what's going on.' His brows
were drawn together in a frown.

'Nothing you need to worry about.'

'I do worry. You've not been yourself for weeks. Sit down.'
He took her shoulders and pushed her down into one of the
fireside chairs, then seated himself opposite, leaning forward
intently. 'You've not been eating properly, you're tense all
the time, and you're not sleeping much at nights.'

'Nobody sleeps very well these nights. Mrs Borland was
just saying a while back that if we're not wakened by the
sirens we're lying awake listening for them to start that
terrible wailing—'

'What's wrong, Julia? For God's sake tell me, before the lads come charging in and interrupt us.' He took her hands in his. 'Whatever it is, we'll see it through together.'

His grip was strong and warm and reassuring. Julia drew a deep breath and then said, 'It's about Thomas Gordon. He died this morning.'

There was a short silence, then Frank let his breath out in a long sigh. 'So that's it, then. He's finally out of our lives once and for all. How did you know? Did you get a letter from Glasgow?'

'He didn't die in Glasgow, Frank. He was in the Royal Alexandra.'

His eyebrows shot up towards his hairline. 'Here in Paisley? What the blazes was he doing in Paisley?'

'He moved here a few weeks ago, when he discovered that he was dying of the consumption. It was Mirren Hepburn who got him into the infirmary.'

A tremor ran through Frank, and from his hands into hers. 'I still don't see why he was here!'

'Because he didn't have anyone else to turn to. His sister was killed in the Clydebank blitz and there—'

She stopped as he pulled his hands free of hers and got up, pacing to the window to look down at the backcourt, then turning to lean back against the wooden surround that framed the small sink. With the light behind him, his face was in shadow.

'How long had he been in this town?'

'About five or six weeks.'

'Did you arrange it?'

'No, of course not! The first I knew of it was when he came here.'

'Thomas Gordon came to Glen Street . . . to this flat . . . this room?'

She nodded. 'I had to ask him in. The man was clearly ill, and—'

'Did any of the children see him? Did he see them?'

Frank's voice had gone flat and expressionless, as hard to read as his shadowy features. Julia shivered; it was like being interrogated by a stranger. She cast her mind back to Thomas's one and only visit, trying to recall the details.

'Duncan was just going out to play. He met Thomas at the door and came to tell me I'd a visitor. Then he went out. That was all.'

'So, how did the man know where to find you?'

'He was trained to find folk, Frank. We always knew that he could track us down if he really wanted to.'

'After all these years, I thought we were safe from him.'

'But we're safe now, that's what I'm telling you! He died in the infirmary this morning and I've spent the whole day seeing to his funeral. It's over, Frank!'

'What do you mean, you've been seeing to his funeral?'

'I was still married to him. That's why he came to Paisley when he realised that he wasn't going to get better. He took a wee room in Clarence Street . . . he wanted me to look after him because there wasn't anyone else. I was at my wits' end, Frank, and I didn't know what to do. So I told Mirren Hepburn, and she was such a help. She got him into the infirmary, and—'

'Who else knew about him, besides Mrs Hepburn?' the flat voice probed.

'Just Nan Megson from upstairs; and that was only because she happened to be on duty in his ward and she saw me during visiting hours. But when I told her the truth of it, she promised not to say a word to a soul. She's a good woman, she—'

'You visited him while he was in the infirmary.'

'I couldnae desert the man, not in the last days of his life. You'd surely not have wanted me to do that?'

He gave a short laugh. 'I doubt if what I might or might not want ever came intae it.'

'Frank!'

'Weeks, you say. Five or six weeks he's been here, in

our town, and you've been seeing him and talking about
him to Mrs Hepburn and Mrs Megson. And you never said
a word to me?'

'I didn't want to upset you.'

'Upset me?' His voice began to rise. 'For God's sake,
woman, I've been out of my mind with worry about you. I
thought you were ill, and I was convinced that if you couldnae talk tae me about it, then it must be something serious.
I was so afraid in case you were going tae die . . .'

His voice broke on the last word, and Julia got up and
went to him, only to be fended off.

'No, leave me be, I don't want tae . . .' He raked a hand
through his brown hair. 'I don't want you tae touch me, not
just now. I didnae have anyone tae talk to about my fears,
Julia. No Mirren Hepburn, no Nan Megson. I just had the
worry, gnawin' away at me. And all the time you were
seeing that man, talkin' tae him, helpin' him. Keepin' him
a secret from me.'

'I wanted to tell you, but you'd enough to do, what with
your work and the Home Guard. And anyway . . .' She tried
to swallow, but her mouth was too dry. ' I didn't know what
you might do.'

'You surely didn't think I'd beat a sick man the way he
thrashed me, did you? After all these years, d'ye not know
me better than that?'

'Of course I didn't think you'd hurt him, I just felt that
it was best that I kept quiet about him. And I'm sorry about
that, Frank, I can see now that I was wrong.'

'That makes everything all right, does it?' He pushed
past her and snatched his jacket from the hook on the back
of the door.

'Where are you going?'

'Out. I need some fresh air . . . a drink, mebbe.'

'Frank!' She followed him out into the tiny hall. 'Can
we not sit down and talk about it?'

He paused, his hand on the door handle. 'We went

through a lot just so's we could be together, you and me. As far as the world's concerned we've been man and wife for . . . how long? Over sixteen years now. We've had three bairns together. I thought we'd no secrets from each other, Julia, and it sticks in my craw tae find out that for all these weeks you've not said a word . . . not once asked for my help or my advice. You've managed fine on your lone, with the help of your friends. You don't need me, Julia. And that's what angers me most of all!'

The boys and Chloe were all in their beds when he finally arrived home, surly and with the smell of drink on his breath. He turned his back on her as soon as they got into bed, and when the sirens went in the early hours of the morning and they had to hurry down to join the others in the shelter, he sat apart, scarcely talking to anyone.

'Is Daddy not well?' Chloe asked anxiously after he had gone to the India Tyre Company the next morning. 'He's not like himself at all.'

'He's fine, but he's just got a lot of work on. Best to leave him in peace for the time being,' Julia said calmly, while inside her heart was breaking. Only now was she beginning to realise what a terrible error she had made in keeping the news of Thomas's arrival in Paisley from Frank.

She and Mirren Hepburn were the only mourners at the funeral. Dry-eyed and numb, Julia watched the coffin containing her lawful wedded husband being lowered into the ground. If this was the end, if Frank refused to forgive her for what she had done, then it would mean that after all those years, Thomas had won. She could not bear the thought.

She said nothing to Mirren about Frank's reaction to the news, and Mirren did not ask any questions. On the way home in the train, Julia opened her bag and brought out the envelope containing the money left over once the funeral expenses had been paid.

'Here.' She put it into Mirren's hand. 'This is what

Thomas left, to be disposed of as I see fit. I want it to be put to good use. You'll know best where it should go.'

The other woman opened the envelope, glanced inside, and looked up again, startled. 'My dear, this is a considerable sum. Even if you don't want it for yourself, it could come in very handy for your children.'

She held out the envelope, but Julia shrank back in her seat, shaking her head. 'I'll not touch a penny of his money,' she insisted, and Mirren had no choice but to put it away, and promise that it would be used wisely.

In the middle of August George Fulton wrote to tell his wife that he was coming home on leave at the beginning of September. 'With any luck,' he wrote, 'I'll be there when the bairn arrives.'

It was the letter that Lena had been dreading. She scanned the single sheet, crumpled it up, smoothed it out again, read it for the second time and glanced over at the quilt, spread over a chair. It was a considerable size now, and she had become so involved in its creation that she had almost forgotten that George did not yet know about the miscarriage.

Panic formed itself into a lump in her throat and she snatched up her dressmaking shears and hurried into the bedroom. Opening the door of the big mahogany wardrobe, she searched through the clothes hanging there. There was scarcely anything left of hers, and now every one of George's shirts had had patches cut from them. She was running out of materials.

She surveyed the bed, covered as always by a beautiful damask quilt, which had been made by her mother-in-law. On the occasion of her marriage the woman had presented it to her, carefully wrapped in tissue paper. 'I made two of them when my two lads were just wee,' she had said. 'One for William's wife, and one for George's wife, that was what I intended them for all along.'

It had been like receiving a sacred trust and on the few occasions they had had visitors, George had made a point of taking them into the bedroom to show off the quilt, made with his mother's own hand.

Now Lena gathered it up and took it into the kitchen, where she spread it over the table and began to cut out the patches she needed. Her quilt had to be completed before George arrived. There was a lot of work still to do.

Over the next two weeks she concentrated solely on the patchwork quilt, ignoring the other work she had undertaken. Occasionally, someone knocked on the door – a customer, or perhaps Dennis – but she was too busy to pay any heed, and after a while, the knocking always stopped.

In the larder, milk turned sour, bread grew mould and her cheese ration dried and hardened. She raided the store of tins that George had started to amass when talk of war first started, and when she ran out of tea-leaves she drank water. She dozed occasionally in a chair, but most of her time, day and night, was devoted to the completion of the quilt.

'All the way tae the depot,' the woman in the unbecoming black velvet hat snapped when Cecelia went to collect her fare. She stamped the ticket, and then returned to her place on the platform, glad of the breeze generated by the bus's movement. It was a hot August day, and the lower deck in particular was so stuffy that she had had to open all the windows. She and Harry had one more run to do before the shift ended, and she was looking forward to getting home, and changing out of her uniform.

When the remaining passengers left the bus at the final stop the woman with the black hat stayed where she was, and Cecelia had to make her way up to the front of the bus to tell her, 'This is the final stop before the depot.'

'I know that.' Beneath the hat, which resembled a pudding basin with a small brim, the woman's face was flushed with

heat, and her eyes sparked fire. 'I said I was goin' all the
way, and that means intae the depot.'

'But passengers have to—'

'I've got business there, so the sooner ye get a move on
the better for you and me . . . and him.' The passenger
nodded at Harry, who was beginning to twist round in his
seat, wondering about the delay. Deciding that it would be
better to give in and let someone else deal with the matter
once they reached the end of their journey, Cecelia belled
her driver, and returned to the platform.

As soon as Harry turned the bus into the depot the woman
got up and stumped down the aisle, her large leather
handbag swinging from her arm.

'Right, hen,' she said as Harry brought the bus to a stand-
still and Cecelia prepared to jump off and start directing
him into his parking slot, 'where are they?'

'Who?'

'My man and that floozie o' . . . never mind,' the woman
said as a group of drivers and clippies emerged from the
canteen. 'I've found them for mysel'. Here, hold that.' She
thrust the handbag at Cecelia, and then, showing a surprising turn of speed, given the heat, she leapt off the platform
and went charging across the yard, yelling, 'Right, Les
Nisbet . . . !'

The group by the canteen door stopped and stared. From
her vantage point on the platform Cecelia saw the colour
drain from Les's face as he saw the woman bearing down
on him. Hurriedly, he disentangled himself from Nancy,
who had been hanging on to his arm as usual, while the
others began to drift aside, out of the way.

'Didnae expect tae see me back so soon, did ye?'
The woman's voice soared through the air, every word
as sharp as a knife. 'Didnae think I'd hear about yer shenani-
gans, eh?' She came to a halt in front of him, arms akimbo.

'What the blazes is goin' on?' Harry wanted to know,
arriving on the platform. 'And who's that?'

'I think it must be Les's wife. She came in on our bus.'

'Jeeze oh,' Harry said gleefully, 'this should be inter-estin'.'

'Mary . . .' Les was protesting shrilly, 'ye cannae come in here. This is Glasgow Corporation property!'

'I can go wherever I want!' She glared about the yard. 'Unless anyone wants tae try tae stop me?' she invited, and it seemed to Cecelia that everyone present took a step back, while Harry muttered into her ear, 'Speakin' for mysel', I'd as soon try tae stop a Nazi Panzer division.'

'So . . .' The woman turned and looked Nancy up and down. 'This is yer tart, is it?'

'Les . . .' Nancy shrilled. 'Are you goin' tae let her talk tae me like that?' Then, facing her rival, chin up and bosom thrust forward. 'If ye must know, Mrs Nisbet, me and Les—'

'Oh, I know all about you and my Les, hen. I've heard all about it. Ye stupid lummock,' Mary Nisbet turned on her husband again, 'bringin' that . . . that creature intae my house, where all the neighbours could see what was goin' on. Makin' a fool out of me when I was away on an errand of mercy!'

'Mary, come intae the canteen and we'll talk about it, eh?' He stepped in front of Nancy and then yelped as his wife knocked him to one side with a well-placed blow from her fist. He staggered back, arms flailing in an attempt to keep his balance, as she lunged towards Nancy.

'C'mere, you!' she snarled, and began to drive the girl back under a barrage of open-handed slaps.

'Harry, someone should stop them before Nancy gets hurt!'

'You do it then.' The driver folded his arms. 'Nancy got herself intae this mess and as far as I'm concerned she can get herself out of it.'

Even as he spoke, the clippie, recovering from her initial astonishment, ripped the hat from Mrs Nisbet's head and sank her red-tipped fingers into the woman's dark springy hair, holding on tightly while at the same time swinging around like an athlete tossing the caber. Mary Nisbet, screeching at the top of her voice, crashed into the wall of the canteen with one shoulder before managing to clamp both hands about Nancy's wrists. She broke the younger woman's grip, and immediately fastened her own fingers into Nancy's hair, ripping off the uniform cap and tearing apart the sleek chignon that the girl spent hours perfecting in the women's toilets at the start of each shift.

By now, word of the fight was spreading. All work had stopped and a crowd was gathering in the yard. People pouring from the canteen to see the fun were forced to skip aside as the two women, clawing and slapping and punching at each other, reeled about the yard. Les, keeping well out of the way, gnawed at the knuckles of one fist as he watched his wife and his girlfriend fighting for his favours.

'What's going on here?' The inspector on duty burst out of his office. 'Stop that at once,' he ordered the two women. 'This is a bus depot, no' a boxin' ring!' Then, as they paid no heed, 'For pity's sake, someone stop them!'

There was a general shaking of heads. 'I'm paid tae drive buses, no' tae risk my life,' Harry said as the man's eye alighted on him. Just then, Mary Nisbet managed to trip Nancy up and the two of them crashed to the ground, screaming like banshees, with Les's wife on top.

'Right!' The inspector pounced, gripping the woman round the waist and hauling her back inch by inch from her prey. As soon as she was freed, Nancy scrambled to her feet and would have continued the attack on her rival, who now had one arm pinioned by her side, if a burly older driver had not stepped between them.

'Fair's fair, Nancy lass,' Cecelia heard him say, 'the woman cannae hit back now.'

'Fair?' Mary Nisbet screeched, struggling as the inspector managed to pinion her other wrist. 'Fair, did ye say? What's fair about stealin' another man's wife? Tell me that!'

Nancy's attack had left her thick hair standing on end all about her red face. A scratch down one cheek oozed blood, and most of the buttons had been ripped from her coat, which was half off and skewed awkwardly round her shoulders.

Nancy had not fared much better; her long black hair was hanging in rat's tails and the makeup she applied so skilfully had been smeared and streaked, so that her face resembled an artist's palette. Her uniform, too, was dishevelled and missing buttons.

'Whose wife? Who's stealin' who?' the bewildered inspector asked, and then, as a dozen voices began to explain and a dozen hands to point, his eyes landed on Les, cowering among a group of drivers.

'You're the cause of this business, are you? Right, you three intae my office! And the rest of you, get on with your work. There's passengers waitin'!'

'What d'you think will happen now?' Cecelia asked Harry when they stopped at the terminus for a break after their first run.

'I reckon Les and Nancy'll be lookin' for new jobs by now, and it serves them right for no' bein' a bit more careful. As to which of them he'll end up with, that's his problem. If it was me, though, I'd not touch either of them with a bargepole.'

'I've never seen women fighting before.' Cecelia gave an involuntary shiver. 'I never knew they could be so vicious.'

'Oh aye, there's nothin' like a good catfight,' the driver said with relish. 'See, lass, men use their heads as well as their fists when they fight. They think ahead and plan things out. But women . . . they get the blood lust and they just go for the kill. That's why a catfight's much more interestin'.'

The depot was still buzzing with excitement when they

returned from their final run. As Harry had predicted, both
Les and Nancy had been dismissed on the spot.

'He went off lookin' right sorry for himsel', with Nancy
and his wife still tryin' tae snatch him from each other,' one
of the other drivers said gleefully. 'And if that's what it
means tae have two women after ye, I'll be happy just tae
keep tae the one I've already got.'

'It's my belief that he'll stay with his wife,' a clippie
predicted sagely. 'He's got a home with her, and he'd have
tae start all over again with Nancy. Anyway, she'd leave
him soon enough. With Nancy, it's more likely tae be the
pleasure of nabbin' someone else's man than keepin' him.
You're wanted in the office, Cecelia, by the way.'

'Me? What's it about?' she asked nervously, then when
the woman shrugged, 'I've not been doing anything wrong,
have I, Harry?'

'No, hen, ye've not bashed any of the buses intae the
wall since the last time. And I've got no complaints about
ye. Unless . . .' He paused, then said, 'Mebbe it's because
it was you that brought Les's wife intae the depot on our
bus.'

'I couldn't help that, she wouldn't get off!'

'Whatever it is, ye'd best no' keep the man waitin',' the
clippie advised. 'He's been in a right mood ever since this
morning's trouble.'

'There ye are at last,' the inspector greeted Cecelia sourly
when she trembled her way into the small office.

'Is it . . . did I do somethin' wrong?'

'If ye did, ye'd best keep it tae yersel', for I've had quite
enough for one day. That bottle of whisky ye found on yer
bus six months back . . .' He reached into a cupboard and
brought it out. 'It's no' been claimed, so it's yours.'

'Here,' Cecelia thrust the bottle at Harry when she
emerged from the office on rubbery legs. 'Have it.'

He took it reverently, the tip of his tongue moistening
his lips as she stared at the rich golden liquid sloshing about

behind the glass. 'I thought ye wanted tae keep it for yer man . . . ?'

'After what's been happening today,' Cecelia said, 'I'm not bothered any more. Share it with the other drivers.'

29

Dennis Megson was hovering by Lena's door when Chloe
and her mother came back from doing the Saturday shopping. 'You've not seen Mrs Fulton about, have you?' he
asked.

'Not for a day or two, but she's never out and about
much. We could easily miss each other.'

'I chapped her door a minute ago to see if she wanted
to come down and do a bit of weeding, but there was no
answer.'

'I'll help with the weeding,' Chloe said at once. 'I'll just
go and get changed.'

'Oh . . . right,' he said, after just the slightest hesitation,
then as the girl scurried into the flat he went on, 'She . . .
Mrs Fulton, that is . . . was talking about going to Millport
to join her aunt. I just wondered if she'd gone already. Did
she mention it to you?'

'No, but she might have gone there, or she might just be
doing a bit of shopping, this being Saturday. I'll listen out
for her,' Julia offered. 'If I see her, will I say that you want
to speak to her about something?'

'No, it's not that important. I expect you're right . . . she's
up the town getting her messages in,' he said, and went on
down the stairs. She heard him going through the back close
as she went into her own flat.

Chloe had already changed into casual clothes, her face

alight at the prospect of spending time in Dennis's company. 'Bring Dennis up for a cup of tea later,' Julia suggested, and the girl beamed at her.

'Thanks, Mum,' she said, and then the outer door slammed and Julia was on her own. The boys were out playing as usual, and as for Frank, there was no knowing where he might be these days. He could be working over-time, even though it was a Saturday afternoon, or perhaps having a drink with his workmates somewhere. Up until ten days ago Julia had known where he was every minute of the day, but nowadays he went his own way in silence.

She began to unpack the shopping, her heart heavy. The children had sensed that something was wrong; they went about the flat quietly, watching their parents with anxious eyes.

How long, Julia wondered, before she was forgiven? Or would that never happen? Had she and Frank reached the end of the road? She finished putting away the food and fetched the ironing board, so wrapped up in her own worries that she forgot about her promise to listen out for Lena Fulton.

Lena spread the completed quilt over the bed and smoothed it out carefully, the tips of her fingers brushing over the neatly stitched patches. It was a perfect fit, and a complete history of her life. Her childhood, the happiest time, took up a small space in the middle, with pieces from a party frock, the blouse she wore on an outing with her parents and her brother, a favourite scarf, and her mother's favourite dress. Then the other patches, radiating outwards and taking up most of the quilt, marking George's courtship, their engagement and wedding and married life.

She gave a sigh of contentment, and straightened, both hands pressing into the small of her back to ease her stiff-ness. She was very tired, and now it was time to rest.

Back in the kitchen, she tidied up quickly and took one

last glance out of the window. Dennis Megson was working in the vegetable garden, and the McCosh girl was helping him. Lena smiled, pleased to see that he had found someone to replace her. It put her mind at rest.

She took off her apron and folded it neatly before hanging it over the back of a kitchen chair, then went to the hall cupboard, where George had stored all his brushes and paints.

Taking the bottle of Ligroin, the stuff that Dennis had wanted to put safely into the garden shed, she returned to the bedroom. He had fastened the stopper so tightly after using the Ligroin several weeks earlier to clean his hands that for a few panic-stricken moments Lena though that she was not going to be able to loosen it. But she succeeded, with some difficulty, and proceeded to scatter its contents evenly over the quilt.

When the bottle was empty she returned to the kitchen to fetch the big box of matches she always kept beside the stove. And finally, when she was sure that nothing had been forgotten, she took off her slippers and climbed into bed, fully clothed, to settle herself comfortably below her lovely new quilt. The matchbox was still clutched in one hand . . . the hand that bore George Fulton's wedding ring.

She gave a deep, contented sigh. The quilt had taken a lot of work, but it was done now, and she could finally allow herself a good long rest. She was ready for a rest, Lena thought as she took a match from the box. She was wearying for peace and quiet, and an end to worry.

She nestled her head on the pillow, untroubled by the reek of Ligroin, and struck the match.

It was like talking to a brick wall, Chloe thought, glancing over at Dennis, who had replied to everything she said with a grunt, or a brief 'yes' or 'no'. She took a deep breath and tried again.

'You're digging there as if you're trying to get to China.'

'Eh?' He stopped and straightened his back for a moment. 'Australia, isn't it?'

'What is?'

'Where you'd get to if you dug all the way from here.'

'Mebbe it is. I was never much good at geography at school.'

'Nor me.'

At least he was talking now. Emboldened, she said, 'It's nice, being grown up and out of school, isn't it?'

'It's all right. You missed a dandelion over there.' He returned to his work, and Chloe, feeling a little more cheerful, launched a vicious attack on the dandelion.

Ellen Borland yawned and settled herself more comfortably in her chair. She and Donnie and Jessie had had a nice midday dinner, after which the old woman had gone back to her own flat for a lie-down while Ellen started work on a pile of darning.

By the time she had finished a pair of Donnie's socks and started on a second pair, the soothing rhythm of her husband's snores had begun to have an affect on her. Her eyelids drooped, opened, began to droop again, and the sock she had been darning gently drifted down to her lap. Her jaw sagged open and a slight snore escaped . . . and then she frowned and stirred, opening her eyes and sniffing the air. There seemed to be something . . . but mebbe it was just her imagination. The pleasant aroma of the chops and onions they had recently eaten still hung around the kitchen. That must be what she smelled, she thought, then sniffed again.

'Donnie?' When her only answer was another snore, she raised her voice. 'Donnie!'

He jerked suddenly in his chair. 'Eh? Wha . . . ?'

'D'you smell somethin'?'

'God, Ellen,' he mumbled. 'Ye're no' goin' tae start fussin' about me takin' my slippers off, are ye? A man's entitled tae wear his stockin' soles in his own house.'

'It's not yer feet I'm talkin' about! It's . . .' She heaved herself to her feet. 'Can you smell smoke?'

'How can there be smoke when there's no fire in the grate?' he asked, settling back into his chair and closing his eyes. Throwing a half-exasperated, half-affectionate glance at him, she got up and went into the hall, sniffing as she went. There was definitely a trace of something in the air, she thought. Then she opened the door of the bedroom she shared with Donnie, and her face went blank with shock as she realised that she could scarcely see across the room for smoke.

'Donnie!' She slammed the door and raced back into the kitchen. 'Get up, man!' she yelled, shaking his shoulder. 'There's a fire somewhere. We have tae get out of here!'

'Eh? He sniffed the air. 'By God, ye're right,' he said, then leapt to his feet, showing surprising agility in a man who had not moved at more than a snail's pace for years.

'Get Jessie!' his wife ordered, snatching the canary's cage from its stand. 'Bang on her door and tell her tae . . .' Then she screeched as one of Donnie's stockinged feet skidded on the polished linoleum surround, and he smacked into the doorframe and then collapsed backwards on to the floor. 'Donnie! Oh my God! Get up, Donnie.'

'I cannae!' He writhed at her feet, clutching an ankle. 'I've busted my leg. Ye'll have tae get help!'

'There's no time for that, we have tae fetch Jessie and get her downstairs.' She grabbed his arm, trying to pull him to his feet, and he howled in pain.

'It's no use, I cannae get up.'

For a few moments Ellen ran about like a squirrel in a trap, going from Donnie to the door, then back to Donnie, the birdcage swinging wildly from her hand, and its occupant hanging on to its perch for dear life. Then she ran to the window, from where she had earlier seen Ralph's interfering brother working in the backcourt. To her relief, he was still there, and the McCosh lassie with him.

Ellen tried to open the window for the first time in years, but it refused to budge, even when she used her strength, honed by years of manual labour.

The smell of smoke was stronger now; whimpering in panic, she banged on the windowpane, shouting, and when the young people below worked on, oblivious, she slammed the birdcage on her polished table, heedless for once of the danger of scratches, and then snatched up one of the upright chairs by the table and pushed it, legs foremost, at the glass.

It finally shattered, but the anti-blast tape held it in place, and she had to swipe at it several times with the chair legs before she managed to create a space. She leaned across the sink, heedless of the danger from jagged glass, and bellowed at the top of her voice, 'Fire, there's a fire and my man's hurt! Ye've got tae come and help him!'

'It's Mrs Borland, she's broken her kitchen window.' Chloe pointed up at the woman, who was gesticulating frantically. 'There's something wro . . .' Then as the spade fell from Dennis's hands and he sprinted for the back close, she followed hard on his heels.

She smelled smoke as she chased up the stairs after him, and when she gained the first floor she could see pale grey tendrils twisting lazily in the air.

Dennis was hammering on Mrs Fulton's door, screaming her name.

'It's coming from in there,' he said frantically as she reached him. He pointed at the ground, and she saw the smoke oozing out from below the door. 'And I don't know if she's in the flat!' He thudded his fist against the door. 'Lena! For God's sake, Lena, if you're in there, open the door!'

'Help me!' Mrs Borland roared over the stair railings. 'My man's hurt and I have tae get Jessie out.'

'What's going on?' Julia asked from her own doorway,

and then began to cough as the smoke caught at the back of her throat.

'There's a fire. Go down to Mr Binnie's shop and tell him to telephone for the Fire Brigade, then stay out in the street,' Dennis ordered. 'Go with her, Chloe.'

'I'd better help Mrs Borland, and I can knock on the other doors and warn folk.' She was already scrambling up the next flight of stairs.

'No! Chloe, come back!' Julia shouted, while at the same time Dennis bellowed, 'Damn it, lassie, get out of here when you're told!'

'You can't do it all on your own,' she shouted back at him. 'I'll be out in a minute, Mum. You do as Dennis says.'

Dennis gave up on her. 'Someone's got to fetch the Fire Brigade,' he told Julia. 'Go on now. I'll see that Chloe's safe.' Then he turned away from Lena's door and began to follow Chloe.

As soon as he reached the next landing Ellen Borland grabbed him. 'Thank God ye're here, son! It's my man, he's fallen. He's on the kitchen floor and I cannae get him ontae his feet. Ye have tae get him out of there!'

Dennis looked after Chloe, already halfway up the next flight and out of his reach. 'Where's Mrs Bell?'

'In her own place.' The woman's face was distorted by fear.

'Get yourself and her downstairs and outside as fast as you can!'

'Donnie ... !'

'Leave him tae me, and just do as you're told!' he shouted at her, and then plunged in through the open door of the Borlands' flat.

Feeling his way through the smoky hall, he touched each of the doors as he passed. None was hot to the touch, which indicated that although the flat was filling rapidly with smoke, the seat of the fire was elsewhere, He knew already that it was located in the flat directly below ... Lena's flat.

In the kitchen, he almost fell over Donnie Borland, who immediately clutched at his legs.

'It's my ankle, son, I think it's broke,' he wheezed as Dennis tried to untangle himself.

'It's all right, Mr Borland, I'll get you out, but you'll have to get on to your feet.' Using the techniques learned at the fire station, Dennis almost got the man upright, before Donnie let out a scream and slumped down again, almost pulling his rescuer down with him.

'Ye're hurtin' me!'

'You'll get more than hurt if ye don't get off that floor and out of here!' They were both coughing now, and their eyes were streaming. 'Here . . .' Dennis grabbed at a kitchen chair and swung it away from the table. 'Try to get on to this.'

Donnie Borland was large, well-fed and almost twice Dennis's weight, but finally Dennis succeeded in getting him on to the chair. 'Now . . . stand up on the foot that's not hurt, and put your arm about my shoulders.' Then when Donnie, whimpering with pain and fear, managed to do as he was told, 'That's grand, well done. Now we're goin' to get out of here. Just keep thinking of moving forward, and let me take most of your weight.'

As the two of them inched along the hall, smoke curled up through the floorboards to twine itself about their ankles like a horde of friendly cats. Dennis's stomach lurched as he remembered the tins of paint and bottles of thinners, relics of George Fulton's civilian work, crammed into the cupboard of the hall in Lena's flat . . . tins and bottles he had meant to store safely in the garden shed, and had forgotten. Please God, he prayed behind clenched teeth as he and Donnie Borland lurched towards the open door, let Lena be at the shops, or safe with her aunt in Millport!

From outside the open door, he could hear voices calling out and feet pattering down the stairs as the tenement evacuated. Just as he and Donnie gained the landing, Ellen

Borland, the canary cage still clutched in one hand, came out of the door opposite, with her free arm about Jessie Bell. The old woman, wrapped in a quilt, was blinking and confused, still half asleep.

'My insurance books,' she said suddenly, turning to go back into her flat, and then, 'my teef, Ellen, I cannae go anywhere without puttin' my good teef in.'

'We'll get them later, Jessie. Best get down to the street just now, just till the smoke's gone, eh?' Ellen coaxed, and then gave a piercing scream as two figures appeared through the smoke. 'Donnie, ye're safe!'

'My leg . . . I'll never be able tae manage the stairs . . .'

'Dammit man, stop moanin' about your leg and get moving!' Dennis snapped.

'Don't you speak tae my Donnie like that!'

'I'll speak tae him any way I like, and tae you too.'

'Leave me here,' Donnie wailed. 'I've had my life!'

'No! If he stays, I stay with him. Jessie . . .' Ellen tried to push the birdcage into the old woman's hand. 'Take wee Tommy down the stairs.'

'Nobody's staying!' Dennis's voice was beginning to rasp painfully. 'We're all going down, even if I have tae throw you. Now get on with it, woman, and we'll follow.'

'Dennis?' Chloe called from halfway up the flight below. 'D'you need help?'

'Take Mrs Borland and Mrs Bell down. My mother and the girls and . . . ?'

'They're all down in the street . . .' She clutched at the banister as a fit of coughing bent her double, and then continued when it was over, 'and the fire engine's been sent for.' Then she struggled up the rest of the stairs to take Mrs Bell's free arm.

'Lena?'

'I don't know. Nobody knows where she is. Are you all right?'

'We're fine, we'll be right behind you.'

As the three women descended the stairs, linked together and shuffling sideways like crabs, Dennis followed with Donnie, who was now coughing uncontrollably as the smoke penetrated his lungs. They had just gained the next landing when three men sped up towards them. One stopped to help the women while the other two squeezed past and continued up.

'Anyone else in the building?' one of them shouted.

'Just the one woman, mebbe, but I don't know for sure if she's there. Here, take him.' Dennis relinquished his heavy burden and as the men began to ease Donnie Borland down the final flight of stairs he threw himself across the landing towards Lena's door. The paintwork was blistering now and the panels, when he beat at them with his fists, were burning hot. Then they suddenly quivered beneath his hands, and to his horror, he heard a series of explosions within the flat as the fire found George Fulton's tins and bottles.

'Lena!' Her name tore itself from his throat over and over again. He took a few steps back and ran at the door, but it was solid enough to resist his shoulder. He tried again and again, even though he knew that, if she really was inside, it was almost certainly too late.

He was still trying to force the door in, still screaming her name, when the first fireman came racing up the stairs.

30

The McCosh and Megson children had been playing in the street when the alarm was first raised, and now the smaller children were huddled close to their mothers. Even Ralph, white and shaken and looking more like the child he still was, stayed close to Nan.

'Look, Mammy!' Amy pointed up at one of the windows. Following her gaze, the two women saw flames dancing behind the taped glass. Smoke was already curling out of the cracks.

'It's Mrs Fulton's flat,' Nan said; and then, swiftly, 'She's not in it, is she?'

'I don't know. I hope not.' Even though it was a mild day, Julia found herself shivering. She drew the boys closer.

'Mrs Goudie's at work, I saw her going out,' Ralph offered.

'Dennis . . . where's my Dennis? He was in the back-court . . .'

'The last I saw of him he was on his way up to help the Borlands,' Julia said. 'Chloe was with him. She said she'd knock on all the doors . . .'

'It was Chloe that told us what was happening,' Nan said.

'Where is she?' Julia asked in sudden panic. 'Did she come out with you?'

'She started down the stairs after us, but I don't see her now.'

'Chloe . . . ?' Julia looked wildly around at the people now pressing in all sides, but could see no sign of her daughter. She should have stayed with Chloe, should have insisted on dragging her outside instead of letting her run off to warn the rest of the tenants. How could she ever face Frank again if anything happened to Chloe?

'I want my daddy.' Leslie's voice quivered, and he looked up at his mother, tears glittering in his eyes. 'Where's my daddy?'

'He'll be here soon, pet.' Her own voice shook, while her eyes kept flickering from face to face in search of Chloe.

'Come on intae my place,' a neighbour from across the street offered. 'There's nothin' you can dae here, and the brigade'll arrive any minute now.'

'My daughter . . . I have to make sure my daughter's safe.'

'She will be,' Nan told her firmly. 'Dennis won't let any harm come to her. Or to any of them if he can . . . look!'

She pointed across to the street to where Chloe was emerging from the close, together with Ellen Borland and Jessie Bell. The three of them were coughing and choking.

'Chloe!' Julia started to cross the street and then drew back as the fire engine, bell clanging, screeched to a halt outside the close. As the firemen began to disappear into the building, Frank McCosh shouldered his way through the crowd and made straight for his daughter.

'Chloe, are you all right?'

'Oh, Daddy,' the girl choked, while Ellen, anxious about her husband, argued with a man who was trying to lead her away from the close. 'Daddy, I'm so glad to see you!'

'Here . . .' Frank put one arm about her and the other about Jessie Bell, leading them across the street to where his wife and sons waited.

'You're safe now, Mrs Bell,' Nan soothed the old woman. 'It's all over.'

'I've no' got my good teef wi' me,' Jessie whimpered.

'Never mind that, pet, at least you've still got your gums,' said the woman who had offered hospitality earlier. 'Come and have a sit down. All of ye,' she added over her shoulder as she swept Jessie and the Megsons into her close.

'On ye go, pet.' Frank gave Chloe a gentle push. 'And take the boys with you.'

She hung back, her reddened eyes searching the front of the tenement. 'Dennis is still in there . . .'

'The firemen'll see that he's safe,' he said, and she went, with one last anxious look at the building opposite. Just then, two men came out of the close, half carrying Donnie Borland. Ellen pushed the birdcage at one of the men, and gathered her husband into her arms.

. 'Our home, Frank . . .' Julia wailed, almost at the end of her tether. 'What are we going to do if it's burned down? Where are we going to go?'

'It'll be all right, pet.' He put an arm about her shoulders and began to lead her into the nearby close. 'Everything's all right now. I'm here.'

Lena Fulton's flat had been more or less destroyed by fire, and the flooring in the Borland's flat, immediately above Lena's, had been badly damaged, and would have to be replaced. Mrs Clark's sweetie shop on the ground floor had suffered some ceiling damage, but the other flats were still habitable, though reeking of smoke.

Ellen and Donnie Borland went to stay with their daughter Chrissie, taking Jessie Bell with them. A few days after the fire, the entire street watched open-mouthed as an apparently endless procession of Borland relatives trooped in and out of the building, carrying away furniture, ornaments, and carpeting.

'Stuff that looked more like what ye'd have found in a palace instead of a tenement flat,' the women who had watched from windows and close entrances gossiped. 'That Ellen Borland must have been ontae a good thing with her money lendin' and all the other bits and pieces she was intae.'

Nobody knew if the Borlands or old Mrs Bell would ever be back. There were those, Dennis Megson among them, who had reason to hope that they would settle elsewhere.

George Fulton, who had been due to come home on furlough in any case, was given compassionate leave and arrived in time for his wife's funeral.

'I'm told that you tried tae get my wife out,' he said to Dennis who, along with his mother, Chloe, Julia and Frank, had attended. 'Thank you for that.' He held out his big hand, and after a moment's hesitation, Dennis shook it.

'I'm grateful tae ye all for comin',' George told the others in the little group, then turned on his heel and rejoined his family. Chloe, who missed nothing where Dennis was concerned, saw the muscles stand out along the line of his jaw, and the hand that had clasped George Fulton's being scrubbed along his jacket as he followed his mother from the cemetery.

She had arranged to go out with Marion that evening. Making some excuse, she went home early, slipping through the close and out the back to tap on the shed door.

'Dennis?' she said softly against the rough slats of wood. 'Are you in there? It's me, Chloe.'

'What d'you want?' His voice was gruff and unwelcoming.

'I have to talk to you.'

'Not now!'

'Yes, now. I'm coming in,' she said.

He was sitting on an upturned crate, his face in shadow, and as she went in, he scrubbed his hand over it from forehead to mouth. 'Well?'

'Are you all right?'

'Why wouldn't I be?' He fumbled in his pocket for his cigarettes, then after taking one he hesitated before holding the packet out to her. 'Want one?'

Chloe had tried smoking at school, and then with Marion, but had never cared for it. Now, she nodded. 'Yes please.'

As he lit her cigarette and then his own, the flare of the match showed that his eyes were reddened.

'So . . . say what you have to say and then leave me in peace.'

'I'm . . .' she began, and then choked on the tobacco smoke. It was just like being in the fire again, with her lungs stinging and tears gushing into her eyes. A few minutes passed before she was able to speak. 'I'm sorry about what I said that time we were working in the garden.'

'What time?'

'When I said that you and Mrs Fulton were getting to be too friendly. It was none of my business and I should never have said it and I'm very sorry,' she said in a rush of words, then waited nervously for his reaction.

For a long time he said nothing, and then, just as Chloe was beginning to wonder if she should go, and leave him on his own, he said, 'Lena . . . she was special.'

He dropped his cigarette on the floor, grinding it out under his boot as he went on, his voice rising, 'I know that she didnae care for me as much as I cared about her, but that brute of a man didnae deserve her. It fair sickened me today, havin' tae shake his hand and hear him thankin' me for trying to save her. What the hell's the sense in thankin' anyone for that? The point is that I didnae manage it!'

'Nob'dy could have got her out alive, son,' Tom MacIntosh had told him. 'I probably shouldnae be tellin' ye this, but for some reason of her own the woman must have soaked the beddin' with somethin' inflammable, then set it alight.'

'She'd not do a thing like that!'

'We can never know what's goin' through other folks' heads, Dennis. Whatever caused that lassie's death, it was her decision and she'd made no effort tae escape. The shock of what was happenin' would have stopped her from feelin' any pain, though, and it would've been over quick. Believe me, son, I know what I'm talkin' about.'

'Dennis . . .' Chloe's voice brought him back to the present, and to the small shed. She reached over and put her hand on his, tentatively, half expecting him to fling it off. Instead, he burst into tears.

Chloe sat motionless, paralysed with shock and not knowing what to do for the best, then after a moment, Dennis's hand turned beneath hers, his fingers twisting about hers and clinging so tightly that it hurt.

The deep, wrenching sobs were finally beginning to quieten when a sudden sharp pain in her free hand made her jump. At first she thought that she had been bitten by a rat, and then she realised that the forgotten cigarette had smouldered down until the lit end was against the delicate skin on the inside of her index finger.

'Dennis?' she said cautiously through gritted teeth. 'Dennis, my cigarette's burning my fingers . . .'

'What? For goodness' sake!' He snatched at her hand, stamping out the cigarette end when it fell on to the floor and then blowing on the scorched skin. 'Are you daft? You should have put it out if you werenae going to smoke it!'

'I forgot I had it!' Tears of pain and humiliation made her voice shake.

'Go home and run your hand under the cold tap,' he ordered, his own tears gone, though his voice sounded thick. 'And tell your mother to—'

'I'm not going to tell my mother anything! She'll give me what for if she thinks I've been smoking.'

'You'll have to pretend that you're washing your hands, then. Rub soap over the burns and leave it on. Bicarbonate of soda's good too, and if it blisters, you'll need to prick them with a needle and then use more bicarbonate. And put a clean cloth round them before you go to bed.' The words whirled round her head as he bundled her to the door. 'Go on now,' he ordered, and she scurried through the backcourt, nursing her stinging fingers in her other hand.

'D'you want me to find somewhere else for you to live?' Fergus Goudie asked his wife as they walked along Glen Street. He was on a four-day leave, and she had managed to get two whole days off work. Earlier in the day they had survived a visit from Cecelia's father and his new wife, and after seeing the older couple off on the Glasgow train they had gone to see a film.

'Why should I want to move away from Glen Street?'

'After all that's happened ... the fire, and that poor woman being killed ... I thought you might want to go back to Glasgow, now that you've made it up with your father.'

'I'd not dream of it. I like my neighbours and I like my job.' She twined her fingers through his. 'This is home and I'm staying, at least until this war's over and we can look for that nice wee house with the garden that you keep talking about.'

They turned in at the close, meeting up with Chloe McCosh, who was hurrying in from the back of the building.

'Hello,' Cecelia called, and then, as Chloe swung round guiltily, 'What's happened to your hand?'

'It's just a wee burn ... a cigarette burn.'

'I didn't know you smoked.'

'I don't,' Chloe confessed. 'That's why I got the burn. I was just trying it out.'

'We all do that. Let me see ...' Fergus took the damaged hand in his and peered at the fingers in the dim stair light. 'It looks sore.'

'I was just going to put some soap on it. I don't want my mother and father to find out. My dad'll say that I'm too young to smoke.'

'Come to our flat,' Cecelia said at once. 'Then you can get it seen to without them knowing. At least it hasn't blistered,' she said five minutes later, inspecting the burn under the kitchen light. 'Hold it under the tap for a wee while. Soap, did you say?'

'Or bicarbonate of soda.'

'You seem to know quite a lot about treating burns,' Fergus remarked, and Chloe blushed.

'We got it at school once . . . first aid.'

'Fergus, put the kettle on, will you? I think there's enough water in the kettle. There's some bread in the bin that would be better for toasting, too. Now then . . . soap, and bicarbonate of soda . . .'

'I don't know when I'll ever get the stink of smoke out of the flat, or out of our clothes,' Julia said from where she stood at the ironing board.

'At least we've still got solid walls, and a roof over our heads. There's a lot of folk much worse off than us,' Frank said, and then, putting the paper aside, 'Julia, I've been thinkin', there's nothin' tae stop us getting' wed now.'

The iron slowed and stopped, then she set it aside. 'There's nothing to stop us just going on as we have been all these years, either.'

'Does that mean that you don't want tae marry me?'

'No, I'm saying that you don't have to feel obliged to make an honest woman of me. I'm content to go on as I am.'

'Well, I'm not. I'm a right fool, Julia, gettin' so jealous of Thomas Gordon even though I was the one you chose over him. And I'd like us tae resolve the matter once and for all. So . . . will ye marry me?'

She paused in the middle of ironing the collar of Duncan's shirt. 'You know I will, you daft man.'

'I'll see to the arrangements, then. Just a quiet affair, so's nob'dy knows about it. We'll need witnesses . . . d'you think your friend Mirren Hepburn would do that for us?'

'I'm sure she will. And mebbe her man'll be willing to stand as a witness too.'

Frank grinned. 'I never thought I'd have a former Paisley Bailie as a witness at my weddin',' he said, and then buried himself in his paper as the landing door opened and shut.

'You're late,' Julia said as her daughter came into the kitchen.

'I met the Goudies on my way in and they asked me into their flat for some supper.' Chloe had taken off her coat; she still carried it over one arm, draped so that it covered her entire hand. 'So I'm not hungry now. I think I'll just get to my bed.'

Workmen moved in to repair the fire-damaged flats and the ground-floor shop. The building rang to the sound of hammering and sawing, the stairs were liberally sprinkled with sawdust, and the smoky smell began to give way to the more pleasing aroma of fresh timber and paint.

Dennis kept his eyes averted each time he went past the flat that had been Lena's. Despite what Tom had told him, he still felt that he could, and should, have saved her.

The sight of George Fulton at the funeral, staring down without any apparent emotion at the coffin that held his wife's remains, had almost made him sick. He had even made up his mind to forget about the Fire Brigade and enlist so that he could get as far away from Paisley as possible. He had gone as far as visiting a recruitment centre, but at the last minute he had turned away and caught the next bus home, realising that he would be punishing his mother rather than himself. So he chose the harder path, and stayed where he was, in the building where Lena had died.

Charlie had changed; Chloe could tell as soon as she saw him on his first leave. He was more confident than before, and full of talk about the people he had met, the rigorous training he had been through, and life in the big RAF camp.

To his delight, he had been selected to take a training course for aircrew in London.

'You're enjoying yourself,' his father accused, and Charlie grinned at him.

'Tae tell the truth, I am.'

'And long may that last, since you're enlisted and it's better to enjoy it than hate it,' Mirren put in swiftly, shooting her husband a warning look as he opened his mouth. He closed it again, shrugged, and said, 'Well, everyone tae their own choice, I suppose.'

'Exactly,' Mirren said crisply. 'So read your paper, Joe.'

Charlie had had his photograph taken while he was away, and brought several copies home . . . two to be sent to his relatives in America, one for his mother, and one for Chloe. 'Will you put it beside your bed?' he asked hopefully as she stared down at his likeness. He looked handsome in his uniform, the cap set at a jaunty angle on his dark head.

'Of course I will, and I'll give it a big kiss every night.'

'Now you're just being sarcastic.'

'Well, mebbe about the kiss,' she admitted. 'But I'll keep it on the cupboard by my bed.'

'I keep yours on my locker.' He had taken a framed snapshot of her with him – a photograph that Marion's boyfriend Robert had taken with his box Brownie camera in the Fountain Gardens, with the main fountain as a background. In the picture she was laughing as she put a hand up to push back a strand of hair that had blown across her face, and she was wearing her favourite dress, v-necked and in pale blue cotton sprigged with pink and white flowers.

'What . . . on your locker for everyone to see?'

'We all have pictures on our lockers,' he said defensively. 'The other lads think you're pretty.'

'Do they?' Despite herself, she was flattered.

Charlie had changed in another way; as Chloe had anticipated, the new lifestyle was broadening his horizons, and
although they enjoyed the time they spent together during
his leave, it seemed clear to her that they really had become
just friends.

31

———————————•———————————

The first booking in a while, the chance to play at a dance in the Co-operative Halls, came along in October, and the band gathered in the McCosh's front room for a practice.

It was a pleasant October evening, and neighbours gathered in the street, the close and on the stairs to listen as Frank ran his small group through its paces. Despite the fact that they had not played for a while, everything fell into place and there was scarcely any need to stop and replay sections time and time again.

Frank and Julia had chosen all the favourites . . . 'Talk of the Town', 'String of Pearls', 'Stardust', 'Music Maestro, Please', 'Chattanooga Choo Choo', 'Who?', and the rehearsal ended with a trumpet solo rendition of 'I've Got the World on a String'.

Chloe sat in her usual corner, knees drawn up to her chin and arms wrapped about them, her eyes, as usual, on Dennis as he stepped forward on her father's nod to take a solo. Raising the trumpet's mouthpiece to his lips, he breathed into it, coaxing the notes into life, using sound to create pictures.

Chloe was careful to keep her face still and her mouth soft and relaxed, but inside her head she was singing the words, her voice as true and beautiful as Vera Lynn's.

She wondered if trumpet players were better kissers than most. As yet, she had not been able to find out, but she would, in time. She had known that since the night she

had burned her fingers in the old shed, the night Dennis
had cried. On her way to the back close afterwards, her
hand stinging as though it had landed in a bed of nettles,
she had suddenly remembered her mother saying, 'It's not
really in your body or your head or even your heart. It's
something that happens, and when it does happen, you'll
know.'

It had happened that night, in the shed, and she knew it.
Dennis would know it too, one day. Not yet; perhaps not
for a long time, but suddenly he would know, the way she
had. And when he did, she would be waiting.

She sang on behind still lips, each note in perfect harmony
with Dennis's playing.

'Our turn'll come, if the war keeps going,' Marion prattled
on. 'You could go into the Woman's Auxiliary Air Force,
then you might meet up with Charlie somewhere. You never
know. I'm going into the ATS myself, because of Robert
being in the army.'

'I might be a land girl.'

'Why?'

'So that I can learn about gardening.'

'They don't garden on farms, they work in fields and
drive tractors and they have to tramp about in horrible
smelly mud in all weathers.'

'Some of them do horticulture. I'd like to try that,'
Chloe said. She had been reading about the Land Army.
'Anyway, the war'll probably be over by the time we're
old enough. D'you remember how that new dance goes?
The one that couple danced last night at the Templar
Halls?'

'Ballin' the Jack? It's a daft name!'

'But it's a good dance.' Chloe jumped up and began to
dance in the paved section before the fountain, humming
the tune and waving her arms, bouncing and dipping,
swaying and side-stepping while Rabbie Burns, leaning on

his stone ploughshare, watched with solemn approval from atop his plinth.

'You look daft,' Marion criticised from where she sat on the bench.

'That's because I'm on my own. Come on, Marion.'

'Why should I look daft too?'

'Och, come on!' Chloe held out a hand and Marion glanced nervously around.

'Folk'll see us.'

'There's scarcely a soul about, and anyway, who cares? There's no law against dancin', is there? C'mon!' Chloe wiggled her fingers impatiently and then, as Marion hesitated, she darted forward to haul her friend off the bench. 'We'll start off facing each other and holding both hands, all right? Now, you just need to do what the song says – stand with your two knees together.' She started to sing.

They both had a good sense of rhythm and a good ear for music, and it was not long before Marion relaxed, and they began to get into the dance. Throwing caution to the winds, they whirled around the fountain, singing to the four sea lions as well as to Rabbie. A few children gathered to jeer, and Chloe stuck her tongue out at them and kept on dancing, snatching at Marion's hand when she would have stopped, and dragging her back into the dance.

Two footsore housewives, wearied from queuing and taking a short cut through the gardens with their message bags full of small, hard-gained parcels, stared as they went by.

'Daft lassies,' said one.

'Ach, it's only a bit of fun,' said the other, wistfully. 'Leave them be, they'll grow up soon enough.'

They trudged on through the park, oblivious to the beauty of the trees and the flowers, absorbed instead with talk about the coming winter and the miseries of the recently imposed coal rationing, while Chloe and Marion danced on, bouncing, dipping, swaying and twirling and side-stepping.

The sun was shining and they were still young, and for the moment, at least, life was still sweet and brimming over with promise.

Bibliography

Images of Fire – 150 Years of Fire Fighting by Neil Wallington, published by David and Charles, London, 1989

What Did You Do In The War, Mummy? – Women in World War Two by Mavis Nicholson, published by Chatto & Windus, London, 1995.

McAdam's Women

1

Although she had been watching the doorway intently
for the past five minutes, Isla felt a sense of shock, like
a fist slamming into her breastbone, when the girl she
had been expecting arrived. They had never set eyes on
each other before, but she would have known immediately who the newcomer was, even if they had only
glanced at each other in a crowded street in passing.

From beneath a black cloche hat clear blue eyes
swept the busy tearoom, halting as they reached the
table in the corner, and Isla's tentative, half-raised hand.

They flared, just as Kenneth's did whenever he was
astonished. Black-gloved fingers reached out to grasp the
door-frame for a moment, and then, wiping the shock
from her face with a deliberate effort, the girl came
across the room, skirting tables, side-stepping waitresses.

Isla had intended to rise to meet her, but instead she
stayed where she was, pinned to the small chair by this
reminder of her recent loss. The paralysing agony had
hit her several times since Kenneth's death; just as she
thought that she had accepted it and come to terms with
it, sudden realisation and a wave of desolation swept
anew through her.

Now her first sight of Kenneth's daughter – his older daughter – had revived it.

The girl had his clear, steady, somewhat pale blue eyes, though in her case they were fringed with gold, instead of Kenneth's more stubby lashes. She had his strongly marked brows, his mouth – without, of course, the red-gold moustache above it – his straight neat nose. Beneath the black velvet hat she wore, Isla glimpsed hair the vibrant glowing bronze of autumn leaves. The colour Kenneth's had been. Her face was oval, her chin neatly rounded where his had been square. Slim and straight, dressed in a high-necked black knitted suit, black stockings, black shoes, she even had Kenneth's walk, lithe and quick and easy, though constricted at that moment by the tables in the room.

Isla's throat tightened, and for a moment tears prickled behind her eyes. She fought them back, telling herself sternly that she was not going to let herself weep in this public place, in front of this young woman who looked so familiar to her, yet was a stranger.

Swallowing hard, she regained her own self-control as the girl arrived beside her table, suddenly hesitant and unsure. 'You can't be—' she began, then stopped, folding her mouth round the next two words as though to hold them back.

Isla got to her feet. 'I'm Isla Mc—' She hesitated, then said clearly, 'Isla McAdam.'

The girl's eyes flared again, this time with arrogant anger, and she ignored the hand that was held out to her. 'You've got no right to that name!'

'Please believe me when I say that I thought I had,'

Isla said steadily, letting her hand fall back to her side. 'And you're Ainslie.'

'But you're so young!'

'I'm twenty-six.' Twenty-six for the past week. Her birthday had come one short week after hearing of Kenneth's death.

'My God!' There was anger in Ainslie's voice. 'You're only five years older than I am – and he was forty-six!' She swayed slightly, groped for the back of a chair, found it, and sank into it.

'I knew Kenneth's age, but I never felt that it mattered.' Isla took her own seat again, still fighting to keep her voice level. She had made up her mind that she wasn't going to be afraid of this girl, but despite herself, the fear was there. Without knowing it, she had been part of a terrible wrong committed against Ainslie McAdam and her mother and brother.

Colour rose to Ainslie's cheeks and contempt honed her voice. 'How could he do this to – to us?'

It was numbing to look into eyes so like Kenneth's, yet cold in a way his had never been. Under his daughter's antagonistic stare Isla might well have given way to her grief and her terror of the unknown future, but it was the contemptuous note in the girl's voice that saved her from possible weakness. She wasn't to blame for what had happened, she had nothing to be ashamed of. She would not allow this young woman to make her feel like a criminal.

'Ainslie – Miss McAdam, it was you who suggested this meeting. If you've changed your mind, you're free to go, though I've ordered tea for us both.'

It arrived just at that moment, brought to them by a

middle-aged woman so plump that her small white frilled apron looked like a postage stamp stuck on to her black dress. She deftly transferred the cups and saucers and the nickel-plated teapot and sugar bowl and milk jug to the spotless white table-cloth, then scurried to a huge sideboard and brought back a tiered plate-stand filled with plates of cakes and biscuits. Her eyebrows rose and she looked hurt when Ainslie McAdam impatiently flapped a hand at her and said, 'Take these away!'

'Madam? The cakes've just come up fresh from the bakery below . . .'

Isla forced the corners of her lips into a placating smile. 'They look delicious, but I don't think we're in the mood for them today.'

The woman's eyes swept from one to the other, taking in Ainslie's black suit and the black armband on the sleeve of Isla's grey woollen coat. Her own face fell into solemn lines.

'Of course, madam,' she murmured, and went off, leaving them alone and silent in a roomful of chattering, brightly dressed women.

Ainslie McAdam watched, her brows drawn together in a straight line above brooding eyes, as Isla drew off her gloves and began to pour tea. She shook her head when Isla lifted the milk jug, and pulled her own gloves off, lifting a hand to flick the flowing end of the black silk scarf that served as a hatband back from her shoulder.

Carefully, aware of the unblinking gaze opposite, Isla poured her own tea, added milk and more sugar than she would normally have taken, and stirred the liquid. The hot sweet tea helped to steady her nerves.

'This is very difficult for us both,' she said as she returned the cup to its saucer.

'I asked you to meet me here because I won't have you calling on my mother. She's never been strong, and now she's ill with worry and shame over this – this business. I'll not have her upset any further!'

'I've no intention of forcing myself on your mother, or on any other member of your family.'

Ainslie's eyes said that she didn't believe that. 'Why would you come here to Paisley if you weren't out to make trouble for us?'

'I came at my—' Isla stopped herself just in time from saying, 'my husband's,' and changed it to, 'your father's lawyer's invitation. There are matters we have to discuss.'

'You – talk to his lawyer?' Ainslie's voice rose, and one or two people at neighbouring tables turned to look at the two sombrely dressed young women. She noticed the curious glances, and lowered her tone. 'But there's nothing to talk about. You weren't his wife!'

The words stung against Isla's cheeks like small stones, raising spots of colour. 'I thought I was.'

'You thought wrong!'

'I know that now. And I didn't ask Mr Forbes for this meeting – as I said, I'm in Paisley at his invitation.'

'I don't see why,' Ainslie McAdam said with open hostility.

'Nor do I, until I see him.'

Ainslie's right hand, having dealt with the troublesome hat-ribbon, was rubbing nervously at the third finger of her left hand. Her gaze dipped to the gold band on Isla's wedding finger, and her mouth tightened.

'Mr Forbes said' – she hesitated, then went on as though the words were wrenched out of her throat, 'he told me that there were – children.'

'We – I have a four-year-old daughter and a baby son.'

The girl's eyes darkened. She drew in her breath sharply, then said in a burst of anguished rage, 'I wish he knew how much misery he's caused with his selfishness! I wish I could tell him! He's ruined everything for me – for us!'

Tears sparkled among her lashes, diamonds in a mesh of gold, and Isla automatically stretched a comforting hand across the table towards her. Ainslie jerked back, rising to her feet with an awkward motion that set the china on the table jangling and the tea slopping in the cups.

'Don't touch me!'

'My dear—'

'Keep away from my mother! Keep out of Paisley!' Ainslie McAdam blurted the words, her face crumpling, then almost ran out of the room, heedless of the faces that turned to watch her go then swung back to where Isla sat, alone, at the table.

She reached for her cup and discovered that she was trembling so much that she had to use both hands to lift it from the saucer. Head bowed, she sipped at the tea again, but now its warmth held no comfort for her. The waitress appeared as she put the cup down, her face creased with concern.

'Is something wrong, madam? Isn't your friend coming back? She's scarcely touched her tea.'

'No, she's not coming back.'

6

'Oh dear, your saucer's wet. I'll fetch a clean one.'

Her fussing was irritating, yet comforting. Nobody had fussed over Isla, until Kenneth came into her life. She smiled her thanks at the woman when the clean cup and saucer arrived, and after she had poured out more tea she opened her envelope handbag and drew out a single, folded sheet of paper. The letter had been handed to her by the solicitor when he came to her home to break the news of Kenneth's death – and the news about his other wife and children, living in Paisley.

Although she knew the few words off by heart, Isla smoothed the sheet out and read them slowly, carefully, one by one.

'My darling Isla,

By the time you read this you will know the truth about me. Please, my dearest, forgive me for what I have done, and what I must now do. I can see no other way. You have given me more happiness in the past few years than I have ever known before, though you will know now what I always knew – that I had no right to it. Kiss the children for me, and I hope that you can find it in your heart to let them think kindly of me.

I love you all, Kenneth.'

The letter had been in her possession for only fourteen days, but already the creases where she had folded and refolded it were beginning to bite into the paper, and the fainter lines, where she had impetuously crumpled the page up and thrown it away in the first angry throes of her grief, were fading.

She smoothed it yet again, carefully, before tucking it away in the small pocket that held her return train ticket to Gourock, the Clydeside town where she lived. Then she signalled to the waitress to bring the bill.

After fumbling in her purse for the necessary coins to pay the smart, aloof cashier in her raised box by the entrance, she went into the ladies' room, unable as yet to face the busy pavements. The mirror, lit discreetly, reflected a thin face, normally with a smooth olive glow to the skin, inherited from her Italian mother. Since Kenneth's death, the glow had gone, leaving her skin almost sallow. Her brown eyes, tilted slightly at the outer corners in an almond shape, were large and expressive, and her surprisingly full mouth, her best feature, was pale. She stared intently into the glassy depths, noting that grief ill became her, thinking of Ainslie McAdam's creamy skin and blue eyes against the unrelieved black clothes she wore.

Fumbling in her bag, she found a pale pink lipstick that Kenneth had bought for her. Isla had never made her face up until she met him, but he had persuaded her to try some lipstick, and she had to admit that it enhanced the colour of her skin and improved the mouth that she had always considered to be too large, but Kenneth had described as beautiful, and eminently kissable.

The memory of his words almost brought tears to the surface again. She forced them back and applied the lip colouring lightly, but it didn't do as much for her as it had in the days when she had been happy and fulfilled, a woman in love, a woman who knew that she was loved in return.

After tidying an errant strand of black hair away beneath her plain woollen cloche hat, she went downstairs and through the bakery on the ground floor, wondering, as she stepped out on to the pavement, how the May sun could shine, the small fluffy clouds drift calmly across the sky, the people around her go about their business as though nothing had happened. How could a world suddenly robbed of her beloved husband's presence – for to Isla he was still her husband, despite what she now knew of him – continue to function?

Even the discovery that she was not his legal wife couldn't dull the edge of her love for him, her need of him. She felt like a widow. She was a widow, no matter how the law stood in the matter.

A clock chimed. She looked up and saw it atop the imposing Town Hall on the other side of the wide bridge spanning the river that ran through the town centre on its way to the Clyde. It was a quarter to three, and her appointment with the lawyer was at three o'clock. She had already ascertained that Moss Street, where he had his office, was only a short distance away. A few minutes would take her there.

Taking advantage of a break in the traffic, she made her way to the other side of the bridge, mildly curious as to what lay beyond the stone balustrade edging the opposite pavement. The Town Hall was to her left, rising from the river bank; on the opposite bank, to Isla's right, people walked through well-laid-out public gardens, or sat on the wooden slatted benches facing the bright flower beds. A handsome statue of Queen Victoria stood on a plinth in the middle of the gardens, her back to Isla.

9

She smiled faintly at the stone figure, thinking that it was little wonder that even the likeness of the dead Queen should be turned away from her. She was a fallen woman now, with no right to the gold band that Kenneth had put on her finger. She briefly touched her left hand with her right, and, under the material of her glove, felt the ring's outline. She wasn't going to take it off; she had decided that almost as soon as she heard that their marriage had been bigamous. Even the thought of that word, harsh and ugly, made her wince.

Below, a stick, once part of a tree or a bush, circled lazily in the water and was almost caught in the long grasses fringing the river. It broke free at the last moment, disappearing beneath the bridge, drifting with no will of its own. Isla sympathised with that stick. She too was drifting, alone and with no power, it seemed, to control her own life.

She would have liked to go down the stone steps further along the pavement and into the gardens, moving among the flowers, perhaps sitting on a bench, defying Queen Victoria's stony disapproval, but there was no time for such luxuries. Instead, she turned away from the water and re-crossed the road.

Thin strands of music met her as she neared the handsome war memorial on open paved ground. A handful of men stood below it, faces hollowed by lack of nourishment. One played a penny whistle, one had an accordion, another beat on a child's toy drum with a stick. A fourth man jigged from foot to foot in a pale imitation of a dance as he played the fiddle. Lying upside-down on the ground at their feet was a well-worn cloth cap. They were almost certainly ex-servicemen, learning the hard way that their country's gratitude for their service during the most appalling war the world had ever experienced didn't stretch as far as guaranteeing them the right to earn their own livings once they returned home.

Pausing to search in her purse, Isla thought of her own adored father, who had been killed in action in April 1915, shortly before her twelfth birthday. Her mother had died three years later, an early victim of the great influenza epidemic that shadowed the ending of the war.

She tossed a coin into the cap and the man with the drum said hoarsely, 'Thanks, missus.'

It might well be the last time she would be able to help poor souls such as these, Isla thought as she went on her way, passing another group, this time idling on a street corner, hands in pockets. A grim smile twisted her mouth as she pictured herself entertaining people in the streets in order to feed and clothe her children. She had no musical talent at all, unlike her father, with his rich baritone voice, or Aunt Lally, his sister, who had taken her into her Edinburgh home after she was orphaned.

It struck her that while it had become commonplace in the 1920s to see men playing musical instruments or singing in the streets in the hope of making a few pence, she had never seen women taking it up. Surely there must be many women in the position she now found herself, alone and destitute, with small children to care for. They tended to work for their more fortunate sisters, taking in washing or sewing, or scrubbing stairs and other women's houses.

Isla wondered if that was what she would have to do. If so – she drew a deep breath and squared her shoulders – she would do it. She would do anything, rather than lose her children, all that was left to her of the happy years she had spent with Kenneth.

The words 'Forbes and Son Limited' glinted at her from a polished brass nameplate on the wall of the building she was passing. She walked through the close and up the spotlessly clean stairs, whitewashed in two broad strips down the sides, to find out what lay in store for her.

2

The woman in the reception area looked at Isla with more than passing interest when she introduced herself.

'Take a seat, Mrs – er . . .' she said, a sudden flush coming to her face as she stumbled over the name. 'I'll tell Mr Forbes you're here.'

She disappeared into one of the rooms flanking the square hall. The door closed quietly behind her, then opened again a moment later. A fair-haired young man came out, looked at Isla with unexpected hostility, then walked past her without a word and disappeared into another room. She was still staring after him, puzzled by his attitude, when the receptionist said, 'Mr Forbes will see you now.'

After the hostility she had encountered from Ainslie McAdam – and from the young man who had recently left this office – Isla felt that Gilchrist Forbes, coming round his large desk to meet her, hand outstretched, was an old friend. He had been remote and stilted early in their first meeting, but once he had realised that she was completely unaware of her husband's other life he had mellowed, treating her with a comforting courtesy that was still evident in his manner as

13

he seated her, then went back to his own place behind the desk.

'You found your way here with no trouble?' As before, the well-educated voice brought a lump to her throat. He spoke just like Kenneth. Kenneth's voice had attracted her the very first time they had met in the ward of an Edinburgh hospital, where he had been admitted with appendicitis after being taken ill on a business trip to the city, and she had been undergoing her nursing training. 'It's fortunate that we're only a short distance from the station.'

'I arrived by an earlier train. Kenneth's daughter had written, asking me to meet her first.'

His thick brows, dark and speckled with grey, rose sharply. 'Ainslie contacted you?' His voice was disapproving.

'I presume she got my address from you.'

'Yes, she did wheedle it out of me.' Gilchrist Forbes frowned down at the papers on his desk. 'But I advised her to leave matters be, and I thought she had agreed. I should have known better where Ainslie's concerned.'

'I imagine that her curiosity got the better of her,' Isla remarked dryly, drawing off her gloves. 'She'd got it into her head that I might call on her mother and cause trouble.'

He glanced up with a quick motion of the head, concern in his eyes. 'You'd not do that, surely.'

His reaction, coming on top of Ainslie's attitude, suddenly angered Isla. 'I assured her, and I can assure you, Mr Forbes, that I have no intention of doing such a cruel thing,' she said sharply. 'I may not have been legally married to Kenneth, but I believed that I was. I love—'

her voice broke and she brought it under control at once, digging her fingernails into the palms of her hands. 'I loved him,' she corrected herself, and saw embarrassment in his eyes. This man didn't belong to a generation that spoke of love. Neither had Kenneth, though with her he had managed to overcome his reservations. 'I would do nothing to harm him or his family. I even stayed away from his funeral, though that was very hard. I shall always regret not being able to see him laid to rest.'

'I'm sorry, my dear, but, like you, I'm in a very difficult situation. Kenneth McAdam was one of my closest friends. Our two wi— our families know each other well, and it came as a great shock to me to learn first of his death, then of your existence.'

Isla nodded, smoothing her gloves out on her lap. The fingers of her right hand stole across to touch her gold wedding band for comfort. She was reminded of much the same movement made by Ainslie a short while earlier.

'Would you like some tea?'

'I'd rather attend to our business, then get back to my children.'

'Of course.' He cleared his throat, and rustled the papers on the desk. 'I'm afraid that I can give you nothing but bad news.'

'I expect little else, these days,' said Isla, then listened intently while he explained that Kenneth had taken an overdose of laudanum because the hitherto comfortable Glasgow-based business he had inherited from his father had crashed due to financial problems. She had already been given that information, on his earlier visit to her home, but then she had been too distraught to take it all in.

'Why?' she asked now. 'Why should he have been in such distress that he could see suicide as the only way out? It wasn't like Kenneth. At least, not the Kenneth I knew.'

Gilchrist Forbes paused, compressing his lips tightly together, reluctant to betray his dead friend.

He had glossed over the situation when talking to Catherine McAdam, and she, wrapped up in her own thoughts, had accepted what he said without question.

Ainslie, however, had come to his office later and insisted on hearing in detail about her father's financial troubles. Forbes found himself thinking that Ainslie and the young woman now facing him had a lot in common. They both had a way of looking directly at him, of wanting to know everything, no matter how much it might hurt them. They even shared the same expression in their eyes, one of deep loss, and a determination to survive. Neither would turn away from the truth, however hard it might be. He wondered if Kenneth himself had ever noticed the similarity between daughter and consort.

Isla's brows tucked down in a slight frown as the silence lengthened. 'Mr Forbes?' she prompted, and the solicitor was jerked back to the present.

'I'm sorry – I was trying to think of how best to explain matters to you.'

'I believe that the time to soften blows is long past, Mr Forbes. I know very little about business, but I'm sure I can deal with a straightforward explanation. I understand that my husband was an insurance broker, though he never spoke of his work.'

'He was well thought of in the city, but to be frank,

it would seem that he had taken to speculating somewhat rashly with his clients' money.'

'It can't have been easy, running two families. I
wish,' Isla said, 'that he had confided in me. It's hard
for me to know now that he was so worried, and I did
nothing to help because I was in ignorance.'

Forbes blinked at her. Her attitude was so unlike
Catherine McAdam's that for a moment he floundered.
Catherine had turned her head away when he tried to
explain about Kenneth's financial problems, had flatly
refused to accept a word of it.

'Under the circumstances,' he said at last, 'he could
scarcely have confided in you, of all people.'

'If he had, I would surely have tried to understand,'
Isla told him steadily. At least she would have heard the
truth from Kenneth's own lips of why he had drawn her
into an illegal marriage, and how he had managed for
five years to live a lie. Now she would never know the
answers.

She said aloud, 'I imagine that there is very little
money for anyone to inherit. And of course his legal
family will have first right to anything he left – including the house my children and I inhabit.'

'That, like most of his estate, will be sold and the
proceeds will go to his creditors. Catherine, his . . .'

The man's voice faltered, and Isla said clearly, 'His
wife.'

The papers rustled sharply. 'As you say. Catherine
has money of her own, enough, perhaps, to cushion the
worst of the blow. Do you yourself have private means?'

'I have nothing. I was training to be a nurse when I
met Kenneth.'

'Is there no family to assist you?'

'I was an only child, and my parents both died several years ago. I have an aunt, but I'm quite certain that she only has enough to support herself.'

She was relieved that Aunt Lally, in Edinburgh, was too far away to know anything of the situation. Not that she had ever been interested in Isla's problems. 'If I'd wanted a man and children you can be sure I'd have got them,' she had said often during the few years Isla had lived with her. 'But I'd no intention of tying myself down. Life's for living, not for fretting about others.' It was quite impossible to imagine Aunt Lally, who loved spending money, having any savings.

'There's a tenement block here in Paisley, in George Street, that Kenneth owned. I handled the purchase for him, years ago, and the rent collector's a man I use myself for other properties. It seems that Kenneth signed the building over to you several months ago. Did he not tell you?'

Isla looked at him in astonishment. 'Not a word.' Then, with sudden hope, 'Does that mean that the rent it has made since he signed it over will come to me?'

He cleared his throat, and a slight flush appeared over his cheekbones. 'Kenneth re-invested the proceeds in his company – I assume that he did it on your behalf, to make the money work for you.'

Isla saw her hopes of a nest-egg fade away. 'But it would have been lost when the company folded.'

'Sadly, yes. The rent it has made in the past few weeks is, of course, yours, but it amounts to very little, because it's an old property and the tenants don't necessarily pay promptly, though I can assure you that the

18

collector we use is very conscientious.' Gilchrist Forbes riffled through the papers before him until he found the right one. He studied it, stroking his chin. 'One of the dwelling-houses is lying vacant at the moment, but I'm sure that we can find tenants for it. I could put the building on the market on your behalf.'

'How soon would you expect to find a buyer?'

His brows lifted slightly at her forthright question and she knew with grim amusement that because of her youth and her accent, more broad than his own prim, educated speech, he had instantly assumed that she was no businesswoman.

'Frankly,' he said after a slight pause, 'I wouldn't be too optimistic. Businessmen are finding these times hard, and it is, as I said, an old building. But there's no harm in searching for a buyer.'

'Then we must do so,' said Isla briskly, adding as an afterthought, 'that empty flat – I could live there in the meantime.'

Concern flashed into Gilchrist Forbes' eyes. 'I scarcely think that it would be the most suitable place for your children.'

'There's nothing wrong with tenements, Mr Forbes. I was raised in a Glasgow tenement, and I survived the experience.'

'But – but this is an old building—' Consternation made the man stammer over his words. 'And with Catherine and her children already living in this town—'

'How much time do I have before I must move from the house we're in now?'

'No more than another month, I'm afraid. If I can manage to sell the tenement for you in that time you could use the money to buy somewhere else to live – perhaps in the area where you live at the moment.'

'And if not, I've no option but to move into the empty flat. I'd be grateful if you would retain it for me, just in case. I must keep a roof over my children's heads somehow,' she reminded him as he opened his mouth to argue.

The Town Hall clock could be heard chiming the half hour, and he automatically consulted the watch pinned across his waistcoat. Isla, suddenly feeling stifled, got to her feet. 'I must go.'

'But there are still some matters to discuss.'

'Perhaps we can meet again. Next week?'

'Certainly. I'll call on you – shall we say Wednesday, at three o'clock? I'm sorry, my dear,' he went on, going ahead to open the office door for her. 'This must be extremely difficult for you.'

'I shall manage.' Then, as they crossed the hall, she asked, 'That young man who was in your office when I arrived – who is he?'

'My son, Colin. He and Ainslie McAdam are' – he paused, then said – 'were to be married.'

Recalling the way Ainslie had touched the third finger of her left hand, feeling for the consolation of a ring that was no longer there, and the girl's bitter, 'He's ruined everything for me!' Isla felt a flash of contempt for the young man who had cared so little for his fiancée that he had abandoned her at the first whisper of scandal.

'Indeed? I take it that he ended the engagement because of her father's shameful death?'

Something of her condemnation must have sounded

in her voice, because Gilchrist Forbes was cool when he retorted, 'Indeed not. It was Ainslie who ended it, very much against my son's wishes.'

The rapport that had been growing between them had vanished with her criticism of his son, and his voice was formal when he wished her good day and closed the door behind her, leaving her to walk alone down the stairs to the street.

Emerging from the tearoom after her disastrous confrontation with her father's secret 'wife', Ainslie McAdam walked aimlessly along the street, weaving her way around pedestrians without seeing any of them. Someone called her name, and she looked up to see a former schoolfriend, her round, rosy face suitably solemn, but her eyes bright with curiosity. Clearly she had heard the rumours that had begun circulating despite all Gilchrist Forbes' attempts to keep the details of Kenneth's suicide quiet.

'Ainslie, I meant to write to you. I was so sorry to hear about your father.'

'Thank you, Christine. I'm – I'm in a terrible rush,' Ainslie said, and hurried on, knowing full well that Christine was gaping after her, taken aback by her coldness. But she couldn't talk to anyone while her mind was filled with pictures of the woman she had just left. She had expected – had hoped – to see someone much older, a plain elderly spinster, perhaps, who had somehow embroiled Kenneth McAdam in her clutches. Instead she had been confronted by a young woman only a few years older than herself. At that moment, for the first time in her life, she hated her father with all her heart.

21

She was glad that he was dead, she told herself fiercely, swinging round a corner and almost bumping into a great crowd of women straggling along the pavement, moving in the opposite direction from Ainslie herself. Young, old, fat, thin, all dressed in working clothes with scarves wound round their heads, they talked and laughed and called to each other loudly as they poured along the pavements past her. Drifts of cotton clustered on a coatsleeve here, a mop of hair there, and Ainslie realised that she had walked right through the town and was nearing Ferguslie Mills as it was disgorging its workers at the end of a shift.

She glanced at her watch and discovered to her astonishment that, somehow, the afternoon had passed, and she should have been home an hour earlier. She turned the next corner and kept walking, this time with purpose, past the cricket ground and the neat double row of back-to-back housing built to accommodate some of the mill workers, then under the railway bridge and up the hill to where a row of comfortably large houses stood back from the road, separated from it by their neat gardens.

Her heart sank when she saw the small car, its chocolate-brown paintwork and chrome gleaming in the late-afternoon sun, standing in the driveway of her own home. Letting herself in quietly at the front door, she tried to escape upstairs to her room, but her mother's voice called her name as she passed the drawing-room's closed door. Ainslie hesitated, then decided to pretend she hadn't heard the summons. Just as she gained the staircase the drawing-room door opened.

'Ainslie?'

She stopped, turning towards the man she had once promised to marry. 'Hello, Colin.'

'Your mother wants to see you.' His voice was gruff, and his hazel eyes, when she met them, still carried the hurt of her rejection.

There was nothing else for it. Ainslie stepped back down into the hall and walked past him and into the room.

'Ainslie, where have you been?' Catherine McAdam wanted to know as soon as her daughter appeared. She lay on a chaise longue, a rug over her legs and cushions piled behind her back. The windows were curtained against the daylight, and fringed standard lamps glowed feebly in the twilight within the room.

'I went out for a walk. I thought you were resting in your room, Mother.'

'I was, but I had to come downstairs to see to some business.' The rings on Catherine's limp hand sparkled in the electric light as she indicated the open desk. Colin moved to it and began to gather the spilled papers together neatly, his back towards mother and daughter. 'I could have done with your help,' Catherine went on reproachfully.

'What d'you want me to do?'

'It's too late now, I had to see to it all myself, with Colin's help. Now I'm trying to persuade him to stay for tea.' A warm note crept into Catherine's voice. She had been delighted when her daughter and Colin Forbes became engaged, and furious when, only days after her father's death, Ainslie had taken it upon herself to return the handsome diamond and emerald ring that had been specially made for her.

'I expect he has to get back home.'

'I've already explained that to your mother,' Colin said stiffly, turning away from the desk. 'Goodbye, Mrs McAdam.' He took Catherine's hand in his for a moment. 'Remember that you only need to telephone myself or my father if you need help. Goodbye, Ainslie.'

'Goodbye.' She opened the door for him, and her mother said sharply, strength coming into her voice, 'Ainslie, have your manners deserted you entirely? You might at least see Colin to his car, since I'm not fit to do so.'

'I expect he remembers where he left it.'

'Ainslie!' A cushion tumbled softly to the floor as Catherine, outraged, struggled to sit upright.

Colin's face had gone quite white. 'I can find my own way out, Mrs McAdam. I know this house well,' he said, looking at Ainslie, who glanced away. Still shocked by her meeting with the woman who had been part of her father's secret life, she didn't feel strong enough to deal with Colin's pain as well as her own.

'Nonsense, Colin, I hope that we've not entirely forgotten our manners in this house, despite all that's happened.'

Catherine put a hand on the rug over her legs as though about to throw it back and escort her guest to the door personally, and Ainslie said, 'Stay where you are, Mother. I'll see Colin to his car.'

3

They walked through the square hall and down the stone steps in silence, blinking as they emerged into the sunny garden. The familiar scent of petrol and sun-warmed leather upholstery filled Ainslie's nostrils as Colin opened the car door; his car was so familiar to her that she knew just how hot the leather passenger seat would feel against her calves on such a day.

He tossed the brief-case into the car then straightened and said, his hand on the door-frame, 'Something's troubling you.'

'My father's killed himself and left us with the shame of knowing that he had another wife and family hidden away,' she retorted tartly. 'Is it any wonder that I'm troubled?'

He reddened under the sting of her sarcasm. His fair colouring and his tendency to flush easily was a great burden to him, Ainslie knew. It was one of the qualities that had once endeared him to her. 'I mean that something else is troubling you. I was at the window, I saw you charging in the gate and up the drive as though you were about to do battle with some poor soul. Your eyes' – he hesitated, then swallowed and said, 'Your eyes are very bright, and that means that you're angry.'

She bit her lip and scuffled the toe of one of her smart black strapped shoes in the gravel, heedless of scratch marks. 'I met her this afternoon.'

'Who?' The question was automatic, followed immediately by, 'You don't mean your father's—'

'His *woman*!' Ainslie spat the word out. 'Colin, she's quite pretty. And she's young, not much older than I am!'

'I know. I saw her outside my father's office. That's why I had to come here, instead of him. He'd arranged to meet with her.'

'You didn't tell Mother that, did you?'

'Of course not – d'you take me for an utter fool? I said he'd had to call on a very old client who needed his advice urgently.'

Ainslie gave a bark of harsh laughter. 'Scarcely a very old client. How could he? How could he take up with someone not much older than I am?'

'How did you happen to meet her?'

'I wrote to her, when I heard that she was coming to Paisley to see him. We had tea together.'

His jaw tightened. 'You shouldn't have done that, Ainslie.'

'I had to see her for myself.' She rushed on, her voice suddenly choked, tears gathering behind her eyes, 'They even had children together, Colin! A girl and a boy, just like Mother had. Only they're still very s-small—'

His hand closed over her arm. 'Come for a spin – we can talk about it, away from here.' He looked beyond her bent head to the drawing-room window, worried

26

that her mother might see them and assume that he was upsetting her daughter. But there was no movement in the narrow space between the curtains.

Ainslie drew away from him, shaking her head. 'Mother would only think that we were making up. She'd start expecting me to wear your ring again.'

'Would that be so terrible?' His voice was low, but vehement. 'Ainslie—'

'The past is past, Colin. Nothing can ever be the same again. Everything's changed!'

'I see no reason why we should change too. I love you, Ainslie, yet you've not even given me the chance to—'

'Hello, Colin,' Ainslie's young brother called cheerfully from the gate, and Colin, inwardly cursing, turned to smile at the boy as he and his closest friend, both in the neat blue blazer and striped blue and silver tie of Paisley Grammar School, came up the short gravelled drive.

'Hullo, Innes – Gordon.' He hoped that the boys would continue on round the side of the house to the back door to coax something to eat from the cook, but instead they stopped, letting their schoolbags drop to the ground, their hands and eyes hungrily reaching out to the car.

'I'm going to get one just like this when I'm old enough,' Innes announced, and Gordon gave him a scornful look.

'You're only eleven! By the time you're old enough to drive, this'll be out of date. I've got a cigarette card of the new Delage sports car. That's the sort of car I'm going to get when I'm old enough.'

'You didn't tell me! Why didn't you bring it to school?'

'And let everyone put their grubby fingers on it? I'm keeping it at home, in my album.'

Ainslie, who could have kissed the boys for arriving at just the right moment, saw that her young brother's eyes were bright with avarice.

'What would you swop for it? I'll give you my Swift open tourer card.'

'And your Alvis?'

The boys began wrangling, and Colin, with a resigned shrug, got into the car.

'You couldn't take us for a run, could you?' Innes asked at once. Colin started to shake his head, but Ainslie cut in.

'Go on, just a short spin.'

'Your mother—'

'I'll explain to Mother,' she said, and with whoops of glee the boys jostled their way, schoolbags and all, into the rear seat.

Colin shot an angry look at her and then, resigned to his fate, started the engine. Ainslie waved as the car reversed down the short drive, then went back indoors to where her mother was still lying on the sofa.

'You took your time – the two of you must have had quite a lot to talk about.'

'Innes arrived, with Gordon. Colin's taken them both out for a short drive. We didn't think you'd mind.'

Catherine shifted restlessly. 'He's such a nice young man. I can't think why you gave him back his ring.'

'I told you, Mother – this isn't the time to think of marriage.'

A sharp note came into the older woman's voice. 'Don't be so silly, girl, it's the perfect time. The Forbeses are comfortably off, and one day Colin will take over the business. A connection with them just now would put us in better standing with the town than we are at the moment, after what your father did. Anyway, I can't afford to keep you indefinitely, you know that. Not now that I've got Innes's school fees to see to.'

'You won't have to keep me. I shall find a job.'

'You're not trained for anything other than marriage!' Catherine said irritably.

'I'll find something.'

'You sound more like your Grandmama McAdam every day! She was always a difficult, stubborn woman. I can't think why your grandfather married her.'

It was a chant that Ainslie had heard over and over again. 'Won't you let me open the curtains? It's such a lovely day—'

'Leave them!'

'Very well.' Her hands dropped from the curtains. 'I'll take the tray to the kitchen, and find out how dinner's coming along.'

'Tell Cook not to make anything for me. I don't feel like eating.'

'But you must eat, Mother.' Ainslie regarded the older woman with concern. Catherine's greying fair hair was drawn back tightly, accentuating the harsh lines of her face and the droop of her mouth. Her cheekbones jutted sharply beneath her pale skin. 'You have to keep your strength up.'

'I can't think why,' Catherine said bleakly. 'There seems to be little point, now.'

As Ainslie carried the tray out of the room, she marvelled that her mother hadn't realised why she had given her engagement ring back to Colin. After what her father had done, she herself no longer had any desire to marry, to become tied to a man, dependent on him, open to the humiliation and hurt her mother was suffering. She had loved her father, almost worshipped him, despite the fact that he showed little interest in her. Now, she would never trust men again.

Although she had told the lawyer that she had to hurry back home, Isla turned away from the station when she left his office. She walked back towards the Cross, where she asked a passerby for directions to the cemetery, and was directed to one of the tram-stops. The ex-servicemen were still playing their reedy music as she passed the war memorial. Only a few coins lay in the pathetic cap.

Paisley, she realised as the tram rocked along, was built on three terraces. The High Street ran along one of them, with all the streets on Isla's left swooping downhill, and the streets on her right running uphill. She glimpsed a handsome church with a great broad sweep of steps leading from the pavement to the arched doors; it was very like a church she had seen in Paris, where she and Kenneth had spent their honeymoon.

And all the time, a small voice whispered in her ear, Ainslie and her mother and brother had been going about their lives here in Paisley, no doubt believing that Kenneth was away on business. Was that what he had told them? She tried to close her mind to the malice in the voice, not wanting her precious memories to become soured and blackened.

The conductress tapped her on the shoulder. 'This is the cemetery, hen,' she said cheerfully, pointing. 'Just across the road there.'

Inside Woodside Cemetery's stone gates Isla made enquiries at the small office, then walked up the wide driveway between the gravestones, some of them so elaborate that they were like miniature war memorials. Kenneth's grave had yet to be marked by a headstone; the earth was still raw above him but the dead funeral flowers had been cleared away and someone – Ainslie? The real Mrs McAdam? – had recently put some carnations into an urn at the foot of the grave.

Isla stood for a long time looking at the mound. She had expected to weep, had wanted to weep, to ease the pain that had been gnawing at her ever since Gilchrist Forbes, hat in hand, face sombre, had come into her comfortable home to tell her that Kenneth had left her for ever. But her eyes remained obstinately dry. The man she had loved, still loved, wasn't really here, in this quiet, green graveyard where the dead slept in peace beneath the trees. He was still with her – and yet not with her.

She turned away, and started on her journey home.

After their quiet marriage in Edinburgh, Isla and Kenneth McAdam had settled in a comfortable little house in Gourock, by the River Clyde. Isla had come to the place as a stranger, and had not made many friends. For one thing, she wasn't used to having friends and therefore didn't feel the need of them, and, for another,

31

Kenneth didn't care to see people when he was at home, claiming that he had enough contact with others in his office.

Isla had been happy to go along with his wishes. During her training she had lived in the nurses' quarters and spent her off-duty time with Aunt Lally, a garrulous woman who usually had her tenement flat filled with people. At times Isla had ached for peace and quiet, and at last, in Gourock, she had found it.

Although Kenneth was often away – on business, he had told Isla, and she had had no reason to doubt him – she had never felt lonely. She enjoyed gardening and sewing and reading, and when first Barbara and then Ross were born, she had had more than enough to do.

Grace, the maid, opened the door as her mistress went up the front path between the hydrangea bushes. 'How are the children?' Isla asked as soon as she got indoors.

'Miss Barbara was frettin' for ye, but she got over it. Pearl took them both out for a walk this afternoon. I'll make ye a nice cup of tea.'

'I don't want—' Isla began, but Grace had already vanished into the little kitchen at the rear of the house. Wondering why it was that the Scots felt that everything could be cured by tea, Isla hung up her coat and went upstairs, towards the sound of splashing and squealing. Barbara loved bathtime.

Before going in to see her daughter she opened the door of the small nursery. The room was quiet and smelled of baby powder and clean clothes airing before the guarded fire. The coverings were folded back invitingly in Barbara's small bed in the corner, and Ross was already in his cot, clean and contented, almost asleep. She bent over the cot, resisting the temptation to lift him into her arms and bury her face in him, and he lifted heavy lids to smile drowsily at his mother, his lips parting to reveal four pearly little teeth, then slid back into sleep.

He was his father's child, fair-skinned and red-haired and blue-eyed. And very like his grown half-sister, Isla thought, as she straightened up from the cot. Kenneth had taken such delight in his children, claiming that it was because he was so much older than the average father, and had had longer to wait.

Isla wondered if he had been as devoted to Ainslie and her brother as he was to his second family. Part of her mind told her that she should hate him for deceiving her, trapping her into a tissue of lies, then leaving her with two children who were, in the eyes of the law, illegitimate. One day, perhaps, when she could look back over the years to this time in her life, she would feel anger against him, but not now, not yet. Now, she knew only terrible loss.

The bathroom was steamy and smelled of the floral soap Barbara loved. Pearl, who had come to help Isla after Barbara's birth, was lifting the little girl out of the water.

'Mummy!'

Barbara wriggled with excitement, reaching dripping hands out to her mother, and Pearl shrieked, 'For any favour, bairn, will ye stay still. Mind yer mammy's nice clothes, ye'll get her all wet!'

'Never mind about my clothes, they'll dry.' Isla dropped to her knees and gathered the plump, towel-swathed body close. Water trickling from Barbara's hair, making it look much darker than its usual fiery bronze, ran down beneath the collar of Isla's blouse, but she paid no heed to it.

'Did you bring Daddy back with you?'

'Not this time, darling. He'll be away for – for a long time,' Isla said, and over her daughter's wet head she saw Pearl's eyes fill with sympathetic tears.

'I missed you,' Barbara said into her ear. 'I cried for you.'

'You knew I'd come back, surely.' Isla squeezed her eyes shut to fight back her own tears. She didn't want her own grief to touch her children. 'You know I'd not leave you and Ross,' she said. 'Not ever, whatever happens.'

4

At the end of June Isla's home was repossessed to pay Kenneth McAdam's debts, and as nobody had bought the tenement building he had left her, she had no option but to move herself and her children to its empty ground floor flat.

She left her home without looking back. Although the house was small, it had been the grandest she had ever lived in. She had loved having a garden, and a front door that opened on to a path, instead of a landing or a close. Now she was returning to tenement life.

Mr Forbes had warned her that the building she now owned was old, but even so, she hadn't realised just how old, or how small and cramped it would be. Her parents and Aunt Lally had lived in modern tenements, with tiled closes and stairs that were scrubbed down each week then carefully edged with white pipeclay to give them a smart appearance, but this building was small and sad and neglected.

The outer wall, facing on to the street, looked dark and damp, and when Isla ventured in, Ross clutched in one arm, her free hand holding Barbara's, she saw that the stone floor of the narrow close was cracked and broken and uneven. The centre of each of the steps rising into the darkness of the upper floor was hollowed almost to the level of the step below, and she was thankful that she lived on the ground floor, and didn't have to climb into that unfriendly darkness above. The paintwork on the door of her new home was faded and scratched, the wood itself furrowed with deep ravines, as though some predatory beast had once clawed at it in a frenzy. The entire building smelled of damp and stale food and too many years of human habitation. A child wailed from somewhere at the back of the close, and Isla felt that the misery in the sound matched her own feelings.

The empty flat was situated at the front of the building. When Isla released Barbara's hand to search for the large clumsy key the lawyer had given her, the little girl stayed by her side instead of running off to explore as she usually did.

The door had to be pushed hard before it creaked open. Isla, peering into the gloom before her, almost lost her nerve and scurried back to the street; she had to force herself to move forward instead, the floorboards squeaking underfoot.

The door opened straight into a small empty room. Isla went towards the only window with a sense of purpose that was put on for the children's benefit, and pulled aside the dingy curtain stretched across the window. The very touch of the material, stiff and clammy, sent a shiver down her spine, and she found herself rubbing her hand against her skirt afterwards.

The window was filthy. A cool breeze from the gaps in the frame brushed her face and she breathed it in with relief. A small sink leaned against the wall below the window as though tired out, its single tap weeping slowly and sadly. Barbara, clutching a brightly coloured rubber ball that had been Kenneth's last present to her, stood in the middle of the floor and stared round at the mottled walls.

'Where's the bedroom?' she wanted to know. There were two narrow doors, one on either side of the small fireplace. Isla opened them to reveal cobwebbed shelves, only a few inches in depth. Glancing round she saw that half of the wall opposite the window was covered by wooden folding doors. The hinges complained as the doors were pulled open, and dust showered down on her. The bed was there, a high metal frame supporting a solid wooden platform. The space below it was dark and forbidding.

'There isn't a bedroom, love. This is called a wall-bed. You'll sleep here with me.'

Barbara scampered over to stand by her mother, going on tiptoe to inspect the dark space. 'It looks dirty.'

It did. Isla remembered wall-beds as clean, comfortable places, with piled pillows and soft quilts. Her parents hadn't had much money, but they had been thrifty, and her mother had always kept a clean house and had taken great care of the possessions bought, one by one, when they could be afforded. Even Aunt Lally, who was more of a 'feast and famine' person, enjoying money when she had it, and coping cheerfully with spells of enforced poverty, took a pride in her small home.

'We can clean it,' Isla said with a cheeriness she

37

didn't feel. 'And we'll wash the window to let more light in, and once our furniture arrives it'll look fine.'

Barbara gave her one of her direct looks. 'There isn't a bathroom.'

'The water closet's outside, but that doesn't matter. When I was a little girl we didn't have a bathroom inside. We used a tin bath, all cosy in front of the fire.'

Now that her eyes were growing accustomed to the gloom she could make out the handle of a chamber-pot that was lurking beneath the bed. 'Look, we can use this at night if we have to, then empty it into the privy in the morning.'

With difficulty, because Ross was squirming in her arms, she bent and pulled the chipped, stained delft pot out from under the bed. A little puddle of gritty dust lay on the bottom, and Isla only just managed to smother a scream when a long-legged spider scuttled into the interior from under the rim. She set the pot down hastily on the wooden bed so that Barbara, shorter than the bed, couldn't see into it. Her daughter, head tilted back, doubtfully surveyed the bulge of the pot from below, then announced, 'We're going to have to clean that, too. We'll have to clean everything,' she added, glancing over at the filthy little gas-cooker beside the sink.

'It'll all look better when the furniture arrives,' Isla said hopefully, giving in to Ross's noisy demands and putting him down to ease the strain on her aching arm. He took two steps away from her, then fell over on to cracked linoleum that was so faded that it was impossible to see what the pattern had been. He broke into an angry roar and as Isla picked him up again, Barbara put down her ball. It rolled across the floor to disappear under the cobwebby gloom beneath the sink.

'See? It was the floor that pushed him over,' she said accusingly. Then she clutched at her mother's skirt with one hand and added, her voice suddenly uncertain, 'I want Pearl.'

'Barbara, you know that Pearl couldn't come with us,' Isla coaxed, doing her best to keep a cheerful note in her voice. 'We're going to be all by ourselves now, just you and me and Ross, all cosy in our new little house.'

Barbara stuck the thumb of her free hand in her mouth. 'I still want Pearl,' she said around it, indistinctly. 'I want to go home.'

Isla, bouncing Ross in her tired arms to calm him, looking round the small, bleak single room, agreed wholeheartedly with her daughter. But she couldn't say so, or give way to the tears that were building up in her throat. For the children's sakes, she had to be strong. She had to manage, though at that moment she didn't know how she was going to do it.

The furniture arrived a few minutes later, trundled along the street from the station on a cart. The man and the boy in charge of the cart edged the pieces one by one along the narrow stone close and into Isla's new home, beneath the interested stares of the women and children lounging around in the street outside. She had let almost all of the handsome furniture that she and Kenneth had chosen between them go with the house, and kept only what she considered to be essential. But the room was so small that when the cart was finally unloaded it was crammed.

'Ye'll have tae sell most o' it, missus,' the man observed as Isla fumbled in her purse for the money to pay him. When he had left she tucked Ross, who had fallen asleep in her arms, into the only armchair that she had brought with her, then searched the jumble of boxes until she found bedding for the cot, which was wedged into a corner beside the wall-bed. The little boy tumbled into the cot bonelessly, without waking, and she drew the blanket over him, deciding that it was better to leave him undisturbed than to try to change his napkin and wash him. It was only then that she discovered that Barbara had gone.

'Barbara?' she said hopefully, peering at the clutter around her. There was no answer, nor had she expected there to be. It was difficult to miss Barbara when she was around; almost from birth she had made her presence felt, first with a cheerful babbling, then, as she grew older, with words that swiftly became sentences, sentences that became paragraphs, paragraphs that became great spiels of continuous chatter.

Isla racked her brains, and recalled that she had last seen her daughter while the last pieces of furniture were being delivered, standing nose to nose outside the close with a ragged little girl of about the same age. They had been studying each other intently, silently, as children did when they first met.

She ran out to the close-mouth, careful to leave the door on the latch so that she could get back in, and gazed up and down the street. Groups of children played in the gutter, and the women who had come to close-mouths and windows to stare openly at the furniture being carried in from the cart had gone back to their gossiping. There was no sign of the familiar bronze curly head.

Panic-stricken now, Isla ran back through the close and burst out into the back court, a gloomy and over-grown walled-in area. The section nearest the tenement was paved with broken slabs, weeds thrusting up between them, edged on one side by a row of shaky-looking dustbins and coalsheds with sagging doors. A small outhouse opposite the bins probably housed the water closet, and just beyond it stood the washhouse. Then came two broken steps leading to what looked like a very small neglected field.

'Barbara?'

'Is it yer wean yer lookin' for?' a voice said, almost at her elbow. The window beside the back door was open and a young woman sat just inside the room, her head bound up in a scarf knotted at the top. Her blouse was unbuttoned and a small bald baby was fastened to one breast, sucking steadily and noisily. A cigarette smoul-dered in the woman's free hand.

'My – my little girl.'

The turbanned head nodded towards the steps. 'She's behind the washhoose there with oor Greta. She's fine,' she called after Isla as she hurried up the steps and peered round the outhouse.

Barbara was sitting on a sagging, slimy, wooden bench, her favourite doll on her knee. Beside her sat the child Isla had seen earlier, a thin little waif dressed in a frayed jersey that had been made for someone larger, and almost covered the skimpy little skirt beneath it. The two children were undressing the doll, their heads close together.

'Barbara! I was worried about you!'

Barbara looked up, unrepentant. 'Greta wanted to see Bella's frilly knickers coming off. I didn't go far away,' she added defensively, after another look at her mother's anxious face. Greta, tossing a disinterested glance over her shoulder, went back to the doll.

'Ach, leave them alone, they're no' doin' any harm — for once,' the woman's voice called from the open window, and Isla hesitated, then went slowly back to the close. As she walked past the open door of the water closet, the smell from the interior hit her.

'I suppose she's as well there as under my feet,' she said, as she reached the window.

'Ye'll have enough tae dae, with just movin' in,' the other woman agreed, hauling the baby away from her breast. It came free with a loud sucking noise, eyes and milk-flecked mouth opening wide with indignation. Before it could utter a yell, the small mouth was clamped against the other breast.

'That'll keep ye quiet,' the woman said, then, to Isla, 'Ye'll be ready for a cup of tea? Come on in an' I'll make one.'

'I'll have to get back to the baby.'

'On ye go, then, an' I'll bring the tea through in a wee minute. It's no bother,' the woman said airily when Isla tried to protest.

In the tiny room that was now their home, Ross was still asleep. Isla started trying to tidy the place, but hadn't got far when knuckles rapped at the door. Seen in her entirety, her new neighbour was small and broad, with button-bright black eyes set on either side of a button nose. She walked into the room with a

42

rolling gait that reminded Isla of a sailor accustomed to the moving deck of a ship, and looked round with open curiosity. A mug of steaming tea was clutched in each fist and the baby, asleep now, was fastened against her breast by a shawl deftly wound round her shoulders and hips, and formed into a snug little hammock.

'Ye've got some bonnie furniture.' She settled herself in the armchair and thrust a mug at Isla. 'I put condensed milk intae it, an' two spoonfuls of sugar. Ye'll be needin' yer strength.'

Isla sipped at the tea, and tried not to wrinkle her nose. The liquid was strong and very sweet, with an underlying flavour of grease, as though the mug had been washed in dirty water.

'I'm Magret,' said her first caller.

'I'm Isla Moffatt.' Isla had decided to revert to her maiden name. She had no legal right to Kenneth's name, and neither did the children.

'Isla? That's nice. I wish I'd heard it afore we named her Daisy.' Magret indicated the bald-headed baby with a dip of the chin. 'She's cried after a flower. Have ye ever seen a daisy? Bonny, isn't it?' she went on when Isla nodded. 'Oor Greta's cried after a flower tae, her real name's Magret like mine, with a Rita added on to it. We cry her Greta because he' – she jerked her chin in the general direction of her own home – 'says her real name's too much of a mouthful for a wee skelf like her.' She hesitated, then said delicately, 'I saw ye were wearing a mournin' band when ye arrived.'

'My husband died recently.' Isla spoke with difficulty round a lump that had suddenly come to her throat.

Magret sucked in her breath. 'Ach, that's a shame, so it is. Where did ye used tae live?'

'Ayrshire.'

'I thought ye sounded different from most of us here. More posh.' Isla, who had been raised in Glasgow and didn't have an Ayrshire accent, said nothing. 'Don't fret, hen, ye'll be all right here. The folks is decent enough – most of them. He –' her chin gave another spasmodic jerk towards the back of the building – 'works at the mills. How'll ye keep yersel' and the bairns? Widows don't get much – the folk that pay out the money seem tae think women an' bairns can live on air,' she added, with a sniff.

'I'll need to think of something.' Isla decided to say nothing about the few pieces of jewellery she possessed, some inherited from her mother, some given to her by Kenneth. She planned to sell them to raise money for food for herself and the children. She wasn't entitled to any widow's pension because strictly speaking she had never been married in the first place. The responsibility for seeing that her children survived rested solely on her own shoulders.

'Ye could start by pawnin' some o' this,' Magret suggested, looking round the room. 'There's a pawn-shop not far from here, in Canal Street. He's a fair man tae deal with, no' like some.' She reached out a rough red hand and stroked a handsome chest of drawers. 'That's bonny, but it's out o' place here. The more furniture ye've got, the more corners for the weans tae hurt themselves on. Better tae ask at the grocer's shop for orange boxes – they're grand for keepin' stuff in. Anyway' – she lowered her voice and narrowed her eyes – 'if the rent man sees this lot on top of the posh way ye talk, he'll think ye're a toff and mebbe put up yer rent. Ye'd not want that. The rent's high enough for a flea-pit like this.'

Isla, recalling that she herself was the landlady, felt a guilty pang. Her face warmed and she bent it over her tea. She had discovered that once she got used to the taste, the hot sweet liquid was comforting.

Magret chattered on, thankfully more interested in telling Isla about the other tenants than in asking questions. Isla learned that old Granny Thomson lived alone 'through the wall', and that the McNabs occupied the flat directly across the close from hers.

'He's younger than she is. Her husband drank himself tae death last year an' left her tae run their wee baker's shop, three doors down,' Magret confided, adding, 'they make good pies and she's a clean woman, and fair wi' the prices. Her new man started as the message boy in the shop, and she wed him just months after her man died. He was a bad-tempered pig, so he was. At least she never carries bruises now. There's three lots live up the stair, and it'll be your turn tae use the clothes-lines on Wednesday mornings. Don't hang anythin' out there on a Tuesday or Mrs Leach'll have the nose off ye. She's awful snappy, thinks she's above the rest of us.' She gave a sudden bellow of laughter, and Ross jumped and muttered in his sleep, though the baby on Magret's breast didn't stir.

'She does live above us, come tae think of it! I meant that she's awful snooty, but she's got more bark than bite. Here, I'd better be going, or he'll be in looking for his dinner, and me with the tatties not even peeled.'

She drained her mug, and, after a struggle, levered herself and her baby out of the chair, easing her way round the table to peep at Ross, still sound asleep. 'My, look at that head of hair! Ye could warm yer hands at it!'

When she had gone, Isla studied the furniture, knowing that Magret was right – most of it would have to go. She decided to call on the pawnbroker in the morning.

Barbara arrived, looking more cheerful now that she had found a friend, and announced that she was hungry. After a search, Isla found the food that she had carefully packed that morning in Gourock. She filled the kettle, trying in vain to turn the tap off hard enough to stop its persistent dripping, and lit the tiny gas cooker, making a mental note to start scrubbing the layers of grease off it first thing in the morning. It looked as though the previous tenant had never even attempted to clean it.

Ross was irritable when she roused him, and after feeding him and washing him sketchily, she put him back into his cot then cut the string that held the mattress firmly in a roll, and found pillows and blankets. She attacked the wall-bed vigorously with a stiff-bristled handbrush, raising clouds of dust, then made it up, and she and Barbara climbed in. It was still early, but Isla was bone-weary, and there was no reason to stay up.

'It's cosy here, isn't it?' she said when the two of them were snuggled together in the bed.

'You won't close the doors and leave us in the dark, will you?' Barbara asked anxiously.

'Of course not.' A chill crept up Isla's spine at the very thought. Heaven alone knew what might be lurking in the shadows below. She tried not to let her mind dwell on it.

Exhausted though they both were, they were kept awake by footsteps and voices and laughter as people went up and down the street outside. In the building itself, doors banged, people scuffed their way along the close, and feet tramped back and forth above their heads. Something scuttled behind the skirting board, and Barbara clutched at her mother fearfully.

'What's that?'

'Nothing, pet, nothing at all,' Isla comforted her, while the skin at the back of her neck crawled.

The two of them waited, holding their breaths, but the sound wasn't repeated. Gradually, Barbara's fingers eased their tight grip on Isla's arm.

'I like Greta,' she said, her voice drowsy. 'She's going to teach me to play peevers.' Then, mercifully, she fell asleep.

Isla, too, slept, and dreamed of Kenneth; of walking with him along the shore at Gourock, sitting by the fire with him, lying in his arms in their marriage bed. A drunken voice raised in song startled her awake during the night, to darkness, Barbara's knees digging painfully into her side, and the realisation that Kenneth was gone for ever.

She turned over and wept her loneliness into her pillow, until it and her face and her hair were all soaked with tears.

5

'I think it was most unwise of you to move to Paisley, Mrs – er—' Gilchrist Forbes paused uncomfortably.

'I'm calling myself Mrs Moffatt now. I have a right to the name, I was born to it,' Isla assured him tartly. 'And I wouldn't dream of raising my children in that tenement if I'd any other option, I can assure you of that.' She was tired after a night's broken sleep, depressed at the prospect of having to live in the old tenement. The lawyer's cool disapproval was more than she could take.

'Did my – did Kenneth know what the place was like? Did he know the conditions his tenants have to live in?'

The man looked offended. 'George Street is in an old part of the town, and the tenements there have been standing for some time. I understand that they now enjoy gas lighting and running water, and of course the rents are very low, to compensate for the lack of other amenities.'

'I'd hardly call life there enjoyable, even with gas lighting and water that sometimes won't stop running,' Isla told him, tightening her grip on Ross, who was struggling to get down from her lap. 'Barbara, don't touch!'

'I was only looking,' Barbara said at once from the desk, folding her hands behind her back. 'Not touching.'

There had been nobody for Isla to leave the children with. Now, realising the impossibility of carrying on a conversation with the lawyer while trying to cope with them both, she gave in and got to her feet, putting the little boy down, but keeping a tight hold of his hand. 'I only came to let you know that I was installed, and to make arrangements about the rent.'

'It's collected every Friday evening. I can arrange to have it delivered to you on Monday mornings.'

'I think it would be best for me to call here for it. And as I don't want anyone to know that I'm the land-lady, I suggest that your collector knows me only as an ordinary tenant, and collects rent from me every week as well as from the others. You can leave the money in the outer office on Monday mornings, then I won't have to trouble you. Good day, Mr Forbes.'

'My dear—' Gilchrist Forbes reached the door before her, almost falling over Barbara in the process. Although it was clear to Isla that her presence in his office – in Paisley, come to that – made the man feel most uncomfortable, he nevertheless seemed to be genuinely concerned about her well-being. 'It's a difficult business, collecting rents from that type of building. Many of the tenants tend to be in arrears, and I can't guarantee a fixed sum every week. How will you manage?'

'I shall have to do the best I can – like my fellow tenants,' Isla told him, and he bit his lip. Barbara, impatient to be out in the street again, scurried out of the door as soon as he opened it, and ran across the hall to the outer door. As she reached up for the handle, the door opened almost in her face, and she recoiled with a squeak of surprise, tripping over the edge of the carpet and landing, with a thud, on the floor.

The newcomer, the fair-haired young man Isla had seen on her first visit to the office, dropped to his knees beside her.

'Are you all right?'

'I'm fine.' Barbara sat up and beamed at him. 'I bounced like a ball.'

He laughed, and took her hands in his. 'Let's see if you can bounce back up again, then. Up you come – one, two th—' His voice trailed away as the little girl got to her feet and he looked beyond her to see Isla.

'This is my son, Colin. Colin, this is Mrs . . .'

Gilchrist Forbes hesitated, and it was left to Isla to say shortly, 'Mrs Moffatt. I've decided to return to my own name.'

The laughter had gone from Colin Forbes' face, and as he let go of Barbara's hands Isla was fixed, once again, by an unfriendly look. She returned it as their hands touched briefly, then fell apart.

'I like the one that knocked me down,' Barbara said as they went down the stairs to the street, 'but I don't like the old man, 'cos he doesn't like us, much, does he?' Then as they emerged on to Paisley Cross again, she asked hopefully, 'Can we go back now? Greta's waiting to teach me how to play peevers.'

Before returning to George Street they called in at the pawnbroker's in Canal Street, where Isla arranged for someone to come and have a look at her furniture. She then spent most of the money she had left, buying food and cleaning materials, and when they got back to the tenement she settled Ross in his cot with his toys while Barbara scampered out to play. Isla rolled her sleeves up, put on an apron, tied her hair up in a scarf, and tackled the gas stove.

The pawnbroker arrived two hours later and arranged to take most of the furniture off her hands for what seemed to be a very small amount of money. Half an hour after that, two boys arrived with a handcart and almost all the furniture left from the Gourock house was taken away.

The women standing round the entrances to the closes watched, their sharp eyes appraising every item and judging its value, probably to the penny, Isla thought. She smiled nervously at one or two of them, and received blank stares in return. Someone made a remark about snobby folks who liked to show off their possessions, and there was a general snigger of agreement.

'Pay no heed, missus,' the man with the cart muttered. 'Some folks is just jealous of everyone else.'

Isla bit her lip, and tried to ignore the stares.

'Folk never take kindly tae new neighbours,' Magret told her when she called in, Daisy tied to her by the shawl, and a cigarette – the same cigarette as yesterday, for all Isla knew – in her free hand. 'They'll come round in their own good time. Just don't be snobby with them when they dae talk tae ye. Ye'll need tae try tae redeem yer furniture when the ticket falls due, then just leave it in and take out another ticket. That way it stays yours. That's what we do with a bonny clock his auntie gave us when we got married.'

By now Isla had realised that the mysterious 'he'

Magret kept referring to was her husband. Magret sighed, then said wistfully, 'I'd like fine to see that clock on our mantelshelf just one time, but it's never been there, for we can never afford tae bring it out. The money's always needed for somethin' else.'

‧ Daisy was less flower-like than any baby Isla had ever seen. Beneath her bald little pate she studied the room with close-set black eyes, clearly inherited, along with the snub nose, from her mother.

Magret puffed at her cigarette and looked on while Isla scraped at the stove with a broken knife she had found lying near the dustbins in the back court. Ribbons of solid grease peeled off and fell on to the newspaper she had spread out on the floor.

'I don't know why ye're botherin', hen. It'll only get dirty again. That's what I hate about housework – it always has tae be done again.'

Daisy whimpered, and Magret settled herself in the armchair and opened her blouse, chattering on over the baby's head about the time when she had worked in Coats' mill, not far from George Street.

'It was nice, the way we all worked taegether. That's where I met him. It was noisy, right enough, and the fluff went for some of the women's lungs, but everyone was pally and we all had a good laugh. I'll mebbe get back there some day, when Daisy's older.'

'You might have another baby by then,' Isla ventured, and Magret gave a husky laugh.

'No' me, hen, not after the time I had with these two. I'd tae stay in the Infirmary for a week when I was carrying Daisy, and I near lost her the way I lost the two that came after our Greta. It's the rickets, ye see.

The nurse said the rickets was making it awful difficult for me tae carry weans.'

She hauled up her skirt unselfconsciously to reveal curved, vein-clustered legs, and Isla realised that the young woman's rolling walk and solid stocky body were due to the cruel disease, brought on by malnutrition, that distorted growing young bones.

'They said there'd be no more weans for me,' Magret explained, pushing her skirt down again.

'I'm sorry.'

'Ach, it suits us fine, for weans cost money and we've scarce got enough for the two we have already. He doesnae get a big pay. See my sister Agnes? Six weans she's got – and there'll be more afore she gets too old for it. She's never done carrying an' birthing weans, and worryin' about where their next meal's comin' from.' Magret shook her head and took another puff at her cigarette. 'I'd not want tae be her, poor soul. Anyway, I'd not want tae go back into that Infirmary – there was a terrible smell stingin' at my nose all the time from all that disinfectant they used. Cleaning like dafties day and night, so they were!'

'How could you agree to such a thing?'

It had been a long day. At the end of days like this, Gilchrist Forbes wondered if the time had come to hand over the business to his son and retire to the soothing pleasures of his books and his garden.

'I didn't agree to it,' he said wearily. 'There was no question of that. The woman owns the building and she has a right to live there if she wishes.'

Colin glared at his father across the over-furnished

drawing-room. 'But here in Paisley – scarcely more than a mile from the McAdams' home! She could have chosen to live anywhere in Scotland – why settle so close to Ainslie and her mother?'

'It takes money to buy or rent a place to live, and Kenneth McAdam left nothing but debts.'

'Surely she has money of her own – or family she can turn to?'

'Apparently not.' Gilchrist filled his glass almost to the brim, then tilted the decanter enquiringly. When Colin shook his head, his father set down the decanter and sipped at his own whisky.

'I find it hard to believe that she's entirely alone in the world.' The younger man's normally cheerful face was set in hard lines, his eyes stormy.

'There's an aunt in Edinburgh—'

'Well, there you are, then!'

'But Mrs – Mrs Moffatt tells me that she has no wish to throw herself and her children on this woman's mercy.'

Colin snorted. 'No doubt she'll have no hesitation in throwing herself on Mrs McAdam's mercy.'

'She claims that she has no intention of doing so.'

'And you believe her?'

Gilchrist took another swallow of whisky and tried to keep his own temper under control. 'Colin, I don't know what she has in mind. Nor do I have the power to order her out of her own property.'

'You must reason with her, Father! Point out that it's wrong for her to—' Colin stopped abruptly as his mother came into the room.

'What's wrong for who?' Phemie Forbes asked at once. She loved gossip and had ears as sharp as a bat's,

54

particularly when it came to things she wasn't supposed to hear.

'Nobody, my dear,' Gilchrist started to say, but Colin blurted out, 'We were talking about Kenneth McAdam's . . .' Under his father's suddenly hard gaze he paused, biting back the words he had been about to utter, then said sullenly 'Kenneth McAdam's other woman.'

Phemie's round, good-natured face wrinkled with concern. 'Poor Catherine, all those years as a good wife to the man, and now this terrible shock on top of his death. It's changed her beyond recognition, Gilchrist. She's refusing to put a foot over her own doorstep, convinced that the whole town's whispering and pointing.' She sat down in her usual armchair by the fire and reached for her embroidery. 'I keep telling her that folk forget quickly, but she'll not listen to me.'

'I'm wondering if they really will forget, with the woman moving to Paisley,' Colin said.

'Moving to—' Phemie, about to plunge her needle into the heart of a half-stitched rosebud, plunged it into her own finger instead, and gave a choked shriek of pain. 'Look what you've made me do!'

She held her hand well away from the material in the embroidery ring and her husband hurriedly set down his glass and dropped to his knees beside her, whipping a crisp white handkerchief from his breast pocket to mop the bead of blood from her finger.

'Gilchrist, you'll ruin your handkerchief!' Phemie pulled her hand back and sucked at the injured finger. Round it she said, 'In Paisley? In this town?'

'In a tenement building in George Street that Mr McAdam left to her,' Colin confirmed.

'But surely the property should pass to Catherine?'

Gilchrist Forbes' knees cracked like winter twigs as he straightened up. 'Kenneth signed it over to her legally some time before his death. I can't force her to give it up, or to move away from the town.'

'But what'll happen if poor Catherine gets to hear of it?'

'The young woman's calling herself by her own name – Moffatt. I don't think she intends to make life difficult for Catherine.'

'I'd not be so sure about that,' Colin put in, and his father glared at him.

'She has two children to support, Phemie. It's my belief that she merely wants a roof over their heads until such time as she can make other plans.'

'There are children?'

'A boy and a girl.'

Tears came into Phemie's eyes. She loved children, and had always mourned the fact that she herself had had only one. She had been looking forward to Colin's marriage to Ainslie McAdam, and the hope of having many grandchildren in the future. 'The poor wee souls, what a start to have in life!'

'She seems to be a caring mother, I'm sure she'll do her best for them.' Gilchrist Forbes stared down at his handkerchief, then, guiltily, started refolding it to hide the bloody stain.

'I think you're being altogether too kindly in your attitude, Father,' Colin told him shortly. 'The woman may well be more ruthless than you think. Ainslie's very concerned about it all.'

'If Catherine hears that this woman and her children

are here, in Paisley, it may well be the final straw,' his mother agreed. 'She's in quite a state of depression as it is over Ainslie's latest news.'

'What news?' Colin came across the room towards his mother, bumping into an occasional table in his haste. 'What about Ainslie?'

'Did you not know? She's found work for herself.'

'Where? What's she doing?'

'Let me see that handkerchief, Gilchrist.' Phemie held out a hand and her husband reluctantly relinquished the folded square. She shook it out and tutted. 'Just as I thought – you've managed to get blood on it. It must be soaked in salt and cold water at once.'

'Mother, what sort of work has Ainslie found?' Colin persisted.

'She's taken on a position at Blayne's the auctioneers in MacDowall Street. Catherine's most upset about it, but Ainslie's not trained for anything, after all, and with Innes's school fees to find, not to mention the house to run, there's little Catherine can do about it. You know Ainslie, she can be very deter— Colin, where are you going?'

'Out.' Her son threw the word over his shoulder.

'Colin,' Phemie began, but he had already gone. She sighed, crumpling the handkerchief in her hand. 'Poor boy, he's still very upset about Ainslie returning his ring.'

Gilchrist Forbes picked up his glass of whisky. 'No point in fretting about it, my dear. They must work out their own problems, as we had to do at their age.'

'We didn't have such bad problems, though, Gil.' Phemie's voice was wretched. 'Who'd have thought of a level-headed man like Kenneth McAdam killing himself, then turning out to be a bigamist?'

Her husband shook his head. 'I wish he'd come to me when his business started going wrong. I would have done all I could to help. It should never have come to this.'

'What's this other woman like, Gil?'

The sound of his son's car starting up took Forbes to the window. He watched the vehicle roaring out of the gate, scattering gravel to left and right. 'Young, much younger than Kenneth. She has dignity, I'll give her that. I don't think she's out to cause more trouble for Catherine. I can't understand why he did it – took her through a marriage ceremony, I mean. I'd never dream of doing such a thing.'

Phemie, setting aside the handkerchief and picking up her embroidery, smiled fondly at him. 'I don't think you would, my dear. But this whole business has just proved that we never know what's going on behind other people's walls, hasn't it?'

He swung round from the window. 'Are you telling me that the McAdams weren't happy in their marriage?'

Phemie sighed. 'Even though she's a friend I'll admit that I've always sensed a coldness in Catherine. I think she put appearance before anything else. Kenneth, now – I'm not sure that he was strong enough for her. From what Catherine's said about her father-in-law, I get the impression that he was a much stronger man than poor Kenneth. She seemed to admire him greatly. What was he like, Gil? I never knew him well – he died not long after I became friendly with Catherine.'

'I remember him as being very able, in every way. Kenneth worshipped him.'

'Perhaps,' said Phemie shrewdly, 'he lived in his father's shadow.'

'Surely not.' Then, tiring of the turn the conversation was taking, Gilchrist Forbes said, 'As to Ainslie, I think she may well rue the day she decided to earn her own living. She could come running back to Colin yet.'

'I'd not be too sure of that, she's a very determined girl. Stubborn, Catherine says, like her grandmother.'

'In that case,' her husband returned to his chair and reached for the evening newspaper, 'we can only hope he gets over her quickly, and finds someone more suitable.'

6

Within two weeks Isla let her few remaining pieces of furniture go to the pawnshop, realising that the room was too small for them. She bought an old fireside chair from the pawnbroker, scrubbing it well before covering its slippery, worn seat and back with remnant material bought cheaply from a draper's shop. She bought more cloth to make curtains for the window, and another curtain to stretch on string across the storage space below the bed. She crawled reluctantly into the space first, poking a long-handled brush ahead gingerly, and found a dirty tin hip-bath which served herself and the children very well, once it was scrubbed out with disinfectant.

An orange box obtained from the local greengrocer made a serviceable cupboard for their few dishes, turned on its side and with a scrap of bright material hung on a string along the top to curtain it off. Searching the waste-ground at the back of the building, she found two bricks of the same size and used a piece of wood to scrape off the slimy creatures adhering beneath them, holding the bricks at arm's length as she worked, her face twisted with disgust. When she was satisfied that the bricks were free of pests, she scrubbed them with Jeyes Fluid and sat the orange-box on top of them to keep it clear of the floor.

Her own clothes and the children's clothes were hung from nails hammered into the walls, and another curtain on a string beneath the sink closed off an area for the cleaning utensils. She scrubbed the shallow wall-cupboards and lined their shelves with an unwanted roll of wall-paper bought for two pence from a paint-shop, and after finding a spider in the flour crock, made sure that all the food kept in the cupboards was well covered.

The rent money, which she collected every Monday morning from Mr Forbes' front office, was spasmodic, and barely enough, at times, to see her through the week and pay her own rent on a Friday evening, but as soon as she could, she bought paint to brighten up the warped woodwork round the window. Gradually the room began to look cleaner and brighter.

It was impossible to get rid of the smell of sweat and urine and stale cooking that had soaked into the fabric of the entire tenement, but Isla did her best, blocking up mouse-holes in the skirting and swabbing Jeyes Fluid into the cracks in the floorboards to deter the cockroaches that emerged at night and sometimes were to be found during the day, wandering across the hearth. Once, she and Barbara collapsed shrieking into each other's arms after a particularly large cockroach marched across the table before their horrified eyes during a meal.

She worked from morning to night on the small room, falling into bed bone-weary after each day's efforts. The work helped to ease her deep sense of loss;

Kenneth was never far from her mind and she cried herself to sleep most nights, longing for the warmth of his arms, and the security that his love and strength had given her. She talked about him to the children, determined that they wouldn't be allowed to forget him. But there was nobody she herself could talk to about him, and about what he had meant, and still meant, to her. So she worked instead, driving herself on.

'This place smells like the Infirmary,' Magret complained one day, fanning the air before her. Isla, on her knees in a corner of the room, brushing disinfectant into a particularly bad crack, straightened her aching back and rubbed a hand across her forehead.

'If I don't get rid of those insects I'll go mad.'

'Ach, ye'll never get rid of them,' Magret told her. 'They was here before us, and they'll be here long after we've gone. 'Sides, they don't do any harm.'

That same evening, noticing Barbara scratching furiously, fingers buried in her thick bronze hair, Isla investigated, and recoiled in horror as she saw tiny lice scurrying over her daughter's scalp, weaving through the hair like natives bustling through a jungle. She snatched Ross up from the floor, where he was placidly playing with a toy motor car, and saw that his scalp, too, was alive with vermin.

'What's the matter?' Barbara asked apprehensively, eyeing her mother's face.

'N-nothing.' Isla put Ross down and filled the kettle at the sink with shaking hands. 'I think it's time you both got your hair washed, that's all.'

'You washed it yesterday.'

'I know that.' Isla suddenly realised to her horror that

she had absent-mindedly raised her hand to scratch her own head, and snatched it back. She could have burst into tears. She had done her best to make sure that the children were clean, but now it seemed that she was fighting a losing battle. It would have done no good to insist that they stayed away from the other children. Thanks to Greta, Barbara had settled into her new life and had been accepted by the other children in spite of the fact that she 'talked posh' and wore better clothes than they did. She had learned to play peevers and spent most of her day hopping and skipping and jumping over chalked squares and symbols on the pavement.

A natural mimic, she had fallen quickly into her new friends' speech patterns, and although Isla did her best to make sure that she spoke properly in the house, she knew that Barbara had to be free to talk to the other children in their own language. The little girl had, fortunately, adjusted to the sudden changes in her life, and it would be cruel to isolate her from the rest of the youngsters in the street.

The children yelled their protests when she scrubbed hard at their heads that night. The next day she went out and bought a fine-toothed comb and a large cake of coal tar soap, which added its own pungent aroma to the strong smell of disinfectant.

Magret sniffed at the air on her next visit, and said knowledgeably, 'Nits?'

Isla stared at her in horror. 'How did you know?'

'It's the smell of the soap. No need tae look so worried, hen – all the kids has got nits round here. Some worse than others – have ye not seen the poor wee souls with the shaved heads? It doesnae mean ye're dirty,' she hurried to assure her stricken friend. 'I've heard that nits can be found in grand houses tae.'

As the weeks went by, Isla got to know the other people in the building – old Granny Thomson, a tiny wizened creature, bent and twisted with arthritis, who crept in and out of her own door like a mouse and never spoke to anyone; Lena McNab, a striking-looking woman who ran the tiny baker's shop a short distance along the road, and her husband and former messenger-boy Peter, thin and clearly younger than Lena, peering at life through a pair of thick wire-framed spectacles. Lena had a warm heart, and sometimes gave her neighbours pastries and loaves that had become too stale to sell. Broken up and soaked in a mixture of milk and water, then covered with a scattering of sugar, the stale bread and pastries made a nourishing meal for the children.

Two of the flats upstairs were tenanted by the Kellys, a shy young couple, and Mrs Brown and her son, recently out of school and apprenticed to a joiner's shop. There was no sign of Mr Brown – Magret said that he had run away with 'the woman from the Co-op'. The third flat, a single room sandwiched between the others, which both had two rooms, was the residence of the formidable Mrs Leach, a gaunt widow who wore her grey hair twisted into a small tight bun at the back of her head, and made it her business to see that the other inhabitants behaved themselves.

The first time Isla hung out clothes to dry Mrs Leach came forging her way up the steps from the close to inspect them.

'Ye're not used tae hangin' out a washin', are ye?' she said with a disparaging sniff.

'I know fine how to do it,' Isla snapped back, aware that it would be fatal to give in to a bully.

To her astonishment, Mrs Leach reached up, unpinned a garment from the line, and flipped it about. 'Ye shouldnae hang yer bairn's trousers from the waist like that,' she said, her hands re-pinning the small garment so rapidly that they were blurred. 'Ye hang them from the legs, then the waistband can blow in the wind an' get dry. Here, I'll give ye a hand.'

She delved into the basket and proceeded to hang the clothes on the line, driving the wooden pegs into place so strongly that Isla expected them to snap in two.

'Ye've got some bonny things,' the woman commented as she worked. 'It's nice tae see things like that hangin' on our lines.' She wiped her hands on her wrap-around pinny and bent to Ross, who was watching, wide-eyed, clutching at his mother's skirt.

'How old is he?'

'Fourteen months.'

'He's a bonny wean.' Mrs Leach bared her yellowed teeth in a smile at Ross, who retreated further into Isla's skirt, pushing a thumb into his mouth.

'An' ye don't want him doin' that,' Mrs Leach snapped, straightening. 'His teeth'll grow in crooked.'

When Isla told Magret about the encounter her friend nodded sagely. 'If she helped ye tae hang yer washing, it means that she approves o' ye,' she announced.

It was a surprise to find that young Mrs Kelly was Mrs Leach's only child.

'That's why the wee soul never opens her mouth – she's never had the chance,' Magret said. 'They came down in the world after Mr Leach was killed in an accident at his work, and they'd nowhere else tae go but here. The lassie worked in an office, and when she insisted on gettin' married tae one of the lads she worked with, no matter what her mother had to say aboot it, Mrs Leach got them the house through the wall from her, so's she could keep an eye on them.'

She drew her breath in sharply through pursed lips and shook her head. 'Poor souls – the old woman gave them a right hard time when he lost his job last year – not that it was his fault that the place where he worked closed down. Ye'd have thought he'd done it just tae spite her, the way she went on. I think that's why they've no' got any weans yet – he must be scared tae touch the lassie, with her mother only the thickness of a wall away from their bed. If ever I treat my lassies the way she treats hers, I hope they've got the sense tae push me under a tram.'

Gradually, Isla began to settle into her new home. She managed to clear the lice from the children's heads and also managed, by dint of careful budgeting, to keep the three of them nourished and still have enough left over to pay the rent-collector when he called every Friday. He was a tall, sour-faced man who spread the coins out over his palm and counted every one carefully before stowing them away in his leather pouch and writing the date and the amount down in a large book, licking his pencil before he began. He had the look of a man who wouldn't take kindly to people being behind with the rent.

Magret had confirmed Isla's instincts from the beginning. 'Ye don't want tae get intae his bad books, hen.

He'd no' care about you being on yer lone with the weans tae look after – he'd take yer last penny out of yer hand and think nothin' of it.'

Isla grew to hate her Monday morning trip to Gilchrist Forbes' office to collect the rent-money, because she was taking money from people she knew, people who had little enough to spare and found it difficult at times to raise the rent. But she had no option, for she had her own children to care for. The little she made by keeping her furniture in pawn helped, but not much, and as the summer crept along she had to pawn first one piece of jewellery, then another, to make ends meet.

A previous tenant had left a rusty old garden fork by the bins. Seeing it lying there, Isla thought of saving money by growing vegetables. She already knew that a patch of the weedy stretch of ground at the back of the tenement officially belonged to the single room she and the children now lived in; she marked it off carefully with rows of stones so that nobody, particularly Mrs Leach, could accuse her of taking over anyone else's weeds, and carefully went over it, picking up stones and rubbish, which she piled neatly in one corner before fetching the fork.

The ground hadn't been dug for years, and it was as hard as the mysterious bits of iron she kept finding in it. Stopping to catch her breath, she saw that several people were at their windows, watching her, and even the dingy net curtain at Granny Thomson's window was twitching. Soon there was a row of children peering over the wall at her.

'Heh, missus,' one of them shouted. 'Are ye buryin' some'dy?'

'I'm going to grow things,' she told him, and the children howled with laughter, as though she had said something very funny.

After struggling for an entire afternoon Isla had made very little impact on the ground. Nevertheless, she went back to it again and again whenever time and weather permitted. Magret watched, fascinated, Daisy straddled across her hip.

'Ye'll never dae it.'

'I'm doing it now.' Isla proudly indicated a square foot of exposed earth. Magret peered at it, and sniffed.

'Even if ye dae manage tae get somethin' planted, it'll vanish as soon as it appears,' she argued, nodding towards the next tenement, where a large, rowdy father-less family was known to survive mainly on the proceeds of the children's thefts. 'That lot'd steal a dead cat out of a gutter, so they would.'

'I'd like to see them try,' Isla said grimly, plunging the fork into the ground and leaning her weight on it. 'I've got my children to feed, and nobody's going to stop me!'

At the beginning of August Barbara celebrated her fifth birthday. When she and Kenneth had talked about the forthcoming event, not long before his death, Isla had suggested buying a doll's house for their daughter.

'I used to have one when I was a little girl – a lovely house, with stairs to the bedrooms and a cook in the kitchen,' she recalled, the pleasure of playing with the dolls' house flooding back to her. 'I wish I'd been able to keep it, for my own little girl.'

Kenneth had put his arm about her. 'She shall have a new one all to herself,' he promised. 'We'll choose it between us, and you can have the enjoyment of decorating and furnishing it for her.'

Remembering, Isla blinked back tears and looked round the shabby home she now shared with her children.

There was no room for a fine doll's house here, nor the money to buy one. She must find some other gift for Barbara, something she could make herself, for she couldn't afford to buy presents.

She was working on her gift a week before Barbara's birthday when someone rapped on the door. Isla, assuming that it was Magret, called out, 'The door's on the latch,' then jumped to her feet, showering clothes-pegs and scraps of cloth on to the floor, as Ainslie McAdam walked in.

'What are you doing here?'

Ainslie's mouth tightened as she looked at the mourning band on Isla's arm, then her gaze travelled on around the room. She was clearly shocked by what she saw. 'So it's true – you are living here!'

'I am – not that it's any business of yours.' Isla was stung by the look on the other girl's face as she took in the shabby room. At their last meeting she had felt herself to be in the wrong, ignorant though she had been of Kenneth's other family. This time, though, she wasn't going to allow Ainslie McAdam to dominate her. 'Who told you we were here?'

'Colin Forbes.'

'I might have known. He'd no business to tell you anything about me.' Isla stooped to gather up the clothes-pegs and the scraps of material she had been working on.

'It is my business, if you're living in Paisley. I told you already that—'

Isla straightened up. Ainslie was the same height as herself and she met the girl's blue eyes unblinkingly. 'This was the only place we could come to. I had to get out of the house I was in, and I've no money of my own. Ken— your father,' she amended, seeing the way the other girl winced at her familiar use of his first name, 'left me this building. We were lucky one of the rooms was lying empty.'

Ainslie's curl of the lip intimated that nobody living in such a place could consider themselves to be lucky. 'You could have sold it and used the money to find somewhere further away,' she said aloud.

'And starved my children under some hedge while we waited to find out if anyone wanted it?' Isla's voice was scathing. 'It's for sale now, but not a soul's made an offer.' She saw that her hands were shaking, and busied them in smoothing out the pieces of cloth she had laid on the table.

Ainslie moved forward, and her foot caught against something. She bent and picked it up, her brows wrinkling as she studied the clothes-peg in her hand. A piece of white rag had been tied round the knob at the top of the peg and a face stitched on to the cloth. Round blue eyes stared back at her, and there was the suggestion of a neat nose and a smiling rosebud of a mouth.

Isla, reddening, almost snatched the peg from Ainslie's hand. 'Don't worry,' she said dryly, 'I'm not a witch, making effigies of you and your mother. It's a doll for my daughter's birthday.'

'Is that the red-haired child I saw playing in the str—' Ainslie flinched as Ross, disturbed from his sleep, shifted and whimpered from his cot in a shadowy corner of the room. Isla went to soothe him, then, when the whimpering rose to a wail, she lifted him from the cot.

'You haven't told me yet why you've called,' she said as she turned. A shaft of light from the window turned the baby's sweat-damp curls to flame as she carried him over to the chair by the fire.

'You know fine why I called. You'll have to find somewhere else to live!' Ainslie's voice was harsh and loud, and Ross, still half asleep, clutched at his mother and cringed away from this angry stranger, pushing his hot face into Isla's neck. The smell of ammonia from his wet napkin soured the air.

'It's all right, love, Mummy's got you safe.' Isla soothed him, then over his head she asked Ainslie McAdam, 'Where d'you suggest we go?'

'Anywhere but Paisley! I'll not have you upsetting my mother . . .'

'I've already told you that I've no intention of going anywhere near your mother.'

'But she might hear about you. Someone might tell her.'

'I doubt if we move in the same social circles,' Isla pointed out, and the younger girl flushed at the contempt in her voice.

'I'm working now – I don't earn much but I could probably give you some money in a few weeks' time if you—'

'Miss McAdam, you may not think much of my

home, but at least it's mine and I'm not beholden to anyone. I wouldn't take a penny of your money, not even if you were the wealthiest woman in the country and I was starving.'

'You took my father's money. You had his children.'

If she hadn't been holding Ross, Isla would have launched herself at the girl and known the satisfaction of bundling her out of the room by force. Instead, she said, her voice shaking, 'At the time, I thought I had the right, as his legal wife. Now, will you please get out of my house?'

Ainslie's fists clenched by her sides. 'Don't you care about how terrible it's been for us, for my mother, with the whole town talking about what my father did? Isn't that bad enough, without having his – his—' she choked, then rushed on, 'you living right here in Paisley!'

Her selfishness infuriated Isla. 'D'you never give a thought to the suffering he must have gone through, to be driven to do what he did?'

'Why should I? He made sure that he was well out of it, well away from the whispering and the glances!' the girl said bitterly.

'It seems to me that it must take a great deal of misery to cause any human being to put an end to his life. As to my presence here in Paisley' – Isla's voice was as sharp and as cold as an icicle as she got to her feet, holding Ross close, and swept past Ainslie to the door – 'I'm here only because my bairns and I have nowhere else to go. I'm using my own name, not your father's. I've said nothing to anyone about my past life, and I don't intend to.' She lifted the latch and the door swung creakily open. 'Now – I'd be grateful if you would just go away and let me and my children be.'

Ainslie hesitated, then walked past her and into the close. Isla closed the door at once, then waited, clutching Ross, her ears straining for the sound of the young woman walking out of the close. Eventually it came, the tap of well-shod feet moving out into the street and away.

Isla went slowly back to the fireside chair, Ross weighing heavily in her arms, and collapsed into it. The baby, frightened by something he couldn't understand, clutched at her and burst into tears.

'It's all right, pet,' Isla tried to reassure him. Then her own tears came, and the two of them wept together.

7

Ainslie McAdam was in turmoil as she left the old tenement. She had gone there with the intention of talking
things out once and for all with the woman who had
brought such shame down on her family, making it
clear to Isla how impossible it was for her to stay in
Paisley.

But as she stepped out on to the pavement she felt
that she had failed miserably, and had only succeeded in
making herself look foolish.

A gaggle of toddlers played contentedly in the sun-
splashed gutter, most of them barefoot and wearing
dirty, ragged clothing. One or two were naked from the
waist down. Ainslie shuddered and averted her eyes –
and found herself looking at the little red-haired girl she
had seen on her way in. The child, better dressed than
most of her companions, was energetically swinging one
end of a rope, her brown eyes sparkling with enjoyment.
Another little girl held the other end, while a third
child, in the middle, leapt high with both feet clamped
together to allow the rope to swing beneath her. As
Ainslie watched, she mistimed a leap, and was sent

sprawling on the pavement as the rope tangled her ankles, bouncing up again almost at once.

'My turn!' Isla's daughter – and her own half-sister, Ainslie realised with sudden horror – pushed her end of the rope into the defeated child's hands and took her place. 'Ready? One, two, three, a-leary,' she chanted, feet together, skirt flying as she leapt into the air, up and down, her feet scarcely brushing the pavement before she was airborne again, the rope smacking against the stone slabs beneath her.

Ainslie turned and almost ran from the place.

When she got home her mother was in her usual place, on the sofa in the drawing-room, a glass and a half-empty bottle of tonic wine on a table close to hand.

'You're late,' she said as soon as her daughter went in.

'I had some work to finish,' Ainslie lied. Crossing the carpet to kiss Catherine, she realised that compared to the small room she had recently visited, the drawing-room was enormous. She had always taken her home, with its large, high-ceilinged, carpeted rooms and its comfortable furnishings, for granted, and had never been in any other type of house, until today.

'How are you feeling, Mother?'

'Oh . . .' Catherine shrugged one shoulder, and let her voice drift into silence.

'Did anyone call?'

'Don't be silly, Ainslie, who would call on us now?'

'Mrs Forbes, for one.' Ainslie tried to keep her voice cheerful.

'She did look in,' Catherine acknowledged, reaching

for her glass, then, 'what do you mean, you had work to finish?'

'Some items that came in this afternoon had to be catalogued.' It was the truth, she had had to work very hard to make time to visit George Street, but she had managed it.

'See to the fire, will you? Your father would turn in his grave,' Catherine went on as her daughter obeyed, 'if he knew that you were working as an ordinary clerkess, after all the money he spent on your education.'

'I don't know how to do anything else. I can't type, or sew, or cook.'

'You were brought up to be a lady, and to run your own house efficiently when the time came.'

Ainslie, poking at the coals in the grate, gave a soft sigh, recognising the build-up to a spate of reproaches over her broken engagement. 'It's a lovely day, Mother – too warm for a fire. Why don't you go into the garden and sit in the sun for a little while?'

'I prefer to be indoors,' Catherine McAdam said flatly. 'That reminds me – Innes is in the garden and he should be working at his homework now. Fetch him in, will you?'

Ainslie did as she was asked, glad of the chance to escape from the stuffy drawing-room. The garden at the rear of the house was brilliant with colour from the rose-bushes her father had planted. They massed the flower-beds, filled a small circular bed in the middle of the lawn like a jewelled brooch set against green velvet, and swarmed up the red brick wall that hid the veg-etable garden from sight.

Innes was crouched down by the wall, studying a

butterfly that had settled on his hand. 'Look,' he said as his sister approached. 'Isn't it beautiful?'

She bent down, steadying herself with one hand on his back, careful to avoid letting her shadow fall on the insect and startling it. The rich colour of its spread wings glowed in the sunlight.

'Beautiful,' she agreed.

'It's a Red Admiral. Look, its wings are the same colour as your hair. I wish mine wasn't so gingery.'

'There's nothing wrong with your hair.' Ainslie ruffled it affectionately, recalling that the baby she had seen that afternoon in George Street had the same fiery red head. 'Mother says it's time for homework.'

He groaned. 'Already?'

'You'd better go in.' She watched as he coaxed the butterfly on to a cluster of yellow nasturtiums fronting the flower border, then followed him as he made for the back door.

'I suppose I should let her know I'm in.' Innes trotted into the drawing-room while Ainslie went upstairs to change out of the black skirt and jacket she had worn to the auction house.

A large portrait of the first Innes McAdam, her grandfather, hung on the half-landing beside the bathroom door. He had been a handsome man, with piercing eyes below a thatch of crisp white hair, a neatly trimmed moustache and beard hiding the lower part of his face. He had died when Ainslie was only a month old, leaving the successful business he had started as an ambitious young man to his only child, her father.

'He was so disappointed to have a granddaughter instead of a grandson,' Catherine had told Ainslie so frequently that, as a child, she had believed that her arrival in the world had been the sole cause of her grandfather's departure from it. 'I wish he had lived to see Innes.'

In her room, Ainslie stripped to her petticoat and poured water from the flowered china ewer into the matching basin. As she washed she heard Innes come upstairs and go into his own room, then her mother's bedroom door opened and closed. Ainslie put on a black crêpe de Chine dress and brushed her curly hair until it crackled. The house was hushed, as always, and she found herself missing the bustle and excitement of the auction house.

To her surprise, she had discovered that she enjoyed working in the auction house. She liked the bustle of the place, and the continual coming and going. She found satisfaction in neatly listing the goods that came in and noting the possible value of each item.

She sat on the bed and picked up a fashion magazine, then tossed it down almost at once, rising to wander listlessly about the room. She was in mourning – there was no sense in looking at bright-coloured clothes that she couldn't wear.

Almost an entire wall of the bedroom was taken up by a long low bookcase topped with ornaments and toys that had been dearly loved in their day. Every book she had ever owned was on the shelves, from her first picture book to handsomely bound editions of favourites such as *The Wind in the Willows*, and the works of Dickens and Jane Austen. Most of them had been gifts from her father, who had himself been a keen reader.

Looking at them now, Ainslie wondered if the books

proved his love for her, or merely his desire that she should understand literature. She had wanted so much to be able to love her parents openly, and had always envied those school friends who talked about cosy chats with their mothers, and hugs from their fathers. Her parents' desire that she should be well fed and well dressed, their concern over her childhood ailments, showed that they cared about her, but neither of them had been demonstratively affectionate.

It embarrassed her now to remember how she had followed Colin Forbes around as a small child, desperate for any sign of kindness, grateful for it. Deep down, she knew that she had become engaged to Colin because he was the only person who had ever said that he loved her. Because of that – and because their engagement had pleased her parents.

Then, just when she had begun to hope that she could change her world, setting up a home with Colin, having children who would grow up knowing that they were loved and cherished, her father had ruined everything. And Ainslie, crushed beyond belief by his final desertion, his final betrayal, had decided that it only proved that no man, not even Colin, could be trusted.

She thought of the dark little room she had been in earlier that day, the tiny scraps of cloth on the table and the clothes-peg with a face drawn on to a piece of rag, the young woman who had criticised her sharply for not giving any thought to her father's misery. She wished now that she had kept away from George Street.

She turned from the bookcase with a swift twist of the body, and sat down again on the bed, thinking now about her mother. Catherine McAdam had always seemed to be such a strong character, a woman more than capable of standing alone. She had run her home with great competence, taken her rightful place in local society, known just what to do and what to say in any situation.

She had turned to nobody for help when her husband died, arranging immediately after the funeral for all his clothes to be sent to a charitable organisation, and packing his personal possessions away until such time as Innes was old enough to inherit them. She had had his bedroom door locked, and then, with everything seen to, she had become an invalid.

'Let your mother work through her grief in her own time,' the doctor had told Ainslie when she voiced her concern about Catherine's listlessness. 'She'll come to terms with her loss when she's ready.'

But as the weeks passed Catherine hadn't shown any signs of recovery. Sometimes Ainslie wondered if she was genuinely grieving, if she had perhaps been closer to her husband than Ainslie had thought. That possibility didn't comfort her at all, but merely added to her growing terror with the fear that her mother, too, might kill herself rather than go on alone.

She jumped up from the bed and smoothed the coverlet briskly, trying to smooth her worries away at the same time, then went into her mother's room. Catherine, in a long-skirted black evening dress and a light wrap over her shoulders, sat at the dressing-table, staring blankly into the mirror. Even in the midst of mourning, even in her depression, she insisted on dressing for dinner, although only her children were there to see her.

'Mother, would you like me to brush your hair?'

Catherine's body rippled as though a shiver had run through it. Her mirrored eyes lifted to stare at Ainslie blankly, then blinked, recognition drifting into them.

'Very well.' She sat straight-backed as Ainslie carefully removed the pins from her hair and let it drop over her shoulders, then began to draw the brush through it. The room was immaculate, as usual, with Catherine's silver-backed brushes and mirror neatly laid out on the dressing-table. The small studio portrait of Catherine and Kenneth McAdam that had always stood on the dressing-table was gone, replaced by a photograph of Ainslie's grandfather Innes and his wife, a woman with character in her features rather than beauty. Looking from the portrait in its elaborate silver frame to her own mirrored reflection, Ainslie had to acknowledge that her mother was right – there was a look of Grandmother McAdam about her features.

'Perhaps you should have a change, Mother – go away for a few weeks,' she suggested as she worked.

'Why should I want to do that?'

'It might do you good. Helensburgh, maybe. There are some pleasant hotels there, and the sea air can be very bracing.'

Catherine shook her head impatiently, almost tangling her fine greying hair in the brush. 'How can I go away just as Innes is about to start the new school year?'

'I can see to him.'

'You?' Catherine gave a short, bitter laugh. 'You've got your work to attend to now.'

'I'm not there all the time. And the servants are very

81

well trained, they can be trusted to look after him when I'm not at home.'

'No.' Catherine snapped the word out, then folded her lips tightly. Ainslie, who knew better than to argue, said nothing more.

When her mother's hair was pinned into its usual twisted plait at the back of her head, she went downstairs to see that the table was set for dinner and the meal ready on time. As the clock chimed seven Catherine came in to take her place at the foot of the table. Innes, his face shining from a recent bout with his face-flannel, scampered into the dining-room a few minutes later.

'Sorry, Mother, I had to finish the sentence before I forgot what I was writing about,' he said breathlessly, his bright hair introducing light and movement into the room.

Catherine smiled, and held her arms out to him. 'Come and give Mother a kiss, darling.'

As he smacked a kiss on her pale cheek, her arms encircled him tightly. Watching, remembering how Isla had comforted her own red-haired son earlier that day, Ainslie suddenly felt very lonely.

Isla made two dolls out of clothes-pegs, wrapping pipe-cleaners round them to make arms, clothing them in long dresses and giving them mob caps. She bought a small orange box from the greengrocer's and hid it beneath the wall-bed. In the evenings, while the children slept, she covered its interior with scraps of wall-paper, drawing a large kitchen range on the back wall and a dresser on one of the side walls. A circle of cardboard nailed on to an empty wooden bobbin made a table, and other bobbins covered with cloth served as stools. With Plasticine, she made some plates for the table, finishing the single-roomed house off with a curtain stretched across the front on string.

Barbara was delighted with her gift. 'It's a house just the same size as ours, isn't it?' she said in wonder, kneeling before the orange box house. 'This is the mummy and this is the little girl.'

'She's a big little girl.'

'Not as big as her mummy.' Barbara stood the two peg dolls side by side and sure enough, one was a fraction smaller than the other. 'Where's the daddy?'

'You don't get daddy dolls,' Isla told her, and the little girl's lower lip trembled.

'Yes you do,' she insisted. 'Of course you do! Where is he?'

'At work?' Isla suggested, her mind on her sewing box. There was still some white material left that would do for a shirt, and a scrap of black that could be turned into trousers, and perhaps some kind of cap.

Barbara's face cleared, and she nodded. 'All right, but he'll be coming home. He'll be coming home soon.'

'Tomorrow.' Isla hugged her daughter. Barbara scarcely ever asked about Kenneth's whereabouts now, but clearly he was still in her mind.

Magret, invited with her children to share the small dumpling Isla had made for the occasion, was enthralled by the little house.

'Who'd've thought ye could turn an old orange box intae a house, and a clothes-peg intae a dolly?' she marvelled, studying one of the dolls closely. 'It's bonny, Isla.'

'It's not difficult.'

'Not for you, mebbe, but I'd never manage it.' Magret handed the doll back to her elder daughter, who bustled importantly over to the orange box and knelt down, pushing the top half of her body into it as she replaced the doll. Catching a glimpse of skinny little buttocks, Isla realised that Greta didn't wear drawers.

When Barbara woke up the next morning the daddy doll was in residence, much to her delight. The next day, over a mug of tea, Magret asked Isla to make a peg doll for Greta.

'She's been on at me for one ever since she saw Barbara's.'

Isla sipped the tea, realising that she was now used to its strength and sweetness, and to the mingled taste of condensed milk and grease.

'I could show you how to make it,' she offered, but Magret shook her head.

'I'm not good with my hands, like you,' she coaxed, and beamed her delight when Isla gave in.

8

Isla had begun to admit to herself that in trying to wrest a vegetable patch from the weedy backyard she was fighting a losing battle, but her pride wouldn't let her give in. She well knew that almost everyone living within sight of the back court was watching her progress, and, like Magret, none of them thought that she would succeed. So she battled on, glancing up one evening to see a young lad watching her from beside the wash-house.

Isla smiled at him, recognising Mrs Brown's son Drew, and he looked away in embarrassment, then looked back at her.

'What're ye growin'?'

'Potatoes, if I ever manage to clear enough land.'

He spat on his hands, then held them out. 'I'll give ye a hand. See's the fork.'

She handed it over, stepping back to let him get to the pitifully small amount of earth she had won from the grasses. He drove the tines of the fork deep into the ground with more force than she had thought possible from his slight frame, then leaned on the handle, lifting a solid clod of earth free. It had been bound into place by generations of grass roots that stubbornly held on to it, and he had the sense to work patiently at it until all the roots had snapped. He dumped the clod on the ground and smashed at it with the side of the fork, then drove the tines into the ground again.

Isla left him to it and went into the building. When she came back with a mug of tea in each hand, he had got into the rhythm of it, and had learned the sense of trying to gain only a little ground at a time.

He straightened up and accepted the tea with mumbled thanks. Together they sipped in silence. 'It might not work,' Isla said at last, 'but I don't think there's any harm in failing as long as you've tried.'

'Aye.' The lad drained the last of the tea, his Adam's apple bobbing in his thin throat, then handed the mug back and got on with his work, digging steadily until a cloud of midges, those tiny maddening flies that persecuted Scotland, arrived and made further work impossible.

'I could do more for ye, if ye want,' he said diffidently as the two of them retired to the close.

Isla hesitated, then decided that frankness was the only way. 'I can't afford to pay you.'

'Doesnae matter. I like diggin'.'

'What'll your mother say?'

'It was her that sent me down. I'd nothin' tae dae.'

'I tell you what – if you want to help, I'll share the potatoes with you and your mother.'

For the first time, he looked fully at her, and grinned. 'Aye. That'd be fine.'

By the time Barbara started school, Isla and young Drew Brown had dug over more than half the patch of ground between them, and a succession of women up and down George Street had asked Isla to make peg dolls for their daughters, just like the dolls Barbara and Greta had been showing off to the other children.

Isla, aware of the importance of building up a good relationship with her neighbours, refused nobody, and soon almost every little girl playing out on the pavement had become the proud owner of a peg doll. Some of the women offered her money in exchange for her work, while others brought half a dozen home-made scones, or a fruit loaf, or a good soup-bone with fragments of meat still attached, or a piece of material.

By the time she started attending the West School, only ten minutes' walk away from George Street, Barbara had made a number of friends, though Greta was her closest confidante. Barbara admired Greta; in her eyes, the child could do no wrong. This led to some conflict between mother and daughter, especially over the business of underwear.

'Greta doesn't need to wear drawers,' Barbara protested after being caught playing in the street with nothing on underneath her skirt. Her rolled-up knickers were substituting for a pillow in a battered dolls' pram that Greta had inherited from an older cousin.

'She would if she was my little girl.'

Barbara's lower lip slid forward mutinously. 'Drawers just get in the way when you want to pee in the yard.'

'When you want to – *what*?' Horrified, Isla stared at her daughter. 'But you always use the privy, like a good girl. Don't you?' she added, as Barbara shrugged her shoulders and scuffed the toe of one shoe over the floor.

'Sometimes someone's in the privy and I can't wait,

and anyway, every time I use it that old Mrs Leach comes running down to make sure I didn't make a mess,' Barbara muttered, adding, 'anyway, the grass is nicer, it's not all dark and smelly like the privy, and it tickles.'

'Barbara!' It was all that Isla could do not to shake the child. 'You must never ever use the yard as a privy, d'you hear me? No matter what anyone else does. If you do, I'll – I'll give you such a smacking!'

Barbara stared up at her, wide-eyed. Isla rarely hit her, and never hard.

'D'you hear me?' Isla insisted, and the child finally gave a sullen nod. When she had been sent out to play, with firm instructions to keep all her clothes on, Isla went back to her ironing, gnawing at her lower lip, aware that it was going to be hard to continue to insist on certain standards when the children Barbara played with had their own way of looking at life. The little girl had settled in well, even accepting her new surname without question, and as far as she was concerned the future would be like the present, living in one small room playing out on the pavement or in the rubbish-strewn backyard.

Isla still hoped that one day she and her children would be able to move out of George Street and back into the sort of home Kenneth had once provided for them. It was a hope that had begun to turn into a dream, for not one person had made an offer so far for the tenement building. But she refused to accept that she and her children were going to remain in George Street for ever.

Ross, playing on the hearth-rug with a wooden toy, lost interest in it and grabbed the leg of the fireside chair for support while he hauled himself upright. He toddled across the floor, moving from one piece of furniture to the other, until he got to the door, then banged on it, whimpering.

'You're too wee to go out and play,' Isla told him. As he continued to grizzle, she fetched the bag of clothespegs and offered it to him. He snatched at it and sat down on the floor, turning the bag upside down and emptying its contents out.

'Whatever would we do without pegs?' Isla wondered aloud, lifting the flat-iron from the gas ring and putting her finger in her mouth to damp it so that she could test the iron's heat. Barbara had started walking at an earlier age than Ross, but Magret had assured Isla that boys usually took longer than girls to get on their feet. Isla saw it as a blessing. All too soon Ross would be insisting on going out to play in the street like his sister, and then there would be two of them to deal with.

She thought of the little boys who played in the gutter, naked from the waist down, and the older boys, up to all sorts of mischief, from knocking on doors then running away to stealing from the local shops. Would Ross grow up to be like that? The responsibility of raising her children on her own weighed heavily on her shoulders, reviving the aching misery of Kenneth's death. At times like this, she would have sacrificed everything in the world, except Barbara and Ross, to bring Kenneth back again.

On the first day of the school term Magret and Isla saw their daughters settled in a large classroom noisy with the wails of children thrown into panic at the thought of being abandoned by their mothers. Barbara and Greta had no such qualms. Seated side by side, they were both enchanted with the double bench and the two desks with lids that could be raised to reveal an inviting space within, waiting to be filled.

'Thank God,' Magret said with all her heart as the two women made their way home. 'I made such a fuss the first day I started school that my mammy had tae take me home again. I got a right hammerin' when we got there, too. Black affronted, she was. I never liked the school. See the very smell of the place? When I went in there today I nearly turned and ran out again, the memories of my own time were that strong.'

Isla nodded. 'It helps when they've got each other. I was sorry for that woman whose wee boy wouldn't let go of her legs.'

Their smug pleasure at having such well-behaved children didn't last long. At half-past ten that morning, when Isla answered an imperious thumping at the door, Barbara marched past her into the room. 'I'm back,' she announced, tossing the shabby little school-bag that Isla had bought from the pawn-shop on to the floor.

'What are you doing here? You're supposed to be at school!'

'I've been,' said Barbara. 'We played with boxes of sand and sang a song, then they let us out, so me and Greta came home.'

Magret burst in just then without waiting to knock, towing a puzzled Greta by the wrist. 'Isla—'

'I know.'

'What would ye make of them?' Magret asked in exasperation, while Isla explained to her daughter, 'You were only let out to play for a wee while. Then you were supposed to go back in again until I came to take you home for your dinner.'

'Back again?' Barbara asked in astonishment.

'Aye, my lass, and tomorrow tae. Isla, we'll need tae take them back, an' me with the wean sleepin' in her cot . . .'

'Tomorrow?' Barbara and Greta squeaked in unison.

'You didn't say about tomorrow too,' Barbara accused her mother.

'Hen, ye've got years o' it ahead o' ye,' Magret said with heart-felt sympathy, adding to her own daughter, 'and you too, wee imp that ye are, what's yer daddy goin' tae say about this?'

'He'll have a good laugh about it.' Isla was beginning to see the funny side of the situation herself. 'You look after Ross, Magret, and I'll take them back. You'll come with me, won't you, Greta?'

'Uhuh,' Greta said round the thumb she had stuck into her mouth, while Barbara gave a huge sigh of irritation over the contrary ways of adults.

'You didn't say anything about going back in,' she pointed out as she and Greta were shepherded out of the room and through the close. 'You should have said!'

Ainslie McAdam had never been happier in her life. Charlie Blayne, her employer, was a broad-shouldered middle-aged man with twinkling blue eyes and a head of thick curly hair that had once been rich brown and was now well sprinkled with grey.

'I see myself as a working man's auctioneer, lass,' he told Ainslie when she applied for the post as his office clerkess. 'Folk die, an' their relatives want to get rid of a houseful of stuff, some of it pure rubbish. So they send for me, and if it can be sold, I'll sell it for them. Or mebbe they need a bit o' money, so they bring their granda's clock, or ornaments they never liked anyway – stuff they don't want back, or else they'd pawn it.'

He tipped his chair back and looked with satisfaction round his small office. It was filled with papers and ledgers and boxes crammed with books and spoons and pipe racks and pots and pans. A rag doll stared blankly at Ainslie over the top of one box.

'Folk all want different things. A picture frame or a nice wee ornament for the mantelpiece – or a toy for the wean,' Charlie went on, nodding at the doll. 'An' mebbe they're looking for a bit of a gamble. In a shop they must pay the price asked, but here, they might get just what they want for less, or have a bit of fun out-biddin' the next man.' He beamed at Ainslie. 'D'ye see what I mean?'

'I think so.'

'Ye never get bored in this job, lass. Ye never know from one day to the next what'll come in – or who. Now . . .' He swung his feet down from the desk and became more businesslike. 'What I need is someone to keep the paperwork tidy. There's lists to be sorted out and valuations to record, and letters to write and books to keep. There's not much to it, but I'd as soon be free to get on with the business of seein' to the sales and the stores and going out and about, valuing stuff. D'ye think ye could manage it?'

'I was good at arithmetic at school, and I can deal with lists,' she said cautiously.

'Can ye use a telephone?'

'Yes.'

'What about a typewriter?'

'I'm willing to try it.'

'Aye, well, that suits me. We'll see how things go for a week or two, will we? If ye don't like it, say so, an' if I don't think ye'll fit in, I'll have to tell ye, lass. No point in either of us wasting our time over something that won't work. I can start ye off at six shillin's a week.'

It wasn't much, but Ainslie had never worked before, and beggars couldn't be choosers. She nodded, and he ran a thoughtful eye over her neat black skirt and jacket. 'Ye'll be in the store-rooms sometimes, lass, an' it's awful mucky there. It's mucky in the offices, come to that,' he added frankly. 'That's somethin' else ye could mebbe try to see to. It's not easy keeping a place like this clean. Ye'll get into a mess.'

'I'll bring an overall.'

'Aye, that'd be wise,' said Charlie Blayne.

The offices, Charlie's and Ainslie's, both small and both cramped, stood at the end of a long gallery that ran the length of the auction-room below and was connected to it by a stair at the far end. The gallery was crammed with items, particularly before a sale, and at times there was little more than a narrow passageway between the offices and the stairs, between high walls of tea-chests and crates and tables and roped sets of chairs. Double wooden doors with a smaller door set in one of them led from the auction rooms to the cobbled yard and the street, and two other doors at the opposite side opened into the large store-rooms where the goods were kept. Before each sale it was Ainslie's job to see that the goods on offer were clearly listed and marked, so that they could be brought into the saleroom in the correct order.

A narrow door and dark wooden stairway led directly from her office to the street outside, so that she could come and go each day without having to enter through the saleroom. Each morning, as soon as she arrived, she wrapped herself in an overall she had bought for work. The old building seemed to ooze dust through every chink and crack, and a number of women were specially employed just to keep the furniture for sale dusted and polished. Ainslie saw to the two offices, sweeping and dusting and cleaning out the fireplaces every morning before clambering up on to a high stool to work at the sloping desk. When the day was done, she had to wash her hands and often her face before leaving, because of the dust.

Charlie Blayne was an easy-going employer, with the knack of turning the men and women who worked for him into a second family. From the first day, Ainslie loved her work, and after a few weeks it seemed to her that she only truly came alive while she was busy in the tiny office, or down in the rooms, lists in hand.

While she was working there was little time to think of anything else, but as soon as she stepped out on to the narrow dreary street and set off homewards she started fretting about Catherine, who was still refusing to go out or to take an interest in life again. She also refused to let Ainslie tell her anything about her work.

'If your father knew – and your poor grandfather . . .' She gave a shudder of disgust. 'Auction rooms!'

'Auction houses can be very respectable, Mother,'

Ainslie protested, more hurt for Charlie Blayne's sake than her own.

'Yes, they can. Christie's, for one, or Sotheby's – but you're not employed by them, are you?'

'I doubt if they'd want me, since I have no qualifications.'

'You have to work in some nasty little place, when you could have done so much better for yourself!' Catherine ranted on, and Ainslie held her tongue, knowing that her mother would never change her views.

Innes, who was at the adaptable age where life always goes on, was doing well at school, and clearly relieved to be back there after a summer spent in a house in mourning.

'Will Mother ever get better?' he asked his sister once, wistfully.

She hugged him. 'Of course she will.'

Innes inspected his large-knuckled bony hands. 'She says she wants me to be just like grandfather McAdam when I'm old enough. Does that mean dying, too?'

Ainslie felt a chill creep up her spine. 'Of course not. She means she would like you to go into business.'

'Work in an office?' He wrinkled his freckled nose. 'I'd rather do something with cars. Or p'raps go to Africa to collect creatures for a zoo.'

'Best not to tell Mother that. There's plenty of time yet, you might think of all sorts of things you want to do before the time comes.'

'I won't ever want to be in business,' Innes said firmly, then added, 'but whatever it turns out to be, it'll be something that makes a lot of money for us all, so you and Mother needn't worry about that.'

9

In October an Indian summer, an unexpected spell of golden warm weather, descended on the west of Scotland, and one of Ainslie's former schoolfriends invited her to a tennis-party. The invitation was waiting on the drawing-room mantelpiece when she returned from the auction rooms; she read it and stuffed it back into the envelope without comment, but her mother, watching her, asked with studied casualness, 'What was that?'

'Lena Gillespie's having some people in for tennis on Saturday.'

'I think you should go,' Catherine said at once.

'But we're still in mourning, Mother.'

'Even so, you've not been anywhere this year, and it's not right for young people to shut themselves away for too long. It would do you good to see your friends again.'

'I don't really think I want to play tennis. For one thing, I'm out of practice.'

'Nonsense.' Catherine sipped at her tonic wine – the bottle, Ainslie noticed, was almost empty. It had been full that morning when she left. 'Phemie Forbes was

96

here this afternoon, and she recognised the envelope, because Colin got one this morning. Phemie says he's going, and she's sure he'll be happy to drive you.' A smile brushed her lips briefly. 'She and I were just recalling the tennis parties we went to when we were your age. We enjoyed them so much.'

For the moment, her interest in the forthcoming social event had brought colour to her cheeks, and a lilt to her voice. For her sake, Ainslie agreed to go.

When the day came, her tennis dress felt very light and flimsy after the sombre black clothes she had been wearing. Surveying herself in the mirror, smoothing the crisp snowy skirt over her hips, Ainslie realised with surprise that the dress was loose. She must have lost weight since her father's death. The grandfather clock in the hall – a longpiece, auctioneers called it – chimed the hour, and immediately afterwards Catherine called up from the hall, 'Ainslie, Colin's here.'

As she went downstairs, Ainslie felt rather as though she had forgotten to put on her outer clothes and had come from her room in her petticoat. But her mother, waiting in the hall with Colin Forbes, nodded approval as she reached the bottom step.

'You look very nice, dear. Don't you think so, Colin?'

Colin cleared his throat and muttered something, and Catherine picked up her daughter's racquet, waiting in its press on the hall table, as Innes appeared from the kitchen.

'Can I come?' he asked hopefully. He had been taking lessons the year before, and showed promise, but the lessons had been cancelled after his father's death.

'No you can't, this party is for grown-ups. You can

stay here, with me. We'll have a lovely afternoon together.'

Innes's face fell, and Ainslie wished that she could have sent him in her place. She had borrowed a book on furniture from Charlie Blayne, and would have enjoyed an afternoon with it.

Catherine accompanied them as far as the steps, and stood in the doorway, waving, as the car went down the short drive. Ainslie, glancing back, noticed with concern that she wasn't the only member of the household to lose weight. Her mother, who had always been slender, was now almost stick-like.

'I wish Mother would start going out again,' she said, settling herself in the familiar bucket seat. 'She badly needs fresh air and company.'

'My mother's done her best to coax her, but it doesn't seem to be any good.' Colin steered round a car parked too near a corner, then added levelly, 'It's not easy to get the McAdams to co-operate.'

Ainslie opened her mouth to argue, then closed it again. They drove the rest of the way in silence.

Lena's father owned a local engineering firm, and the family lived in one of the largest houses in Paisley. There were almost twenty young people gathered round the tennis court, and Ainslie, on her first social outing since her father's death, was greeted with squeals of pleasure from the girls she had grown up with.

Lena hugged her. 'You poor darling – has it all been terrible?' Her large brown eyes were soft with concern.

'Not too bad.'

'I heard you'd had to find employment,' someone else chimed in, a girl who had been one of Ainslie's closest friends in their final year at school. 'I can't imagine how I would manage if I had to do such a thing!' She gave an exaggerated shiver, and lifted a hand delicately to her cheek in order to show off her new engagement ring. Her fiancé, the son of a man who owned a chain of successful groceries throughout Scotland, put a protective arm about her shoulders, and she snuggled back against him – just like a kitten in a basket, Ainslie thought, wondering why she had ever admired the girl.

The afternoon dragged by. She took her turn on the court, and found that although her skill swiftly returned, her heart wasn't in the game at all. She drank tea on the flagged terrace, ate tiny sandwiches and creamy cakes, went with the others to admire the new lily-pond, then played tennis again. And at last, to her relief, it was time to go home.

Most of the others were changing in the house before driving to Glasgow to attend the theatre, but since Ainslie was still in mourning, it was not possible for her to join them. For that, she thought as they all walked round to the front of the house, she was grateful.

'There's no reason why you shouldn't go to the theatre,' she pointed out to Colin.

'Yes, why not?' Lena chirped. 'The chauffeur can drive Ainslie home.'

He shook his fair head. 'I brought her here and I'll see her home again,' he said, ushering Ainslie to where the car waited on a wide sweep of gravel.

As the others went into the house, a group of carefree moths in their white tennis outfits, he tucked her into the bucket seat then went round to the driver's door. 'Did you enjoy yourself?' he asked as he got in and switched on the engine.

'Oh yes,' Ainslie lied.

Colin eased the car between huge gateposts and turned on to the road. 'So – tell me about this place where you work.'

She described it all in an impersonal way, reluctant to let her enthusiasm show, or to let him know that walking into her cramped little office was like pulling on a cosy, much-loved dressing-gown on a winter's night. She had a superstitious notion that if she let the two very different areas of her existence get too close to each other, they might collide, and cause some sort of damage to themselves, and to her.

Colin listened in silence, his square capable hands steady on the wheel. When she glanced at him she saw that his face was expressionless, and that he was staring straight ahead, never glancing sideways at her as he had so often done in the old days.

'I'm beginning to get a grasp of the ledgers, though the first time I saw them it was like reading Greek— I didn't think I would ever be able to make sense of them. I'm very slow when it comes to using the typewriter, but Cha— Mr Blayne doesn't seem to mind, and the letters do look more official when they've been typed.'

She caught at the dashboard as the car suddenly swerved round a corner and she was thrown against Colin. He had tossed their jackets on to the back seats, and for a moment, as their shoulders touched, she felt his arm hard and warm against hers, bringing back sudden memories of another time, another life, when being

100

with Colin had been the most exciting thing that had ever happened to her.

'What are you doing?'

'Taking another route.'

She glanced at the small wristwatch her parents had given her on her twenty-first birthday. 'Mother will be wondering where I've got to.'

'She knows you're with me. She knows you're safe,' he shot back at her, his voice abrupt. They were driving out into the country now, instead of continuing through the town. The car swerved again, this time towards a layby, then stopped.

Colin killed the engine, then turned in his seat and said, without any preamble, 'Ainslie, will you marry me?'

She stared into his eyes, only inches away from hers. They were best described as hazel, but they changed colours according to his mood. Today, they were grey, the colour of the River Cart on a stormy day. 'Colin, we've been through this before—'

'There's no harm in going through it again. I'm asking you, in all seriousness, to become my wife. And don't answer without taking time to think about it,' he added swiftly as her lips parted. 'You owe me that, at least.'

She did, but at the same time she knew already what her answer must be. She had ended their engagement, and she had no intention of changing her mind. He must have known that himself, for he slammed a hand on the wheel and said, the words pouring out, 'I hoped you'd hate that job, hate having to earn your own living. I hoped that you'd have realised by now that your future lies with me. It always has, Ainslie. I want nothing more than to look after you, and give you everything you want and deserve, and make you happy. And if you're worried about your mother and brother, there's no need, for I'll gladly take them on, too. Look . . .' He turned in his seat, fumbling in the pocket of the jacket in the back seat, withdrawing a small white box. 'I brought this with me today. It's rightfully yours.'

His hands, Ainslie noticed, were trembling as he snapped the box open. 'I love you – did I forget to say that?' Colin asked huskily. 'I love you, and I want you to take this back, because it's yours, and so am I.'

The engagement ring blazed against its white satin bed. She remembered how snugly that ring had fitted on her finger, how happy she had been to see it there. But it belonged to another world, a world that could never be brought back. Afraid that the jewels might draw her down into their depths and drown her senses until she was unable to think clearly, she looked away, to the tumble of bushes edging the road. Other jewels gleamed back at her – glossy red rosehips, fat blackberries, ripe and bursting with their sweet purple juices, set among emerald green leaves. She stared at them until they blurred and merged and she realised that there were tears in her eyes. She still loved the man by her side, but as a very dear friend, not as a future husband.

'Colin, I'm very fond of you, but I'm not going to marry you.'

'But I thought . . .' he began, then stopped, finally saying angrily, 'where's the sense in punishing us both because of what your father did?'

'I'm not punishing anyone. It's just that everything's changed.'

'It needn't.'

'But it has. There's no sense in pretending otherwise.'

'It's that damned woman's fault – the one who's come to live in George Street. If she'd kept away from the town everything would have been over and forgotten by now!'

'I don't need her presence to remind me of what my father did,' Ainslie shot back at him. Then, seeing the bleak look in his eyes, she added lamely, 'I'm – I'm sorry, Colin.'

'So am I.' He snapped the box shut, tossed it into the glove compartment. 'I've made a fool of myself, haven't I?'

'No!' She reached out to him, but he drew his hand back sharply.

'For God's sake, Ainslie, don't start pitying me now!'

She wished that she could be anywhere but where she was. 'You've always been my best friend, Colin. I'd hate it if you turned your back on me.' Then, as he sat mute, staring through the driver's window at the other side of the road, she added, 'If you'd rather, I'll walk the rest of the way home. It's not far.'

'Don't be daft!' Colin snapped, and started the car. He said nothing more until they drew up in the McAdam drive. Then, leaving her to open her own door, he said, his voice still clipped, 'I promise I won't propose to you again. I'll not make a nuisance of myself.'

She shut the door and stepped back, watching as he turned the wheel to take the car past her along the short stretch of driveway in front of the house, then reversed noisily until the rear bumpers almost touched the locked doors of the garage where her father had once kept his own car. It had been sold immediately after the funeral, despite Innes's protests that one day he himself would need it.

Throwing up a spray of gravel, Colin went off down the drive, stopping the car with a jerk at the gate, then taking off into the road to a scream of protest from the tyres.

As Ainslie turned towards the front door she glimpsed a movement at the small gap between the drawing-room curtains, and realised that her mother had been watching for their arrival. Catherine came into the hall as she closed the front door. 'Well? Did you have a lovely afternoon?'

'Yes, thank you.' Ainslie made for the stairs and started to ascend.

'Why didn't you bring Colin in for tea? You know he'd have been very welcome.'

'He was in a hurry.' Ainslie threw the words over her shoulder and kept climbing. She had just laid the racquet down when the bedroom door opened and her mother walked into the room without knocking.

'What happened?'

'We played tennis, we had afternoon tea, then I came home.'

'Ainslie, don't be annoying! Why didn't Colin come in with you?'

Suddenly Ainslie, standing before the mirror, taking off the ribbon she had used to tie her hair back, remembered Colin's reaction to her refusal, remembered him saying, 'But I thought . . .', then choking the words back. Suddenly, she knew. She turned to face her mother, tossing the ribbon down on to the bed. 'It was all planned, wasn't it?'

'What was?'

'You and Mrs Forbes decided that this would be the perfect opportunity for Colin to ask me to change my mind about marrying him, didn't you?'

A slender hand went up to Catherine's throat. Her eyes widened, and Ainslie saw that her cheeks had gone quite pink. 'He proposed? Oh, Ainslie, how wonderful!'

'No need to pretend, Mother – you knew. That's why you urged me to go to the tennis party with him.'

'Well, I – Phemie did say when she was here the other day that Colin's been pining ever since you gave his ring back.'

Ainslie felt quite sick with shame and pity as the full realisation of the situation hit her. 'Did his mother hint to him that I'd changed my mind? How could you? How could you be so cruel?'

'I don't know what you're—' Catherine's eyes fell on her daughter's left hand, bare of rings. She whimpered faintly, and sat down suddenly on the bed. 'You turned him down? Again?'

'I told him what I had told him before. What I've told you, again and again. I don't want to marry anyone.'

There was a short silence, during which Ainslie could almost hear her mother's fury crackling in the air between them, then, 'I spent the entire afternoon praying – praying!' Catherine burst out. 'Hoping that you would come to your senses and accept him. How many men have the courage to face humiliation twice? Do you realise what you've done to that poor boy – to me?'

'What *I've* done? I didn't lead him to believe that I had changed my mind. You did that – you and that scheming mother of his!'

'How dare you talk about my friend like that! How dare you presume to know better than your elders and betters—'

'Mother, I will not marry in order to please anyone, even you.'

'If your father could hear you!' Catherine's hand, which had gone to her throat, now moved to her mouth, as though pressing back a sob. Round her slim fingers she said, 'He was so pleased when you and Colin announced your engagement. What do you think he would make of you now?'

Ainslie linked her own fingers behind her back and took a deep breath. 'My father didn't stop to wonder how I might feel about it before he took his own life – or before he became husband to another woman and father to another family. Why should I concern myself with him?'

The colour drained from Catherine's face. 'How dare you?' she said again, in a harsh whisper.

'I'm sorry to vex you, Mother, but I'm only trying to make you understand about my own feelings.'

'Your feelings? That's been the trouble all along. You're selfish, Ainslie, you always have been, from the moment you were born. Selfish and obstinate and uncaring, just like your Grandmother McAdam. She ruined her husband's life, and now you're ruining mine. You're no better than she was.'

'Then perhaps it's as well that I've turned Colin down. I might have ruined his life as well, and I care for him too much to do that.'

Catherine gave a bitter little laugh. 'You flatter yourself, my dear. You don't care for anybody but yourself, do you? You don't care that people in this town are wondering what sort of mother I am, letting my daughter go out to work in some nasty little auction room. Or what sort of wife I must have been, for my husband to take another woman behind my back—' Her voice broke, then changed to an eerie banshee wailing. Her hands went up to clutch at her head, fingers digging into her scalp. Ainslie went to her, alarmed by such behaviour from her normally emotionless mother, but Catherine pulled away from her touch.

'Leave me be! The only one who truly cares is Innes,' she said with sudden, almost frightening dignity. 'One day he'll make up to me for everything you and your father did.'

She rose from the bed and walked, straight-backed, out of the room, leaving Ainslie shaken and confused. She and her mother had had disagreements for as long as she could remember. She recalled, frequently, occasions when she stood obstinately silent, taking the sting of her mother's sarcastic tongue, refusing to let herself weep. But they had never had such an ugly, venomous quarrel before. And never, until now, had Catherine lost control.

Guilt welled up. She had allowed herself to hit back, had behaved very badly towards her mother at a time when Catherine wasn't herself. Although Ainslie's anger was justified by the fact that Colin had been cruelly deceived by his mother and hers, she would have to apologise.

She leaned forward until her forehead was resting against the cool mirror, closing her eyes. There seemed to be no way to please her mother, other than by giving up her job and agreeing to marry Colin. But if she did that, she would betray herself. It was too high a price for anyone to pay for other people's happiness.

With a flash of insight, Ainslie realised that she had spent the first twenty-one years of her life betraying herself. She had tried, really tried, to do what others wanted – her parents, her teachers, her friends, even Colin – but she had always fallen short of their expectations, because pleasing them meant displeasing herself.

Her father's death had put an end to it. Torn from the life she had always known, cast into an uncertain future, she had changed far more than even she herself had suspected before that moment. She had become a different person, a woman who was learning, slowly and painfully, how to make her own way in the world. Independence was beckoning, and she had started the long journey towards it. Having started, she must continue, and that meant never again allowing herself to be hurt simply in order to make others happy.

Nor, she realised, did she have the right to interfere in other people's lives. She had been no better than Catherine when she went to George Street and tried to order Isla out of the town and out of their lives. Isla had been her father's business, not hers.

When the maid came to remind her that dinner was on the table, Ainslie, still in her tennis dress, sent word downstairs that she wasn't hungry. She stripped, washed, and brushed out her curly red hair until it crackled. During the day she restrained it in a long plait hanging down her back, but when she was at home she liked to leave it loose. After changing into her night-dress and dressing-gown, she took *The Wind in the Willows* from the shelves, and turning to her favourite chapter, the one about Mole and Rat seeking shelter far from home on a cold winter's night, she settled down to read.

Almost at once she fell asleep, tired out by fresh air and exercise, followed by the stress of the scenes with Colin and then her mother, then wakened with a start to find Innes standing beside her, a tray in his hands.

'I got you this from the kitchen.'

He had brought a roast beef sandwich and a glass of milk. Ainslie still wasn't hungry, but, touched by his concern, she nibbled at the sandwich and sipped the milk while Innes sat on the side of the bed and watched. 'How was the tennis party?'

'All right. I'll probably be stiff tomorrow, not having played all summer.'

'I miss it,' he said. 'I miss everything. D'you think we'll ever get back to normal again?'

'Of course we will, next year.' She put down her sandwich, unable to take another bite. 'I ate too many sandwiches this afternoon. I'm still full up.'

'I'll finish it if you like,' he offered, and ate the food as though he hadn't had any dinner at all. Innes had always had a huge appetite.

'Mother sat with a face like thunder all through dinner, then went to bed with a headache,' he said round a mouthful of bread and meat. 'I might as well be honest,

I heard you both rowing after you came back from the tennis party.'

'She's still angry because I won't marry Colin.'

'I thought you liked Colin.'

'I do, but I don't want to spend the rest of my life married to him.'

'If you did marry him, he'd probably teach you to drive his car. He'll probably give you a car of your own.'

'Marriage is about more than cars, Innes.'

'I wonder if it'll happen to me one day.' Innes licked his fingers then lay back on the bed beside her and linked his fingers behind his head. 'Marrying, I mean, not learning to drive. I'm definitely going to do that as soon as I'm old enough.'

'Time you were in bed.'

'In a minute.' He yawned, then said, 'I don't like you and Mother quarrelling, Ainslie. We've only got each other now, the three of us.'

She put her arm around him. 'I'll apologise to her in the morning. It'll be all right.'

'That's good.' There was a pause, then he said sleepily, 'Tell me again about the place you work in.' His red hair was soft against her chin and his body solid and comforting within the circle of her arm. Ainslie was tempted to drop a kiss on his cheek, but held back, knowing that he would hate it.

'Outside my tiny office there's this long wide gallery, stacked with all sorts of furniture . . .' she began.

10

Once she realised that school was a five-days-a-week occurrence, Barbara took to it like a duck to water. She loved the sand trays, where the children used their fingers to write out figures and letters, and the importance of having a desk of her own. She loved the games in the school-yard at playtime, the chanted multiplication tables, the stories and songs and poems. She and Greta played schools in their spare time, commandeering Ross and Daisy and any other small child they could get hold of as pupils.

With Drew Brown's help, Isla cleared the patch of earth in the backyard, but the soil was poor, soured by years of neglect, smoke and soot from the chimneys, and by the cats and dogs who roamed the area, using the backyards as lavatories. Every weekday morning, after she had watched Barbara and Greta run in through the school gates to mingle with the other children in the playground, Isla, pushing Ross in the little perambulator she had brought to Paisley with her, walked on past the huge bulk of the Ferguslie Mills, where the machinery gave out a continual muffled roar, towards the open moors on the outskirts of the town.

Here, while Ross toddled around, she hunted out molehills, carefully scraping them up with a battered tablespoon and stowing the rich soil away in an old shopping bag kept specially for the purpose.

'It's dung ye want tae feed the earth,' Drew said when he found Isla emptying the battered old bag over the newly dug patch, shaking it vigorously to make sure that not a speck of good soil was lost.

'Where can I get it?'

The boy shot a surprised look at her, as though wondering if she was pulling his leg. 'From the horses that go up an' down the street, of course. It's the best thing ye can use for growin' things. I'll get some for ye after work if ye want, or ye could ask any of the laddies round here tae gather it for ye in a bucket, for a ha'penny, or one or two empty bottles tae take tae the wee shop.'

Isla felt colour rise to her face. She was well used by now to the sight and sound of the great cart-horses pulling wagons and carts along George Street, but even so she had never thought of using their droppings for her vegetable bed. She gave the bag a final vicious shake, cursing her own stupidity. What sort of example could she set her own children when she didn't even remember that manure was good for growing things, she chided herself, then a giggle bubbled to her lips as she realised that not knowing about manure was scarcely likely to damage their young lives.

She followed Drew's advice the next morning, impatient to get on with planting the old potatoes she had been carefully hoarding under the bed for weeks. As soon as she stepped tentatively out of the close, bucket in one hand and shovel in the other, a grubby little boy arrived at her side.

'Is it dung ye're after, missus? I'll see tae it for ye!' He grabbed the bucket and shovel, and was off before she could say anything. Isla looked after him helplessly, convinced that she had seen the last of her precious possessions. Thieving was rife in the street, and she had been well warned by Magret never to leave Ross's little perambulator outside on its own.

'It's not all badness, it's just that some poor souls have nothin' at all, except what the weans can lay their hands on,' Magret had said. 'Folks has got tae live.'

Ten minutes later, the boy thumped on the door and handed Isla her shovel and a steaming bucket, filled to the brim with richly smelling manure. 'I kenned there was a cuddy just turned intae Castle Street,' he explained. 'I had tae run tae catch up wi' it.'

She gave him a halfpenny, which he folded tightly into his fist as he followed her through the close and into the yard. The bucket was heavy, and she marvelled at such a small boy being able to carry it all the way from Castle Street on his own.

'What're ye doin', missus?' He gave a huge sniff and swatted at his nose with the back of his hand.

'Growing potatoes.'

'Tatties? When'll they be ready, then?'

'Mind yer own business,' Magret snapped from behind him. 'Get back tae yer own close – go on, now! Ye don't want tae tell the likes of him too much,' she went on when he had gone, his bare feet slapping hard against the steps and along the close, the hems of his ragged trousers flapping about his knees. 'He'd be wantin' tae know when the tatties'd be ready for him tae steal.' She wrinkled her nose as Isla, after a struggle, managed to upend the bucket, and a solid lump of manure thumped out on to the turned earth. 'God bless us, what a reek!'

'I'll soon have it dug in.' Isla sniffed the air then said thoughtfully, 'It's a good healthy natural smell.'

Magret, used to the stink of blocked drains and broken sewage pipes and human beings crowded together in old, unsanitary housing, gave her new friend a puzzled look.

'I don't know how ye can say that – it's chokin' me,' she complained, waving her hand before her nose while Isla seized her fork and began spreading the manure over the earth.

Over the next few days Drew obtained several more bucketsful of manure for her, and helped to dig it in. 'I think it's as ready as it can be,' she said at last, and went to the house. When she brought the old tin tray out from under the wall-bed, she saw that the potatoes she had saved for the garden were already sprouting. Putting the vegetable knife into the pocket of her pinny, she carried the tray out.

'Now we need to cut each potato in half, and plant each half with the sprouting side up.'

Drew took a penknife from his pocket and reached for a potato. When they had all been cut and planted in rows, Isla fetched her bucket and Drew found an abandoned tin can, and together they carried water from the wash-house to give the soil a good soaking. Then, side by side, they surveyed the smooth weed-free bed with satisfaction.

'With any luck, we'll have good new potatoes to eat next spring,' Isla said.

Drew, now comfortable in her presence, beamed and said, 'Aye!' just as Barbara, playing in the wash-house with Greta and the peg dolls, came hurrying up the steps, her face screwed up.

'Mummy, my dolly's lost her face!' She brandished the little doll, now with an ordinary peg-head atop her dressed body.

'Bring the cloth here and I'll fasten it back on.'

'But I don't know where it went,' Barbara wailed. 'I want her face back. I don't want her to have an old peg-face!'

'Give it here.' Drew, who had struck up a friendship with the children, took the peg from her and sat down on one of the steps beyond the wash-house. 'I'll do a new face for her, if you like. I've got some wee tins of paint upstairs that'll finish her off nicely.'

Barbara sat beside him, fascinated, as he started working at the peg with the tip of his knife. 'Two eyes – and a nose – and a nice smiley mouth,' he said as he worked. 'And curly hair, too, with a bit of a fringe at the front, like yours.' The knifepoint moved deftly, the peg twirling about in his fingers, then he gave the doll back to Barbara, said, 'Back in a tick,' and hurried into the close, whistling tunelessly.

'Look at what Drew's done, Mummy.' Barbara handed the peg to Isla, who took it and was still studying the neat little bland face and the swirl of curly hair that the lad had carved from the plain wooden knob when he came back, some tiny paint tins and a brush and an old bit of rag in his hands.

'Now then,' he said, taking the peg doll back and opening one of the tins. In a few minutes the little face had sprung to life, with blue eyes, tilted up at the corners, a neat little rosebud mouth, and brown curly hair.

'Careful,' Drew cautioned as he handed it to Barbara. 'Let her get dry, or she'll smudge into all the colours of the rainbow.'

'I didn't know you were so clever, Drew,' Isla said, astonished, and he blushed, then shrugged.

'Och, it's nothing. I like making wee things out of old bits of wood. It gives me something to do with my hands.'

There had been no further visits from Ainslie McAdam, and Isla, greatly relieved, allowed herself to hope that the girl had decided to leave her alone. She hadn't seen Gilchrist Forbes or his disapproving son either, and that suited her. Each Monday morning she went to the lawyer's office, where she received a sealed envelope from his receptionist. She signed for it, and left the office as quickly as she could, feeling very like Judas as she pushed the envelope, with its ill-gotten gains, deep into her pocket.

Back home, spreading the money out on the table, she felt as though she was stealing it from them, particularly from Mrs Brown, after all Drew's help with the potato bed. But she had no option. One day, she kept promising herself, she would make amends. One day when – if – she ever had money she would do all she could to improve their living conditions, although for the life of her she couldn't see what could be done. The entire row of tenements was old and should have been pulled down long since. What these people needed was rehousing.

Often there was a brief note with the money, recording

a tenant's inability to pay the full amount, or any money at all, and informing her that if she wanted action to be taken against the non-payer she should notify Mr Forbes. She threw the notes on the fire, feeling as though she was prying on her neighbours. She had no intention of taking action against anyone simply because they were too poor to pay the rent on time. Poverty wasn't a crime, although people like Gilchrist Forbes seemed to think it was.

Often, it was Granny Thomson who hadn't paid her rent. Old as she was, the woman did some cleaning in one of the shops to augment her tiny pension, but she suffered from rheumatism and bronchitis, and often she couldn't get out of bed, let alone work. When that happened, Isla and Magret took it in turns to see that the old woman didn't starve, taking a bowl of soup or a cup of tea and a bit of bread and butter in to her stuffy, cold, dark little room until she was on her feet again. It hurt Isla to know that Granny Thomson lived in constant fear of someone else being given her job while she was unable to do it, and of ending her days in the poorhouse. Her mingled gratitude and choking shame at 'being a burden' to her neighbours almost broke Isla's heart. She wished that she could tell the old woman the truth, and assure her that as long as she owned the building, Granny wouldn't be put out. But she had to stay silent.

Sometimes the Browns were unable to pay all the rent, and once the Kellys were defaulters, because there had been a strike at the factory that employed Mr Kelly and he had been laid off. Both he and his wife aged with worry over the two-week strike, and so did Isla, on their behalf, then to their mutual relief the strike was settled and the rent money slowly made up during the following week.

It was a hand-to-mouth existence, and she often wondered if Kenneth had had any knowledge of the struggle his tenants went through simply to survive, or about the conditions they had to live in. It disturbed her to think that he might have known, and yet not cared enough to do anything about it.

November came raging in with strong, bitterly cold winds that found every chink and crack in the old tenement. Rags and newspaper had to be stuffed round windows and below doors, and at night the flames within Isla's fragile gas mantles often flickered in the draught. It rained all the time, which meant that the washing had to be dried indoors, the smell of wet wool and the steam of its drying adding to the stuffiness and humidity of the single room. It became difficult to get close to the fire, because the washing had to take priority.

'I wish I was a vest,' Barbara grumbled more than once. 'Then I'd get to be nice and cosy in front of the fire.'

All Isla's energies were concentrated on keeping the children as healthy as possible. She fed them plates of thick porridge morning and night, because it was a cheap and nourishing way of filling their stomachs. Scattering precious sugar as thickly as she dared over it, she remembered her own childhood, when her mother had poured generous spoonfuls of honey or golden syrup over her porridge, then added cream. Her father, a true Scotsman, salted his porridge, but Isla and her mother liked theirs sweet and rich.

She learned from Magret that it was best to delay a visit to the greengrocer's until it was almost closing time, when he was anxious to sell off any vegetables that might not be fit for sale the next morning. Carrots and potatoes and turnips, chopped up and simmered with a handful of lentils and barley and a bone, made a nourishing broth that lasted for a few days. If there was meat on the bone, it was carefully pared off to add a savoury flavour to platefuls of potatoes.

Survival became the centre of Isla's existence. She lay awake at night listening to the rain sloshing down the gutters at the side of the street, worrying about the cost of calling in the doctor and paying for medication if one or both of the children took ill. She didn't even dare to contemplate the thought of any illness touching her, making her too weak to care for Barbara and Ross. But the porridge and home-made soup, with fish whenever Isla could afford it, kept the three of them well.

Poor little Greta wasn't so fortunate. In mid-November she took a sore throat and had to miss school and stay at home, one of her father's socks, filled with hot salt, tied around her small neck. Isla took Ross to fetch Barbara from school, keeping an eye on the clouds racing overhead as she hurried the children out of the school gates, anxious to get them indoors before the rain started to fall again. Her clothes-horse was already groaning under the weight of drying clothes; she didn't want to have wet coats and shoes to deal with as well.

'Come on, Barbara – don't pull at me like that!'

Barbara, undeterred, gave another tug on her mother's hand. 'Mummy, that lady over there looks funny.'

Isla's eyes followed her daughter's pointing finger.

The school stood opposite West Station, and in her rush to get the children home she hadn't noticed the black-clad figure leaning against the station wall, head bowed. The woman's unfashionably long skirt hung down below her coat, and on the ground by her booted feet stood a basket. One or two neatly wrapped parcels had spilled from it.

Nobody else seemed to have noticed her. Isla pushed Ross's perambulator across the road and bumped it up on to the pavement, turning it with its back against the bitter wind.

'Are you all right?' She put a hand tentatively on the woman's shoulder and a paper-white face swung towards her.

'So silly,' the woman whispered. 'Came over faint. I'll be – all right in a minute.'

Isla looked up and down the street, but it was almost empty. Nobody wanted to loiter on such a day.

'D'you think she's going to die?' Barbara asked in her clear voice, staring up into the old lady's face.

'Sshh! Of course not!' Beneath her hand Isla felt the bony shoulder ripple in a half-laugh.

'At least I'll die with – my boots on!' the frail voice commented.

'Can you tell me where you live?'

' 'Course I can. Not stupid, just a bit – breathless. It's just round the – corner there. I'll go on in a minute, when – when I've caught my breath.'

Isla stooped and scooped the parcels into the basket, then straightened and put an arm about the woman. 'Barbara, can you manage to push Ross's chair for me while I help this lady?'

'Of course I can.' Barbara stooped in her turn, picking up a folded umbrella that Isla hadn't noticed. 'Here, Ross,' she told her brother, 'you can carry that.' She swung the chair round with a bit of an effort and began to push it towards the corner.

'Put your arm over my shoulders, and I'll put my arm around your waist.' Isla organised the old lady, who was taller than she was, and drooped over her. Slowly, they made their way round the corner, past the entrance to the West Station, then followed the road in a gentle downhill curve towards the large houses opposite the cricket ground. Barbara had difficulty in manoeuvring the push-chair, especially as the furled umbrella clutched in Ross's chubby little hands stuck out on either side and tended to hit off the wall, but she managed it, concentration making her tongue protrude beyond her teeth.

'Round here,' the woman said feebly, and Isla saw to her dismay that the road they had turned into led uphill. There were high walls on either side, and no sign of a house, and she doubted whether Barbara, or she herself, burdened as she was, could manage to keep going to the top of the hill. But there was nothing else for it but to grit their teeth and forge on. To her surprise, the old lady stopped only a matter of yards further along, outside a small faded green wooden door set in the high wall.

'Here we are. I can take the basket, my dear, if you'll open the door.'

Barbara, forsaking the pram, squeezed past her mother's legs to stare through the opened gate. 'It's a magic place!' she said with delight, and the woman laughed, a wheezy, rusty sound ending in a fit of coughing.

'That's what I used to think when I was your age,' she said when she had caught her breath again. 'I'd forgotten that.'

The gate opened on to a small quiet road. On their left, flanked by tall trees, stood the high wall that divided this road from the main road, and on the right a series of gates led to gardens and houses. Even the wind had lost some of its power in this sheltered place; while it buffeted and howled against the other side of the wall, the little road seemed untouched, only the tops of the highest trees swaying before it.

'Just a few gates along, dear – not far to go.'

When they reached the right gate, Barbara wrestled with the latch, finally managing to open it. 'Use the umbrella for the – children, or they'll be soaked – by the bushes,' the elderly woman advised Isla. 'I'm much better now, I can manage.' Isla opened the large black umbrella and put it into Ross's hands. He held it high as Barbara, her head ducked forward beneath its shelter, pushed him up the flagged path, edged on either side by dripping bushes. Between the bare twigs, Isla, taking up the rear, could see small leaf-strewn lawns on either side.

'Now I'm for it,' the woman said gloomily, edging round the pram to mount the two steps into the small, open, glass-sided porch. Her legs, impossibly thin and looking like saplings planted in the sturdy boots she wore, just managed the climb. She tugged at a brass bell-pull set by the side of the front door and the bell jangled in the depths of the house.

'Will your mummy be angry?' Barbara asked, wide-eyed, deserting the pram and skipping up into the porch, which had a bench running down each side. The woman chuckled again, and again ended up coughing and spluttering. She dug into her coat pocket and produced a handkerchief, which she held to her mouth.

'I've not got a mummy,' she said through the folds. 'I've got an Annie, and she's far worse.'

As she spoke, the door opened to reveal a stout woman with iron-grey hair curling out from under a frilly white cap. Her sturdy body was clothed in a black dress and white apron, and her round, ruddy face was wrinkled with concern.

'Miss Flora, where have you—' She stopped, her gaze travelling down to Barbara, then to where Isla wrestled with the umbrella, trying to get it down, hampered by the basket and the push chair. 'What's happened?'

'Nothing, nothing. I took a little turn in the – the street, that's all, and these young people - kindly helped me back home.'

'I told you, didn't I, Miss Flora? I told you that you weren't strong enough to go out on your own. But would you list—'

'You were right, Annie, as usual. Now,' said Miss Flora, 'are we going to stand here – all day, or are we going to get indoors out of the cold and – offer these kind people some refreshments?'

Isla had succeeded in closing the umbrella, showering herself with rainwater in the process. 'No, really, we must get home before the rain starts,' she began, but Miss Flora interrupted.

'Nonsense, my dear, you've saved my life and I insist – on giving you a cup of tea, at least.' Stronger now that she was back home, she swept into the hall, Barbara scampering after her.

11

Isla, realising that there was no help for it, began to unfasten the straps that held Ross into the chair.

'Here – I'll get it,' Annie said as she lifted the little boy out and began to wrestle one-handedly with the push-chair. She surged down the steps and lifted the chair, muttering as she did so, 'Never pays a blind bit of notice to what I say. Oh no – off she goes and what happens? She very near kills herself!'

'Come in here, my dear,' the elderly woman called from beyond an open door to the right as Isla followed Annie into the hall, 'There's a nice fire.'

Barbara stood in the middle of the room, turning slowly, her eyes and mouth open as she took in every detail of the polished furniture and the pictures on the walls.

'You should go straight to your bed,' the maid told her employer sternly. 'You'll make yourself ill again. She's just getting over a bout of bronchitis,' she explained to Isla. 'She should never have gone out on a day like this, but try telling her that.'

'I was bored. I needed the fresh air. And now I'd like a cup of tea – if you don't mind. And some bread to toast, and whatever you think the children would like to drink.' Now that she was safely home, Miss Flora's breathing was easier. 'Take off your coat, my dear, and sit down here, by the fire.'

Annie, muttering under her breath, peeled her employer and then the two children efficiently out of their coats, while Isla took her own off.

'I don't know what I'd do without her, but she fusses,' the old lady said as Annie, arms piled high with coats, went out of the room. 'I'm Flora Currie, by the way.' A large bony hand was thrust out towards Isla. She shook it and introduced herself and the children, then allowed herself to be coaxed into a cushioned chair by the fire.

Ross, intimidated by the strange room, pulled at her skirt and she lifted him on to her lap, saying automatically, 'Barbara, don't touch anything.'

'Nonsense, children need to touch things. She'll be sensible, I'm sure.' Miss Currie – Isla had noticed that both hands were free of rings – sat down in the chair opposite. She had kept her hat on; it was a woollen black turban, and its slightly Eastern look suited her hawk-like nose and angular features. The colour had come back into her face. 'D'ye see that large, pink shell, little girl? Fetch it over here, will you?'

When Barbara did as she was told, carrying the shell carefully in both hands, Miss Currie took it and held it to the child's ear. 'If you listen, you can hear the sea. Hear it?'

Barbara concentrated, frowning, then the frown faded and her brown eyes widened in astonishment. 'I can! I can hear the sea, Mummy!' She brought the shell over and held it first to Isla's ear, then to Ross's, then to her own again.

'My father brought that home for me when I was about your age,' Flora Currie told her. 'He was a sea captain, sailing out of Greenock.'

'My daddy's going to bring one just like it for me when he comes back to us,' Barbara said at once.

Miss Currie's eyes flicked swiftly to Isla's face, a mute question in them. She read the answer, then said calmly, 'I expect he will. Until then, you're welcome to come and listen to my shell now and again. It likes people to listen to it.'

Annie came in with a large tray and set out the tea things on a low table between both women. She had included sturdy mugs of milk for the children, and piled a plate with slices of bread. While Miss Currie showed Barbara how to spear the slices on a brass toasting fork and hold them close to the bars of the fire until they were browned, Isla drank the hot tea gratefully, and ate buttered toast and Madeira cake, feeding Ross, still perched on her knee, mouth open like a little fledgling.

As they ate, Flora Currie talked about her childhood, spent in the house where she still lived, and about her father and mother and two older brothers.

'I'm all that's left now – apart from some nephews and nieces scattered about Scotland and too busy to visit me.'

She asked few questions, only enough to learn that they lived not far away, in George Street.

'But it seems like a hundred miles away,' Isla told her. 'I'd no idea that this road existed so close to where we live.'

Ross, growing bolder, wriggled to get down, and she handed him over to Barbara with instructions to behave themselves.

'Oh, let them explore a little, I'm sure they won't hurt anything. My brothers and I and the other children who lived here when we were young enjoyed popping in and out through that gate,' Flora Currie said. 'After I read *Alice in Wonderland* I felt that the gate would have fitted well into the story. I'd forgotten all about that until your little girl reminded me. The road opens out at the other end, of course, so that vehicles can get through. My papa had a carriage – the double gate just a little bit along from where we came in leads into our drive and up to the carriage-house, but the gates haven't been opened in years, and the carriage-house is filled with rubbish.' She leaned forward, her eyes on Isla. 'You don't speak like the people round here.'

'I was brought up in Glasgow, then I lived in Edinburgh for several years, then on the Clyde coast. We've only been in Paisley for a few months.'

'You've still got a trace of that pretty East coast lilt to your voice. I used to love excursions to Edinburgh – it has such an air of timelessness about it.'

As though on cue, the clock on the mantelshelf chimed softly and Isla said, 'We must go . . .' just as rain spattered on the bay window behind Miss Currie.

'Better stay here until this shower passes,' she advised, just as Barbara's clear little voice called from the hall, 'Mummy, come and see this!'

'Barbara, what are you up to?' Isla jumped up and hurried towards the sound of her daughter's voice. The children were standing at an open door on the other side of the hall, towards the back of the house.

'Look!' Barbara disappeared into the room, towing Ross behind her.

'Barbara!'

'They've found my secret vice,' Flora Currie said, moving past Isla to the open door. 'We all have our failings, I suppose.' She gave Isla a lop-sided, shamefaced smile. 'This used to be my mother's sewing room, but since my parents died and my brothers married and moved away, I've taken it over as my own. Come and see.'

Isla stopped on the threshold, staring. The room was filled with dolls' houses, sitting on counters that had been built around the walls. Large elaborate houses and smaller modest dwellings jostling together, some wide, some narrow, some high, some single-storey. Barbara was moving along the counters, hands clasped behind her back, the tension in the curled fingers and small shoulders indicating a repressed urge to open each house front and look inside.

For a long moment Isla gaped, then she said huskily, 'How wonderful.'

'So you don't think I'm a stupid old woman who's never properly grown up?'

Isla turned, and realised that Miss Currie's eyes were green. 'I think you're very lucky.'

A gust of wind hurled rain against the window, but nobody noticed as, one by one, Miss Currie opened the fronts of the houses, revealing doll families in parlours and nurseries and kitchens and studies. Ross, too small to see, found a box half filled with miniature furniture and dolls and tiny animals tucked away beneath one of the counters, and squatted happily on the floor to empty it.

'I've got a dolls' house,' Barbara told Miss Currie proudly. 'My mummy made it out of a box. And she made clothes-peg dollies for me and Greta and some of the other wee girls in our street.'

'Indeed? You've got a very clever mummy.' The old woman smiled at Isla.

The grandfather clock in the hall chimed the hour, and Isla, suddenly noticing the mess Ross was making, stooped to put everything back into the box. 'We must go – I have to get to the shops.'

It was still raining, with no sign of an improvement now, and Miss Currie offered her the large black umbrella. 'You can hand it in some time,' she said, and waved from the porch as they set off into the November gloom, Isla negotiating the push-chair with one hand and holding the umbrella with the other.

'I like that lady,' Barbara said as Isla filled the tin bath before the fire that evening. 'When I'm old like her I'm going to live in a big house.' Her brows wrinkled in thought, then she said, 'We had a house like that once.'

'Something like it.' Isla refilled the kettle at the tap and put it on to the stove, then caught Ross up as he toddled past her and settled into her chair to take his clothes off. 'Come on, young man, time for your bath.'

'When can we go back to our house?' Barbara persisted. Isla looked at her over the top of Ross's red head.

'I don't know, love,' she said, and the longing that swept over her for Kenneth was so great that she had to blink back tears.

*

She returned the umbrella on the following day, intending to hand it in and then hurry away. But Flora Currie herself opened the door, the knitted turban still pulled firmly down over her ears, and insisted on giving her a cup of tea.

'Annie's doing the shopping today, so we'll have to manage on our own,' she said, leading the way through the hall to a door hidden in the shadows behind the stairs. It opened into a kitchen fragrant with the smell of baking and warmed by a large range.

'How are you, Miss Currie?'

'Oh, completely recovered from that silly nonsense yesterday. Annie's quite right, of course, I should never have ventured so far after being in bed for two weeks. But sometimes I feel the need to defy her, just to prove to myself that I'm still alive. Sit down there,' Flora ordered, and Isla obediently sat at the white-scrubbed table that took up most of the room. Ross wandered about fingering the knobs on the cupboard doors.

'Can I help?'

'No need, my dear, I know how to fend for myself.'

Flora measured tea into a small teapot then eyed the huge kettle simmering on the range, and added, 'Though I'd be grateful if you could see to that monster for me.' She held out her large bony hands to reveal swollen knuckles and some slightly twisted fingers. 'Rheumatics,' she explained, scowling at her hands. 'I might tip the kettle too far and scald myself, and then I'd never hear the end of it from Annie. She insists on being the servant, and wearing that ridiculous uniform,' she went on, setting out cups and half filling a mug with milk for Ross while Isla poured boiling water into the teapot. 'I've tried to get her to settle for a skirt and cardigan like mine, but she never will.'

She produced a plate of spiced scones, still warm from the oven. 'I have to do my baking when Annie's out at the shops. She won't admit that I've got a lighter hand than hers when it comes to pastry, in spite of the rheumatism. My mother, bless her, believed in her children learning how to cook and bake.' She slit the scones and spread them generously with butter. 'Being a seaman, my father agreed with her. My brothers could cook and sew – not that their wives allowed it, for the very thought shocked them. My brother Arnold did that.' She nodded at a framed sampler on the wall, the words, 'The Heart of A House Is The Kitchen', surrounded by neatly stitched forget-me-nots. 'In secret, when his wife wasn't around, just to prove to himself that he could still manage it.'

She poured the tea and sat down. 'I take it that you're a widow.'

'My husband died six months ago.'

Flora nodded. 'I thought as much, the way your little girl talked about her daddy. How d'you cope, with two children to look after on your own?'

'I manage.'

'I'm sure you do.' Flora Currie pushed the plate of scones towards Isla and poured out more tea for them both. 'Tell me about the dolls' house you made for your daughter.'

'It's just a wee orange box with a curtain over the front.'

'I'd like to hear all about it all the same – what you did for furniture, and how you made the dolls.'

She listened with interest, breaking in with an occasional question, as Isla described the making of the orange-box house. 'I used to try to make houses myself,' she recalled. 'But I wasn't good at it. I lack your imagination.'

Then, planting her hands flat on the table, she levered herself to her feet. 'Come and have another look at my collection. It's not often I get to show them off. Annie complains about the dust they collect, and thinks I'm a stupid old woman. It's good to meet someone who understands.'

In the room that held the dolls' houses, Ross made for the box he had been playing with on the previous day. 'Leave him be,' Flora said when Isla tried to stop him. 'It's only broken furniture and dolls that were never repaired. I'm no good at throwing things out. I'd some notion of giving the houses to my nieces, but my brothers tended towards sons, and the only two girls were given handsome dolls' houses by their parents before I got round to making the offer.' She looked round the room, and sighed. 'They should really be given to a hospital or something. They'll just be a nuisance to my heirs one day, and they're meant to be played with, after all.'

'Not that one.' Isla pointed to the grandest house, a Victorian mansion complete with a butler's pantry, and servants' quarters in the attic. 'That's a collector's item.'

'That was my own, when I was small. My grandmama gave it to me, and I was only allowed to play with it when my nurse or my mother were there to see that I didn't do any damage. I used to long to be allowed to spend just ten minutes with it on my own; I think that's why I was so determined to do as I pleased once I had the freedom.' She sighed, touching the house lovingly. 'Poor thing, it's been neglected. It was put away in the attic when I got older, and not brought out until long after my parents died. I kept meaning to have it renovated, but I never got around to it.'

The front door opened and closed. 'We're in here, Annie,' Flora Currie called, and the maid, in her outer clothes, glanced in at the door, sniffing when she saw Isla.

'You're here again, are you?'

'Mind your own business,' her mistress snapped back at her, while Isla, suddenly afraid that she was outstaying her welcome, knelt to replace the toys that Ross had taken out of the box.

'We must go.'

'Would you like to choose one of the houses as a Christmas gift for your little girl?' Miss Currie asked abruptly as they were about to leave the room. Isla was taken aback by the suddenness of the offer, but rallied.

'It's very kind of you, but she's fine with the one she's got.'

'You said it was made from a box, and I thought she might like . . .'

Isla felt hot colour surge into her face. 'She's fine,' she repeated, and regretted the sharpness in her voice as soon as she saw the stricken look on Miss Currie's face.

'My dear, I'm so sorry if I offended you.'

'You didn't. It's just that . . .' Isla's voice trailed away and they surveyed each other in an awkward silence. Ross, between them, looked up at their faces, puzzled by the sudden tension in the little room. Miss

133

Currie bent and scrabbled in a corner beneath one of the tables, bringing out a shabby little dolls' house.

'This is the one I had in mind, it seemed to me to be the right size for a child of your daughter's age. It needs doing up, but from what you've told me, I'm sure that you could do it very well.'

Isla wished that she had never come back to the house. 'I don't mean to be rude, Miss Currie, but,' she bit her lip, then said in a rush of words, 'it's just that I'll not take anything from anyone unless I can pay for it. And I can't afford to buy a dolls' house just now, not even a wee one.'

The older woman's flush deepened. 'Oh my dear, I should have realised.'

'It was kind of you to think of Barbara. No, Ross!' Isla seized his hand, which was reaching out hopefully towards the box. 'We have to go now, pet.' She escaped thankfully to the hall to collect her coat and Ross's small jacket, hating herself for depriving Barbara and for hurting the old lady, but knowing that she couldn't, wouldn't, accept charity.

To her astonishment, Annie, still hanging up her own outdoor clothing, muttered out of the side of her mouth, 'For any favour, let her give the lassie the wee house.'

'What?'

'Go on,' the woman hissed, putting a large cold hand on Isla's. 'She's got nob'dy of her own, and she's fair desperate to do somethin' for somebody. It surely couldnae do any harm to give in to her just this once!'

Isla's resolve faded as she looked into Annie's round face and saw the pleading look in her eyes. She swallowed hard, her hand falling away from the hook that held her coat, then turned and went back into the room, where Flora Currie stood, looking lost and alone, still clutching the little dolls' house.

'Miss Currie – if you're sure that you really mean it—'

The green eyes lit up. 'I do! You'll accept it, then?'

'Yes, but I'll not take it without paying for it. I can't afford to pay in money,' she added hurriedly as she saw the older woman open her mouth to protest, 'but I could do some renovation work on your Victorian house in return, if you want me to.'

'Oh my dear, that would be so kind of you. I accept.'

'I'll need to work on the wee house here, for there's no room in my own place.'

'Och, that's no trouble at all. I'm sure there are some wee pots of paint around that you could use – and there's the furniture in the box. You're welcome to it, if you can do anything with it,' Flora Currie enthused.

From the doorway, Annie said heavily, 'I suppose that'll mean a mess for me to clear up.'

But the faintest of smiles tugged at the corners of her mouth.

12

Because their year of mourning still had five months to run, there could be no Christmas or New Year celebrations in the McAdam household. Christmas trees, becoming more fashionable now, could be seen here and there in their neighbours' bay windows as December matured, and Ainslie, alighting from the bus each night, liked to look at the trees with their pretty decorations as she walked home.

It was a custom that the McAdams had never taken up, but Colin's family had a tree each year, and she recalled with pleasure the fresh pine smell that had pervaded their large drawing-room the year before, and the way the light from the tall red candles on their dinner table had gleamed on green pine needles. She and her mother and brother had had dinner with the Forbeses last Christmas Day, and she had become engaged to Colin on New Year's Day, at a dinner party in the McAdam house.

Her father had been present at the engagement celebration, but not at the Forbeses' dinner table, because he was always busy at Christmas. Now, Ainslie knew where he had been.

Although they didn't make much of Christmas Day themselves, the family did give gifts to each other, and it was Catherine McAdam's custom to present small gifts to the servants. Ainslie had had a generous allowance since leaving school, but that had stopped with her father's death, and it occurred to her that she might buy presents for her mother and brother from the auction house. Nervously, she approached Charlie at the beginning of December and asked if she could purchase a pair of china figures for her mother, and a boxed set of model cars that she knew Innes would love.

He squinted up at her from his desk. 'This is an auction room, lass, not a shop.'

'I know that, but I thought that if I paid the reserve price . . .'

He tutted and shook his head. 'They might go for more than the reserve price if they're auctioned, and if I sold to you instead, I could be depriving my clients of money – and myself of commission. If you want 'em, lass, you must go into the auction room at the right time and bid for 'em.'

Her mouth went dry at the prospect, and a gleam of amusement came into the eyes surveying her. 'Scared, are you? No need to be – I'll not let you buy a wardrobe by mistake. Go on and bid for 'em – it'll be good experience for you. When it's your turn to run an auction you'll know what the other folk in the room feel like.'

'When I—? I'm not going to be an auctioneer. I'm office staff.'

'Think so?' Charlie Blayne tilted his chair back, openly grinning now. 'Everyone turns their hands to

everything here, and I think ye'd do well as an auctioneer, once ye learn the ropes.'

The thought of Catherine McAdam's reaction if her
daughter was ever to run an auction made Ainslie feel
faint. 'I'll maybe just have a look round the shops.'

'That's the coward's way out, and ye never struck me
as a coward, Ainslie McAdam. Go on,' Charlie urged,
'I'll be auctioning the items ye want later this week, and
the office can look after itself for an hour. I'll expect ye
to be there – and that's an order, young lady.'

Ainslie scarcely slept on the night before the auction.
She told herself a dozen times that she couldn't go
through with it, and her stomach started churning
when, looking down from the interior office windows
the next day, she saw the public surging in through the
street doors. Still unsure as to her final decision, she
finished the work she was doing, blotted and closed the
big ledger, then took a deep sustaining breath and went
down the outer stairs, into the street, and into the auction room via the public door.

She had watched a few sales from the safety of the
gallery, and had been aware of the surge of excitement
wafting up from the floor below, but being in among it
all was quite different. There was a tingle in the air, a
sense of anticipation. Some people stood about in
groups, heads together, arguing, dissenting, sometimes
agreeing, all the time eyeing each other slyly, measuring
up the opposition. Others drifted in ones and twos
around the room, examining the stacked furniture and
rolled carpets, running their fingers over the china or
through drawers of cutlery, making notes on scraps of
paper. Ainslie, too, walked about, studying items she

had no intention of buying, carefully ignoring the pieces she was interested in, trying to look as though she was an old hand when it came to attending auctions.

There was a buzz of excitement as Charlie swept down the stairs from the gallery, dressed in his usual auction-day clothes, a smart lounge suit with a bow-tie at the collar of his crisply starched shirt. Leonard, his clerk, was in close attendance, his arms filled with ledgers and lists.

Some people moved to the rows of chairs below the platform, but Ainslie remained on her feet at the rear of the room, ready to slip out through the street door if her nerve failed her. To her horror, Charlie, after casting a quick glance round the room, saw her lurking in the background and rapped his gavel on the lectern, booming, 'Order now, ladies and gentlemen – and make way for the young lady at the back there. Come forward, madam, and take a seat. Don't worry, we won't expect ye to bid for it.'

A ripple of appreciative laughter ran through the crowd, and there were hearty guffaws from the furniture movers as they recognised Ainslie. The bidders standing in front of her looked over their shoulders, then stepped aside. Blushing, she had no option but to walk through their midst like Moses moving between the parted waves, to take a seat. Charlie gave her the ghost of a wink, then rapped again on the lectern, and the auction began.

He was good at his profession, taking his audience neatly through the lots, occasionally tossing out a joke to set them at their ease. His eyes seemed to be everywhere, and no bid, no matter how unobtrusive, went unnoticed. Beside him, Leonard scribbled furiously, keeping pace with each and every bid and the names of the successful bidders, while the aproned men responsible for putting each lot on view without any time-wasting worked smoothly and efficiently.

Ainslie's terror ebbed away as she watched the proceedings, fascinated, then her mouth went dry when Charlie, giving her a meaningful look, announced, 'Lot twenty-six, ladies and gentlemen – a handsomely boxed set of model cars, every detail correct. An excellent buy for the car enthusiast. What am I bid?'

Ainslie put a hand up and called out an amount that she knew to be well below the reserve. Charlie's eyebrows rose.

'The young lady knows a good bargain when she sees one,' he told his audience smoothly. 'Any other bids?'

Somebody at the back of the room put in a bid. Ainslie topped it, then had to top it again, and again. They were over the reserve price and approaching her limit when, to her astonishment, the other bidder dropped out, and Charlie slammed the gavel down once, twice, and said, 'Sold to the young lady in the front row.'

The unexpected success boosted her confidence, and when the china figures she wanted for her mother were brought out half an hour later, she bid with more confidence, again starting below the reserve price. This time, though, the bidding was rapid, quickly going beyond her limit, and she had to concede the figures to a plump woman further down the row. During her look around before the auction, she had noticed a set of china wall plates, so she waited, and managed to buy them when their turn came. Then, flushed with success, she escaped back to the office.

'That was a dirty trick to play on me – starting the bidding below the reserve price,' Charlie said when he came up to the office later. Ainslie shot him a quick sidelong glance, and was relieved to see that though the words were grim, he was smiling.

'I thought that that was what bidding was all about, Mr Blayne,' she told him demurely. 'If I'd started at the reserve price, I might not have got the cars.'

He laughed. 'Ye're quite right. Well done, lassie, ye got a bargain both times, and my clients still got a price they'll be happy with. D'ye see now what I meant about not selling at the reserve price?'

Ainslie nodded. 'I didn't know an auction could be such a challenge.'

'It can be enjoyable, but it can be like gambling, too. It's amazing the folk who come in and buy stuff they don't need, just for the fun of bidding.'

'And the folk who bid, then can't pay,' chipped in Leonard, a small, elderly man who, with his large hooked nose and sharp eyes, looked like the picture of Punch in one of Ainslie's childhood books. He put the plates and the box of model cars down on a table, and gave her a broad wink as Charlie continued on into his own office. 'Ye did all right, hen,' he whispered. 'Good for you!'

Ainslie and Innes attended the midnight church service on Christmas Eve, debating over the following day's routine as they walked home. It had always been the family custom to take their presents downstairs and put them on the dining-room sideboard to be opened after breakfast, but this year everything was different.

'I think we should,' Ainslie said firmly.

'But if Mother stays in bed we can't open the presents.'

'Then we'll leave them there until dinner. She'll be at the dinner table.'

'But that means that I'll have to wait all day to open them!' Innes's voice was anguished.

'That can't be helped. We should do as we've always done.'

To their surprise, Catherine was already seated at the breakfast table when they went into the dining-room in the morning, and there were two wrapped parcels on the sideboard. Ainslie and Innes, who had met on the stairs and entered the room together, exchanged glances.

'Merry Christmas, Mother.' Ainslie kissed Catherine's cheek. 'It's good to see you downstairs at this time of day.'

'One must make an effort, I suppose, on special occasions.'

When they had finished eating and the dishes – Catherine's scarcely touched – had been cleared away, the servants were summoned to the dining-room to receive a sealed envelope each from their mistress. They curtsied and scurried out, then it was the family's turn. Innes tore at his parcels and exclaimed with delight over the model cars and the *Boys' Own Annual* he received from his mother. Catherine unwrapped the parcel he had given her to reveal a wooden teapot stand.

'I made it in school,' Innes said proudly. 'Yours too,

Ainslie, but I didn't have time to finish the other one.
I should have it done by February.'

Ainslie put the book-end down and went round to
his side of the table to give him a hug. 'Thank you,
Innes, it's beautiful.'

He wriggled out of her embrace. 'Aren't you going to
open your other presents?'

Catherine had given Ainslie a pair of leather gloves.
She herself glanced at the decorated plates and said
vaguely, 'They're very pretty,' then put them aside,
and excused herself, saying that she had a headache
and must go upstairs to lie down.

Unlike the English, the Scots worked through
Christmas and holidayed on New Year's Day, their own
special celebration. There was an air of excitement about
the auction rooms when Ainslie went in that day, a
holiday feeling. Charlie Blayne presented a small box of
chocolates to each of the women on his staff, and a
miniature bottle of whisky to each of the men, and as
the day drew to a close he summoned them all together
in the auction room, where a table covered with a white
cloth held trays bearing small glasses of whisky and
ginger wine, and plates filled with thick slices of dark
fruit-cake.

When they had all taken a glass, Charlie raised his.
'A good year it's been, and a better one to come. My
thanks to all of ye,' he said, beaming round at them.
'Drink up, now, and eat up too. My missus made the
cake and she'll have something to say if I take any of it
back home.'

Going home at the end of the day, Ainslie could still

taste the sharp tang of the ginger wine on her tongue, and feel its fire in her stomach. Her spirits sank as she let herself into the house and breathed in the usual funereal atmosphere. It was as though Christmas had been shut out, left on the doormat.

As soon as she went into the dining-room she saw that Innes's teapot stand had gone, but the plates she had given her mother still stood untouched on the sideboard. They ate in the usual silence, broken only by Innes as the dessert was cleared away.

'Mother, may I go to the matinee in the Glen Cinema on New Year's Eve?'

'Certainly not,' Catherine said at once. 'Cinemas are dirty, unhygienic places. You don't know who you'll be sitting next to.'

His face fell. 'But it's Tom Mix! You let me go last year, and I'm a whole year older now.'

'I said no, Innes.'

'But Douglas is going, his parents said he could.'

'Douglas isn't in mourning,' Catherine snapped, and he flushed scarlet and said no more, excusing himself a few minutes later and going up to his room.

'He's still a little boy, Mother,' Ainslie ventured when they were alone. 'It's hard on him, keeping a whole year of mourning.'

Catherine gave her an icy look. 'It's hard on us all, and it has been much harder on me than it should have been. When are you going to stop this foolish nonsense?'

Ainslie kept her eyes on the table-cloth. She had made herself apologise abjectly to her mother after their bitter quarrel on the day of the tennis party; Catherine had acknowledged the apology stiffly, but ever since then the wall that had always stood between them had been noticeably stronger. 'I'm not going to tie myself to marriage for the sake of living a comfortable life, Mother,' she said doggedly, for what seemed like the hundredth time.

'It's what you were raised to do!'

'It's what you were raised to do as well, and it's brought you nothing but grief. Why try to make me follow in your footsteps?'

As soon as the words were out she regretted them. Catherine's face went bone-white. She got to her feet so abruptly that for a moment Ainslie thought her mother was going to come round the table and strike her. Instead, Catherine walked to the sideboard, reaching out to clutch at its dark solidity for support.

'That,' she said in a low voice, 'was a cruel thing to say.'

'Yes, it was. I'm sorry.' Was she going to spend the rest of her life apologising for speaking her own mind? Ainslie wondered wearily. 'But we've already been over it all, Mother, and we'll never agree.' She heard the pleading in her own voice. 'Even if I did change my mind, Colin has his pride. He wouldn't marry me now.'

'There are other eligible young men, but none of them will want you either, if you don't pull yourself together soon.' Catherine's voice was tight with anger. 'Do you want to become an old maid? Do you want to lose what looks you have and skivvy away in that stupid auction house until they decide they don't want you any more? And you needn't think I'll support you then, for Innes and I will have better things to do!'

Her hand swept out in a strange groping motion, catching the three plates Ainslie had bought for her, sweeping them on to the floor. One bounced on the thick carpet, but the other two crashed against the chair Catherine had just vacated, and fell to the floor in a shower of fragments. For the space of a breath mother and daughter stared at each other, then Ainslie got up and walked out of the room, brushing past the maid, who had come running at the sound of breaking china.

After the maid had swept up the pieces of china Catherine McAdam sent both servants to bed and sat huddled in the drawing-room, staring into the fire while the house settled around her for the night.

Through no fault of her own, everything in her life had gone wrong. Catherine had been raised to be a good wife, and was quite certain that she had fulfilled her purpose in life admirably. She had never enjoyed Kenneth's attentions in the privacy of their marriage bed – it had always been her belief that no well-bred woman could ever go through such a business without feeling disgust and repugnance – but the thought of him sharing a bed with another woman while she herself wore his ring was more than she could bear. He had dealt her the final humiliation by killing himself, making her the object of vulgar gossip in the town and among her neighbours.

And as if that wasn't enough, she was now cursed with a daughter who might as well have been born into a working-class family for all the gratitude she ever showed. An ungrateful, uncaring girl with no sense of duty, no feeling for anyone else but herself.

She took the brandy decanter from the cupboard and poured a generous measure into a glass. The doctor had prescribed brandy with a raw egg whipped into it to keep her strength up, but in recent months Catherine had found that she preferred the brandy on its own. It soothed the bitterness and dulled the memories of Kenneth's and Ainslie's faults. She refilled the glass, and by the time she had emptied it again the fire was a silver-rose glow in the grate, and the room was chilly. Stiffly, she got to her feet and went into the hall and went up the stairs, holding tightly to the banisters, halting as she neared the top to study her father-in-law's portrait.

It, like the brandy, always soothed and calmed her. The landing light had been left on, and its glow brought his painted face to life, picking out the twinkle in his blue eyes, the crispness of his snowy hair, the firm planes of his face. Catherine stood motionless for some time, drinking in each detail, then went up another few carpeted stairs and reached out to the cool glass, running the tips of her fingers over the outline of his mouth, then up to touch his cheek.

Innes McAdam had been able to transform a room simply by walking into it, she thought, her stiff, ageing limbs becoming fluid at the memory, just as they had each time she saw him, all those years ago, when she was sixteen and he twenty-five years her senior. Her father's friend, quite unaware of her, other than as one of Kenneth's friends; unaware that she only came to his home whenever she could in the hope of seeing him. Even if he was away from the house she was content just to be there, touching door-knobs he had touched, books his hands had held.

His wife, Kenneth's mother, had never been worthy of him in Catherine's opinion. She was generally acknowledged to be a woman of strong character, an intellectual who sat on committees, raised funds, and was known for her work among the poor. Catherine had merely seen her as a bad wife, content to spend her time with others instead of devoting it to her husband's comforts, and spoiling her only son when she should have encouraged him to grow up to be as strong and as noble as his father.

Catherine's smile faded, and her hand stilled on the glass. Marrying Kenneth had been the closest she could get to marrying Innes McAdam himself. At least it gave her his name, made her part of his family. But he had died just over a year after the marriage, shortly after Ainslie's birth. And tragically, Ainslie had inherited her grandmother's nature rather than her grandfather's. Her mother-in-law, Catherine thought bitterly, would probably have approved of the girl's stubborn foolishness.

But at least there was another Innes, young and now hers alone, who would be raised to be a worthy successor to his grandfather. At the thought, Catherine's smile returned. Her Innes would carry on the family name and make it mean something in Paisley again. He would atone for all the mistakes his father had made.

Soothed, she let her hand fall away from the portrait and continued on to the upper landing. As long as she had Innes, nothing else mattered.

13

In the weeks before Christmas, Isla went along to Flora Currie's house every day to work on the little dolls' house. She had decided to turn it into a country cottage, painting the roof to resemble thatch and giving the exterior walls the look of rough white-washed stonework.

She added mock timbering, and climbing roses all round the walls. Then, using scraps of wallpaper and linoleum and carpet that Flora provided, she papered the interior and covered the floors.

Digging about in the box, she found furniture that could be adapted, cutting out rockers for the chairs from strong cardboard then glueing them on and painting them, making tiny cushions, curtains that tied back with ribbon, frills for dressing-tables and stools.

Flora was overcome with admiration. 'Where did you learn to do all that?'

Isla, making a cradle from a matchbox, cardboard, and glue, smiled up at her. 'I enjoy finding ways of making things.'

Flora raked through drawers and cupboards, finding broken necklaces, bits of ribbon, scraps of material for

Isla to use. She insisted on contributing a family of little china dolls, and Isla dressed them – a dress and apron for the mother, smocks for the two little girls, overalls and a work shirt for the 'daddy doll' she knew Barbara would insist on. Strands from an old summer hat of Flora's were deftly woven into straw hats for the family, and in the cradle lay a tiny baby wearing a white lacy gown.

The work took time, and Magret soon wanted to know where she got to in the mornings. Isla, knowing instinctively that it was best to keep her two lives apart, said that she had managed to find some cleaning work in one of the houses at Castlehead.

Barbara, too, was fully occupied. With Christmas approaching, her class was rehearsing for its part in the school Christmas concert, and Barbara, who had always loved singing, was in her element, warbling carols in her clear, sweet little voice all the time she was at home. Ross, not to be outdone, sang along with her, much to her annoyance.

'He keeps getting it wrong,' she protested.

'But he's learning the words quite well. Aren't you, my clever lad?'

Ross beamed up at his mother from where he sat on the fireside rug. 'Oil city,' he agreed.

'It's Royal – David's – City, not oil city,' his exasperated sister snapped, and flounced out to practise her carols with Greta in the wash-house.

Isla finished the little doll's house in good time, and was able to spend the last few days before Christmas studying the Victorian house and planning the renovation work. She was nervous about undertaking it, but Flora Currie was adamant. 'You said you would do it, and I have every faith in your ability. In fact, I insist!'

On the last day of the school term, Isla and Magret, dressed in their best, attended the concert, which was staged in the large gym hall. They went alone, because Tommy was on the late shift at the mill.

'Not that he'd have gone anyway,' Magret said as they walked to the school. 'The men always leave that sort of thing tae their womenfolk. Ye'll mebbe get some grandads, though.'

Sure enough, the few men among the crowd flocking into the large hall tended to be older – retired men, bored and looking for any diversion that might brighten the monotonous days. A lot of the women had brought small children with them, for there was nobody to look after them at home. Ross clung to Isla's hand while Magret carried Daisy, bound snugly to her by a shawl, as usual.

The large echoing hall was decorated for the occasion: Ross stared about, enchanted, while Daisy reached grasping fingers up towards the brightly coloured paper streamers criss-crossing over the ceiling and walls. A small decorated Christmas tree stood at one side of the stage, and there was a vase of paper flowers on the piano at the opposite side. As the hands on the clock above the stage reached the time announced for the beginning of the concert a self-conscious young teacher in a low-waisted wool stockinette grey dress, her hair plaited into braids curling like shells around her ears, crept out of the wings to take her seat on the piano stool and flutter through the sheets of music before her.

'That's Miss Wilson,' a hoarse voice said from behind Isla. 'She taught our Myra last year. Awful nice lassie, but awful shy.'

'She looks as if she's wearing her mother's dress,' Magret whispered loudly into Isla's ear just then. 'She'd be pretty if she just wore something more modern.'

Miss Wilson, uncomfortably aware that the entire audience was staring at her, cast an imploring look into the wings, and then, at a hidden signal, raised her hands high and crashed them down on to the piano. Daisy, now slumbering contentedly against her mother's soft pillowy breasts, jerked violently, while Ross, on Isla's lap, clutched at her sleeve for reassurance. A small child somewhere near the front of the hall let out a wail of fright. The hall lights went out, the curtain opened to reveal a row of carol singers clutching paper candles with scarlet crayoned flames, and the concert was under way.

When the 'babies' ' turn came, Greta lurked shyly in the back row, while Barbara was right at the front, singing lustily and beaming down at the audience, her cheeks pink with excitement. Ignoring her teacher's frowns, she waved happily at her mother and brother when she spotted them, and her voice soared above the others as they launched into, 'Once in Royal David's City'. Ross, kicking his heels painfully against Isla's shins, joined in with great enthusiasm.

'I told you not to sing, it was just the schoolchildren that were supposed to sing,' Barbara nagged huffily when she joined her mother and brother later for tea and mince-pies in one of the classrooms which, like the hall, was decorated with paper streamers. Ross bit into a mince pie, ignoring her.

'Nobody could hear him,' Isla said in his defence.

'I could, all the way up on the stage,' said Barbara, then, hopefully, 'Could you hear me? Was I good? Was I the best?'

Filled with mince-pies, they walked home in the dark, the lights going off one by one in the school behind them. It was long past the children's bedtime, and Ross grizzled to be carried. He fell asleep almost at once, his sticky little face nuzzling into Isla's neck, and his breath, sweet with mincemeat, puffing warmly against her chin. Barbara and Greta ran hand in hand ahead of their mothers, singing snatches of carols, shrieking with laughter, then suddenly falling silent as a drunk man lurched out of a pub and towered over them, telling them in a slurred voice that they were bonny wee lassies, so they were.

Isla felt her stomach tighten. She often heard intoxicated men lurching home past her window at night, sometimes singing, sometimes quarrelling, their voices loud and their words ugly and menacing. She had seen them in the street now and then during the day, but she had never before had to confront one.

Magret had no such qualms. 'Now you leave the lassies be,' she ordered sharply as the man reached out a hand towards Barbara's bright hair.

He jerked round towards her voice. 'Who d'ye think ye're . . .' he started to say, then the tone of his voice changed. 'Is it yersel', Maggie? How are ye, hen?'

The light from the pub window caught his face, gaunt and stubbly. Hair stuck in tufts from under a peaked cap, and he stank of drink.

'I'm fine, Willie, and so will you be, when ye've slept

153

it off. Away home, now, for I've got more tae dae at this time of night than stand in the cold talking tae ye.'

'Aye, right ye are, pet. Nae harm done, eh?' the man said, and lurched off along the road. Barbara, subdued now, came hurrying back to Isla's side and took a firm grip on her coat.

'I didn't like that man.'

'Ach, there's no harm in him, pet,' Magret assured her. 'But it's as well no' tae talk tae men that smell of drink, eh?' To Isla she added, as they hurried towards their own close, 'Poor soul – he was a gaffer in the mills when I worked there. A good, sober man he was too, then his wee boy died of the diphtheria and his wife went off with someone else. Look at him now. It's a shame, so it is.'

'Drunk men scare me,' Isla admitted.

'Ach, they're all right, most of them. They drink for comfort, but the pity of it is that some of them don't have the sense tae settle for one or two glasses. My own father was drunk more often than he was sober, and my poor mother had a time of it tryin' tae keep us from starvin' tae death.' Magret huffed air angrily out of her nostrils. 'The publicans never have that worry, though! They're happy tae line their pockets with other folks' hard-earned money. I'm fortunate that my own man knows how tae take a sociable drink then call it a day.'

The dolls' house was smuggled into the George Street flat on Christmas Eve and hidden beneath the bed. On Christmas Day, Barbara's astonishment and delight made Isla feel that her hard work had been well worth while.

Greta was summoned at once to admire it. 'You can

have my other house,' Barbara announced graciously, and Greta's thin little face lit up.

'She must be a real nice lady ye're workin' for, Isla, tae give ye a house like that for the wean,' Magret marvelled. Then, as Ross charged across the space between them, towing his Christmas present, a brightly painted, jointed wooden dog that nodded its head and moved its legs when pulled along on a string, 'He'll wear your oilcloth out by New Year.'

'It's already worn out. I doubt if it'll last another six months,' Isla said in despair. Small though the room was, there always seemed to be something that needed replacing.

Daisy, allowed down on to the floor more often now that she was two months from her first birthday, squirmed after the wooden dog on her stomach, with no hope of catching it. Magret scooped her up and planted a loud kiss on her head, now covered with fine downy brown hair, then sniffed the air appreciatively. 'That smells good.'

'It's a boiling fowl I put on to simmer on the stove for our Christmas dinner. I made a dumpling, too.'

'We always have our special dinner at New Year.' Magret's bright little eyes twinkled with anticipation. 'Wait till the New Year, Isla – that's a grand occasion here. Everyone gets the day off work, an' there's parties in just about every house, with dancing and singing – out in the street tae, if the weather's no' too bad.' Her twinkle broadened into a grin. 'Ye'll not get much sleep on Hogmanay, for the noise.'

Kenneth had always claimed to prefer celebrating Christmas, and Isla was keeping the custom alive for his children, although now she realised that Kenneth must have established the custom because his other family had naturally expected him to be with them for New Year – a time, he had told her, when his office was at its busiest. Staring absently at the two little girls down on their knees by the dolls' houses, she wondered why she had always believed every word he said, never questioned him about those busy times when he had to be away from home for days and occasionally weeks. She supposed that it was because she had loved him too deeply to do otherwise.

'Magret, why don't you and the children have your dinner with us today?' she suggested, anxious for company on a day that held so many memories for her.

'That'd be grand – if ye're sure there's enough for us all.'

'Of course there is. That's what Christmas is about – sharing.'

Even with Magret's cheerful company to dull the edge of her memories, Isla was glad to see Christmas Day past and eager to get to work on Flora Currie's Victorian dolls' house on Boxing Day. She felt a tingle of anticipation as she unhooked the catch and the front of the house swung open like double doors, to expose the rooms within.

Ross, used to Miss Currie's house by now, went happily to the kitchen with Annie, who shrugged Isla's protests aside with, 'Ach, I'd plenty wee brothers and sisters when I was a lassie. I can surely manage tae see tae just the one.'

Fired by enthusiasm after the school concert, Barbara

156

had decided to organise her own carol concert, and was too busy coaxing some of the street children to form a choir to accompany her mother to Castlehead. Magret had agreed to keep a watchful eye on her.

'She's got quite bossy since she started school,' Isla told Flora as her fingers worked confidently at glueing a length of fringing round the canopy of a double bed for the master bedroom. The original canopy had come unstuck in several places, and it was easier to renew it than replace it. 'To think that I was worried when we first moved to George Street in case the other children ostracised her and broke her heart! But it was never easy to keep Barbara down. I can't think where she gets her determination from.'

Flora, a willing assistant, was sifting through a box of old costume jewellery, sorting beads into sizes and laying aside lengths of chain. Isla had earlier discovered part of a necklace which included tiny crystal drops, and had decided to try her hand at making a chandelier, if she could find enough fine chain.

'She gets it from you, my dear. It takes determination and courage to face life with no money to speak of, and two small children to care for.'

Isla arranged fringing on a sheet of paper and brushed glue carefully along its length. 'That's not courage, it's necessity. I was such a timid child – nothing like Barbara. I'm sure she's got her strength of mind from her fath—'

She stopped abruptly, and Flora Currie flicked a sidelong glance at her, then said casually, 'I wonder what the thirties will bring. It seems no time at all since we were approaching 1920. I used to think when I was

157

young that time would slow down as I got older, but it doesn't. It gets faster and faster.'

'I've found the years rushing by since the children were born,' Isla said, relieved that they had moved on to a safer subject. 'A few years ago they didn't even exist, yet in no time at all they'll be into their teens, and thinking of what they want to make of their own lives. What's that wee box you've got there?'

Flora held it up. 'I remember keeping bits and pieces in it as a child. I can't think where it came from – my father may well have brought it back from one of his trips.'

Isla wiped her fingers on a cloth, then took the little box from her and studied it. 'You know that nice laquered chest you've got in your front hall? I could paint this up to look just like it for the dolls' house hall. And I could make a nice vase to put on it, with a spray of flowers . . .'

In return for the shared Christmas dinner, Magret had invited Isla and the children to eat their New Year's Day dinner with her and Tommy and their children.

'It'll be steak pie, same as we always have, with tatties and carrots. That's what we like best,' she said, her eyes bright with happy anticipation. 'There'll probably be some folks comin' in after – my mam and my sister, and her lot. I love New Year, so I dae, we always have such a good time!'

New Year's Eve was always a busy day for Scottish housewives, for tradition demanded that every house had to be rid of the old year's dirt and dust, ready to start a new year afresh.

As well as cleaning out every nook and cranny, the womenfolk also had to make sure that there was food for the flood of visitors they might expect. The children, roped in to help, were sent to the shops with long lists wrapped round the money to pay the shopkeepers, or set to minding smaller brothers and sisters or beating carpets and rugs in the backyards and helping their mothers to shift furniture so that every corner of every room could be cleaned thoroughly.

Wash-houses were in great demand for the final few days of the old year, and the clothes-lines in every yard were crammed, as were clothes-horses indoors. Smaller items of clothing bubbled and steamed in metal pails and tubs on top of stoves and ranges, cheek by jowl with 'clootie' dumplings, tied in clean dish-cloths or pillow-cases, simmering in pans of water. Flat irons were fitted in among the pots and tubs wherever room could be found for them, so that they would be hot enough for use once the clothes were dry. There was scarcely an oven in the town that didn't hold at least one steak pie in the making.

It was the men's task to see that there was enough drink available in the house for all who might call in after the bells rang to welcome the new year. Those men with dark hair were expected to 'first foot' other houses, arriving as soon as possible after the bells rang, armed with a bottle of whisky, a large wedge of black bun – a rich cake crammed with fruit – and a lump of coal to bring plenty and good fortune to the household for the coming year.

The Hogmanay cleaning usually brought a rich harvest to the children, as empty bottles and jam-jars that had lain forgotten in cupboards came to light, some to be borne off to the nearest shop and exchanged for halfpennies and farthings, some carefully set aside for the penny matinee at the Glen Cinema, down at the Cross, a welcome haven from parental tyranny on Saturday afternoons, and every Hogmanay.

By early afternoon on that final day of 1929, many of the mothers were beginning to lose patience with their offspring, and deciding that they could probably manage to get on with the work faster on their own. Gradually, the children returned to their play, banished to the street with thick wads of bread and jam and instructed not to come in again until summoned for the obligatory bath, hair-washing, and change into clean clothes. The lucky ones were despatched to the cinema, some of the older girls carrying the baby of the family, a dummy stuck in his or her mouth.

One of Greta's older cousins, an eight-year-old girl, called to take her to the cinema, and Barbara, who had heard of the delights of the moving pictures from the older children in the street, begged to be allowed to go too. When Isla refused permission, Barbara flew into a tantrum and, on being smacked, climbed on to the box bed, drew the curtains shut, and sulked. Isla left her to it, wondering if she was being over-protective, yet uneasy about letting the little girl go.

'Mebbe next year, when you're six,' she opened the curtains to tell Barbara, who flounced round in the bed so that her back was to her mother. Sighing, Isla got on with her work.

She was on her knees by the cooker, trying to reach right under it with a brush to coax every bit of fluff out of hiding, when Magret burst into the room, her face white and strained, Daisy in her arms.

'Take the bairn for me,' she gasped, 'There's somethin' happened at the Glen – I'm away tae look for our Greta!'

Isla scrambled to her feet. 'What do you mean—?' she began, but Magret bundled the baby into her arms, and with a wail of, 'Oh God – my wee lassie!' she was out of the house, through the close and out into George Street, running as fast as her curved legs and stocky body would allow.

14

Ross, who had been put into his cot to play and had fallen asleep, woke in fright. With her free arm Isla scooped him out on to the floor, and he staggered drowsily after her, still grizzling, as she carried Daisy outside.

Women had come to the close-mouths all up and down the street, and some had started running in the direction of the Cross, still carrying dusters or floor brushes. Others hung out of windows, loudly demanding to know what had happened.

'It's the Glen!' The news was passed from mouth to mouth along the street. 'It's on fire!'

A woman who had appeared at the next close dropped her metal bucket with a clatter as the words reached her, giving a cry of pure anguish. She started to run, kicking off shabby down-at-heel slippers and running on in her bare feet, lurching clumsily from side to side, sawing her clenched fists through the air. 'My bairns!' she screamed as she went. 'My bairns are in there!'

'Mummy, what is it? What's happened?' Barbara arrived on the pavement. Just as Isla opened her mouth to reassure her, a boy came hurtling past, yelling, 'The Glen's burnin'! The bairns is all killed!'

'Greta?' Barbara's eyes filled with tears. 'Where's Greta? I want to see her . . .' Her voice was an anguished wail that set Ross to crying again and started Daisy off. Up and down the street people were weeping, and more and more of them were taking to their heels. Mrs Leach and her thin, pale daughter joined Isla on the pavement, along with Mrs Brown and Granny Thomson. Drew Brown was there too, clutching a carpet beater. His mother put a hand on his arm when she heard the news.

'Thank God you didnae go this year, son. These poor, poor bairns!'

'Greta was there – Magret's gone to look for her.'

'Mebbe they all got out in time,' young Mrs Kelly ventured, and her mother sniffed.

'That's no' likely, is it? Now ye know,' she nagged at the young woman, 'why I would never let ye go. If it's no' fleas, it's fire!'

Men began to appear round the corner of Maxwellton Street, earlier than usual, come from the mill as word of the fire spread. One or two stopped to question the women at the close-mouths before hurrying on to the Cross in search of their children, or to see if they could help.

Numbly, Isla shepherded her three tearful charges back into the tenement. There was no sense in standing out on the pavement, and Daisy was heavier than she looked. She sat the little girl down on the rug, and Daisy promptly fell over and lay there, breaking her heart. Isla picked her up and sat down so that she could hold Ross as well. Barbara insisted on burrowing into her arms too, and the four of them huddled together, cramped in the small armchair, waiting for news.

An hour dragged by before Magret came back, her husband Tommy with her, carrying Greta, her face streaked with dirt and dried tears, a bruise purpling one cheekbone. At sight of her, Barbara burst into tears, setting off Greta and Ross and Daisy.

'If ye'd seen it, Isla,' Magret choked against the background of wailing children. 'All the folk screamin' and shoutin' for their bairns, an' the firemen an' the polismen carryin' these poor wee souls out, some of them just lyin' there and not movin'. Not even cryin' . . .'

Tommy clumsily patted her shoulder with his free hand. They were both ashen.

'Was the whole place on fire?'

Tommy shook his head. 'We never seen any flames. They'd stopped the trams, an' we found her on one of them.'

'A polisman wanted tae take her tae the Infirmary, but she's all right – not like some of those other poor wee pets. She just needs tae be safe with her mammy and daddy, don't ye, my wee hen?' Magret reached up and stroked her daughter's face gently.

'What about Greta's cousin?'

'She's – she's all right.' Tommy's voice was husky, and choked on the first word. 'They was both lucky. Come on, pet, we'd best get her tae her bed,' he urged, and Magret nodded and held out her arms for Daisy.

'I'll see ye later, Isla.'

'You're wet, Mummy,' Barbara said when they had

gone. She sniffed tears back and pointed to the large damp patch on Isla's skirt, then looked down at her own skirt. 'I'm wet too – so's Ross.'

For the first time Isla noticed the sharp smell of urine hanging in the air. 'Poor wee Daisy, I never thought to change her.'

More washing to do if she wanted everything to be clean for the new year, she thought. But at least Greta was safe, and so were her own two. She knelt and gathered them both into her arms. If she had let Barbara go – if she had lost her in the same year she had lost Kenneth –

The thought was more than she could bear.

Contrary to rumour, the cinema had not caught fire. A reel had started to smoulder in the projection room and the smell of burning celluloid had permeated the packed cinema. Before anything could be done to reassure them, the children had panicked, rushing to the exits only to find that they couldn't open the doors. Those who reached them first were the victims – crushed and smothered as the frantic children behind them struggled to escape from the building forcing them to the ground, clambering over them in search of safety.

Sixty-nine children died needlessly, and at midnight the bells that rang in 1930 tolled, too, for the lost children, and a town in mourning.

Magret insisted on her Ne'erday dinner going ahead as planned. 'We've still got tae eat,' she said, and so Isla and Barbara and Ross, together with Granny Thomson, who had no relatives of her own, crowded into the small one-roomed flat. With the resilience found only in children, Greta had recovered from the previous day's ordeal, though it would be at least a week before the bruising on her face disappeared. The children ate heartily, while the adults picked at their food, still numbed by what had happened.

'It's a terrible way tae start a new year, losin' a bairn,' Magret voiced all their thoughts as she carefully mashed potatoes for Granny Thomson then ladled gravy over them. 'More than one for some folk – I heard that four were lost from the one family, an' one of them a bairn just about the same age as your Ross, Isla.' Her voice shook on the last few words, and Isla noticed that she and Tommy kept glancing at Greta, as though reassuring themselves that she was still with them.

'There ye are, Granny,' Magret went on with determined cheerfulness, 'you eat that up. The poor soul's no' got a tooth left in her jaw,' she mouthed to Isla across the old woman's head. 'Cannae manage the meat.' Aloud, she said, 'I did custard an' stewed apple for after, ye'll enjoy that, won't ye?'

Granny Thomson nodded, loudly sucking the purée of potatoes and gravy from a spoon, her face almost touching her plate, her back hunched and the bones of her spine pushing against the material of her dress. She left not long after the meal was finished, her thin colourless lips stretched in a toothless smile of gratitude, and Isla made her own excuses a little later, when members of Magret's and Tommy's families began to arrive. The small room was becoming unbearably crowded, and the talk was all about the cinema disaster. Isla felt that she couldn't bear to hear about it any more.

Not that it could be avoided. Everywhere she went, people were talking about the tragedy. Early in January the pavements were thronged to see the small coffins go by on their way to Hawkhead Cemetery for burial in a communal grave, some of them children who had been in Barbara's class at school. Many of those who had survived were still receiving treatment in Paisley Alexandra Infirmary. Funds were set up to help the bereaved families and the victims, and the cinema manager was arrested in connection with the closed exits that denied safety and life to so many small victims.

Even Flora Currie talked about the tragedy when Isla went back to her house to work on the Victorian dolls' house.

'I heard that there were riots outside the Infirmary, with people wanting to get in to see what had happened to their children, and the police trying to hold them back. Those poor, poor souls. In my childhood a little girl we played with was killed in the street when a cart ran over her – I can still remember the shock of hearing the news. I'd been so sure until then that only old people died. It was dreadful – and it still is – to realise that it can happen to little children too. I recall my mama trying to write to that child's parents and saying to my papa, what comfort can one give to people who have lost a child?' She sighed. 'And now I must find the right words myself.'

'You knew one of the children?'

Flora nodded. 'Innes McAdam, the son of people I used to know.'

They were taking tea in the parlour. Isla, about to sip from her cup, set it back in the saucer with a faint clash of china. For a moment the room seemed to shift around her, then to her relief it steadied. Flora Currie didn't notice.

'I only knew the boy slightly. Such a nice child, and so polite, even as a little tot. His father was very friendly with one of my brothers at one time. They grew apart after they left school, long before Arnold left Paisley. Arnold was a bit of a perfectionist, and I believe that eventually Kenneth McAdam just didn't match up to his standards, though I thought him a very pleasant youth. As it turned out, my brother's judgement may have been correct.'

Her voice rattled on and Isla, quite unable to stop her, had no option but to listen.

'Kenneth's problem was that he grew up in his father's shadow. His father was a fine man, very well thought of in the town, but I always pity children who have to follow perfection. After all, we're all as God made us, for better or worse. Unfortunately, Kenneth didn't inherit his father's strength of character as well as his father's business. I remember Arnold saying that Kenneth tended to take the easy way out of a dilemma instead of facing up to it.'

She paused, and Isla frantically sought for some way of changing the subject. Before anything came to mind, Flora went on, every word a spear plunging into Isla. 'Poor man, I'm not so sure that he did take the easy way out in the end. Apparently his business began to fail, and he speculated foolishly with clients' money in a bid to save it. Instead, inevitably, he lost good money after bad, then took his own life. It was a terrible blow to his wife. She's a very proud woman.'

'Miss Currie—'

But the old lady was well into her subject now, her eyes cloudy as she looked into the past. 'As if she didn't have enough to bear, she discovered that he had set up a second wife somewhere else, a woman much younger than himself, and had two children by her. So poor Kenneth ruined the lives of another three people when he decided to put an end to it all. Such a tragedy, and now his own son's gone as well. He looked like his father, too. Kenneth was a handsome young man, with vivid blue eyes and red hair that seemed to light up any room he was in. I can see it yet – like autumn leaves on a sunny—'

Ross was playing on the carpet, in a patch of January sunlight that made his downbent head glow. Flora's eyes had been resting absently on the little boy as she spoke. Now her voice stopped abruptly, her eyes clearing and widening, flying up to meet Isla's frightened gaze.

'Oh, my dear,' she said on a breath of sound. 'What a very stupid old woman I am, talking about Kenneth's other wife and two children, never stopping to wonder where they might be, or what they might be doing . . .'

'It's—' Isla choked and tried again. 'I—' But the words wouldn't come. She put down the cup and saucer, blundered to her feet, and ran from the room.

The dolls'-house room was comforting and familiar, a haven where nothing bad could happen. Isla picked up the four-poster bed she had been working on before the New Year, blinking hard to clear the mist from her eyes. The new canopy was firm and straight now; she found the curtains that had been hemmed for it, then began to glue each one into place so that it could be gathered back later and tied to the bedposts. Her mind was numb and she left it in peace, concentrating on her fingers, shutting the rest of the world out.

Half an hour passed before Flora Currie tapped on the door and came in, cup and saucer in hand.

'I made some fresh tea. Annie's taken the children out for a walk. I hope you don't mind.'

Isla stared at her, startled. For once, she had forgotten about her children. 'I'm sorry, I shouldn't have just walked out and left them like that.'

'You needed time on your own – and Annie loves being with them,' Flora said timidly, then, 'Oh, Isla! Oh, my dear, I wish someone had broken into the house and cut my tongue out while I was asleep last night. My mama always said that I spoke before I thought, but the things I said today were quite inexcusable!'

'You weren't to know.'

'But I should have guessed!'

'I was hoping that nobody would guess. A lot of Scots have red hair, and you wouldn't have expected to find us right here, in Paisley.'

Now that her secret was out and she had got over the first shock of it, it was a relief to tell someone about it all. Once she started, though, she couldn't stop; the words poured out, and Flora Currie had the sense to let her talk without interruption.

'My dear child, what a hard time you've been having – and nobody to turn to,' she said when Isla had at last come to a stop.

'I'm managing, and the children are thriving. And I've good memories of the time I had with Kenneth.'

'You don't resent what he did to you?'

'Resentment doesn't come into it. I loved him.'

'I really didn't think I'd missed out on anything, staying single,' Flora said after a moment. 'Now I'm beginning to wonder.' Then her tentative smile faded. 'Now that I know, I hope that you'll continue to come here, and go on working on my little house.'

'Are you so sure that you want me to? It could be embarrassing for you, having me around,' Isla explained, when the older woman looked puzzled. 'After all, you know the McAdams.'

'Scarcely at all, now, and anyway, why should I let the past hinder a good friendship? Annie and I would miss you and the little ones sorely if you stopped coming, so I hope we'll hear nothing more about that,' Flora said firmly. 'And I give you my word that nobody, not even Annie, shall know what you've just told me.'

She beamed at Isla, who summoned a wavering smile in return. Then Flora rubbed her bony hands together vigorously.

'I do hate sentiment,' she announced. 'It embarrasses me. Now then – what plans do you have for today's work?'

Charlie Blayne called at the McAdam house on New Year's Day to tell Ainslie to take as much time off as she wanted. Standing on the step, twisting his cap round and round in his big hands, he said, 'We'll manage fine till you get back, lass. Your poor ma'll be needin' you.'

She stared at him through the cotton-wool haze that

had wrapped itself around her since Innes's death. 'I'm sorry I can't ask you in,' she heard herself saying.

'I'd not expect it – not at a time like this.' He stumbled backwards down the steps to the gravel drive. 'I just wanted you to know – for as long as your ma needs you.'

But Catherine McAdam didn't need anyone but Innes. She didn't want anyone but Innes. Time after time, as she served tea to the few people allowed into the house, or tried to coax Catherine to eat, Ainslie caught her mother looking at her with eyes that told her, clearly and coldly, that the wrong one had died.

'She could have borne my death better than his,' she said through frozen lips to Colin when he called at the house. Her mother, who couldn't sleep at night, had fallen into one of her sudden, exhausted dozes on the drawing-room sofa, and the two of them sat in the dining-room, at either side of the polished table.

'Don't say that.' He reached across the table and covered her hand with his. His fingers were warm and real; Ainslie, who had had the eerie feeling since Innes's death that she wasn't really there, and that her own flesh had become transparent, half expected his hand to sink through hers on to the surface of the table, but it didn't.

'It's the truth. She never cared for me, it was always Innes – and I didn't blame her, because he was such a – such a nice little boy, wasn't he?' She hadn't cried before, not even when she saw her brother in the Infirmary, pale and calm, looking as though he was asleep, the only sign of the violence that had ended his life a large bruise at his temple, flaring up into the red hair

172

that someone had carefully combed. But now the tears spilled down her face, and Colin came round the table and held her, not as a would-be lover, but as a friend, someone she could lean against, a support and a comfort.

'Why did he do it?' she wept into his jacket. 'Why did he defy Mother and go to that beastly cinema?'

'Because he was young, and restless, and because he'd had enough mourning.' His hand was gentle on her hair. 'Ainslie, kids always do impetuous things. Innes wasn't to know what was going to happen any more than anyone else.'

By the time he left, she felt as though she had been completely emptied of tears. She looked in on her mother, who still slept, then went quietly into Innes's room, feeling a need to sit among his possessions for a while.

Catherine McAdam's eyelids fluttered and lifted, and she was wide awake. Since Innes's death, she only knew that she had been sleeping when she woke, for there was no drifting, no drowsiness or sense of letting the day go and slipping into rest. She was either asleep in a deep black pit filled with nothing, or awake with unbearable anguish tearing at her, sharp-toothed and bloody-clawed.

She sat up slowly and lowered her feet to the floor, then stood up carefully, holding on to a nearby occasional table, feeling very old and very frail.

'You must eat, Catherine,' Phemie Forbes had coaxed that morning. 'You must keep your strength up.' She had visited every day since the cinema disaster, bringing beef tea and calves' foot jelly and urging the red-eyed servants to make nourishing broths that Catherine could scarcely touch. 'You have to keep going, dear, for Ainslie's sake.'

She was like an irritating housefly, buzzing and droning and refusing to go away. She didn't understand, Catherine thought impatiently as she made her way across the room, moving from one piece of furniture to another, testing the carpet with each step as though it was a marsh. None of them understood. The pain she felt had nothing to do with lack of food. In any case, why keep going for Ainslie's sake, when Ainslie had done nothing for her?

She groped across the precarious, furniture-free desert of the hall, finally clamping a hand tightly on the newel post with a grunt of relief. After a pause to gather her strength, she started to climb the stairs one step at a time, the beast inside her snapping at her heart as she recalled Innes going upstairs in exactly the same way when he was learning to walk, his nurse by his side. She remembered the way he swatted the woman's protective hand aside and insisted on climbing on his own. So determined, so like his grandfather!

She paused for breath, clinging to the banister, misery washing over her in fresh waves as she looked up at the portrait. Now there would be no McAdam to carry on the name and make amends for Kenneth's sins.

As she opened the door of Innes's room Ainslie looked up, startled, from where she sat on the bed, her eyes swollen. The two women stared at each other, then Catherine said harshly, 'How dare you come into his room!'

'Mother—'

'Get out!' She stepped aside, holding the door open, and the girl went without another word. Closing the door behind her, Catherine erased her presence from the bedcover with swift, angry movements of her hands, muttering angrily to herself as she worked.

When she was satisfied that the covering was free of Ainslie's presence, she moved about the room, touching Innes's possessions to calm herself. The model cars Ainslie had given him at Christmas annoyed her, so she swept them off the top of the bookcase and into the waste-paper basket. Finally she settled in an armchair and closed her eyes, soaking in the atmosphere of the place.

Innes was still very much a part of this room. It didn't know that he was dead, and while it waited for his return, he was still alive.

15

Most of the small victims of the New Year tragedy were buried together in Hawkhead Cemetery, but Innes McAdam was laid to rest beside his father in Woodside Cemetery. Catherine refused to attend the funeral service, and it was left to Ainslie to travel with her young brother on his last journey, Gilchrist Forbes and his son by her side.

There was a great throng of people around the open grave, some of them friends of the McAdam family, many of them strangers from all over the town, united in their sorrow. As the minister's voice droned on, Ainslie remembered the last time she had stood by this grave. Then, she had been filled with shock and bitterness, but now there was only a deep, aching grief.

Glancing up, she saw Charlie Blayne among the throng, unusually sombre and serious in black. The sight of him brought a little warmth to her heart. He was a reminder that although her past had been shattered beyond repair, she still had some sort of future.

A small reception was held for close friends in the McAdam house after the funeral. Catherine, with Phemie Forbes hovering protectively by her side, received her guests in the drawing-room, a bleak-eyed ghost of the gracious hostess she had once been. They stood around in uncomfortable groups, eating sandwiches, drinking tea, trying to make conversation in hushed voices. The funeral of a child was so much more harrowing than that of an adult. Ainslie, moving among them, trying to make sure that everyone present was thanked for their attendance, bent over her mother's chair.

'Can I get you anything, Mother?'

Catherine shook her head without looking at her.

'At least, dear,' Ainslie heard someone say to her mother as she moved on, 'you still have Ainslie. She must be such a comfort.'

'So one would have thought.' Catherine's voice, strengthened with bitterness and contempt, rang out. 'But it seems that my daughter cares far more for her place of employment than her home, or her family.'

There was a sudden, uncomfortable silence. Heads turned, and all eyes fixed on Catherine, who gazed back at them arrogantly, then on Ainslie, who looked as though she had just been slapped hard in the face. Colin Forbes stepped forward to put a hand on her arm, his fingers tightening; she looked up at the mingled anger and pity in his gaze, forcing her lips into a smile, then moved on, away from him, saying something banal to one of the staring faces. The woman blinked, answered, and the soft hum of voices started up again, with an undertone of relief.

Ainslie went back to the auction rooms two days later. There was no sense in staying at home. It was clear that her mother had no need of her presence.

*

Isla had become so involved in working on the Victorian house that even when the snow came she made a point of struggling along to Castlehead, wrestling Ross's push-chair over frozen, slippery humps of snow, glad of its support as her shoes skidded on the ice. He was almost two years old now, and well able to walk, but not for long distances.

She had been working hard since Christmas and the dolls' house was almost finished. A cook in a volumi-nous white apron ruled over a little scullery maid in the well-stocked kitchen, the master sat in his armchair in the library, while his wife, in plum-coloured silk, occu-pied the drawing-room, busy with her embroidery, which was stretched over a curtain ring Isla had found in one of Flora's boxes of odds and ends. There were two children and a baby in a lacy cradle in the nursery, under their nurse's watchful eye.

In the hall stood the small wooden box Isla had noticed several months before, painted to make a pass-able copy of the inlaid chest in Flora's hall. She was still working on the chandelier, which was proving to be a long-drawn-out, difficult task.

'We could hang it in the dining-room,' she suggested one Monday afternoon. She had come on to Castlehead after collecting Barbara from school; Greta was at home nursing toothache, so Isla had taken advantage of her absence to spend some extra time on the dolls' house. Both children were in the kitchen with Annie, who had become a firm favourite.

'You'll have finished that house in a few more weeks.'

'Yes.' Isla had enjoyed every minute of the task. It

had given purpose to her days, and the thought of being without it saddened her. They were having tea in the drawing-room; glancing at the window, she saw that the snow had stopped falling.

'We'd better go, before it comes on again.'

Someone tugged at the bell-pull just then, and they heard Annie bustling along the hall, then after a moment the parlour door opened and Ainslie McAdam walked into the room. She stopped in her tracks as she recognised Isla, the rosy glow that the cold weather had brought to her face deepening.

Isla, as horrified as the other girl by this unexpected encounter, struggled to her feet as Flora said, 'Ainslie, my dear, how good of you to call. This is my friend, Isla Moffatt; Isla, this is Ainslie McAdam.'

'How do you do?' Ainslie came further into the room reluctantly, unable to do anything else, short of turning on her heel and leaving the house she had just entered. She pulled her glove off and held a hand out. Isla took it and they exchanged a brief clasp of fingers, Isla's warm, Ainslie's icy.

'You'll have some tea?'

'I – I think not, Miss Currie, I must get home. I just called to thank you for sending the basket of fruit to my mother.'

'My dear girl, of course you must have tea – I'll not have you going back out into that snow without something warm to drink.' Flora put her hand to the bell-pull just as Annie came in with fresh tea and an extra cup.

'Sit down, both of you,' Flora instructed, pouring tea. Watching her, admiring the calm, unhurried way in which she guided the conversation, bringing first one of her guests in, then the other, making it seem that they were conversing with each other when, in fact, she herself was acting as go-between all the time, Isla admired her fluent ability, recognising the years of training Flora had undergone while growing up in her mother's house. She would have made a grand wife for some ambitious businessman.

But not even Flora's skill could bridge the gap between herself and Ainslie McAdam; unable to bear the tension in the room a moment longer, Isla shook her head when Flora went to fill her cup, and stood up.

'I must go, Miss Currie – please, stay where you are,' she added as Flora began to get up. 'I'll collect the children and Annie can see me to the door.'

'Very well, my dear. I'll see you soon.'

'I came at a bad time,' Ainslie said when the door closed.

'Not at all, Isla was about to go home anyway. She brings the children to visit me often.'

'Really?' Ainslie couldn't hide her surprise.

'Oh yes. She saved my life one day – helped me home when I'd gone out too soon after a bout of illness, and wasn't able to get back under my own steam. She's a considerate young woman, and I admire her very much,' Flora said calmly, giving her visitor a swift sidelong glance. 'Life's extremely difficult for her, poor girl. It can't be easy for a young widow, raising two wee ones on her own like that, with hardly any money, but she never complains.'

Ainslie remained silent, staring at her fingers, which

were crumbling a piece of Annie's excellent fruit loaf. Flora took pity on her.

'How is your mother, my dear? I thought of calling, then I decided that it might be best to leave it for a while. She probably has more visitors than she can cope with.'

Ainslie looked up, her face shadowed. 'She's started eating again, though scarcely enough to feed a bird.'

'It's a terrible thing, losing a child,' Flora agreed.

Ainslie nodded, then said, as though unable to stop herself, 'I'm worried about her, Miss Currie. She sits in Innes's room for hours at a time, and she insists on making the servants lay a place for him at the table at every meal. She keeps looking at his chair all the time we're at the table, as if she's listening to something he's saying.' Her lower lip trembled, and was brought under control. 'The housemaid's given notice – when I asked her to reconsider, she said that my mother frightens her.'

'Have you spoken to her doctor?'

'I tried, but he just says it's her way of dealing with her loss, and she'll come out of it in time. I'm not so sure.'

'We can only hope that he's right. It must be a terrible thing, losing a son.' Flora paused, then went on gently, 'Losing a brother's a terrible thing, too, though sometimes other folk forget that. But once the edge of the grieving dulls, my dear, you'll have all the years of knowing him to sustain and comfort you.' After letting silence hang between them for just the right amount of time, she asked briskly, 'Would you like to have a look at my collection of dolls' houses?'

'Dolls' houses?' Astonishment swept away the tears that threatened to spill from Ainslie's eyes.

'It's a daft hobby for an old woman like me, I know, but I like to show them off now and again – when I meet someone I think will understand. This way . . .'

The girl's amazement turned to admiration when Flora unlatched the front of the big Victorian house.

'This is perfect!'

'You should have seen it before Isla started on it.'

'Isla?'

'Oh yes indeed, she's been working very hard. She's making a chandelier just now, and look at the family portraits she cut out of magazines. She made the frames herself, and this rocking chair,' Flora told her proudly. 'The thing is – what do I do with it when it's finished?'

'Oh, you must keep it and enjoy it.'

'Nothing's enjoyable, my dear, when there's nobody to share it with. Besides, I have so many.'

'Not like this one. It's a collector's item.'

'Then perhaps some collector should have it. I feel that all Isla's hard work should be seen, and admired.'

'If you ever think of selling it, let me know,' Ainslie said earnestly. 'I'm sure my employer would like to have a look at it – he's a good valuator.'

'Really?' A light came into Flora's eyes. 'Ainslie, I've just had an idea – what about asking your employer to auction it for me, then the amount raised can be handed over to the Glen Cinema fund?'

'You mean that you'd give away that beautiful wee house?'

'Why not? I've had my pleasure in watching it come to life again, and I intended to make a donation to the fund in any case. This seems to be a fitting way to do it.'

'If you're quite sure . . .'

'Oh I am,' said Flora. 'Quite sure. The more I think of the idea, the more I like it. Would you ask your employer to call? And come with him – I'd like to see you again, my dear.'

Later, when she had seen her guest out, Flora returned to the back room to study the Victorian house.

'A very fitting contribution,' she said to herself, well satisfied.

Isla finished the Victorian house a few weeks later, but refused to be present when Ainslie brought Charlie Blayne to see it.

'But, Isla, you must be here! After all, you've made such a wonderful job of renovating it, and I'm sure Mr Blayne'll want to meet you.'

'It's your house, and your idea. I think it's a very generous idea, but I'd as soon not be involved,' Isla insisted, and wouldn't be swayed. She did, however, agree to go along the day after the auctioneer's visit to find out what had happened.

Flora met her at the door, glowing with excitement. 'My dear, Mr Blayne was very impressed indeed, and most disappointed not to meet you. He came back this morning in person to pack the house up and take it away. It's to be auctioned next week, and I've been invited to attend.' She drew Isla and Ross into the hall, talking all the time. 'Apparently they fix what's called a reserve price on things that are auctioned, and they won't sell below it—'

When she named the reserve price Isla gasped, then said faintly, 'Well, it is an old house, and very well made.'

Flora brushed the words aside with a wave of the hand. 'It was the work you put into restoring it that's brought the value up.'

Annie brought a tea-tray into the drawing-room, heavy-footed as usual. 'I don't know,' she grumbled as she set it down. 'Strangers tramping in and out the place, auctioneers carrying things out to a van – the neighbours'll think you're having to sell everything you own to make ends meet.'

'Away with you,' Flora retorted. 'You're enjoying the excitement as much as I am. We've been a pair of old fogies for too long – we need a bit of a stir in our lives.'

'We don't need footprints all over my newly scrubbed doorstep,' Annie shot back, and held a hand out to Ross. 'Come on with me, son – there's still some sanity in my kitchen, thank goodness.'

'I'm going to miss the pleasure of bringing that wee house back to life,' Isla said later as they gazed at the gap left by the Victorian house.

'I haven't had such a good time for years,' Flora admitted. 'Of course, there are the other houses.'

'Miss Currie, I doubt if Annie could stand any more of our nonsense.'

'Och, away with you, lassie, she's had the time of her life. There's nothing she likes more than a reason to grumble. Besides, she's taken to your wee ones. She'd miss them as much as I would.'

'And I'll miss coming here. I've enjoyed having

something to do apart from housework, and looking after the children.'

'We all need some sort of interest in life. I feel ten years younger myself, and you look better. When you first came here you were worn down by worries. Now there's colour in your face, and a sparkle to your eye. You've filled out a bit, too.'

'It's all Annie's home baking.'

'I think it's a sense of fulfilment. And it's not all one-sided, you know. Look at me – not a sniffle or an ache have I had since that day you had to half carry me home. We're good for each other – we mustn't give up now.'

Flora looked around the room, then pointed to a modest little house. 'That one could do with a bit of cheering up.'

'D'you know what that one always reminds me of?' Isla asked. 'Have you read *Little Women*?'

'Many times.' The older woman looked puzzled, then understanding dawned. 'Are you talking about the house that Jo and Beth and their sisters lived in? An American dolls' house? Could you do that?'

A tingle of excited anticipation ran through Isla. 'I'd like to try.'

Flora beamed at her. 'I've got the book somewhere – come and help me to look for it.'

The Victorian house fetched a very good price at the auction rooms, and resulted in considerable publicity for Flora Currie. She came straight from the auction to George Street, throwing Isla into a panic when she arrived on the doorstep. Flora swept into the small room and beamed at Magret, who was sitting by the fire.

'How d'you do?'

'This is Miss Currie, Magret, my . . .' Isla swallowed hard, then said, 'My employer, the one I've told you about. This is my neighbour, Mrs McDougall.'

With the merest hint of a raised eyebrow in Isla's direction, Flora shook Magret's hand while with her free hand she patted Ross's head when he came to throw his arms affectionately about her knees.

'I'll be going, then.' Magret gathered Daisy up and edged towards the door, and Isla, completely thrown by Flora Currie's arrival, nodded.

'I'll see you later. I'm sorry,' she added as soon as the door had closed. 'I had to tell her that I was working for someone at Castlehead. She was wondering where I got to every day, and I didn't want to say about the dolls' houses.'

Flora, more interested in the room than in Isla's dealings with her neighbours, was at the orange-box cupboard, fingering the curtain across it. 'What a sensible idea. Isla, I just had to come and tell you . . .' She launched into a description of the auction, and the interest the Victorian dolls' house had attracted before finally going to a collector who had paid an amazingly large sum of money for it.

'Everyone wanted to know who had restored it, but I didn't give them your name,' she said reassuringly. 'I merely said that it had been done by a very talented young friend. A young man from the Paisley *Daily Express* spoke to me, he's going to put something in the newspaper about it.' Her eyes were shining and her voice rattled on; Isla had never seen her so animated.

Almost as soon as she had gone, Magret returned, her face concerned. 'She didnae come tae turn ye off, did she?'

'No, nothing like that.'

'That's all right, then. She seems tae be a decent woman, for all her posh talk,' Magret said. 'It's good tae be appreciated, isn't it?'

16

In March, Barbara and her friends presented their concert in the wash-house to an invited audience of mothers and little brothers and sisters. Heedless of the fact that Christmas was long over, the gathering of little girls, many with dirty faces and bare feet and runny noses, bawled their way through a selection of Christmas carols, followed by some Great War songs, most of them sung by Barbara herself.

The women enjoyed every minute of it, clapping loudly at the end, while the little girls curtsied low, the smallest falling over and being hauled to her feet by those on either side.

'That Barbara's a right clever wee lassie,' Magret enthused afterwards. 'She'll mebbe go on the music halls when she's old enough.'

Barbara had wanted to invite Flora Currie, but Isla managed to dissuade her. Instead, Barbara ran through the entire repertoire on her own before Flora and Annie in the drawing-room at Low Road. Drunk on their praise, she then danced along the pavement all the way home, clutching a silver sixpence and a bag of sweets she had been given as a reward for her hard work.

Flora Currie's donation of the entire amount raised by the auction of the Victorian house to the Glen Cinema fund had created quite a stir in the town. Both local newspapers, the *Express* and the *Gazette*, had written articles about it, and Mr Leckie, owner of a big toyshop in New Street, had called.

'He did all he could to get your name out of me, but he didn't succeed,' Flora told Isla later. 'However, I did tell him about your plans to make a *Little Women* house, and he's shown an interest in buying it when it's finished. If he does, you must overcome your shyness and start charging for your work. In fact, I could advance some of the money to you now.'

'No! If he buys it you can pay me part of the money – but not until it's finished and paid for,' Isla said warily. She could have done with some extra money, but she couldn't take payment for work that hadn't been done. Secretly, she didn't believe that the sale to Mr Leckie would ever go through. The man would have lost interest, surely, long before the house was finished.

In April, when work was under way on the *Little Women* dolls' house, Ross had his second birthday. Isla bought him a toy delivery van, and baked a cake for the occasion, inviting Magret and her daughters in for tea.

A few days after the little birthday party, Isla lost the rent money. There were few hiding places in the single-roomed flat, and she felt safer with the little money she had tucked into her bag. On that particular Friday, she had spent an hour or two window-shopping along the High Street and through the Cross, the busiest area of the town, returning home via St Mirrin Brae and Causeyside Street. Barbara and Greta were old enough now to make their own way home from school, so they didn't have to be fetched.

When they got back to George Street Ross ran ahead of her into the close and out into the backyard. Isla fetched the old hoe that Flora Currie had given her and went to work on her little garden, where the first potato shoots were beginning to show. When Barbara arrived home, she put the hoe away and went into the house to make tea. It was then, going into her bag to get the packet of tea she had bought on her outing, she realised that her shabby purse had gone.

Panic blossomed as she checked her coat pockets, then the pocket of the pinny she wore in the house, then looked under the cushion on the chair and even, futile though it was, in the cot that was getting too small for Ross, and on and under the wall-bed.

'My purse – it's not here—'

'Have we been burgled?' Barbara asked, wide-eyed.

'No, pet, but your mummy's been very careless.' Isla fought back panic. 'Run and ask Mrs McDougall if she'll keep an eye on you and Ross while I go out to look for my purse.'

Barbara did as she was told, and returned with Magret, whose expression mirrored Isla's sick fear. Nobody in George Street could afford to lose money, that scarcest of commodities. 'How much was in yer purse?'

'Everything I had. I'll need to go back along the

street – mebbe I left it in the shop where I bought some tea.'

Isla ran all the way back to St Mirren Brae, but the grocer and his assistant shook their heads when she asked breathlessly if a purse had been handed in.

'I mind ye comin' in earlier, hen,' the grocer said, 'but I never saw what ye did with yer purse after ye paid me.'

Isla retraced her steps along the High Street and down Castle Street, peering into the gutter and along the foot of the house walls, returning to George Street empty handed.

'I'll just have to tell the rent man I'll pay him next week,' she told Magret, who retorted, 'He'll not like that.'

'He'll just have to like it. I've never been behind with the rent before.'

'Can ye not ask that woman ye work for tae pay ye next week's wages in advance?'

Isla shook her head, appalled at the thought of asking anyone, particularly Miss Currie, for financial help.

'I couldn't do that.'

Magret sniffed. 'See these rich buggers? They'd not give a crust tae a dyin' dog, most of them. I wish I could help ye, Isla, but we've not got much more than our own rent.'

'Don't worry about it, I'm sure Mr Reid'll be willing to wait for one week.' It would be hard to make up two weeks' rent next Friday, but she would do it somehow. The thought of explaining the situation to Gilchrist Forbes and asking him to have a word with the rent collector came to her, and was dismissed. For one thing, she couldn't rid herself of the feeling that it was wrong to be treated differently from the other people in the tenement, and for another, the older Forbes might not be in the office, and she couldn't, wouldn't, ask for favours from that cold-eyed son of his.

The children were both asleep when the rent collector arrived that night. He scowled and pushed his lower lip out when Isla explained the situation, taking a step into the room so that she had no option but to retreat before him.

'My employers'll no' like that.'

'I told you, I'll make it up next week.'

He continued to move forward until he was in the middle of the room. 'An' how dae I know that? How dae I know ye'll no' do a moonlight flit and be out of here by next week?'

'I've no intention of leaving.'

'Have ye got nothin' ye could pay on account? Somethin's better than nothin'.'

'Every penny I had was in my purse.'

His eyes travelled over her, then he said, 'I could mebbe put it in the book that ye'd paid somethin'.'

'I'm not asking you to lie for me, Mr Reid, or to use your own money. I'm just asking you to wait for a week.'

The man blinked rapidly, then said, 'That'd be fine with me, hen, but ye see, it's the man that owns this place that's not very patient. He likes tae get his rent in time, and it's me that'll get intae trouble if it's not. So . . .' his tongue moistened his lower lip and he noted something in his book, ignoring her protest.

'That's the entry made, all nice and tidy like,' he

announced, stuffing the book into his pocket. 'The thing is, hen, what can ye dae for me in return?'

'I didn't ask you to lie, Mr Reid. I don't owe you anything.'

'Aye ye dae . . .' He stepped towards her again and Isla, suddenly realising what he meant, retreated behind the fireside chair.

'I've said I'll pay you double next week.'

'Mebbe so, hen, but it seems tae me that there's still that wee bit on account tae be settled.'

'Mr Reid, if you don't get out of here, I'll—'

'Ye'll what?' The chair was scooped aside, then the man was crowding Isla against the wall, his hand on her arm, the stubby fingers squeezing into the soft flesh. 'There's always another way for lassies tae pay their debts. It suits them – an' it suits me.'

Isla tried to drag back on the grip that was drawing her towards him. The smell of the man was thick in her nostrils, a mixture of tobacco and spirits and hair-oil and clothes in sore need of washing. 'Let go of me!'

'I will, hen – in my own time.'

'I'll scream,' she warned, knowing even as she said it that she couldn't shout for help, couldn't waken the children.

He laughed, moving in on her, confident of himself now. 'Go ahead, hen, scream all ye want. Folk round here know how tae mind their own business.'

Isla, caught between his body and the wall, tried to bring her knee up sharply, but he was too close. Instead, she managed to stamp hard on his instep, causing just enough pain to make him step back for a moment. He swung in towards her almost immediately, but she had gained enough time to slide sideways along the wall and reach the poker, which she had propped up against the fireplace before going to answer his knock at the door. She gripped it between both hands, forcing it up towards his face. 'If you don't get out of my house, I'll use this on you. I mean it!'

He stepped back, his gaze flicking between her face and the poker. 'There's no need to be like—' A whine came into his voice as Isla took the advantage and followed him, still clutching the poker. 'I only wanted tae help ye.'

'And to help yourself,' she said between her teeth. At that moment, she would have swung the heavy poker without hesitation, would have done anything she had to do in order to rid herself of him. 'Get out of my house, Mr Reid.'

'It's you that'll be gettin' out, ye wee bitch. I'll see tae that. I'll see you and yer brats out on the street!'

She pulled her arm back as though to swing the poker, and he ducked instinctively, then ran for the door, his nerve broken. Isla slammed it shut behind him and leaned on the panels, her heart pounding so hard that she thought it would burst out through her ribs.

'Mummy?' Barbara, startled awake by the slamming door, sat up in bed, knuckling her eyes. Ross, a heavy sleeper, didn't stir.

'It's all right, pet, I – I opened the door to shoo a fly out and the wind slammed it.'

'Did the fly get hurt?' Barbara asked drowsily. The thought of her daughter's concern for a fly after what had almost happened brought a sudden spurt of laughter to Isla's throat.

'No,' she said on a giggle. 'The fly's fine.'

'Good.' Barbara slid back into sleep as Isla groped her way to the chair by the fire and sank into it, the poker still clutched tightly in her hand.

'He'll complain about ye. Ye'll mebbe be put out,' Magret fretted the next morning.

'Put out for refusing to let him molest me? It's me that'll be complaining about him.'

Magret's eyes darkened with alarm. 'Don't go makin' trouble, Isla, they'll no' listen tae ye. They always believe their own.' She twisted the dish towel between her hands into a rope. 'I was that worried about ye last night. I'd've asked Tommy tae sit with ye till the man had gone, but . . .' She stopped, and looked away, embarrassed. Isla understood. Magret couldn't risk losing her own home, even for a friend.

'Has this happened before?'

'Of course. It happens all the time.'

'Has it happened to you?'

Again, Magret's eyes slid away. 'There was one time, when he was laid off and there wasnae enough money.' She shivered, then said, 'I made sure after that that the rent was paid, even if it meant us goin' without.'

'Does Tommy know?'

'Of course not!' Magret was shocked at the very idea. 'Men have their pride, the shame of it would've near killed him. Either that or he'd've killed Geordie Reid, then we'd've lost the room for sure.'

'I wish now that I'd hit him with the poker, instead of just threatening him,' Isla said between her teeth. 'A

195

man like that shouldn't be allowed to go round bullying women and – using them.'

'Ach, it's just life, hen. Plenty women have tae face worse than that, day in and day out.'

'Your envelope's not ready yet. You'll have to wait, or come back later,' the receptionist told Isla when she presented herself at the offices in Moss Street first thing on Monday morning.

'I'm not here for the envelope, I'm here to speak to Mr Gilchrist Forbes.'

'Mr Forbes isn't in the office this morning.'

'What about his son?'

'He's here, but—'

'Then I'll see him,' Isla said. Since the father wasn't available, the son would have to do. She wasn't going to leave the office until she had had her say.

The woman hesitated, then shrugged and went away.

A few minutes later she reappeared, and Isla, clutching Ross by the hand, followed her into an office smaller than Gilchrist Forbes', but just as cluttered.

Colin Forbes' expression showed it clear that he, too, deplored this meeting. 'Mrs – Moffatt. Won't you sit down?' He made no move to shake hands, but stayed on his feet until she was seated.

Isla drew Ross to her side, taking some comfort in his nearness, and instructed him in a whisper to be a good boy. Then over his red curls she told Colin Forbes, clearly and calmly, exactly what had happened on the previous Friday evening. The event was burned into her mind – she had thought of little else all weekend – and she repeated everything George Reid had said, every move he had made, in detail.

Colin Forbes listened with growing distaste. 'I find it hard to believe that one of our employees . . .' he began when she had finished.

'I'm sure you do. I'm also aware that you're more concerned with protecting your employee's interest than mine.'

Colour rose beneath his fair skin. 'I assure you—'

'And I assure you, Mr Forbes, that every word I've told you is the truth. Not only that – I've been making enquiries over the weekend, and it seems that I'm not the only woman in the street to have had this experience.'

'Nobody has ever complained to us before about Mr Reid.'

Isla gave a short laugh. 'Tell me, Mr Forbes, would you complain if it meant being thrown out of your home? I've heard of one poor young woman who was left with three children to feed after her husband had to go into the Infirmary. She didn't pay any money at all to Mr Reid for a few weeks, but I'm quite sure that his book says differently. Mr Reid puts in the money himself, then claims his reward for keeping a roof over their heads. When – or if – the tenants can afford to pay back-rent he makes them repay to the last penny. That way, he gets his enjoyment without having to pay for it.'

The young man was almost crimson now, one hand fiddling with a pencil. 'Mrs Moffatt, all you had to do was to let my father or me know that you were unable to pay the rent this week, and we would have had a word with Reid.'

'Why should I seek favours that my own tenants can't have? I believe that every landlord should try living in their own property now and again, Mr Forbes. They may well learn something to their own disadvantage.'

They glared at each other across the desk, openly hostile now, then he asked, 'You realise that this may well mean that George Reid will lose his job?'

'In my opinion, he deserves to.'

'Very well. My father will be in the office this afternoon,' he said stiffly. 'I'll tell him about your visit.'

'Please do.' Isla got to her feet. 'And you can also tell him that if Mr Reid should call for the rent in future, I'll not be opening my door to him. Nor will my neighbours, if I have my way of it.'

17

In spite of her brave words, Isla grew more and more nervous as the week passed, and on Friday evening she kept the poker close at hand.

She was breaking stale bread into a bowl for the children's supper when someone knocked at the door, and Barbara, washed and in her nightdress, scampered to open it before Isla could stop her.

'Come in,' she said hospitably, and stepped back. Isla's fingers, reaching frantically for the poker, fell to her side as Colin Forbes walked in.

'Good evening, Mrs Moffatt. I came to assure you that Reid won't be troubling you again.'

Relief flooded over her, but, stubbornly, she didn't want to reveal it to young Forbes and let him think that she was being pathetically grateful. So she went on with her work, picking up the kettle and pouring warm water from it into the bowl. 'You mean he'll be troubling the poor souls in another area?'

His voice sharpened. 'My father and I looked into your complaint very thoroughly, and as a result of our investigations the man no longer works for us. Until we find someone more trustworthy, I'll collect the rents.'

Isla added milk to the bowl, then divided the mixture between two smaller bowls and put them on to the table. 'Barbara, stir these for me – carefully, mind, no splashing.' As the little girl scrambled importantly on to a chair, she bent to lift the tin bath to the side.

'Let me do that for you.' The young man put the rent book on the table and hoisted the bathtub up, moving towards the sink.

'Not there,' Barbara told him sharply. 'Mummy empties it in the backyard, over the potatoes, 'cos it's not been raining and they need water.'

He put the tub down by the sink then straightened. 'You're growing potatoes?'

'It's cheaper than buying them,' Isla said dryly, fetching her purse.

'Mummy's mixed a lot of dung into the earth,' Barbara told him blithely as she stirred at the bread and milk. 'It smells, but it's good for the potatoes. Would you give me the sugar, please?' She indicated the paper bag on a shelf by the cooker, and he handed it to her.

'Thank you. Dung comes out of horses,' Barbara explained as she dipped a dry spoon into the bag.

'So I've heard,' he agreed solemnly.

'Here you are.' Isla tipped coins on to the table and sorted them out, pushing most of them over towards him.

'There's too much here.'

'I wasn't able to pay last week's rent,' she reminded him, 'so I must pay it this week.'

He coloured. 'Aren't you being unnecessarily exact, Mrs Moffatt? How much have you left yourself to live on?'

200

'We'll manage.' She had had to pawn Kenneth's last Christmas gift to her, a bracelet that she had been hoping to keep. Even so, the next week was going to be difficult, but she had no intention of admitting it to this well-dressed man who had never in his life known what it was like to have to do without.

He glanced at Barbara, dribbling sugar, grain by grain, into one of the bowls, then at Ross, who stood by her side, craning up to watch the procedure, his blue eyes bright with anticipation, and said, low-voiced, 'D'you think you're being fair to your children?'

Isla fisted her hands on the table.

'We'll manage,' she repeated. Overhead, someone walked across the floor, and the ceiling gave out a series of creaks. Colin Forbes glanced up involuntarily, then looked round the room. Isla bridled as she saw that, unlike Miss Currie, who had noted only the attempts to improve it, all he saw was the shabbiness, the cracks in the ceiling, the damp patch in the corner.

'It's not much of a place, is it?' Isla asked, watching his face. 'It doesn't seem fair to me to take rent from the folk that have to live here.'

'People must pay their way.'

'Did my – did Kenneth McAdam own many other properties like this one?'

He had opened the rent book and was noting the amount she had paid. His hand faltered, then moved on. 'A few.'

'D'you think he ever visited them, and looked at the leaking windows and the draughts and the water running down from the backyard and into the close when it's been raining?'

201

'I'm sure my father could find something better for you.'

'I doubt if I could afford it. And as you just said yourself, Mr Forbes, people must pay their way.'

'Good night, Mrs Moffatt.' He snapped the book shut and swept the coins up, then turned on his heel.

As he opened the door, Barbara said cheerfully, 'Bye!'

'Bye,' Ross sounded like an echo.

Colin Forbes's face softened into a smile. 'Bye,' he said, and left.

She followed him into the close, closing the door behind her so that the children couldn't hear. She must have been left to the last, for he was on his way out of the close. 'Mr Forbes, why do you dislike me so much?' she asked his departing back bluntly.

He swung round. 'I beg your pardon?'

'I asked why you dislike me so much. I think I have a right to know.'

The close was only dimly illuminated by a gas lamp in the street, and Colin Forbes was a vast black shadow blocking out most of the feeble light. 'I get the distinct impression that the feeling's mutual, Mrs Moffatt.'

'Only because you made it very plain that you disliked me intensely from the first moment you saw me, at your father's office. If you have a reason, I can't think what it is.'

There was a pause, then he said bitterly, 'Ainslie McAdam and I were engaged to be married.'

'So your father told me. I understand that she ended the engagement.'

'She did – because she was ashamed over the way her father had betrayed his family with you.'

Isla stared, then began to laugh. She was shocked by her own reaction, but the laughter bubbled up of its own accord, filling the space between them, before she could stop it.

'I'm glad someone's amused,' she heard Colin Forbes say coldly above her mirth. 'At least the whole sorry business hasn't been wasted entirely.'

'I'm – I'm sorry.' Isla pressed her fingertips against her mouth to quell further laughter. She swallowed hard, then said, 'It's just that I've never been held responsible for so many crimes in my life. All I did was marry the man I loved in the belief that he was free to marry me. Yet Ainslie's convinced that I plotted to tear Kenneth from his family, you're certain that somehow I forced her to end your engagement – and now Mr Reid's lost his job because of me. I'm beginning to wonder if I started the Great War without realising it.'

'You're being ridiculous, Mrs Moffatt,' the shadow looming against the street light told her coldly. 'Ridiculous and childish.'

'Possibly, but I'm not the only one, Mr Forbes. From what I know of Ainslie McAdam, I'd say that she's an intelligent young woman, with a mind of her own. You make her sound like a lassie with a powder puff for a brain, someone who could be easily pushed into ending her engagement.' Anger began to replace the amusement. 'If she gave your ring back to you, Mr Forbes, it wasn't just because of me. She must have had her own reasons, and perhaps it's time you began to ask yourself what they might be.'

She heard him draw his breath in sharply, then

without another word he strode out of the close and along the street.

Isla sagged against the clammy, peeling wall for a moment, then pulled herself clear and stood upright. She had been cruel – but he had asked for it. 'Him and his disapproval!' she said aloud, the words echoing through the dim close, then with a quick, decisive gesture she spun round and went back into the house.

'For goodness' sake, Barbara!'

'What?' Barbara asked blankly, looking up from her bowl. Ross had clambered up on to a chair and the two of them were relishing their bread and milk. No wonder, Isla thought, peering into the sugar bag as she put it away. In her absence, Barbara had used up almost the entire week's supply.

'Did you have to talk like that to Mr Forbes?'

'I said please when I asked for the sugar, and thank-you when he gave it to me.'

Isla wiped milk from Ross's chin. 'I meant, did you have to chatter on about dung?'

Barbara, unperturbed, dug her spoon into her bowl and scraped up the last of the mush. 'Oh, that. I thought he might want to know about how to grow potatoes,' she said.

On the first anniversary of Kenneth McAdam's death, Isla didn't go to Flora Currie's house. Instead, she stayed at home, cleaning the room from top to bottom, throwing herself into hard work in a bid to keep her memories at bay. When the children were asleep that night and the tenement had creaked into silence, she wept into her pillow. The edges of her grief had dulled, but she still missed and wanted him.

The next morning Barbara, visiting the privy before going off to school, came hurrying back. 'Mummy, someone's dug your garden up!'

It was Mrs Leach's turn for the wash-house, and her washing was already on the line. Isla ducked beneath it and went to the far corner, where the tumbled earth was draped with stripped plants; when she picked one up it lay limply across her fingers, already dead. The thief must have struck the night before, after dark. Looking up at the building, she glimpsed Drew at a window, watching her, and a moment later he came hurrying out in shirt and trousers, thumbing his braces over his shoulders. Mrs Brown and Magret arrived at his back, with Greta and Daisy in tow.

'After all your hard work – it's a shame, so it is.' It was the first time Mrs Brown had directly addressed Isla.

'And after your Drew's digging, too.'

'I hope they were all bad,' Barbara announced. 'I hope that whoever ate them got a sore tummy.'

'Barbara! What's done's done, so we might as well hope that whoever took them was in real need of them.'

'The shaws were still small,' Drew mourned. 'The potatoes must have been like wee marbles.'

Isla nodded. 'I know. Could they not at least have left them until they could steal a decent meal?'

'Ach, most of the folks round here would never think of that.' Magret glanced up at the surrounding windows. 'It could have been anyb'dy.'

Mrs Leach came out of the wash-house with another basket of washing, her daughter at her back. 'I knew it wouldnae be worth the bother,' she said without sympathy as she began to peg out the clothes. 'Ye were askin' for trouble.'

'It was nice to see things growing, though,' Mrs Kelly ventured, and her mother gave a snort.

'It was a waste of time, that's what it was.'

Isla pounced on Ross, who had scampered into the yard dressed only in vest and trousers, and, Daisy at his heels, was approaching the looted bed with the clear intention of plunging his bare feet into the soft earth. As she pulled him away, struggling and protesting, she heard Mrs Leach say, 'Catch me workin' my fingers tae the bone just tae give some thief a meal!'

A few weeks later Isla was putting a batch of scones into the oven when the door, on the latch, was pushed open and Ross, now old enough to play outside with the other children, came hurrying in and made straight for her. His free hand locked on to her apron and his fiery head butted at her thigh as he attempted to get as close to her as possible.

She dusted flour off her hands. 'What's wrong, pet?' Ross was still learning to cope with the rough and tumble of street life, and often came running to her for comfort when things got too much for him.

'Lady . . .' he whined as someone rapped on the door. Isla moved to open it, but the little boy was like an anchor, holding her back, and she had to gather him into her arms before she could get to the door.

Despite the mildness of the day, the woman who stood in the close wore a heavy black coat reaching almost to her ankles. As soon as the door opened she moved forward imperiously, so that Isla had no option but to step back and let her into the room.

'What d'you want?'

The newcomer's head tilted back slightly, the brim of her hat lifting to reveal a pale, haggard face dominated by cold grey eyes.

'I am Mrs McAdam – Mrs Kenneth McAdam. And this' – the grey gaze moved to Ross – 'must be Kenneth's son. I saw him out on the pavement.' She was well spoken, but her voice was harsh, the words falling like stones from her thin mouth.

Icy water seemed to trickle down Isla's spine. 'What do you want?'

'The boy, of course.'

'The—?'

'I've come for the boy,' Catherine McAdam said slowly and clearly, as though talking to an idiot. 'He's my husband's son—'

'He's my son!'

'—and naturally, he must be raised in my husband's house,' the woman went on as though Isla had not spoken. 'Not in this' – she looked round the room, her lip curling in disgust – 'this hovel.'

'Mrs McAdam.' It was strange, addressing another woman by the name she had once thought to be hers. 'This is my son, mine! And you and I have nothing to discuss.'

Catherine McAdam surveyed her dispassionately, then dismissed her, looking back at Ross. The pale lips shaped a slight smile. 'He's a true McAdam. He's going to grow up to look just like his grandfather.'

Isla began to have the eerie feeling that the woman

who had invaded her home wasn't even aware of her as a human being, only some sort of mechanism that had produced Kenneth's son. His second son, she thought, and knew why Catherine McAdam was there. She had lost her own child, and she was looking for a replacement.

'Nobody's going to take my bairn away from me.' As Ross tightened his grip on her neck she put a hand up to his curly head, over one ear, wondering if he understood what was being said.

Catherine looked surprised. 'But he's a McAdam, with the McAdam blood in his veins. I can give him everything – a comfortable home, a good education. His room's waiting for him, with toys and books in it. I can teach him to follow in his grandfather's footsteps.'

'No!'

'Would you deny him all that, when you yourself can give him nothing?'

'Mrs McAdam,' Isla fought to keep the growing fear from her voice, 'I have every sympathy with you in the loss of your own son, but you can't walk into my home and demand mine to take his place.'

In answer Catherine took an impatient step towards her, coming close enough for Isla to catch the faint scent of brandy on her breath. She held her arms out towards Ross, and Isla backed away. This woman represented a threat far more terrifying than the blundering, lustful rent collector had. She could scarcely take a poker to her supposed husband's legal wife, she thought wildly.

'You're – you're not yourself, Mrs McAdam. You should be at home.'

Ross began to whimper and struggle; his weight was

almost too much, but she daren't even shift his position lest Catherine McAdam took the opportunity to lunge at her while she was off balance, and snatch him from her arms.

The woman's hands fell back to her sides. 'If it's money you want, you can have it,' her harsh voice said. 'I have no objection to paying you for the time you've spent caring for him.'

'I don't want a penny of your money, I just want you to get out of my house!'

'My dear, your sort of woman always needs money,' Catherine told her with sweeping contempt. 'I shall instruct my lawyer to have a legal agreement drawn up and delivered to you tomorrow. As for now . . .' she held her thin arms out again. 'Give him to me.'

'No!' Isla's voice rose above the little boy's frightened wails. 'Don't you touch him!'

For the first time, Catherine McAdam looked puzzled. 'If you didn't want me to have him, why did you bring him to Paisley? It was meant to be – don't you see that? You were sent here to help me in my time of need.'

'Please – go away!'

Again, Catherine's reaching arms fell away. 'I must have him, and I will have him, though not today, since you've seen fit to upset him.' She turned and walked unhurriedly to the door, opening it with only the tips of her fingers as though afraid that the wooden timbers might contaminate her. Then she turned.

'My lawyer will contact you tomorrow. He will pay you an adequate sum, and you may hand the child over to him.'

18

When Catherine McAdam had gone, closing the door quietly behind her, Isla dropped into her fireside chair, still clutching Ross, murmuring reassurance. His sobs gradually died down; he was hot, and sticky with sweat and tears, but Isla, almost out of her mind with terror, couldn't bring herself to ease her grip on him.

Just when everything seemed to be working out for her, her world had begun to shatter. Losing the rent money, having to fight the rent collector off, then being robbed of the potatoes she and Drew had so carefully tended. And now this, the most frightening threat of all. She should never have come to this town. Ainslie McAdam was quite right, she should have found somewhere else for herself and the children. They would have to leave at once, go where nobody knew them and where Ainslie's terrifying mother would never find them.

Her mind raced like a mouse caught in a cage, hurling itself from side to side but unable to find a way through the bars that held it captive. She couldn't just leave Paisley, much as she wanted to. For the children's sake, she must first have somewhere to go. She thought fleetingly of asking Flora Currie for help and shelter, then dismissed the idea. Flora had been kind, but her family and the McAdams had known each other socially, and Isla herself owed Flora too much to drag her into the dreadful situation. She suddenly remembered Aunt Lally in Edinburgh. She could go there, but first she would have to find money to pay for the journey.

She and Ross both jumped as Magret came barging in from the close. 'Isla? Somethin's burnin', can ye no' smell it?' Then, after one swift look at Isla, 'God, lassie, what's happened? Ye look as if ye've seen a ghost!'

Snatching a towel from the nail by the stove, she opened the oven door, then gave a wail. 'Look at them, they're all spoiled – did ye no' smell them?' She put the tray of blackened scones on top of the cooker and flapped the towel to waft the smoke away. For the first time Isla became aware of the acrid stink of burning.

At the sight of Daisy, standing in the middle of the kitchen, her fine hair wispy round her small skull and one index finger stuck firmly into a nostril, Ross reverted to his normal self and struggled to get down. Isla resisted, but finally gave in when he began to kick and pummel at her.

'Never mind the scones.'

'Never mind? Since when did any of us have money tae throw away like that?'

Isla got to her feet stiffly, feeling as though she had aged years in the past half hour. She had to do something before Catherine McAdam changed her mind and came back for Ross. She took the towel from Magret and wet one corner under the tap, then wiped her son's sticky, protesting face.

'I have to go out. Could you fetch Barbara from school, and keep her with you until I get back?'

'But the weans is old enough to find their own way home—'

'I don't want her left to come along the street by herself,' Isla interrupted sharply, snatching her coat from the nail on the door. 'I'll be back as soon as I can – just keep an eye on her till I get home.'

Ross was getting too big for his go-chair now, and he had begun to hate it. There was no time to struggle with him, so Isla scooped him up into her arms and hurried out, regardless of her friend's baffled face. By the time she reached Moss Street and turned in at the close that bore Gilchrist Forbes' gleaming brass plate, she was staggering beneath the little boy's weight.

The receptionist, seated in her small office behind its sheltering glass window, was speaking on the telephone. She flicked a cool glance in Isla's general direction, then her eyes widened and she began to scramble from her chair as Isla, ignoring her, marched round the corner into the open waiting area outside the offices.

Sunlight poured in through the windows of Gilchrist Forbes' large office. He and his son, bending over papers on the large desk, looked up as Isla burst into the room.

'Nobody's going to take my child away from me – nobody!'

Colin's exasperated, 'For goodness' sake, not again!'

clashed with the receptionist's, 'I couldn't stop her, Mr Forbes, she just—'

Gilchrist Forbes held up a hand for silence, looking at the distraught young woman who had just invaded his office, realising that she was on the verge of hysteria. 'Sit down, Mrs Moffatt. Miss Lang, could we have some tea? And perhaps you could take the little boy into your own office and keep him amu—'

'No!' Isla glared at him over Ross's head. 'He's staying with me!'

'Very well.' Forbes nodded at the receptionist, who withdrew with an offended sniff, then he picked up some blank sheets of paper and a pencil from the desk, and held them out to Ross.

'Would you like to draw pictures, young man? Over here, where your mother can keep an eye on you.' He took a stool from a corner and placed it in a puddle of sunlight. Isla hesitated, then released the little boy, who went at once to the stool and knelt down on the carpet, reaching for the pencil the lawyer held out to him. The sunlight turned his downbent head into a mass of dancing flames and the sight of the nape of his neck, soft and innocent, wrenched at Isla's heart. She couldn't bear the thought of losing him.

'Mr Forbes, you're not going to take my son away from me. I won't let you!'

Father and son exchanged puzzled looks. 'Why should we want to do that?' the older man said mildly.

'Mrs McAdam . . .' Then, seeing that both men were bewildered, Isla said, slowly and carefully, 'Mrs McAdam came to my house this afternoon. She w-wants . . .' The horror of the meeting swept over her again and her voice began to waver. 'She wants Ross.'

'You mean that she offered to adopt your child?' Colin asked.

'She just wanted him! She said that he was a McAdam, he had Kenneth's blood in him and she could give him things that I couldn't. She said that you'd – you'd come for him tomorrow, with an agreement for me to sign. She wants to b-buy . . .' Despite the warmth of the room Isla had begun to shiver.

The door opened and Colin Forbes hurried forward to take the tray from the receptionist. He poured tea then put a cup into Isla's hand and said, in the gentlest voice she had ever heard from him, 'Drink this, Mrs Moffatt.'

The hot sweet tea began to revive her and the shivering eased. She looked up to see Ross sinking his small white teeth into a biscuit, the crumbs glittering in the sunlight as they sprayed towards the carpet.

'Ross, look at the mess you're making . . .' she began automatically, but Gilchrist Forbes put a hand up to stop her.

'Never mind the mess, m'dear, just tell us exactly what Mrs McAdam said to you.'

Isla forced her mind back to the confrontation, speaking haltingly at first, then faster as she relived the scene. By the time she had finished she had begun to shake again.

'Nobody can make me give up my children. I won't let them!'

'You've got nothing to fear, Mrs Moffatt,' Gilchrist assured her. 'Nobody can take your children from you without your permission.'

'I've heard of folk in George Street who've had their bairns taken from them.'

'Only if they were unable to care for the children, or if they ill treated them. Only if it was in the children's interests, surely?' He spoke gently, but to Isla's ears the words were condescending, easily voiced by a man who had never known the insecurity caused by hardship or the gnawing worry over where his next meal was to come from.

'It's not as simple as that, Mr Forbes,' she told him sharply. 'Not if you've got no money behind you and the folk with the power decide otherwise. Mrs McAdam, for instance – she's right when she says that she can give Ross more than I can, but that doesn't mean that she can love him more than I do.'

Ross, his cheeks bulging with biscuit, came over to lean against her. She put her arm about him and hugged his small body to her. The thought of him, ill or alone in a strange big house, calling in vain for her, was more than she could bear. 'She doesn't look to me like a woman who could love a wee bairn properly,' she said to the two men, the tears beginning to flow again. 'She doesn't look to me like a woman who could love anyone.'

At his father's request, Colin Forbes drove Isla back to George Street in his smart car with its smell of leather seats. The children playing in the street and the women leaning against the close-mouths, arms folded, gaped as first Ross then Isla got out.

'Are you all right?' Colin Forbes asked from the car's interior. 'Do you want me to come into the house with you?'

'We're fine, thank you.' He had been kind to Ross, courteous towards Isla, but the irritation was still there, every time he looked at her or spoke to her. The last thing she wanted was to spend more time in his company.

'My father will be in touch with you tomorrow,' he said, and drove off as soon as she closed the door.

Barbara sped out of the close, Greta at her heels. 'Mummy, where've you been?'

'I goed in a motor car,' Ross bragged to her, pulling back on Isla's hand to watch the car disappearing along the road as she hurried him into the close, away from prying eyes.

'Phemie,' Gilchrist Forbes asked as soon as he got home, 'did you tell Catherine McAdam where Kenneth's other – other wife lives?'

'Of course not – as if I'd do a cruel thing like that!'

'But she knows?'

His wife, setting the table for the evening meal, paused in her work. 'She told me that she'd heard about the woman, though I can't think how, since she never goes out.'

'What else did she say?'

'Nothing.' Her eyes brightened with curiosity. 'Why? Has something happened?'

'Nothing of any great importance.'

Phemie almost stamped a plump foot on the carpet. 'It has – it must have. Gilchrist, are you going to give me that nonsense about lawyers' confidences again?'

'No, my dear—'

'Because if you are, mebbe it's time I started thinking about lawyers' wives' confidences too. I don't know,' Phemie said, thumping knives and forks down on the table, 'it's one thing when you want to know something from me, and quite another when I ask you anything—'

'Dinner smells good, mother,' Colin said from the doorway.

'It'll be ready in twenty minutes. Colin, what's your father hiding from me now?'

'Hiding?' her son asked, his face expressionless.

'Men!' She glared, then shooed them out of the room. 'If you're not going to tell me what's going on, you might at least have the decency to get out from under my feet when I'm busy!'

They went willingly to the small library, where Colin said as soon as he closed the door, 'You surely don't believe what that woman told us today?'

Gilchrist was already pouring whisky into two glasses. 'Mrs Moffatt is a client of ours, Colin, and she has a name.'

'She had another name before that – but it turned out to belong to someone else.'

'That's enough,' Gilchrist said sharply, handing a glass to his son. 'I don't know why you have to be so disapproving. If an old fogey like me can accept the idea of a bigamous marriage without blinking, I don't see why a modern young man like yourself should make such a song and dance about it.'

Colin, suddenly reminded of Isla Moffatt's laughter in the dark, smelly close, her voice pointing out that Ainslie must have other reasons for ending their engagement, swallowed down a mouthful of fine malt whisky. 'Being modern has nothing to do with it. She should never have come to Paisley.'

'But she did come to Paisley, and she's our client, and we must do our best by her. Whatever his faults, I believe that McAdam cared for her, and as his friend as well as his lawyer, it's my place to do the best I can for the girl. She's got nobody else.'

'Being the mother of his children doesn't give her the right to make accusations against his lawful widow.'

The older man walked to the window and looked out on the side drive where a red brick wall was covered with yellow climbing roses. After a long moment he said, 'Colin, Catherine McAdam telephoned just after you and Mrs Moffatt left the office. She told Miss Lang that she wanted me to call on her tomorrow morning at eleven o'clock.' He emptied his glass and turned to look at his son. 'To deal with an urgent and very important personal matter on her behalf.'

Colin stared for a moment, then asked, 'What are you going to do?'

Gilchrist Forbes sighed, and moved to his favourite chair, suddenly feeling very weary.

'I think that I must have a talk with Ainslie first,' he said. 'Tomorrow, at her place of work, so that Catherine knows nothing about it.'

Isla took both children into the wall-bed with her that night and lay sleeplessly staring into the darkness. It was a warm night, and the little room was stiflingly hot; the children tossed and mumbled in their sleep, faces and hair damp with sweat, throwing their arms and legs wide, digging sharp little knees and elbows into her.

Every time footsteps approached the close-mouth, or a car or cart came along the road, she sat upright, convinced that Catherine McAdam had sent someone to steal Ross away from her.

She walked to school with Barbara and Greta in the morning, then went along to Castlehead, where Flora immediately whisked her into the dolls'-house room to show her some bits and pieces she had found that might be of use for the *Little Women* house, which was already coming along well.

'She's been ferretin' in every cupboard and every drawer,' Annie said gloomily from the doorway. 'I'm at my wit's end, following her round and tidying up after her.'

'Nobody asked you to,' Flora snapped. 'I'm not in my dotage yet – I can do my own tidying.' She laid ribbons and buttons and costume jewellery and cardboard before Isla, who looked on listlessly, reacting only when Annie tried to take Ross into the kitchen.

'He's fine here, with me.' She put an arm about the little boy and drew him to her, lying to the two puzzled faces, 'He was a bit crabbit this morning. I think he might be coming down with a chill.'

Annie and Flora looked at Ross's clear eyes and happy grin, then at each other.

'Whatever you think best, dear – Annie can bring his drink of milk in here, then.' Flora signalled to the servant, who withdrew, a hurt expression on her round face. 'Is there something worrying you?' Flora ventured when the maid had gone.

'No, nothing,' Isla told her, and Flora said no more. When she took him back to George Street, Isla couldn't bear to let Ross play outside with the other children. He stormed and stamped, then bawled when she smacked him, and she gathered him up in her arms and cried along with him, rocking and kissing and soothing him until he fell asleep.

'What's amiss with ye?' Magret wanted to know when she came in and found the two of them huddled in the chair.

'I'm fine.'

'Ye've been out of sorts since ye burned those scones yesterday.' She waited, then when no explanation was forthcoming said, 'I'll make us a nice cup of tea.'

'Where's Daisy?'

'She's fallen sound asleep on the rug by the fire, bless her. She was up half the night with her teeth. She'll be fine on her own for a minute,' Magret said comfortably. Watching her as she gathered the cups together and took the muslin cover off the milk jug, Isla envied the other woman her placid assumption that Daisy, alone, was safe from harm.

Ross woke just then, and again demanded to be allowed out to play. 'Ach, let him go,' Magret advised. 'He needs the fresh air, don't ye, pet?'

'I'll go outside too. It's a nice afternoon . . .' Isla picked up one of the chairs standing by the table.

'Aye, all right, on ye go. I'll bring the tea out, and fetch Daisy.'

The afternoon was pleasantly warm and there were quite a few women enjoying the sun, some sitting on the close steps, some on chairs and stools they had brought out, others 'windae-hingin' ', leaning out of open windows, their forearms supported by cushions or blankets laid on the window-sills. While they gossiped and laughed and lifted their faces to the sun and yelled at their children, Isla kept her gaze fixed on Ross.

Catherine McAdam had spoken the truth when she said that she could give the little boy much more than Isla could. Was she being unfair to him, she wondered, craning her neck round the bulk of a woman who happened to move between them, afraid to lose sight of him for a minute. Should she put her own selfish need of him aside and let him have the chance of growing up in a big house and getting a fine education? What would Kenneth have wanted for his son? She had a terrible suspicion that he would have wanted Ross to have all the things that his legal wife was offering.

'It's all right, hen, yer wean'll no' catch somethin' nasty just 'cause he's mixin' with the likes of our bairns,' the woman who had blocked her view said sharply, and Isla drew back, flushing.

'I just – Ross, come back here,' she called as he ventured a few yards further along the pavement. Magret and the other women exchanged looks, and exchanged them again when the time for the schoolchildren to be let out drew near and Isla got up and announced that she was going to fetch Barbara.

'Ye don't want tae go runnin' after yer weans all the time, hen,' someone advised. 'They'll only get spoiled.'

'I feel like the walk. Come on, Ross.'

'Ach, let him play,' Magret said comfortably, from her seat on the hollowed stone step leading to the close. 'I'll keep an eye on him.'

'No, he's to come with me. Ross, did you hear me? And stop dragging your feet like that, you'll ruin your shoes!' Isla ordered as the little boy left his friends reluctantly and went to her, his bottom lip sticking out and his toes scuffing along the pavement. She took his hand, pulling him along behind her as she hurried towards the corner of Maxwellton Street, where the West School stood.

'Yew'll ruin yewr shoes,' she heard someone mimic as she went, and there was a ripple of laughter from the women at the close-mouth. Most of their children played barefoot in the summer, and a few went barefoot through the winter too.

'Hoity-toity!' someone else said loudly. The tears that were never far from the surface now burned Isla's eyes as she walked on. It had been hard enough to win the friendship and trust of those women. If it hadn't been for the peg dolls she had made for their daughters, some of them would still be ignoring her. She was aware that her sudden possessiveness towards her children would only remind them that she was indeed an outsider, but what else, she wondered in despair, could she do? Gilchrist Forbes had been reassuring on the previous day, but his wife was a friend of Catherine McAdam's. He might be put under pressure to help Catherine rather than Isla. His son would have no difficulty in deciding between herself and Ainslie's mother, Isla thought bitterly.

By this time even the most possessive of mothers had stopped coming to fetch their children home, so she and Ross waited alone outside the school railings. Isla fidgeted, looking up and down the road every few seconds, half expecting to see Catherine McAdam, all in black, bearing down on them.

At last, a handbell clanged within the school, and a few seconds later one or two children came running out of the main door. More and more followed, until the playground was seething with them. Isla, clutching Ross with one hand and the railings with the other, strained for a glimpse of Barbara's tawny head, waving and shouting when she finally saw it.

Barbara, like Ross, came to her reluctantly, not at all pleased to see her mother waiting for her. 'What're you doing here?' she wanted to know, brows drawn down between hostile brown eyes. Greta trailed at her back, as usual.

'We thought it would be nice to walk back with you.'

Barbara gave her mother a withering look. 'Nobody's mummy comes to fetch them home! Come on, Greta,' she ordered, and ran ahead, heels flying and her curly hair, now quite long, bouncing on her shoulders. Ross, who had dragged behind Isla all the way to the school, made a futile attempt to break free of her imprisoning hand, then, unable to get away, tried to pull Isla along in an effort to catch up with his sister and Greta.

As they went, Isla turned her tired mind to Magret. It wasn't possible to keep secrets from her neighbour, she knew from experience. The safest course was to tell her something, though not necessarily everything. Isla began to put together the story of a nameless woman who had lost her son in the Glen Cinema tragedy, and after seeing Ross playing out in the street, had recognised a similarity to her own dead child and offered to raise him in the other boy's place. Isla knew that by telling that story she could enlist Magret's support in her struggle to keep Ross safe.

Her life, she thought wryly as Ross hauled her round the corner and into George Street, was beginning to sound like a novelette.

Gilchrist Forbes himself arrived not long after Isla got home, stepping out of his car, tipping his hat courteously to the staring women still gathered round the close-mouth.

Isla, in the middle of making the evening meal, motioned him to a chair, wiping her hands nervously on her pinny. He put his hat and cane on the table and smiled at her. 'I've come to put your mind at rest.'

She sank into a chair. 'You mean she can't take Ross away from me?'

'There was never any question of that, my dear. Mrs McAdam is – unwell. None of us realised just how unwell she was, until now. She got it into her head that you had been sent to Paisley by some higher agency, so that she could adopt your son in place of her own. I've explained to her that she cannot possibly do this.'

'But did she listen to you? She might try again—'

He held up a reassuring hand. 'I've already made arrangements for a nurse-companion to care for Mrs McAdam until such time as she recovers from her illness.'

He looked strained, Isla thought with compassion. 'Can I make you some tea, Mr Forbes?'

'It's a kind thought, but my wife expects me home. Besides . . .' he smiled down at Barbara and Ross, 'You've got your hands full. The companion I mentioned will take up her duties tomorrow, and in the meantime Ainslie will stay with her mother.' He got to his feet, saying as he reached for his hat and stick, 'She's asked me to tell you that she's extremely upset over the worry you've had.'

'Ainslie?' Isla was scarcely able to keep the disbelief from her voice.

'I can assure you, Mrs Moffatt, that she was very upset when I spoke to her this morning. Like the rest of us, she had no idea that her brother's death had had such an effect on her mother. I feel very sorry for Ainslie,' he said thoughtfully, as he left. 'She's not had an easy life lately.'

19

A few nights later, when the children were in bed and asleep, someone knocked at the door. Isla, who hadn't recovered from the fright Catherine McAdam had given her, felt her heart turn over beneath her ribs with a painful wrench.

The trousers she had been darning for Ross fell from her limp fingers to her knee, then to the floor as she pressed her body back into the chair, hoping that whoever waited outside would go away and leave her in peace.

The knock came again, more insistently. Afraid that the children would be wakened, she got up and opened the door an inch, peering through the small space, ready to slam it shut again if need be.

'Who is it?'

'Ainslie McAdam.'

'Go away,' Isla said against the crack. 'I want nothing to do with you or your family. Leave us in peace!'

'I've not come to cause trouble. I have to talk to you.'

Reluctantly, Isla opened the door, and the girl came into the room, pulling her close-fitting hat off to let her red hair fall loosely about her face.

'Are your children asleep?'

Isla nodded, watching her warily. The arrogance had gone out of Ainslie McAdam's face; as she stepped into the pool of light shed by the gas mantles above the fireplace Isla saw that her eyes were shadowed, and the skin beneath them was shaded a delicate violet, as though she too had been enduring sleepless nights.

The official year of mourning for Kenneth McAdam was over, and Isla had discarded her black armband. She would have thought that Ainslie would now be in mourning for her brother, but the girl wore a slim skirt in a deep violet shade, with a silky tailored jacket patterned with small violet and white squares. On any other redhead, violet might have been garish, but on Ainslie, it looked stylish.

The two young women eyed each other warily for a moment, then Ainslie lifted her hands away from her sides, palms out, in a helpless gesture. 'I'm sorry. I'm so sorry. I had no idea of what was in my mother's mind, none at all, until Mr Forbes told me.' Then, as Isla said nothing, 'I don't blame you for not believing me, but it's the truth. She's been in a bad way since my brother's death, but she seemed to be coming out of it. I thought that she was improving. Instead she was thinking up this – this nonsense about replacing him with your wee boy. You'll hear no more about it, I promise you.'

'How can I believe you? How can I be sure?'

'I don't blame you for mistrusting me. You've had a bad time at the hands of the McAdams, haven't you?'

'You needn't presume to speak for your father. I don't regret a moment of the time I shared with him.'

Ainslie's eyes flared with surprise – just as Kenneth's did, Isla thought, as she had thought the first time she and Ainslie set eyes on each other. Her lips tightened, and for a moment she was the Ainslie that Isla knew, arrogant and bitter. Then the look was gone. She dipped a hand into her jacket pocket, then laid a small paper-wrapped package on the table.

'This is for the children,' she said, then went past Isla towards the door, leaving the faint scent of floral perfume in her wake. At the door, she paused. 'May I call again, when things have settled down?'

'I don't see that—'

'Please,' Ainslie said. 'I need to talk to you. I need to talk about my father.'

'If you want to,' Isla said, against her own instincts.

As the click of Ainslie's smart shoes faded away along the pavement, she hoped that that might be the end of the matter. She didn't believe that the girl would come back. She herself would prefer it if Ainslie stayed away, for she had had more than enough of Kenneth's other family. They might hold her to blame for their own troubles, but they themselves had caused her more heartbreak than she wanted in one lifetime.

She picked up the small packet from the table. It smelled faintly of moth-balls and the light scent Ainslie had worn. When she pulled at the ribbon tied around it, the wrapping paper fell away to reveal two books. The first was a sturdy, brightly coloured picture book, designed for a child of Ross's age, depicting balls and kittens, kites and building bricks. The second had imaginative, well-drawn pictures and a simple story that Barbara could read for herself.

Opening it, Isla caught her breath as her eyes fell on a few words in a firm, familiar handwriting that she would have known anywhere. The few short, treasured notes Kenneth had written to her in that same hand during their brief courtship were still in her possession.

'To Ainslie Isobel McAdam,' the words said. '12th October, 1912, from her father, Kenneth Innes McAdam.'

A gift from Kenneth to his daughter. A gift that had clearly been cherished and cared for over the years, and had now been handed over as a peace offering to his other, secret daughter.

The promises made by both Ainslie and the lawyer held. Catherine McAdam didn't come back to George Street, but Isla had had such a fright that it was several weeks before she allowed herself to believe that the threat no longer existed, and Ross could safely play with his friends without her constant supervision. By then the damage had been done; although Magret remained loyal to her, the other women in the street had decided amongst themselves that Isla Moffatt thought herself better than they were, and they took to turning away when she walked down the street, or making loud asides to each other in her presence about folk who thought they were something they weren't.

'Ach, it's just the way they are,' Magret said. 'Pay no heed.'

Fortunately, the antagonism towards Isla didn't extend to the children, who continued to be accepted by their friends. The school summer holidays began and Barbara, at home all day, passed the time by organising another back-court concert.

Lena McNab, the handsome woman who lived across the close and owned the little bakery down the road, went regularly with her young husband to the Paisley Theatre in Smithhills, and took great pleasure in teaching Barbara the songs she heard at the music hall, even coming round the counter, if the shop was quiet, to dance a few steps. Barbara often came back from the bakery with another song.

'Hello, hello,' she would warble, setting down the loaf she had been sent to buy and dancing across the floor, Ross jigging up and down in her wake. 'Who's your lady friend? Who's the little girlie by your side?' Or, linking her arm with some difficulty through his, she would break into, 'Roamin' in the gloamin'.'

Unfortunately, willing though Ross was, he had none of his sister's sense of rhythm, and when he was involved, the songs usually ended with the two of them falling over because Ross had moved the wrong way, or Barbara being put off the melody by his enthusiastic, noisy off-key renderings.

'She's a natural wee music-hall turn, that lassie of yours,' Mrs McNab told Isla when she went into the bakery. 'She should go on to the halls herself one of these days.'

Isla smiled, and nodded, and wondered what Kenneth would have made of it all.

To her surprise, Ainslie came back again, and as the summer went on, her visits took on a weekly pattern. At first they talked about Paisley, Barbara and Ross, books, the auction rooms, Flora Currie's dolls' houses, circling round each other warily, keeping well away from any subject that affected them deeply.

Noticing how relaxed and animated the girl became when she talked about her work at the auction rooms, Isla suspected that life wasn't easy, had perhaps never been entirely easy, for Kenneth's elder daughter. She couldn't understand why this should be, because Kenneth had been a loving and demonstrative father to Barbara and Ross. She had often asked him teasingly what his business colleagues would say if they saw him playing with the children, or cuddling them both on his lap while he read to them.

Now that she thought of it, he had never really responded to those questions, fobbing them off with a smile, or changing the subject.

The sight of Ainslie walking down the road and into the close, smartly dressed and clearly from a different world, only added to the other women's suspicions that Isla was a 'neb in the air'. She explained her new visitor to Magret by saying that Ainslie was the daughter of the household where she worked, and then had to admit the lie to Ainslie herself.

'Just in case the two of you meet, and she says something. I sometimes feel as though I'm living two separate lives, but if the people round here knew that I owned this building they'd never accept me, and there's nowhere else for us to go just now.' She looked round the shabby room. 'It's still up for sale, but who would want it?'

'My father would be turning in his grave if he knew that his flesh and blood were living in a place like this.'

'It's not his fault.' Isla immediately went on the defensive. 'He signed the building over to me so that I'd have some income coming in – he didn't dream that we'd have to live in it.'

'He should have taken the trouble to think things through.' There was suddenly more than a hint of Ainslie's former arrogance in her voice. 'Because of him you're having to struggle along on hardly any money and tell your neighbours all sorts of untruths.'

Isla was ironing, using the table in place of an ironing board, with an old blanket folded on it to protect it from the heat. Now she set the flat-iron on its end with a thump. 'If you're going to insult your father's memory, this isn't the place to do it,' she said quietly. 'I'll not allow anyone to speak ill of him in my hearing, especially his own daughter.'

'You're beginning to sound like all the rest. Just because he was my father it doesn't mean that I have to idolise his memory. Folk should earn respect, not take it for granted.'

'Earn it? The man educated you, clothed you, fed you – and provided a nice home into the bargain. If that's not earning respect, I don't know what is!'

Ainslie's fair skin flushed crimson at the criticism. 'Are you saying that having money makes everything all right?'

'I'm saying that you should be grateful for what Kenneth did for you, and give some thought to what he must have gone through in the last weeks of his life.'

'He brought it on himself. If he hadn't been trying to support two families—' Ainslie stopped, a hand flying to

232

her mouth, then said, 'I'm sorry, I shouldn't have said such a thing, not to you.'

Isla pushed a straggle of black hair back from her forehead. Now the truth was coming to the surface. 'Yes, you should. It's why you came here, isn't it? To try to understand your father?' The words that had gone through her mind again and again in the past thirteen months came easily to her lips. 'If only he'd told me about his worries, I'd have done all I could to help.'

'How could he tell you, of all people?'

'That's what makes it worse – thinking for five years that everything was open and honest between us, then discovering that it was all—'

'All lies?'

Isla shook her head and sat down at the table, the ironing forgotten. 'He didn't lie. He made up a story in his own mind about the way he wanted things to be, and then he tried to live it, with me.'

Ainslie, in the fireside chair, looked down at the hands clasped round her knees. 'And my mother and Innes and I were left outside, in the real life that he didn't want.'

'I didn't mean that. You were his daughter.'

'But that doesn't mean that he loved me! Oh, he liked Innes well enough, but that was because he was a boy.'

'What about the lovely books you gave the children? They were his gifts to you.'

'Where we live, everyone has nicely bound books on show. My father wanted me to have the right books, that was all.'

'You're wrong, Ainslie. Kenneth loved his children. I

mind the patience he had with Barbara, spending hours with her on his knee, reading stories to her—'

'How nice for Barbara.' The girl jumped up and reached blindly for her bag and her gloves. 'At least he cared for one of his daughters—'

'Ainslie, I didn't mean – Ainslie!'

But the door had opened and closed, and Isla was alone.

'Tell me about Kenneth McAdam.'

Flora Currie blinked at Isla, then said, 'You surely know more about him than I did.'

They were working on the *Little Women* dolls' house, Flora, with glue and cardboard and narrow strips of beading, making a frame for a tiny sampler that Isla had drawn with coloured crayons, Isla brushing pieces of wall-paper with flour and water paste and pressing them into place on the parlour walls.

She told Flora, briefly, about her conversation with Ainslie on the previous day, ending with, 'I'm not asking you to gossip, or tell tales. I just think it's time I knew more about the man I thought I was married to for five years.'

'We all present different faces to different people, my dear.'

'I know that – goodness knows I do it myself all the time these days,' Isla said wryly, 'what with paying myself rent for a building I own, and changing my name. But for my own sake – and the children's – I have to understand him better. For instance, *my* Kenneth wouldn't have made money out of renting rooms in tired old buildings to folk who have no choice but to live there. But the Kenneth that Ainslie knew did that.'

'A lot of folk make money out of owning homes they'd not live in themselves. It's the way of the world,' Flora said evasively.

Isla, realising that the older woman heartily disliked talking to her about Kenneth, changed tack. 'Tell me about his – about Ainslie's mother, then.'

'Catherine? Her people were well off, and I mind that everyone thought it a very suitable match, though my brother Arnold – you mind I said he and Kenneth had been friends – was surprised at Catherine choosing Kenneth. He said that she'd not had much time for him before. I saw her on her wedding day, and she looked radiant. The next time I saw her was at her father-in-law's funeral, and then she looked quite ill. She wasn't long past Ainslie's birth at the time, as I remember.'

She paused to collect her thoughts, then said, 'When Catherine's parents died, I heard that she wanted to move into their big house, but Kenneth would have none of it. I don't think he could have afforded the upkeep. Catherine could – she inherited quite a lot from them – but he'd not have wanted to live on his wife's money. Come to think of it, that might have been what finished his own business, trying to show Catherine that he could make a lot of money. I always felt a bit sorry for Kenneth – I don't think he ever felt comfortable with the life he led.'

Flora Currie's words fitted in with what Isla herself had said to Ainslie about Kenneth inventing a world, and sharing it with her. Waiting for sleep to come that night, she mulled over them. He seemed to have been so many things – a husband who wasn't a husband at all, a loving father who hadn't, it seemed, shown much love towards his older children, a caring man who charged rent for sub-standard housing he had made no effort to improve.

Ross muttered, and she got up and looked into the cot. He was sound asleep, twisted in the sheet, the pillow wedged alongside him. Lifting his head and slipping the pillow beneath it, she wondered if she had ever really known Kenneth at all.

20

Mr Leckie, the toyshop owner who had spoken to Flora at the auction sale, called on her unexpectedly one day to see the half-completed *Little Women* house, and met Isla.

'You have an interesting talent, Mrs Moffatt. I wonder – would you be interested in decorating another little house for me when you've finished this one? Something simple and straightforward, that I can put on show to advertise the furniture and houses I sell.'

'Surely you could do that yourself.'

The man shook his head. 'I'm not talking about just putting furniture into a doll's house, Mrs Moffatt. Anyone can do that, but you have the ability to create a home in miniature.'

'I quite agree,' said Flora. 'Of course you must do it, Isla.'

'I'll supply the house,' the shopkeeper added as Isla hesitated. 'And the furniture, though I'd leave the choice of furnishings entirely to you, and pay for any other materials you may need.'

'But I haven't got anywhere to work on it.'

'Yes, you have,' Flora said firmly. 'You'll work here. She'll do it, Mr Leckie.'

'I can't use your home as a workplace,' Isla protested when the man had gone.

'Nonsense, I enjoy seeing you and the children, and so does Annie, though she'd rather die than admit it. And now you'll be earning some money – you can do with that, surely.'

'At least it means that I can afford to pay you for the use of your premises.'

Flora looked shocked at the very idea. 'My dear girl, it's me who should be paying you for the interest you've brought into my life. Your visits are the only thing that have kept me going, since poor Agnes passed away.'

Flora's neighbour, a woman she had known for many years, had died after a long illness, and now the house next door lay silent and empty, waiting for the next-of-kin to decide what was to be done with it.

'It reminds me of my own mortality every time I see the closed door and the curtains pulled across the windows,' Flora Currie had told Isla with a shiver not long after the funeral. 'Poor Agnes was such a lively woman before her illness, always popping in.'

Young Mr Kelly upstairs lost his job again and couldn't get another. He and his little wife began to look more and more desperate, and Mrs Leach looked more and more like a dragon.

Going into the wash-house one day, Isla hesitated as she heard the woman's voice from inside, nagging and complaining. She turned and went quietly back into the close. 'She was going on at poor Mrs Kelly about how she should never have married him,' she told Magret later.

'She's a right bitch, so she is. I'm heart-sorry for that

lassie. It's bad enough havin' yer man out of work without yer ma going on and on about it. It's not her fault, poor soul – or his.'

The Kellys fell behind with their rent, and Isla refused to let Colin Forbes, who was still collecting the rents, threaten them with eviction. 'He's doing his best to find work – where's the sense in making their lives more difficult by making threats, or putting them out?' she asked.

'People have to pay their way, Mrs Moffatt.'

'The Kellys have every intention of paying their way. They're not deliberately trying to cheat – they're not committing a crime, so why punish them?'

Colin Forbes glared. 'Mrs Moffatt, you keep asking me about repairs – when can the roof be fixed, when can the close be lit. D'you not understand that nothing can be done unless you yourself have the money to do it? And you'll not get the money while you protect tenants who don't pay!'

'In that case, wouldn't it make more sense to try to find work for Mr Kelly than to put him out of his home?' she shot back at him. 'The man's an office worker, and from what I know of him I'm quite sure very conscientious. Is there any chance of finding him a place with Forbes and Son?'

'Not at the moment. And even if there was, would it be wise to put him where he might learn who owns this building?'

She hadn't thought of that. She stuttered for a moment, confused, then rallied as she saw the cold smile on his lips. 'There are other offices. You might be able to place him elsewhere.'

'I'm a lawyer, Mrs Moffatt, not a nursemaid,' he said, and slapped the rentbook shut.

Without Gilchrist Forbes' help, Ainslie would never have been able to persuade her mother to let the nurse-companion into the house. Gilchrist, under the guise of bringing papers for Catherine to sign, talked of a respectable woman of his acquaintance, fallen on hard times through no fault of her own, searching for a position as a useful companion to some lady, and by the time he set down his empty teacup, Catherine herself had suggested that, with Ainslie busy about her own affairs, it would be pleasant for her to have someone else in the house, other than the servants.

Ann Dove, a woman of about Catherine's own age, calmly and with just the right amount of meekness, submitted to being ordered about, but Ainslie was acutely embarrassed by her mother's high-handed attitude.

'You're a nurse, not a servant,' she protested to the woman when Catherine was out of earshot.

'Your mother doesn't know that, does she? She's a very sad woman, Miss McAdam, and a lonely one – through no fault of yours,' Miss Dove added swiftly as she saw the stricken look on Ainslie's face. 'It's just part of being the sort of person she is. She needs someone to order around, and it's better that it's me and not you. And don't worry,' she added with a faint smile, 'if things get too bad, I can look after myself.'

Her presence in the house eased Ainslie's life a great deal, giving her freedom to concentrate on her work. She hadn't gone back to Isla's house since leaving it in a rage a few weeks earlier. She wanted to, but at the same time, she was wary at what she might find out if she and Isla really talked to each other.

Colin called, and found her in the front garden, weeding a flower bed. Walking up the drive, he looked beyond her kneeling figure and saw that the curtains were looped back from the windows. Daylight had at last been permitted back into the house.

At the sound of footsteps on the gravel Ainslie looked up, then scrambled to her feet, smiling. Her hair was escaping from the green ribbon that tied it back, to curl round her face like little flames.

'Are you here on business?'

'Strictly for pleasure, to see you.'

'Would you like to come in? Or we could sit in the summer-house.'

He opted for the summer-house, and as they walked round the side of the house together she dusted the soil from her hands then took off the heavy apron she had been wearing.

'Mother isn't pleased,' she said as she saw him glance at her white and green dress. 'She thinks I should be in mourning black for Innes, but I've had enough of mourning. In any case, I don't think Innes would have wanted us to dress in black for him.'

'How is your mother?' he asked as they stepped into the summer-house's cool shade.

'The nurse is very good with her. I'm grateful to your father for finding her.' She flicked a sidelong glance at him, then asked, 'Did you know that Mother had been drinking?'

'What?' He stared at her in disbelief.

'I knew that she was taking rather a lot of the tonic wine the doctor recommended to get her strength up, and that she had a glass of brandy sometimes. But I didn't think that . . .' She stopped, then said, 'It was Miss Dove – the nurse – who told me. Apparently the servants knew, because they were the ones who bought the bottles for her, and disposed of them. But they couldn't bring themselves to tell me, poor souls. I thought your father might have said something to you.'

Colin was appalled at the thought of Mrs McAdam, always the lady, turning to drink. 'Not a word. He probably wanted to protect your mother, but I wish I'd known, for your sake. You've been through hell over the past year or so, haven't you?'

'If it hadn't been for the auction rooms and the people there, I would probably be fighting Mother for the brandy bottle,' Ainslie agreed, with a faint laugh. She picked a leaf from her skirt and smoothed it between her fingers, staring intently down at it. 'Isla Moffatt says that my father loved her children,' she said suddenly. 'He played with them.' She began to shred the leaf, tearing tiny neat strips from it. 'It wasn't that he didn't have any love to give, Colin. He'd just chosen to give it to another wife and other children.'

'Everything comes back to Isla Moffatt, doesn't it?' Colin rose abruptly and paced to the door. After the shadows, the sun was almost like a blow against his face and arm. 'If she hadn't come to Paisley—'

'That's what I thought at first. But now,' Ainslie said, 'I'm not so sure. It hurts to learn the truth, but it's the only way forward. And that's the way I'm going from now on, Colin. Forwards.'

In the shade of the summer-house, her face swam like a water-lily within the glow of her hair. Looking down on her, Colin Forbes accepted, at last, that there was no chance now of Ainslie marrying him.

The day after Colin's visit, Ainslie went back to George Street, stepping round groups of children squatting on cracked paving stones warmed by the sun, forging her way through the huddle of women snatching what fresh air they could at the close-mouth. She stood at Isla's door, fists thrust into the pockets of the sleeveless jacket she wore, and said, 'No matter how it hurts, I want to know the truth about my father.'

Isla had been washing clothes at the sink, and her face was flushed with heat, her hair wisping across her cheeks. She stepped back, drying her hands on her crossover pinny. 'Come in,' she said.

'I wanted him to love me,' Ainslie told Isla an hour later, getting the words out at last. 'All my life I tried so hard to earn his love. That's why it hurt when I realised he'd given it freely to your daughter. Now, I'm beginning to think that my mother stood between us, for reasons of her own. She tried to stand between me and Innes, even after he died. She's always wanted to possess people, and she's always been afraid of them loving each other, because she thought that that would shut her out.'

'Poor soul. It must be terrible to be afraid all the time.'

Ainslie shot Isla a startled glance, then said, 'They should probably never have married. Mother was disappointed in my father, and perhaps he withdrew because he knew it. So she turned all her ambition on Innes instead.'

Isla, wringing out the last of the small clothes she had been washing, shivered inside at the thought of the misery Ross might have suffered in Catherine's hands. 'People aren't made of Plasticine. Try to shape them against their natures, and you'll only end up misshaping them.'

Ainslie ran a hand over the back of her neck, lifting her hair to let what little air there was cool her. It had been a long afternoon and she felt bone-weary, but also as though she was on the road to recovery after a serious illness.

She and Isla had been ruthlessly honest with each other; Ainslie had heard about the human side of her father, a side she had never been privileged to see in all the twenty-one years she had known him, while Isla had discovered the darker side of his nature, the cold, reserved husband and father, the ruthless businessman.

'That's probably why he wanted another marriage, with you,' Ainslie said now. 'You knew nothing of his background or his family. You accepted him as he was, without criticism. What are you doing?' she added as Isla opened out the ungainly wooden clothes-horse and began to hang the wet clothes on it. 'It's a lovely day, they'd dry in half an hour if you put them outside.'

'You've never lived in a tenement, have you? This is Mrs Kelly's day for the washlines.'

'She might not be using all the line.'

'Even so, this is her day, not mine,' Isla said, and went on with her work.

Ainslie watched for a moment, then asked, 'D'you feel any differently towards my father now that you know more about him?'

Isla took time to consider. It had been hard to face the fact that her Kenneth had been so different, so uncaring, in his other life. But she still had her own memories of him to offset these pictures.

'He was a human being,' she said at last, 'and no human being's perfect.' She glanced up at the cracked, stained ceiling then at the warped window frame and the dripping sink, and the corners of her mouth turned down. 'I'm a fine one to talk – this place is mine now, and I haven't done any more to improve it than he did.'

'That's another responsibility he put on your shoulders – looking after this place. We're all what he made us, when you think of it,' Ainslie said thoughtfully. 'You and me, and Mother too. All McAdam's women. And there's your Barbara as well.'

'I doubt if anyone could influence Barbara,' Isla told her dryly. 'She's got a mind of her own.'

'Are you going to tell the children the truth about Father?'

'Mebbe one day, when they're grown up, if I think they can take it and understand. But not for a long time.'

As though on cue, the children arrived at that moment, hot and grimy from play, in search of food, but hanging back a little at the sight of Ainslie.

'I haven't had time to make anything yet,' Isla told them, fetching a loaf and a half-full jar of jam.

'I'm thirsty,' Barbara whined, and Ross, his eyes fixed on Ainslie, joined in.

'Make up your minds.' Isla paused, about to cut

slices from the loaf. 'I can't do both things at once.'

Ainslie got to her feet and took the breadknife from her. 'You get them something to drink,' she said. 'I'll see to the bread and jam. After that, I wouldn't mind a cup of tea. I think we've both earned one.'

In September, the *Little Women* house was finished and borne off by Mr Leckie, who brought with him another house for Isla to work on, and a box of furniture. He gave her a fair price for the finished house, and Flora insisted on Isla taking all the money.

'All I contributed was bits and pieces that were already here,' she said when Isla protested. 'The Victorian house was a gift, and I can't even remember where the other one came from. You did all the work.'

Isla, who badly needed the money, finally gave in, and they started to sift through the box of furniture from the toyshop.

'It's awful plain,' Isla said when they had finished.

'Make your own furniture, then, the way you did for the others. Mr Leckie said you could alter it if you wanted.'

'The other houses were just for show, but this one's supposed to be played with, so it needs good solid furniture. But I'd like something better than this. Something – different.' She frowned down at the sturdy little table she was holding.

'Mebbe we could find someone who's good with his hands,' Flora suggested. And suddenly Isla remembered Drew Brown, sitting on the steps in the back court, using the point of his penknife to shape a proper face for Barbara's peg doll.

She took the table back to George Street with her, and went up to his flat that evening, while the children were playing with Greta and Daisy in Magret's flat. It was raining, and too wet for them to be outside.

Isla had never gone to the upper floor before. The stone steps were hollowed in the centre, and she had to feel her way up, her outstretched hands pressed against the chill, damp walls. Drew himself opened the door, peering into the gloom. 'Mam, it's Mrs Moffatt,' he called, and his mother appeared at once, looking anxious.

'Come in,' she said, then, as Drew moved back to let Isla in, 'is there something wrong?'

'No, it's Drew I really came to see.' Isla stepped into the little flat, and instantly recognised the smell of damp. A metal bucket stood on newspapers, yellowed with age, against the outside wall near the sink, water dripping into it with a continuous, steady tinny little beat.

'You've got a bad leak there.'

'Only when it rains,' Drew said with a bleak grin, while his mother explained, 'The roof's rotten.'

'Have you not complained about it?'

Mrs Brown shrugged. 'Early on I did, but it wasnae any use. Now I just don't bother.'

'When did it start?'

'Och, three or four years ago,' the woman told her vaguely. 'We're used tae it. Ye'll have a cup of tea, Mrs Moffatt?'

'I can't stay, the children'll be looking for me soon.' Isla remembered why she had called, and held out the little table she had brought. 'Drew, could you do something with this for me? Mebbe carve the legs into a

247

better shape, full at the top here, then tapering down, with the feet curved.'

'You mean like a bandy-legged woman with nice neat ankles? I've seen that sort somewhere. Table, not woman,' he added hurriedly as his mother, shocked, said, 'Drew!'

'Could you do it?'

He studied the little table, running his thumb down over the legs. 'I think so.'

'I'll pay you for it.'

'Wait till we see if I can do it first,' the boy said, but his face was alight with interest as he studied the tiny table, and she could see that he was longing to start work.

'I think you should have another word with the factor,' she said as she left.

'I don't want to be a nuisance . . .' Mrs Brown began.

'I keep tellin' her that the man that owns this place'll be living in a grand house that doesn't leak when the rain comes,' Drew said.

The contempt in his words rang in Isla's ears as she felt her way back down the dark stairs. When the roof first started leaking, Kenneth had had the money to repair it, she thought. But there was no sense in dwelling on the faults of a man who was dead and no longer able to defend himself. She was the landlord now, and it was up to her to do what she could.

21

After careful calculation Isla divided the money Mr Leckie had given her into three lots. One was for Drew, if he managed to alter the table for her, another for herself and the children. She took the third sum with her when she went on the following Monday to collect the rent money. When she asked if she could see Mr Forbes, the receptionist shook her head.

'He's not in the office just now. Mr Colin's here, though.'

'I'd better see him, then,' Isla said without enthusiasm.

Colin Forbes stared at the coins she put on his desk. 'What's this?'

'Mrs Brown's ceiling's been leaking since I first moved here. The roof badly needs repairing.'

He frowned. 'Mrs Brown's not complained to us.'

'If she had, what would you have done?'

'I suppose we'd have had to pass the matter on to you.'

'The poor soul's scared that if she makes too much fuss she'll mebbe be put out. It's easier for her to keep emptying a bucket, and do without the use of that part of her living-room. Her son sleeps in the other room, and I've a suspicion that the rain gets in there too.'

He pushed the coins around with a forefinger. 'There's not nearly enough here to get the work done.'

'I know, but you can keep that safe for me until I can afford to give you the rest.'

'Mrs Moffatt,' he said, the familiar exasperation in his voice, 'your money would be better spent on your children.'

'I can assure you that my children are well cared for, Mr Forbes.' Isla indicated Ross, who had climbed on to a chair and was looking out of the window. 'Does he look under-nourished and neglected?'

'No,' he admitted, then, leaning forward and eyeing her, 'but you don't look as well as you might be.'

'There's nothing wrong with me!'

'A few days by the sea might do you good. You could use the money for that.'

'I'm too busy earning the rest of the money for the roof repairs.'

He looked as though he was going to go on arguing, then shrugged. 'Very well, if that's what you want, I'll see that it's put away safely, and recorded.' As she rose to go, he added, 'By the way, a friend of my father's with an office in Incle Street has an opening for a clerk. I've passed Mr Kelly's name to him.'

To Isla's delight, Drew managed to carve the plain little table into something graceful and delicate, even varnishing it before handing it over. More and more dissatisfied with the solid, unimaginative furniture Mr Leckie had given her, she asked the boy if he could make a chaise longue for one of the rooms. Together, they pored over a book he had brought from the library, then, using scraps of wood from the workshop where he was employed, Drew managed to provide just what she wanted.

Isla padded and covered the little piece of furniture, working at nights after the children were asleep. She had to work standing at the mantel on most nights, for the gas light above the mantelshelf was poor, and the work she was doing was very fine. By the time she fell into bed her legs and ankles were sore and stiff. But the chaise longue was perfect, and Flora's admiration the next day made all the work worthwhile.

Spurred on by the need to get the roof repaired before the winter came, Isla gave Drew more furniture to work on, and spent as much time as she could on the new doll's house. Her eyes felt sore and tired, and she began to suffer from headaches caused by the amount of time she spent on the detailed work of stitching tiny cushions and curtains.

'Ye'll make yersel' ill,' Annie said bluntly, leaning against the frame of the dolls'-house room door, arms folded, and Flora nodded.

'She's right, my dear, you look pale. You need to take a day off now and again. Why not take the children up to Brodie Park for some fresh air?'

'They're outside most of the time, and I get plenty of fresh air walking round here and home again,' Isla told them. Now that the little house represented much-needed money, she lay awake at nights, planning the next day's work, and hurried round to Castlehead as soon as she could in the mornings.

Magret nagged at her about not eating properly.

'It's too hot to eat,' Isla told her shortly. The early autumn was unusually warm and dry, and although the continual smell from the drains didn't seem to affect the children as badly as it affected Isla herself, she fretted in case they caught some disease from the poor sewerage. It seemed to her, sometimes, that she worried about everything. She finished the little house for Mr Leckie, and the toyshop owner, delighted with it, had promised to put more work her way. Even so, Isla fretted. Earning some money of her own, even a little, had made all the difference, and there was no jewellery left to pawn. If Mr Leckie didn't give her more work, she didn't know what she would do.

It was because her mind was full of such concerns that she didn't see the tram bearing down on her as she crossed the High Street on her way to collect the rent money one Monday morning. Alerted by a sudden jangling of bells, and shouting from the driver, frantically leaning on his brake, she finally looked up, too late.

Colin Forbes had just arrived in his office and was opening the window to let some air into the stuffy room when he glanced down in time to see the cowcatcher in front of the tram hit a young woman. Her body was tossed through the air like a discarded rag doll, and as it landed in the gutter her head glanced off the kerb.

'My God!' He ran from the office, almost knocking the receptionist over as she came through the door, a pile of envelopes in her hand.

'Telephone for the ambulance wagon,' he shouted into her startled face, and ran on, through the door and down the stairs and across the road to where a policeman was pushing his way through the gathering crowd. The officer knelt down beside the woman in the road, slipping an arm under her shoulders.

Her head lolled against his sleeve and Colin, breaking through the people who had gathered, recognised Isla Moffatt, her eyes closed and her face as white as paper, apart from a ribbon of shining crimson blood that crawled, slowly but steadily, down her face from the wound in her forehead.

'Slight concussion,' the ward sister said briskly. 'Nothing to worry about, but the doctor wants you to stay with us for a few days.' Her professional smile faded when Isla, dazed and confused, struggled to get up. 'Now don't be silly, dear.'

'My children – I have to see to my children!'

'They're fine.' The sister tucked Isla back into bed, pulling the blankets tightly over her. 'A Miss McAdam came to visit you earlier, while you were sleeping. She says you're not to worry, the children are being well looked after.'

'Better do as she says, hen, they're a bossy lot in here,' a voice said from the next bed as the sister moved away on silent feet. Isla began to turn her head, but stopped as pain washed through it. Putting a hand up to the source of the pain, she felt a padded bandage across her forehead, then sleep came, and she drifted away from the big, high-ceilinged room into nowhere.

Pictures came to her as she floated in and out of sleep – uniformed nurses crossing and re-crossing her line of vision like ships in sail, a balding man in a neat suit with a gold chain strung across his waistcoat bending over her, a woman with an elaborate feathered hat perched on her head marching past, carrying a bunch of flowers – they had come and gone before she could register them. It reminded her of her childhood, and rides on the merry-go-round's painted horses when the shows came. Up and down and round and round, clutching tightly to the pole that grew out of the back of the horse she rode, daringly freeing one hand to wave to her parents as they came into sight then fell away again.

'I must take the children to the shows,' she said aloud, and was startled when a familiar voice replied, 'That's a good idea.'

Isla's lids lifted and she looked up into Flora Currie's green eyes. 'What are you doing here?' she asked, confused and still thinking of the merry-go-round.

'I'm visiting you. You had a nasty accident crossing the road, but you're fine now, and so are the children. They're staying at my house – you'll see them in a day or so, when you're better. Annie sent some home-made scones, they're on your locker. And Ainslie will be in to visit you tomorrow.'

When she had gone, Isla slept again, wakening once or twice during the night to the sound of snoring and an occasional groan or mumbled sentence from the beds around her. A voice called a man's name plaintively further up the long ward and a nurse went past, a silent ghost in the dimly lit ward. The voice stopped, and Isla slept again, until she was wakened to face the day.

Her head still ached, but the confusion had left her, and when the doctor made his rounds she begged to be allowed home.

'You had a nasty crack on the head, and we want to

be quite sure that you're over it. Besides,' a frown crossed his face, 'you're in sore need of rest and nourishment. You've not been feeding yourself properly, have you?'

She started to protest, but he cut in with, 'It won't hurt you to be cosseted for a day or two,' and turned back to the group deferentially waiting for him at the foot of the bed. As they moved off, Isla heard him murmur something about women who allowed themselves to become rundown.

The woman in the next bed heard it too. 'It's all right for the likes of them to criticise,' she said with a sniff, then lowered her voice slightly, as the ward sister turned and looked sharply at her before hurrying after the doctor. 'They don't know what it's like, do they? What sort of mother would feed herself and leave her kids hungry?' Then, settling herself comfortably, 'But what can't be cured must be endured, eh? Make the most of it, hen – that's my advice.'

The long narrow ward, with its double row of beds and its uniformed nurses, brought back memories of Isla's training in Edinburgh. All she had wanted then was to become a nurse, perhaps rising to the post of ward sister or even matron, one day. But Kenneth McAdam had been brought into her ward from the operating theatre when she was halfway through the course, after being struck down with appendicitis during a business trip to Edinburgh. And from that moment, her life had changed.

Ainslie came in that afternoon, turning patients' and visitors' heads as she walked up the long ward. She was dressed in a blue knee-length skirt with knife pleats at the front, and a long V-necked blouse in the same colour, with a geometric pattern in gold, and a gold leather belt around her waist. Her vivid hair was tied back at the nape of her neck with a blue ribbon, and a beret dipped rakishly over one ear. She had developed new confidence, Isla thought, watching her approach the bed. Ainslie was coming to terms with herself.

She put a small basket of fruit on top of the locker. 'I'd have brought flowers, but you're not going to be here long enough to enjoy them.' Her eyes swept over Isla and she said bluntly, 'I hadn't realised that you'd got so thin.'

Isla hurriedly tucked her arms beneath the sheet. 'I'm not thin!'

'The ward sister told Miss Currie that you were under-nourished.'

'It's just this hot weather. Nobody feels like eating when it's hot. How are the children?' Isla asked anxiously. 'Have you seen them?'

'I saw them last night, and this morning too. Your neighbour told me what had happened when I called on you, and where the children were, so I went round to Castlehead. They're very well. Missing you, of course, but they know you'll be back soon. Isla, we've been talking – me and Miss Currie and Annie – and we all think that you should have a wee holiday when you come out of hospital.'

'How could I afford that?'

'Colin told me about you giving him money to have the roof repaired. You'd be better spending it on yourself.'

'But the work needs to be done. And it needs to be done before the winter comes.'

Ainslie fidgeted, then said, almost guiltily, 'Miss Currie's written to your aunt to tell her what's happened.'

'She hasn't!'

'She found the address in your house when she was getting the children's things. It's all right,' she added hurriedly, 'she just said you'd been widowed, and that you're living in Paisley now. And you'd had a wee accident, but you're fine.'

Isla stared at her in dismay. She didn't want Aunt Lally to know the truth about Kenneth, or about the struggle she had had since his death.

Ainslie and Colin Forbes took her home on the following day. Barbara, waiting on the pavement, jigging from one foot to the other in a frenzy of impatience, threw herself at Isla as soon as she got out of the car, but Ross hung back for a moment, finger in mouth, unsure of this white-faced mother with a sticking plaster on her forehead.

'We've been staying in Miss Currie's house,' Barbara said in a rush of words. 'We had a bedroom all to ourselves and a big bed, where's your bandage, Miss Currie said you'd have a bandage . . .'

'I don't need it any more. Ross?' Isla held her hand out to the little boy, just as Magret arrived at the close-mouth, her round face wreathed in smiles. Ross ducked his head and whirled round to bury himself in Magret's apron. Daisy, not to be outdone, followed suit.

'Ross!'

'Ach, they forget quick at his age,' Magret soothed. 'Come on in, hen, and sit down. I've got the kettle on. There's enough for everyb'dy,' she added, looking beyond Isla to where Ainslie and Colin stood.

'On you go, Isla. Barbara, carry your mother's case.' Ainslie handed the small cardboard case to the little girl. 'I'll come and see you this evening, when you've had time to settle in,' she said, and turned back to the car as Isla went into the close, Barbara clutching her hand and chattering like a little monkey. As she went, she was aware of the women at every window and every close-mouth up and down the street.

Ross released Magret's apron and shot across the room to climb on to his mother's lap as soon as they got into Magret's flat, while Magret herself, reaching for the condensed milk tin, confessed, 'It's just as well they couldnae stay, for there's no' enough cups. I didnae like tae say, though. Mind yer mammy's poor sore head, Ross,' she cautioned, but Isla hugged the little boy tightly.

'My head's all better. I'm all better,' she said, smiling at her children's anxious faces.

Even so, she was glad to go to bed early that night, and she felt so listless the next day that the thought of walking round to Castlehead was too much. Instead, Flora called on her, her face wrinkled with concern.

'I'll be fine tomorrow,' Isla assured her, but she wasn't. It was as though she had come up against a brick wall that refused to allow her to get on with her life. She recalled that the ward sister had warned her about this just before she left the Infirmary.

'It'll take some time before you get back to your old self, Mrs Moffatt. The accident wasn't serious, but you've worn yourself out, and you need a longer rest than you've had here.'

'I've not been doing nearly as much as most women,' Isla had argued. It was true – some of her neighbours had large families to cope with, some had sick parents or in-laws staying with them, others went out to work or took in laundry or sewing in addition to caring for their husbands and children.

'Mebbe not, but there are other ways of exhausting yourself, and continual worry's one of them. You'll have to be kind to yourself for a while,' the woman had advised.

Isla felt that the kindest thing she could do for herself was to get on with her life, but the harder she tried to spur herself on, the more difficult it became.

When a letter arrived from Edinburgh, informing her that Aunt Lally would like to see her again, and to meet the children if she cared to bring them to Edinburgh for a short visit, both Ainslie and Flora Currie urged her to accept.

'But what about Barbara's schooling?'

'She could stay with me,' Flora suggested, but Isla had got such a fright over almost losing Ross that she refused to go to Edinburgh without Barbara.

She thought that that was the end of the matter, but Ainslie went with her to the school, where the headmistress agreed, under the circumstances, to let Barbara take two weeks off.

'She's a quick learner. If you take her school books with you, Mrs Moffatt, and undertake to see that she does some work while she's away, that would be acceptable.'

Colin Forbes called to hand back the money Isla had given him for the roof repairs, and suggest that Forbes and Son should advance the money needed to cover the most essential repairs, recovering it from the proceeds when a buyer came forward for the building.

'But it's been over a year now, and nobody's put in an offer,' Isla pointed out, adding suspiciously, 'has Ainslie put you up to this? Or Miss Currie?'

He had been pleasant to her on the day he drove her home from the hospital, but now the usual edge came into his voice and the usual irritated gleam darkened his hazel eyes. 'It's often done in business, Mrs Moffatt. You'll get more for the place if it's seen that some work's being carried out on it, and it's in our interest to try to sell at a good price because of our commission. Since you're determined to get the roof repairs done soon, my father and I feel that we should do what we can to help. But only insofar as the essential work is concerned,' he added hastily. 'It would cost more than the whole building's worth to have all the roof repairs carried out.'

'As long as Mrs Brown and her son can escape the worst of the rain when it comes,' Isla said, and couldn't help adding, 'at least you'll get a bit of peace while I'm in Edinburgh.'

He flushed. 'I don't know what you mean, Mrs Moffatt.'

That night Isla wrote to Aunt Lally to let her know that she and the children would arrive the following week.

'You're no sooner back home than you're gone again,' Magret lamented.

'That's what I think too, but so many folk are nagging at me to go to Edinburgh that I might as well give in. Anyway, Aunt Lally seems to be eager to see the children. Mebbe she's mellowed in her old age.'

Magret offered to lend a battered old suitcase for the journey. 'It's only used to keep the bairns' winter jerseys in below the bed,' she explained, 'and they'll not come to any harm wrapped up in paper for a wee while.'

22

Barbara and Ross gaped in amazement as their great-aunt Lally Moffatt came sailing towards them in Edinburgh's Waverley Station. She had scarcely changed in the six years since Isla had last seen her. She was still tall and commanding, straight of back and large of bosom, and she still favoured startlingly bright colours and floating, wispy scarves.

On this occasion, she was dressed in a scarlet calf-length dress topped by a pale-grey overtunic splashed with embroidered roses. Crimson feathers drifted from her grey hat, and a red feather boa rustled round her throat and floated in her wake.

'Isla, my dear!' Isla was enveloped in a perfumed embrace, her face briefly smothered against the boa, then released, to be held back at arms' length and studied through narrowed blue eyes. 'Your friend was right when she wrote to say that you needed a holiday. You look like something the cat dragged in,' Lally announced in ringing tones that had once reached to the back of theatre galleries with ease. Heads turned all up and down the platform.

'And these are your little ones! Darlings, come to your auntie!' Lally stooped with an ominous creaking of stays and swept a child into each arm. When she released them, Ross sneezed.

'It's the feathers,' Barbara explained, bright-eyed. 'They got up his nose. Mine too.'

'How sweet!' her great-aunt trumpeted, and spun round, her eyes searching the platform. 'Porter!'

More heads turned. 'We only have two small cases,' Isla protested, embarrassed by the attention they were attracting. 'I can carry them.'

'Nonsense, a lady should never carry her own luggage – remember that, little girl,' Lally added to Barbara, who nodded eagerly, standing on one leg and bending the other back to catch her foot in one hand.

'I can hop. I can hop all down the platform.'

A porter was already scuttling eagerly up to them. 'Kangaroos hop, young ladies walk, head up and shoulders back,' said Lally. 'Come along!' And she set off down the platform, Barbara forging along by her side, and the porter trotting behind her.

Following, Ross's hand clutched in hers, Isla began to wonder if she had the strength to spend two weeks in Aunt Lally's company.

Lally Moffatt had lived in the same first-floor flat in a handsome tenement building ever since Isla could remember. Climbing the stairs, she recalled her aunt's claim that the flat had been bought for her by a wealthy admirer during her days in the music hall chorus, and wondered again if it was true.

The flat hadn't changed much, and the children's

mouths rounded, as well as their eyes, when they went inside. The living-room walls were covered with framed paintings, photographs, decorative plates, bows, bunches of dried flowers, fans, and programmes. Every piece of furniture held more photographs, albums, books, vases filled with more dried flowers, gloves, more decorative plates, and fancy little boxes. Even the mirror over the cluttered fireplace had its share of cards and pro- grammes pushed into the frame. Footwear – shoes and slippers in patent leather, kid, suede, satin, velvet, buck- skin, lizardskin, and snakeskin – stood in rows along the skirting board.

'Nothing's changed,' Isla said in wonder.

'I believe I've collected a few more mementoes.' Lally unpinned her hat and tossed it carelessly on to a chair already overflowing with hats, gloves, and long scarves. Her hair, which Isla remembered as daffodil yellow, was now pure white, still cut short, level with her ears. Her mouth was a bright pink cupid's bow, and her eye- brows had been plucked out and replaced by delicate arches, pencilled in. 'Now then' – she clapped her hands briskly together – 'let's have some tea!'

'Yes!' said Ross, and trotted after her as she marched off to the small kitchen. Barbara stayed where she was, still turning round slowly to take everything in.

'Look, Mummy, a piano!' She pointed to a corner of the high-ceilinged room where a small piano was almost hidden by the shawl that had been tossed over it. Barbara drew in a deep breath and let it out in a sigh, her eyes bright.

'I'm going to like staying here!' she said.

*

264

'I don't remember you making a fuss over me when I was small,' Isla said that night when the children had been put to bed and she and her aunt were sipping sherry on either side of the fireplace. Lally's raised eyebrows disappeared under her fringe.

'Don't tell me you're jealous of your own children!'

'Of course not, just making an observation.'

'For one thing I'm much older, and old age tends to yearn towards youth. For another, your two are really quite beautiful, whereas I remember you as a quiet, dark, sallow little girl. Such a pity you didn't take after me and your father, instead of your mother.'

'Mother was lovely.'

'She was, wasn't she, bless her,' Lally remembered, her face softening. 'But she was of Italian parentage, my dear. She still had the Mediterranean sun on her cheeks, like the bloom on black grapes. You never had that at all. You still don't.'

'We don't get a lot of sun in Paisley,' Isla said dryly.

'Your hair doesn't help – all that dark stuff round that wee pale face. You should get it bobbed.' Then, seeing Isla's involuntary glance at her own uncompromising short cut, Lally said, 'Don't worry, it'll not look like a chopped field the way mine does. You've got nice soft hair, it would lie in well round your face.'

'Mebbe so, but I've got more to do with my money than spend it on myself.'

'There's a friend of mine . . .' Lally had always had friends who could turn their hands to everything, Isla remembered. 'A dresser she was, but she could cut hair very well. She once trimmed Marie Lloyd's hair in an emergency, and there was never a complaint. She'd do it for nothing.'

'I'll think about it.'

'Your little ones, now – what wonderful hair! Their father was a very handsome man, as I remember from our two brief meetings. What happened?' Lally asked so abruptly that Isla was disconcerted for a moment.

'He – he died. If you remember, he was older than I was.'

'Why take up your own name again?'

'I just wanted to,' Isla said shortly.

Lally gave her a long shrewd look from beneath darkened eyelashes, then shrugged, and sipped at her sherry. 'You always were secretive – now that, you got from your mother. D'you have plans to marry again?'

'Who would want a penniless widow with two children to support?'

'You'd be surprised.' The blue eyes studied her face. 'Whatever's happened to you, you've had to walk a hard road. But you're still young enough to attract men.'

'I've no wish to attract men.'

'Nonsense, there isn't a woman alive who doesn't want to look her best,' Lally said briskly. 'You need fattening up – and some stimulating company.'

'What I need is some peace and quiet.'

'Away you go, lassie,' said Lally Moffatt. 'At your age?'

Later, in the small, crowded spare bedroom, Isla tucked the blankets round Ross, who slept on a small truckle bed, then turned out the gas mantle and climbed into bed beside Barbara, who murmured sleepily and turned over. Gradually her eyes became accustomed to the dark, and the silhouette of a macabre headless body, the tailor's dummy Lally had used in the old days to make her stage costumes on, outlined against the window.

Outside, she could dimly hear the hum of traffic passing along the main road two blocks further down, and the occasional motor car chugging its way along below the windows. With surprise, she realised that she felt homesick for the single room in George Street.

The bracing winds of Scotland's east coast seemed to blow Isla's cobwebs away. During the day she and Lally took the children to visit Edinburgh Castle and the Palace of Holyrood House, strolling down the narrow cobbled Royal Mile and along Princes Street to look in the shop windows, exploring Princes Street gardens and the warren of streets and closes in the Old Town.

Almost every night some of Lally's friends dropped in, for she loved company, and had always been famed for holding open house. Dressed in crêpe de Chine frocks with bold patterns and loose sleeves and floating sashes and scarves, a cigarette in a holder and a headdress thick with paste jewellery clamped on to her short white hair, Lally held court.

Most of her friends had been on the stage, or connected with the theatre, and almost every sentence began with 'D'you remember?' They laughed a lot and talked over each other, and spoiled the children outrageously.

Sometimes during the day Barbara and Ross went off with Lally and some of her friends, leaving Isla to enjoy some time to herself, and sometimes their great-aunt kept them amused in the house, teaching them songs and letting them dress up in the trunkfuls of stage clothes she had kept, so that Isla could wander round the streets and through the shops without worrying about them.

She never knew what would meet her when she came back from those trips. It could be a dramatic play, with the children tottering about in Lally's shoes, with dresses and jackets far too big for them falling off their shoulders and threatening to trip them up at every step. It could be a music hall turn, with Lally thumping out a song on the piano and the children strutting around the room with canes, Ross with his head tipped back so that he could see from under a top hat stuffed with newspaper, Barbara with her top hat wedged on by her hair, which had been bundled up for the occasion.

Once or twice Lally took the children to an afternoon matinee. Ross tended to fall asleep, but Barbara came back with eyes like saucers, able to recite most of the show, with some prompting from her great-aunt.

'She's got a marvellous memory, darling,' Lally enthused, 'And such style! She must have inherited it from me.'

Watching her daughter, a sailor hat tipped saucily over one eye, strutting across the living-room and bellowing out 'All the Nice Girls Love a Sailor', Isla had to agree with her. Barbara certainly hadn't inherited her outgoing personality from either of her parents.

Egged on by the children, Isla finally gave in to her aunt's insistence, and had her hair bobbed. She sat with her eyes closed, listening to the crunch of the scissors and the soft regretful sighing sound her hair made as it fell in clumps to the floor, where Barbara gathered it up. She thought, as Lally's friend worked, of how Kenneth had loved to loosen her hair at night and brush it for her, stopping now and again to bury his face in its softness, or lift it aside so that he could kiss the nape of her neck. A shiver ran through her at the memory, and the woman said at once, 'Did I hurt you?'

'No.' No sense in living in the past, Isla told herself. Lally was right, her hair would be easier to care for now, and that was all that mattered.

Even so, she was reluctant to open her eyes when the cutting was finished, despite the two women's assurances that she looked lovely. Barbara finally climbed on to her knee and said, her nose bumping Isla's, her breath tickling Isla's top lip, 'Look, Mummy, you're beautiful!'

Isla opened her eyes and found herself staring into her daughter's face. 'You're not made of glass, Barbara. I can't see through you.'

The little girl giggled, and squirmed round until she was sitting on Isla's lap. Looking into the mirror, Isla saw a neat, wide-eyed face, framed with dark wings that curved softly round on to her cheeks, staring back at her in astonishment.

'I look like a different person!'

Lally's friend, standing behind her, nodded her satisfaction, while Lally herself said, 'It's about time!'

In their second week in Edinburgh, Lally, who loved parties, held one to mark their visit, inviting all her theatrical friends. Barbara provided the entertainment all on her own, glowing at the applause that greeted each song.

Halfway through the evening, watching her children, particularly her daughter, being fussed over by all the adults, Isla knew that it was time to go back to Paisley, back to their usual life. Lally pouted when she announced the next day that it was time to start making plans for their return.

'But you've only just got here!'

'We've been here for almost two weeks, Aunt Lally, and that was the arrangement. Besides, Barbara has to get back to school.'

'Talking of Barbara,' Lally said slowly, flashing a quick look at her niece from beneath her lashes, 'she's a very talented little girl, Isla. Bertie was just saying the other day that she'd be a natural on the stage.'

'That depends on what she wants to do when she grows up.'

'But she ought to start as soon as possible. I was at elocution and dancing by the time I was her age.'

'Aunt Lally, I can't afford to pay for these things for Barbara, and even if I could, it would only set her apart from her friends. She's managed to make a place for herself in Paisley, and it wouldn't be fair to her to change things now.'

'Paisley! What chance will she have there? There are some excellent classes here in Edinburgh, and you can't deny that we have good schools – look at your own education.'

Isla put a hand up to the nape of her neck, and was astonished, as always, to touch skin instead of a heavy mass of hair. 'I've no intention of uprooting myself and the children again.'

'I'm not talking about the entire family being uprooted. Why don't you leave Barbara here with me, just for a year, until we see how things work out? I'll bear the cost of her education and her dance classes and singing classes. And for elocution too, she'll need that,' Lally went on as Isla stared at her. 'I still have some influence, you know. It could all be done on very little, and she deserves—'

'No!' The cold terror Isla had known when Catherine McAdam tried to take Ross away from her returned. The older woman looked at her in astonishment.

'My dear child, I'm not suggesting kidnap! I've no intention of coming between you and your daughter, I'm only asking you to give her one little year, to see how she does. I can guarantee that with the proper training now, she'll be a star in ten years – we'll be so proud of her—'

'No!' Isla, aware of the children in the next room, trying on Lally's clothes, fought to keep her voice calm. 'We've been through enough as it is, and all I want for Barbara is an ordinary upbringing.'

'But—'

'She's only a little girl, Aunt Lally. She has years ahead of her to make up her own mind. But not now, not yet – and don't try to persuade her,' she added swiftly as she saw her aunt's eyes narrowing. 'I'll not have it, no matter how much she pleads.'

'Do you realise what you're denying that child? She may well grow up to resent you for it.'

'That's a chance I have to take. I want her to grow up like any other child, and I know that that's what her father would have wanted, too.'

They eyed each other, then, 'Oh, very well,' Lally said at last, huffily. 'But I warn you, Isla, you're being most unfair!'

Barbara sulked when she was told that they were going home. 'But I like it here! Why can't we stay with Aunt Lally?'

'Because holidays don't go on forever,' Isla told her sharply, aware of her aunt's hurt looks.

The old fear of losing one of her children had been re-awakened, and she didn't feel entirely safe until the train was pulling out of Waverley Station, leaving Lally alone on the platform. Sinking back into her seat, Isla struggled to justify her decision to take Barbara back to Paisley. Lally was getting older, she couldn't possibly be expected to care for an active little girl, she told herself. Besides, she had had difficulty in getting Barbara to do her lessons every day. Barbara had objected, and Lally had supported her. If she left the child in Edinburgh for a whole year, she told herself as the train moved westwards, the child would be quite illiterate.

But she knew that the truth was that the children were all she had in the world, all that was left of her life with Kenneth. And that, quite apart from the deep love she had for both of them, was very important to her.

'Ye'll never guess,' Magret said almost as soon as Isla got home. 'They've repaired the roof above the Browns' flat! Ye could have knocked the lot of us down with a feather when the men arrived and began to put up ladders.' She handed Isla a cup of her strong, sweet tinned-milk tea. 'I don't mind anyone doing any repairs on this place in all the time we've been here. Mrs Brown's fair thrilled about it.'

That evening, Drew came down to show Isla a small wardrobe that he had made. The interior was hollow, and the double doors opened. 'I minded you sayin' that you didnae like that solid wardrobe you had for the wee house, so I thought I'd see what I could do,' he explained, glowing with pride in his success and her pleasure. 'The hinges came from a box my mam had. And I've found another book in the library, and bought myself an exercise book so's I can copy the pictures down.'

'Look, it's even got a rail! Now I can make some clothes, and some cardboard hangers to put them on. You're clever, Drew!'

When she took some coins from her purse and insisted on paying for the wardrobe, Drew protested.

'Och no, you didnae ask me tae make this for you. You can just keep it.'

'I'm buying it,' she told him firmly. 'You deserve payment, and anyway, it means that I can feel free to ask you to do more, if I get another order for a house.'

'I enjoyed it,' he said as he gave in and took the money, then, 'did you hear that there's been some work done on the roof?'

'Mrs McDougall told me.'

'My mam's fair pleased,' Drew said happily. 'She cannae wait for the rain tae come, so that she can enjoy being dry.'

23

Annie beamed – a rare event – when she saw Isla on the doorstep. 'It's grand tae see ye back. She'll be fair pleased.' She nodded at the parlour door. 'She's in by.'

'Isla!' Flora Currie came forward with hands outstretched. 'My, your holiday's done you good – I've never seen you look so well. Your hair's very smart!'

Isla put a hand to her short hair. 'It was my aunt's idea, not mine. It still feels . . .' Her voice trailed away as a man got up from the chair by the window, his long body seeming to unfold in sections.

'Come and meet Philip Hannigan,' Flora said briskly. He towered over both women as she made the introductions, his teeth flashing white in a tanned face.

'My friends call me Phil. I'm very pleased to meet you.' He spoke in a soft, attractive drawl and her hand seemed to disappear into his.

'Phil comes from Canada,' Flora said proudly, as though she had made him all by herself. 'His great-aunt was my dear friend Agnes from next door. He's inherited her house.'

'You're going to settle here?'

'No, ma'am, I've got a timber business back home in

Ontario, and that's where I belong.' Philip Hannigan smiled down on his hostess. 'Miss Flora's been my guardian angel ever since I got here.'

'Och, away with you, man!' Flora flushed like a young girl. 'I just did what Agnes would have done for my kin if things had been the other way round. He's insisted on staying in that house on his own,' she explained to Isla. 'So of course I said he must have his meals with us. Ainslie McAdam's been a great help with sorting out the house – she's arranged for her employer to have a look at the furniture to see what should go for auction.'

'I'd like some of the furniture to be sold along with the house,' Phil put in. 'They sort of belong together, but Ainslie – Miss McAdam – thinks there's too much of it, and some of it should be disposed of separately.'

'Where are the children, Isla? I was looking forward to seeing them again.'

'Barbara's back at school, and Ross wanted to stay and play with Daisy. Barbara's learned a lot of new songs from Aunt Lally,' Isla said, half-ruefully. 'She's planning another back-court concert.'

'I told you that Isla's little girl was musically gifted, didn't I?' Flora asked Philip Hannigan.

The Canadian dipped his head in agreement. 'I'm looking forward to meeting both of them.'

'Isla, Mr Leckie's got a special order in for a dolls' house, from a customer who wants you to furnish it.'

'That's wonderful!'

'I said I was sure you'd want to do it, so he brought it the other day. His customer wants it for Christmas, and you can decide on the style.'

'I've heard all about your talent, Mrs Moffatt,' Phil
Hannigan put in. 'It sounds to me as though you've got
yourself quite a business there.'

'It's just a hobby.'

He shook his head. 'Don't you believe it. Finding out
what folk want, then supplying it – that's how busi-
nesses begin.'

It would have been very easy to sit back and drown
in that soft drawl, but Isla was longing to see the new
house. When she excused herself Philip unwound himself from his chair, reaching the door before she did and
holding it open for her.

'I look forward to meeting you again, Mrs Moffatt.'

'Isla.'

'Isla,' he agreed. 'It's a very pretty name.'

As she crossed the hall Isla glanced in the mirror and
saw that she, too, was blushing. The man had that sort
of effect on women, she decided, as she opened the door
of the doll's-house room.

On the following Saturday, when Isla and the children
arrived at Castlehead, Philip Hannigan and Ainslie were
both in Flora's drawing-room, Ainslie equipped with a
notebook and pencil.

'We're going to start making a list of the furniture
that's going to auction. Come and have a look around,'
the Canadian suggested. Isla hesitated. She had planned
to spend her time at Castlehead making a mirror by
glueing some tiny jet beads from an old necklace round
silver paper stuck on to cardboard.

'I'm not going, because the house holds too many
memories for me. But you should, Isla, you'd enjoy

seeing round it,' Flora urged and she gave in.

Outside, Phil lifted the children over the hedge then swung his long legs over without any difficulty. Isla and Ainslie declined his offer of help, and took the longer route through Miss Currie's gate and along the pavement.

'He's a good-looking man, isn't he?' Ainslie murmured.

'Probably married.'

'Actually, no. Your holiday's done you good.'

'I ate far too much in Edinburgh.'

'You suit a little more weight.' Ainslie herself looked more relaxed. She wore a summer dress in pale blue, the same colour as her eyes, with an open jacket in navy to match the braiding at the dress's neck and hem.

'How is your mother?' Isla asked, formally, and a shadow passed over Ainslie's face.

'Her health has improved, but her mind . . .' She stopped, her hand on the gate leading to the neighbouring garden, then said, 'She seems to live in a world of her own making. She talks of nobody but Innes and my grandfather. She doesn't seem to be aware of my existence.'

'I'm sorry.'

For a moment Isla saw hurt in the other girl's gaze, then it was gone, hidden behind a mask of indifference as Ainslie opened the gate, then closed it behind them.

'It's that nurse I'm sorry for. Mother's become very arrogant, and she orders poor Miss Dove about all the time. Fortunately Miss Dove doesn't seem to mind, she treats Mother with just the right mixture of deference and firmness.'

'Come on, you two,' Phil called from the porch. As she went up the steps Ainslie tripped and Phil put out a hand to steady her.

'I'm all right,' she said hurriedly, pulling herself away. He raised an eyebrow.

'Do all Scottish girls hate being touched?'

She coloured. 'I don't hate it. I mean . . .'

'Only teasing. Come on in.' He stood back to let them pass, winking at Isla.

The house smelled musty, as though it hadn't been lived in for some time. The children were already on their way upstairs, Ross puffing in Barbara's wake.

'Let them go where they want,' Phil said easily when Isla called them back. 'Kids like to explore. I understand that Great-Aunt Agnes more or less lived in the drawing-room,' he went on, opening the door.

Isla, fascinated, moved about the stuffy room, edging round occasional tables, plant-pot stands, chairs and cabinets. She studied the massive sideboard, laden down with ornaments, then tipped her head back to look up at the ceiling and the cornices. The room was similar to Flora Currie's drawing-room, but not as square. There were alcoves on either side of the fireplace, and the window had more of a bay.

'It's a very graceful room, isn't it?' she said thoughtfully. 'This' – she put a hand on a small cabinet – 'suits it, and so does that corner cupboard, while this sideboard's out of place.'

'The room's big enough to take it,' Phil said.

'Yes, but the piece itself's far too big and clumsy for the lines of this room,' Isla told him, moving around, rejecting and selecting, while the other two watched.

'Try to imagine it with only a third of the furniture in it and most of the ornaments gone,' she said at last. 'Think how light and airy it would look then.'

'I quite agree,' said Colin Forbes from the doorway. She turned, and saw his eyes widen as he recognised her. 'Mrs Moffatt! I thought it was – you've done something to your hair,' he said feebly, and Ainslie laughed.

'Did you think we'd brought in an expert? I believe we have, at that. I didn't know you knew about interior design, Isla.'

'I don't, it's just that I . . .' Isla stopped on the verge of saying 'I learned a lot when Kenneth and I were furnishing our house', and changed it to, 'I like houses, and furniture.'

'I never did have any imagination,' Phil Hannigan admitted. 'I can only see what I see.'

'I understand what Isla means,' Ainslie said. 'You should shift most of this furniture out, Phil, but keep the pieces she mentioned. That'll make the house look more attractive, and easier to view as well. If the buyer doesn't want them, they can be auctioned off later.'

Forbes and Son were handling the sale of the house, and Colin, like Ainslie, had come on business, bringing notebook and pencil with him. They moved upstairs, and after taking a quick look round Isla left them there, Ainslie listing the furniture, Colin thumping walls and jumping on the floors, with the children's enthusiastic help, to test the joists. She slipped back down to the kitchen, where she washed the few dishes Phil had left in the sink. She was rinsing the dishcloth when Ainslie arrived.

'Here you are. Colin and I are going to drive Phil down to the Clyde coast this afternoon. Come with us.'

'I couldn't possibly . . .'

'The children too, they can sit on our laps, and I'm sure they'd love to see the sea,' Ainslie coaxed. Isla was shaking her head firmly when Barbara and Ross burst in, shouting, 'Mummy, we're going to the seaside!'

'Ainslie! You told them without asking me first!'

'I must have let it slip out,' Ainslie said guiltily, then brightened. 'You'll have to say yes now, won't you?'

They went to Barassie, where the car could be driven right on to a wide stretch of firm sand and the children could shed their socks and shoes and paddle in the shallow water. Ainslie went with them, while the two young men stayed by the car with Isla. They were from different worlds, she thought, looking at them. Colin Forbes, formal in a blue suit, with shirt and tie, stood staring out at the glittering water, while Phil, dressed casually in cream-coloured trousers and an open-necked checked shirt beneath a sleeveless tan pullover, sprawled bonelessly on the sand, completely at his ease.

'Look at the way the light catches their hair – they've all got the same colouring,' he marvelled, watching the three figures at the water's edge. 'They look more like Ainslie's kids than yours, Isla.'

There was an awkward silence, broken by Colin saying easily, 'Red hair's common among the Scots. By the way, Mrs Moffatt . . .'

'Is stuffiness common too? Calling Isla Mrs Moffatt,' Phil explained when Colin looked puzzled.

'Mrs Moffatt is a client.'

'So am I, but you call me Phil. What's the matter, don't you like each other?' The Canadian looked from one to the other, then grinned. 'Personally, I can't imagine anyone not liking Isla.'

If Isla hadn't been just as embarrassed as he was, she would have laughed at the mixture of expressions that chased each other across Colin Forbes' reddening face. Finally he said stiffly, 'As I was saying – Isla – I think we may have found a buyer for the tenement building.'

'Really?'

'I should be able to give you further details when you come to the office on Monday, but I need to be able to tell the prospective buyer whether the building's fully tenanted or not. Will you be moving out if you sell?'

'I don't see how I can.'

'Surely you'll be able to buy another place with the money you make from the sale?' Phil asked. His interest was so sincere that it didn't occur to Isla to feel annoyed at the question.

'I've already spent some of the money I'd get from a sale, paying for essential repairs. It would probably be wise to stay where I am, and invest the rest.'

'Why not make an offer for my great-aunt's house? It would be a great place to raise kids, with that backyard and all. And you'd have room to develop that dolls'-house business of yours.'

'I couldn't begin to afford a house like that!'

'Make me an offer,' he invited, and when she laughed, he persisted. 'Go on – I've not had any offers yet. You might as well be the first.'

'Five shillings is as much as I could afford.'

'Five shillings. There you go, Colin – the first bid's in.'

Colin Forbes grunted, and ran a finger round his constricting collar. He stooped and picked up a stick, flicking at the sand with it as he wandered down to the water's edge, where Ainslie and the children were playing.

'What's troubling Ainslie?' Phil asked when Colin was out of earshot. 'She flinched away like a startled deer when I tried to steady her back at the house. Made me feel she'd rather have been left to fall flat on her face.'

'She's – not had an easy time lately.'

'Uh-huh?' He settled his back more comfortably against the car wheel. 'I can't imagine why anyone would want to cause problems for a girl like that.'

The offer made for the tenement was lower than Isla had hoped.

'It's not a good time to be selling,' Colin Forbes explained. 'Ordinarily, we'd advise waiting in the hope of the market improving, but . . .'

'I can't afford to wait.' The repair bill for the roof was still haunting her. 'I'll have to take it.'

'And remain as a tenant?'

'I've no option. At least I can stop feeling guilty about the state of the place if I don't own it.'

'Then I'll get the papers drawn up, and let you know when they're ready for signature.'

Phil always seemed to be around when Isla went to Castlehead, and Ainslie was there often too, helping him to clear out cupboards and get the house ready for sale.

The lanky Canadian took a liking to Barbara and Ross, who both adored him, and somehow, without Isla knowing how it happened, the three of them – Phil, Ainslie and Isla, had fallen into the habit of taking the children on outings. Colin often accompanied them – so that he could be near Ainslie, Isla assumed.

To her consternation, Phil even turned up at Barbara's back-court concert with Ainslie, causing more than a ripple of excitement. The women were far more interested in him than in their children's talents, nudging each other and whispering amongst themselves. Phil, unabashed, tipped his hat and beamed at them all, then settled down to enjoy the concert, applauding each song loudly, and handing out coins afterwards to all the performers, who immediately ran off to the corner shop to buy sweeties.

'Ye've got some strange friends, Isla,' said Magret after he had gone, adding with a coy giggle, 'mind you, he's a fine-looking man, is he no'?'

'I think he's the nicest person in the whole world,' Barbara, flushed with the success of her concert, said indistinctly round a large peppermint ball.

One windy day, they all drove up to the top of the braes flanking Paisley to fly Colin's old kite.

'Phil likes your company,' Ainslie said as the two of them sat on the springy grass, watching the children jump about with excitement as the kite soared.

'He likes everyone, he's got that sort of nature. And if you're trying to matchmake you're wasting your time. I've become used to my independence, and I like it fine.'

'But think of it, Isla – life in Canada! The children would love it. Phil's got his own business, and a fine house, with beautiful countryside around it, and Lake Erie not far away.'

'He's been telling you a lot about himself, hasn't he?'

'I'm not the marrying kind,' Ainslie said at once.

'Neither am I, now.'

'Hey, look at this – it's going up to the sun!' Phil called as the two men skimmed past, Colin controlling the kite while Ross, on Phil's shoulders, reached up towards the dancing, colourful kite with one hand, and clutched Phil's thick hair with the other. Barbara raced alongside, her ribbon long since lost and her red hair streaming in the wind.

Following Isla's advice, Phil had the surplus furniture removed from his great-aunt's house and sold at auction. Left with only the smaller furniture, the house looked just as Isla had visualised it – spacious and elegant, despite the clean patches on the wallpaper where the furniture had stood for many years.

Phil, in plus-fours and a casual jacket, attended the sale, lounging at the back of the large auction room. Whenever Ainslie, who was assisting the clerk, found a moment to glance up from the lists she had to follow meticulously, he caught her eye and winked. Afterwards, he stayed behind and gave the men a hand to clear the room, carrying lots outside to pack on to carts and lorries, putting unsold goods back into storage. Then he joined them for a mug of strong tea.

'You did all right,' Charlie told him, and Phil shrugged. He was leaning against a wall, mug in hand, looking, as he always did, as though he belonged.

'It wasn't bad. To tell the truth, it goes against the grain, making money out of someone else's possessions. I prefer to know that what I've got was earned by my own efforts.'

Ainslie, eyeing the rangy Canadian, was taken by his relaxed self-confidence, his ease with his surroundings. Compared to him, the Scots seemed to be confined in invisible boxes, limited by self-imposed rules of behaviour.

'How do you get home?' he asked as they left the auction rooms together.

'By bus from the Cross.' Then she said impulsively, 'But today, I think I'd like to walk.'

'To the other side of the town? Won't your mother wonder where you've got to?'

'She won't notice,' Ainslie said, then, as they stepped out briskly together, she found herself telling him about her mother and about Innes. He was a good listener, and it seemed natural to go on to talk about her father, about giving Colin back his ring, about Isla, and her own guilt at having treated the other woman so badly when she first came to the town. She spoke freely of her need to make amends, to her half-brother and sister as well as to their mother. As she talked, the pavement seemed to skim past beneath their feet, and suddenly they were standing at her gate. She felt tired after the long walk, but it was a good, healthy tiredness, as though all the talking had cleansed and eased her.

'I wish I could invite you in for tea, Phil, but . . .'

'I understand.' He looked beyond her, to the garden and the house, then back at her face. 'This doesn't look like the right sort of place for you. It's too closed in.'

She turned to study the house where she had been born and raised. 'I feel that way too, whenever I'm in it.'

'Tell me, d'you feel bad about breaking off your engagement to Colin?'

'Yes, but I still think that it was the right thing to do.' She held her hand out. 'Thank you for being such a good listener, Phil.'

His hand was reassuring as it clasped hers. 'Any time,' he said, then released her, flipped a finger at the brim of his soft hat, and swung round, walking away with that long, unhurried step she had found easy to adopt.

For once, there was no feeling of apprehension as Ainslie went through the front door. She felt warm and at ease – and safe.

24

Isla handed the pen over, and watched as Colin Forbes scribbled his own name as witness to her signature. Over the past week or two, thrown into his company more than before, she had discovered that he could be much nicer than she had thought possible.

She had seen him glancing at Ainslie when he thought he was unobserved, and had recognised the look on his face. It was clear, in those brief, private glances, that he knew that he had lost Ainslie McAdam for ever, and was still coming to terms with the truth. Isla knew what that was like. By selling the tenement she herself had broken another of the few, delicate strands that still linked her to Kenneth.

'When the money comes through, we can discuss what you want to do with it.' His voice broke through her thoughts.

'I'm hoping that we'll be able to live on it for at least two more years. Once Ross goes to school, I'll be free to look for paid employment.'

The little boy, standing by the window where he could look down on the passing tramcars, turned at the sound of his name and came to her. She smiled down at him, smoothing back his hair.

'You'll not make much from the sale.'

'I've learned a lot about managing on very little money,' she said wryly, getting to her feet. 'Most of the folk in George Street are experts at that.'

It was ironic that just as Isla had sold the tenement, Mrs Leach discovered that she had owned it.

The woman came storming down the street, battered shopping bag in hand, just as Isla and Magret, on their way back from the bakery, reached the close.

'So – what's like tae be a landlord, then?' she shouted from several yards away. Mrs Kelly, her daughter, trotted just behind her, pale and anxious. 'You – I'm talkin' tae ye!' A hand caught Isla's shoulder, pulling her back as she was about to step into the close. Ross, who had been running ahead with Daisy, came back to his mother, his small face tight with concern.

'Let go of me!'

'Did ye know?' Mrs Leach swung round on Magret. 'Did ye know that it's her that owns this building? It's her we pay our rents tae—'

'Ach, away wi' ye,' Magret scoffed. 'Don't be so daft. Isla's in the same boat as the rest of us – she's tryin' tae raise two weans on her own.'

'Mam—' Mrs Kelly plucked at her mother's sleeve. Mrs Leach threw her off with a twitch of the arm.

'Her that's let the place fall down about our ears while she lives on our money!'

'Ye're haverin'!' Magret was getting angry. 'Look at the lassie. Does she look like a landlord?'

'She looks like a sly wee besom, that's what she looks like,' Mrs Leach roared back. By now there wasn't a window without a face framed in it, not a close-mouth without its group of staring women.

'I don't own anything!'

Mrs Leach sniffed. 'Not now ye don't. But ye did, didn't ye? Oh, ye thought ye were so clever, pretendin' tae be a poor wee widow. But I've found ye out – I've got yer measure now, milady. There's no' much can be kept hidden from me!'

'Tell her she's haverin', Isla,' Magret said contemptuously.

'Haverin', am I?' Mrs Leach caught her daughter's arm and pulled the distraught girl forward. 'And what about her man, was he haverin' tae, when he heard in the very office where he works that she's the one that owns this building?'

'Mam, I told ye that in confidence,' Mrs Kelly whimpered, but her mother wasn't interested.

'Tell the truth and shame the devil,' she shouted to the gathering audience. 'That's the way I was brought up.'

Magret began to waver. 'It's no' true, is it?' she asked Isla. 'It cannae be true!'

Ross, clinging to Isla's legs, started to wail, and she put a hand on his head. 'It's all right, pet.'

'See? She'll not answer ye,' Mrs Leach told Magret. 'She's scared tae answer ye!'

'But she pays her rent, the same as the rest of us.'

'Aye – and then she goes tae the factor's every week an' gets it back, along wi' our hard-earned money!' Mrs Leach's hard finger rammed into Isla's shoulder, forcing her to retreat. Her ankles collided painfully with the step, and she almost fell, but managed to stay upright, stumbling on to the step. Ross was almost hysterical now, and she scooped him up in her arms, retreating to the safety of her own room. Mrs Leach followed her along the close, her bulk shutting out the light, her voice hounding and nagging.

'We don't want the likes o' you livin' here,' she brayed, her voice rolling like thunder round the narrow close. 'The folks that live here's decent! We've no time for liars. Ye can just get out of this building – you an' yer weans!'

Even when Isla reached the safety of the room and slammed the door in the woman's face, her fist pounded on the panels and her voice kept bellowing on, magnified by the enclosed passageway.

Trembling on the other side of the door, hugging Ross to her and trying to hush him, as though afraid that his weeping would somehow give them both away, Isla heard Magret arguing, and Mrs Kelly pleading with her mother to come away. At last, Mrs Leach allowed herself to be led upstairs, after one final thump at the door. After a moment, there was another, gentle tap at the door.

'Isla?'

She put Ross down and opened the door. Magret came in, Daisy gawping at her side. 'She's bletherin'. The woman's gone clean off her head – I knew it would happen one day.'

'It's true, Magret.'

Magret's mouth opened and shut. Finally she said feebly, 'The landlord? You?'

'I did own the place, but I've sold it now. I didn't want to say anything because—'

Magret looked dazed. 'I'll have to see what he thinks about all this business,' she said, then caught Daisy by the hand as the little girl made a move towards Ross. 'I'd – I'd best be gettin' his tea ready. I'll see ye later,' and she almost ran out of the room.

Isla turned away from the door, just in time to see faces at the window, peering into the room. She managed, for Ross's sake, to swallow back her involuntary yelp of fright, then went across to pull the curtain shut. As she did so, something thumped against the glass, but didn't break it. Ross jumped at the sound and ran to her.

'It's all right, pet, it's all right,' she soothed him, but she didn't dare to venture out, or to draw back the curtain. They sat in the gloom, listening to the sound of voices outside as the news was relayed from one person to another, until Barbara came home from school, tears in her eyes, wanting to know why the women in the street had pointed at her and shouted nasty things about her mummy.

From that day, life in George Street became impossible. None of the other children were allowed to play with Ross, and Barbara, bewildered, wanted to know why the children at school had turned against her.

'Have you been bad?' she asked suspiciously.

'No, love, it's just that – this tenement belonged to your daddy, and he gave it to us when he – had to go away. But the neighbours didn't know that, and they're angry with me for not telling them.'

Barbara's eyes were like saucers. 'The whole building? Did they think he should have given it to them instead?'

Isla tried to explain, but Barbara got it into her head

that the neighbours had somehow taken the tenement away from her mother, and arrived home next day with her snub nose bloody and her blouse torn after a fight in the playground over the issue.

Isla couldn't stay in the house all the time. When she went out, people stared and pointed and made loud asides to each other about rich folk slumming, and poor folk unable to trust their neighbours. The curtains stayed closed, because every time she opened them, people stared in. The owner of the corner shop, a friendly man who had previously been willing to put Isla's purchases on the slate until the beginning of each week, refused to sell her anything until she had cleared her debts.

'But you give credit to most of the folk round here.'

'Aye, missus, because I want tae keep my customers,' the man said. 'If I serve you, most of them'll go elsewhere. I cannae afford tae let that happen.'

The other women in the shop stepped aside ostentatiously to let Isla out, muttering amongst themselves. She had no option but to go to the lawyer's office to ask Colin Forbes if she could take some money out at once.

'Is there something wrong?' His gaze moved from her to Ross, unusually silent and clinging.

'No.' She was too ashamed to tell him about what had happened. It was her problem, and she must cope with it. She was sure that if she and the children could just wait out the storm, it would die down. Once the George Street folk realised that, like them, she was struggling to support her family and worrying about where the next meal was coming from, they would surely come round.

She arrived home to find a pile of horse manure outside her door. She fetched the shovel from the back court and cleared it, then scrubbed the close out. After sluicing the water away down the street drain she came back into the close to find Magret lurking there.

'Oh, Isla, it's a rotten shame, so it is. I'd have cleaned it up for ye, but Tommy says I've no' tae talk tae ye, and the bairns cannae play together. I'm sorry . . .'

'It's all right, I can understand why he's so angry.'

Magret held back Daisy, who was trying to reach Ross. 'Why did ye keep it a secret, Isla?'

'Because I knew that if the folk round here knew the truth, they'd do just what they're doing now,' Isla told her, and went into the house.

Drew tapped on the door that night; when she was certain he was alone, she opened the door, closing it quickly behind him.

'I've finished that wee sideboard.' He handed it over and she ran her fingers over it.

'It's lovely, Drew.'

He reached into his pocket and brought out a small parcel, fragrant-smelling and still warm. 'My mam's just baked these scones. She thought you and the bairns'd like them. And here's a wee pot of raspberry jam to go with them.'

Tears of gratitude stung Isla's eyes. 'Thank you – and thank your mother for me.'

'It was you that got the roof fixed, wasn't it? If there's anythin' we can dae for ye, mam an' me, ye just have tae let us know. It's no' right, the way folks is treatin' ye,' the youth said hotly. 'It's that old Leach that's got the rest of them stirred up against ye. It'll be forgotten in a week.'

As he stepped out into the close again, she heard him say, with a boldness that she never would have believed of Drew, 'Evenin', Mrs Leach. Is there somethin' wrong wi' yer eyes? They look awful stary.'

The old woman's scandalised sniff reverberated through the close as Isla closed the door.

Drew was wrong – Isla's betrayal, as Mrs Leach and her cronies saw it, wasn't forgotten in a week. Instead, the persecution became increasingly worse, until finally one night, someone threw a stone through the window, shouting, 'See how long ye take tae repair that, land-lady! Nob'dy wants your sort here!'

The children, who had just been put to bed, screamed with fright, and Isla, working at the sink, jumped back as shards of glass flew into the washing-up water. She caught Ross up out of his cot and jumped with him into the wall-bed, where the three of them crouched together.

'Look, Mummy,' Ross said suddenly, wide-eyed, pointing at the back of her hand, which was bleeding freely. There was blood on the blanket, and on Ross's clothes.

Isla put her hand to her mouth, tasting the saltiness of her own blood. Round it she said reassuringly, 'It's just a wee cut,' to the two frightened little faces peering up at her in the wall-bed's gloom. She wound her hand-kerchief around the cut to stop the bleeding. They all stayed in the wall-bed that night, for Isla was afraid to put Ross into his cot. The children went to sleep quickly, but Isla lay awake, jumping at the slightest noise from outside, her mind conjuring up alarming pictures of people smashing the door down, robbing her, harming the children. Her hand throbbed all through the night.

Isla had been going to Flora Currie's house in Castlehead every morning as usual, and had managed to persuade Ross to say nothing about the trouble in George Street.

The day after the window was smashed was a Saturday, and after boarding the broken window up with cardboard, Isla took the children to Flora's, braving the walk along George Street, under hostile eyes. It was a relief to turn the corner into Maxwellton Street.

Barbara had been safely tucked away in her classroom during the week. Now, as they passed the West Station and made for the gate in the wall, Isla did her best to tactfully suggest to her daughter that nothing should be said about what had happened in George Street. Barbara, looking forward to being cosseted by Annie and as glad as Isla was to get away from the unfriendliness in George Street for a little while, agreed cheerfully.

Ainslie, who had become a regular caller at Castlehead, was already in the house when Isla arrived, and so was Phil. His sharp eyes fell on the bandaged hand at once. 'Been in the wars?' he asked, and before she could say a word, Barbara, completely forgetting all that she had promised, launched into a dramatic story about the broken window.

Flora tutted. 'Those children that throw stones! Do their mothers never think to teach them how dangerous it is?'

'It was a man,' Barbara chirruped. 'I heard him

shouting, "Nobody wants your sort here!"' Her clear little voice dropped to mimic the harsh taunt she had heard the day before.

'A man?' Flora asked. 'Why would a man do a thing like that?'

'It's because my daddy didn't give them the tenement,' Barbara explained, ignoring her mother's glare. 'The folk are all angry with us, and nobody'll . . .' She stopped and gave a gulp, then went on, her voice wobbling slightly, 'Nobody'll play with me and Ross—'

She stopped as Phil jumped to his feet, staggered, clutched at a chair, then limped theatrically towards the door, opening it then clutching at it for support.

'Oh, my leg – it's gone again,' he said dramatically. 'Barbara, would you and Ross go to the kitchen and ask Miss Annie if she knows what I did with my spare wooden leg?'

'You haven't got a wooden leg,' Barbara said, the threatening tears vanishing.

'Sure I have. I've got two, and this one's giving out on me. Tell Miss Annie that I think I might have left it in the biscuit tin,' he called after them as they scampered out, giggling.

'You'll drive Annie daft with your silliness,' Flora told him as he closed the door.

'Not her, she loves a bit of fun. Now . . .' Phil came back into the room, his face suddenly grim. 'What's going on, Isla?'

'It's nothing important.'

'Sounds pretty important to me.'

'She's not been herself for the past week,' Flora fretted, 'but I didn't want to pry.'

'I think you should pry,' Phil told her. 'I think it's time we all pried.'

'It's not your worry.'

'Nonsense. Anything that harms you and your bairns is my worry. Out with it.'

'Better do as the lady says,' Phil drawled. 'She can be mean when she puts her mind to it.'

'I wish Agnes could have met you, Philip. She'd have loved you! Come on, now,' Flora added with a change of tone, and Isla shrugged helplessly and started to talk.

'They can't treat you like that,' Phil exploded when she finished. 'Who do they think they are?'

'You should go to the police,' Ainslie chimed in, and Flora nodded.

'I certainly will not. They're hurt because I deceived them, and I can't say that I blame them.'

Phil's eyes were blazing with suppressed fury. 'You don't blame someone for smashing your window and terrorising your kids?'

'No – I mean yes – I mean,' Isla said helplessly, looking at her friends' tense faces. 'The trouble is that now they think I'm wealthy, when I'm not. I'm no better off than they are. It'll blow over.'

'You think so? And how many broken windows d'you think it'll take?' Phil made for the door, but Ainslie's voice stopped him in his tracks.

'Going to George Street and making a fuss won't help matters, nor will reporting it to the police. It'll only make things worse for Isla and the children. They'll have to move out.'

'I can't afford to move!'

'Colin's father owns property in Paisley. He might have a flat you could rent.'

'It'd have to be the same rent as the place I'm in now. I didn't make much money from the sale of the tenement, and part of that went to pay for the repairs. We'll have to live on the rest until Ross goes to school and I'm free to look for a job.'

'You've already got a job, doing up those dolls' houses.'

'That doesn't bring in much, Phil,' Ainslie said absently, staring into space, her neat brows drawn together in thought.

'Why don't you move in here? There's enough room.'

Isla reached out to pat Flora Currie's hand. 'It's kind of you, but I'm not going to impose two active children on you.'

'I love the bairns!'

'I know you do, but they're more lovable in small doses, believe me.'

'What are we all fretting about?' Phil said. 'There's my aunt's house, lying empty right next door.'

'I couldn't afford to pay rent on a house that size!'

'Who said anything about rent? I need to sell it and get back home. I'm not interested in renting.'

'Then it's out of the question.'

'You already made an offer for it a few weeks ago.'

'Phil, that was just a bit of fun!'

'What was it again?'

'Five shillings, and that's still as much as I could—'

'Done.' The Canadian strode over to take Isla's hand and shake it firmly. 'You've got yourself a deal, Mrs Moffatt.'

'But—'

'Don't tease the lassie, Philip,' Flora snapped, but Ainslie, her eyes bright, touched the older woman's arm.

'Wait a minute, Miss Currie, I don't believe he's teasing her at all. You mean it, don't you, Phil?'

'We shook hands on it. I've never in my life gone back on a handshake.'

'But . . .' Isla said again, feeling as though the world had been turned upside down like a snow scene in a glass ball. 'You can't sell a house for five shillings!'

'Sure I can. I can do anything I want, as long as it's not breaking the law. Listen, I've got everything I want back home – well, almost everything,' Phil added, with a swift sidelong glance at Ainslie, who coloured slightly and looked away. 'I didn't come over here to make money out of my great-aunt's death, I came to try to make up in some way for not having come over earlier, while she was still alive. I reckon that having folks like you and your redheads living in her house, and you working in it at those dolls' houses, is as good a way as any of making amends.'

'Isla, you could put a room aside for your dolls'-house work,' Ainslie said excitedly.

'Great, I've got an ally!' Phil put an arm about her shoulders. Even in her confusion, Isla noticed that Ainslie didn't break the contact as before, but stayed within his casual embrace.

'Well now, Isla,' said Flora Currie, sounding as dazed as Isla felt, 'it looks as though you've just bought yourself somewhere else to live.'

25

Isla had fully expected Colin Forbes and his father to show Phil Hannigan the error of his ways, and explain to him how ridiculous his scheme was. But to her surprise, both men were willing to let the five-shilling sale go through, though Colin was tight-lipped.

'Mr Hannigan has quite made up his mind that this is what he wants, and therefore it stands as a proper business arrangement,' Gilchrist Forbes said. 'For your part, it's clearly advantageous, and the papers will be drawn up as soon as possible. I understand that Mr Hannigan wants them to be signed as soon as possible, and the matter brought to a conclusion.'

'But I can't just buy a house that size for five shillings!'

'Normally, I would agree with you, but this is not a normal transaction. For five shillings, the house is yours. And from what Ainslie and Colin tell me,' the lawyer added, 'the sooner you move out of George Street and into Castlehead, the better.'

The George Street folk gathered to watch the 'flitting' in sullen silence. Both Phil and Colin were there to help carry Isla's few pieces of furniture out to the van that had been hired for the occasion, and their presence acted as a deterrent to those who might have made something of the occasion.

As the van drew away from the kerb and Phil helped Isla and the children into Colin's car, Mrs Leach, who had been standing by the close watching every move, said loudly, 'Good riddance tae bad rubbish!'

The tall Canadian immediately turned, cupping a hand behind his ear. 'I didn't quite catch that, ma'am, you've got such a quiet voice,' he said politely. 'Can you speak a little louder?'

Mrs Leach went crimson as some of the onlookers tittered, and flounced back into the close with a loud sniff. The titters strengthened into a laugh as she disappeared. The George Street folk had united against someone they saw as an outsider, but on the other hand, Mrs Leach herself wasn't popular, and many of them relished the sight of her being bested.

Phil had insisted on including the furniture still in the house in the deal, pointing out that Isla herself had said that it belonged there, and Flora donated two small beds from her attic for the children. Ross was overcome with excitement at having a real bed, instead of a cot that had become too short for him.

Isla, who was living in a daze, had thought of turning the small room beside the kitchen into her workroom, but Ainslie talked her into taking one of the two big front rooms instead.

'You may well end up with quite a lot of work, and if so, you'll need the space,' she pointed out. Isla, seeing the sense of her argument, decided that one front room should be the living-room while the other, formerly the dining-room, became a workroom. She would have no need for a separate room to eat in, the kitchen was as large as the room she and the children had lived in at George Street. She took one of the three bedrooms upstairs, and put both children into another room. It was too soon for Ross to be on his own. Once he was old enough, he could move into the smallest bedroom.

'As far as they're concerned, the most exciting place in the house is the bathroom,' she said wryly to Ainslie, who had insisted on helping her to get the workroom ready. Annie was making up beds upstairs, with the children hindering more than helping. 'I can see that I'm going to have trouble keeping Ross away from that running water.'

Ainslie, whisking a handbrush along the skirting board, sat back on her heels and looked round the room. 'This place has so much space. I never noticed until recently how dark and crowded our house is.' She hesitated, then said slowly, 'My aunt's here from the Border on a visit. She's suggested finding a small place there for Mother, so that they can see more of each other.'

'D'you think she'll agree?'

'I think she feels the same way I do – that that house has too many memories. She and her sister always got on well. I believe Mother would be the better for a move.'

'What will you do? Go with her, or stay in Paisley?'

'Mother and I both know that we can't share a house. As to staying in Paisley . . .' Ainslie hesitated again, fidgeting with the brush in her hands.

A sudden thought struck Isla, but it was so delicate that she daren't put it into words, in case she blundered. Instead she kept her voice light when she said, 'Phil's going to see what Mr Blayne has in the way of long tables and a good chest of drawers for this room. I shall miss him when he goes back to Canada.' She sneaked a glance at Ainslie. 'He's very good at knowing just how to make people happy, isn't he?'

'Yes, he is.' Ainslie looked up, her lips curved into a determined, but wavering, smile, her eyes sparkling. 'Isla . . .'

Isla decided that she wouldn't be blundering after all. 'He's asked you to go to Canada with him. He's asked you to marry him!' Then, as Ainslie nodded and burst into tears, Isla dropped to the floor beside her and hugged her. 'That's wonderful!'

Ainslie caught and held her so tightly that she felt her ribs creak.

'No it's not, it's ridiculous!' she wept into Isla's neck. 'I said – I swore – that I'd never marry. And I meant it! I scarcely know him – I might hate living with him in Canada!'

'That's not what you said when you were trying to persuade me to consider it.'

'Yes, but you're you and I'm . . .' Ainslie gave a huge sniff and sat back, scrubbing a wrist across her face just like a child. She was so like Barbara, Isla thought. Even when they cried, they both looked beautiful. 'I'm such a difficult person, Isla, such a mixture. I'd probably be a terrible wife!'

'Phil doesn't seem to think so.'

'I might not even l-like Canada!'

'You're quite right. It's all ridiculous, and you'd both be very unhappy, and Canada will probably turn out to be the most dreadful place on earth.'

'Isla!'

'Ainslie! If you love the man, marry the man!'

Ainslie burst into tears again and, this time, Isla joined her. They sat on the floor, in each other's arms, and cried their eyes out.

Ainslie McAdam and Philip Hannigan were married quietly in Oakshawhill Church on a crisp, sunny December day, just before Christmas, with Isla and Colin as their witnesses. The date of their wedding had been carefully planned to ensure that eight days later, on the anniversary of Innes's death, Catherine and Ainslie would both have left Paisley, one moving to the borders, the other on her way to Canada with her new husband.

Colin watched impassively as Ainslie, beautiful in a suit of deep green with a huge sable collar and sable at the cuffs of her jacket and round the hem of her skirt, became Phil Hannigan's wife, and even managed a cheerful smile and a kiss for the bride as they left the church. Isla, watching, felt heart-sorry for the young man.

At Catherine's insistence, a small reception was held in the house. Isla, given her own way, would have gone back to Castlehead, where Annie was looking after the children, when the ceremony was over, but Ainslie and Flora both persuaded her to see the occasion through to the end. 'The children'll be fine with Annie, and I'm going to be at the reception,' Flora said. 'We'll be company for each other.'

Even so, Isla faltered at the front door, and might not have managed to step over the lintel if Colin Forbes hadn't taken her arm and drawn her into the long rectangular hall by his side, murmuring, 'If I can go through with the wedding, Isla, you can go through with the reception.'

It was the first time he had spontaneously used her given name, and Isla was so taken aback by the sound of it on his tongue that she was inside the house and being greeted by Flora, striking in a yellow and black dress beneath a black coat, before she knew it.

Catherine McAdam sat in state in the drawing-room, graciously receiving her daughter's guests. She proffered her cheek formally for Ainslie's kiss, then Phil's, only coming to life when Colin's turn came to greet her.

'My dear boy!' She took his hands in hers, smiling warmly up at him.

'This must be a very happy occasion for you, Mrs McAdam.' He bent to kiss her, then drew Isla forward. 'I'd like you to meet Mrs Isla Moffatt.'

Kenneth's first, legal wife and his second, unlawful wife looked into each other's faces, and Catherine's gaze swept over Isla without recognition. 'How d'you do.' She touched Isla's hand briefly, then turned back to Colin. 'Unfortunately, my daughter's chosen a Colonial,' she told him, her voice ringing out. 'She never does the right thing. But at least he's wealthy.'

There was an audible, collective gasp, as everyone within earshot swivelled towards the bridal couple, avid to record their reaction. The colour drained from Ainslie's face, and Isla sensed Colin tensing beside her, ready to jump to his former fiancée's defence. Then Philip Hannigan, an arm about Ainslie's shoulders, drawled in a voice just as clear and carrying as

Catherine's, 'Well I'll be darned. I thought that I was the one marrying money!'

Ainslie laughed, a peal of genuine, unselfconscious amusement, while Catherine stared coldly at her upstart new son-in-law and the cream of Paisley society blinked and murmured and bridled, sensing that it had just been mocked, and not sure what should be done about it.

'Phil's done that girl the world of good already,' Flora approved, arriving beside Isla. 'She's learning that cattiness doesn't matter, even when it comes from her own mother.'

Later, someone came and swept Flora away to meet someone else. Isla, on her own, sipped at the glass of champagne offered by one of the maids, looking around the drawing-room, trying to imagine the Kenneth she had known at home in it. It was impossible. There had been so many Kenneth McAdams.

'Mrs – Moffatt, isn't it?' Two stylishly dressed women bore down on her. 'The Mrs Moffatt who made that delightful *Little Women* house?'

'Yes, that's right.'

'Dolly McNair bought it from Leckie's toyshop,' the speaker informed her friend. 'It's really quite sweet. I wonder if you would do one for me?'

'I'd be happy to. If you let Mr Leckie know what you want, he'll pass the information on to me.'

'I'll do that,' the woman gushed, then, eyes sharpening, 'I understand that you bought Agnes McFall's house in Castlehead. For five shillings, someone told me, but of course they must have got it wrong.'

'Five shillings? Surely not,' her friend chimed in.

'My dear, I can assure you – the five-shilling mansion, people are calling it.'

'But nobody sells a house for that price – are we getting confused with your dolls' houses?'

Their eyes were bright, greedy with the desire for some lucrative gossip. Isla, taken aback by what she now realised had been a planned attack, stammered, her mouth going dry. She was looking from one face to the other, searching wildly for something to say when a hand closed on her arm and Colin Forbes said smoothly above her head, 'Pardon me, I couldn't help overhearing. Mrs Moffatt and Mr Hannigan came to a private agreement regarding the sale of his great-aunt's house, and as Mrs Moffatt's solicitor, I can assure you that everything was in order.' Then, turning his back on the two women, who had begun to quack out protests, 'Isla, my mother is anxious to meet you.'

Gilchrist Forbes stood by the window with a plump, maternal-looking woman.

'Mother,' Colin said, 'this is Isla Moffatt. I've just rescued her from that pair of nebby old crows.'

He jerked his head towards the women who had been talking to Isla, and Phemie Forbes, followed the movement, gave an outraged gasp. 'You're talking about two friends of mine. Gilchrist, speak to him!'

'Colin's too old to be spoken to, Phemie,' her husband said calmly. 'In any case, I'm more likely to agree with him than disagree. Mrs Moffatt, this is my wife.'

'Tchah!' Phemie glared at her menfolk, then turned her attention to Isla, her gaze swiftly evaluating the sage skirt and long tailored jacket with dark green trimmings that Ainslie had insisted on buying Isla for the wedding. She held out a ringed hand. 'How do you do, my dear. I hope you've settled into your new home?'

'We have. I think we're going to be very happy there.'

'I must say, though, that it's a very strange situation. Did you really only pay five—'

'Phemie!' her husband cut in hurriedly, while Colin said, 'I'd wondered where these old biddies got their information from.'

'Are you suggesting that . . .?'

'What, Mother?' Colin smiled down on the woman, who glared back at him. It was clear to Isla that there was affection between the three members of the Forbes family; it reminded her, achingly, of the bond there had always been between herself and her own parents.

'Men can be quite impossible, can't they?' Phemie turned to Isla to include her in the general conspiracy of womanhood, then her still-pretty features blurred and her eyes widened. 'I mean – that is . . .'

Suddenly, Isla knew that for all the older woman's apparent friendliness, in Phemie Forbes' eyes, she herself was outside the conspiracy, a woman apart, wife yet not wife, widow yet not widow.

It was a relief when Ainslie and Philip marked the end of the reception by leaving. They had decided to spend a few days on honeymoon before sailing to Canada. Catherine McAdam stayed in her chair, announcing that she was too tired to accompany her daughter and son-in-law to the gate. Once again, she accepted Ainslie's kiss without any show of emotion, and Phil's arm went protectively about his new wife as she turned to leave her home for the last time. She pressed her head briefly against his shoulder in recognition of his gesture, while Isla, watching, swore to herself that she would never allow anything to destroy her own small family as the McAdams had been destroyed.

As the couple made their farewells out on the driveway in a flurry of kisses and handshakes, the last of the day's sunlight struck rich copper glints from Ainslie's hair. At the gate, she left Phil's side to hug Isla.

'Write to me – long letters telling me every single thing that happens. And I'll write back, I promise. Kiss the children for me.'

She released Isla and turned to hug Colin as Phil caught Isla up in a brief embrace. 'Be happy in great-aunt Agnes's house,' he said.

As the car moved off, and Ainslie's hand fluttered from the window, the final rays of the sun sparkled on the gold wedding ring. Isla, hanging back from the press of people crowded at the gate and spilling on to the pavement, saw that Colin was beside her, his face expressionless.

'It must have been hard for you, today.'

He blinked down at her as though he had never seen her before, then his eyes cleared. Today, she saw, they were the green of deep water. 'I think she's married the right man. She's never looked at me the way she looks at him.'

The guests had started to move back towards the house. An involuntary shiver ran through Isla at the thought of going back inside.

'I think I'll just go home.'

'D'you mind if I walk with you?' Colin asked. 'I'd welcome a change of scene.'

'I don't expect to be long, Robert,' Phemie Forbes told her chauffeur as he opened the garden gate for her.

Walking up the flagged path between small neat lawns, each with its circular rosebed, she forced back the fluttery feeling that invaded her stomach and told herself that she was doing nothing wrong. She was merely safeguarding her son's interests; any good mother would do the same. She gave the bell-pull a smart tug, and almost at once saw movement through the stained-glass upper half of the door.

When it opened, Phemie, fully expecting a maidservant, was taken aback to see the lady of the house herself. Isla Moffatt, for her part, looked just as astonished to find Phemie on her doorstep, but quickly produced a welcoming smile.

'Mrs Forbes, what a pleasant surprise. I haven't seen you for some time. Please,' she stepped back, 'come in.'

'I've only dropped in for a moment,' Phemie said as she stepped inside and followed Isla into a room to the right of the hall, noting the young woman's blue crêpe de Chine blouse with a large bow at the throat, and the navy skirt that fitted snugly over slender hips, then flared out.

'You'll have some tea, of course.' As protocol dictated in the west of Scotland, the phrase was more of a statement than a question. It was a standard joke in the west that in the Edinburgh area, where the people were reputed to be more formal, the greeting to a casual caller was, 'You'll have had your tea?'

'I only called in for a few minutes . . .'

'But I was about to have one myself, and I'd welcome the company.'

'Well, perhaps a quick cup.' Phemie allowed her hostess to relieve her of her sealskin wrap.

'I'll not be a moment,' Isla promised, and hurried out.

Taking advantage of her absence, Phemie set about a close scrutiny of the room as she drew the gloves from her plump little hands. In the five years since moving to Castlehead, Isla Moffatt had done very well for herself. It had become the fashion in Paisley and further afield to have one of her dolls' houses on show in one's home. Many of Phemie's friends had bought them, and she herself had two, both presented to her by Colin. One was based on Haworth Hall, the home of the Brontë sisters, while each room in the other house depicted a scene from *Alice in Wonderland*.

Isla's home reflected her financial success. The room Phemie stood in was furnished in modern style, with walls of pale rose, not papered, but painted, and bearing only two paintings, whereas Phemie's drawing-room walls were crowded with pictures. Long curtains in a deeper shade of rose hung at the bay windows, and the carpet was patterned in rose and pale green against a creamy background. The wooden surrounds were highly polished, and the rest of the woodwork was cream. The soft, inviting sofa and chairs were covered with a rose and pale green patterned material, with small cream and gold cushions scattered over them.

The room was fragrant with the smell of roses from a large bowl on a table by the window. Their rich colours reflected in the table's gleaming surface, and they also filled another bowl set on the hearth, in front of the empty grate. Phemie recalled noticing more flowers in a tall vase in the hall, by a telephone.

The few pieces of furniture in the room were made of polished walnut, and the overall effect was one of space, light, colour and comfort.

The door opened. Caught in the act of studying the high ceiling, which, like the walls, was painted soft rose, Phemie jerked her chin down so sharply that pain shot through the back of her neck. 'Won't you sit down?' Isla put the tray down on a small table before the fireplace as Phemie sank into one of the chairs. It was extremely comfortable, and she wondered, a trifle grimly, how often her son had sat in this very same chair.

The tea service was patterned with geometrical shapes filled in with bold colours. It looked very like a dinner set that a friend of Phemie's had recently shown to her, boasting that it was designed by Clarice Cliffe, one of the leading designers of the day.

Isla talked about her garden as they drank their tea, apparently unaware of her guest's silence. Phemie, sneaking little glances over the rim of the cup that she was now quite certain must be Clarice Cliffe, recalled how sorry she had felt for the girl at Ainslie's wedding, with her pinched, sallow face. Feeling sorry for her, she had invited Isla and her children to her home several times, and had even begun to like the little family. But gradually, as she noted the growing friendship between Colin and Isla and began to sense problems ahead, the invitations had ceased, and for the past three years the two women had only encountered each other occasionally in the town, exchanging brief greetings and moving on.

Now, five years after their first meeting at the wedding, Isla's face was nicely rounded, her skin like smooth ivory, with just a touch of dusky rose over each cheekbone. Her brown eyes, once anxious and apprehensive, sparkled with life, and her dark hair fell sleekly to her jawline, curling inwards slightly at the bottom. She looked positively pretty, Phemie thought, with a pang that gave her the courage to introduce her reason for calling.

'I understand that your little houses are doing very well, Mrs Moffatt.'

If the younger woman had noticed the deliberate condescension in 'little houses', she gave no sign of it. 'I'm continually surprised by the number of orders that keep coming in,' she confessed with a smile. 'I fully expected interest to have fallen away quite early on.'

'My son tells me that they're even selling in England, and abroad.'

Isla picked up the teapot, then put it down again when Phemie gave a decisive shake of the head. 'Ainslie took some leaflets and photographs back to Canada with her the last time she and Phil were over here, and managed to obtain several orders for me, for both decorative and practical houses.'

'By practical, you mean houses that are to be played with, rather than to be put on show?' When Isla nodded, Phemie forged on. 'Several of my friends have bought your practical houses for their little granddaughters.' She smiled, a smile that didn't touch her eyes. 'I'm hopeful that one day soon I'll be able to give you a similar order.'

'Really?' Isla looked up, interested. 'Is Colin planning to marry?'

The time had come. Phemie drew in a deep breath and dusted an imaginary crumb from the lap of her tan woollen skirt. 'I thought you might know more about that than I do, Mrs Moffatt. He seems to spend a great deal of his time in this house. I expect he confides in you – since you're an older woman.'

The barb went home; she saw the colour in Isla Moffatt's cheeks deepen. 'He does call in frequently, but he's said nothing to me. And I'm quite sure that he doesn't keep secrets from you.'

Phemie's hand again whisked across her skirt. 'The fact is, Mrs Moffatt, my husband and I would both like to see our son settling down, instead of gallivanting around with this girl and that. He never used to be so – so flighty.'

Amusement danced into her hostess's eyes, and was suppressed. 'I never thought of Colin as being flighty,' she observed mildly.

'Nor I, until recently. I take it he talks to you about his thoughts, his hopes for the future?'

'From time to time, as friends do.'

Phemie pounced. 'Friends?'

Isla Moffatt regarded her for a moment, then said, 'You might as well speak your mind, Mrs Forbes, rather than dancing around your reason for calling.'

Phemie, who had been raised to believe that 'dancing around', as the younger woman put it, was the correct thing to do, blinked, then rallied. 'Very well, if you prefer it. It seems to us, Mrs Moffatt,' she stated, invoking Gilchrist's support, confident that if she had told him what was on her mind, he would have agreed with her, 'that Colin spends altogether too much time in this house. Folk are beginning to talk.'

'I'd have thought that with all the troubles in the world just now folk would have more to gossip about than friendships.'

'There's bound to be talk when one of the friends is a respectable young bachelor of good family, and the other an older woman with—'

'With a past?'

'With two growing children!' Phemie snapped. 'It's time Colin was settling down.'

Colour surged into Isla's face, and her hands, bare except for Kenneth McAdam's gold band on one finger – a ring he had had no right to put there, Phemie reminded herself – gripped the arms of her chair. 'I can assure you, Mrs Forbes, that there has been no talk of marriage between your son and myself. We've never even considered such a thing.'

'It's time Colin did consider it, and there are plenty of young women in Paisley who are eminently suitable.' Over the past five years Colin had brought some of them home – pretty girls of good family, just the right age to start bearing his children, and in many cases clearly willing to walk down the aisle of Paisley Abbey by his side. But one by one they had drifted away, married other women's sons, presented other women with grandchildren. 'You must tell him to stop calling and look elsewhere for his – friends,' Phemie said flatly, and Isla Moffatt put her cup down and got to her feet.

'Now that you've said what you came to say, Mrs Forbes, I think you should go.'

'I intend to.' Phemie began to struggle out of the chair, which showed a tendency to want to keep her within its soft depths. Eventually, she had to suffer the indignity of taking her hostess's proffered hand, and being helped to her feet.

In the hall, accepting her wrap, she said with as much dignity as she could muster, 'I hope that you'll pay heed to what I've had to say.'

'I can assure you of that,' said Isla Moffatt, opening the door.

Comfortable living had piled weight on Phemie Forbes as the years went by. As a result, her self-righteous, straight-backed march down the path to the waiting car appeared, from where Isla stood on the porch, more like the waddling of an elderly, contented bear; a bear with short legs and only a patch of gleaming fur left across the shoulders.

But Isla was in no mood to be amused by the thought. She was embarrassed, confused, and very angry, although she wouldn't for the world have let Colin's mother know that. As the car drove off with Phemie, in the back seat, resolutely staring ahead,

Barbara arrived at the gate, her schoolbag dangling from one hand, her skirt swirling round legs that seemed to be growing longer by the month. Ross was immediately behind her, and as Barbara opened the gate he tried to squeeze past. The two of them, jammed in the narrow gap, squabbled briefly before breaking free and scurrying up the garden path, both starting to talk about their day at school as soon as they saw their mother standing on the porch.

They were unmistakably Kenneth McAdam's children, Isla thought as she watched them come towards her. Although twelve-year-old Barbara's eyes were brown, like her own, her expressions were Kenneth's. She also had his enthusiasm for life, and the same swinging, easy stride that had caused the breath to catch in Isla's throat the first time she saw Ainslie walking towards her. Isla's dark hair had tempered Kenneth's red-gold head to produce, in their daughter, a rich, striking auburn.

Ross had Kenneth's blazing red hair and pale skin and light blue eyes, and he also had the more serious side of his father's nature. There were times, when he pulled at his lower lip and drew his brows down in thought, when strong memories of the man she still thought of as her husband flooded back to Isla.

'That was Colin's mother, wasn't it?' Barbara asked as she reached the porch. 'I remember seeing him with her in the town.' Her gaze was direct, just like Kenneth's. 'What did she want?'

'She was just visiting.'

'Why?' asked Ross. 'She's never visited you bef—'

'Upstairs, the two of you, and change out of your

school clothes.' Isla scooped them before her into the house. 'I've got work to do.'

'I'm too weak with hunger to climb the stairs,' announced Barbara, who possessed an excellent appetite, yet never seemed to put on any weight. Her brother was already on his way to the kitchen, where Nan, who had moved in as housekeeper when Isla's work had begun to take up most of her time, would be putting out milk and scones. The children always came home from school hungry.

'Five minutes – then upstairs and get some work done before teatime,' Isla called after them, then went into her favourite room, the dolls'-house workshop opposite the living-room.

Its cream-painted walls were lined with counters holding a variety of miniature houses, boxes of materials, small pots of paint or glue, and books on furniture and fashions. In the window recess Mabel Torrance, the seamstress who had worked full-time for Isla for the past eighteen months, sat at one of the two sewing machines. She smiled at her employer, then went back to her work. Isla sat down at the desk in one corner, where she had been planning a new house when Colin's mother had interrupted her.

She picked up her pencil, put it down, and started riffling through one of the books, staring blankly at the pages without seeing them. Instead, Phemie Forbes' visit played itself over and over again in her mind, like one of the films she occasionally took the children to see.

The whole episode had been just like a film, she thought – unreal, the sort of thing that didn't really happen. Only it had happened. She gave up all pretence of looking for something, and let the book in front of her lie where it had fallen open. After Ainslie's departure for Canada, Colin, in the double role of Isla's lawyer and Ainslie's friend, had helped Isla to settle in the Castlehead house. He had advised her on business matters as the demand for her work grew, suggesting and drawing up a contract between her and Mr Leckie, the toyshop owner.

It was Colin who had suggested having leaflets advertising her work printed and distributed to attract more clients, Colin who had taught her how to cope with the paperwork as orders started to come direct to her home. He had somehow drifted into the habit of calling in once or twice a week, occasionally taking them out in his car, even helping now and again with homework. As Ross grew from toddler to schoolboy, Colin had become, in some ways, the father-figure Ross had never known.

But nothing more than a friend. In the years following Ainslie's departure for Canada, he had plunged into the local social life and, to his mother's delight, had become one of the town's most eligible bachelors, often bringing the latest conquest to visit Isla and see the dolls' houses.

'It's more comfortable here,' he had said when she pointed out that his mother might prefer to play hostess to his friends. 'Mother would pry and simper, and probably start planning wedding outfits. Anyway, I need someone like you to tell me who should be taken to meet her, and who should be kept well away from her.'

After each introduction, he inevitably asked for Isla's

opinion of the latest girl. She enjoyed meeting them all, and became genuinely fond of one or two, but steadfastly refused to criticise any of them, insisting that he must make his own judgements. After a few weeks, or, at most, a few months, the current girl would disappear, to be replaced by someone else.

'She was too possessive,' Colin would say vaguely, sprawling at his ease in Isla's comfortable living-room. Or, 'She giggled too much,' or perhaps, 'She began to get that engagement-ring gleam in her eyes.'

'You must stop comparing them all with Ainslie,' Isla told him one day, and he stared at her, astonished.

'You think I do that?'

'Of course you do. It's not fair to them, Colin. People deserve to be judged on their own merits.'

'Mmmm,' Colin said, and gradually, fewer girl-friends had been brought to Castlehead for Isla's inspection. She hadn't even realised that, until now.

'People are bound to talk – a respectable young bachelor of good family – an older woman . . .' Phrases the older woman had used came back to her as she stared down at the open book, taking on new meaning, turning an easy, happy friendship into something suspect and distasteful.

'I'll see you tomorrow morning, Mrs Moffatt.' Isla came back to the present with a jerk. Mabel was covering the sewing machine, which meant that it was five o'clock.

'Yes, Mabel, thanks.' She rubbed a hand over her eyes, then panic flared through her as she heard a man's voice in the hall, talking to Mabel. Colin sometimes looked in on his way home from the office.

Isla stood up, almost knocking the book to the ground. She couldn't face him now – she needed time to think things through—

But when the door opened it was Drew Brown who came in, pulling his jacket on over his overalls. 'That's me away home. I've varnished the table, it'll be dry by tomorrow.' He looked down at the open book and gave a low whistle. 'That'll take some work. Still, I reckon I could manage it.'

Isla, glancing down, saw that the book had fallen open at the picture of an elaborate three-seated chair in green velvet.

'I've not decided, Drew, so don't worry your head about it yet.' She closed the book. 'You go off and enjoy your evening at the theatre with Mary.'

'I will. G'night, then.' He went off, whistling cheerfully.

Only days after Isla had left George Street, Drew had come shyly to Castlehead to offer to go on making furniture for her.

'I'd not want to get you into trouble with your neighbours, Drew.'

'Ach, what happened was just a storm in a teacup. My mam and me both think it's only right for me tae go on helping ye, seeing as it was you that got our roof fixed,' he had said, standing in the hall, twisting his cap round and round in his hands. 'Anyway, I like making the wee furniture.'

For three years he had worked for Isla in the evenings and weekends. As the orders began to flow in she had become increasingly dependent on the young man's talents, and when he was dismissed from the joinery shop after finishing his apprenticeship, Colin had suggested that she employ Drew herself.

He had scribbled figures on paper, convincing her that she could afford to pay Drew, suggesting that the carriage-house, still packed with its former owner's rubbish, could be pressed into service.

Between them, Drew and Colin had turned the carriage-house into a decent workshop, and Drew had settled in happily. Now, two years later, he had become an essential part of Isla's life, thanks to Colin.

Isla bit her lip realising that, unbidden, Colin had managed to steal back into her thoughts. He would have to go, not just from her mind, but from her life. It would be hard to turn her back on him, for although she knew a lot of people now – neighbours, clients, acquaintances – her only close friends were Colin, Ainslie, far away in Canada with her husband and twin sons, and Flora Currie, who had become frighteningly frail during the past year. But if, as his mother had said, folk were gossiping, a break had to be made. Since Kenneth's death, Isla had developed a dislike, almost a fear, of being talked about.

She heard the children leaping down the staircase on their way to the kitchen for tea, and was grateful beyond measure for their existence, their casual conviction that life would never change. As long as Ross and Barbara were in her world, she would never be alone, or lonely.

Cheered by that thought, Isla squared her shoulders and went out to meet her children in the hall.

27

With relief, Isla remembered during tea that that evening Colin, who had joined the Territorial Army as Britain uneasily watched the steady growth of strength and power in Germany, would be attending the weekly meeting in their headquarters, and wouldn't come to Low Road.

Too restless to sit and read after the evening meal, she went into the garden with the intention of tiring herself out with some brisk weeding. Ross was playing with several other boys in a garden further along the road, and as she worked, Isla could hear their voices on the soft evening air, while the beautiful, sad strains of 'Ol' Man River', floated from the open window of Barbara's room. A steady stream of girls, like a line of ants, had begun to converge on the house immediately after tea, trotting up the stairs to Barbara's room to rehearse yet another of her concerts.

Aunt Lally had died in 1934, leaving everything she had to Barbara and Ross. Isla had put the proceeds of the sale of the flat and the furniture, together with the little money her aunt had left, into trust for the children, but Barbara had insisted on keeping all Lally's scrapbooks and sheet music. A cupboard had had to be bought specially to house it all in her room. She used the music for her concerts, which had already raised considerable sums of money for various charities.

After her sudden, enforced move to Low Road, Isla had decided – largely on Colin's and Flora's advice – to keep Barbara at the West School, rather than unsettle the child by moving her elsewhere. Once they were away from George Street, the animosity Barbara had begun to experience in the school playground had ebbed away, and in no time at all she was bringing her former friends from the street home to play at the end of each school day.

Greta and, once she began to go to school, Daisy, were among the group. Only weeks after the 'flitting', Isla had encountered Magret in a shop, and her former neighbour had greeted her as though nothing had happened.

'Ach, life's too short tae bear a grudge,' she had declared, her face wreathed in smiles. 'It's only sour-faces like that Mrs Leach that never forget. Mrs Leach, and elephants, eh?'

Since then, Magret had called in at Low Road now and again, refusing to sit anywhere but in the kitchen, where she and Isla and, eventually, Nan, enjoyed many a cosy gossip over a cup of tea. With Daisy at school, Magret had gone back to work in the mills, only five minutes' walk from Low Road. She was saving hard in the hope of moving to a better house. There was a good chance, being overcrowded, that the McDougalls would get a house in the new scheme at Ferguslie Park, but Magret wanted to stay near the mills and near her friends and neighbours. She had her eye on a rented flat further along George Street, on the other side of Maxwellton Street.

In June, Barbara's stint at the West School had come to an end, and now, in early September, she and Greta had just started attending Camphill Secondary School. Most of the Low Road children were attending the John Neilston Institution or the Grammar School, both fee-paying, but Barbara insisted on staying with her former classmates, and Isla, who would have found it difficult to pay school fees as well as wages for Drew and Mabel, had been content to go along with her daughter's wishes.

All Barbara asked of her friends was that they were willing to take part in her back-court concerts, now back-garden concerts. As a result, the children who marched up the path most evenings and weekends were a mixture from the Paisley schools, and at each of Barbara's concerts, held in the garden in fine weather and the living-room in bad weather, mothers from comfortable homes and cramped tenements gossiped and laughed and applauded side by side.

Isla straightened up, rubbing at her back. It was almost dark now, and the house-lights looked inviting. There was just a touch of autumn in the air, the slightest hint of approaching winter. As she gathered up her trowel and fork and locked them in the little shed, then walked down the path towards the house, the turmoil Phemie Forbes had caused began to fade away.

'I don't know, Drew,' Isla said the next day, studying the sketches Drew had made of the three-seater chair he had seen in the furniture book the day before. 'It looks very complicated to me.'

Glancing up at Drew, she could tell by the gleam in his eyes that he had already made up his mind. Drew loved a challenge.

'Not when you think of it piece by piece. It'd look bonny in that fancy house you're doing for – oh hullo, Mr Forbes.'

Isla, taken off guard, spun round to see Colin leaning against the frame of the open carriage-house door, grinning at her. 'What are you doing here at this time of day?' she asked sharply, and his eyebrows rose.

'I'm running the old man home for some lunch because his own car's having some work done on it. I thought I'd look in and ask if you and the kids want to go to the Regal tonight.'

'John Gilbert,' Drew said enthusiastically. 'I've seen it, it's good.'

'No, I don't think so.'

'It's Friday – no school tomorrow.'

'We're already going out.'

'Where?'

'Just out.' She bustled Colin out of the workshop, blinking in the sunshine. 'Look, I'm really busy, and your father's waiting . . .'

'Is there something up?'

'Of course not.'

'Then come to the cinema. The kids'll enjoy it—'

'I told you, I'm busy, we're going out.' She had managed to get him as far as the gate, but as she moved to open it, Colin put his hand on the top rail, preventing her.

'There *is* something wrong.'

'It's nothing – just . . .' she wavered, then said in a

326

rush of words, 'you spend too much time with us, Colin.'

This time his eyebrows soared. 'I enjoy your company, and Barbara's, and Ross's.'

'But we've all got our own lives to lead. We can't be in each other's pockets all the time.' She glanced up at him, and saw the smile die out of his eyes.

'In other words, I've outstayed my welcome.'

'Colin, I'm very grateful for all you've done for me – for us – but—'

'But you'd prefer not to be – pestered.'

'I didn't say . . .' Isla began, then, realising that he had offered her a way out of her dilemma, and she must take it, she said lamely, 'well, yes.'

'You should have said something.'

'I just have,' she said to a spot just beyond his right shoulder.

'So you have.' His voice was cold now. She risked a swift glance at him, and saw that he was looking at her just as he had at their very first meeting. Then, she hadn't understood why. Now, she did.

'Colin, I really am very grateful for—'

'Good day, Isla,' he said, and turned away, striding out of the garden and along the road towards the gate that led to the main road and his car and his father and his real life.

It was over, just like that. She had expected an argument, perhaps even a quarrel, but now she realised that that wasn't Colin's way. He had his pride, and if he felt that he wasn't wanted, that was that. It had happened swiftly and easily, and as she turned back to the carriage-house and Drew, she told herself that she should be glad of that, at least.

Before she reached the carriage-house, the sun had gone in behind a cloud.

A week dragged by. The invigorating tingle that had been in the air as summer's dying blended with winter's approach vanished, washed away by drizzling, constant rain. Barbara and Ross came home from school each day soaked to the skin, and squabbled a lot because Ross hated to be indoors all the time. Drew was depressed because the little Victorian loveseat had proved to be too difficult for him after all, and a very particular customer made a fuss over a dolls' house that wasn't ready on the agreed date. It seemed to Isla that everything was going wrong, and the low cloud and persistent rain made her feel tired and despondent.

The previous winter had laid both Flora and Annie low with 'flu; Flora had battled her way through it, but despite all that Isla and the doctor could do, Annie had developed pneumonia and died.

Isla had found another housekeeper, kindly and efficient, but although the woman did everything she could to make Flora comfortable and content, it wasn't the same, and a lot of Flora's old fire and drive had evaporated.

'It's the fighting I miss,' she confided in Isla when she paid her usual daily visit. 'Whenever I snap at Betty her lip trembles and she almost turns cartwheels trying to please me. Annie knew how to give as good as she got.' Her green eyes, still lovely although the sparkle had gone from them, were wistful. 'You know you're still alive when you're having a good quarrel.'

Then she leaned forward in her chair and fixed her

gaze on Isla. 'You've heard my grouse against life, now tell me yours.'

'I don't have any, other than being tired of this wet weather.'

'Something's been troubling you for the past week, lassie, and it's not the rain. Anyone living in this part of the world should be used to that. Come on now, what is it?'

'It's nothing.'

'Fiddlesticks! But if you won't say, you won't. Go ahead and treat me like a stranger, see if I care,' Flora said with an echo of the little girl she had once been.

'You do so care,' Isla mimicked the childish note in the old woman's voice, and Flora grinned at her.

'Of course I do, you daft lassie. Is that not what friends are for?'

'I'm just being silly. Colin's mother called on me last week and she's got some daft notion in her head that I'm getting in the way of him finding himself a suitable wife. It upset me a bit.'

Flora snorted. 'Phemie Forbes was always kind-hearted, I'll give her that, but as thick as a plank, even as a young woman. You're surely not going to take any heed of what she says?'

'Flora, she said that folk have started to talk. I don't want to be the subject of gossip, I've had my share of that.'

'Gossip should always be ignored, even if it's telling the truth,' Flora said blithely. 'Have you talked to Colin about this?'

'I've spoken to him, but I couldn't bring myself to tell him what his mother had said. I just said that I didn't want him to come to the house so often.'

'That's a fine thing to say to a man whose got his pride. So he's not been back since?'

'No.'

'I'm not surprised. So that's why you've been going about with a face like a wet washing. You're missing him.'

'I'm not – but I enjoy his company, and the children like him. They've been asking about him, and I don't know what to tell them. I didn't mean that he shouldn't come at all, just that he shouldn't come so often.' Under the steady green gaze, Isla floundered, then said feebly, 'Mebbe I didn't make myself clear.'

'And mebbe you don't even know what you want yourself,' Flora said dryly.

'I just want to live my life in peace, without folk talking about me.' Isla got to her feet and roamed about Flora's drawing-room restlessly. 'Oh, I wish his mother had never come near me!'

'Poor Phemie.'

'Why? She's got what she wanted. She must be really pleased with herself.'

'For the moment, mebbe. But she'd have been well advised to tend to her own business and let Colin tend to his. He's old enough. Sometimes,' said Flora, 'if you throw a stone in the wrong place, it comes bouncing back and hits you. Phemie should have thought about that before opening her mouth.'

Mercifully, the rain stopped on the following day and the weather brightened. Over the next two days the sun, together with a fresh, drying wind, made it possible for the once-a-week gardener Isla employed to gather up the fallen leaves and old vegetation and burn them at the bottom of the garden. The bonfire smouldered all afternoon, scenting the air with its smoke, and after the children had gone to bed Isla went out to make sure that it had died down.

Dawdling back up towards the house, she stopped halfway to sink down on to the swing that Colin had put up for the children years earlier, resting her heels on the grass and letting the swing drift to and fro, trying to slough off the lethargy that was still troubling her.

She was just beginning to feel the tension easing from her body when a voice from the darkness said, 'Isla Moffatt, just what the hell are you playing at?'

Her startled reaction sent the swing spinning, and she might have hit her shoulder against the wooden supports if Colin hadn't caught at the ropes and steadied her. Still holding them, standing so close that she could smell the familiar, comforting smell of soap and tobacco from him, he said again, 'What are you playing at?'

'What are you talking about?'

'Don't pretend. Did Ross not tell you I met him this afternoon?'

'No.' Trapped by his body, she had to crane her head back painfully to look up at him.

'He stopped to watch me playing cricket on his way home from school. I went over to talk to him and he happened to mention that my mother had called on you last week – the day before you decided that you didn't want me hanging around any more.'

His head was a dark mass, surrounded, from her viewpoint, by stars. 'I did not say—'

He gave the ropes a little shake, and the swing jiggled. Their knees were pressed together, and she could feel the warmth of his legs against hers. 'That's what it sounded like. I thought . . .' he stopped, then said, 'I thought you must have met someone, some man.'

'It was nothing to do with another man! You've been very good to us, Colin, but you've got your own life to live, and your own friends and interests—'

'And my own right to choose my friends?'

'Yes, but . . .'

'Thank you for that concession, at least.' At last he released the ropes and took a turn away from her, towards the edge of the lawn.

'Poor Mother,' Colin said out of the darkness as Isla got up from the swing, rubbing at the back of her neck, 'she never could understand that actions must have consequences.'

A breeze rustled the bushes and Isla shivered. 'I'm going indoors. D'you want some tea?' she asked automatically.

'I want you to hear me out first. You listened to my mother, so it's only fair that you listen to me.' Colin took her place on the swing. 'It wasn't until Ross told me about Mother's visit that I realised how wise she had been.'

'Wise?'

He edged the swing seat back until he was almost upright, supported by his feet on the ground. 'Very wise. She'd sensed something that I hadn't, fully. That I'm in love with you.'

'You – what?' Isla couldn't have been more astonished if the stars had suddenly swooped down to turn the garden into a circus ring.

'Think about it, Isla. Would I have kept coming here all those years if I didn't love you?'

'That's nonsense,' she said briskly, sounding, to her own ears, just like Flora. 'You think of me as a – an older sister. Why else would you bring all your girlfriends to this house and ask for my opinion about them?'

'Exactly. I put that very question to myself, and the answer was so obvious that I can't think why neither of us saw it before. You once accused me of looking for another Ainslie, remember?'

'Yes,' Isla said cautiously.

'Yet none of the girls I brought here were redheads, were they? They were all dark, like you. I suppose,' Colin mused, 'that I must have been making comparisons, and each time I found the others lacking, and stopped seeing them. The only woman I kept on seeing was you, Isla Moffatt, because the only woman I wanted to see was you – and my clever little mother was the first to see it.'

'Have you been drinking?'

'Not a drop. Oh, I thought about it, after you sent me away and I thought that perhaps you'd found someone else. But I didn't get around to it, thank God. Nor did I realise why I felt so miserable until I met up with young Ross. Talk about babes and sucklings,' said Colin with sudden jubilation. 'I'm going to take that lad out on Saturday and buy him a Knickerbocker Glory, whether you approve or not.'

'You have been drinking! And I'm going indoors n—'

Colin lifted both feet and the swing, released, soared through the air. As it reached the end of its curve, he let the ropes go and landed lightly in front of Isla, who was turning towards the house. Before she had time to utter more than a faint squeak, she had been spun round and into his arms.

Her first thought was that it was all wrong to be kissed by a man who was almost like a brother. Her second thought, arriving almost immediately on the heels of the first, was how wonderful it was to be kissed passionately after all those years of abstinence, and to want to dissolve in the kiss and return it fourfold.

'It's all wrong,' she said shakily when he finally released her.

'No it isn't, it's all very right,' Colin whispered, and kissed her again.

'You're younger than I am,' she protested a few minutes later.

'Only by a couple of years. And before you think of any more objections, let me say that I like your children, and I'd enjoy being their stepfather. Think about young Ross, surrounded by women,' he urged, his mouth moving against her ear, sending ripples of desire through her awakening body. 'It's your duty to bring a man into his life, and I'm recommending myself for the position. Officially, on Forbes and Son headed office notepaper, if you insist.'

'Your father—'

'Who cares?' Colin kissed her again, and again she melted into his arms, her mouth softening and opening beneath his. The past week's depression had vanished, to be replaced by joy that seemed to bubble up from the depths of her body to fill her with golden fire.

'Your mother,' she protested weakly, 'will be dreadfully upset.'

'I'll buy her a Knickerbocker Glory too,' Colin promised. 'If it wasn't for her, heaven knows how long it would have taken us to realise how much we needed each other.'

'You can't be serious,' Phemie Forbes whimpered the next morning, a piece of toast falling from her fingers.

Colin beamed at her. 'I've never been more serious in my life, Mother.'

'But – an older woman, with two children! A woman who's—'

'Who's what? Who's struggled against incredible odds to raise her family with no help from anyone? A woman who's built up a business and earned respect from the community?'

'She's tricked you into this!'

'I'm thirty-two years old, Mother. If I was as easily led as you seem to think, I'd have been married to some scheming minx years ago. As for being tricked, it took me some time to talk Isla into accepting me.'

'Gilchrist,' Phemie appealed frantically, 'make him come to his senses before it's too late!'

'You've already done that yourself, Mother,' Colin told her, then, as she stared blankly, 'because of your visit, she sent me packing, and that was when I realised how much I wanted to be with her. I'll never be able to thank you enough for that.'

'Gilchrist!' Phemie almost screamed through the lacy handkerchief clutched to her mouth. 'I demand that you speak to your son!'

'My dear, Colin's old enough to make his own decisions,' Gilchrist Forbes pointed out, then, as the door slammed behind his wife, he laid down his fork and sighed. 'God knows if she'll ever get over this.'

'She'll have to. I meant what I said, Father, I won't give Isla up.'

The older man's brow was furrowed. 'Colin, you'll be taking on all the responsibilities of a ready-made family. Are you quite sure that Isla Moffatt means that much to you?'

'I've no doubt of it. I'd like you both to be happy for me, but if needs be, I can do without your approval. I'm going to marry Isla, as soon as possible.'

Gilchrist pushed back his chair, eyeing his half-eaten breakfast with regret. 'In that case,' he said, 'the sooner I can bring Phemie round to the idea, the better.'

28

Isla opened her eyes to darkness and the soft murmuring of the River Clyde breaking against the shore across the road from the Helensburgh hotel where she and Colin had spent their three-day honeymoon. In a few hours they would be on their way back to Paisley, back to Low Road and the children and their new life together.

Although their bodies weren't touching in the large bed she could feel his warmth lapping against her just as the broad river outside lapped the shore. Isla smiled drowsily and wriggled across the mattress until she could feel his body against hers. In spite of the chill November weather they had had three wonderful days, walking and driving together, talking, laughing, getting to know each other in an entirely new way. And there had been three wonderful nights, too, rediscovering the joy of lying in a man's arms, of loving and being desirable and loved, a luxury that she had thought would never be hers again.

They had been married quietly in the vestry of Oakshaw West Church, the church Colin's parents worshipped in, with Barbara and Ross present, and Mabel and a friend of Colin's standing as witnesses. They

337

would have liked Ainslie and Phil to be their witnesses, but the Hannigans' twin sons had just started school, and Ainslie was reluctant to leave them with Phil's sister at such a time.

The reception had been held at Low Road. Phemie Forbes, who had no option but to accept the marriage once she realised that her son wasn't going to change his mind, had wanted to hold the reception in her home, but Colin refused.

'Miss Currie isn't strong enough to go to Stanley Drive, and we both want her to be there, so it has to be in Low Road,' he said firmly, and Phemie had no option but to give in, and be a guest at the home of her new daughter-in-law.

'You look very – pretty, my dear,' she said graciously, eyeing the pale blue wool and angora dress that Barbara had helped Isla to choose. Barbara had insisted on the hat to go with it – a slouched felt decorated with a jaunty curve of dark blue feathers. Isla had settled it at an angle on her dark head with foreboding, but when she saw the look in Colin's eyes when she stepped from the hired car at the church, she knew that Barbara had been right.

Phemie presented a powdered cheek, and Isla dutifully kissed it, knowing that Colin's mother would never fully accept her as a member of the Forbes family.

Flora, on the other hand, had regained all her former animation for the wedding reception, her cheeks flushed and her green eyes sparkling. 'I knew you two were right for each other,' she said smugly, surveying the couple before her. Colin, laughing, put an arm about his wife's shoulders.

'I wish you'd told me, then, instead of letting me waste all those years blundering about in the dark.'

'Och, I knew you'd find out for yourself eventually. Best to let things work out naturally. Anyway, you've got the rest of your lives together.'

Isla, recalling the words in the dark hotel room, smiled drowsily and brushed her lips against her husband's warm, naked shoulder. He wakened at once, turning over to scoop her into his arms. His face, already scratchy with the night's growth, snuggled against her neck.

'What time is it?'

'Go to sleep,' she whispered. 'It's not morning yet.'

'Good.' His hands slid over the silky nightdress she wore, rousing her body to an instant response. As they met and merged in the bed's warm nest, Isla felt that nothing could ever hurt her again.

In the summer of 1938, Catherine McAdam took a bad stroke and Ainslie, summoned to Scotland, arrived too late to see her mother. After the funeral she and Phil, together with their twin sons, came to Paisley.

'If I'm honest, the only emotion I have is pity,' Ainslie told Isla during one of their long talks together. 'She wouldn't let me love her, but she couldn't stop me from feeling sorry for her. She didn't really have much of a life, did she?'

'By her own choice. She could have got some pleasure out of seeing Mike and Jamie.' Isla had been appalled to hear that when Ainslie offered to bring her sons on a visit while they were still small, Catherine had refused. Ainslie had never made the offer again.

Now, she shrugged. Over the past seven years, she had absorbed much of Phil's easy-going nature. She was more relaxed than Isla had ever seen her, happy in her marriage, and delighted with her active sons. 'That was just Mother. I never could understand her, any more than she could understand me.' She stretched luxuriously. 'Isn't the house lovely and quiet?'

'For once,' Isla agreed. Phil had taken all four children down to the seaside for the day, and Colin was at work. The two women were in the kitchen, Ainslie sitting at the table, Isla icing a cake for the twins, who were to celebrate their sixth birthday in Scotland.

'What affected me most, after the funeral, was realising that I'm the only one left. There we were, the four of us, Mother and Father and me and poor little Innes – I thought that we were there for ever, and now there's only me.'

'And Phil, and Jamie, and Mike,' Isla reminded her. The boys were clearly Phil's sons, wiry and cheerful, but they both had their mother's blue eyes, and Jamie, the younger and slightly smaller twin, had red glints in his thick brown hair.

'And Barbara, and Ross,' Ainslie said. 'I'm their half-sister, remember?' She hesitated, then said carefully, 'They don't know about their father yet, do they?'

'Only that he died when they were both very small. They get on so well with Colin, and I don't want to throw any stones into the pond.'

'But isn't it time they knew the truth? Barbara at least is old enough to understand. She'll be fourteen soon.'

Isla put the icing knife down and wiped her sticky

fingers on a towel. 'I want to be sure that it's the right time – and I want to tell them myself, in my own way.'

Ainslie gave her a long look, then had the sense to change the subject. 'You and Colin are perfect together. I've never seen a couple who looked so right together. You're like—'

'A set of book-ends?'

'What I'm trying to say is that you fit each other. Colin wouldn't have been nearly as happy if he'd married me. I can be prickly at times, but Phil copes so well when I'm being difficult. He knows when to steer clear, and when to tell me to shut up and calm down.'

'He's wonderful. I just wish he would let us pay the proper price for this place.' After their marriage, Colin had tried to persuade Phil to take the market price for Isla's house, but the Canadian refused point-blank.

'We made a deal, and we shook hands on it. If I went back on it now I'd never live it down,' he drawled.

'But when you made the deal Isla was on her own, with very little money. Things have changed now. We can afford to pay the proper price.'

'No way,' Phil said flatly, then added, a gleam in his eye, ' 'Sides, at the time I got a real kick out of telling the folks at home that I'd sold a house for a few dollars. I don't want to ruin my reputation.'

'He's got no intention of taking a penny more for the house,' Ainslie said now. 'As far as Phil's concerned, the deal was fair. Do people still call it the five-shilling mansion?'

'Some, sometimes. It used to bother me, but not any more.'

'Good.' Again, Ainslie stretched her arms catlike over

her head, then gave a lazy laugh. 'If anyone had told me eight years ago that I'd move to Canada and settle happily into marriage, I'd have called them a liar. Isn't life strange?'

'Mmmm. But it's good, too.'

Ainslie used a finger to scoop up some icing that had fallen from the knife.

'Very good,' she said indistinctly, but enthusiastically, round the fingertip in her mouth.

The Hannigans tried to persuade Isla and Colin to return to Canada with them for a visit, but Gilchrist Forbes had retired shortly after his son's marriage, and it was difficult for Colin to leave the business just then. Instead it was agreed that the family would spend the following summer in Canada.

But while Isla was enjoying the happiest phase of her life for many years, clouds had begun to gather over Europe. German soldiers had marched into Czechoslovakia; Jews in Germany were being systematically terrorised and stripped of all rights, and by the summer of 1939 it looked as though war was becoming inevitable. The Territorial Army was being strengthened, and as well as finding the task of running the office without his father's presence demanding, Colin found himself spending more time than ever before at Army headquarters as 1939 progressed. Isla, too, was flooded with orders from clients, and before the school holidays arrived it became clear to them both that the planned Canadian holiday would have to be cancelled.

Barbara and Ross, who had been looking forward to

the trip, were heart-broken at the news. 'You promised!' Ross said accusingly, a tremor in his voice.

'I know, but that was before we realised how busy we were going to be,' Isla tried to explain, while Colin chimed in with, 'We'll go next year.'

'That's what you said last year,' Barbara pointed out, tossing her long red hair back over her shoulders.

It was pleated into pigtails for school, and combed out when she came home. Colin reached for a handful and tugged it gently.

'We'll go to North Berwick for two weeks instead. You like it there, don't you?'

'Not as much as we'd like Canada,' she told him sharply, twitching away and jerking her hair free.

'You promised!' Ross said again, his voice breaking and the gathering tears spilling over, despite all his attempts to hold them back. He scrambled to his feet and ran out of the room, banging the door.

Colin put out a restraining hand as Isla began to get to her feet. 'Leave it, love. Let him have a good bawl without being fussed over.'

'Why can't we go on our own?' Barbara persisted. 'I'm old enough to look after the two of us.'

Isla's temper began to rise. She was as disappointed as the children about their cancelled plans. Like them, she had been looking forward to seeing another country, and visiting Ainslie's home. 'For goodness' sake, Barbara, don't be so silly,' she snapped. 'We couldn't possibly do that!'

Barbara scowled, her lower lip pushing itself forward. 'I think it's very unfair!' she said hotly, and flung herself out of the room.

Listening to the sound of her daughter bounding up the stairs, Isla sighed. 'At times like this, you must regret marrying me.'

Colin reached out and raised her hand from the arm of her chair, squeezing it hard. 'Not me. They're disappointed, and who can blame them? But they'll get over it.'

But the children refused to get over it. They moped to school in the mornings and moped back again in the afternoons, long-faced and sulky. They squabbled with each other almost all the time, and refused to become interested in any plans Isla and Colin tried to make for the summer.

Isla had already written to Ainslie to explain the situation, and her reply arrived while both children were still sunk in gloom. 'We're really disappointed about your change of plans, particularly the twins. Phil and I have talked it over, and we think that you should let Barbara and Ross come for the summer anyway. You needn't worry about them travelling alone, it would give me a marvellous excuse to come to Scotland, to bring them back with me. You and Colin could surely take a little while off at the end of August to come over and take them home. It would be better than nothing. Please say yes.'

Luckily, Barbara and Ross were at school when the letter arrived. Isla kept it in her pocket, out of sight, and showed it to Colin that night when the children were in bed.

'I think we should agree,' he said when he had read it.

Isla gaped at him. 'Of course we can't agree! For one

thing, we can't have Ainslie coming all the way here just to fetch them, and for another, it would mean them being far away from us for at least six weeks.'

'I'd rather be apart for six weeks and know they're happy than have them sulking around all summer because we ruined their holiday,' Colin said reasonably. 'It's Ainslie's own idea to come for them, so we're not imposing on her. It sounds as though she'd like the chance to make the trip, and it would be good for them – and for us – to spend a little time apart. You know they'd be safe as houses with her and Phil, and they'd have a wonderful time.'

'But what if the war comes while they're away?'

'I don't think it'll happen all that quickly. We'll have time to fetch them back. I think I should be free by the end of August – it only means asking their schools to let them start the autumn term two weeks later than usual. They'll probably agree to it under the circumstances.'

'But they've never been away from me before,' Isla argued in growing panic. Colin put the letter aside and came to kneel by her chair, his hand warm against her cheek.

'Darling, I know how much they mean to you, and I've not forgotten that time Ainslie's mother tried to take Ross away from you, but that was a long time ago. Barbara's going to be fifteen in August, and Ross is eleven. You can't tie them to your apron-strings for ever.'

'I don't!' she said at once, vehemently. Then, as he said nothing, 'Do I?'

'Not exactly, but you do have a tendency to worry over them like a mother hen.' Colin's voice was light, but with a serious undertone. 'It's understandable, but at the same time, it's not good for them to be over-protected, Isla.'

'I'm going to bed.' She got up quickly, the movement knocking his hand away from her face. Alone in their bedroom, brushing her hair, she stared into her own eyes in the dressing-table mirror. Colin's words had hurt, but they had to be faced.

For years, between the time of Kenneth's death and her marriage to Colin, the children had been her sole responsibility, all that she had. Every meal they ate, each day they survived, had been the result of her efforts. She could still recall, as though it had happened only the day before, the terror of almost losing Ross to Catherine McAdam, and the lesser, but still frightening, threat of losing Barbara to Aunt Lally. But as Colin had pointed out, these fears belonged to the past, to a time of deep insecurity and uncertainty. The children were growing up now, Colin was part of their lives, and Ainslie was nothing like her mother. There was no threat as far as she and Phil were concerned.

The brush slowed, and stopped. When Colin came into the room some time later Isla was still at the dressing-table, gazing into her own reflected eyes. She jumped slightly at the light touch of his hands on her shoulders, looking up to meet his gaze in the glass.

'You're right, I do tend to fret about them too much,' she said slowly, reaching her fingers up to cover his. 'It's time to start letting go.'

The cloud that had been hanging over the household lifted as soon as Barbara and Ross were told that they could spend summer in Canada after all. They immediately began to shower Isla with assurances of their very best behaviour during the visit to Ainslie and Phil.

'If they keep their vows, you'll find yourself playing hostess to a pair of saints,' Isla said wryly to Ainslie when she arrived in Scotland a few days before Barbara and Ross were due to finish school.

'I hope not, I couldn't take the strain. Try to come over before the end of August,' Ainslie coaxed. 'If you wait until then you'll have very little time with us, and I've been so looking forward to introducing you to all our friends.'

'We'll try. But Colin's really busy, and for some strange reason everyone wants to buy dolls' houses – I've never had so many orders all at once.'

'Mebbe they're trying to hold on to the good things of life while they can.'

'You sense it too?'

Ainslie was curled up in an armchair in Isla's living-room, her feet tucked beneath her. She was still lithe, though motherhood and maturity had softened and rounded her body. Her curly red hair had been cut short, framing a tanned face with freckles sprinkled like a drift of gold dust across nose and cheekbones. The twins were also freckled, but much more heavily. 'With more freckle than face,' Barbara had teased them the previous summer.

'It's hard to ignore the atmosphere in this country at the moment. People don't actually come out and talk about the possibility of a war, but I can see it in their eyes, hear it in their voices.' She gave a sudden, involuntary shiver. 'We talk about it in Canada, too, but the threat of it seems to feel closer here. Britain's such a small country, and everything's more concentrated in a place that's surrounded by water.' She shivered again, then, said briskly, 'Listen to me – all gloom and doom. It probably won't come to anything, and the children'll have a wonderful time with us, I promise.'

Upstairs, a door opened and shut loudly several times. Voices clamoured shrilly above the noise of feet thundering down the stairs and across the hall. The front door opened, then closed, and the voices rocketed past the window, fading as the group of boys, led by eleven-year-old Ross, ran round the house to the back garden.

'Are you quite sure you want to take on the responsibility of my two?' Isla asked as the noise died away. 'Ross never seems to tire, and Barbara can be quite an insufferable little madam at times.'

'It'll be fine, don't worry. There's lots of space at home to run wild in, and Phil's great with kids. He knows when to put his foot down without stamping on anyone. As for Barbara – I'll enjoy getting to know my kid sister,' Ainslie said.

She and the children sailed from Greenock a week later. Ross, who hadn't quite shaken off the little-boy look, and was chubbily cherubic in grey shorts and a grey jacket over shirt and tie, couldn't wait to start the great adventure that lay before him. He gave Isla then Colin a strangling hug, then raced up the gangplank of the steamer waiting to take the passengers out to the Tail of the Bank, where the liner lay. One sock, Isla noticed as she watched him go, was already coming down, and his ginger hair had broken free of the cold-water combing she had given it not much more than an hour earlier.

Barbara, already a stranger in her first grown-up costume, hugged her mother, then Colin, more sedately, but with warmth.

'I'll write every week – I'll tell you everything that happens,' she promised.

'And I'll make sure she does – that they both do,' Ainslie said. 'Don't fret. And take good care of yourself, and each other.' She hugged them both, then said in a choked voice, 'Come on, Barbara, let's go and get it over with. I hate goodbyes. They make me cry, and I hate crying even more than I hate goodbyes!'

As the two of them went towards the gangplank, Barbara's flared skirt swung round slim, sleekly stockinged legs and the sun sparked red lights from her hair, peeping out from beneath the green beret set stylishly to one side. Isla had never felt so desolate in her life. She clung to Colin's arm, convinced that if she didn't restrain herself she would run up the gangplank and snatch her children back.

'They change so quickly,' she said tearfully as she and Colin drove home after watching the liner move regally down-river towards the open sea, tugs fussing round her. 'They'll be entirely different by the time we see them again!'

'It won't be all that long. We'll be joining them in a matter of weeks,' Colin reassured her. 'In the meantime, just think about the fun we're going to have, with some time to ourselves for a change. It'll be like being newly-weds. We'll start tonight – I'll take you out for dinner in a restaurant, somewhere special, with candles on the table.'

That summer seemed to pass more swiftly than any other. In August, Barbara celebrated her fifteenth birthday in Canada, and Ainslie and Phil gave her a big party. Judging by the letters they wrote every week, both children were having a wonderful time.

But the news from Europe grew more ominous, with the Germans poised to march into Poland. Towards the end of August it became clear that Colin wouldn't be able to get away from the office after all, and Isla would have to go to Canada on her own. But when she tried to book a passage, she discovered that all the shipping lines were busy because of a flood of bookings from Canadians returning home, and parents sending their children away from Britain to the safety of another country.

Reluctantly, because she had never flown before, she tried the airlines, only to find that they were in the same situation.

'If it comes to it, you could go on a one-way ticket,' Colin suggested. 'I'd rather have the three of you safe in Canada if we do go to war.'

'I don't like the idea of leaving you here on your own for goodness knows how long,' she said, then tried to make light of the situation. 'Your mother would probably start introducing you to eligible young women as soon as my back was turned.'

'Oh, I think she's realised by now that I'm a very married man.'

'I'm not so sure,' Isla said dryly. Since the wedding,

she and Phemie Forbes had only met each other when they had to, and on those few occasions there was still a coolness in the air. It was clear that Phemie could not get over her disappointment at her son's choice of wife.

'Isla, I may not be here for long.'

'But you're thirty-four, Colin. They'll be calling up younger men, surely.'

'I'm not exactly Methuselah,' he protested, then, his smile fading, 'I'm in the Territorials, love. I've been trained, and if they want me, I'm willing to go.'

'What about the business?'

'My father's going to come out of retirement, so that he can take over when the time comes. We've already discussed it and I think he's quite excited at the thought of being in the office again. So you see, you might be left here alone. At least in Canada you'd be with the children.'

'If it comes to war, the children will be fine with Ainslie. And if you do go away, I'd want to be here for you when you have leave. Anyway, there's Flora to consider – I'd not leave her now, after all she's done for me.'

Ainslie phoned, her voice crackly and distant, coming and going as though the telephone cable was being swung to and fro on waves, to say that she had investigated the possibility of bringing Barbara and Ross back to Scotland herself, only to find, as Isla had, that liners and aeroplanes alike were fully booked. Ross and Barbara both spoke to their mother, sounding excited at the prospect of staying on in Canada for longer than planned. Ainslie had taken the first step towards enrolling them in local schools, just in case, and Ross was looking forward to that.

'It won't be like being in school at home, because of them sounding different because they're Canadians,' he explained.

Barbara at least had the tact to say, just before the call ended, 'We miss you both, Mum, but everything's fine here, and it won't be for long, will it?'

'Not long,' Isla agreed, praying that she was telling the truth.

Colin, struck to the heart by the look on her face as she put down the phone, redoubled his efforts to get her to Canada, and almost managed to get her a berth on the liner *Athenia*. But even as Isla was packing for the trip the booking fell through, and the liner sailed without her.

Two days later, the German army marched into Poland, and Britain declared war.

'There's still the chance of getting the children back,' Isla said hopefully as Colin switched off the wireless, Neville Chamberlain's war announcement still ringing in their ears. 'Surely nothing will happen for a little while. I'll keep trying.'

On the following evening Colin came into the kitchen where Isla and Nan were getting the evening meal ready, his face like stone.

'Look . . .' He held his newspaper out and Isla took it, sinking into a chair as she read the headlines. The *Athenia*, packed with passengers, had been torpedoed on the previous day, only hours after Britain had declared war on Germany. More than a hundred people had died, including children on their way to safety in Canada.

'That's that,' Colin said flatly. 'You stay here, and Barbara and Ross stay with Ainslie, until this business is over.'

Later, in the privacy of their bedroom, he said wretchedly, 'Isla, I'm so sorry. I should never have talked you into letting them go. If it hadn't been for me, they'd be here, with us. I should have known better!'

'You weren't to know that things were going to happen so quickly. And you were right – it was time they learned to spend time away from me.' She summoned up a smile. 'We're more fortunate than some of those poor souls that are having to send their children away from the cities without knowing who they're going to. Barbara and Ross will be fine with Ainslie and Phil – they'll look on the whole thing as an adventure.'

But behind the smile was the icy realisation that the die was cast, and her children thousands of miles away from her, perhaps for years. There was no chance, now, of getting them back until the matter was resolved. Isla kept on smiling reassuringly into Colin's worried, guilty face, but inside, she felt as though her heart was breaking.

Paisley, like every other town in Britain, seethed with preparations for war. Policemen were to be seen on the streets with gasmasks hanging at their sides and tin helmets slung over their shoulders, and Isla stood in long queues to obtain heavy black curtaining for the windows, and sticky netting which she and Nan and Colin, with Drew's help, put over every window to prevent shards of glass flying into the rooms in the event of the windows being smashed during air-raids. As there was no basement to shelter in if a raid came, she bought a large solid table from Charlie Blayne's auction room and had it placed against the back wall of the living-room.

'It's hideous,' Colin said flatly when he saw it.

'But it's solid. If there's a raid, Nan and I can pull the couch across in front of it and even if the whole window comes in we'll be safe.'

'And if the house collapses about your ears?'

She banged on the table with her knuckles. 'It won't, but even if it does, Nan and I and Flora, if we can get her under it, will be quite safe beneath that table until we're dug out.'

'For God's sake, woman, don't say things like that!' Colin pulled her into his arms and held her tightly. She clung to him, knowing, though she would never admit it to him, that the thought of his going away from her, possibly being badly hurt or killed, was far more fright-ening than the fear of anything happening to her. For the time being, at least, she had lost her children; she couldn't bear the thought of losing Colin, too.

First Aid posts were set up, one of them in the West School, and Drew came back from registering for the services and proposed to his girlfriend, who accepted him.

'We're not going to get married before I go,' he explained to Isla, shyly but proudly. 'But when I'm away from Paisley it'll be good to know that she's mine. It'll give me something to stay alive for.'

'I hope you both have a very long and happy life together.' On an impulse Isla reached up and kissed Drew, who went crimson and escaped to his workshop as soon as he was released. He was twenty-five now, but, to her, he was still the shy teenager who had helped her to dig the potato patch in George Street. Isla watched him hurry from the room, and hoped that the war might be over soon, before too many young lads like Drew were dragged into it.

A blackout was imposed at once, and by the end of the year a number of local people were among the first victims of the war, some of them knocked down in the darkened night streets by cars and buses and tramcars, others killed or injured by tumbles down narrow stone stairs in unlit tenement buildings. Gas masks were issued and after trying hers on, Isla hurriedly tore herself free of the constricting straps, dragging in gulps of air.

'I'd rather take my chances with the gas!'

'You'll wear that mask if you're told to, for as long as you must,' Colin told her grimly.

'But I couldn't breathe!'

He caught her by the shoulders and shook her. 'Listen, Isla, I've been through a gas tank in training, and believe me, you're much better off with the mask. So wear it!'

Magret, too, hated the gas masks. 'It doesn't seem to bother the lassies,' she said mournfully on a visit to Isla's kitchen. 'They go off every day with their masks over their shoulders in wee cardboard boxes, and not a care in the world, and there's me worried sick, wondering what would be worst – me choking in that nasty smelly thing, or them coming home to find me gassed on the floor,'

'I'll be wearing mine,' Nan said firmly. 'I'm all for

staying alive.' Nan had already volunteered for duty in one of the town's first-aid posts, and was an avid collector of silver paper and waste paper and cardboard for the war effort.

Shy little Mrs Kelly, Mrs Leach's daughter, had given birth to a son almost a year earlier, and to George Street's astonishment, Mrs Leach, the dragon who had been the bane of the street children's lives for many years, had become a doting grandmother. When 'baby helmets', the small compartments intended to hold the entire child and protect it against gas attacks, were made available, Magret's account of helping to fit little Boyd Kelly into his helmet had Isla and Nan in tears of laughter.

'Honest tae God, ye'd need at least a week's warnin' tae get that wean ready,' Magret insisted, elbows on the kitchen table. 'As fast as we got an arm in, a leg popped out. It was like trying tae fit a chicken back intae its egg three days later. What with the wee soul roaring his head off, and Mrs Leach giving orders, the place was in an uproar. Finally she pushes the lot of us out of the road and says she'll dae it herself – you know what she's like, Isla, aye has tae be in charge. Then she lifts the bairn up and starts tellin' him that Gran wants him tae be a good boy and let her tuck him intae the contraption.' She beamed at her listeners. 'That was when his nappy fell off and he peed all down the front of her good blouse.'

Despite all the haste of the war preparations, a strange lethargy fell on the town as 1939 gave way to 1940. Men who had registered for call-up continued to work, and for a while life went on as before. Orders stil came in for dolls' houses, and in the little spare time he had, Colin, following exhortations to dig for victory, helped the elderly gardener who came once a week to dig up most of the back lawn and plant vegetables for future consumption. It was like waiting for the starter's gun to start the race, Isla thought, and being unable to move until it was fired.

Canada, too, had declared war on Germany, but to his chagrin, Phil was unable to sign up because of a knee injury he had sustained shortly after the twins' birth, when he had been caught in the path of some timber that had broken loose in his yard.

'He's needed here in any case, because the yard's important to war work,' Ainslie wrote. 'Several of his friends are going, and I've given them all your address in case they ever find themselves in Scotland. Barbara and Ross have settled in very well at school. Barbara's keeping her piano lessons going, as well as studying dancing. She wanted to take singing lessons, too, but Phil and I thought that that might be too much for her to cope with on top of everything else. A music teacher I know heard her sing, and says that she has a natural talent that shouldn't be suppressed, so thankfully Barbara's given up on that idea.'

For their part, Ross and Barbara's letters were filled with enthusiasm and excitement.

'It's all a big adventure to them,' Isla told Magret bleakly. 'They're having a wonderful time.'

'Bairns is like men and pet dogs, hen,' her friend said knowledgeably. 'As long as there's someone around tae keep their bellies filled and give them a fireside tae sit by and a roof over their heads, they're happy enough.

But that doesnae mean they're no' missing ye. They will be, but they'll no' want tae say too much about that, because they know that it'd worry ye. Everything'll turn out fine, you'll see.'

Busy though Colin was with the garden and further training with the Territorials, and with organising the office so that his father could run it in his absence, Isla sensed a growing restlessness about him.

'You can't wait to go, can you?' she asked one evening as they stumbled home arm in arm through the pitch-black night, with only a pencil-thin line of light from a hooded torch to guide them. At Colin's suggestion, they had been to the Regal Cinema to see the Ritz Brothers in *The Three Musketeers*, but even during the film, with people laughing all around them, she had been aware of his tension.

'In one way I don't want to go at all, but in another – well, I've got this daft notion that if I can just get away and do something, the whole rotten business might be over and done with and we can all get on with our lives. I hate all this waiting!'

Isla, who had put her name down with the Nursing Reserve and was waiting to hear from them, understood how he felt. But they had no option but to wait.

Greta reached her fifteenth birthday and went to work in a shop in the High Street. Not long after that, Magret achieved her greatest ambition when she and her family moved into a two-bedroomed flat in a more modern tenement further along George Street. There was a tiny scullery, only large enough for one person at a time, and a bathroom.

With three of the family working, Magret achieved another long-term ambition, and got Tommy's auntie's clock out of the pawnshop. It sat on her new mantelshelf in pride of place – a huge and hideous black marble creation like a Greek temple, complete with a roof and pillars. Magret was in her element.

Isla and Colin celebrated Christmas quietly with Nan and Flora Currie, and early in 1940 the dolls'-house business was put into mothballs when Drew was called up and Mabel went into the Women's Auxiliary Air Force.

In April, Hitler's army invaded Denmark and Norway. Colin was summoned to Aldershot for further orders and Isla started nursing in the Craw Road Sanatorium, about ten minutes' walk away from Low Road.

Suddenly, the starter had fired his pistol, and the grim race to win the war was on.

29

All the sanatorium patients who were well enough to be sent home had gone by the time Isla started work there, and the remainder were put into two small wards. The other wards dealt with a mixture of patients, so that the Royal Alexandra Infirmary, Paisley's largest hospital, could be freed for incoming wounded, or people injured in the air-raids that were already hitting southern England.

As a partially trained nurse, Isla was given the more mundane tasks, fetching and carrying, emptying bed-pans, helping to clean the wards and serve meals and bathe patients. But despite that, and despite an aching back and feet that were so sore at the end of a shift that they could scarcely carry her home, she enjoyed being back in a hospital routine. For one thing, it kept her occupied, easing the helpless frustration of missing Colin and the children and worrying about them continuously.

Colin was sent to France, and had scarcely landed there when the German tanks broke through and the British Expeditionary Forces found themselves outnumbered and in retreat. He came home only a month after leaving for Aldershot, with one arm in a sling after being hit by flying shrapnel at Dunkirk, embarrassed at being wounded before he had had a chance to do any fighting, and bitter with memories of the nightmare on the French beaches, where men under fire from the enemy clawed their way desperately through the shallows, trying to scramble aboard the mongrel flotilla of ships and boats that had come to snatch them to safety. Two short weeks later he returned to his regiment, fit for action again.

Letters arrived regularly from Ainslie, Barbara and Ross. Ainslie sent photographs, and parcels of tinned meat and fruit that were gratefully received, for rationing was already biting deep into civilian life. Isla shared the food with Flora Currie, and with Magret and, through Magret, the residents of the old tenement. Although she no longer lived there, Magret still took a keen interest in the place. She had even persuaded young Mrs Kelly, whose husband had been called up, to secure a job in the mills, and now the two of them worked beside each other.

Only Mrs Leach, who looked after her grandson while his mother was at work, declined to take anything from Isla. She did her best to make her daughter follow suit, but Mrs Kelly, with a growing son to feed, defied her mother and accepted her share of the tins gratefully, as did the others.

'Is that no' what life's all about?' Magret asked. 'War or no war, if we don't help each other we deserve all we get. Never mind that Mrs Leach, there's no understanding her at all, but the lassie's really nice, when ye get her away from the old woman. She must take after her da, rest his soul.'

Phemie Forbes threw herself into war work with enthusiasm. She joined the Women's Voluntary Service, and in her spare time she knitted for the troops. She was hardly ever to be seen these days without knitting needles in her hands and a half-finished garment in khaki wool on her lap. Isla, who for Colin's sake made a point of calling on Phemie at least once every week, sitting on the edge of a chair in the Forbeses' drawing-room and making small talk to the background of clicking needles, often thought that her mother-in-law looked like a fly perched in the middle of a khaki web.

Gilchrist, guiltily revelling in the luxury of having the reins of the business in his own hands again, referred to his wife's continual industry as knitting for victory, or stitching up the war. He and Isla got on well together and he often called in on her on his way back from the office, sitting in the living-room with his feet sprawled over the carpet, just as his son had once done.

Colin, in England for the remainder of 1940, was able to come home on leave fairly regularly, but at the end of the year his regiment was sent overseas and Isla was forced to settle down to a life bereft of husband and children. Throughout 1940, radio broadcasts had conveyed reports of the horror of the interminable raids on London and Coventry and Liverpool; once 1941 arrived, Paisley's sirens started sounding more frequently, and Isla and Nan, both busy with their war work, saw little of each other.

Clydebank, a shipbuilding town not far from Paisley, was almost destroyed by a devastating two-night air raid in March. Isla was on duty both nights, and as most of the patients were kept awake by the unnerving wail of the sirens, the sound of wave after wave of German planes rumbling through the sky, and the distant thump of anti-aircraft guns, all the staff on duty had a hard time of it. Hurrying from one building to the other on the first night of the raid, Isla saw the searchlights weaving back and forth across the sky. A faint rosy glow on the horizon, almost like the early promise of a beautiful sunrise, marked Clydebank's agony by fire.

Some of the 'Bankers' who had been bombed and burned out of their homes came to Paisley, and a family of four, a dazed young mother and her three children, spent a few weeks in Isla's home. It was like the old days, when Barbara and Ross were home. Both Isla and Nan revelled in the luxury of having children around, and Nan, the most efficient person that Isla had ever known, worked wonders when it came to finding enough food to keep ever-hungry little stomachs content. They were both sorry when the family moved on, to stay with relatives in Stranraer.

Early in May it was the turn of Greenock, another Clydeside town famed for its large shipyards. It, too, was bombarded for two nights, and again, the enemy bombers flew over Paisley, but this time they didn't pass by harmlessly. On the first night, an incendiary bomb landed not far from Low Road, on the railway embankment close to Ferguslie Mills.

On the following night, Isla, who was off duty, was wakened by the mournful wail of the sirens. Nan was on duty that night, and Isla was alone. She dressed hurriedly and ran through the dark to Flora's house, blundering into bushes, fumbling impatiently with the stiff catch on Flora's gate.

Betty, the housekeeper, opened the door to Isla. 'Thank goodness you're here, Mrs Forbes. She refuses to let me help her to get dressed. She'll not leave her bed!'

'I'll see to her.' Isla hurried across the hall to the little room that had once housed Flora's dolls' houses. Not long before the war began, they had been moved upstairs so that the ground-floor room could be turned into a bedroom for the old lady, who was finding it increasingly difficult to cope with stairs. Colin had supervised the installation of a small ground-floor bathroom adjacent to the kitchen.

In spite of all Isla's pleading and coaxing and threatening, Flora refused to leave the comfort of her bed. 'After all those years, I see no sense in trying to prolong my life by making it a misery,' she announced. 'Squatting beneath a table isn't dignified. I decided the last time you got me to do that that I'd never do it again. I'm fine where I am.'

She could scarcely be heard over the noise of the planes passing overhead. The sky must be thick with them, Isla thought, glancing fearfully up at the ceiling. It was hard to credit that so many could crowd into such a small patch of sky. The mind-picture of big heavy machines colliding with each other and falling on the houses beneath came to her, and refused to leave. 'Flora, you might get hurt if you stay here. You're right beside the window. It's far safer in the living-room.'

'If my end's coming, it'll come no matter whether I'm cowering on the carpet or lying comfortably in my bed.'

'What about Betty? And me? If you insist on staying here, we'll have to stay with you.'

'No you don't.' All that could be seen of Flora were bright eyes, grass-green in the lamplight, peering over the edge of the quilt gripped in her two hands. Her voice was muffled, but determined. 'I don't want your deaths on my conscience, but I'm not stirring one step. I'm too old to be bothered by all this palaver!'

'Flora Currie, if you don't let us help you up right now, we'll just have to drag you out of your bed and carry you into the living-room.'

There was no reply. Isla and Betty looked helplessly at each other, knowing that they couldn't leave her, or risk a heart attack by forcing her into safety.

Isla thought wistfully of the big solid table in the living-room next door, then said slowly, 'There's that old folding screen we found in the attic and put in the drawing-room.'

After a struggle, the two women managed to fit the large, ungainly screen between the window and the bed, then settled down in the dim light of a torch to wait the raid out. Flora dozed, and was still asleep when there was a great blast of sound from somewhere and their empty teacups, placed on the bedside table, jangled together with the vibration. The entire house shook, and Isla threw herself across the bed to protect the old woman against breaking glass. Betty screamed, then went scrambling after the torch, which had rolled from the bedside table to the floor, as Flora, waking with a start, hit out with her fists at the sudden weight across her.

'In the name of God, lassie, I thought I'd been attacked,' she said reproachfully when the torch was found and order restored.

'I was trying to keep you from getting killed.'

Flora tutted. 'It's you that needs saving, not me. Didn't I say that if my time's come, it's come? There's a man and two bonny children that'll be wanting to see you safe and well when this nonsense is over.'

'D'you think it landed in Low Road?' Betty whispered when Flora had drifted back into sleep.

'It wasn't that close. Maybe the mills – or George Street.' The day before, the railway embankment close to the mills had been set alight by incendiary bombs. Some thought that the mills had been the real target.

'Whatever it was, it was close,' Betty said. 'And it was big.' They stared at each other, wondering what the dawn would bring.

They finally slept, huddled in armchairs by the bed, sleeping right through the All Clear and waking to blessed silence, broken only by the birds' dawn chorus.

Leaving Betty to snatch an hour's sleep in her own bed, Isla went back home. It was early yet to expect Nan home; if the night's explosion had meant death and injury to some poor souls, she might be later than usual, kept busy at her first-aid post.

Isla went to bed, but couldn't sleep. Finally she got up again, dressed, and made breakfast, expecting to hear Nan's key in the lock at any moment.

She was drinking her second cup of tea when Mr Smith from further up the road came to the door, wearing his official ARP tin helmet and armband. He looked as though he hadn't slept for a week.

'Mrs Forbes, I'm afraid I've got bad news,' he began. 'Colin—'

'No, no, it's got nothing to do with your husband,

he said hurriedly, then, 'that explosion last night – a landmine scored a direct hit on the first-aid post at Woodside . . .'

The church at the foot of New Street had been set aside as a temporary mortuary. Isla walked to it down George Street, her feet crunching on broken glass, and waited in line to go in to identify Nan. War meant queuing for everything, she thought drearily. Buying food, buying clothes, identifying the dead. She caught snatches of talk from the others waiting with her. The landmine had been clearly seen, drifting down through the search-lights, swinging from its parachute. If the wind had only carried it a hundred yards further on, it would have landed on the cemetery where Kenneth and his son lay. Almost immediately after the landmine had hit the first-aid post, killing doctors, nurses, ambulance drivers, and helpers like Nan, another bomb had landed on the east wing of the West School, used as an auxiliary fire station, killing several firefighters. Again, the general belief was that the mills, so close to both explosions that most of their windows had been blown in, had been the target.

When her turn came, and the corner of the blanket was lifted aside, she looked down at Nan, eyes closed, mouth slack, her greying brown hair, always in such a neat roll, untidy and darkly clotted at one side. 'Yes, that's Nan – Mrs Agnes Urquhart,' she corrected herself.

'Is she from Paisley?'

'Her sisters live in Stirling. She's been widowed for years. I'll write to her family,' Isla said. Her guide nodded and dropped the blanket.

'Ninety-two killed in all,' he said as he escorted her from the church, 'and every last one of 'em decent folk doing their duty. When's this terrible business going to stop?'

Isla left the building, passing the people who still waited outside, to claim their own dead, and walked home, heedless now of the broken glass under her feet. At that moment, she was glad that Barbara and Ross were safe in Canada, where the bombs couldn't reach them.

The house seemed very empty when she let herself in. Once there had been Colin and Drew and Mabel and the children – and Nan, who had, in her own way, been the very heart of the house. Now there was only Isla. She paused at the foot of the stairs, the newel post solid beneath her hand, and looked up towards the landing, remembering all the times she had stood there in the past, calling to the children to make less noise.

For a moment she knew blind, suffocating panic, wondering how she was going to be able to keep going on her own, then, quite unexpectedly, the tears came. She clung to the polished post, letting all the grief come out, crying noisily like a child, because now there was nobody there to be disturbed by her misery. When the tears finally ebbed then stopped, she went into the kitchen – Nan's kitchen – and sluiced her face with cold water, then made herself a cup of tea before going to tell Flora about Nan.

At the end of the year, the Japanese bombed Pearl Harbor, and America came into the war. And the terrible business continued.

*

'Here, let me give you a hand.'

Isla, who had assumed that she was alone in the garden, jumped and almost sliced off the toe of her wellington boot when she heard the voice. For a moment she thought that the easy drawl was Phil's, then as she spun round she saw a stranger advancing towards her from the corner of the house.

'Sorry, did I startle you?' He took the spade from her and eyed the rows of green shoots. 'They're too small to be dug up.'

'I know, but I wanted to give my neighbour some new potatoes.'

'Okay.' Effortlessly, he buried the spade to its shaft in the earth. Isla stepped aside and left him to it. She had no idea who he was, but she was glad of the chance to straighten her aching back.

The man bent to the spade, then heaved it up with a soft grunt. The potato shaw keeled over and small pale potatoes gleamed through the crumbling earth. He put the spade aside and knelt to run his hands through the soil, gathering the frugal harvest.

'There aren't many.'

'There's enough.' Isla held out her basket and he put the potatoes into it, then dusted his hands together as he stood up.

'Are you Isla? Isla Forbes? Phil and Ainslie told me to look you up if I was in the area.'

'You're Canadian?'

A grin split his thin face. 'Most folks can tell that the minute I open my mouth,' he said, then thrust his hand out. 'Gregg Marshall.'

A sudden April shower began to fall, and Isla, who

hadn't slept well earlier in the day despite being exhausted by her busy night on duty, smothered a yawn and collected her wits. 'I was just going to make myself a cup of tea. Would you like one?'

'That'd be fine, if it's not too much trouble.'

She led him into the house through the back door and put the basket of potatoes down on the dresser, then began to ease her first wellington off.

'Sit down.' He knelt before her, taking her muddy foot in his hands, levering the tight boot off skilfully. 'There we are – now the other one.'

'That one's always hard to get off.'

'I've never yet met the boot that could get the better of me. Tod, my eldest, has the darnedest knack of getting his socks wedged down inside his boots, so I learned at a hard school.'

Sitting on a wooden chair, clinging to the seat to avoid being pulled off by the final tug on the boot, Isla looked down on a mass of curly light brown hair. The boot came off and he tipped his head back to smile triumphantly at her before setting it to one side with its companion, then washing his hands at the sink. Isla, padding barefoot across the kitchen in search of her slippers, was uncomfortably aware that she didn't look her best in one of Colin's jerseys and an old skirt. She hadn't been expecting anyone to call.

'D'you mind if I get these potatoes ready for Flora?' She eyed the clock. 'We'll be eating in an hour, because she likes to get to bed early and I'm going on duty.'

'Not at all. Can I help?'

When she declined the offer, he peeled off his leather jacket then sat down at the table. 'I'm stationed down at

Prestwick Aerodrome, and Ainslie said that if I found myself in Scotland I had to call and say hello from the Hannigans, and from Barbara and Ross.'

Isla, washing the tiny potatoes, turned from the sink, heedless of the water dripping from her hands. 'You know the children? How are they? Are they happy?'

'I know them well. We live pretty close to Phil and Ainslie. You've got a couple of nice kids, Mrs Forbes – and they're doing fine, believe me. Barbara has a wonderful voice. She sang in a concert for the troops just before we left for Europe. She's doing a lot of singing, helping to raise money for the war effort as well as singing for the troops.'

'She's always loved music.'

As she put the potatoes on to cook and made the tea Isla told Gregg Marshall about the back-court concerts Barbara used to run, and he listened with genuine interest, then said, 'You know she's been on radio a few times?'

'Oh yes, she wrote to tell me all about it.'

'Pat – my wife – envies you, you know. She always wanted a girl, just like your Barbara, but after three boys she's given up hope. Maybe when this is all over . . .' He paused, lost for a moment in his own thoughts, then said, 'You must miss them a lot.'

'I do. I miss them dreadfully,' Isla said, fussing over the potatoes in order to hide the tears that had gathered in her eyes.

Luckily, she had managed to make some buns the day before. She put them out on a plate, together with a precious pot of raspberry jam Nan had made a year earlier from Flora's raspberry bushes, and watched with

371

carefully hidden concern as Gregg Marshall spooned precious sugar into his cup. She herself had learned, like most civilians, to get used to drinking tea without sugar.

'Ainslie told me your husband's in the Army.'

'The artillery. He's with the Fifty-first Highland Division now, in Egypt as far as I know.'

'I thought most of the Fifty-first were captured in France?'

'They were, after Dunkirk. They were cut off, trying to get to the beaches. But the regiment's been rebuilt with men seconded from other regiments. That's how Colin came to be with them.'

Gregg put the sugar bowl down and started stirring his tea, then stopped suddenly. 'Oh heck!' He looked across the table at Isla, his eyes, very clear blue, concerned. 'I've just realised – is this all the sugar you're allowed?'

'It's all right, I don't use much.'

His thin, rugged face flushed. 'I should have thought – we're not used to this rationing you folks have to deal with. I'll bring you some from the base.'

'You don't need to do that, I can manage very well.'

'You live alone?'

'Our housekeeper, Nan, used to share the house with me, but she was killed last year by a landmine.'

'I'm sorry.'

'So am I.' Isla felt the tears threatening again, and blinked hard. 'I still miss her very much.'

'You must get very lonely, with your husband and kids away.'

'Not really. Most of the time, I'm working at the sanatorium, or with my neighbour. Life's so frantic at times that on the few occasions I'm on my own here, I've learned to quite enjoy the solitude.'

'Pat would hate it. She could never stand her own company, not that she gets the chance now, with three boys to raise on her own.' Gregg reached for his jacket and brought a handful of photographs out of an inner pocket, proudly showing off his pretty blonde wife and his three sandy-haired sons. To Isla's delight, Ross was in a few of the photographs, squinting into the camera as he always did, and seventeen-year-old Barbara was in one, long-legged and mature in trousers and a blouse, perched on a wall, laughing into the camera, her mane of curly hair blowing about her face.

Isla studied the children she hadn't been able to touch for almost three years, hungry for every detail. Ross, who had lost the last trace of infant plumpness, was only a week away from another birthday. She had posted a long letter to him, and a book inscribed on the flyleaf, 'To Ross on his fourteenth birthday, with much love from Mum and Dad. April 1942.'

When she relinquished the photographs to Gregg he separated those with Ross and Barbara in them and gave them back. 'They're for you.'

'But your own boys are in them, and Ainslie's been very good about sending letters and photographs. I'm filling my third album now.'

'Keep them anyway, I've got plenty of snapshots of the boys.' He looked at his watch. 'I'd better be going.'

'Come next door and meet my neighbour first. She doesn't get out now and she loves company. Stay and have a meal with us,' Isla urged.

'If you're sure—'

'I'm quite sure. It won't be much, but we'd both be glad of the company.'

The rain had stopped when they left the house, but enough had fallen to give the earth a fresh, cool smell. As they walked out of her gate, then along the pavement for a few yards and in at Flora's gate, Isla tried to work out how to stretch the meal to cover another person. She had made some vegetable soup, and had handed her meat ration over to Betty so that she could make a stew for the three of them. They often pooled their resources.

Flora, looking almost like a faded photograph of the woman Isla had first met outside the West School, was in her usual chair in the front room, a blanket that Isla, Barbara and Nan had knitted for her tucked over her knees. Her white hair covered her skull in soft wisps and her face was gaunt, but her green eyes were still able to sparkle up at the tall airman when Isla introduced him.

'It's just like having Phil here again. So you're at Prestwick? A pilot?'

'Nothing as grand, ma'am. I'm ground crew – a mechanic to trade.'

'You'll have some whisky,' Flora stated. 'The bottle's in the sideboard, Isla, and the glasses. No need to worry, young man, we'll not send you back to the aerodrome drunk. There's not that much whisky left, so you'll only get enough to make you thirst for more.'

Gregg took the tiny glass from Isla and looked at its spoonful of amber whisky. 'I see what you mean, Miss Currie.'

'It's the thought that counts – and I can assure you

that the thought's worth half a tumblerful of Scotland's finest malt,' Flora told him. His laughter followed Isla out of the room as she went in search of Betty to tell her that there would be a guest for dinner.

'But, Mrs Forbes, there's scarce enough to feed us, let alone a man!'

'We'll manage. We'll have to – I thought it would be good for Flora to have some new company for a change, and anyway, it was good of the man to come and visit.' Isla lifted pot lids and peered inside. 'We can use small plates for the soup, and with Flora eating the wee new potatoes, there'll be enough of the others to go round. If I'd known he was coming I could mebbe have got a rabbit,' she fretted, studying the stew that would be hard put to it to stretch to four helpings. 'D'you have any corned beef left?'

'Just a slice, but I was keeping it for Miss Currie's lunch tomorrow.'

'I can let you have some of mine for her lunch,' Isla said rashly. 'Break the slice up and mix it into the stew, and beat a slice of bread in as well, to make it look more. Add some water to the gravy, too. I brought the rest of the buns, so we can fill up with them afterwards, with a cup of tea. He's heavy on the sugar, but we'll get by.'

Even though she and Betty served the meal on the smallest plates they could find, it didn't amount to much. Gregg Marshall made no comment, but Isla noticed that he took only one spoonful of sugar with his tea.

'She's a wonderful old lady,' he said when the two of them left Flora's home.

'She enjoyed your company. You must visit us again.'

'I surely will – and I'll bring you some sugar.'

'There's no need for that.'

'I feel bad about taking your supply. Can I give you a lift to your hospital?' he asked as they stepped on to the pavement. Isla eyed the motor-cycle propped on its stand outside her gate, and explained that the sanatorium was just a step away, and she would walk there. When the machine had roared off up the road, bringing one or two neighbours to their windows, she went into the house to get ready for work.

Flora was in bed, her eyes still bright, when Isla looked in, as she always did on her way to and from the sanatorium.

'It was nice to see a new face, wasn't it? He was just like Phil – these Canadians seem to get such enjoyment out of life. Not like the dour Scots at all. I hope some of that rubs off on your bairns, Isla. It'd be good for them.'

30

Gregg came back often, roaring up to the gate on his motor-cycle, bringing delicacies such as sugar or a small packet of butter, and occasionally some delicious crunchy doughnuts from the canteen. These gifts, like Ainslie's food parcels, were shared with Flora and Magret and the people in the tenement in George Street. Tommy McDougall had been called up now, and was stationed in England.

Isla's gardener had had to give up work because of ill-health, and she hadn't bothered to find anyone else. Gregg willingly helped her in the garden when he called, or sat for hours in the kitchen talking about his home and his family, frequently introducing Barbara and Ross into his reminiscing until Isla felt as though she had been present with her children at the sledging parties in the winter, the picnics, the visits between the Hannigan and Marshall houses to view new kittens or puppies. These word-pictures of her children in Canada made the temporary separation more bearable for her, and went a long way to easing the pain of being without them. Gregg also spent a lot of time with Flora, who had developed a new interest in life since his unexpected arrival.

'You've done her so much good,' Isla told him gratefully. 'She needs company, and I can't spend as much time as I'd like with her these days.'

The Canadian tipped the kitchen chair back and stretched his legs across the linoleum floor. 'I'm the one who's getting all the favours. You and Miss Currie have been like family to me, and it's great to be able to visit a real home.'

Isla looked around the kitchen, which had grown noticeably shabbier since Nan's death. 'I'd scarcely call this place a real home nowadays. The house used to be full of people coming and going, and now I almost live in this room. I hate to see the place so – alone.'

'You're like my Pat – wherever she happens to be is home to me. I get that same feeling when I'm around you.' Gregg smiled at her, then asked, almost shyly, 'Could I have a look at those dolls' houses I kept hearing about from Ainslie and Phil and the kids?'

Isla rarely visited the dolls'-house room now. Walking into it with Gregg, she felt for a moment as though time had looped back. As far as this room was concerned, the war had never happened, her family hadn't been scattered far and wide, and Nan was still alive, bustling round the kitchen pouring out milk and putting fresh-baked scones on a plate, ready for the children's return from school.

Gregg, unaware of the memories she was experiencing, was moving carefully round the tables, fascinated by the little houses and the miniature furniture. 'I wish more than ever now that I had a daughter. It would have been great to give her something like this.' He stopped in front of one with a murmur of delight. 'Hey, this is just like the place my grandparents used to have!'

'It's supposed to be from *Anne of Green Gables*. I'm hoping to complete it one day, but at the moment my furniture maker's in the Navy.'

'He certainly loved his work,' Gregg marvelled, his fingers gently caressing a tiny rocking chair in pale gold wood. 'Listen, would you make me a house just like this, to give to Pat?'

'Of course, but you'll have to wait until after the war. Even if I had the time, I can't get the materials just now. Anyway, I couldn't do it without Drew to make the furniture.'

Gregg was still admiring the little chair. 'I can't get over how perfect this is. I can almost see my grandma sitting in it!' He held the miniature piece gently, lovingly, just as Drew would, Isla thought, and on an impulse she took him out to see the workshop.

Despite being locked up, the place still smelled of fresh wood and paint and glue and textiles. 'Your carpenter certainly cares about his trade. These tools have been well looked after.' Gregg turned his head and smiled at her, and suddenly she was looking at Drew, hearing her long-ago voice saying, 'How are things coming along?' and his voice replying, 'Fine. I'll have time to finish this before I go home for my tea, and it'll be dry in the morning, ready for the handles to be put on.'

Drew was thin, whereas Gregg was as lean and strong as a whip. Drew had serious grey eyes, Gregg's were blue and full of a love of life. Both had light brown hair, but Gregg's was fairer, and curly, whereas Drew's was straight and often flopped over his eyes. The two men were unlike each other in many ways, yet their shared love of fine craftsmanship, and the way Gregg had just turned and smiled absently at her, reminded her so strongly of Drew that to her horror, she burst into tears.

At once he was beside her. 'Isla? What is it? Did I say the wrong thing?'

She shook her head and tried to explain, then gave up and rested her head on his shoulder, letting the tears have their own way. Gregg said nothing more, just stood and held her while she sobbed out her grief over Nan's violent and unnecessary death, her longing to see Barbara and Ross again, her fears for Colin's safety, her exhaustion and loneliness, and her continuous, strength-sapping fear.

When at last the weeping had slowed to sniffs and hiccups, he mopped her face dry with his handkerchief, then locked the workshop door and led her into the house, where he sat her down at the kitchen table and made some tea.

'I shouldn't have asked to see your workplace. It brought back too many hurtful memories.'

'It wasn't that – I'm just being daft.'

'You're not daft,' Gregg told her, the Scottish word sounding so different on his lips. 'You're worn out with work and worry and not getting enough to eat.'

Isla flopped in her chair like a rag doll, completely drained, shaken by an occasional involuntary shudder. When he put the cup into her hands she sipped at it then wrinkled her nose.

'It's t-terrible!'

'I'm not used to making tea,' Gregg said matter-of-factly, taking a seat at the other side of the table. Eyes closed, he inhaled the steam rising from his cup, then sipped. 'It tastes fine to me.'

'It's too strong, and too sweet, and . . .' She sipped again, then it was her turn to sniff at the brew. 'You've put something in it.'

He dipped into the pocket of his leather jacket, hanging from the back of his chair, and held up a small silver flask. 'A few drops of brandy, that's all.'

'No wonder it tastes terrible!'

'Don't look a gift horse in the mouth, that's what my grandma used to say. Drink it up, it'll do you good.'

Although she grimaced at every mouthful, she had to admit that she did feel better when she had drained the cup. She got up to put it in the sink, then gave a gasp of horror as her gaze fell on the small mirror hanging nearby. Her face was stained, her eyes and mouth swollen with weeping. 'I look awful!'

'Everyone looks awful when they've been crying as hard as you were. Splash cold water on your face.'

She did, and looked marginally better, though her eyelids were still puffy. Gregg rinsed the cups and set them on the draining board while she was still peering into the mirror and making small sounds of horror. 'Take a couple of aspirin and go to bed with a hot-water bottle. You'll feel fine after a sleep.'

'But I said I'd call in on Flora this afternoon. She'll know at once that I've been crying, and it'll upset her.'

Gregg dried his hands and reached for his jacket, moving about the kitchen comfortably, as though in his own home. 'I'll go. I'll tell her you've got a headache and you've had to go to bed.'

'Gregg,' she said as he opened the back door. 'I've never in my life made such a fool of myself. You've been very kind.'

'What are friends for? Listen, Isla, nobody can be strong for ever, not even you. Don't be so hard on yourself – you needed a good bawl, and today just happened to be the day for it,' he said, and went out, closing the door.

In July, Colin came home on leave. Isla had been living for that day, but as he stepped off the train at the West Station and came towards her, his nutbrown face almost split in two by his grin, she suddenly felt ridiculously shy. He was like a stranger, bronzed and more muscular than when he had first been called up, his teeth astonishingly large and white against his tan. Then she was swept up into his arms and despite the rough khaki uniform and the bronzed skin, she knew that he was still the man she had married.

She had worked hard in preparation for his return, putting in extra hours at the sanatorium in order to win some time off, cleaning the house from top to bottom with Betty's help, saving her coupons and the extras Gregg had brought so that she could feed him well.

He paused for a moment in the hall. 'The house hasn't changed a bit. I've dreamed of the smell of that furniture polish you always use.'

'Is that all you thought about while you were thousands of miles away? Furniture polish?'

He caught at her hand as she started to move towards

the kitchen, spinning her round and into his arms. 'Oh, I've thought of other things as well,' he murmured against her mouth, then scooped her into his arms.

'Colin, your parents are coming round in a little while!'

'And we'll be the perfect host and hostess when they arrive,' said Colin, marching up the stairs as though his wife weighed nothing at all. 'First, there's a little matter I've been dreaming about since the last time I was with you.'

'I've missed you,' he whispered later as they lay together in bed. 'Looking up at all those beautiful stars in the sky at night, and wishing that you were there to see them with me.'

Isla trailed her fingers down the side of his face and he caught at her hand and nibbled on her fingertips, then stretched and yawned. 'I suppose we'd better get ready to entertain our guests.'

She lay for a moment, watching him dress. His body had been tanned all over by a sun much more fierce than the sun that shone over Scotland.

'D'you think we'll ever get back to the way we were?'

He grinned down at her, his fingers moving nimbly down the front of his shirt, popping buttons into buttonholes with practised speed. 'Back together as a family? Of course we will, there's no doubt about it.' The grin faded. 'Though we're all going to miss Nan such a lot.'

'Yes, we are.'

'I felt even worse about persuading you to let Ross and Barbara go away when I heard about Nan,' Colin said sombrely. 'Now you're all alone and I can't do a damned thing about it. I often wish I could turn the clock back.'

'I'm managing – and they're fine where they are.

Mebbe it was for the best after all. At least I don't have to worry about a bomb mebbe falling on them at school. It's helped to hear so much about them from Gregg Marshall.'

'When am I going to meet him?'

'At the weekend. He offered to stay away and let us have time to ourselves while you were home, but I said you'd want to meet him. You'll like him, Colin, he's a very nice man.'

'I'm sure I will.' Then, stooping to kiss her nose, he added, 'But if you don't stop lying there, Mrs Forbes, looking so desirable and so tempting, I'll not be in a fit state to meet him, let alone my parents in about ten minutes.'

As Isla had expected, Gregg and Colin got on well together, and the Canadian paid several visits before Colin had to report back. When the time came, Isla found it hard to let him go, to step back and watch the train carry him away, knowing that his regiment was being sent to North Africa, where the fighting had been fierce and the Eighth Army forced back almost to Alexandria by Rommel's troops.

She missed him even more this time. The big bed was an island of loneliness, and she often lay awake, despite being exhausted by her work at the hospital, yearning for Colin. She knew, from the talk she heard from the rest of the staff at the sanatorium, that she wasn't the only woman to have such feelings. One or two of the nurses confessed, sometimes defiantly, sometimes tearfully, that they had found comfort with some other man.

For her part, there were times, particularly in the

first weeks after Colin's leave, when Isla found herself glancing at Gregg as they worked together in the garden, or sat on opposite sides of the kitchen table. She found herself wondering what it would be like to be held in his arms, caressed by those large, well-shaped, sure hands. She thrust the thoughts away as soon as they arrived, embarrassed and angry with herself. Once or twice she considered asking him not to come back, but he got such pleasure out of the visits that she couldn't bring herself to be so cruel.

Drew came home, no longer a gawky lad but a man in his naval uniform with the cap tilted jauntily over his eyes. He came to tell Isla that his sweetheart Mary had agreed that on his next leave they would marry.

'Our mums are going tae save their coupons, and their clothes coupons too, tae give us a smashing wedding,' he said happily, 'I can't wait to see my Mary as a bride. She's a lovely dresser – makes all her own now. She even knows how to paint her legs to look as if she's wearing stockings – the seam down the back and all!'

In the workshop, he ran his hands lovingly, just as Gregg had done, over the tools awaiting his return. 'It'll be good to get back to work again.'

'I'm not going to lose you to the Navy after the war?' Isla asked, and he looked round and grinned – again, just as Gregg had done.

'Not a chance. I'm enjoying the life, but I'm looking forward to coming home, too, and settling down. I've been sketching furniture in my spare time. I've got all sorts of plans – just you wait and see.'

For her part, Isla was afraid to look too far ahead. All her thoughts these days were with Colin, in North

Africa. His letters home made no mention of the life and death struggle for supremacy that they both knew couldn't be far away now. Instead, he wrote about everyday life in the desert.

'I suppose the flies were here before we were, but you'd think they'd be willing to have discussions with us about what should be theirs and what should be ours. They're even more obstinate than Rommel, and insist on being my food tasters, often getting eaten themselves if they don't get out of the way in time – and if I don't spot them in time. As to the sand, I wonder if eating and drinking sand with everything means that my teeth will benefit? They're constantly being scoured with the stuff. You'll be heading into winter now. It's cooler here, thank goodness, but still hot compared to home. I wish I was an artist, and able to capture the sunsets on paper and send them to you, my darling. They're beautiful, but they'd be even more beautiful if we could only be watching them together. Perhaps one day, when this war's over, I'll take you to Africa and show you those sunsets.'

The inevitable battle came in October, a fight that, once started, had to be fought to the bitter end. Even after the news came through that the Eighth Army had succeeded, at El Alamein, in forcing the enemy back and winning a massive victory, Isla couldn't rest until Colin's letter arrived, telling her that he had come through without injury. Then, and only then, she allowed herself to weep with relief.

Early in December, while Gregg and Isla were playing cards with Flora in her drawing-room, Gregg asked Isla to go with him to the Christmas dance at Prestwick Aerodrome.

'It'll be fun,' he coaxed when Isla refused. 'It's time you had some fun in your life, and you'd be doing me a big favour.'

'I'm not a dancer.'

'That doesn't matter, it's just a case of moving with the music.'

'On you go, Isla,' Flora urged. 'Everyone needs time off, and if you're not at the sanatorium you're dancing attendance on me. It's time you enjoyed yourself. It's Christmas!'

Isla finally gave in and agreed, then wished she hadn't when she surveyed her wardrobe in search of something to wear. The two evening dresses she possessed were rejected as being too formal, and all she could find was a pale pink silk blouse, and a dark blue evening skirt. They still fitted, but a glance in the mirror showed that they looked dated and uninteresting.

Magret called in at least once every week after her shift at the mills, since there was no longer any need to have 'his' dinner ready on time each evening, so Isla put on the blouse and skirt and paraded round the bedroom for her friend's benefit.

'I see what you mean,' Magret said. 'They've no' got much life tae them, have they?'

Isla lifted a handful of skirt, then released it. It fell limply against her thigh. 'I haven't time to make anything, and I'm not going to waste coupons on something I'll probably never wear again. Besides, I told Drew that I'd save some clothing coupons to help towards his wedding. I'll have to tell Gregg that I've changed my mind.' Peering in the mirror again, this time at her face, she added, 'Anyway, I'm thirty-nine, not nineteen. Far too old to go gallivanting off to dances.'

'Ach, ye're only as old as ye feel.'

'All right – forty-nine.'

'If that's the truth, it's probably time ye had a good night out. I tell ye what, I'll bring our Greta over tonight tae have a look at them. She's awful clever at making things over.'

'She'll have to be a miracle worker to make anything of this outfit.'

'Don't give up hope yet, hen,' Magret advised, and later that evening, she arrived on the doorstep with Greta.

Isla hadn't seen the girl since Barbara had gone to Canada, though she frequently heard from Magret about Greta's job in a draper's shop, and about her boyfriend, who was on important war work in the India Tyre factory at nearby Inchinnan. To her astonishment, the thin, plain little girl who had always been in Barbara's shadow had blossomed into a self-possessed young woman, casually smart in a red woollen jersey that showed off her full breasts and slim waist to advantage, worn over a snug-fitting tweed skirt. Greta's hair, once nondescript brown, had a chestnut glow to it, and was swept up to form a halo round her skilfully made-up face.

'How's Barbara?' she asked.

'She's fine – she's singing with a band now.' Isla produced some photographs that had just arrived from Canada, and Magret went through them, exclaiming over each one.

'My, wee Ross's nearly a man now, isn't he? Oh, Greta, look, isn't Barbara just beautiful?' She handed her daughter a photograph that Isla had looked at again and again, unable to believe that the lovely young woman standing at the microphone in a tight-bodiced, long-skirted dress with a sweetheart neck and short puffed sleeves, her long hair curling on her shoulders, could be the schoolgirl who had gone off with Ainslie.

'I like the frock,' Greta said. Later, in the bedroom, she eyed the pink blouse and navy skirt critically. 'I see what ye mean.'

'I haven't got anything else.'

'Mind if I have a look?' Greta riffled through the wardrobe and drew out a summer dress in navy, with large white spots, navy buttons down the bodice, and a cluster of artificial navy and white flowers pinned to the collar.

'The buttons are pretty, I could use them, and mebbe the flowers, but it'd mean spoiling yer dress. The skirt hangs well, though, ye could still use it, with a new waistband.'

'I doubt if I'd be wearing that dress again anyway. Do what you want with it – keep the skirt for yourself, if you can use it.'

'Oh, great!' For the first time, Greta looked animated. 'That Peter Pan collar on the blouse'll have tae go. All right if I change it about a bit?'

She took the clothes home with her, and returned them the day before the dance. When Isla put on the blouse and skirt she was stunned by the difference. The blouse now had a plain round neck, enlivened by a row of navy blue flowers from the bunch on the dress,

alternating with pink flowers that Greta had made from
the discarded collar. The plain pink buttons down the
front of the blouse had been replaced by decorative
navy buttons from the dress, and the starched skirt and
underskirt swirled and rustled as Isla moved around
the bedroom.

'Ye look bonny, Isla,' Magret marvelled, adding with
justified pride, 'I told ye our Greta was clever with a
needle, didn't I? Have ye noticed her skirt?'

Greta gave a twirl. She wore the same red jersey as
before, but tonight her skirt, snug-fitting over the hips
then full to the hem, was navy with white spots.

'Nothin' tae it, I just made up a waistband from the
bodice,' she said casually. 'Sit down and I'll cut yer
hair.'

She was as good with scissors as she was with a
needle. Isla's dark hair was neatly trimmed, then washed.
Then, using a poker heated in the kitchen range, Greta
curled the ends under.

'Ye're gettin' a bit grey at the temples,' she said
matter-of-factly. 'Wearing yer hair like this'll help tae
hide that.'

She tore up some newspaper into strips and used it
to put Isla's hair into curlers before she left.

'It'll be uncomfortable in bed tonight, but it'll be
worth it.' Then, delving in the large shoulder-bag she
had brought to produce bottles and boxes, 'Now I'll
show ye how tae do yer face.'

31

Greta was right – the newspaper curlers meant that Isla spent an uncomfortable night, but on the following evening, when she went over to show Flora her outfit, she had to admit that her suffering had been worthwhile. Her hair had brushed out into a soft bell about her face, and the blouse and skirt looked as though they had been made for each other.

For once Gregg had left his beloved motor-cycle in Prestwick and borrowed a car. When he arrived at Flora's, as arranged, to collect her, he stopped in the drawing-room doorway, staring. It was the first time Isla had seen him in uniform; they gaped at each other for a long moment, then caught each other's eyes and laughed.

'Stand side by side, and let me take a look at you,' the old woman commanded, nodding her satisfaction when, self-consciously, they obeyed. 'Very nice indeed. You make a smart couple. Now mind and give her a really good evening, she deserves it,' she commanded Gregg as he helped Isla into her everyday navy serge coat.

'I surely will, ma'am,' he promised solemnly.

In peace-time, Isla and Colin had often taken the children for summer holidays to Troon, close by to Prestwick. It was a pleasant part of the Clyde Firth, with great stretches of sand, and shallow water just right for paddling. She hadn't been back there since the war began, but had heard that the sandy beaches were covered with rolls of barbed wire to defend the Clydeside towns against invasion, and most of the hotels and gift shops and tearooms and ice-cream kiosks were closed and shuttered.

They drove down in the dark, so Isla had no chance to see the changes for herself. The dance was held in the canteen, which Gregg called the PX. It was a long wooden hut, with paper chains looped over the ceiling and walls, and a Christmas tree on either side of the stage where the band sat. They stepped through the dark entrance into a dazzle of light and a clamour of music and voices, and for a moment Isla hesitated. Gregg put an arm about her and steered her confidently round the edge of the dance floor, crowded with men in uniform and women, some uniformed, others in their best dresses, to a table where they were clearly expected. Chairs were hauled out for them, and Isla was introduced to more people than she could possibly remember.

'Now before she sits down, I'm taking her off to give her a few words of advice on how to handle you lot. Get her a drink, Gregg, we'll be back in a minute.' A young woman with blond hair swept up into a mass of curls at the top of her head took Isla by the hand and led her to the ladies powder room, where she leaned against a wash hand basin and took out a cigarette packet, lighting one for herself when Isla shook her head.

'I'm Doris, you're staying at my house tonight.' She blew a smoke-ring and studied Isla with bright blue eyes. 'I know they're a bit much when you're not used to them, but they're all nice lads. Far from home, and desperate to have as good a Christmas as they can, bless 'em.'

'You've been here before?' Isla combed her hair, then studied herself in the mirror.

'Here . . .' Doris took the comb from her and deftly flicked a stray wisp of hair into place. 'I work here, so I know them all. Gregg's one of the nicest. He's talked about you a lot – I'm glad you agreed to come to the dance, he didn't think you would.'

'Neither did I. I'm not used to socialising any more, it terrifies me.'

'There's no need, none of us bite. He really wanted to give you a good night out, in return for all the kindness you've shown him.'

'He's done more than enough, bringing us things, and helping in the garden.'

'But you've provided a home he can feel comfortable in, and that means a lot to all those lads out there. He's a real family man, is Gregg. It's a shame, what this war's done to his sort. Ready to go out and face them now?' Doris paused at the door and winked reassuringly. 'Just give yourself time to get used to us all, and make up your mind to have a good time.'

She was right. As Isla began to concentrate on the people around her, her nervousness faded. It returned when Gregg drew her on to the dance-floor, but he was a good dancer, and in his blue-uniformed arms she learned how to relax and follow the music. During the evening she danced with several of the men, but discovered that she was most comfortable with Gregg. They danced well together, moving in easy unison, and it came as quite a shock when the band struck up 'Auld Lang Syne' and she was whisked on to the floor to squeeze into a great circle, arms crossed, one hand in Gregg's, the other in the grip of Doris's partner, a navigator called Mike, to mark the end of the evening.

Gregg and Mike drove the two women to Doris's house in Prestwick, but didn't come in, because Doris's parents were asleep, and her father, a baker, had to get up early the next morning to start work in the bakehouse.

Declining Doris's whispered offer of a cup of tea, Isla followed the girl upstairs on tiptoe, carrying the small case she had brought with her. There were two beds in Doris's room, one of them the property of her sister, who was in the WAAC.

'I hope it didn't spoil your evening, having to come back here with me,' Isla said into the darkness when the two of them were in bed.

'No goodnight kiss from Mike, you mean?' Doris chuckled softly. 'Don't worry about that, we're just mates. My boyfriend's in a German PoW camp.'

'I'm sorry.'

'So am I.' For the first time Doris's voice was bleak, devoid of laughter. Then she said firmly, 'But he'll be home soon, you wait and see. Winnie says we've reached the beginning of the end, and I think he's right. G'night.'

Gregg drove Isla home on the following morning and they had lunch with Flora, who was waiting to hear all about the dance. Gregg, who had to go on duty that evening and would remain on duty over Christmas, presented Flora and Betty with their Christmas presents, a soft woolly bed-jacket for Flora, two pairs of stockings for Betty, and enthused over the hand-knitted scarf and the bottle of whisky he received in return.

'I'll savour this drop by drop,' he said, eyeing the whisky, but Flora snorted.

'Nonsense, man – half a tumblerful at a time, and don't forget to drink a toast to me.'

'Miss Currie, I'll be doing that for the rest of my life, believe me,' Gregg said sincerely. Later, in Isla's kitchen, he took a wrapped packet out of his pocket. For her, too, there were stockings, as well as a small box containing a butterfly brooch. She gave him a tie-pin, with matching cufflinks.

'Thank you for a lovely evening,' she said as he reluctantly got up to go.

'It's me who should be thanking you. You looked beautiful.' Then, as she began to move past him to open the door, he stopped her with a hand on her arm, and bent to kiss her, his mouth warm and hard on hers. In a reflex action, Isla's arms went round him, and his own embrace tightened. Suddenly overwhelmed by the need to be close to someone after all the months of abstinence, she clung to him, and he responded. When they finally stood back from each other, she saw her own hunger, her own need, mirrored in his rugged, normally laughing face.

As they stared at each other, their faces only inches apart, thoughts spun giddily through Isla's head. She wanted him to go away and never come back. She wanted him to kiss her again, to stay with her. She wanted to be able to turn the clock back, only five minutes, to the time before the kiss and the turmoil it had caused.

Finally, 'I have to go,' Gregg said, his voice husky, unsure of itself. 'Have a happy Christmas.'

'You too,' she said, and stood looking at the door long after he had gone through it.

'The man's a fool!' Flora glared at the wireless, where the Radio Doctor's fatherly voice was giving Boxing-Day advice on how to deal with the discomforts of overeating on Christmas Day. 'Overeating indeed – it seems to me that a fragment of chicken and a spoonful of potatoes followed by mashed parsnips with banana flavouring's not that far away from bread and water. How can anyone overeat on the rations we get? Switch him off, Isla, for goodness' sake!'

Isla obeyed, and silence fell on the room. Flora seemed to be dozing, as she often did these days, and Isla was startled when the old woman said abruptly, 'I've a feeling I did you a wrong when I persuaded you to go to that dance.'

'What?'

'Isla, we've known each other long enough to be honest. You've not been the same since you went to Prestwick.'

'There was nothing wrong with Prestwick, the folk there were very nice. I just miss the children, and Colin. Christmas is a bad time to be apart from your family,' Isla said shortly, burying her nose in the magazine she had been pretending to read.

She had been in a panic all through Christmas Day. Gregg's kiss had altered their relationship for ever. The memory of his mouth on hers, his arms about her, had haunted her ever since. Everything had changed, and suddenly he was no longer the friendly, likeable Canadian she had grown to depend on. He was a man, a very attractive man, who had succeeded in stirring up emotions that had lain dormant since Colin's last leave.

'It's more than just Christmas,' Flora said. 'I'd no worries about coaxing you to go to the dance with Gregg, for he could never be anything but a gentleman. But now I've a suspicion that that very thing might be the trouble.'

'Are you sure you didn't overeat? You're talking a lot of nonsense.'

'Am I? You're two decent people, and you've both been away too long from those you love. I should have thought of that, instead of just telling myself how nice it would be for the two of you to have a break from all this war business.' Flora's fingers twisted restlessly at the blanket about her knees.

'Flora, you've got nothing to reproach yourself about. Nothing happened!'

'No? There was a glow about the two of you when he brought you back the next day. I thought it was just the pleasure of the dance, but you've been ill at ease ever since, lassie, worried about something.'

'Who wouldn't be worried with her man . . .' Isla's voice wavered and she got up and made a business of stacking the used tea things so that Flora couldn't see her face. 'Her man away fighting?' she finished, gaining control over herself.

'One man away fighting, another nearer at hand, and both of them good caring souls,' Flora said from behind her. 'I nearly married once, you know.'

'You?'

Flora nodded. 'The marriage was all but settled, then a friend of my family's who'd been away from Paisley for years came back, and suddenly everything was changed. I swithered from one to the other, and I swithered too long. They both lost patience and looked elsewhere.' Flora gave a soft chuckle. 'It's as well for them that they did, for if they'd had the patience to wait, they'd be waiting still. To this day, I don't know myself which I wanted the most. But one thing I do know to my cost, Isla – it's possible for a woman to love two men.'

'In all the years I've known you, you've never said a word about this before,' Isla said suspiciously.

Flora's eyes, normally heavy-lidded now, flashed emerald fire at her. 'That's because I've never had need to,' she said.

Letters arrived early in January from North Africa, where Colin expected to remain for some time, and from Canada. Barbara, who at eighteen had left school and was singing with the band every week, wrote excitedly about their regular slot on radio. Ross, still at school, working for Phil at weekends and holidays, wrote about the timber-yard. Colin wrote about the flies and the sand and the other men. Isla had little to tell them in her replies, other than that she had been moved from nightshift to dayshift. Her days off were always the same, filled up with gardening, queuing outside food shops, visits next door, the petty annoyances of rationing and queues and having to do without, and the endless longing for peace and a return to normality.

She had dreaded meeting Gregg again, but when he roared up on his motor-cycle a few days after Christmas he was his usual relaxed self, and his visits continued as usual, though Isla noticed that, like her, he tended to avoid any physical contact with her, no matter how small or how innocent. By mutual, unspoken consent, they spent most of his time in Paisley with Flora.

Returning on a pleasant April afternoon from a dutiful visit to Colin's mother to find Gregg's motor-cycle on its rest at the front gate and Gregg himself working in the back garden, his jacket slung over the clothesline, Isla stood for a moment at the corner of the house, unnoticed, watching him. She knew that his father had been a farmer, and that Gregg had expected to follow in his footsteps. But a growing interest in machinery had led him to leave the farm in his late teens and set up his own business, supplying farm machinery. He still had a deep love of the land and enjoyed working it, no matter how small the scale. He was digging now to an easy rhythm, his lean body bending and swinging, his arms tensing then relaxing as he worked. As Isla watched him, she knew that Flora was right – it was possible to love two men, to want to be with one as much as the other.

He looked up just then, and the broad grin that was never far away spread over his face when he saw her.

'Hi there – I got an unexpected afternoon off, so I thought I'd get some work done on this ground before the weeds take over.'

'You shouldn't have bothered.'

'Why do the Scotch always say that?' Gregg asked.

'Scots. Scotch is the drink.'

'We learn something every day. You look very nice.'

Isla looked down at the suit she was wearing, a misty blue-grey check that Colin particularly liked. 'I always try to look smart when I visit Colin's mother. She expects it of me. I'll get changed.'

Later, working alongside him, sharing his country-man's pleasure in the good dark soil that slid from their spades, she felt soothed by his companionable silence. One day, she might have to face up to her feelings for him. But not yet.

They walked round to Flora's for tea, then returned to finish the digging, completing the task just as dusk brought out the clouds of tiny midges that made life outside unbearable. Then they drank cocoa in the kitchen and listened to the news broadcast on the radio, then to *ITMA*, which Gregg loved. He was roaring with laughter at something Tommy Handley had said when the back door burst open and Betty erupted into the room, heedless of the need to prevent the lamplight from spilling out of the door.

'Thank God you're still here, Mr Marshall.' Her face was as white as paper. 'It's Miss Currie, I think she's fallen in the bathroom and I can't get the door open—'

Gregg was on his way out of the kitchen before she had finished. The two women caught up with him just as he put his shoulder to the locked bathroom door. It flew open to reveal a small slight figure huddled on the floor.

'Let me by!' Isla pushed past the Canadian. Flora

was unconscious but still breathing. Her pulse was erratic and the area round her mouth had gone blue.

'Betty, telephone for the doctor.' Isla deftly drew Flora's nightdress and dressing-gown, which had rumpled up in her fall, down over her skinny legs, then Gregg carried the old woman across the hall and laid her gently on the bed.

'He's coming right away,' Betty said. 'He should be here in ten minutes.'

Isla, her fingers on Flora's pulse, laid her friend's hand down very gently on the bed, then tucked the blanket round Flora as though to protect her from the chill that was already on its way and would not be denied. 'There's no hurry,' she said.

32

Flora's family had been Baptists, and had worshipped at the Coats' Memorial Church, the church with the great sweep of stairs that Isla vaguely remembered passing on her way to visit Kenneth McAdam's grave, the first time she came to Paisley. That day seemed to belong to another life entirely, she thought, as she climbed the stairs to attend the funeral service, Gregg by her side.

The church's interior was beautiful and spacious, but even so it was quite well filled with people who had come to pay their respects to the last member of a family well respected and remembered in the town. Isla spotted Charlie Blayne, the auctioneer, among them and later, after Flora had been laid to rest in the imposing family plot not far from Kenneth's grave, she introduced him to Gregg.

The auctioneer's hair, a mixture of brown and grey when Ainslie had worked for him, was now a mass of tight silvery curls. He beamed at Gregg and shook his hand enthusiastically, then introduced his wife, a small neat woman almost hidden by his big sturdy body.

'How's Ainslie?'

'Very well, and busy looking after my two as well as her own boys. The twins'll be eleven next month.'

Charlie shook his head in wonder. 'Time flies when ye measure it against youngsters growing up. Give the lassie my regards the next time ye write, and tell her we still miss her at the auction-rooms. She could've done very well as an auctioneer if she hadnae lost her head and run off to Canada.'

'I think it was her heart she lost, Mr Blayne,' said Gregg, amused.

'Call me Charlie, son, everyone does. Aye, well, I suppose we all let our hearts away with too much.' Charlie put an arm about his wife and hugged her. 'Eh, Lizzie?'

'Aye, we all have a daft streak in us,' she said dryly, then to Isla and Gregg, giving Charlie a dig with her elbow, 'this is mine, and the older he gets the dafter he gets.'

Once again Gregg had borrowed a car from someone at the aerodrome. As it moved down the cemetery drive Isla asked him to stop for a moment. 'I'll not be long,' she said as she got out.

It was only a short walk along a side path to where Kenneth and his son lay. Catherine, at her own wish, had been buried in Dumfries. Isla stood for a moment, wishing that she had thought to bring flowers, even a single blossom, from those heaped round Flora's grave.

'Someone special?' Gregg asked as she went back to the car and settled herself beside him.

'Someone very special.'

The nieces whom Flora had never been able to give dolls' houses to were at the funeral, and so were the

403

nephews. Because none of them belonged to Paisley, Isla had offered to hold the reception at her own house where, by dint of a lot of careful planning, and help from Betty and from Gregg, who brought provisions from the PX at Prestwick, she managed to provide everyone with food and drink.

Nobody stayed long, for many of the mourners had come from outside Paisley, and were anxious to get home before dark because of the blackout.

'We're grateful to you for all your help,' one of the nieces said as she was leaving. 'We'll be back next week to clear the house out and see Mr Forbes about selling it.'

Betty, who was going back to her family in Bishopton, a nearby village, was the last to leave. 'I'll never forget Miss Currie,' she said at the door, tears in her eyes, then she left, and Isla went back to the living-room, where Gregg was gathering up cups and plates.

'I'll help to clear things up,' he offered. 'I don't have to be back at the airbase for a few hours yet.'

After washing the dishes, they put the living-room to rights and Gregg got out the carpet sweeper while Isla made tea. It was growing dark, and he made sure that the blackout curtains were all in place before joining her in the kitchen. 'She had a very happy time, that last day,' he said gently, after a long silence. 'We all did, remember?'

Isla nodded, remembering how Flora had had them both laughing, Gregg until the tears ran down his cheeks, with some story of friends of her parents. 'I'm not being malicious, you understand,' she had said, her

404

green eyes gleaming. 'Just a wee touch wicked – but that makes for a better story, doesn't it?'

'It's good to spend your last hours in life with friends,' Isla said now, summoning a smile.

'Are you sure you'll be all right on your own tonight? You look worn out. I can phone the base and tell them I can't get back until morning.'

'Of course I'll be all right,' she said at once, and knew by the way the colour rose in his face that her voice had been too sharp.

'I didn't mean . . .'

'I know. I'm sorry. I'll be fine.'

'Take some whisky before you go to bed, it'll help. Here . . .' he started to reach into his jacket pocket for his flask, but Isla stopped him with an upraised hand.

'Not brandy in my tea again, thank you, I remember the taste from last time. I've got some whisky, I'll make myself a hot toddy before I go to bed.'

'Okay.' Silence fell between them, companionable at first, almost like the old days, then gradually taking on a meaning of its own. It couldn't be allowed to continue, Isla thought, and jumped up to switch on the radio. A man's voice came through, talking about architecture in Italy. She twirled the dial in search of some music, or a comedy programme, but tonight every station she could find had people talking. All except one, but it was playing gloomy funereal music that she knew would reduce her to tears on such a day. She wished that she had thought of sitting in the living-room, where there was a gramophone.

Instead of sitting down at the table again she picked up her cup and drained it, then took it over to the sink.

'I'm so tired that I don't think I'll need that whisky,' she said over her shoulder.

Gregg brought his own cup to the sink. 'In that case, I'll clear out and leave you in peace.'

Isla took the cup from his hand, almost dropping it in her eagerness not to let their fingers touch, and started washing it vigorously, listening to the sounds he made as he picked up his jacket and put it on.

'I'm going to miss Flora a lot,' he said, his voice sombre. 'You've both been family to me since I came over here. She was like a favourite aunt, and you . . .' He stopped, then said slowly, 'Isla, we have things to talk about.'

'Not tonight.' She swung round from the sink, and pulled the tea-towel from its hook so roughly that the material caught and tore.

'You know what I mean, don't you?' Gregg asked. 'We've been scared to look at each other ever since the dance.'

'I don't know what you're—'

'For God's sake, Isla,' he suddenly burst out. 'Don't start behaving like a flirty teenager! That's not you at all. We're grown-up people, old enough to face up to what's happening.'

'We're married people too, with growing children, and responsibilities.'

'I know that.' He sounded so defeated that she wanted to go to him and hold him and comfort him. Instead, she folded the towel with great care, hung it over the back of a chair, and sat down at the table, so weary that she could no longer stay on her feet.

'I know,' Gregg said again, quietly, letting his lean

body fold down into the opposite chair, resting his curled fists on the scrubbed wooden table. 'I love Pat – but now I love you too.' The fists tightened. 'I never thought there could be room in my life for another woman, but there is. A great empty hole I knew nothing about, just waiting to be filled to the brim by you.'

'I wish I'd never gone to that dance!'

'I wish I hadn't asked you. I wouldn't have, if I'd had any idea of the harm it was going to do. But there's no use in wishing the past away. One kiss,' he said in wonder. 'One little friendly Christmas kiss between friends. That's all it was supposed to be. But I've not been able to get you out of my mind since, not for a minute.'

'It would have been better if you hadn't come back.'

'I know, but I couldn't have stayed away. Isla . . .'

He looked up from his hands, catching her gaze before she could turn away. His look seemed to light up the kitchen, his love was like a soft blanket, waiting to enfold and cherish her. She wanted to draw its warmth around her and stay in its folds for the rest of her life. But she couldn't, she mustn't.

He read her thoughts, and tried to lighten the tension between them. 'Of course, there was another reason why I couldn't stay away. I knew that the vegetable bed needed digging.' For a moment, as they laughed together, the clock was turned back and everything was all right again. Then, watching the laughter fade from Gregg's eyes, seeing the bleak despair that replaced it, Isla knew that, like her, he knew what must be done.

'There's no future for us, is there?' It was a statement, not a question.

'No future at all, Gregg. My Colin, your Pat – they don't deserve to be hurt.'

'I don't want to hurt you either.'

'At least I'll know why, and I'll know it's for the best.'

Gregg suddenly lifted his fists then slammed them down hard on to the table. 'God damn it, how can it be so wrong to love somebody and want to be with them. I could wring Adolf Hitler's damned neck! If it wasn' for him, I'd never have come to Scotland, or met you . . .'

'If you want to wring his neck, you'll have to stand in a very long line,' Isla said wryly, and he gave a grunt o laughter that was almost a sob. The sound of it hurt her unbearably.

'Right. Anyway, I guess I'd prefer knowing you and losing you to not knowing you at all.' He put his hands flat on the table and studied them. 'We seem to have talked ourselves into a decision.'

'Yes, we have.'

He got up, reached for his cap, then turned, his eyes pleading. 'Isla, can I stay here tonight? Just one time, once to remember for the rest of my life?'

It would have been so easy to say yes. Nobody need ever know, nobody would be hurt. But against all her own instincts, Isla shook her head. 'I think you should go now, Gregg. And I don't think you should come back.' I struck her that this was the second time she had sent a man away. The last occasion had had a happy ending but that couldn't, wouldn't happen again.

Gregg gave a long defeated sigh, then got to his feet Isla stared down at the table, praying that he wouldn' touch her, knowing that one touch from a finger-tip would be enough to destroy the wall she had managed to build round herself.

'You know something? I'm glad I took you to the dance,' Gregg said. 'At least I got to hold you in my arms, even though there were about a hundred other people round us.'

The door opened, then closed swiftly, to keep the light from spilling out. Isla got up and fumbled her way through the dark hall and into the living-room to the window, bumping into furniture as she went. She drew the blackout aside, but it was so dark outside that she could see nothing. She stood clutching the folds of material, hoping that he would change his mind and come back, but at the same time praying that he would just go away and get it over with.

Outside, a car engine hiccuped, then roared into life. The sound dwindled away into the distance, and faded to nothing.

The days trailed by, each just like the one that had gone before it. Gregg stayed away, and didn't make any attempt to get in touch with her, and with the house next door lying empty, Isla felt completely alone. Several times she found herself hurrying down the path on her way to visit Flora, and had to turn and trail back to the house. The only bright moments in her life came when she received letters from Colin and the children and Ainslie. She carried their letters and photographs around with her, reading and re-reading the written words until she could have recited every single one of them in her sleep, running the tips of her fingers hungrily over the photographs. Her longing for the children, assuaged a little by Gregg's descriptions of them, came back as strong as ever, to torment her.

Flora's relatives returned to clear everything out of the house, and a 'For Sale' sign went up in the garden.

'Heaven knows why,' Gilchrist Forbes said when Isla paid her weekly visit to him and his wife. 'It's not a through road, so there's no passing traffic to see the sign. But it's what they wanted, and the client is always right.'

Isla fell heir to Flora's dolls' houses, because nobody else wanted them. 'I don't know what she collected them for,' one of the nieces said when she made the offer. 'They just gather dust. I understand that you like that sort of thing, Mrs Forbes, so perhaps you'd care to take them. I seem to remember that there was a very nice Victorian house – you don't happen to know what happened to it, do you?'

'It was refurbished and auctioned to raise money for the families of the children killed in the Glen Cinema disaster.'

'Oh yes, I remember hearing about that,' the woman said vaguely. 'What on earth made her think of selling the little house, though? It must have been worth quite a bit – why couldn't she have just donated a pound or so to the fund and be done with it?'

The houses, together with a few boxes containing a jumble of furniture and dolls, had to be stacked on the upstairs landing, because Isla couldn't get them up into the loft by herself, and Gregg was no longer around to do it for her. One of them, Isla noticed, looked quite like the house next door. She took it into her bedroom o that she could study it, and decided that once the war was over, she would furnish it and turn it into a copy of Flora's house, just for herself.

The thought cheered her and gave her something to do in her spare time, sketching the rooms in Flora's home from memory, and sorting through the boxes of odds and ends in search of pieces she might be able to use for the task.

In May, the Allied forces, Colin among them, took Tunis, and it began to look as though the war was beginning to swing, slowly, in the Allies' favour.

Drew came home on leave, and as soon as Isla opened the door and saw him standing in the porch she knew that there was something wrong. He was wearing civilian clothes this time, and all his jauntiness had vanished. He followed her through to the kitchen, but declined her offer of a cup of tea.

'Mary's married,' he said bluntly.

'Married? Oh, Drew, I'm so sorry!'

'Not half as sorry as I am,' Drew said between clenched teeth. 'She met up with some damned Geordie soldier in the NAAFI and off she went. She'd only known him a matter of weeks, her mum said. I knew she should never have gone to work in that NAAFI, I said so at the time. But she wanted to do her bit.' He drooped over the kitchen table, the picture of misery. 'She did that, all right. Sent me one of those "Dear John" letters.'

'Mary's not the only girl in the world. You'll find somebody else, somebody more worthy of you.'

He wasn't impressed. 'That's what my mum says, but I don't want anyone else, I just want my Mary.

411

She'll be sorry, you know. I reckon she married the uniform, not the bloke. He'll look a lot different in civvies doing a nine to five job and moaning because his tea's not ready.'

In an attempt to take his mind off Mary, Isla asked him to store the dolls' houses in the attic for her. He agreed in a lackadaisical way, but had brightened up a little by the time the job was done, even going out to his workshop to give some of his tools a good cleaning. Standing by the door, watching him at work, Isla was able to pretend for a little while that the war had never happened, that Nan was bustling around the kitchen and Colin was in his office and the children were due home from school at any minute, fighting to be first through the gate.

When Drew had finished they went back into the house, where he downed a mugful of cocoa and ate a jam sandwich as they made plans for future dolls' houses once he was back on civvy street.

Drew liked the idea of the Flora Currie house. 'She was a nice old soul, Miss Currie. I was sorry when Mum told me she'd gone.'

On the doorstep on his way out, he stopped to say 'Mum and me are going to have a slap-up meal before I go back, with the coupons she was keeping for the wedding. And I've given her some money and told her to go out and put the clothing coupons she was keeping towards a fur coat for herself. They'd have been wasted on that Mary anyway.' And he went off with the slightly rolling step common to all seamen, leaving Isla to struggle with the mental picture of little Mrs Brown, thin and stooped, creeping along George Street in a fur coat.

Colin had survived the desert, and the taking of Sicily, and his letters had grown confident and cheerful, certain of victory now that the list of Allied victories was steadily increasing. In Canada, Barbara had gone on tour with the band, to Isla's consternation, though Ainslie's letters were reassuring.

'Phil and I felt that it would be wrong to insist on her staying here instead of going. She'll be nineteen in two months' time, Isla, she's not a child any more. The band leader's wife is travelling with them, a sensible soul who can be trusted to keep an eye on Barbara. Anyway, you've got a level-headed daughter, and I'm sure she's well able to make her own decisions.'

It seemed to Isla, who still tended to think of Barbara and Ross as she had last seen them, that she was caught in a time warp. Even with the photographic proof before her, she found it hard to think of Barbara as a young woman and Ross, now fifteen, as a youth on the brink of manhood.

Gilchrist Forbes sold Flora's house in September to a couple with a young family. A lot was done to it before they moved in, and the quiet road, which had once known the roar of Gregg's motor-cycle, now echoed to the sound of hammering and sawing, and workmen calling to each other.

Another letter came from Ainslie, a thick envelope. Isla knew, just by looking at it, that it carried bad news. She had recently received Ross's usual fortnightly letter, but nothing from Barbara, who had fallen into the habit of sending cards from wherever she and the band were playing, and photographs of herself and the grinning musicians. There were usually some fans in the photographs too, young men, and the occasional young woman, autograph book in hand.

She carried the envelope into the kitchen and laid it on the table. If Flora had been alive, she would have gone next door to open it, but Flora wasn't there any more, Colin was far away in Sicily, and Isla was on her own. After five minutes, during which her imagination ran riot, she opened the envelope.

Ainslie's writing, normally neat, sprawled across the pages, launching into the story she had to tell without wasting time on chat about the weather. Because the Canadian government had become somewhat edgy about the number of British children evacuated to their country and left there for much longer than had first been anticipated, they had recently been checking on all the British people temporarily resident in their country. Ainslie had explained that Barbara and Ross were not technically evacuees, but her half-sister and half-brother, visiting her on an extended stay.

This had been accepted without comment, but unfortunately, now that Barbara required a work permit in order to travel with the band, she had had to deal with some paperwork on her own, and had seen, in black and white, the details about her relationship with Ainslie.

'She managed to get time off, and came here in quite a state,' Ainslie wrote. 'I explained that you had thought it best to leave things alone until you were able to tell her in person, but I'm afraid she was in no mood to accept that. She's very hurt, Isla – she wouldn't discuss it with me, just went storming back to Ottawa. She's since written to Ross, but not to me. Ross, by the way is quite pleased to find that he's related, through me, to Phil and the boys, and not in the least bothered. I suppose Barbara's just more emotional than he is.'

Isla groaned softly as she reached the end of the letter. She should have told Barbara the truth earlier, but by the time the girl reached the age when she might have started asking questions about her real father, she was in Canada and involved in a new life.

She waited and worried for a few weeks, hoping that her daughter would write, reluctant to burden Colin with her problems when he was so far away and engaged in the day to day business of just staying alive. But there was no word from Barbara. Ross wrote, bubbling over with the joy of discovering that he had a whole set of relatives. 'I think it's great,' his untidy scrawl said. 'It makes me feel as if I'm really part of the Hannigan family. I expect Ainslie's told you that Barbara's not so happy about things, Mum. I can't think why, because she really likes Ainslie. I suppose it's something to do with being female. Don't worry, she'll come round to it.'

But Barbara didn't come round to it. Eventually, deciding that she could wait no longer for a letter from the girl, Isla steeled herself to sit down at Colin's desk on one of her days off, and start writing a long letter to Barbara.

The only way, she thought, chewing the end of the pen, was to tell the whole story, from the first day she had set eyes on Kenneth McAdam in the men's surgical ward of the Edinburgh hospital where she was a probationer. She wrote steadily for several hours, keeping nothing back, forcing herself to go once again through all the pain of Kenneth's death, and the discovery of his other marriage and the first, terrible, meeting with Ainslie. It was even harder than she had expected it to be, but Barbara already felt as though she was being deceived, and now she needed, and deserved, every bit of the truth.

She stopped to eat and to rest her hand and wrist, which were stiff and painful, then drove herself back to the desk. 'I meant to tell you and Ross when you were old enough to understand, but by the time you both reached that stage, you were in Canada. Your real father loved you very much, Barbara, and so do I. Colin thinks of you as his own daughter. I know it must be hard for you to discover that your father and I were never legally married, but surely you must see that the important thing is that you're part of a family, and nothing will ever change that.'

It was late when she finished, signing and sealing the letter without reading it over, partly because she was afraid that she might then lose the courage to post it, partly because having just relived years of her life on paper, she couldn't bear to go over it all again. She had even taken Kenneth's final letter, the letter Gilchrist Forbes had given her when he came to tell her of Kenneth's death, from the tiny drawer below her jewel box, and copied it out word for word.

She slept badly that night, and went out to post the letter as soon as the post-office opened, before walking to the sanatorium.

It was a difficult day. For some unknown reason, the patients were all irritable, and two of the nurses on her shift were ill and off work. A group of officials chose that day of all days to inspect the place, and the matron took her nervousness out on her staff. Worn out though she was, Isla welcomed the hard work, because at least it kept her from fretting about Barbara, and reliving the submerged memories that had been released by the letter, and thrown up to the surface of her mind.

She stayed on duty for a few hours longer than necessary to help the night staff, also short-handed, to settle the patients down, then walked slowly home through a dark night lit, now and again, by the moon glancing through scudding clouds. She was halfway down the hill when she saw a sudden tiny flare of light appear then disappear as someone at the foot of the hill pulled on a cigarette. Isla stopped, listening, but there was no sound of footsteps either approaching or walking away from her, and no voices. She stared into the night until her eyes were aching, and eventually glimpsed another tiny glow, just where the first had been. Someone was standing near the wooden door she had to go through to reach Low Road.

Isla fumbled for the torch she always carried in her bag. She hadn't used it on the walk because the batteries were low, and she knew the way from sanatorium to Low Road so well that she could have walked it blindfold. She switched the torch on, but the light was so weak and wavery that it was no use to her at all.

She bit her lip. The moon had been hidden for the past few minutes, and she was in total darkness. She was on her own, faced with the prospect of trudging back to the hospital, or going on. Home was nearer. It had been raining when she left the house that morning, and she was carrying her folded umbrella. She gripped it firmly and walked on, the tap of her heels on the roadway loud in the silence.

She had almost reached the door when she heard the sound of movement, the heel of a shoe scraping on the pavement as someone turned. Just then the moon slid out from the clouds and shone on the man turning towards her. It was Gregg Marshall.

'Isla,' he said, 'I couldn't stay away.'

33

Gregg lit a fire in the living-room and they talked half the night, sitting on the rug before the fireplace. He had applied for a transfer to an air base in England, and it had come through. He was leaving in a few days' time.

'When it came to it I couldn't just leave without seeing you, just one last time,' he said, and Isla, happy for the first time since Flora's death, unable to believe that he was really there, really with her, reached out and allowed her fingers the luxury of touching his face. He put his own hand on hers, turning her hand so that his mouth could brush over her palm. 'How've you been?' His eyes travelled over her face. 'You look worn out, Isla. What's wrong?'

She told him about Barbara, the words spilling out. It was such a relief to be able to talk about it. He listened in silence, and when she had talked herself out, he took his handkerchief and dabbed gently at her face, drying tears that she hadn't even noticed.

'Isla, Barbara's a very nice girl who's growing up to be a very nice, very beautiful, very sensible woman. I've got no doubt of that. You're going to have to give her time, honey – as much of it as she needs. She'll come to terms with everything, and while you're waiting, just keep on writing to her. She's been hurt, but she needs to know that this doesn't make any difference to the way you love her. What does Colin have to say about it?'

'I haven't told him. He's got enough to worry about.'

Gregg's eyebrows rose. 'Honey, he's the only father Barbara's ever known, and she's his daughter now. Don't try to cut him out of what's happening; if you do he'll resent it when he finally finds out.'

Isla looped her hands about her knees, staring into the fire. 'Oh, Gregg, I've made a terrible mess of things!'

He shifted so that he could put an arm about her. It was good to be able to lean back against a man's shoulder again. 'You haven't made a mess of anything, you've just been trying to save other people from grief. You've been so used to coping on your own all the years you were raising your kids that you've forgotten how to let others help.' He squeezed her shoulder. 'You need to loosen up, lady. Nobody can take the cares of the world on their shoulders, not even Isla Forbes.'

'Oh, Gregg, I'm so glad you came to Paisley tonight.'

She felt a laugh rumble through his body. 'I aim to please, ma'am.'

They sat together in silence for a long time, looking into the fire. Then Isla stirred, turned, and found his mouth waiting for hers.

Loving Gregg in the firelight, being loved by him, was inevitable and natural and, in its own way, right. At the beginning they were hungry for each other, hungry for contact, demanding and taking, almost devouring each other. Then, with the first urgent need satisfied, their lips and hands and bodies gentled into true loving and giving and receiving in mutual pleasure, both anxious, in this first and last time together, to give as much happiness to the other as possible. They spoke to each other with their bodies, their mouths, their hands. Questions were asked and answered, pledges made, assurances given, without a word being spoken aloud.

The years seemed to drop from them, and they loved like teenagers, rather than the parents of growing children. Isla felt no self-consciousness at all over exposing her aging body to his gaze and his touch, nor was there any guilt. Colin had always been an enthusiastic lover, though considerate; Gregg brought a form of poetry to his lovemaking, worshipping and celebrating their union with every part of himself, finally flowing into her and around her, enclosing her, merging the two of them into one being.

She sensed, as she responded with a fluidity that she had never known before, that this was not the way he and his wife made love, just as it was nothing like the way she and Colin coupled. This was unique, belonging only to the two of them, and only for this one magical night. It was a primitive celebration of their meeting at a time when their great need of each other surpassed everything that had been in their lives before, or would come again.

At last, they slept in each other's arms, lying on cushions, wrapped snugly together in the large woollen shawl that was normally draped along the back of the couch. Isla wakened to find Gregg kneeling by her side, his lips moving slowly, gently, across her breasts. The fire had gone out, and because of the blackout, the room was dark, but she could hear birdsong outside.

'It's five o'clock, honey,' he said against her shoulder. 'I'll have to go.'

She wrapped her arms about him, drawing him close. 'Not yet . . .'

'Not quite yet,' Gregg agreed, his body responding to the movement of her limbs. This time the magic of the night before had gone, and they made love comfortably, completely, like a man and a woman who were dear friends, as well as sharing a mutual physical attraction. But his leaving couldn't be put off for ever; they dressed swiftly in lamplight, then walked to the door, their arms around each other. It was almost daylight outside, the air fresh after the previous day's rain.

'Are you sure you won't have something to eat before you go?'

'If I stay any longer, I'll never leave.' He kissed the tip of her nose, and said, 'I'll wheel the bike to the end of the road, otherwise the neighbours'll start talking about you.'

They looked at each other, a long look that they both knew would have to last the rest of their lives. 'I won't write,' Gregg said. 'I mean, I will, often, but I won't send any of the letters. Best to end it here and now.'

'When the war's over, we might go to Canada to visit Ainslie.'

'If you do, I'll stay away. I don't think I could bear to see you and not be able to touch you.' He kissed her, his mouth hard on hers. 'Take care,' he said, then she was alone, straining for one last glimpse of him through

422

the bushes as he kicked the bike off its stand and wheeled it along the road.

When he had gone, Isla bathed in the few inches of tepid water allowed by the war regulations, dressed, and had breakfast before going into the living-room to open the blackout and restore the spilled cushions and shawl to their rightful places. She cleaned the ashes from the fireplace, washed the mugs and plates they had used, then set off for the sanatorium.

Although she had had very little sleep she strode briskly up the hill and along the road, ignoring the heavy rain-filled clouds that had begun to gather over-head. She felt fit and well, refreshed and renewed by Gregg's loving. Catching sight of her reflection in the glass panel of the sanatorium door as she was about to go in, she made a face at herself, then smiled.

She was forty years old, but she felt as young as Barbara. She would never cease to be grateful to the big Canadian for blessing her life, reminding her what it felt like to be young again, and happy. A mere fifteen hours earlier she had felt old and tired and depressed. Now, stepping into the sanatorium, she felt strong and opti-mistic. Although she had no knowledge of what lay ahead, she was sure that everything was going to be all right.

At last, in September, Barbara sent a letter. It was brief and somewhat cool, but at least it was a letter.

'I feel as though after all these years of being me, I'm not me at all,' she wrote. 'I'm a different person alto-gether. You should have told me, or Ainslie should have told me, instead of leaving me to find out the way

I did. I still don't know right now how I feel about it all, but I guess I should thank you for finally telling me everything.'

Although she wanted to reply at once, Isla restrained herself for a week, then wrote a chatty and affectionate letter, making no further reference to Kenneth other than to assure her daughter that she understood how Barbara felt, and would leave her to sort out her own feelings in her own time.

Christmas came and went, bringing with it bitter-sweet memories of the dance at Prestwick aerodrome the year before, and Christmas Day with Flora. This year Isla worked during Christmas Day and visited Colin's parents in the evening. On Boxing Day she went to Magret's to admire Greta's new engagement ring and meet her fiancé, a plump, fair-haired, shy young man content to sit in a corner and watch his beloved with adoring brown spaniel eyes. He and Greta didn't plan to marry for a year, at least. They had already put their names down for a Corporation house in one of the housing schemes built before the war.

'We don't mind which,' Greta told Isla. 'Whitehaugh, or Lochfield, or Ferguslie Park. The houses are all very nice.'

The Gillespies, the couple who had bought Flora's house, had moved in just before Christmas. They had two young children, a boy and a girl, and Isla welcomed the sound of the children's voices as they played in the garden. Early in January Janice Gillespie appeared at the dividing hedge as Isla walked up the path to her own door and invited her in for a cup of tea that afternoon.

Isla hesitated. 'I've got rather a lot to do,' she lied, reluctant to go back into a house which held so many memories.

The young woman looked disappointed. 'Just for a little while,' she begged. 'I wanted to ask you about something.'

So Isla agreed, then discovered when she nerved herself to step over the door lintel that it wasn't so difficult after all, because the house had changed out of all recognition. All Flora's dark wallpaper had been stripped off and replaced by pale distemper, 'stippled' with clusters of colour applied by dipping a sponge in paint then dabbing it over the walls. The furniture was modern and lightweight, and the couch and chairs in the living-room were covered with dark brown material, heaped with small cushions in vivid colours and patterns.

Janice Gillespie, pouring tea from an elegant, pale green fluted china pot into matching cups, suited her surroundings. She, too, was smart and modern, with short, well-cut dark hair, and red fingernails. She wore a dark green linen dress beneath a short-sleeved yellow coatee. Isla had heard that Mrs Gillespie came from a wealthy family, and her husband held down an important job at the munitions factory in Bishopton.

'Won't you have a biscuit? You'll probably think this is very impertinent of me, Mrs Forbes,' the young woman said a little nervously, putting the plate down. 'But I understand that you run a very successful business, furnishing dolls' houses.'

'I did, before the war. I'm nursing at the Craw Road sanatorium now, but I intend to start the business up again when I can.'

EVELYN HOOD

'Oh, I see.' Janice Gillespie looked disappointed. 'My daughter Angela's going to be six years old next month, and my sister's offered us the dolls' house her own daughter used to play with. But it's all very shabby now, and I'd hoped to persuade you to furnish it for her.'

'I do have some furniture, but it's rather ordinary,' Isla said hesitantly. 'I usually use specially made pieces, but my craftsman's in the Navy.'

Hope came into her neighbour's face. 'We wouldn't want anything too elaborate at this stage. Angela's too young to appreciate it, so we thought – just an ordinary little house that she can enjoy—'

'Ask your husband to bring it round tonight, when she's in bed,' Isla told her impulsively, 'and I'll do my best.'

Clearly, there was a genuine mother beneath Mrs Gillespie's sophistication. She beamed her delight. 'That's so kind of you!'

Later, showing her visitor out, she said, 'I understand that you knew the previous owner well. It must be strange to see how much we've changed the house.'

'I'm glad you did.' Isla looked round the hall and said, 'I think it rather likes the changes.'

'Really? We loved the place the moment we set eyes on it. It has a good feeling about it. I hope the children haven't disturbed you, playing in the garden. They're thrilled to be able to get out – we were in digs before, and there was nowhere for them to go. We had to spend most of the day in the park.'

'I enjoy hearing them – it brings back memories. My own children are in Canada for the duration of the war.'

'How dreadful for you, being apart from them!'

'They're not really children any more, almost grown up. But yes, I miss them very much, so it's good to hear your youngsters. And I think,' Isla said warmly, 'that the previous owner would be pleased if she knew that there was a family in the house again.'

Walking home, taking the old familiar route down one path, along the pavement, and up the other path, Isla was glad that she had thought of doing a copy of Flora's house eventually. Although the real house had changed out of all recognition, she would have her replica full of memories.

Mr Gillespie brought the dolls' house round that evening. When he had gone Isla eyed it thoughtfully. It had four rooms and an entrance hall and a flight of stairs to the upper floor, and once it had had a cheerful red roof, now scratched and faded. She ferreted in the cupboard in the workroom, unearthed some small pots of paint, brushes, items and furniture and scraps of material, and got to work.

The little house kept her happily occupied in her spare time over the next four weeks, and when she handed it back to the delighted Gillespies, fresh and colourful and furnished, she began work straightaway on what she now thought of as the Flora house, doing what she could and leaving the more difficult tasks until the day when Drew would be back in his workshop.

Another letter arrived from Barbara, still cool, but a little longer than the last letter, with some news of the band tour. Ainslie wrote to say that Barbara had asked her for photographs of Kenneth, which had been sent to her.

In March, Colin came home on leave, and insisted on taking Isla to Largs for a holiday by the Clyde. He booked a comfortable room in a comfortable hotel, and they spent most of their days braving the weather, walking along the front, wrapped up in their warmest clothes. Colin looked, on those outings, as though he was about to set out on an expedition to the North Pole. Largs, an attractive and very popular holiday town, was noted for its stiff sea breezes and Colin, used now to a much warmer climate, felt the cold intensely.

Isla had wondered, nervously, in the time between hearing that he was coming home and his actual arrival, if Gregg would come between them, if Colin might somehow taste the Canadian on her skin, read about him in her eyes, sense him in her touch. But once she was with him, held in his arms, she knew that there had been nothing to fear. Like Flora, she had learned that it was possible to love two men deeply. What had happened between herself and Gregg had come about because they had had a great need of each other at a certain stage in their lives. It had been written into their stars at birth, and it had also been written that, physically, their union would be brief. In every other way, it was real, and lasting, and guiltless.

Gregg would always be with her, locked away in a deep, secret compartment that nobody else would ever know about. But Colin was her husband, her love, her future, her life. He had asked, casually, about Gregg, and Isla had told him, just as casually, that the Canadian was in England.

'I dreamed of wet streets at night,' he said as they leaned on the rail on their first day in Largs, watching the waves race each other down the Firth of Clyde and the small boats at anchor rocking and tugging on their cables like horses trying to break free, 'with lamplight shining on puddles, and of the way falling rain dimples water, and sometimes I dreamed about snowball fights and zooming down a hill on a sledge. We must take the children sledging the first winter we have together.'

'They'll probably feel that they're too old for that sort of thing by then. Anyway, they've had lots of snow in Canada. Ours might be a comedown.'

'I don't care what they think – we're all going sledging in the first peacetime snow, and that's that,' Colin said stubbornly, then shivered and pulled the brim of his soft hat down as another gust of wind came chasing along the front towards them. 'I can't say I missed the gales, though.'

'We should have stayed at home.'

'No we shouldn't. You badly needed a holiday, and I wanted us to spend some time alone together. If we'd stayed in Paisley my mother would have been knocking at the door every day.'

'She's missed you, too.'

'I know, and I promise that I'll make a fuss of her when we get back, but you come first,' he told her. 'I want you to get the sea air into your lungs. Breathe deeply, or you'll end up as a patient in that sanatorium of yours.'

'I'm perfectly well!'

Colin put an arm about her and held her close, bending to nuzzle his cold face against hers. 'I don't know how you've been able to stand it. At least we're well fed, and we get the feeling that we're getting things done, bringing an end to this damned war. It's you and the other folks left at home who've had to bear the brunt of it – not knowing half the time just what's going on, coping with rationing, worrying about air-raids and about whether I'm all right and not seeing your kids for years.' His other arm wrapped itself about her and he kissed her. 'I'll make it all up to you one day, darling,' he whispered when he lifted his mouth from hers. 'I promise!'

'Colin, people are looking at us!'

'Let them,' he said, and kissed her again.

Later, in bed, he started to laugh. 'No wonder people were staring at us this afternoon. I'm as brown as a berry and you're white as a ghost.' He caught her hand and raised their bare arms in the air, pressed together. 'The two of us must look like a half-eaten chocolate cream when we're out together.' Then, as their hands, still linked, fell back on to the bed he added, 'Isla, I'm not going back to Sicily. I've to report to a unit down south.'

Relief swept over her. 'You're staying in Britain?'

'For a while, anyway. There's something special on the way, and they're reorganising things so that the older men can relieve the youngsters to prepare for it.' He turned his head on the pillow and kissed her shoulder. 'In military terms I'm a has-been. God, the very thought makes me feel old.'

Isla raised herself on one elbow and looked down at his tanned face, familiar, yet not familiar. There were lines there that she had never seen before, some caused by laughter, some by squinting into a fiercer sun than she had ever known. But most of the lines were grim

and hard, engraved deeply into his skin by sights and
sounds and experiences he would probably not talk
about for many years.

'You're not old. You'll never be old,' she said
fiercely, and he reached up to pull her close.

'If this war's taught me anything, Isla, it's how much
I love you and treasure you.'

The week in Largs was like a honeymoon. They spent
every minute together, talking, walking, loving, rediscovering each other.

Following Gregg's advice, she had told Colin about
Barbara. Now that they were together, they were able to
talk about it in depth. Colin, like Gregg, believed that
the girl should be left to her own devices. 'I don't think
you'll lose her, darling. You did the right thing, telling
her the whole truth once she'd found out about it.'

'If I could just talk to her face to face, answer all her
questions, I'd feel better. Oh, Colin, it's been so long
since I last saw them both!'

'I know, love, but I don't think it's going to be much
longer now.' He gave her a sidelong glance, then said,
'Has it occurred to you that they might want to settle in
Canada? They've both enjoyed their stay, and Barbara
seems to have established a career there.'

She looked at him in dismay. 'They wouldn't do
that, surely?'

'They might. If they do, it's not the end of the
world. We could settle there ourselves if it came to it.'

'But what about the business?'

Colin gave a short, grim laugh. 'After what we've all
been through in the past five years, the business doesn't

seem to be all that important any more. Not nearly as important as being with you and Barbara and Ross, and being happy. If it comes to it, I'm game.'

Isla thought of Gregg, of living in his country, perhaps meeting him, seeing him with his wife and his sons. He had said that he couldn't bear a meeting under such circumstances, and she knew that she felt the same way.

'They'll want to come home, I know it,' she said obstinately, and Colin shrugged.

'No sense in crossing our bridges. I just thought I'd mention it.'

34

In June, Allied forces stormed the beaches at Normandy, the 'something special' that Colin had spoken of in Largs, and began to drive the Germans back. British losses were comparatively light, but that meant little to Isla, because Drew Brown was among them. Her letter to Colin was smudged with tears that had refused to stop trickling for days.

'I went at once to see Mrs Brown, but the place was filled with neighbours, so there wasn't much left for me to do. The poor woman was just sitting there, huddled in her chair, lost and bewildered by what's happened. Drew was all she had. The only thing she said while I was there was that perhaps it was for the best that he hadn't got married after all. I'm not so sure. At least if he had, she would have had a daughter-in-law to share her grief. Now, she's got nobody.'

She stopped writing in order to dab at her eyes with a handkerchief that was already damp, then, seeing that some tears had splashed on to the paper, she tried to blot them and only succeeded in smudging the ink. She contemplated starting the letter over again, but it was almost time to set out for the sanatorium, and she wanted to post it on her way there. She sniffed hard, gave her eyes another swipe with the handkerchief, and went on.

'Magret has done a lot for Mrs Brown since the news arrived, and Mrs Leach was a tower of strength while I was there, so gentle with Mrs Brown that I could scarcely believe it. She's older now, of course, which might have mellowed her. And poor Mr Kelly's death in Italy might have had something to do with it. Magret says that since then, Mrs Kelly has become much stronger, and won't allow her mother to bully her any more. Her little boy is a beautiful child – completely spoiled by his grandmother, who looks after him outside school hours when his mother's at work. Would you believe it, Colin, Mrs Brown even managed to rouse herself when I was saying goodbye, and thank me again for getting her roof mended all those years ago.'

Although the war was swinging in the Allies' favour now, the Germans were fighting back viciously. At the end of June, flying bombs started ravaging London.

'It must be like being attacked by a swarm of bees, only a million times worse,' Magret said, shaking her head and showering Isla's kitchen with the white fluff that always clung to the mill workers' clothes and hair. 'Bees don't stop buzzing then start exploding. These poor souls down south, they've had the worst of it!'

The Allies marched into Paris, then on to Belgium, while rockets being fired from Germany and Holland added to the misery of the flying bombs for the London civilians, and set Isla fretting afresh about Colin. She had thought he was safe in England, but now he was involved with anti-aircraft guns and, she knew from his letters, rarely able to enjoy a trouble-free night.

Unable to do a thing to help him, she concentrated her spare time on doing as much work on the Flora dolls' house as she could. That helped her a little, though every now and again dark depression swept over her as she recalled that once the war was over, Drew wouldn't be there, after all, to create miniature replicas of Flora's massive, dark furniture.

Eventually she set it aside and, buying a plain little house from Mr Leckie, who was still running his toyshop, she turned to copying the room she and Barbara and Ross had inhabited in George Street.

'I didnae know that there were this many folk in Paisley,' Magret bawled into Isla's ear. The two of them stood on the bridge spanning the River Cart at Paisley Cross, at the exact spot, Isla suddenly realised, where she had stood looking down at the river on her first visit to the town.

Only this time she wasn't alone; it was VE-Day, and every inch of the Cross and the gardens on the riverbank was crammed with people singing, dancing if they could find the space, hugging and kissing each other, celebrating the end of the war.

A group of soldiers to one side were bellowing out a Welsh song, on the other, a bunch of girls and servicemen, arms linked, were jigging up and down, singing, 'Pack up Your Troubles In Your Old Kitbag'. Cars and buses caught in the crowd shrilled their horns in celebration, people leaning from the windows of the surrounding buildings waved Union Jacks and cheered, and all the statues in the gardens, even Queen Victoria's, were being used as footholds and handholds for folk trying to get above the crowd.

A burly man in naval uniform, a beer bottle in his hand, set up in competition with other singers with 'Roll Out The Barrel!' in a powerful voice that was soon joined by others, including the Welshmen and the girls and their escorts. Magret roared the tune out lustily, beating time in the air with clenched fists, then broke off and grabbed at Isla's hand. 'I'm dyin' for a cup of tea. C'mon, we'll find the lassies and go home.'

Half an hour later they had only travelled a few yards, to the other side of St Mirren Brae, and there was no sign of Greta or Daisy.

'Hell mend them,' their mother said cheerfully. 'We'll just go on home and let them come back when they're good and ready.'

Together the two women battled down St Mirren Brae, Magret stopping to hug every man she met, with an extra warm hug for anyone in uniform. 'Take yer chances where ye find them, that's what I say,' she said cheerfully after a particularly enthusiastic encounter with a good-looking naval rating. 'There's none of them'll bother tae pass the time of day wi' a middle-aged biddy like me once we get used tae the idea of peace again.'

The crowds were thinning by the time they had reached the end of George Street and begun to walk up its length towards Magret's new home. They stopped at the old tenement to visit Mrs Brown, and Magret tried to persuade her to go with them, but she shook her head and said with an apologetic smile, 'I'd just as soon stay here on my own today.'

'All right, hen – but ye know where I live,' Magret patted her hand. 'Ye'll be welcome there any time ye feel like it. Any time at all, mind.'

They covered the rest of the distance in subdued silence, both thinking of Drew, and young Mr Kelly, and finally arrived at the flat to find that Greta and Daisy were already there, holding an impromptu party with Greta's fiancé and Daisy's boyfriend and several other people, the gramophone the girls had bought between them thumping out a Glen Miller tune.

Magret's usual high spirits returned at the prospect of a party. Towing Isla behind her, kissing and hugging to left and to right, she fought her way through the crowd to the tiny scullery, which she called a kitchenette. 'Won't be long before your two are back, Isla,' she shouted above the noise as she set the kettle on the gas stove. Then, with a swift glance at her friend's face, 'Are ye still frettin' about Barbara?' Isla had told her about Barbara's discovery, but had withheld Kenneth's name. Although there were no longer any McAdams living in Paisley, she couldn't bring herself to betray him. For once, Magret hadn't pried.

'I can't help fretting.'

'Ach, she'll get over it. She'll have tae. And when all's said and done' – Magret, heedless of rationing on this special day, spooned sugar generously into both their cups – 'you're her mammy. It'll be fine, just wait and see.'

In July the blackout curtains were pulled down and the street lights went on again. Isla packed the hated gas mask into a cupboard and out of sight, relieved beyond measure that she had never had to find out whether or not she would have used it in a gas attack, and prepared, nervously, for the return of her son and daughter from Canada. To her relief, Barbara had decided to fly back with Ross, and Ainslie was coming with them.

'I'm more than ready for a reunion,' she wrote. 'Phil, bless him, will stay here with the boys. He reckons that on this occasion, we should be on our own. I can't wait to see you again. Prepare for a shock when you see Ross, he's so like the McAdams, though I would say that he has your temperament, thank goodness. Every time I look at him I'm reminded of poor little Innes.'

Isla, who was still at the sanatorium, and would go on working there until the local Hospital Board got everything sorted out and their nursing staff up to its required level, arranged to take time off on the day they were due to arrive. It had been agreed that they would come to Paisley from Prestwick Aerodrome by train, then get a taxi to Castlehead, where Isla would be waiting. As the expected time for their arrival came near, she was so nervous that she couldn't sit down, but had to pace the ground floor, going restlessly from room to room until she was certain she must have worn a track in the carpets. When at last she heard the taxi stopping at the gate, she rushed to the door, then paused at the top of the porch steps, terrified. It had been so long, and so many things had happened since she had last seen her children.

Ainslie was first out of the vehicle. Sophisticated though she looked in a tailored navy skirt and fur jacket, her red hair still fiery beneath a smart navy and white hat, she nevertheless gave a Red Indian whoop of excitement as she spotted Isla. She fumbled with the gate, then ran up the path as Isla ran down the porch steps. They met halfway along the path, thumping straight into each other's arms.

'I thought today would never come! You look—' Ainslie held Isla back for a moment. 'My God, you look as though you've been through the mill,' she said with brutal honesty, then gathered Isla close for another swift, hard hug before turning towards the two young people coming in at the gate.

'Come on, you two – let your ma see what a disaster I've made of your upbringing.'

Ross came forward first, grinning, and Isla saw with a catch of breath what Ainslie had meant. It was almost like seeing Kenneth again, though Ross's eyes were a darker blue and his face rounder. He caught her up in a bear hug that almost squeezed the breath from her. At sixteen, he was a good head taller than Isla herself.

'You've grown!'

'No, you've got smaller.' His eyes were bright, his voice deep, with just the trace of a drawl to it.

Then it was Barbara's turn. In spite of the photographs, Isla had been unable to think of Barbara other than as the leggy schoolgirl she had last seen going up the gangplank of the steamer at Greenock. Now she was confronted by an elegant young woman in a tan and cream checked costume, her lovely face carefully but lightly made up, her shoulder-length hair a glowing mass against the cream hat perched like a halo on the back of her head. For a moment mother and daughter eyed each other warily, then Isla opened her arms and

Barbara came into them, briefly, dropping a light kiss on Isla's cheek before freeing herself.

'Hello, Mother.'

'It looks so small!' Ross broke the awkward moment, staring up at the house. 'I remembered it as a big house.'

'Your mother's right, you daft lump – it's you that's grown,' Ainslie told him. 'Didn't I keep saying that you were eating too much?'

The taxi-driver, still waiting by the gate with a pile of luggage, cleared his throat loudly, drawing their attention to his patient presence. There was a flurry of activity, paying the man, getting the luggage into the hall, then they were all indoors, the door shut, grinning self-consciously at each other. All except Barbara, Isla noticed, avoiding eye-contact, looking around as she drew her gloves off.

'Same room?' Ross asked, and when his mother nodded he scooped up two cases and ran up the stairs, calling back, 'I'll fetch the others in a minute.'

'Ainslie, I've had to put a bed for you in Barbara's room.'

'Oh, no,' Ainslie said in mock horror. 'The indignity of it, having to share a room at my age with my kid sister!'

Barbara grinned at her, and for the first time, Isla caught a glimpse of the daughter she had known. 'First there gets the best bed,' she said, and ran lightly upstairs after her brother.

'She hates me,' Isla said in a panic.

'No, she doesn't.' Ainslie put an arm round her and gave her a swift hug.

'But she's so formal with me, and so relaxed with you.'

'She hasn't seen you for years, and anyway, she's inherited the McAdam pride, that's for sure. You'll have to give her time, Isla. Come and make me some tea, I've been dreaming about a cup of tea all through the flight.'

As they sat at the kitchen table waiting for the kettle to boil, they could hear Ross running up and down the stairs collecting the luggage, the thump of footsteps above, Barbara and Ross calling to each other, the slam of doors.

'This house has been so quiet, for so long,' she said in awe. 'And suddenly it's come alive again.'

'Everything'll soon be back to normal.'

'It'll never be the same again, but if we're lucky, we can start all over again.'

'Any word of Colin coming home?'

'Next month, he hopes.'

'You'll be pleased about that.'

'So will his father – he's worn himself out looking after the office. This time, he's looking forward to retiring.'

'Gregg Marshall arrived back just before we left, much to Pat's relief. She's missed him terribly. They've always been a very close family. It was good of you to give him hospitality while he was based in Scotland.'

'He's a very nice person.'

'That's exactly what he said about you,' Ainslie said. 'You'll be looking forward to getting back to your dolls' houses.'

'Mr Leckie's had some enquiries already. And Mabel's written – she'll be demobbed soon, and she wants to come back to work for me. I'll have to find another furniture maker.' She swallowed, then said, 'There'll never be anyone like Drew, though.'

'I know.' Ainslie reached over and touched her shoulder. The kettle began to whistle and Isla got up and poured some boiling water into the teapot, then emptied it out and reached for the tea-caddy.

'I was thinking of asking Mrs Brown if she'd like to be our housekeeper.'

Ainslie went unerringly to the right cupboard to fetch cups and saucers. 'Drew's mother? D'you think she'll want the job?'

'I think she might. It'd be good for her to be part of a family. If we are still a family,' Isla added, a tremor in her voice, as she set the empty kettle down.

'Of course you are. It's funny how things that happened years ago keep affecting our lives, isn't it?' Ainslie sat down again, putting her elbows on the table and leaning her chin in cupped hands. 'It's been over sixteen years since my father died, and yet when Barbara started asking about him, and the two of us spent hours going over the photographs I'd found for her, I could almost see the change coming over her. She matured, Isla. She's found qualities in herself that she'd never noticed before. Even though he died when she was little, Father shaped her, just as he shaped us. Remember when we talked it all over years ago, and I said that we were McAdam's women?'

Ross, yelling to his sister to hurry up, came thundering down the stairs and into the kitchen, a camera in his hand. He stopped suddenly, then said, 'I almost expected to see Nan here.'

'So do I, every time I come in,' Isla told him.

'It must have been awful for you.'

'It was – but now you're back home, and everything's going to be all right.'

Ross blinked rapidly, swallowed, then opened the back door. 'Outside, everyone,' he said briskly. 'I want to take some pictures.'

'But I want my tea,' Ainslie wailed.

'Later. I'm preserving this moment for posterity.' Ross tossed the words over his shoulder as he plunged into the garden.

Ainslie, groaning, got to her feet. 'We gave him that for his last birthday, and right now I wish we'd never thought of it. He's camera mad, I warn you. Come on, we might as well fetch Barbara and get it over with.'

They found Barbara in the workroom, standing over the dolls' house that Isla was working on. She turned as they went in, wonder in her eyes. 'This looks just like our old room in George Street!'

'You remember it?'

'Of course I do. That was where I learned to play peevers.' For the first time, Barbara gave her mother a genuine smile, and Isla, heartened, went to stand by her.

'I wanted to keep my hand in, and I thought it would be an easy one to do.'

Barbara reached into the little house and withdrew a matchbox tray, painted creamy yellow to resemble an orange box. Gently, she drew back the scrap of cloth hung on a thread across the opening. 'You've even put the little dishes on the shelves. Can I have it when it's finished?'

'Of course you can.'

Barbara gently replaced the little makeshift cupboard

in the dolls' house, then her index finger, tipped with pink nail polish, touched each of the dolls in turn. 'A mother doll, a girl doll, a boy doll. I insisted on having a daddy doll, didn't I?'

'Yes. You were quite right,' Isla said. 'There should have been one. I'll make one.'

'No, don't.' The silky fall of Barbara's red hair hid her downbent face. After a moment she straightened. 'We seemed to manage well enough without one,' she said matter-of-factly, and swung out of the room.

'She's thawing,' Ainslie whispered as they followed her through the kitchen and into the back garden, where Ross was standing by the edge of the vegetable patch, staring round in amazement.

'The swing's gone. Where's my swing?' he asked in his man's voice.

'You're old enough to make your own now,' Barbara said, and he made a face at her.

'I might just do that. Now, over against the garden wall, the three of you, with Mum in the middle.'

They grouped themselves, and he studied them through the viewfinder, then flapped a hand at them. 'Closer together.'

Barbara's scent, fresh and flowery, wafted towards Isla as they obeyed, arms about each other.

'That's good. Hold it,' Ross instructed.

'McAdam's women,' Ainslie murmured, just as the camera shutter clicked, freezing the three of them, Isla, Ainslie, and Barbara, entwined in an embrace for all time.